Y0-BQQ-423

by Bruce Palmer

HECATOMB
HORSESHOE BEND
MANY ARE THE HEARTS
FLESH AND BLOOD
BLIND MAN'S MARK

HECATOMB

a novel by
Bruce Palmer

Simon and Schuster
New York

For Herbert Lobsenz

HECATOMB

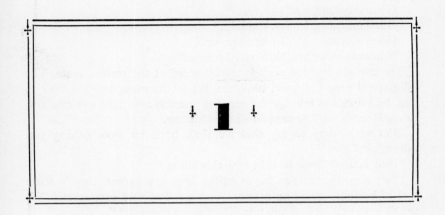

LIVERMORE leaned over the rail and watched the pilot
boat come alongside. The morning sun was already warm on his neck
and shoulders. The pilot boat wallowed and spluttered, and gulls
shrieked and swooped for the breakfast garbage. The pilot, stocky
and very dark, swung nimbly up the boarding stairs, and the pilot
boat cast off and roared ahead toward the harbor, churning a white
wake in the slick water. Livermore selected a cigarette from his case
and walked forward. Heavy, rapid footsteps sounded on the deck
behind him, and Livermore turned.

"Good morning, Mr. Dunkel."

"Morning. Going to be a scorcher."

"Yes, I'm afraid so. They seem to have only two kinds of weather
here. Hot and hotter. I was just stepping up to the bridge. Won't you
join me?"

"Fine. Maybe we'll catch a little breeze up there."

Livermore nodded. Dunkel was a big, fleshy man, the kind that suffered in the tropics. Already his broad pink forehead was damp with perspiration. The two men climbed to the bridge. The second mate touched the bill of his cap.

"Good morning, sir."

"Good morning, Miller. Captain."

"Good morning, Mr. Livermore, sir."

"You remember Mr. Dunkel, of course."

The captain nodded politely and glanced at the second mate. The pilot stood near the brass binnacle. When the mate stepped over to him, he broke out into harsh-sounding Spanish and flung out one arm toward the shore. The captain stroked his jaw.

"I'm very sorry to say that we shall be a bit slow getting you ashore, sir."

"Why is that? Some trouble with this fellow?"

"Not him, sir. But, as far as Miller here can gather, there's some sort of business going on ashore. A strike, I should say, myself. We shan't have our tugs, at any rate. They won't come out."

"I see."

Dunkel mopped his face and stared at the pilot.

"What's next? Can you put us ashore in a boat?"

The captain smiled and shook his head.

"That wouldn't do, I'm afraid. Mr. Miller?"

"Sir?"

"Tell him to take us on in. Deckhands fore and aft to set lines. Rig the gangway. Tell purser to notify all passengers that the customs officials are waiting in first- and third-class dining rooms."

"Very good, sir."

The pilot began to protest, but the second mate cut him short. Dunkel raised his bushy eyebrows.

"Your people going to dock her by themselves, Mr. Livermore?"

"I daresay."

"Should be something to see. A ship this size."

"I daresay."

The pilot muttered an order, and the engine telegraph rang for one-quarter ahead. The bow of the ship swung toward the shining shore. Livermore walked out on the wing of the bridge and finished his cigarette. The low coast gleamed in the morning sun. As they drew closer, the reflection from the beaches would be dazzling, the silver

8

coast that gave the country its name. Dunkel joined him. The American was smoking one of his cigars.

"Have you been often to Costa Plata, Mr. Dunkel?"

"My first time. I understand he speaks English."

"Very fluently."

"The captain says the strike started this morning. The longshoremen walked out, too. I guess we'll have to smash our own baggage, eh?"

"I'm sorry, I don't . . . oh, no, I expect the crew will handle our luggage."

"Funny smell."

"The marshes. South of the city. Unhealthy."

"Smells like it."

"I've been told the duck hunting is excellent, though. That's why the marshes have never been drained. They keep them for the sport."

Dunkel nodded and gazed at the shore.

"That's it, eh? Just the one city. Good-sized, though."

"The capital is large. There are some fair-sized towns inland, scattered through the hills, up into the mining territory. West is the *campo*."

"What's that?"

"The farms. Cattle, for the most part. Very little of interest to the south. Villages, that's about all."

"There's the kraut."

"Where?"

"Down there."

Livermore looked down at the foredeck. A man in shirt-sleeves bent over the steam winch. Some members of the crew stood around him. A thick hawser snaked across the top of the fore hatch. The man became aware that he was in the way and stepped back, nodding his head.

"Yesterday he was down in the engine room. All day long."

"Herr Herzler is very thorough, very competent."

"And pretty chummy with Vizarra, to hear him tell it."

"Herzler helped install the mining equipment twelve years ago. He has been here ever since."

"As long as he isn't too chummy."

"We have no cause for concern. Not from Herr Herzler."

The liner moved steadily toward the harbor. The pale mass of the city broke into fragments, sharp-edged blocks of buildings, low, smutty warehouses, the gilded cup of the cathedral.

"What's the big place on the hill, Mr. Livermore?"

"The palace. We will be received there. He generally lives at his villa outside of the city, especially at this time of year."

"Quite a place."

"If you care for official Spanish architecture."

"I guess so."

‡

Fingel bent over his rumpled bunk, packing his suitcase. He locked it, then unlocked it. He patted the breast pocket of his coat. His papers were there. The cabin was hot and fuggy, even with the ventilator working. The four Belgians sat, two on one lower berth, two across the aisle. They talked in low voices and seemed to be dividing up a wad of flat paper packets. One of them held four passports. Fingel waited until they finished their business, then edged between them. He murmured an apology and held his derby against his chest. He gazed out through the disc of grimy glass. The dock was very close. The tarred piles slipped past. The dock was empty. Then he saw a group of soldiers with rifles. The ship shuddered, slowed and stopped. The propellers threshed, and the dirty water whitened. The ship touched against the dock, very gently, a soft, ponderous nudge. The Belgians stood up and shook hands with each other. Fingel waited until they left the cabin, then picked up his valise and briefcase. The corridor outside was crowded and noisy. Fingel slipped out and was carried along toward the third-class dining room. He waited in line, pushing his valise forward with his foot, fanning himself with his derby. The Belgians, he noticed, were scattered. They had separated themselves. Yet they had been together all during the long voyage from Liverpool, sharing the same cabin, eating by themselves at the same table, drinking beer and playing cards. Fingel shrugged, stepped forward, and placed his passport on the table. The uniformed official glanced at it, checked the passenger list and handed it to another man in uniform. The second man examined the passport very carefully, turning the pages and holding them up to the light. Fingel began to sweat, and his hands grew cold. The second official stared at him. Fingel smiled feebly.

"Français?"

"Oui. Oui, oui!"

The man shrugged and carried the passport away to a clerk at another table. The clerk copied the information into a black notebook. The passengers behind Fingel began to mutter. He turned and shrugged, smiling at them. The man at the table wrote out an embarkation card, stamped the passport, and waved him on. Fingel picked up his valise and hurried out onto the deck. He whuffed with relief. That had been close. The four Belgians stood at the rail, talking together. Fingel looked down and blinked slowly, surprised.

Two black official limousines stood on the quai. Blue-and-silver pennons fluttered from flagstaffs set in the front fenders. Some soldiers stood around. Three army trucks had been drawn up in the shade of a warehouse. Through a large arch Fingel could see a line of taxis. The customhouse was to the left, a low, metal-roofed building. But there was no crowd of relatives and friends, no shouting mob of porters. The cab of the nearest crane was empty. Twice before, Fingel had landed in Costa Plata, once as a Pole, once as a German. Both times the dock had been crowded, colorful and noisy, with shouting men, women in bright, tight dresses, and uniformed pages from the big hotels. Fingel touched his French passport and shook his head slowly. The gangway slammed down on the dock, and members of the crew ran down to make it fast. They called to each other, their voices loud and harsh in the damp heat of the still morning. Some ship's officers came suddenly out through a door, accompanying three men in dark suits. A fourth man, carrying baggage, followed them. The officers smiled, and shook hands with a tall, thin man, who looked English to Fingel. The doors of the limousines on the quai popped open. A group of officials dressed in blue double-breasted suits and broad Panama hats walked stiffly to the foot of the gangway. A number of police followed them and ringed them, facing in toward the customhouse, the archway, and the waiting rank of taxis. One of the officials took off his hat, and one of the Belgians muttered something. The others nodded. Fingel fanned himself with his derby and craned to see. It was Colleo, the Prime Minister, a thin, dark scholar with silver hair. Fingel's collar stud popped. He watched in dismay as the metal bit fell between the ship and the pier. A tiny spray of dirty water rose without a sound and vanished. Fingel clutched his collar and smiled apologetically at no one.

The three men in dark suits walked together down the gangway to the dock and there met the officials. They were introduced in turn to Colleo, shook hands and smiled. One of the Belgians said something

11

very loudly. Fingel picked up his valise and sidled away, still watching the quai. He settled again, a safe distance from the Belgians. The party with the Prime Minister walked toward the limousines. An officer of the National Guard supervised the blocky heap of luggage. Three soldiers carried the suitcases across the quai out through the arch to another sedan. The men vanished into the great, shining automobiles that moved at once out through the arch. A loudspeaker rasped, announcing that first-class passengers could now disembark. There would be a long wait, Fingel knew. He sat down on his valise, fanned himself for a moment, then opened his briefcase to examine his papers.

✦

Livermore glanced out of the window of the sedan. The narrow streets of the dockyard slums were oddly, quietly empty. Herzler sat to his left, Dunkel to his right. The Prime Minister crouched on a jump seat like an awkward, dark bird. Colleo seemed ill at ease. He glanced hopefully from Herzler to Dunkel, then lifted his thin upper lip at Livermore, exposing his perfect false teeth.

Livermore saw the poster on the building as it flashed past: the square, jowly face with the stiff hair and the eyes that seemed to follow you. The poster had been defaced. A crude scarlet smear in the form of a letter H, joined at the top to form an odd A-shape. He leaned forward and touched Colleo's knee. The old man started and smiled convulsively.

"Yes, please?"

"Don Diego, what was that? Painted back there. On the poster."

"Oh, nothing. Children, perhaps."

"Children? I have seen it before. You see? There's another."

He pointed. Herzler looked, grunted and nodded.

"Axoloqui."

"I beg your pardon?"

The Prime Minister smiled suddenly, very widely, his whole dark face wrinkling. His melancholy eyes shone. He began to speak in a pedantic tenor, marking the air with his long fingers.

"This letter, you mean, no? There is a third, over there."

Livermore saw a red daub across a cinema advertisement. Colleo nodded, still smiling, as though encouraging a dull student.

"As Señor Herzler says, that is the sign of Axoloqui."

"Indeed. I regret to say that I know nothing of Axil . . . him.""

"But that is to be regretted, Mr. Livermore. I have met several of your countrymen who were remarkably well informed on the deities of the several peoples of India, Vishnu and so on, Kali . . .""

"Sorry to say that's never been an interest of mine. But . . . well, will you be good enough to tell me?"

Dunkel suddenly heaved and surged, dragged out a cigar case and offered it to the Prime Minister. Colleo shook his head sadly, tapping his breast over the heart. Instantly, he forgot Dunkel and fixed his dark gaze on Livermore. He spoke slowly, distinctly, like a tour guide.

"An Indian legend. Very interesting. The indigenous peoples of Costa Plata, before receiving God's grace through the hands of the missionaries of the Church, had their own faith, or myths. That letter . . ."

He sketched the shape of it in the air. Herzler silently pointed out another painted on the blinding white wall of a tenement.

". . . is his sign. Axoloqui. He was believed to be the son of God and the force of good. With his hands he built all of the country, all of Costa Plata."

Dunkel grunted and struck a match for his cigar. Colleo coughed discreetly.

"And then he fell in love."

Herzler leaned forward, his pale mouth puckered.

"About the silver. Tell them that, Don Diego."

The Prime Minister picked at his trousers, where the heavy blue cloth clung to his thighs. He nodded and smiled again.

"Axoloqui asked his father—God, that is—for a wife. He had seen and now desired Onati, the woman of the clouds. It was sanctioned by God, and the woman was given to him. I do not think you are a member of the Church of Rome, Mr. Livermore?"

"Of England. Please go on."

"I did not wish to give offense. It is simply an old story, you see."

"I do understand."

"Mighty quiet here for a working day."

Colleo glanced at Dunkel. The Prime Minister's face wrinkled with anxiety. He made an odd little gesture, but said nothing. The American stared at him. The Prime Minister cleared his throat sharply.

13

"Axoloqui took the woman Onati for his own. But at the instant of his pleasure in . . . um . . . coupling with her, in bed, she knew pain and fear and withdrew herself from him. You know, yes? Yes. Well. She withdrew her body, I mean to say. Some of Axoloqui's seed spilled on the earth. The dust heaved to hide it and became the mountains, and the seed became the silver there. In Señor Herzler's mines."

Herzler shifted and nodded. The interior of the sedan was very hot. Dunkel stared out into the streets and chewed his cigar. He glanced at the Prime Minister.

"Sounds like he picked the wrong girl."

"The miners believe it. Each morning they ask his pardon before they begin to work. The priest there, he can do nothing with them. It is just their way."

Colleo rubbed his thin hands together briskly and leaned forward, raising one finger to make his point.

"What Señor Herzler says is quite true. The indigenous peoples are still very superstitious. The archbishop has much distress. The priests are often angry. The people attend Mass, but before, they burn offerings to Axoloqui before the village churches. Nothing can be done, it seems."

"If they do a day's work, why should anyone care?"

"But, Señor Dunkel, they worship false gods still, and that is not correct."

Dunkel grunted and gnawed his cigar. He gestured at an empty square.

"Is that where they're all at today?"

"I don't understand you, señor. Your pardon."

"I said, where are they? Is this all part of the dock strike?"

"Oh, no, no. No."

"But it's ten o'clock. Ten-fifteen, as a matter of fact. It always this quiet, Mr. Livermore?"

"Not to my knowledge."

"Herzler?"

"Eh? No."

"That's what I thought."

The Prime Minister drew himself up and stared over Livermore's head, out through the rear window of the limousine. His tenor voice rapped sternly, striking down the questions of unruly students.

14

"The woman Onati conceived, but she bore an imperfect child. So she called him Vigo, which, in dialect, means ugly, crippled or evil thing. For one hundred and fifty-seven years the Church has struggled night and day to prevent the indigenous peoples from infant murder. They kill malformed children, those born feet foremost and all twins, believing them cursed. But God was displeased with Axoloqui, for Onati had not been forced to submit to the divine will."

"Is that a market there, Mr. Prime Minister?"

"Yes, señor. A market."

"Closed, eh?"

"Your pardon?"

"Nothing, señor. You go right ahead."

The sedan slued around a corner and into the mouth of a broad boulevard shaded by tattered palms. A small group of people, mostly men, stared at the sedan. Livermore saw poor clothes and thin, sullen faces. Dunkel turned to stare at them.

"Well. God summoned Axoloqui and kept him at his side. Axoloqui yearned in his heart to have again his once-bedded bride. His passion to dominate her increased."

Herzler leaned forward, jostling Livermore again.

"And that is why, after a church marriage, there is the beating of the wife. With a stick, so. Pah! Pah! Pah! Three times. So the woman will not be like Onati. I have seen this many times."

"Unfortunately, that is still so."

Dunkel laughed abruptly.

"But God dissolved Onati back into clouds. And every day she drifted across the face and body of Axoloqui, tormenting him."

"Very . . . very interesting."

"Yes, you think so? Meanwhile, Vigo grew and took power. So Axoloqui was forced to suffer double pain . . . how do you say it? Unrequited love? Yes? Ah, good. Unrequited love and the slow ruin of the land he formed with his own hands."

The Prime Minister waggled his own thin, twig-dark fingers. Herzler coughed and batted away cigar smoke. Livermore felt the beads of perspiration on his own forehead. He nodded, once.

"Vigo was volcanoes, drought, pestilence and the madness of war, tribe against tribe. He demanded first the sacrifice of field crops, then of fowls and beasts, and, at last, flesh. For more than a century the people had practiced human sacrifice, before the missionaries of the

15

Church came with Manuel Huelta, the *conquistador* of Costa Plata. This street is named for him. His statue is up there ahead, you see? Very good example of eighteenth-century bronze equestrian sculpture."

"The man on horseback, yes. I should say there is some resemblance between Huelta the *conquistador* and the Caudillo."

"It has often been pointed out, Mr. Livermore."

"There is a space-time unity between the Aztec culture and that of Costa Plata."

"Exactly, Señor Herzler!"

Livermore clamped his jaws together to conceal the yawn that swelled up in him. Something more than a dock strike was in the air. His regional manager, Ferguson, would know about it. Dunkel snorted again, amused, and shook his heavy head slightly. Colleo raised his voice slightly.

"Vigo, too, sought to couple with Onati, in incest, but since God had made her without substance, he could not have her, you see."

"An interesting example of prehistoric Oedipal myth."

Livermore groaned silently. He was hot and bored. Native customs and habits were so often more tedious than amusing. He watched the Prime Minister nod and smile again, very pleased. Obviously, he and Herzler were old acquaintances. How like the Hun to curry favor with the natives.

Colleo made a little vulgar gesture with his hands and smirked.

"Vigo's . . . well, his organ . . . flashed across the skies, standing through the clouds of her. And that is lightning and thunder. Vigo's seed falls as rain. No Indian woman of Costa Plata can be touched by rain without great shame to her. She is not clean then, you see."

Dunkel chuckled and slapped his thigh. Colleo's face stiffened. He mopped his brow.

"A myth, only. A foolish story."

"*Nein!* Scientifically very interesting. Also good. Finish it, please, Don Diego."

"But the other gentlemen do not care, perhaps . . ."

"Not at all, Don Diego. Fascinating."

"There is not much more. The indigenous peoples welcomed—no, received—Manuel Huelta the *conquistador* with the greatest honor, as a god. They had never seen the horses, you understand. Huelta had

16

twelve—one for each month of the year, it was believed. The peoples thought him to be Axoloqui. Only later, too late, did they learn that the guns—the thunder tubes, they called them—were in the hands of the followers of Vigo. Still, you understand, since Huelta was the leader of the expedition, they believed him to be Axoloqui. It was Huelta who discovered the royal mines and forced the first tribute of silver. He returned to his home in Avila and died there of fever. The peoples still believe that he was Axoloqui and will return."

"Like the second coming of Christ."

"Exactly, Señor Herzler. Therefore Christianity, while easily rooted among the tribes, has never been able to quite dominate the minds and hearts of the indigenous ones. The Archbishop, poor soul, suffers the pain of ulcers as a result."

The sedan reached the end of the boulevard and circled the *glorieta*. A fountain splashed in the humid morning air. Livermore felt stifled. He gestured to Herzler to roll down the window. Two motorcycles roared out of a side street and raced ahead up the hill to the Plaza Mayor. The great façade of the Presidential Palace came into view as though dropped like theater scenery. Colleo smiled, mopped his brow again and apologized for the heat. He pointed to the left with such suddenness that Dunkel threshed and broke the tip off his cigar.

"Oh, oh. A thousand pardons, Señor Dunkel."

"That's all right. It's fine. It's all right."

"I merely wished to point out the Arch of Independence."

The Prime Minister dropped his hand and swallowed. On the side of the arch a great scarlet *A* burned like a brand. At the same instant, the motorcycle sirens wailed and sobbed. Herzler tried to shout a question, but the dry, dark old man on the jump seat shook his head stubbornly. A military guard of honor stiffened. The great iron grille yawned in, and the limousine rolled across a vast plain of gray gravel and stopped. The heels of a hundred men crashed in unison. A barrel of maroon carpet plunged out toward the sedan. Two rows of men in shining breastplates, boots and plumes swung forward. Livermore followed Dunkel from the sedan. Colleo looked about, alarmed, until he discovered Herzler on the other side of the automobile and beckoned him forward. A staccato command clapped off the great stone building. A hundred sabers slithered to salute, and a band smashed into "God Save the King." Livermore stood at attention. He strode forward when the smearing brass ceased and halted, flushed and in mid-stride, as a voice barked again and the band played the American anthem. Livermore drew his heels together and stifled another yawn, wincing at the strident final measures. Dunkel was humming, he realized. There was no anthem for Herzler.

The German's face was expressionless. He stared at Livermore, holding the Englishman with his gaze, as Colleo, talking animatedly, led Dunkel up the red runner to the palace steps.

"That letter."

"Yes, Herr Herzler?"

Lesser officials from Colleo's office shifted and scraped in the gravel. The palace guards stood rigid. The damp heat of the city clogged Livermore's chest. The German shook his head slowly.

"That is not for Axoloqui."

"No? I fear we're keeping these gentlemen waiting . . ."

"That letter stands for Alessandro."

"Who?"

"Alessandro Martín!"

Colleo paused and glanced behind. Livermore began walking. Herzler hurried him to keep out of hearing of the slender young men in identical suits from the Prime Minister's office. Colleo smiled fixedly. Dunkel still held the stump of his dead cigar. The German shook his head again.

"There was talk. Before I left. That he had come back to his fatherland. When I heard of the dock strike, I knew. He is here in Costa Plata."

"Is he? You must tell me more about him, Herr Herzler. When we have more time."

"He is frightened."

"Who?"

"Don Diego."

The Prime Minister waited at the first landing of the broad flight of stone steps. Dunkel stood beside him. The American waited until Livermore and Herzler could hear him. The thick irony of his tone made Colleo's face twitch.

"You sure have a quiet city here, señor. Fine place to talk business."

Dunkel stared insolently at Livermore and turned abruptly. The German nodded.

"You see, Mr. Livermore? It can be sensed. It is in the air."

Livermore mounted the stairs. He said nothing. As soon as it was feasible, he would contact Ferguson. Something had gone wrong, quite wrong. Not that it would much matter, but it was always best to avoid unpleasant subjects. The official luncheon might be a most awkward affair.

"You see—"

"Please, Herr Herzler, we are detaining the Prime Minister and his party. Later, perhaps—"

"His party? That is Malata."

In the gloom-backed square of the open doorway of the palace stood a man as slender and dark as a whip. Malata, minister without portfolio, the Caudillo's personal aide. Livermore stretched his long legs, taking the stone steps two at a time. Herzler trailed behind and began talking in guttural Spanish to the lesser officials from the Prime Minister's office.

At the top of broad stone stairs Livermore paused and turned. The honor guard and the brass band had vanished. The limousines were gone. The scarlet runner lay on the gravel, thinned to a ribbon by the distance. The far end of it looked snipped with shears. A sound trembled in the humid air. Livermore lifted his head. Over the dome of the cathedral droned the stiff insects of aircraft, a dozen biplanes flying in groups of three. Their propellers shone like new coins.

Herzler joined him and grunted once.

"The new ones. Purchased last year. From America."

Livermore turned and walked through the great open door of the palace. The Prime Minister bowed slightly. A double row of footmen in blue-and-silver livery waited. The aircraft racketed overhead, drowning Colleo's words. Malata stepped forward and jerked out his hand. Livermore accepted the small, dry palm in his own.

"Welcome to Costa Plata, Señor Livermore. I will conduct you to His Excellency."

↓

The four Belgians sat at four different tables under the awning of the café. Before each man stood a glass of beer. The aircraft droned over the city. The waiter standing out on the sidewalk snapped his towel and wandered back into the café. One of the Belgians drew a newspaper from his pocket and held it before his face. He turned the

19

pages and stared at the smudged photograph of a young woman surrounded by children and nuns. The young woman was assisting at the opening of an orphanage. Her name was Lucía Bosola. Someone coughed at his side.

"M. Voget?"

The Belgian folded his newspaper and placed it on the sticky table. A short, fat man with a greasy, anxious face stood staring at him. His brown eyes bulged.

"Yes."

"Permit me."

The fat man yanked out a chair and sat down. He extended a damp hand and squeezed Voget's fingers fiercely.

"Welcome to Costa Plata, comrade. I am Rota, secretary of the Unión de Trabajadores. The united workers of this country offer you their greetings. A good voyage?"

"Good enough."

"Waiter! A beer."

Rota peered at the other Belgians and nodded.

"Have you been waiting long?"

"No."

Rota spoke slow, careful French. Before the waiter set down the glass, Rota wiped the section of the table before him clean with a handkerchief.

"Take this back. The glass is dirty."

The waiter stared stupidly at Rota and shrugged. Rota pointed at the glass.

"This glass is dirty!"

"They're all like that."

Rota picked up the glass and tilted it. The beer splashed on the floor. He placed the empty glass on the waiter's tray.

"Five centavos."

"I owe you nothing."

"Five centavos."

The waiter folded his arms and tried to look like a man who will wait all day to get what is his due. Rota ignored him. He drew out a small cigar and offered it to the Belgian.

"I don't smoke."

Rota nodded and slapped his pockets. He held out his hand without looking at the waiter.

"Give me fire."

"Five centavos."

"Don't be an idiot."

Rota glanced at the other Belgians.

"Do they smoke?"

"Two of them, yes."

Rota started to rise, then sat down again. The waiter stood there, holding the empty glass on the tray. Rota chewed his cigar.

"Perhaps you carry matches, M. Voget?"

"No."

"No?"

One of the other Belgians lit a cigarette.

"Waiter, ask that man for his matches."

"Five centavos."

Rota stood up and thrust his hands into his pockets. He smiled and drew out a wooden match. He struck it on the tabletop. It fizzed blue smoke and went out. Rota flung it to the floor and sat down again. He dried the cigar and put it back in his breast pocket.

"We must now discuss our affairs."

"Very good."

"We will go in two taxis to the railroad station and proceed by train to our destination. Two compartments have been reserved."

"Aren't they on strike, too? The taxi drivers?"

Rota smiled blandly.

"Of course not, monsieur. There is no strike. It is forbidden to strike in Costa Plata. The purpose of the U.T. is to settle all differences without such provocations. The Caudillo himself is honorary president of the U.T. And that is why we meet here instead of our office. If you understand me."

"I understand."

"And that is why I come alone. I am a very sick man. I have sent a copy of a letter from my doctor to various departments. It is necessary for me to rest. Complete rest."

The Belgian nodded. The waiter stood there gazing stupidly at Rota.

"You will find, monsieur, that the middle class is with us."

"Good. How big is the U.T.?"

"All workers in Costa Plata are members. It is required. Even this donkey is a member. Very effective for security purposes. Two photographs, front and profile. Fingerprints. Since you are foreigners, you will not be required to obtain such a card."

"I was told that the silver miners are not members of the U.T."

Rota shrugged.

"It is true. They are very superstitious. They refuse to be photographed. They believe the camera steals the soul. Also they refuse the fingerprints. For some other reason, equally foolish."

"Then the strike will start in the mines. They are safe."

"He has not yet decided."

"Who has not yet decided? That priest?"

"He is not a priest. He was excommunicated years ago."

"Will he call the strike, though?"

"That has not yet been decided."

The Belgian nodded. Rota pulled a watch from his pocket and glanced at it.

"We must go."

Voget stood up. The other Belgians gathered the suitcases. Two taxis rattled up and stopped. Rota nodded and smiled.

"Right on time."

Voget finished his beer standing up and wiped his mouth with the back of his hand. The other Belgians waited and watched the taxis. Voget jerked his hand.

"Henri, you, Paul and the kid in the first one. Coco, you come with us."

"Right."

Voget pulled out his wallet, but Rota pushed it aside. He dropped four coins to the table.

"There."

"And five centavos."

"M. Voget? We will go now."

"For your beer. Five centavos."

Rota stared at the waiter. His face flushed and his mouth crimped in anger. He reached into his pocket and carefully placed the chewed cigar on the waiter's tray.

"There, *amigo*. That is for you to smoke tonight. The next time, you will turn in your card at the district office, understand?"

The waiter stammered something. Rota walked away through the tables to the sidewalk. Voget followed him into the taxi. Coco, the other Belgian, sat up front with the driver. Rota looked back at the waiter and shook his head.

"You see our problem, comrade. Even our own members lack the necessary discipline. But that will soon change, I assure you. Everything will soon be changed in Costa Plata, comrade. We will create a new era."

The driver let in the clutch, and the taxi shuddered forward down the empty street.

⸸

The train plunged into a tunnel, and Rota's assistants slammed the window shut to keep out the soot. Voget rolled his head on the dry, dusty plush of the seat. He breathed in the smells of soot and spilled wine. The carriage jolted out into the smiting sunshine. Rota clawed at his collar, and his assistants opened the window. The union official was sweating profusely. His bald head glistened like a piece of wax fruit. He sat in one corner of the compartment, surrounded by four young functionaries from the Unión de Trabajadores office. They had all been drinking wine and eating sandwiches. The floor was littered with bits of bread. An empty bottle rolled and clinked under the seat. The four Costa Platans sat down, stood, hung from the luggage racks and leaned out of the window. Rota talked through the dark trellis of their restless bodies. Voget glanced across the aisle at Coco. The young Belgian, flushed with wine, was asleep. Rota nodded his round, shining head at the barren countryside that streamed past the window.

"There has been talk of reclaiming this land. To bring in water. For years there has been talk. But, confidentially, comrade, it has been kept to talk. Without boasting, I may say that I have worked to keep the project limited to so many pieces of paper."

Voget nodded and looked at the rocks, the sandy soil and the brittle weeds. He knew nothing of agriculture. Rota extended his glass. One of the young men bobbed down and up, wrestling a bottle from a paper sack. He poured wine into Rota's glass and glanced, smiling courteously, at Voget. The Belgian shook his head. Rota nodded, serene now from all the wine.

"We must take various fundamental political steps first, you see. I have let it be known in the right places that the U.T. would not eagerly support the irrigation of these lands. For what would happen?

I will explain. The government would merely lease the land to the big owners from the *campo*. We would then have extended the latifundia, big landed estates for the wealthy, in pieces of thousands of hectares. We Party members within the U.T. have been working with certain peasant groups."

"I was not told that the peasants were organized."

"Not officially, no. We are working to create a peasants' union, supported by the U.T. but directed from within by the Party. You can imagine the rest, comrade. The peasants' union makes its demands. The U.T. supports those demands. A realignment of power would be effected. It would be gratifying to feel later that one played a role in such a movement of the people, a truly proletarian movement."

Voget nodded.

"Fine. But it has been my experience that peasants are always reactionary. All they care for is the land. And they're afraid of the landowners. Have you cadres in the field developing leadership through discussion groups?"

"Not yet."

"My information is that the peasants are allied to the Liberal Movement still, the party founded by Felipe Martín, Alessandro's father. That they listen to Alessandro, not the U.T."

Rota swabbed his streaming face and shrugged.

"A difference in tactics, only. Alessandro and his followers go directly into the fields. We work through the produce centers, the wholesale houses. This railroad, this very train, is a method of constant liaison."

"But liaison with kulaks. You are recruiting class enemies!"

The union leader blinked slowly and sipped his wine. Rota's followers listened attentively. Only one of them understood French. He muttered to the others. They weaved and bobbed around Rota, smiling constantly. Rota shook his head.

"One step at a time, comrade. First the peasants who own their own little patches of land, who have a handful of silver. Money talks to them."

"While Alessandro talks to all the others."

"Let him talk. Can a man feed himself and his family with words? Evidently not. We show the independent farmer that the U.T. stands with him, ready to support a peasants' union. We direct. They follow. The landless peasants will follow in turn. The urban workers are the vanguard. All this is quite correct."

24

"In my experience, the kulak follows the landowner, not the urban worker."

"Comrade, your experience is not our experience. We are on the other side of the world from you. I believe we are ideologically correct. We are infiltrating steadily. I suggest myself and these young and faithful Party members as examples to you. At present we are openly cooperating with Alessandro's movement. This is as it should be, no?"

He held out his glass to be refilled. Voget shook his head stubbornly.

"It is unrealistic to believe that Alessandro does not know all of this. Surely you have not forgotten that he was in Switzerland, Germany, Russia itself?"

"Of course we have not forgotten that he is a Trotskyite deviationist, comrade!"

"That is not my information."

Rota raised his eyebrows and smiled, almost contemptuously. The young men smiled and ducked and weaved like prizefighters.

"For the last two years Alessandro has been training his followers in Mexico. That is a fact. Trotsky is in Mexico, I believe?"

"Very true. Alessandro has been training cadres in Mexico. Where does he get money for such work?"

"From certain people. Middle-class people with bad consciences."

"From Trotsky's group?"

"I believe not, no."

"Where do the Party funds come from?"

Rota emptied his glass and shook his head. The union official was enjoying himself.

"Well, comrade, not from the Comintern. It seems you have forgotten us. We are orphans, eh? We are forced to expropriate union funds."

"To give to kulaks? To bribe men who will take your money and betray you? You know, of course, that Alessandro has already distributed arms to these landless peasants. These peasants your Party members have not contacted."

"But we are cooperating, comrade. Now is the time for cooperation. A united popular front!"

"Where are the rifles for Party members?"

Rota chuckled and wiped his face. The young men laughed politely and did not look at Voget.

"Ah, you see, comrade, that's just it! We stand in a superior position. Alessandro's Movimiento Liberal is an illegal organization. They have no method of concealing themselves. The Party on the other hand has infiltrated the U.T., the only legal union of workers in all of Costa Plata. The obvious tactical move will be to distribute arms through the district offices of the U.T. How can a handful of peasants from the villages drive Vizarra out of the capital, eh? The revolution must begin in the city. Or perhaps I have misunderstood the lessons taught in St. Petersburg?"

He laughed comfortably and held out his glass again.

"You see? When the U.T. distributes arms, they will go to Party members. To these young men and many others like them."

"The Comintern is informed as to Party membership in Costa Plata."

"New members join every day, comrade. Every day."

Voget shook his head wearily. Rota was a petty bureaucrat. How had he been permitted to rise to a position of authority in the Party?

"I remind you that in St. Petersburg the Soviet controlled firearms. Alessandro was there to see it. *I* was there to see it. Since Alessandro's M.L. has the rifles now, I do not think they will simply hand them over to the local officials of your union. Or if they do, they will distribute them to union members who do *not* belong to the Party."

"You seem to think that Alessandro has not been confused and corrupted by prolonged association with the Trotskyites."

"All I am saying is that he is *organized*. The M.L. is *organized*. They have contacted and armed the peasants. They are allied with the students and teachers of the university. All the Party has done is infiltrate one union and give money to kulaks! What is the strategy for arming Party members, when it is obvious that Alessandro will not do so?"

Rota flushed and gnawed his lip. He fumbled for a cigar. Two of the young men struck matches. The union official puffed greedily and filled the compartment with smoke that streamed away out the open window. The train swung down into a valley, steel wheels wincing and squealing on the rails. Rota waved his cigar.

"We will purchase arms."

"How? When? There is no time. It would take weeks to smuggle them in from Mexico. You have played into Alessandro's hands, don't you see that?"

26

"Comrade Voget, you are wrong, if I may be permitted to express the opinion both of a devoted Party member and citizen of Costa Plata. You do not yet understand the complexities of the situation here. We do not regret that we have been ignored by the Comintern. This pleases us. The Party here has adapted to the local situation. We are flexible, comrade. This is not Antwerp, not Berlin, not St. Petersburg. Alessandro is not Lenin."

"Nor is he Trotsky. He is—"

"A young man. A few years older than these young men."

"He is an experienced revolutionary. He is in regular contact with the Party. And with the syndicalists. And the anarchists. *And* the middle-class liberals. *And* the army, too. He is *popular* with the people!"

"This is all exaggeration, comrade, believe me. He is an intellectual."

"With the only trained cadres in the whole country. With money. And the peasants with guns in their hands. He is not cooperating with you. You are working for him. Not with him, even. *For* him."

Rota scowled and chewed his cigar. The young men frowned and stared at Voget. Rota pounded his fist on his knee. The wine spilled from his glass.

"He is without influence among U.T. members and Party members, who combine to form the vanguard of the revolution!"

"Alessandro will win the support of the army. We know that certain units are already pledged to him."

"How do you know these things? All this information! I believe they are lies and exaggerations!"

"The Comintern has been studying Alessandro for years. And the work of his father, Felipe. All the history of the Movimiento Liberal. How many members of the M.L. have been purged by Carlos Sánchez in the last two years?"

"Ask Sánchez, comrade. Ask Sánchez."

"I don't have to. Eighty-seven members. Some betrayed to the secret police, others shot. Alessandro's cadres have been in field operation, directed from Mexico. The American, O'Conner, that gangster who runs the secret police of Costa Plata, has been paid fifty thousand dollars just to leave Sánchez alone, so the work of building the M.L. here can continue."

Rota blinked rapidly and mopped his face. He whistled softly.

"Fifty thousand dollars. . . . But why were we not informed, comrade?"

Voget leaned back and said nothing. Rota was too stupid to understand why the Comintern ignored him. The union leader seemed stunned. Good enough. As long as Rota remained bewildered, he would take orders, not give them. Voget gazed out of the window. The young men murmured, dismayed. Coco snored evenly. The train rocked on through the baked and barren countryside. Voget cleared his throat.

"When we get there, it might be a good idea to hold two meetings. One with the U.T. delegates and one with those delegates who are in the Party."

"I was just going to suggest that, comrade. The U.T. must swing gradually in the direction indicated by the Party."

Rota squinted and chewed his cigar, trying to look cunning. He smiled suddenly.

"These young men will infiltrate the student cadres! At once!"

Voget nearly groaned. He nodded agreement. Rota waved his cigar.

"I myself will undertake the propaganda. Massive propaganda! On all levels of class interest. We will distribute through the U.T. offices. Through the national postal system itself!"

His eyes shone with pleasure at the daring program he outlined. The young men writhed about him in enthusiasm. Rota flung his cigar out the window and shook his fist.

"We will direct verbal propaganda to the miners!"

The union official had exhausted his imagination. He sank back in the seat and mopped his streaming face. Voget stared at him. Rota had chosen his own path out of power in the Party. From director of propaganda he would sink gradually to an organizer of new cells. In two weeks he would be cutting out armbands with his wife and daughters. When the right moment came, he would be expelled from the Party. Rota folded his hands on his plump belly.

"There is still time, comrade. Things move slowly in Costa Plata. Perhaps you might . . ."

"What?"

"Well, the propaganda will take much of my time. You might investigate the problem of the firearms, no?"

"My Spanish is not good enough."

"One of these young men here might begin an investigation of the M.L. distributors. Say we located one or two. What would you do then, in Antwerp, for example?"

"Make a raid. Or inform the police and take the firearms from the police when they pick them up. The second way is safer."

"Exactly. Safer. Suspicion is thrown on the M.L. members themselves. They suspect traitors in their own party. I will recommend that at the Party meeting."

Voget nodded. He stirred uncomfortably. He felt dulled and weary.

"I'm going outside for a minute."

"A good idea, comrade. Observe the terrain and the people. Perhaps you will cool yourself, too. Come back in a few minutes. We must plan everything."

Voget slid open the door and stepped outside. Rota's assistants burst into shrill Spanish. Voget unbuttoned his shirt and leaned out of an open window into the hot, rushing air. His countrymen came out of the next compartment.

"How goes it, chief?"

"Not good. This Rota is nothing. A petty bourgeois functionary. He has accomplished so little it's ridiculous. Everything is ideologically correct with him. He has had no practical experience whatever. We'll have to hit the police and the army to get weapons. Infiltrate somehow. The Party has no arms to speak of. We've got to get our hands on guns. Soon."

"What about him?"

"That's not your area of responsibility."

"All right."

"Make your contact outside tonight. They'll have telephones at this place. Tell them we need more money. American dollars and Costa Platan reales. As much as they can send us."

"Anything else?"

"Just say that I'll report in full later this week."

The Belgian called Coco shuffled out into the corridor, yawning and bracing himself against the pitching of the train.

"They woke me up. What a racket. Like a bunch of parrots."

The three men stood, their shoulders touching, leaning out of the window. The dry air rushed at them, a steady buffeting against their faces. They stared at the bare, broken stones, an immense field of tumbled rock that stretched away to heat-shimmered hills in the distance. The sky was as blue and solid as porcelain baked by the sun. Voget's watch hands crept forward.

"When was the last time you were here, Coco? Five years ago?"

"Nearly eight. I was a kid. I worked as a time checker. They were building the southern line then. This line up to the mines is older. You can tell. They don't know how to keep up the roadbed, these people."

The train slowed and shunted drunkenly through a series of switches. Steel parallels swung toward them and away again. Voget squinted against the rush of air.

"What's this place we're coming to?"

"Casanueva. A railroad junction. Where the main and southern lines join. We'll get off at the next stop. Vera Cruz. Where are you going, chief?"

"To see if I can get a map of this place. We may need it. You never know. Want anything? Henri?"

"Some beer, if they have any. This heat dries my throat."

The train crawled forward for a few moments and then jarred to a stop. Voget walked the length of the car and dropped down to the cinder-strewn platform. The heat made him squint. It was like standing in an oven. A conductor in a cheap cotton uniform stood fanning himself with a folded newspaper.

"How many minutes here?"

The conductor shrugged his shoulders.

"Ten minutes. A quarter of an hour. Until we are ready."

Voget strode out of the sun into the narrow belt of shade thrown down by the corrugated roof over the platform. A mixed crowd stood and squatted there, surrounded by their baggage and farm produce. They looked like survivors of a shipwreck on a thin, dark island, marooned in a sea of heat. He stepped over and around them, making his way slowly toward a low, new building of gleaming blue and silver tiles. He pushed open the door and looked around for a canteen. Two big propellers turned slowly on the ceiling, stirring the dead, hot air. The place was half filled with small brown men squatting on the floor, smoking. They stared at the Belgian, their dark, tilted eyes expressionless.

Voget bought four bottles of tepid beer and asked for a map. At first the counterman denied that there were such things. Voget asked him to look carefully. Perhaps in the back room, or along the counter

30

where magazines were sold? The counterman went for his superior. Outside, the heavy locomotive hissed, and voices squabbled. A porter dragged a wagon loaded with wicker cages. Inside the cages crouched dusty chickens, stupefied by the heat.

"Señor."

The counterman placed a fly-specked pamphlet before Voget, a street map of Casanueva, "City of Light and Progress." Voget turned the pages. Most of the streets were indicated by dotted lines, apparently projected or uncompleted construction. But the rail junction and marshaling yards, the switches and bridge locations were carefully drawn. Another page showed the position of Casanueva in relation to both the capital city and the silver mines. Voget placed a coin on the counter and picked up the beer bottles.

An odd sound, half cheer, half moan, swirled through the waiting room. Voget turned. The small brown men were now kneeling on the floor, facing a tall, stooped man dressed in a coarse woolen shirt, canvas trousers bound with leggings, and broken boots. Glittering black hair fell straight to his muscle-humped shoulders. In one dark claw he held a sheet of paper. Voget looked at the counterman.

"A chief of bandits?"

The man grinned and tapped his temple.

"*El padre loco*. The crazy priest. From the mines."

"Ah. The one called Don Ramos."

The counterman nodded and tapped his temple again. Voget stared, impressed and dismayed. This was the man who controlled the miners. Don Ramos, once a priest, long ago excommunicated. Voget had been told only that the man was trusted both by the operators of the mine and the Indian laborers themselves.

He made a sound like someone grinding two stones together. One of the Indians bent forward and touched his brow to the dusty floor. Then he sprang to his feet and stood there, marked like one of the devout on Ash Wednesday. The ex-priest, apparently, was reading their names, telling them off into groups of six or seven. When all the small men stood, all brow-badged with dust, the ex-priest flung out his arm toward the train. At once all the miners ran out of the room, their bare feet slapping the floor. The locomotive bell panged. The ex-priest stalked out through the door. A woman crossed herself as he passed, walking slowly, one leg slightly stiffened, his heavy shoulders hunched. He halted under the shade of the platform roof. The people waiting there edged away. He stood staring down the line of cars. Voget walked in front of him, to see his face. Two eyes like chips of anthracite glared out into the heat. The ex-priest's nose was big and broken thick at the bridge. The left nostril was notched. A full, sensual mouth drooped at the corners, and deep creases gashed his dark skin from the wings of his nostrils to the mouth corners and down into a thin tangle of beard on his blunt chin.

The Indians swarmed aboard the cars, ignoring the shouts and kicks of the conductors. Men bellowed in protest out through the open carriage windows. The compact knots of brown bodies swept down the corridors and forced open the compartment doors. Voget began to run. One of the beer bottles slipped from his hand and plushed into foamy fragments on the platform. A woman wailed, and one of the conductors swung a lantern into the faces of a small gang of miners. Their hard little hands seized him and dragged him down the steps. He sprawled at Voget's feet, cursing furiously and waving the lapel torn from his jacket. The Indians sprang into the carriage, and Voget plunged up the steel steps behind them, one beer bottle held in his hand like a grenade. The locomotive bell beat an alarm.

↓

Fingel dreamed. He lay in a chair in the office of a dentist, but his body was strapped and his head fixed so that he could not move. He could see only a white table. His briefcase lay on it, surrounded by a scatter of tools. A man in a uniform and cap stood with his broad back to Fingel. *What are you doing? I am the doctor. What are you doing? Sir, that's my case. You refuse to open it. I must operate. I must see inside. But there's nothing . . . I must operate.*

The doctor turned and his face was that of the police official in Danzig. He had a knife in his hand. He brought his flat, broad face close to Fingel and raised the knife. *What do you care? You've been operated on once before.* The knife stole across Fingel's brow and the doctor reached up thick fingers and peeled the flesh down over Fingel's eyes. *You are lucky to have such a caul.*

Fingel thrashed awake, clutching his face and sputtering Polish. A tilted dark eye stared into his own. Fingel's hands pressed the handkerchief against his cheeks. A brown face dipped behind a screen of straight, black hair. A hand plucked again at the handkerchief. Fingel struggled to stand up. He was pressed back into his seat. The fat woman with the mustache began to scream that she was being raped. A gang of dark bodies wrestled through the compartment. Fingel struck out blindly, the handkerchief balled in his fist. The hand flashed back at him. He ducked, and the derby sailed off his head. The hand caught it in midair. White teeth flashed and giggled. The dark people plunged out of the compartment. Fingel stood up and stepped on the fat woman's foot. She screamed again. He blundered out into the corridor, waving his briefcase and shouting. He ran heavily a dozen strides and halted. Three Indians, their faces blank of expression, stood blocking the corridor. Beyond them another whirled in a dance, Fingel's derby on his head, his dark hair whipping as he spun.

Bodies came crashing out of the next compartment. A white face, yanked long and howling with fear and rage, hung from a quivering neck. An arm struck the nearest Indian with a loaf of bread. Pieces of crust shattered into the corridor. Glass broke somewhere. The white face shrieked.

"She is my fiancée!"

The miners had abducted a woman! Fingel bounded forward and landed a slapping blow with his briefcase. The Indians fled down the corridor. Fingel bowed politely before a very tall, trembling young man.

"And they have stolen my hat, as well! Let's help each other."

The white face turned toward him. A girl in a scarlet dress cringed in one corner of the compartment. An old man sat on the floor fingering a smashed cigarette. Fingel felt something hard thrust against his belly. He backed away, raising his hands.

"I am a citizen of France."

The young man flung the stump of bread at him and slammed the compartment door. Fingel blinked and dusted crumbs from his shirt. His hat. He would suffer sunstroke without it. He turned and trotted down the corridor, across the steel-slabbed platform and into the next car. A group of men were heaving together there, as though pushing something the length of the car. Voices roared, and bare arms flickered and fell like clubs. Feet pounded, and a police whistle squealed. Fingel was knocked breathless against the door of the toilet. A soldier with a rifle held butt foremost pushed past him and began jabbing the backs of the heaving men. The toilet door snapped open, and Fingel fell into the arms of a stocky man with a revolver.

"Don't! Don't!"

The man kicked the door shut and locked it. He motioned for Fingel to sit down. Fingel perched there, flapping his hands and giggling. The man with the revolver was one of the Belgians from the ship.

"Please. I was just chasing them. They stole my hat."

"Eh? It's you again. My God. What do they want? Have they gone crazy?"

"I don't know. Maybe. I was asleep and dreaming. A terrible dream."

"Shut up, will you?"

"Of course."

"Maybe it's a riot. Who are they?"

"Indians. From the silver mines. This train goes there. To the mines. Listen, there are police and soldiers. Hide that. You'll be in trouble if they catch you."

The Belgian nodded.

"It isn't even mine."

"I should hope not."

"Shut up."

"Of course."

"Why are you following us, eh?"

"Oh, I'm not. Not at all. One of them took my hat. Excuse me, I must go get it."

"Stay here."

The Belgian seemed confused. He passed the revolver from hand to hand, staring around the cubicle.

"The chief will kill me if he knows I took this. The damned taxi driver we had gave it to me. Here, put it in your case."

"Oh, no, no. No, please. I'm just a businessman. They might ask me to open this and—"

"Take it."

The Belgian showed Fingel a big clasp knife. Fingel tried to think of something to say. The Belgian thrust the revolver into his pocket. It lay against Fingel's hip like a rock.

"Is . . . is it loaded?"

"Come on."

The Belgian dragged Fingel to his feet, opened the door and shoved him out into the corridor. A soldier stood there with a rifle. He grinned and shook his head.

"What a time to be doing that! And no towels, either. Get back to your compartments before I arrest you for committing an immoral act."

He laughed delightedly and slammed his rifle butt at the Belgian. It caught him on the tip of the shoulder and drove him against the wall. Fingel ran. At the end of the corridor he turned. The Belgian slumped against the wall, clutching his shoulder, his face puckered with pain. The soldier laughed, bent and picked up a sheet of paper from the floor. Fingel suddenly noticed that the corridor was strewn with paper. The soldier handed it to the Belgian.

"Here, wipe your chin!"

Fingel hurried out of the carriage. A policeman stopped him.

"Where are you going?"

"One of the miners stole my hat."

"Too bad. Back to your carriage."

"I am French."

"What?"

"I say I am a French citizen. I am a tourist. My compartment is this way."

"Oh, pass, then. But be careful."

The floor of the next car was covered with paper, too. Fingel peered cautiously ahead. The corridor was empty. He picked up a sheet. It was marked at the top with a scarlet, blunt-topped letter A. He glanced at the printing. *Freedom . . . a decade of terror and tyranny . . . immediate federation of all provinces . . . the rights of citizens . . . foreign intervention . . . O'Conner . . . brutality . . . land . . . Movimiento Liberal . . . Abajo Vizarra! Viva Alessandro! Arriba Costa Plata!* Fingel dropped the sheet to the floor and wiped his fingers gently on his shirt. A soldier pounded down the corridor toward him, a packet of pamphlets on his shoulder. Fingel dodged aside, his heart fluttering. He could hear the locomotive bell banging like a blacksmith gone mad. He walked down the corridor, trying not to step on the pamphlets, as though he expected the sheets of crudely printed paper to adhere to his shoes. He peeped in through the glass panels of the compartment doors. No one seemed to have his derby.

By the time Voget reached the compartment, the platform was covered with police and soldiers. More soldiers guarded a dozen miners in the corridor. The small brown men squatted, their hands clasped on top of their heads. Rota was yelling out the window, and the four young men were smoking nervously. When the Belgian slid open the door, they sprang at him like hounds. Coco stood on his seat staring down at a policeman and shaking his head.

"Je ne parle pas espagnol . . ."

A voice called from the platform, and Rota bellowed. Voget pushed past the young men. The ex-priest stood on the platform, his ugly hands locked piously at his breast. He said something in his hard, croaking voice. Rota screamed back. The union official's face was crimson. A blood vessel ridged his wet forehead. Voget caught one of the young men by the arm.

"What are they saying?"

"They are discussing the former professions of their mothers."

In one corner of the compartment a miner huddled. He wore a derby, and blood streamed from his split lips. One of the young men kicked him. The policeman grunted. He tapped Voget with his notebook.

"Your name?"

"Je ne parle pas espagnol."

Cadenced footsteps slapped on the platform. A squad of soldiers marched past the window. Formed into a square, they surrounded two men in blue suits. Both men were handcuffed. A truck ground up to the platform. More soldiers began throwing bundles of leaflets into the truck. The soldiers marched out of sight. The police officer scowled at Voget and scribbled something in his notebook.

"Where are the others, Coco?"

"In the next compartment, I guess. What happened, chief?"

"How would I know?"

"Your name?"

"Fingel. Herman Fingel. Tourist. I have come for my hat."

Voget turned around. It was the Jew from the ship. The policeman wrote in his notebook. The Jew smiled uneasily and edged toward the corner of the compartment. The policeman shifted to block him.

"Your passport, please?"

"Right here . . . one moment."

Someone bumped into Voget, throwing him off balance. Coco jumped down from the seat. Everyone talked at once.

"Henri! What happened?"

The Belgian who came in sat down carefully, holding his left shoulder. His face was pale with pain.

"One of these fascists hit me with a rifle."

"Your passport, please?"

"As you can see, he is wearing my hat . . ."

"*Tu madre!*"

"*Y tu abuela!*"

"I think it's broken. The bastard. He was drunk."

"What happened?"

"In a coffin. The pamphlets were in a coffin. The two men are of the M.L."

"Officer, these men are tourists. They have been invited by the Unión de Trabajadores—"

"They will be shot."

The policeman shrugged and spoke with Rota. The ex-priest turned and walked stiffly away. The miner in the corner moaned. Fingel captured his derby.

"I beg your pardon. We meet again. A coincidence. Personally, I dislike violence."

The policeman dragged the miner out of the compartment. Rota sat down and closed his eyes. The four young men surrounded him, offering wine and cigars. The Belgian groaned. Coco took off his belt and made a sling. Voget shrugged.

"You can complain at the consulate, Henri."

"Sure, sure. Listen, chief, that Jew is a spy. I was in the toilet and he broke down the door."

The locomotive sniffed, and the car couplings clashed down the train. A whistle blew three hoarse blasts. The train began to move. Voget dragged the young men apart. One of them hissed at him like a snake.

"What was this madness?"

Rota waved his hands helplessly.

"Anarchy. The movement has collapsed into anarchy."

"What are you talking about?"

"Two men of the M.L. were on the train. With a coffin in the baggage car. Filled with propaganda. And some weapons. Somehow, Ramos found out about it. He is betraying the working classes to the police. But the police themselves refused to act. So he told his miners to find the two men. They traveled together, you see. One had a glass eye. The Indians believe that the blind are evil, they have been so afflicted because they have looked as children into the face of Vigo.

The police would not make an arrest. They had been bribed. But they had not been bribed to ignore a riot. So they arrested the two men. But not the miners. Who can tell? All the Indians look alike. They are reactionary. Ramos is a traitor to his class."

"How well do you know him?"

"Only slightly. Twice he has refused to bring the miners into the U.T. He fosters every superstition. And now he is betraying us. He must be liquidated, comrade, it's the only solution."

The four young men nodded solemnly. Rota smiled at the injured Belgian.

"Have courage, comrade. Where we are going there will be plenty of doctors. And pretty nurses, too. The professional classes have pledged themselves to the struggle against fascism."

The Belgian grinned weakly and shook his head.

"I didn't dare hit him back, chief."

Voget shrugged.

"You can do your work with only one arm, Henri."

"Sure, chief. You can count on me. Is that the beer?"

"What? Oh. Yes. Here."

Voget gave the injured man the bottle. It was nearly empty. He sucked down the tepid suds. Voget rumpled his wet hair. The top of his head was sticky. He had spilled the beer all over himself. He sat down. Something that felt like a stone was under his left buttock. He reached under himself. It was a revolver.

He handed it to the nearest young man.

"Here, comrade, this must be yours."

Coco started to laugh.

"I thought they were monkeys. A whole herd of monkeys."

Voget forced a smile.

"They have nothing to lose but their chains."

The young man thrust the revolver into his pocket and nodded soberly.

"The train stops next at Vera Cruz. A stronghold of Catholics."

"What will *they* do to us?"

"Pardon, comrade?"

"Nothing. Christ, what a country . . ."

"Pardon, comrade?"

"I said soon there will be no Christ in this country."

The young man nodded soberly again.

"And no foreigners, either. Costa Plata for the Costa Platans."

He saluted with a clenched fist. The train jolted slowly up a long grade. Voget leaned back and closed his eyes. He was exhausted.

When the train stopped at Vera Cruz, the fat woman arose and waddled out of the compartment. Fingel followed her, still apologizing for having stepped on her foot. The woman was a widow with a tubercular son at the sanatorium. She had shared her lunch with Fingel and told him how her husband had died in the same sanatorium. Fingel had been moved nearly to tears. The widow lowered herself down the steps, wheezing and apprehensive. Fingel handed her the small suitcase and paper sack.

"Go with God, señora."

"They have collapsed his left lung."

"It must be part of the cure."

The woman tucked the paper sack under her arm, an arm cased in silk like a black sausage. She shook her head.

"The cure is to delay death. The cure is suffering. I pray that God will take him soon."

Fingel opened his mouth, but could think of nothing to say.

Beside the station stood three ambulances. The Belgians were there, with four men in black suits. They stood watching while the attendants loaded the injured one into the back of the ambulance. The other Belgians climbed in after him. The others entered the second ambulance. Fingel stood on the platform for a moment, puzzled. Then he shrugged and went back to his compartment. A young man in a black suit had taken the fat widow's place. Fingel sat down very gently, his heart jerking. The young man smiled.

"Are you going far?"

"To the mines. Just to the mines."

"Ah? You work there?"

"No. I work . . . for myself."

"May one ask what is it you do? This work?"

Fingel told him. He could sense that the young man did not believe him.

↓

Rafael Obregón Vizarra y Salán, Caudillo of Costa Plata by the grace of God, walked slowly through the scented symmetry of the gardens behind the west wing of the palace. The Caudillo was restless. He had never felt at ease in the palace and gardens built in the eighteenth century for the Viceroy when Costa Plata was a colony of Spain. Everything was too big, too blank, in the style the archbishop called Hispanic Anonymous. The reception rooms, dining rooms and private chambers were as mathematical as the flower beds planted outside the heavy stone building. The archbishop had once pointed out that the palace was the product of economy. It had been built not for the first Viceroy but for all of them. Constructed for all, it suited none. It had been built too big, so as to make additions unnecessary. It was a warehouse to store and display imperial Spain. Vizarra had constructed a villa ten miles from the city and lived there, using the palace only for official functions, fewer functions every year.

The Caudillo had plucked a gardenia and wore it in the lapel of his thin, white linen suit. His right hand jerked nervously, touching his gold beltbuckle, his tie clasp, a cuff button, the tip of his pale blue necktie, his beltbuckle again. The diamond ring on his little finger glittered coldly. The Caudillo had been pressed by his Swiss physician to give up cigars. For an irritable week he had not touched tobacco. He longed for one of his thin, dark cheroots. He walked down a gravel path to the trellis where fuschia trailed from hanging pots. He tore off a strand and rolled the red-and-white blossoms between his fingers, mashing the petals and dropping the ruined flowers to the path. His stomach twinged. It was the rich food.

The luncheon had been elaborate, attended by all the members of the Cabinet (except O'Conner) as well as the three foreigners. Jellied consommé with sherry, lobster salad drenched in mayonnaise with Pouilly Fuissé, fried potato puffs, ice cream *bombe* with the finest champagnes, coffee with Costa Plata brandy. Vizarra disliked foreigners in general as exploiters with unpleasant manners and anti-Catholic tendencies. They operated their concessions with unconcealed greed and despised the people they employed. Most of them could not or would not speak Spanish. As a final insult, they forced him to eat foods that distressed him in a building that displeased him. The American drank iced water. Herzler, as usual, ate loudly and overpraised the brandy. Only the Englishman, Duncan Livermore, understood that the luncheon was not really a meal. He had tasted everything, eaten almost nothing, and conversed steadily with calm correctness. His questions had been few, respectfully phrased and to the point. Livermore, obviously, would be the most difficult to persuade. With the Americans one could always make a "deal." Herzler was a known quality, simply more anxious now that his government was in severe economic difficulties. His anxiety could be played upon. A French mining firm had made an offer to run the silver mines. Herzler would have to better their proposal.

The Caudillo sat down on a stone bench, his hands cupping his knees. He stared at the brilliant flower beds without seeing the rich blooms. The sultry air smothered the city sounds. Even for the hour of siesta it was too quiet. O'Conner had called for instructions and had been told to wait until the papers he had forwarded were studied. Vizarra drew out his watch and glanced at it, a gift from Lucía, as slender as a wafer, a perfect little machine with a miniature of herself inside the cover. Light, brisk steps, like the progress of an animal, scratched the gravel. Vizarra looked up. Malata was punctual, as always. He carried two dispatch boxes with him, one in each hand, the blue from the Office of the Interior, the black from O'Conner's secret police. Malata bowed.

"Good afternoon, Excellency."

"They've gone, Julio?"

"Mr. Livermore to visit his office manager, Ferguson. Mr. Dunkel back to the ship for the siesta, for a nap, he calls it. Herr Herzler has gone to eat sherbet with the archbishop and to discuss archeology. The automobiles will deliver them to the villa at four o'clock. Also the Minister of the Interior. Two hours of preliminary discussions of the new agreements and leases. Cocktails from six until seven. Dinner, followed by the dancers, followed by the display of fountains. A light supper, and they will leave shortly after midnight."

"All right. The jewels?"

"They have been removed from the vault and taken to the villa by O'Conner personally. He just telephoned. He sounded in pain. The jewels are such a temptation for him, Excellency. He actually suffers."

The Caudillo smiled and nodded.

"That is why he must carry the jewels himself. Each time he punishes himself, proving his loyalty."

"I do not think he will ever steal them, Excellency."

"If he steals as he has in the past, one day he will steal the jewels. Or try to steal them."

"*Try* to steal them, yes."

"What does he say?"

"There is no evidence of the Unión de Trabajadores having anything whatever to do with the longshoremen's strike."

"He means he has not yet found the evidence. Go on."

"Rota has left the city for the sanatorium. His doctor's orders."

"There is nothing the matter with Rota."

"An X-ray plate reveals a shadow on the right lung."

"Go on."

"Seventeen persons have been arrested for vagrancy. All gang leaders of the longshoremen. They will be bound over by the court until Tuesday of next week, due to the fiesta."

"The fiesta. That's when he will make his move. During the fiesta. They are still looking for him?"

"Of course, Excellency. But in thirteen years he will have changed greatly. There are no records of fingerprints. Only two photographs, the one taken in London, the other in Paris. Everyone in the country recognizes the photographs."

"But no one recognizes Alessandro. How strange."

"Young Carlos Sánchez has definitely left Mexico City."

"He is here, too, then."

"Presumably. O'Conner wishes to know if Your Excellency desires the Minister of Public Education arrested."

"Old Sánchez? Of course not. He is to conduct Mr. Dunkel on a tour of the city schools and orphanages. Herr Herzler declines politely to accompany him. It is just as well. The orphans have already seen Herzler twice."

"General Vola has prolonged the maneuvers of the First Army Group west of Casanueva for no reason whatever."

"He is either drunk or has found a woman or both. Order him to return tomorrow, the troops to follow by train. They are to drill for the parade."

"Yes, Excellency."

"You have notified the National Guard of their duties during the fiesta?"

"Yesterday at eleven o'clock, Excellency. The Red Beret dinner is tomorrow night. The foreigners have been invited, as you requested. The secretary asks for a seating order."

"All three on my right. Livermore, then Dunkel, then Herzler."

"It will cause great offense to the senior members of the Red Beret, Excellency."

"Julio, I have spent thirteen years giving great offense to the senior members of the Red Beret. I do not want the foreigners here any more than they do. Less, most likely. The point is that they are to be kept occupied. Constantly. I want them tired. Is that so difficult to comprehend?"

"Of course not, Excellency."

"Livermore, no doubt, rides horseback. See to it that he observes all-day cavalry maneuvers tomorrow. Have someone invite him during cocktails this evening."

"Perhaps he does not ride, Excellency."

"All Englishmen of Livermore's wealth ride horses, Julio, believe me. It is the fashion. It has been the fashion for years. Therefore it is still the fashion. An Englishman will allow his wife a divorce rather than part with his horses."

"You are very witty, Excellency. But if he refuses?"

"Take him to a rehearsal of the ballet. Take steps for introductions. As for Dunkel . . . I will talk with him. He is from Chicago. I don't know what to do with him, yet. Perhaps a visit to the cattle ranches in the *campo*. I will trust the archbishop to fatigue Herzler. His Grace is an expert. Ten minutes in his presence and I am exhausted. Anything else?"

"The signs have been painted over or removed."

"That is O'Conner's solution, is it? He cannot find Alessandro, so he wipes paint off walls. Tell him to . . ."

"Yes, Excellency?"

"I was going to say have him work through the U.T., cancel the working cards and issue new ones. But that will take weeks. The fiesta is only four days away. Give O'Conner five hundred thousand reales. Tell him to hire more men. Get me the secretary of the Red Beret on the telephone. They might as well start looking for Alessandro, too. They do nothing else useful. Every party member will consider himself personally responsible for discovering the whereabouts of Alessandro. Tell O'Conner to find Alessandro before the fiesta begins! Today! Tomorrow! The next day! Find him!"

"And what if he fails, Excellency?"

"Then O'Conner becomes your responsibility, Julio."

"I understand. Will you consider the proposals from the Office of the Interior now?"

"After I talk with the Red Beret. Bring the box to my office."

Malata bowed.

The Caudillo stood up and paced toward the palace, his hands locked behind his back. He stopped.

"The dress, Julio? It has been sent?"

"It was removed from the ship this morning, Excellency, and delivered to her personal maid. I have the receipts."

"Very good."

The Caudillo walked away. Malata dropped the black dispatch box to the stone bench and plucked a gardenia. He placed it in the lapel of his black suit. He had neglected to tell the Caudillo of the riot provoked by Ramos and his Indian miners. Also at Casanueva. O'Conner was holding both the men. Unfortunately, it seemed that one of the two men taken was a priest. It did not seem the time to bring this to the attention of either Vizarra or His Grace. Perhaps tomorrow. Malata moved, dark and swift, across the gravel walks to the telephone room on the ground floor of the palace.

⊥

The Costa Plata office of the Livermore Lines Ltd. was a four-story whitewashed stone building in Calle Simón Bolívar. A fountain splashed in the cool patio, and from an open window came the clatter of typewriters. Livermore had been shown through the various sections: passage-booking bureau, baggage and freight department, bookkeeping, employee dining room and managerial suites. Even granting that his visit had been prepared for, with Ferguson no doubt making a series of little speeches, bucking up the staff and telling them they must all look smart and step lively, Livermore was fully satisfied. The taciturn little Scot was an ideal office manager. The building was clean, uncluttered and quiet. The work was done promptly with a minimum of fuss. The native employees all spoke English. Ferguson was obviously respected, even liked, by his inferiors. The man had been a purser for years on the *Silver Princess,* the firm's world cruise ship. After that, perhaps anything was easy. More important, though, was that Ferguson had not succumbed to the traditional torpor of Costa Plata. Electric fans blew across great cakes of gray ice that melted in buckets specially fixed to the walls. The manager's own office contained one desk, two chairs, a telephone. On the wall hung an etching of the *Silver Princess*. Livermore sat, accepted a cigarette and a light, and gazed approvingly at his employee. Ferguson struck a wooden match and sucked the flame into the bowl of his pipe.

"I find myself satisfied, Ferguson. Quite satisfied."

"We try to keep things running Bristol fashion, sir. Sorry about the strike. They just popped it on us. Of course, it's not a real strike. A walkout, call it. They'll be back on tomorrow. A few heads will be knocked, but you can't hurt a black that way, you know, sir. I was told Brown brought her in just beautiful."

"Captain Brown is a first-class seaman in every respect."

"He put the laugh on them, anyway. And a good job."

"Have you any thoughts on what provoked the walkout, Ferguson?"

"Yes and no, sir. There's been a lot of hugger-mugger about this Alessandro. I don't know that it's that. These blacks are a techy lot. They row on and off with the customs chappies. There's a dustup from time to time. No more than that, I'd say."

"I see. Have you ever met His Excellency?"

Ferguson raised his brows and sucked on his pipe for a moment.

"I've seen him, sir. Met him never. Nor will I, I think. You must know, sir, he doesn't fancy any but his own people."

"He struck me as very cordial."

"Oh, I daresay, sir. But that's his way."

"The operation of the firm is not in any way disturbed by his government, though. I am sure of that. You would have notified London."

"Twice a year they audit the books. Twice a year we pay them what's due. No more than that."

"I suspect we have you to thank, then. Most foreign concessions are ticklish."

The Scot stroked his chin and nodded.

"Aye, they can be, sir. The mines is that way. There's something you should know about that, sir. *Our* hands is clean, but not everything is . . . well, honest."

"Not honest, Ferguson?"

"It isn't my business to pry, sir. I mind our shop—your shop, that is. I keep a weather eye open and the cotton from my ears, though.

45

You never know in a country like this. Well, I heard . . . I won't say how . . . I've no proof of the matter."

"Go on."

"The major freight shipped out of the city goes along the north railroad line. All the way to the mines. Everything you can think of. A great amount of equipment, parts and so on is for the mines proper. Now, the mining concession pays regular rates, depending on the cars used, both the number of cars and the type. Boxcar so much per kilometer. Flatcar, gondolas, the same. Now, then, the rest is rented. By the government. Passenger carriages and freight wagons, too. It's the freight they've been shaving on. Double-rating, you see. They rents the same cars twice. A boxcar with timber for the mines, say, with rates paid for by the mining folk. The same car rented to, oh, the government cement plant, let's call it. Supposed to be shipped separate. They overload, ship both in the same car. The mining folk and the railroad concession split the rent they get paid by the government. Sometimes they bill the government for rent for empty cars. Usually on the way into the city. Who's to know? Half the time the farmers ride in the empty cars with their stuff down to the markets. Since they don't pay passenger fare, the railroad tacks on a few empties at Casanueva and runs them in, charging the government full rent for the trip from the mines to the city. Casanueva ain't but half the trip, you see?"

"How long has this been going on, Ferguson?"

"Long enough for them to come at me, sir."

"How do you mean?"

"Well, we could rent the government a few hundred cubic feet of air on every bottom in and out of the port, sir. In five years the pounds would add up from the odd shilling taken here, there and the next time round."

"I see. And you're quite sure this isn't being done?"

"Not that I know of, sir. I know to the inch what the holds will take on every ship we've got. We double-check every manifest. We measure deck space, when it's taken. Our hands is clean."

"Does the government know of this? What's being done on the railroad?"

"I should think the Old Man must have slipped if he don't know it."

"The Old Man?"

"His Highness. Vizarra. Him and his Yank bully-boy."

46

"An American? One of Dunkel's people informs against the concession to Vizarra's government?"

"No, it's O'Conner, I mean, sir. He came here some five year ago. He was wanted up there. Murder, I suppose. The local police caught him. The Yanks wanted him back. To stretch his neck. Word went that he drowned trying to escape. The Yank consul was fooled. And O'Conner was made head of the secret police."

"I see. That's very bad, isn't it?"

"It's not good, sir. You can't touch pitch, as the saying goes . . ."

"Vizarra will naturally assume, then, that we have been falsifying rentals along with the others."

"You see how it is, sir."

"I do. And now I wish to know exactly what this office has done to protect the firm against this sort of charge."

"Our Mr. Williams has every cargo manifest, bill of lading, receipt, credit slip from the time we began operations. We also have an approximate figure quarterly on the smuggling in and out of Boca Perro."

"I recall your reports. Go on."

"The fishermen there bribe the Coast Guard and bring in goods from nonconcession bottoms beyond the three-mile limit. We don't carry more than a thousand cases of cigarettes a year. Yet everyone in the country smokes Yank fags."

"You mean that the government is failing to abide by our prior agreement?"

"I mean the firm's loss is fifteen thousand pounds per annum, sir!"

"Times ten."

"Times ten, sir. His High Horse can stop the smuggling, if he's a mind."

"Can he, though? We must be sure of that, Ferguson. I have no intention of charging His Excellency with collusion."

"He might not see it that way, sir. A bit of extra silver in the pockets of the fishermen. He don't care if we're short. Not a bit."

"Well, what do you propose, Ferguson? That we take over the smuggling concession as well?"

"It could be done, sir. Honest, I mean. We've got the dock space for a half-dozen small, coastwise cargo vessels. Shallow-draft for the river to the south. Single-screw. Something like our colliers back home, sir. We'd have no competition."

"Not if we had a coastwise concession. We'd have a monopoly, just as we now have for high-seas freight and passenger service."

"We'd put a dozen so-called captains on the beach for a few months. They'd come to us for work. We could take them on as mates. We'd want our own people as captains, sir."

"Indeed. And the dozen or so little craft now operating we could buy at auction."

"For pennies on the pound, sir."

"All this is excellent, Ferguson, but I fail to see how this would check the smuggling. It would cut our loss, to be sure. Of course, if our little fleet stood out beyond the three-mile limit—"

"With, say, a Royal Navy frigate cruising. Just cruising, you know, sir."

"Simply protecting the property of British citizens . . ."

"A *show* of force ain't *force,* sir. The nonconcession bottoms might think it's a good idea to stand farther out."

"Who are these nonconcession shippers, Ferguson?"

"Ah, Greeks. French. British, too, I think. Carrying whiskey. There's an uncommon amount of whiskey in Costa Plata. Cheap, too."

"Do you purchase smuggled whiskey, Ferguson?"

"Not lately, sir. Not lately, at all."

"I see. Well, I think you've given me an excellent bargaining position, Ferguson. Your company loyalty is to be commended."

"It's my job, sir."

"Quite so. Well, let's see our Mr. Williams about the cargo documents."

"Will you come to tea, sir? My missus has been after me. To invite you, you know."

"That's extraordinarily kind of you, Ferguson, but I'm afraid not today. I'm due at His Excellency's villa at four. I shall just have time to examine the papers here."

"I've had copies made of everything, sir."

"I don't want copies. They can be . . . adjusted, as you know. I'll take the originals along with me, if you don't mind. I'm afraid I'll have to ask you to step along out there with me."

"Well, I've no soup and fish, sir. No dinner clothes. The mold got 'em."

"That won't be necessary. I'm sure arrangements can be made to get you to your home at the end of the meeting. You have a company car, of course."

"Aye."

"Mr. Williams, then."

Ferguson nodded and knocked out his pipe. Both men stood.

"Right this way, sir."

⸸

By the time the full dark draped moist and cool over the city, everyone knew of the incident at Casanueva. The cafés were crowded, and men bent over beaded glasses of beer and talked. In the more expensive and more fashionable places, the talk was cautious, skeptical.

"It's all exaggeration. A few miners drunk on brandy, nothing more."

"But they arrested two men. One of them a priest."

"Who says one of them was a priest?"

"They do. Everyone says so."

"Even the priest?"

"Exactly. A story made up by the police to discredit the Church."

"Impossible. The Church takes no part in politics."

"It is known that the archbishop and Vizarra have never agreed."

"And why should they? Vizarra has separated the Church and the state. There is nothing for them to agree on."

"Besides, both men, if there were two men, were most likely foreigners."

"Man, what would foreigners be doing with a coffinful of pamphlets and firearms? M.L. pamphlets?"

"I have not seen these pamphlets. There was nothing in the newspapers, anyway."

"Do you expect to see such things?"

"Until I see it, I will not believe it."

"But everyone talks."

"Everyone always talks. But do they say the truth? No. When everyone talks, it is always lies. My brother, an official in the Office of the Interior, knows that Alessandro is not even in the country."

"Amazing. Your brother knows more than O'Conner. More even than the Old Mule."

"He knows what he knows."

49

Like certain plants that grow in the Southern swamps, the incident swelled and tangled in the darkness and burgeoned high above as the roots crept deep.

"The entire train set on fire—"

"They shot them both behind the railroad station—"

"The miners turned on Ramos. They nearly killed him. He escaped."

"The coffin was made for Alessandro. Black with silver fittings."

"The priest is the secretary of His Grace."

"All afternoon the miners fought the police. Dozens were killed."

"The miners drove the police away. It took the soldiers to stop the fighting—"

"At once the soldiers joined with the miners against the police."

"There were three men, not two. The third was Alessandro. He was in the coffin. He escaped."

"Both men are priests. Jesuits."

"There were two men. Neither was a priest."

"The railroad station was burned to the ground. Three women were raped."

The lights burned in the office of the Red Beret. Men in street clothes, others in the official party uniform of blue jackets and silver cavalry trousers and black boots, drank coffee. The smoke of cigars drifted through the rooms.

"That Ramos must be held responsible. One miner in five punished."

"The one they call the priest is an impostor. He must be shot as an example."

"Of course the police have not taken Alessandro. They assume him to be clever, rather than the coward he is."

"Clearly it is necessary to the name and sacred honor of the party for Alessandro and his gang to be taken by us. The secret police abuses its powers. The American must be dismissed. It is a moral wrong that the police are headed by a man who is not a Costa Platan."

"It is a question of organization. A house-by-house search in the city and in every village and town."

"And who will search the mountains?"

"The army."

"No, *we* must capture him. That's where he is. In the mountains."

50

"What time is the executive meeting?"

"In thirty minutes."

"I have time to go home and put on my uniform, then."

"It is an intolerable situation. The miners run wild, the Church allies with anarchists, and the police do nothing. It is up to the party to preserve national order and national dignity. His Excellency has ordered it. It must be done. It will be done."

"I say arrest the archbishop, too."

"You are joking."

"No one is joking. This is serious."

"I must go put on my uniform."

"Perhaps we should hold a rally at the football stadium."

"No, His Excellency has forbidden demonstrations."

"Since when does the party dance to every tune played by His Excellency? The Red Beret is autonomous."

"He must be found, that's all. And soon."

Bands of students appeared in the tenement districts near the waterfront. At first they serenaded in the streets outside the brothels, their voices in harmony to the thin music of mandolins. The women screeched down from the windows. The taverns and bars filled and emptied. The narrow streets that lay like slots through the tattered buildings echoed with voices sober and tipsy, shouting and singing songs. Children scuttled through the alleys. The hostile, sullen faces of the workers and longshoremen eased. The students grew loud and friendly over drink. They sang vulgar songs and made remarks, openly contemptuous of the government. A group from the Catholic Student Union knelt on the stones before the university chapel and prayed in unison for the release of the imprisoned priest. Night watchmen forced them away. They slipped into the poor quarter. The night grew clamorous, and the singing stopped. The chanting began. The Catholic students blundered into a fight with another group. Police vans pummeled down the ill-kept streets, the yellow headlights boring through the dark, the sirens sobbing. At ten o'clock all the lights in the city went off. Two dozen young men and three whores were arrested and driven off to the municipal prison. The singing began again, but drifted off, spinning away through the darkness, dissipating in the night. Oil lamps burned in the brothel windows, and business was excellent. The longshoremen drank behind the iron shutters and spoke in grim voices, as though the students had dumped a

51

potion in their glasses. The bars closed at midnight. Police in groups of three and four walked the dark streets, their boots slamming the rough pavement, their flashlights playing down the alley mouths, illuminating the freshly daubed signs: FREE HIM! THE CHURCH IS FREEDOM! PRIEST-MARTYR! CATHOLICS UNITE! There were pictures of O'Conner costumed like a Costa Plata mountain bandit crushing the cross beneath his boot, a dozen crude scribbles of a mule lettered VIZARRA-VENÉREO, and everywhere the letters M.L. and the blunt-topped letter A.

⸸

The waiter stripped off his soiled jacket and hung it behind the bar. He washed his face in the sink and said good-night to the owner. The owner was counting the money and grunted. The waiter pushed open the side door and stepped out into the dark alley. His legs ached, and he was afraid. He stumbled out of the alley into the street.

"Curro García?"

The waiter turned, his heart ramming wildly. He reached in his pocket for his knife. He walked backward. He saw an automobile parked across the street. Hands seized him from behind. He yelled, His wrist was driven up between his shoulder blades.

"Come on. Get him in the car."

"I haven't done anything! I haven't done anything!"

"Shut up, you dirty Red."

They dragged him to the car and flung him into the back seat. A fist punched him in the belly, driving the wind from his body at both ends. Somebody laughed and snapped handcuffs over his wrists. He gasped for breath, helpless. The car doors slammed, and the automobile surged down the street. Tears leaked down the waiter's cheeks.

⸸

The generator hammered in the cellar at the end of the row of cells. Secret police headquarters was lighted; every office, all the long, stale corridors lay under the harsh bath of burning bulbs. The man on the chair wept steadily, squinting into the spotlight.

O'Conner paced back and forth. "Listen, Father, we don't want to hurt you. You understand?"

"Yes."

"All we want to know is—"

"I have told you. I never saw him before. I received a telephone call, that's all. To meet him at the station."

"You knew there was no body in the coffin."

"I thought it was strange, that's all."

"Who called you?"

"I have told you that I don't know. Sometimes by letter, sometimes by telephone. I have never seen anybody. That's the truth."

"How long have you been a member of the M.L.?"

"A few years."

"How did you join?"

"My father was a member. He is dead now, so you can't get at him."

"I don't want him. I want other things. The names of the others at the seminary, Father. There were others at the seminary, weren't there?"

"Oh, I don't know."

"You mean you can't remember?"

"I don't know anything."

"You are lying, Father. I think you know a great deal."

"I know nothing."

"Where is he?"

"Who?"

"Alessandro."

"How would I know?"

"You're not very polite, Father. You're not a very good liar, Father. What kind of priest are you, anyway? Messing with politics. You read Red pamphlets instead of your office. What do you preach in the church? To kill people?"

"Of course not. That's your lesson, not mine. You are in a state of mortal sin."

"And you are in prison, Father."

O'Conner lit a cigarette and stared at the man on the chair. He had been questioning the priest for nearly two hours. The priest was a skinny, sallow-faced young man dressed in a shabby suit and a shirt with no necktie. He kept touching his neck.

"You don't want to see people suffer, do you, Father?"

"No."

"Would you like to hear your friend scream?"

"No."

"You would be responsible, Father—think of that. All I want is a few names. Because you won't give them to me, I will ask the other one. Your friend."

"I have told you that I never saw him before today. I don't even know his name."

"But he is from your parish."

"So it seems. Or so you say."

"We're going to work on him, Father. It's you who will make him suffer."

The priest wiped his streaming eyes. His thin lips curled in contempt. He unbuttoned his cheap jacket and threw it on the floor. He stretched out his arms.

"Work on me. He can tell you nothing. Get your whip, you gringo gangster!"

O'Conner chuckled.

"You're a tough one, eh, Father? You want to get hurt? All right. Take him back and bring in the other."

Two men stepped into the light and lifted the priest from his chair. They half carried him out of the room. In the corridor the priest and his guards met two more guards and the other man. The priest stared at him.

"God give you courage!"

The other man's face was white with fear. The guards opened a door and shoved the priest into the concrete-walled cell. The door boomed shut. The priest stood waiting. He began to sweat. He waited a minute, five minutes, ten minutes. Then he heard the first scream. The sound bit at him, fangs in his chest. Another scream, louder, louder, until it seemed impossible that one man could make such a noise without instantly dying. The voice sobbed and begged incoherently. There was silence. Then another shriek, short, dismayed. Then a low, animal howl that forced the priest's jaws open. The sound cracked and rose to a cry of agony, shrill and terrible. The priest shouted at the top of his own voice, a prolonged maddened yell. It was silent again. The other must have fainted. The priest began to pray, softly at first, but when the screaming began again, he bellowed at full power, trying to drive his words through the wall, down the corridors, past the door and into the very flesh that thrashed helplessly on the table he had seen in that room, a stained table with four leather cuffs, one at each corner, a table that had been used and used, a platform of pain. The priest knelt and clasped his hands in the center of his cell. The screams ripped at him, a muzzle worrying under his rib cage, snuffling for his heart. The priest tried to drown the screams with his own voice, but it was impossible. His prayers faltered, and he rocked on his knees, gnawing his clasped knuckles and shouting.

"Stop it! Stop it! *Stop it! Stop it!*"

He was sickened. He didn't know whether he called to the men standing around the table or to the man lying on it. He heard steps in the hall, and a new man's voice repeating dully the same sentence.

"I haven't done anything. I haven't done anything. I haven't done anything. . . ."

They put the new man in a cell down the corridor. At once they began to beat him. He began to make a high, creaking noise like the call of a strange bird. The priest slammed his fists against the door of his cell.

"Take *me!* Take *me!* Leave them alone, for the love of God!"

†

The *practicante* finished his examination and shrugged.

"No more for him."

O'Conner nodded. They unstrapped him. Someone threw a pair of bloody pliers into a pail of water. O'Conner switched off the spotlight. The *practicante* in his white, starched jacket and pants stood staring at the floor.

"Do you wish me to examine the other one, Señor O'Conner?"

"Clearly. That is your job, no?"

The young intern stared at O'Conner, his eyes gleaming with hatred.

"That is my job, yes."

Three men carried the slack body from the table and out through the door. Another swished a mop over the tiles. O'Conner lit a cigarette and waited. The door opened and a man came in.

"Well?"

"He says they were Belgians or French. Rota talked with one of them in French. But he doesn't know what they said. He says that Rota is a Communist. A cell leader, anyway, maybe higher. Isn't that like Rota? A cheap thief and a Red, too. What shall we do with this one?"

"He's a Red. Just a little fish."

"That's all. So?"

"Dump him back in front of the bar where he works."

The *practicante* stood in the door.

"What do you want?"

"You can't just leave him in the street. He is bleeding . . . inside. Internal hemorrhage."

"He got in a fight. He fell down. Too bad, eh?"

The young intern's face froze.

"Yes, too bad."

"How is the priest?"

"Oh, still praying. What did you learn from the other?"

"Nothing. Yet."

"Let me have him, eh?"

"Tomorrow, Raul. Now we talk to a couple of students, eh? You talk to them. Just *talk,* understand? I'll be in my office."

O'Conner stood up and walked down the corridor. The *practicante* huddled in his dispensary, his face buried in his stiff, white sleeves. O'Conner stopped a guard. He pointed at the glass door.

"That one is on duty until five. Don't let him go home. Lock him up."

"Yes, señor."

O'Conner climbed the flight of stairs and kicked open the door to his office. He poured whiskey from a bottle and drank it.

"Goddam dagos!"

He picked up the telephone, the private line to the Caudillo's villa.

☦

"Rafael?"

"Here, on the balcony, Lucía."

She brushed aside the billowing curtains and stepped out to join him. Her little heels tapped beneath the rustling bell of satin that fell from her waist. She swirled next to him and jerked the mantilla away from her hair. The diamond necklace glittered on her half-bare breast. He placed his large, blunt fingers around her small chin and turned her face to his. Her brow was pale in the moonlight, her eyes very dark, her lips dark too. He stared at the smooth arch of her brows, the unlined forehead. How beautiful she was, how young. His heart ached faintly, with the sadness one feels for a favorite child.

"Well, did you enjoy yourself, Lucía?"

"Yes. Except when you asked me to sing."

"You were very good. They *liked* you! Especially the American."

"Him!"

She made the slum brat's gesture of spitting over her shoulder.

"Please, don't ask me to sing again. For you alone, of course. But when you say 'Sing, Lucía,' something is wrong. I feel . . . that I'm back in some filthy nightclub. All this is a trick that has been played on me. A filthy nightclub with the manager waiting in my dressing room, and I know what I'll have to do to get a contract for another month."

"I am sorry, Lucía. You must forgive me. It is very stupid of me to display you. I only want others to see how beautiful you are. But I have not considered you at all."

"Let's talk about something else. You enjoyed the dancers?"

"As much as I ever do. With that Herzler chattering all the time, explaining the various dances to everyone, whether they want to listen or not."

"Dolores is going to the United States. To Hollywood. To dance in a motion picture."

"Ah. Would you like that?"

"Don't joke, please. You know I wouldn't. I want to be with you."

"You are so very beautiful, Lucía. Don't be sad."

She stared at him, her lashes dark against her moon-paled face. She brushed her warm, soft fingertips against his cheek.

"What is wrong? Something is happening. I feel it. Tell me, please."

"Nothing is happening. How can anything happen? You are tired."

She smiled, a lazy curve of her lips, her face half averted.

"No. I am not tired. Are you?"

Her voice was a soft, sensual drawl that touched him like a caress.

"My beautiful new dress. Very complicated to put on or take off. I have sent Anita to bed. But perhaps you are too tired?"

"Oh, no. Not at all."

She chuckled softly and moved until her dress brushed him and her breath beat softly against his face.

"Then you will undress me? It will take an hour."

"At least an hour."

He tried to draw her against him. She slipped away in a soft wash of satin, spinning until the dress flared, revealing her slender ankles.

57

He wanted to thrust his hands up, to crush through the layers of flimsy petticoats. She danced back to him and kissed his eyes and mouth.

"Now I will have one glass of champagne and wait for you above, *toro mío.*"

She kissed him again, her mouth open and soft, her slender thighs taut and pressing against him wantonly. Her nails nipped the flesh of his thick neck. He buried his face in her perfumed hair.

"Ah, Lucía . . ."

"Hurry to me, Rafael."

"Yes."

"I am nearly in pain. All night I have been unable to touch you, only to see you. When will these people leave?"

He kissed her face, her ears, and stroked her shoulders. He was aroused now and longed to tear open her bodice and fling her to the marble floor. He had once done so and recalled her frenzy, her wild protests and her moans as he ruthlessly took her. He was choking with desire.

"In four or five days . . ."

"Don't. Not here. Not tonight."

He released her. Her voice had sounded so frightened. He muttered something, staring at her hungrily. She cupped her breasts, lifting the bodice of her dress.

"This is so beautiful that I will not let you spoil it."

"I will be very careful. Now. At once."

"Can we go away? After they leave?"

"Yes . . . yes, of course. Where would you like to go?"

"Where this dress came from. Could we?"

"To . . . Paris? Not right away, but soon. Yes, I have . . . some things to clean up here. Some work to do."

"Leave it!"

"Lucía, I cannot! Don't beg it, please."

"Rafael, are you all right?"

"Quite all right. Go, now. I will be up. I will take some champagne, too."

"Excellency?"

Malata, speaking discreetly through the curtains.

"The telephone, Excellency. O'Conner."

"Yes, yes."

The girl slipped by Malata and walked quickly through the long

58

reception room. As she passed the piano, she ran her hand over a few keys, a dull rumble of bass notes. Her heels tapped away over the polished floor. Vizarra could sense his adviser and secretary waiting. He was always there, waiting, always patient, tireless, like a shadow. The Caudillo had grown increasingly cautious concerning Malata, once he recognized the fact that he depended on the young, dark man more than was safe. Gradually he had cut back on some of Malata's functions; certain duties had been handed back to Cabinet members, others he had simply allowed to lapse altogether. Lucía often replaced him at minor receptions, specifically those involving children. She was very good with children. And now she wanted to go to Paris.

The Caudillo released the balcony railing and flexed his fingers. Malata stood in the dim reception room, a telephone in his hands. Vizarra walked past him.

"I will speak with him from the small study."

Malata bowed.

"See that a small bottle of champagne is sent upstairs, Julio."

Malata did not bow. Vizarra walked away. It offended Malata's dignity to be treated as a butler. He did not like to remember the years when he was only the headwaiter of a third-rate nightclub, accepting small tips from an infantry major who came often to drink wine with several other junior officers.

Vizarra opened the door to his study and walked quickly to the bare desk. His eyes swept over the whitewashed walls. An enlarged photograph faced him. Himself, thirteen years ago, sitting in a staff car, a pistol strapped to his hip, a red beret on his head. In those days he had not worn a mustache. He picked up the telephone.

"Yes? O'Conner. What have you found out? Rota. Yes. I'm not surprised. What sort of Belgians? French, then. Hired by the mining concession? What for? A demolition team. Oh, to dynamite for the new dam. Check with Herzler tomorrow. Just to be on the safe side, as you say. Certainly you do not telephone at this hour merely to tell me that. . . . What priest? Speak more slowly. Casanueva? Have you written this up? Then send it here immediately! I don't care what *you* think! It is *you* who care what *I* think! *You* do not think! You act! Now, then, this priest, you haven't . . . good, good. I will speak with the archbishop at once. You will probably release the priest into the care of His Grace tomorrow. Of course, in the meantime proceed as you have been . . . then find someone else. Anyone else. Maybe this priest will talk. You have those dock workers, haven't you? Then beat them, one after the other. Keep the priest awake all night long. No, not the students, of course not. You don't know yet who they even are. You should know those boys always give false names. They don't want the university officials to find out. You got the money? Put it to work. You have discussed the security arrangements with Malata? Very good. You are not to leave the city. Let someone else handle the details. You must find Alessandro. Maintain double police patrols in the area near the docks, single patrols near the university. And telephone again if the priest decides to speak."

Malata drifted down the short hall and stood in the doorway.

"The champagne has been sent up, Excellency."

"What champagne? I don't want champagne. Bring me a coffee with milk."

"Now, Excellency?"

"No, yesterday. Get me the archbishop on the telephone."

"It is very late, but I will try."

"His Grace is an insomniac."

"Yes, Excellency."

The Caudillo finished his coffee and stared at the telephone, a smile still lingering at the corners of his mouth. He brushed his upper lip carefully. Malata stood near the desk.

"There is one weakness all churchmen have, Julio, even His Grace. The whole business of rendering unto Caesar that which is Caesar's and unto God that which is God's. They take it literally. If we don't bother them, they stay out of our way. But when one of their number gets in our way, they get confused. Suddenly they decide that a great deal is Caesar's and very, very little is God's. His Grace is not certain now whether this little priest is God's. His Grace is very embarrassed."

"I thought so, Excellency."

"He will be up all night. Tomorrow morning he will call. He will not be at all cooperative. I will not even be available. You will read to him the transcript of our conversation tonight. Especially the part in which I suggest that he instruct his fellow men of God to examine their consciences in regard to distributing, tolerating the distribution of, or in any way lending support or credence to atheistic philosophies thinly disguised as economic reforms. I believe those will be my words, Julio?"

"Exactly. And His Grace will agree."

"To a *suggestion*. Tonight. Tomorrow he will accuse me of attempting to limit the freedom of debate and investigation within the Church. To His Grace, the Church is Costa Plata. I have informed him more than once that his toleration of lay opinion is so lax as to encourage outright heresy."

"He did not speak to you for six months that time, Excellency."

"I cannot recall being concerned. His Grace talks so much that a half year of silence is a benediction. Insist repeatedly that I may be forced to reconsider the nationalization of all the orphanages if the priests become involved in one more event of this sort. Remind him that there are nearly three thousand nuns in this country. If the orphanages are nationalized, His Grace will have them all on his conscience and all eating up his treasury."

"What is to be done with this one that O'Conner has now, Excellency?"

"I suggest that a young man with a burning desire to reform might accompany the proposed mission to the Brazilian jungles. Instead of stirring up discontent, he can win headhunters for Christ."

A buzzer sounded, and a scarlet stud winked on the wall. Vizarra got up, but Malata lifted off the receiver on the wall telephone.

"The driver from O'Conner?"

"Yes. Malata. Send him on."

"Yes, Excellency."

"Send the papers here."

"You will need me for notes, of course . . ."

The Caudillo stared at the photograph in the frame on his desk. The archbishop, his long, dead-looking upper lip shielding his teeth like a roof, was draping the Order of the Cross of Santa Rosa, Costa Plata's highest honor, around the neck of a strong-shouldered, mustached man in the uniform of a full general. More than once His Grace had complied with the events of history. He would do so again. Anything, almost, was tolerable, as long as the existence of the Church itself was not threatened. The Caudillo had no intention of touching the Church. He regularly attended Confession and Mass, observed all the fast and holy days, participated in the much-photographed Easter celebrations and considered himself a devout Catholic. Once yearly he confessed to the archbishop himself, and humbly endured a harangue lasting over an hour. He dutifully completed his penance and was absolved (very reluctantly) of his sins. He had patiently explained to His Grace that Lucía would not marry him. Lucía refused to see the archbishop, or even one of the more handsome young priests. Between the three of them there now existed an uneasy stalemate, with the burden of guilt lying heaviest on his own shoulders, as usual. His Grace was incapable of understanding why Lucía Bosola, after having lived with Rafael Obregón Vizarra y Salán for nearly six years, should refuse marriage. Forty years' difference in age and the matter of the Caudillo's sterility the archbishop brushed aside. He persisted in believing that the popular name, "the Old Mule," was merely an allusion to the Caudillo's legendary capacity for hard work and an equally well-fabled reputation for stubbornness.

"What did you say, Julio?"

"I said you will need me for notes, perhaps?"

"There is the car."

When Malata left the room, the Caudillo opened the desk with his key and took out the album. There were her pictures. As a girl of eight or nine, a street brat in bare feet and skimpy dress sticking her tongue out at the photographer. The photograph was cracked and faded. The next showed a skinny adolescent perched on a fiesta float, dragging little bunches of flowers from her flat bodice and tossing them into the crowd on the Grand Paseo. A gawky, long-legged girl in a sequined skirt made up to look like a Negro woman. Then the famous calendar photograph, the one entitled "Bridal Night," which showed her slim form sprawled nude on top of a torn wedding gown, her mouth crumpled from kisses, her tender thighs still spread, one hand covering the patch of darkness. The calendar had been prohibited for years. A still shot from her first motion picture, *Amor y Sangre,* in which she had been murdered by her faithless lover to keep her silent so that she might not reveal his perfidy to his still-trusting wife. Three demure snapshots taken in the villa garden, and the breathtaking figure studies, blurred and romantic, she had given him for his last birthday, artistic pornography of the highest quality, executed by a Balkan homosexual, a famous photographer of women. He stared, awed and stirred again by the sight of her body, the astonishing breasts on the slender body, the lovely lean buttocks and tapering legs, the tiny feet, the beautiful lines of the arm draped over the right hip. He slammed the album shut, dropped it into the drawer and turned the key. Malata slipped into the room, a fat envelope in his hands. He placed it on the desk.

"That will be all, Julio."

"Excellency?"

"Wait. Have someone bring me another coffee. And a cigar."

Malata opened his mouth, noticed the Caudillo staring at him, and nodded once.

"Go to bed, Julio. You look tired."

"I assure your Excellency—"

"Go to bed!"

A sleepy servant brought the coffee and a humidor of cigars. Vizarra sniffed greedily and closed the cover with a sigh. With all that lay before him, he must try to follow the recommendations of the doctor. No cigars until after the foreigners left Costa Plata. He opened the envelope and began to read what O'Conner believed to have happened on the train at the Casanueva railroad station.

The dawn sky shone like polished mother-of-pearl when the Caudillo finished the third page of notes and recommendations written in the tiny, fine script and careless spelling that he normally submitted to Malata for copying. He left instructions for the notes to be typed up in his study by Lucía's private secretary, the notes themselves to be burned. He walked through the silent corridors of the villa and out into the garden. He was very tired and strolled only for a moment, breathing deeply. The morning was delicious. He sucked it into his broad chest and flailed his arms. Then he entered the villa again. He slowly climbed the ornate stairway and walked down the hall to the door at the end. He pressed the handle and walked softly inside. Lucía lay in the inner chamber, sprawled on the vast bed, her hair a ruin, the Paris gown crushed and tangled around her legs. One small foot was bare. A champagne bottle, empty, lay on the Persian carpet. A glass stood on the night table beside an ashtray heaped with cigarette stubs. Fragments of the second glass, his own, lay scattered around his picture over her dresser. The diamond necklace circled her throat like a garroting cord. He gathered her into his arms, stroking her tangled hair and murmuring.

"Ah, pobrecita mía . . . my poor little one . . ."

He drew off the dress and draped it clumsily over a chair. He unfastened her silk stockings, her underclothes and laid her in the center of the bed, the light coverlet pulled up to her chin. She made a fretful noise and rolled onto her belly. He smiled at her sadly and stretched out on the divan. He could hear her smooth, light breathing. The birds began to sing in the garden trees. His lids fell and he slept.

2

SÁNCHEZ knotted the cord of his bathrobe and thrust his feet into worn slippers. He shivered slightly and finished the dregs of his *café con leche*. The mountain air was always cold and misty in the mornings. Low clouds hung around the sanatorium, seldom lifting before noon. The weather and the monotonous regimen blunted his purpose; he idled away the mornings in his room, then was forced to skip the siesta after lunch in order to complete his work with the student cadres before dark. After dinner he wrote up his reports, left them with the nurse on night duty in the main ward, then drank brandy until the alcohol and fatigue overcame him.

Ever since he had entered Costa Plata illegally months earlier, Sánchez had felt uneasy, not himself. The sanatorium was a perfect place for the headquarters: modern, well equipped, spacious enough so that the various groups could confer regularly without interfering with the actual patients. The low concrete wings were sheltered against the mountainside, and a single road led to the place through a small village. There Sánchez had established a forward observation post overlooking the main street. The village was three-quarters of an hour away. There was no chance of being taken by surprise. Besides, the secret police would never think of searching in a tuberculosis sanatorium for a group of revolutionaries. It was not the place itself that caused the dull restlessness to seize him. It was the way things were being run.

Alessandro was still in hiding. Twice daily Sánchez received written instructions, carefully typed, brought to him by the orderly who cleaned his room. For more than a decade Sánchez had received letters, cards, pamphlets, lists, instructions, corrections. The boxes and suitcases under his high, white iron bed were filled with sheets of paper, carefully decoded and filed. Sánchez had followed every order without hesitation or question. His loyalty was a habit, like smoking or drinking brandy. The brandy gave him a feeling of well-being, and smoking helped to pass the time. Sánchez knew that his self-discipline had evaporated long ago, and so clung to his habit, his automatic and thorough processing of instructions. Even his imagination had failed. He felt no enthusiasm, despite the fact that every order he put into effect drew the scattered units of the M.L. into closer coordination, equipped them with basic action plans and actual weapons. Surrounded with paper work, numbed by isolation, drugging himself with work and brandy, he felt as though he presided over the liquidation of a bankrupt firm, as if his efforts, directed by some unseen intelligence, served only to disperse the assets so carefully gathered through the years. Sánchez knew that his imagination had failed when he realized finally that he no longer thought of the danger of his activities. He could no longer even conceive of being afraid. The knowledge seeped in him like acid, embittering him. There were times when he hated Alessandro. He had become wooden, a puppet, a thing of jerky movements that imitated life. When he was not working, he simply dangled in the bare closet of his room, a marionette in a bathrobe.

When the orderly came for his breakfast tray, he brought another square white envelope. Sánchez sat smoking in silence, staring out of the window at the drifting clouds. A bell pinged somewhere, and a woman's voice summoned a doctor to the X-ray room. Sánchez stubbed out his cigar and tore open the envelope. It was a list of in-patients admitted the previous day.

Jean Paul Celineau

Charles "Coco" Bobet

Henri Gebel

Victor Hugo Voget, alias Pierre Hugo, alias Paul Victoire, alias Ivan Buber, alias Vladimir Kushenko

These men were sent to us at my request. They are all Communists. Voget is an acquaintance from St. Petersburg. All have had experience in the use of artillery, automatic weapons and demolitions. They have funds in Mexico deposited for their use by the Comintern. I have been assured of their cooperation, and, in turn, have notified the Comintern that the Communist party will be allowed to participate in the government when formed. It is reasonable to suspect that these men will attempt to depose Rota or at the very least force him into a position of little importance. This will be acceptable, at least temporarily.We may expect that Voget will offer to bring more volunteers to Costa Plata, possibly from Mexico, almost certainly non-Communists to give the illusion of a popular front. Cadres in charge of recruiting must be carefully instructed not to accept foreign volunteers other than those men listed on Directive 4578. Voget and his group have been assigned to double rooms in the west wing. They must not be permitted to fraternize with the student cadres, especially the Black Cadre. Since Voget's group is allied with the U.T., all secret meetings of the U.T. must be recorded in full. All meetings of the Communists within the U.T. must be recorded in full and forwarded to me in the usual fashion. When the overthrow of the Vizarra government is an accomplished fact, Voget's group is to be arrested and given safe-conduct to Boca Perro. A fishing vessel there will remove them to a Swedish vessel bound for Liverpool, England. Instructions must be forwarded promptly to the appropriate persons in Boca Perro: no unauthorized personnel are to be brought into Costa Plata via the smuggling boats.

Sánchez lit another cigar and turned to the second page. Two lines were neatly typed at the top of the sheet:

Execute Plan "Masquerade" at 1300 hours.
Black Cadre execute Action Plan 001. 2300 hours approx.
See A-42.

There was, as always, no signature, no message, no human contact. It was as though Alessandro did not exist as a person, a real human being, the oldest friend Sánchez had. Alessandro was an abstract intelligence, a force that dehumanized. A force that was directives, orders, not human ambitions. Sánchez knelt beside his bed and drew out a cardboard carton. "Masquerade" in undecoded form was contained in the body of a yellowed clipping forwarded to Sánchez, originally printed in an American newspaper in the form of a flattering review of Alessandro's second novel, *The Eraser*. Sánchez found the folder. Nine letters in the title, added to the letters of his last name, for a total of fifteen. Reverse the figures. Code 51. Sánchez drew a block of paper and a pencil from his worktable and bent over the clipping. He could read English only with difficulty, but the actual words were of no importance. He patiently searched out the letters which, correctly combined, would indicate the final steps of "Masquerade."

This novel by Alessandro Martín, the second in a planned trilogy, surpasses its predecessor in every manner. The use of obviously autobiographical material has been so heightened by the ringing clarity of the prose itself (prose which in lyric intensity reminds the reader of the author's early verse) that the raw earth, like the dust of his native country, has been transformed to precious metal. The hero, again, is Juan Coronel, the young self-exile, struggling in Europe to maintain his slender contacts with his homeland, despite poverty, the constant threat of arrest and deportation and the pressure of other political philosophies to which he feels himself drawn. The hero's dilemma, amounting finally to an agonized inner debate, is that of the man of action who can act only in the name of ideals other than his own. The scenes, brilliantly illuminated by the clear sense of irony, take place in Paris, the front-line trenches, occupied Berlin and Geneva. The heroism of the European worker-soldier is demonstrated through the subplot, a small masterpiece of naturalistic comedy. To reveal more would be to deny the reader the pleasure of discovering. . . .

Sánchez worked steadily, copying the letters into vertical columns, assigning a numerical value to each and, finally, comparing the numbers with the scrambled alphabet of Code 51. When he had finished, he left his room and walked down the cool, clean corridor. The duty nurse sat behind her low counter. She nodded to him. He handed her a slip of paper.

"Telephone this to 23 in Casanueva. You have the number?"

"Yes, Señor Sánchez."

"Have the instructions confirmed by telegram here. Point by point. Is that clear? They are not to accept the general directive, but point by point."

"Yes, Señor Sánchez."

The nurse watched Sánchez shuffle away down the corridor, his slippers flapping the polished floor. She glanced at the slip of paper: *Teatro Royal has position one male lead in new tragedy "The Masquerade." Can you open in capital on the 15th? Two-week engagement certain. Tour of provinces. Salary arranged. All expenses paid. Advise at once. Eduardo.*

⸸

After lunch Sánchez met five members of Black Cadre in the cardroom of the sanatorium. The sky beyond the big windows had cleared, and only a few cotton puffs of clouds drifted high in the blue sky. The students sat patiently around the table. Sánchez dealt a hand of *vingt-et-un.*

"You will leave in two hours, checked out as outpatients. You will go by ambulance to the railroad station. Two compartments have been reserved. Separate at the city. Go to your homes, stay off the streets. At eighteen hundred hours, Pepe, you pick up the equipment, the package at the post office. At twenty-one hundred hours you meet together in the Café Tres Gatos. In the toilet, distribute the equipment: three pistols, two hand grenades. Leave the café separately. The taxi will be waiting beside the Iglesia Santa Lucía, on the west side, with the hood up, as though there is some trouble with the engine."

Sánchez spoke in a slow, even voice, staring down at the pack of cards in his hand. He did not want to look at the students. Their young, eager faces reminded him of all that had been worn out of him. Pepe Olmega, the cadre leader, wet his lips and leaned forward.

"Who is he? Who do we get?"

Sánchez sighed. They were going to assassinate an old man, a friend of his father's.

"Colleo."

"Colleo! The Prime Minister!"

The five students sat in stunned silence. Olmega nodded. Sánchez glanced at him. The young man's face was set, determined.

"Take that expression off your face. You meet some friend in a café. You talk about girls, going to a brothel. The others aren't interested. You try to persuade them, but fail. It's no fun going there alone. You start home, looking for a girl anyway. You see? You're out for a night of fun, but the others spoil it for you. Don't be serious and don't have anything to drink either. You want to drink at the bordello, see?"

Olmega grinned and nodded, slapping his cards against his palm.

"That's a good idea. I know a place, too. We can go there . . . afterwards."

The others nodded, watching Sánchez. He dropped the deck of cards and lit a cigar. He wanted a glass of brandy, but it was too early.

"We were informed yesterday that Colleo is having dinner tonight with the archbishop—"

"We could get them both!"

"You wish to talk?"

"No, señor. I am sorry. Your pardon."

"Having dinner tonight with the archbishop. About the affair of the pamphlets and the priest. The archbishop is very angry. With everyone—that's his way. Where does Colleo live? You."

"Valleverde 13, fourth floor."

"And how would you go to dinner with His Grace from Valleverde 13?"

"Why, it's just around the corner from the residence. Too short for a taxi. And . . . Colleo doesn't drive an automobile, does he?"

"He'll be walking, then, señor?"

"The last four times he has dined with the archbishop, he has walked. Once it was raining, too."

"It will rain tonight. It will rain bullets!"

"His Grace excuses his guests at twenty-three hundred hours. He will leave Colleo at his doorway. You've seen the residence, Olmega. What happens next?"

"Why, Colleo will come down the walk. To the gate. There are two attendants there. They will let him out onto the sidewalk. He will stand there for a minute, perhaps, then start home. Yes, for a few seconds anyway, he will be under the light at the gate. That's when we—"

"How?"

"We drive up in the taxi. The driver asks if he wants, you know, a taxi. Colleo will refuse. He will stand still, perhaps even come close to the taxi."

"Very good. You and two others will do the shooting. The remaining pair will have the grenades. In case something goes wrong and you are chased. Perhaps there will be extra police in the area. When the taxi is in motion again, wait until you have traveled fifty meters. Then drop one of the grenades. Understand? All right. You others go on with the game. Go ahead. Here, you be the dealer. Olmega, come with me."

In his room, Sánchez offered the young student a cigarette and took one himself.

"A glass of brandy?"

"No, señor, you said—"

"That's later. Tonight. Take one with me now."

Sánchez poured the brandy into glasses.

"*Salud!*"

"*Y Libertad!*"

Olmega drank his brandy at one gulp, like medicine. He looked very healthy, even in the sanatorium bathrobe, pajamas and slippers. Sánchez smoked, looking out of the window and sipping his drink.

"Do you know what A-42 is, Olmega?"

"An attached alternate to 001."

"Have you read it recently?"

"Yes."

"Which member of your cadre is . . . dispensable, Olmega?"

"Jaime, I think. He has little real courage. A good brain, but—"

"Then he's the one."

"But, señor!"

"What?"

"He has affianced himself to my cousin."

"Olmega. Pepe. Your friend has pledged himself, his sacred honor and his life to the Movement. You have taken the cadre leader's oath. You recall the oath?"

"Of course, señor."

"Repeat it."

70

" 'I hereby pledge myself not only to fulfill all nonmilitary duties that shall be required of me, but to execute to the letter, and if necessary personally, the specific orders and commands given to me at any time or place by a duly authorized superior. I will maintain by personal example the highest disciplines of the Movement and further—' "

"You understand, then. Alessandro himself selected Black Cadre. You agreed to do this when you joined us. You have sworn. It is simply required. You have no feelings in the matter. None. You have no friend named Jaime. You have a weak, perhaps dangerous member of your cadre. You must, therefore, expend him. You are the pistol, he is one of the cartridges."

"Yes."

"At the café, take him first into the toilet. Open that box there. Yes. Look at the stuff. The wallet, especially."

"It has a Red Beret card in it!"

"And money. A picture of a girl. Another of his mother. A packet of contraceptives. Give him the wallet. Tell him it contains money to protect you all, and the escape route. I know, I know, you have the escape route already. Tell him there is to be a change in plans. Two changes. He is to have a pistol. When Colleo falls, he gets out of the taxi and shoots Colleo in the head. *Coup de grâce.*"

"And I . . ."

"And you . . . expend your cartridge. It will appear, you see, as though some young fanatic from the Red Beret did the job. Make certain of him, Pepe. He is just as important as the Prime Minister. Do not reveal yourself to him."

"No. I have sworn it and will do it."

"That is what the Movement demands. Loyalty implies sacrifice. Remember that. Go, now. Take this stuff with you."

The boy stood up and raised his clenched fist.

"Trust Black Cadre!"

"We do. May you have good luck. You will be back here tomorrow. Be prepared to give me an oral report and to write one up later."

The boy nodded and walked stiffly from the room and closed the door very carefully. Sánchez finished his glass of brandy and reached for the bottle. The orderly appeared without knocking. Sánchez jerked his hand away from the bottle. He snatched the note.

"Outside, please. There's no answer."

Sánchez stared at the neat handwriting of the duty nurse in violet ink on white paper: *Accept role in "The Masquerade." 15th acceptable date. Two weeks all right, also provincial tour. Minimum salary 200 reales. Plus expenses. Ricardo.*

Sánchez touched a match to the slip of paper and watched it burn in the ashtray. He poured another brandy. He raised the glass in a toast.

"To you, little one. Today we have begun the plans. By midnight you will have killed two of us. How many will it take, little one, how many?"

☩

Lunch was over, and the guests lingered in the shaded patio of the great country house. They lounged in chairs and chatted, still savoring the succulent chicken cooked with rice and onions, the grilled nuggets of beef with peppery sauce and the chilled, crisp melons. Livermore's temples buzzed slightly from too much of the rather nutty-flavored claret. He thanked the host, a broad, bronzed man with an ample white mustache, one of Costa Plata's wealthiest ranchers and proprietor of the broad green acres where fighting bulls grazed. The *patrón* bowed and murmured the conventional politeness. Then his dark, shrewd glance flickered away to where Vizarra stood talking with a group of army officers. Livermore lit a cigarette and strolled toward a fountain that jetted into a fishpond. He stood for a moment, idly watching the golden shapes flick and glide in the transparent water.

"It is a shameful waste."

Livermore turned. Herzler pointed at the fountain.

"A hundred liters an hour. At least. All day and night. And beyond the hills there is nothing but rock and dust. People starve so that one man may have a pool for goldfish."

"They are beautiful creatures, I must say. I have never seen them so large."

The German shrugged. He, too, glanced at Vizarra. Dunkel and the *patrón* were talking about beef cattle. Malata stood between the two big men, dark and alert, translating easily. From time to time his eyes turned in the direction of the Caudillo. Everyone was waiting and watching. Whether or not there would be a siesta depended on Vizarra. When he was hungry, lunch was served. When he was thirsty, wine was poured. When he was tired, everyone dozed. Livermore was used to deference, to the respect his countrymen had for wealth and good breeding. In London the directors of corporations paid him the sort of restrained homage he had lived with so long that it had become something he no longer noticed. No one called him by his first name, not even his wife. It nettled him to see these Costa Platans bow and scrape to a onetime infantry officer from a provincial garrison, raised in an orphanage. They fawned on him as though he were a hereditary monarch. Of course, the Latins were given to all sorts of unhealthy idolatry. Herzler said something.

"I beg your pardon, Herr Herzler?"

"I say, are you fond of caves?"

"Fond? Of caves? I have never seen a cave. Or do you mean a wine cellar?"

"No, no. A cave. In the ground. There are famous caves near here. In the hills. I know them all. They are extremely interesting from all points of view."

"From inside, eh?"

"I do not understand."

"A little jest, Herr Herzler."

"*Ja?* I have no humor, I am afraid. But these caves are interesting from the view of the anthropologist. Also from the view of the student of primitive art. From the view of the architect. From the view of the tourist. I myself visit them often. I could guide you."

Livermore hesitated. If he napped now, he would feel dreadfully fuzzed when he awoke. On the other hand, Herzler was a bore. Vizarra suddenly yawned, his square, brutal jaw dropping to the stiff collar of his uniform. The others in the party stirred as though drawn into motion by the force of the Caudillo's breath. Livermore turned back to Herzler, mildly disgusted by the sight of Vizarra's gold-capped molars so frankly displayed.

"You know a good bit about the country, I daresay, Herr Herzler."

"I have scientific curiosity."

"Indeed. The others are retiring, but I should prefer to walk about some. Are they a great distance away, these caves?"

"Thirty minutes by car. I will arrange everything."

He slipped away to speak with Malata. Livermore sat on a bench and waited, watching the fish slide through the crystal water.

☨

The main entrance to the cave was sealed off by a great iron grille, chained and padlocked. Herzler was obviously known. The guard greeted him in a friendly fashion, routed out two skinny boys to carry the electric torches, and smoothly pocketed the coins Herzler dropped into his hand. The chauffeur and the two army officers hesitated. The chauffeur dropped to his hams in the shade and began to roll a cigarette. The officers flipped a coin. The loser shrugged and accepted another electric torch. The guard loosened the chains, and Livermore stepped through into the dim, cool vault that smelled of dust and bat droppings. The boys carrying the torches submitted to a brief lecture from Herzler who then turned shaking his head.

"They are very naughty, these boys. I have told them to stay close."

"Surely there's no danger."

"In places the floor is uneven. One can fracture a bone in the darkness. It is a waste of intelligence to be looking down. In a cave, one looks up. We go this way."

Livermore nodded. One of the boys walked before Herzler, his torch pointed at the floor. The other shuffled along in front of Livermore, playing his beam on the walls and ceiling. The officer followed, idly turning his torch this way and that, apparently amusing himself with the grotesque leaps of the shadows his light created, typical Latin childishness. The party descended a sort of ramp, broad and level, obviously very old and carefully handworked. Herzler pointed to the big square stones.

"When the streets of London, Paris and Berlin were tracks in the mud, the Xaltopecs of Costa Plata had mastered the art of building in stone. The streets of their cities, even villages, were so paved. Each stone measures one meter, ten centimeters long and wide. Five centimeters deep. They weigh nearly two hundred pounds each, English measure. Notice the grooves cut by wagon wheels."

"Herr Herzler. Does the officer speak English?"

"No. Now we go zigzag, you see. Like the maze at Kew Gardens, no? For purposes of defense and safety. The caves were used first by the Xaltopecs as a treasury. The zigzag allows but one wagon at a time to pass into the rooms beyond. Also, the temple was here. The temple of Vigo. Like the Aztecs in Mexico, the ancient people of Costa Plata practiced human sacrifice."

"He wears a different uniform. Not a Regular Army uniform surely?"

"No. He is a lieutenant in the National Guard."

"Is that the militia?"

"No, no. An elite force. The Caudillo's Praetorian Guard. They have no officers higher than colonel. To prevent jealousy with the Regular officers, you see. Also, they receive less pay. His Excellency is very shrewd that way. He is the general of the National Guard, the commandant. Ah, here is the receiving chamber. Notice, please, the cubicles to the left and right. Chambers for the guards. The inscriptions are Xaltopec hieroglyphics, still undeciphered, although work goes on at the university."

Livermore gazed up at the crumbled cutting in the stone, shapes of animals and geometric figures. Below, he saw an inscription in Latin.

" 'For God, the Holy Mother, and for Spain.' Very interesting, I'm sure."

"Most likely cut by one of the officers accompanying the *conquistador* Huelta. They arrived in Costa Plata in the year 1537, eighty-two men and twelve horses, transshipped from Hispaniola. And three priests. The Xaltopec nation perished in this cave. The Emperor, the high priests, and the nobles. Huelta had a wife and children in Spain, but married the Emperor's daughter. The Xaltopecs believed him to be Axoloqui, you see. He then held the Emperor's son as a hostage and demanded a ransom in gold. It was given to him, and a traitor revealed the location of these caves. There was a great fight. For three days. The nobles sacrificed their servants, finally their own children. Now we go here."

"How did His Excellency take power? There were no Indians, obviously, for him to deceive."

"No. It is not proper history to avoid the chronological process, but it can be given briefly. Costa Plata rose against Spain with the other colonies, inspired by Bolivar. The first Republic was proclaimed with a President General. A series of them, in fact. The last President General opened the country for foreigners. He was very naughty, too, and spent huge amounts on his mistresses, the very daughters of the aristocrats deprived of their titles but not their wealth. The university fell into such decay that Costa Platans went to Europe for education. When they returned, there were no jobs. The foreigners ran everything, even the civil service. The old Movimiento Liberal arose, headed by three men. Old Carlos Sánchez, now Minister of Public Education, Manón Xaltalpa, a leader of the Indians who worked the silver mines, and Felipe Martín, a peasant from the *campo,* self-educated, a bandit of great success and the father of Alessandro Martín."

The officer of the National Guard muttered what sounded to Livermore like curses. He and Herzler exchanged a few sentences.

"What seems to be the matter?"

"He is angry that he has been assigned to accompany the Caudillo. He is eager to join in the search for Alessandro. And young Sánchez."

They walked into a vast circular chamber, paved with stones. Their footsteps came coughing back from the ceiling, and Herzler's voice throbbed in echo. Livermore shivered from the cold. The beams of the electric torches slit the darkness like blades. A boulder, round like a millstone, stood against one walk. Herzler led the group to it.

"The altar of the high priests. Note the hole in the center. The victim was placed so. *Chico, venga.*"

One of the boys lay on the stone, grinning up at Livermore.

"With a flint knife the priest stabbed through the *solar plexus,* ripped up, then down to the pubic bones, then, chanting to Vigo, reached under the ribs and tore out the heart."

When Herzler gestured, the boy screamed so terribly that Livermore jumped, his arms flailing. Herzler cuffed the boy twice, hard, on the head and shoved him off the altar.

"You see? He is a naughty one, always. The blood ran down the hole into a jar at the rear of the altar. Then this very smooth section of wall was painted with blood in various inscriptions, honoring Vigo."

The lights showed a great, leggy daub, a blunt-headed letter A. Herzler nodded.

"Axoloqui. Someone has painted it. The guard, perhaps. He is very ignorant."

The boy Herzler had struck thrust out a skinny arm. His eyes glittered with anger and mischief. He danced with excitement beyond the swing of Herzler's fist.

"No, no. Alessandro! Alessandro!"

The officer brushed by Livermore, grabbing for the boy.

"Hijo de puta! Silencio!"

The echoes beat back through the darkness, hissing and booming like primitive instruments: "Alessandro! Al-dro-aless-andro-ssandro-Alessandro!"

"Basta, basta, Teniente. Enough, eh? *Un chiste, nada mas.* He makes a joke, this boy. You see the letters. *Anno Domini,* and the numerals for the date 1540. The priests with Huelta consecrated this place of blood rites as the first church in Costa Plata. You can still see the holes in the wall there, where with nails was fixed a cross made of a broken horseman's lance covered with plates of thin gold. The cross now hangs in the Cathedral of Santa Rosa in the city. Her story is very tragic. She was captured in 1634 by the degenerate people of unknown origin who had been the slaves of the Xaltopecs. She had converted many of them. However, many more lived in these caves. Troglodytes, technically speaking. She came here, poor woman, to coax them out into the daylight of Christian truth. She was taken, raped by a great many, her breasts cut off with a flint knife, and then she died, of course."

"I daresay."

"Curiously enough, the Xaltopecs also practiced circumcision. All males at the age of three months. The flesh was cooked and eaten by the mother, to encourage the birth of more male children. Paintings of great beauty show this interesting ritual. They are in another room."

Livermore felt his stomach turn queasy. He lit a cigarette and drew the smoke deep into his lungs.

"It would be considered an honor and politeness if you gave tobacco to the lieutenant, sir."

"Oh. Terribly sorry. I never thought."

"Costa Platans have their modern rituals as well. No man smokes without offering tobacco. He will be pleased that you know their habits."

"Perfectly understandable."

"Muchas gracias, señor!"

"Don't give to the boys."

"I hadn't planned to. You were speaking of some movement a moment ago?"

They began walking again, both boys standing clear of Herzler and the lieutenant. The long ribbons of light skipped over stone carvings, a niche or grotto with a rusted grille.

"The shrine of Santa Rosa. Now abandoned. Notice the way the stone has been worked. Cut into the solid rock, the whole structure a monolith in debased Spanish Gothic."

The lieutenant crossed himself as he knelt. The glowing tip of his cigarette shot left to right, forehead to breast in the blackness.

"The three men joined forces on July 17th, 1881, in part of the capital now totally destroyed. The movement for reform was very slow; not until a few years later was a list of grievances submitted to the Cortes, the national assembly, Xaltalpa, Sánchez and Martín hid in the hills. The movement began as bandit raids on government outposts, and isolated attacks on the first railroads. To get the silver, you understand. The army was corrupt and could seem to do nothing. Soon all the north opposed the President General, and the raids began into the *campo*. The peasants rose there and killed the landowners and broke up the latifundia. The army split in two. His Excellency, because of this, was promoted from colonel of infantry in the southern garrison to brigadier."

"And he put an end to the revolution."

"Not at once, no. Manón Xaltalpa went gringo."

"I'm sorry, but I don't . . ."

"Watch your head, now. The Xaltopecs were a rather small people, but beautifully formed. This was the treasury, the storehouse of gold."

Herzler shone his torch on the wall and spoke to the others. The beams illuminated a glittering panel twenty feet above the floor. A figure in a purple robe stood on what seemed to be a ship. His right hand was raised in a salute of greeting or farewell. Herzler cleared his throat.

"This is believed to be the earliest example of genuine mosaic in the world. It depicts Axoloqui, as you see. The Xaltopecs discovered the manufacture of glass, although they used it solely for artistic purposes. Somehow it was treated like stained glass, various chemicals added to color it. The lumps were broken and then the stone cut and pieces fitted into the walls. You see his hair. Long, yellow and curled. His robe. The color of it. I have been, in my free time, you understand, studying this mosaic. When in Berlin last, I consulted

Professor Grünewald. You have no doubt heard of him. I am composing now a monograph. You see, it is my thesis that Axoloqui was a real man. Moreover, he was . . . you cannot guess."

"No, I'm afraid not . . ."

"A Phoenician! Professor Grünewald was astounded, naturally."

"I daresay."

"A most daring, not to say revolutionary, hypothesis. I have his letter at my house. I will show it to you. Those were his words. But the Phoenicians were great explorers. Also they wore purple robes, also notice the face. Although very primitive and stylized, it is a Phoenician face. Also the hair is curled. I believe the Xaltopec calendar and their system of mathematics were given to them by Phoenician explorers. No one believes me. I will publish my monograph anyway."

"A very commendable contribution to knowledge, I'm sure. How did this movement fail?"

"Oh, that. It failed."

"Something about a gringo?"

"*Ja,* Manón, the Indian. Very brave. Very strong in the heart. But not so strong in the head. He got money, of course, and spent it in a foolish way. His followers soon came to believe that he received his money from the President General. Actually, he and his group were receiving certain sums from other revolutionaries in Mexico. Manón Xaltalpa took some for himself. He was not wise. His followers became discontented and protested to a priest. The priest betrayed Xaltalpa's hideout to Vizarra's loyal troops; there was a brief battle and Xaltalpa was shot by his own people. The Indians are very degenerate, courageous and violent. They turned against the movement when Vizarra offered no further reprisals. In so doing he disobeyed the President General, but won admiration. Then he issued the Proclamation of National Unity, appealing to the wealthy, the Church, the landowners and the youth of Costa Plata. Again he defied the President General by the promise of certain reforms— "purifications of the state," a call for moral order. Also he encouraged the formation of what was then an illegal political group, the Red Beret, most of whom recruited themselves into what was soon called the National Army. Those troops in revolt fought for their lives, but they were driven slowly out of the *campo,* away from the mines up into the Sierra del Norte. Then came another betrayal. The

79

hiding place of Felipe Martín was discovered. He was killed. Alessandro, his young son, and young Carlos Sánchez got away. Old Sánchez, *El Feo,* the Ugly One, was arrested, tried and imprisoned for three years. He is now Minister of Public Education."

"I think we must be getting back. It's nearly three-thirty."

"Gott, so late? We mustn't keep His Excellency waiting. What a shame. You have not seen the Emperor's chamber of pleasure with the drinking baths and the pornographic frescoes, the seven positions of Xaltopec pleasure. They are quite famous. I have taken many photographs. Professor Grünewald has declared them the equal to the Hindu sculptures at the temple of—"

"A great pity. Perhaps we can return again."

"Ja. I could show you—"

"How did Vizarra get rid of the President General?"

"But very easy. He was unpopular. Vizarra was a hero. The Red Beret was the biggest party in Costa Plata, though illegal. Vizarra promised free elections. He won easily. Since then, it has been as you see. He served one term in office, four years; then by national vote he was declared perpetual leader, Caudillo. Actually his history is not at all interesting compared with the fate of the *conquistador* Huelta, who, after claiming and seizing all of Costa Plata for Spain, was destroyed by the Inquisition in a plot begun by his half brother, a Jesuit. His *other* brother committed incest with Huelta's sister and drove her mad with remorse—María la Loca. The brother, too, was burned in Granada. Huelta died cursing his king. A great man, Huelta. Why he is not as famous as Cortés, Balboa, Pizarro, I do not know. The Costa Platans are very lazy and unscientific in regard to their own history."

Herzler sighed and played the beam of his torch over the glittering walls. Great, angular birds, stiff-coiled iridescent serpents, kings with square crowns, and blocky tiled temples skidded like fragments tumbled in a kaleidoscope.

"This is the wealth of Costa Plata. The true wealth. The art, the beauty, the tragedy of these Xaltopecs. The tragedy of Costa Plata. They trust. Huelta the *conquistador,* Vizarra the Caudillo. Now, perhaps, they will turn to Alessandro Martín."

"Surely you don't think there is a chance for another revolution? You cannot enter into negotiations with His Excellency if the government will fall. The risk of expropriation, Herr Herzler!"

Herzler's face was revealed by the lieutenant's electric torch. He raised his shoulders and laughed bitterly.

"Expropriation? I have come back to Costa Plata. I have been four months in Berlin. I have seen officials of the Weimar government. I have been granted certain powers, which mean certain responsibilities I must meet. In Germany they pay men once each day, no longer by the month or week. A suitcase of marks for a handful of food. I would negotiate with these naughty boys if I thought it would help Germany."

Livermore stiffened and flung away his cigarette.

"Your people should have thought of that in 1914, Herr Herzler!"

"My people, the Germans, are like the Costa Platans. They, too, trust too much. A Kaiser, a Caudillo, I see little difference."

"And take refuge in cynicism, I perceive."

Herzler looked around the glistening walls and shook his head slowly.

"*Nein*. I take refuge here, in the caves. The Fatherland has no such treasures, no such monuments to tragic fallibility. Even Professor Grünewald doesn't seem to understand. And he is a damned Jew. *Chicos! Vámonos! Teniente?*"

"*A su servicio.*"

"We go this way, Mr. Livermore."

The sunlight at the mouth of the cave was painful. Livermore swayed with his eyes shut, a blood vision swarming behind his lids.

"Thank you, Herr Herzler. That was very interesting. Very interesting indeed."

The German grunted and led the way to the waiting automobile. He rode in silence back to the great country house, staring out at the boulder-black bulls standing in the green fields of the *ganadería*. Dunkel met the car. He was wearing a high-crowned sombrero, a gift from the *patrón,* and smelled of cattle.

"Mr. Livermore, how was the trip?"

"Very informative. Very . . . ah . . . historical and cultural."

"I've got a bit of information, too. They got him. So the fur won't fly after all."

"Got him?"

"Alessandro, this Alessandro fellow everybody's het up about. Some woman turned him in to the police. He's in jail right now."

"Ah. That's . . . news, all right."

"You don't seem very happy about it. His Excellency is real happy."

"I daresay."

"In a way, that's a bad break for us, though. If, you know, Vizarra was still worried about this Alessandro . . . well, I have a hunch he'd be easier to deal with."

"Those are just my thoughts, Mr. Dunkel. So far, all His Excellency has done is to find fault with our proposals on the concessions. I'm afraid we shall soon hear his own. And we can expect no help whatever from the Jerries. They'll take whatever they can get. Where is His Excellency?"

"Gone back to the city. Malata is waiting for us. Can we talk before we get roped into this banquet tonight?"

"I think we had better, Mr. Dunkel. I think we had very much better sit down together before we meet again with Vizarra. We are in for a rough go, I'm afraid."

"Well, so is this Alessandro bird."

"Better him than us, Mr. Dunkel. Better Herr Herzler than us, if I may say so."

Livermore turned away, smiling faintly. *And better you than me, better you than me, if it comes to that.*

☩

"There were no details given?"

"No, Excellency, just that he had been taken alive."

"Good. Very good."

Vizarra leaned back. The heavy sedan rushed along the winding road, the tires pummeling over the spots of broken pavement. A pothole scoured by recent rain jolted Vizarra's spine.

"This road was paved three years ago. Already it is deteriorating. Make a note. The contractor is to undertake repairs at once. At his own expense. Deliver the message to the Ministry of the Interior today."

"Yes, Excellency."

The road curved through low hills tufted with coarse grass and weeds. A small child ran after a scattered herd of jogging sheep. A few scrub pines, twisted by the wind, stood against the blank horizon. The driver shifted into second gear, and the automobile ground through a curve and up into the slot cut between broken boulders, the entrance to the pass. As they climbed, the air grew cooler, streaming

82

into the rear seat of the limousine. The great fractured stones cast angular shadows. The sedan plunged through them and into the sunlight, flicking from black to light like a motion-picture film. Vizarra loosened his necktie. He had changed out of the *vaquero* costume he had worn to please his host, and now wore a light linen suit, white shoes and a broad Panama. The cattleman's sombrero, embroidered shirt and leather pants always made him feel not only hot but awkward and foolish as well, like the costume of a masquerade.

A thought twitched in his brain, synchronizing with the snap of sunlight after a patch of shade. He sat rigid, his senses straining, testing the idea for truth. *It was too easy.* He relaxed slowly. Things happened in unexpected ways. A moment's carelessness, a false friend, trust extended in the wrong direction too long, any sort of accident. But the thought lay taut. *It was too easy.* He had eluded agents in Europe and Mexico for more than ten years. To be captured now, and alive? *No, too easy, too easy.* The sedan slid into gloom and out again into the dry dazzle of the mica-flecked boulders. They had reached the top of the pass. Behind lay the green, irrigated hectares of corn and tomatoes, chick peas and beans, the well-kept farms, dairies, chicken runs and cattle ranches. Ahead the ruined miles of grassless sand and gravel, the grim, fly-blown villages, each a cluster of low stone houses gathered about the well, the life pipe sunk in the dry earth, the secret seep of water, precious stuff, rationed out at so many liters per family. Here was where the Costa Platan proverb "As thirsty as a bachelor" had begun. No one could mistake one area of land for the other. But one man for another? If they had never seen him, could Dunkel and Livermore have singled him out from the other *vaqueros?* O'Conner was an American. Alessandro had more than a dozen aliases, and no photograph of him had been taken for many years. He had lived for extended periods in disguise, once with a set of identification papers so carefully forged that he had been called up by the French Army and had served two years before his wound at Verdun. *No, it was too easy.*

The driver sounded the horn, smacking the button with his palm. A cart drawn by a dusty burro stood in the center of the road. The sedan rushed past. Vizarra pressed his face against the glass and saw a face brown and stiff as leather, wrinkled against the dust. He looked back. The figure bent and lifted something from the road. The dropping of the burro, as precious as silver to these villagers.

"Lucca."

"Yes, Excellency?"

The National Guard colonel turned and looked through the open glass panel into the rear seat.

"Make another note. Also to the Interior. I wish an examination begun and completed on the prospects of establishing a fertilizer plant at Boca Perro, the fertilizer to be processed from fish."

"Fish, Excellency?"

"You are not deaf, I hope?"

"Oh, no, Excellency."

"There must be several species of fish in our waters or farther out that are taken regularly by the trawlers but are too small, perhaps, or too bony to have any commercial value. I wish these species identified and an estimate made of the potential catch in kilograms annually."

The officer nodded, scribbling on a pad he had taken from the dashboard. Vizarra often completed a journey in an automobile and left his aides behind sorting out a fistful of directives, inquiries and suggestions.

"Is that all, Excellency?"

"For the moment."

A sharp report startled Vizarra. He glared out of the window. The speeding automobile swerved and slithered, a burst tire fubbling. They braked and bobbled to a halt; the sedan canted forward. The driver let a long hissing breath out between his teeth. He glanced at the revolver in Lucca's hand and giggled. The National Guard officer frowned and thrust the pistol back into his holster. The back of his neck flushed. Zamal, the other officer seated beside Vizarra, had drawn his pistol, too. Vizarra said nothing, although he was annoyed with them for what their actions implied: another attempt on his life.

"A flat tire, Excellency."

"Yes. Clearly. How long will it take to repair?"

The driver shrugged.

"A half hour."

The air was still, dry and hot. Dust sifted in through the open windows. Vizarra looked ahead. They were on the outskirts, the stone sheep pens and the threshing floors, the tattered vineyard of a small village. He opened the door and stepped out.

"There must be a café. We will wait there."

Lucca raised his brows, but his mouth merely tightened. When the officers joined him, Vizarra began to walk briskly up the road. The driver folded his jacket and placed it on the front seat, then walked to the rear of the sedan and fumbled with a key.

The village was small, a straggle of crude stone dwellings. No electricity, Vizarra noted. No telephone. No hydrant in the foot-pounded little square. Only the main street was paved; the side alleys were rutted clay, cut by hoofs and cart wheels. Clothing hung from lines strung between the houses. A faded coverall dangled in the baking air like a felon on a gibbet. The place smelled of dung, rancid cooking oil, dust and the spicy odors of wildflowers that drooped in weak clusters around the barrels set at the low eaves to catch the precious rainwater. A scruffy burro drowsed in the shade of a building, its legs hidden in the track, the circle worn about the crude pump. Three times a day, blindfolded, the little animal stumbled around and around while the screw lifted the water from the earth, alkaline stuff, barely drinkable. Vizarra looked at the burro. The creature stared back, its eyes dull blobs of gristle. Flies crawled on its lids, stabbing. The burro barely shook its head. Vizarra sighed.

"I know, *amigo,* I know."

Instead of the eagle, the national symbol of Costa Plata should be the pump burro, the half-starved slave of every impoverished village, the scurf-skinned, flea-stung burro, bloat-bellied and weak from green fodder, stumbling the endless circles in darkness in the blazing heat of noon. Vizarra looked right and left. A little platform with a broken railing and a tin roof. Had some enthusiast built a bandstand where a handful of peasants smeared and croaked on battered instruments, trying to lift the parched hearts to dance through a sun-flayed fiesta? Perhaps the rickety structure had been built by the district Red Beret during the last plebiscite. Vizarra walked across the street and climbed the dry, crumbling stairs. The floor was covered with dust fine as talcum. He whisked a place clean with his hat, sneezed twice and sat down. He fanned himself with his Panama. The two officers glanced around dubiously, struggling with the urge to clamp their hands on their pistol butts. The village was very quiet. Behind the shuttered windows and the open doorways hung with bead curtains, faces watched, eyes stared and ears strained to catch any word. Lucca pointed at the faded sign of a bar across the street.

"It might be cooler in there, Excellency."

"Perhaps. I do not wish to disturb anyone."

"Yes, Excellency."

The three men waited, the officers standing on either side of Vizarra. The dry minutes ticked away. No wind stirred. No face appeared. Zamal clicked his tongue thirstily. Lucca fretted.

"May we smoke, Excellency?"

"Of course."

Vizarra nodded when he heard the irregular *tong-tong* of the goat bell. A skinny black gang of them, the leader horned and wicked-eyed, minced and jostled around the corner, heading for the pump. The udders of the females, four-fingered bulbs, swung heavily. The two goatherds appeared, a small girl and an older boy with a matted head of hair black as the goats he drove. The girl ran with a stick; the boy bashed dented two-liter buckets together. At this signal the burro lurched forward. The girl scampered to bind the filthy rag over the burro's eyes. The goats, screwing narrow jaws and frisking tails against the flies, fought for the dribble of water that fell in the stone pan from the pump mouth. The boy swung the buckets, and the sound gnashed off the stone walls. The girl trotted with the burro, then saw the three men and froze, one foot lifted from the dust, pointed elbows out like dirty wings. She whirled and fled to the boy, chirping in dialect like a bird. The boy gaped and half turned, his head swinging from the men to his goats. His face puckered in torment. Even in his fright he dared not leave his father's goats. Vizarra raised his hand and beckoned.

"*Chico!* Boy, is your milk good? How much a liter?"

The boy dragged a bare foot in the dust and hung his head. The little girl ran toward the bandstand, stopped, retreated and came forward another few paces. Her pinched, sun-blackened features disturbed Vizarra. The child looked like some cunning, tormented animal, half mad with hunger. Vizarra felt his heart quail in his chest. The little face thrust forward, almost sniffing. The skinny body poised to flee. Suddenly the child squatted, snatched up her bit of skirt and made a puddle in the dust. Zamal began to laugh. Vizarra shook his head, staring into the child's dreadful eyes.

"Lucca, find a store and buy some candy. Any kind. And some bread. Cheese and meat."

"Yes, Excellency. But the meat in such a place—"

"It is for her. And for the boy. Hurry."

Now there were faces in the windows. Half visible, they glided behind the shutters. Fingers plucked at the bead curtains. Voices whispered like the play of rats. The goats bleated, the thin, stupid distressed noise that was their only sound. A figure appeared in the doorway of the bar, then vanished to return, triple-headed, as two other drinkers peered and blinked over his shoulders. The first man wore sandals, loose black cotton trousers and a torn, dirty blouse. He walked slowly and very carefully across the street, as though the dust might dissolve beneath his feet. His long, dirty hair fell over his brow. He had not shaved in four or five days. Gray stubble fringed his lean jaw. He stopped and hesitated. Vizarra saw that he was trembling violently; terror sweat stood on his forehead. He tried to speak, but the words clogged in his throat. His hands shook. He made a clumsy bow. Vizarra inclined his head and stood up. The man stared at him. Vizarra sprang down the steps. The man shrank and stared dumbly at Vizarra's outstretched hand. Some one tickled a guitar. The notes niddered like ironic laughter. The man drew himself up, pressed his heels together and dropped his hand into Vizarra's clasp. Tears stood in his eyes.

"Caudillo . . ."

"Speak, brother. I am listening."

Vizarra's eyes skidded past the man's face. The bar emptied slowly onto the street, a dozen men, all poorly dressed. A young woman, very bold, thrust open a shutter and leaned out, clapping her hands with delight. People ran into the square, and children sprang out of the doorways to scatter in the dust, racing about madly and darting to the pump to torment the bleating goats. A boy appeared wobbling on an ancient, creaking bicycle. Vizarra smiled, still clasping the man's hand. A few women, dressed all in black, their heads shawled in black, now edged into the crowd. Tears spilled down the man's bristled face. He gestured hopelessly, now bursting with pride and humiliated by the wretchedness of the place and the people.

He stammered, wiped his mouth and cheeks, his face crimson. He struggled to speak again, and Vizarra caught the half-strangled words.

"Welcome . . . each house is your house . . . honor to us . . . we see that God is good . . . loyalty and devotion . . ."

"I thank you. You are the mayor?"

The man nodded and pointed at his bar. Vizarra caught the flutter of the black robe through the crowd that had now formed a semi-circle. Faces thrust at him, dark eyes, severe noses, piercing eyes, mouths that muttered in awe. The crowd broke slightly to permit the priest to pass, a short, greasy young man, terribly out of breath. Vizarra shook hands again, not really listening to the priest's flustered apologies. Vizarra smiled and smiled until his cheeks began to ache. He wished to shake the hand of every man, but knew that he had properly deposited that honor upon the mayor and the priest, both of whom were now speaking at once, apologizing almost hysterically for the lack of ceremony, the inadequate hospitality. Their voices blended to a gabble of sound, confused further by the murmurs and exclamations of the other villagers. Lucca appeared, followed by a boy with a basket. Vizarra beckoned to him. The crowd hushed. The mayor gestured toward his bar.

"It would be the greatest honor to the pueblo, Your Excellency, if you would take something. Anything, anything you wish, Your Excellency!"

The crowd stirred and murmured with wonder and envy, phrases lapping over and against each other, wavelets of sound tumbling on a beach of dust.

"How he calls him! . . . Your Excellency, just like that. . . . What a suit! . . . His shoes are white, see for yourself! . . . Never in my life . . . an automobile, huge, enormous, with an injured foot . . . those with him, they are his sons . . ."

The priest rushed at the crowd, flapping his arms and hissing like a goose. He dashed back.

"Forgive them, Excellency, they are very ignorant, but they mean no harm!"

Lucca stepped up beside Vizarra and ordered the boy to set down the basket. Vizarra clapped his hands on the shoulders of Lucca and Zamal.

"Someone has said these men are my sons. No, not my sons. My friends."

He strode forward and caught the hands of the mayor and the priest and raised them.

"These are my sons! I hope I have two such sons in every pueblo in Costa Plata!"

The crowd sucked in the heat that licked through their shabby clothes, drew up the dust that swirled and sifted and exhaled in a roar of approval.

"Olé! Olé!"

Everyone laughed and smiled. Vizarra stripped off his jacket and handed it to Lucca. He bent over the basket.

"I am hungry."

The crowd laughed automatically.

"But how can we eat together, all of us? I have no knife. I have no wine."

The crowd spread, shouting, as though he had flung a grenade beneath their legs. Men and women dragged tables from the bar and from their houses; others staggered under long benches. The mayor shouted for a keg of wine. A blushing old grandfather presented a knife, an heirloom with a thorn-bush handle inlaid with silver. Vizarra waited until the mayor filled a *bota* from the wine cask, accepted the leather bottle with formal thanks, and squirted the thin, sour red wine into his open mouth. The women applauded quite as though he had performed some special feat requiring great skill and daring; the men nodded approvingly, for even though Vizarra had held the *bota* at arm's length, he had not spilled the wine. His shirt was spotless. He snatched up the knife and clicked the wicked blade open to whet it on his palm. The leather bottle circulated, snatched from hand to hand, the wine jetting into mouths, down jerking throats. Vizarra cut a loaf of bad, doughy bread, began to gnaw a crust, grinding with his white, broad teeth. He spread the pieces before him on a table and offered a bit to the mayor and to the priest at the same time. Another leather bottle was now passed from hand to hand. The mayor, exalted now, drank greedily. The priest began to match him, his mouth crammed with bread. Suddenly he stopped and gazed in dismay at the bread and wine. His greasy face paled, and he thrust the *bota* blindly into the crowd. Some of the young men and boys began to mock him with the high, yapping cry of contempt heard all over Costa Plata.

"Ya! Ya! Ya-ya-ya! Ya! Ya! Ya-ya-ya!"

The National Guard officers stood apart, reluctant to lose their dignity. Vizarra thrust bread at them and stuffed a nearly limp bag of wine into Lucca's hands.

"Drink and eat."

The officers looked from the Caudillo to the people. The villagers waited patiently. Lucca crushed the *bota* expertly; the thin stream splashed down his throat. Zamal ground his bread and nodded thoughtfully. A wooden bowl of small, half-ripened apricots appeared. Vizarra tasted one and passed the bowl. The fruit vanished, snatched by vine-brown fingers. Juice ran unheeded down the mayor's blissful face. Vizarra reached into the basket and pulled out two stale, faded figurines formed of sugar and decorated with bits of paper and tiny gilt crowns, effigies of Santa Rosa left over from the saint's day of the previous year. The priest, suddenly cheerful again, hissed and bobbed his head. Vizarra held a figure in each hand. The sun had already melted the sugar. His fingers were slick with a reddish gum. He walked through the crowd; they sprang back respectfully, no one closer to him than a half-dozen strides. He looked about carefully until he saw the little goatherd. The back fringes of the gathering were attending to everyday affairs; the little girl and the older boy wrung the teats of the goats. Milk hissed into the buckets. Vizarra caught the child gently by the twig-thin arm and drew her from the goat. She whimpered now, afraid again.

"Tsst-tsst, *guapita, paloma mía,* my pretty little one, my dove. Look! Look here! See. Who is that, eh?"

"The Holy Mother."

"Dressed in red? No, the Holy Mother wears blue, always."

"I don't know."

"You don't know Santa Rosa?"

"Yes."

"You do, but you don't, eh?"

The crowd had flowed around them. They laughed. The little girl hid her face against Vizarra's chest and began to cry. She smelled foul, and he could see the flea bites on her scalp. The priest tried to pull her away.

"You bad little girl! She is very ignorant . . . never comes to school. She cannot say her catechism, not a single word! Forgive her."

"I do. She cannot help it. She is poor and must work. Surely God will wait for her a little?"

"I . . . But if she should die?"

Vizarra pushed the child away, looked into her face, those voracious, knowing eyes, and crossed himself. He handed one of the candy figures to the child.

"There. Santa Rosa will protect her."

"Amen. Amen."

The child dropped the sugar effigy into the dust, snatched it up, bit off the head and raced away, the little gilt crown twisted between her fine, pointed teeth. Again Vizarra felt a sluggish drop within his chest, accompanied by a pang that brought tears to his eyes. He straightened and addressed the mayor and a group of men.

"It is for the children that we work. They are the future."

The men nodded. Vizarra gazed about, not quite certain what more to do. He saw a young woman standing in a distant doorway, an infant held in her arms. He walked toward the woman. Her faded yellow dress clung to her body, outlining the curve of her hip, her full breasts. Hair, brilliant and long, plunged nearly to her waist. Her fine, pale lips whispered something to the baby. Her ears, little petals of flesh, vanished beneath her hair as she jerked her head around toward him. Vizarra stopped, his mouth open. The girl with her baby, so beautiful, had eyes like polished blue pebbles. The baby, too, was blind.

"Who is she? Who is this girl?"

The priest scuffled out of the crowd. The people were standing in a dark, disapproving knot, unsmiling. The priest shrugged unhappily.

"That is blind Anna. You must not be offended by her. It is a great shame. She is so beautiful. It is the shame of this village."

The priest, his greasy face scarlet, suddenly rushed at the crowd.

"Yes! The shame of this village! Animals! Animals to do this thing! Not one of you is innocent. Women who refused her comfort, who despised her in your envy! Men who tormented her. Men who . . ."

Vizarra beckoned to the mayor. The priest flapped his arms, still shouting.

"Not one of you confesses to the sin! That is why I have turned you from the confessional! Dogs! Goats and swine!"

"What has happened to her?"

"Ah, Excellency, it is indeed sad. She has no father for the baby. No one would marry a blind girl, so . . . I mean, who knows who is the father? So many men have, you know, and the boys. She said she must find again the first one, it was the only way. With every man, you see."

The priest simply shrieked now, brief, bright pops of fury. He sat down on a bench and began fanning himself and butting his wrist against the foam at the corners of his mouth.

"Lucca!"

"Excellency?"

"Make arrangements. This girl, Anna something, is to be brought into the city. To the clinic, but she is to *reside* there; make certain that is known, completely understood. She is to live with the sisters. If she merely visits the clinic, you know what will happen. In a week, she'll be in a bordello, and the child will be dead."

The priest heard and rose to his feet. He tottered through the dust, choking and wiping his face.

"Your Excellency is a good Catholic."

"I try to be, Father. I very often fail."

"Ah, those are words I shall treasure! You fail. We all fail. But you try! You struggle!"

"Yes. But never hard enough."

"God is merciful. You are acting for Him. If she stayed longer, I don't know what would have happened. Perhaps the women would have stoned her and the baby. Ah, Excellency, there are times, God forgive me, when I wish I had your power."

Vizarra stared thoughtfully into the earnest, oily face pitted with smallpox scars. The priest's cassock was shabby, spotted. Like the mayor, he had not shaved in several days.

"You have a better power, Father. Believe me. I do not govern souls. I do not teach the way to God."

"But you can help her."

"I can try."

"God will bless you."

"What is your name, Father? I will speak to His Grace of your work here." The priest shook his head and raised one hand in a warding gesture.

"Please, no. I wish to stay here. After what has happened to this girl . . . why, I have so much to do. All these men and women, you see, they have sinned and . . ."

"I understand."

Vizarra picked up a three-legged stool, walked with it to the bandstand and set it down on the dusty floor. He sat on it, staring at the villagers. They gazed back, silent, cowed, rapt with fear and wonder. When the Caudillo cleared his throat, they backed away from him. Lucca stood to his left, Zamal to his right.

"Now. You have been good to me. You have been evil to that girl. What shall be done with you? Eh? Speak, someone! Anyone!"

The crowd was silent. The goats shuffled, and the bells *tong-tonged*. The sun seared Vizarra's face. He squinted, his face truculent.

"I will give you a gift. I will give you a pump for the water. Men will come with a truck and drill deeper. One of them will stay. He will stay to run the machine to pump the water. He will know who takes the water. Your fields will flower. You will grow more food. You will have more reales, each one of you. But every head of a family must contribute the tithe. It will be collected by the mayor and given to your priest. He will use the money to better the pueblo. He will give alms to the poorest among you. He will send money to the sisters in the capital to help pay for Anna and the child."

The sedan nosed cautiously into the plaza, great and glittering, the engine rumbling softly like a distant storm. Vizarra accepted his jacket and drew it on. The crowd ebbed away from the bandstand and flowed toward the limousine. The mayor ran on ahead, crying for the children to stand away. Vizarra walked heavily down the dirt street, followed by the two officers. The crowd murmured. At the door of the automobile, Vizarra turned and stared across the plaza. The villagers wadded together, a dark, sullen bundle. The priest had remained back near the bandstand; his head was bowed. In the door-way the beautiful blind girl leaned, her sightless baby balanced on her hip. The children milled, mewing like cats. A goat bell rattled, but he could not see the little girl. He stepped into the car.

"Did you get all that, Lucca?"

"Of course, Excellency."

"Let's go."

The driver let in the clutch, and the sedan surged forward, sliding on the dust back to the main street. Vizarra felt a lump in his pocket. He pulled out the clasp knife the old man had given him. He rapped the side window with the sharp tip.

"How did this crack happen?"

"A boy, Excellency, on a bicycle. Ran into the car. The handlebar, you know, hit the glass. I threw his damned machine down the cliff."

"Ah. Brilliant."

Vizarra fingered the knife. The sedan jolted over a narrow bridge, and the point ripped his left palm. The blood gushed out and spattered his white shoes.

"Ah! I've cut myself. How stupid! Give me a handkerchief, Zamal."

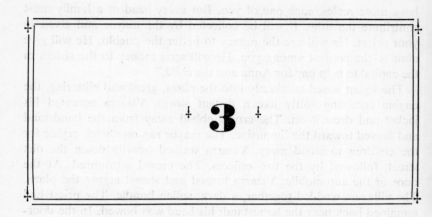

3

Since he has not a *tabula rasa,* but the splotched transcript of ideas that time and effort have transmuted into history, the revolutionary makes his mark with the instrument of writing reversed. He creates by the process of edition; he inscribes a new society with an eraser. He deletes with bold strokes. His revision is often absolute, or absolute in proportion to his will and the social malleability of the people.

—The Eraser, page 127

To be a good Marxist one must possess a cicatrice instead of an imagination. One must love the dreary and be capable of seeing everything in terms of groups, masses and units. One must insist on the supreme significance of money. A copy of Lenin's scribbles is the perfect dowry. How bourgeois!

—Letters From Poland, page 31

"No," André said, straining a blue feather of smoke between his chipped teeth, "political parties are clumps of dissatisfaction more often than they are organisms of creation. Besides, it is only in the compressed societies of today that political parties are really necessary. You shake your head. All right, I admit I oversimplify, but still . . . every man possesses the only two weapons that topple tyranny: the net of love and the trident of laughter. *Ave Caesar!* Remember, the tyrant's thumb is more often in his mouth than turned up or down."

—*Place Bastille,* page 342

⸸

Russia was never wounded by either the Roman Empire or the Renaissance. Neither was the United States of America. As a result, both nations have not aspirations but fanaticisms. They are more alike than any other two nations in the world.

—*The Ebbing Tide,* page 12

⸸

"Juan," she said, tapping my lips with her forefinger (stained to the second knuckle with nicotine) and grinning maliciously, "you like to play the holy one. Both in the party and with women. Don't you ever get bored?"

"No," I said. I stared at my broken foot in its plaster coffin. Why is it that pain does not come with the impact on the flesh, but only later? I knew I was not losing her but thrusting her away. "I haven't the time to be bored."

"What else is boredom but too much time? You are lucky."

"No, I have made my choice, that's all. I can't afford to lose. Not now. Love and politics resemble trench warfare. No, I'm serious. You can hear the opponent—I don't say enemy, you notice—moling in the earth but unseen. When you stand face to face, it is too late for one of you. Also, it is not the frontal assault that one fears but the sniper's enfilade, or the knife in the guts in some cul de sac."

"Very profound," she said, tugging the blanket up beneath my chin with those rude, efficient gestures of the trained nurse. "It is all because I am a married woman. You have some silly religious scruples." All at once I was weary to death of her. I closed my eyes. "Religious scruples may be silly, but they are necessary."

"And love is not?"

"When you say *love,* you mean only the rubbing together. Friction. There are more important things."

I have never been hit in the face so hard in my life. She knocked me unconscious. I had to tell Dr. Previn that I fell out of bed. I am quite sure he didn't believe me.

—*Place Bastille,* page 209

↓

Nature is not cruel but indifferent. One senses this standing among the wind-worn stones, giddy with the height, drunk with the blue distance, staring down on the surf of clouds a thousand feet below. It lies there and seems capable, this curdle of vapor, of either drowning the dry villages below or dropping on them a shower of rain gentle as a sleepy child's caress. One feels capable of flight, that high, of soaring. And the rocks will leap up, if one lets go, leap up like the jaw of Saturn. No, not Nature. Only man is cruel. Down below the clouds that bandage those villages, down in the villages beneath the rippled iron of the marketplace, an old man sells birds. How they sing, the wild thrushes of Costa Plata! One feels that all the silver does not lie clutched in stone. Tiny plates tinkle and ring in the throats of our thrushes. And then you watch the old man heat the wire in the brazier and press it carefully into the beady eyes . . . after that, they sing still more sweetly. To me that is a disaster, not the landslide below the clouds that smashes a hundred houses. The flesh was made rubble before the flood.

—*Sing From the Mountains,* page 177

↓

Despite the recent uproar of the Bolsheviki, there has never been a proletarian uprising. Not even the rebellion of Spartacus. After all, they were professionals, artists of public murder. There have been revolutions that passed into the hands of the proletariat by the blindness and ineptitude of the middle class, with the resulting Reign of Terror or the *bouleversement* in St. Petersburg. But this did not happen in America. The reason? Nearly a hundred years of some sort of self-government. The Americans were not driven to revolt by economic pressures but by the desire to be completely free. No Russian can comprehend this, not even Ulyanov himself, son of a superintendent of schools. Lenin is an example for all time: self-education is socially dangerous, for it produces only autocrats. What the world needs is aristocrats of the heart. More of them. Today they are found only in the middle class. And that is why the middle class is revolutionary. They alone are capable of compassion and possess the willingness to sacrifice. They can imagine a better world. What a sweet gift God has granted them!

—*Letters From Poland,* page 88

‡

The best government . . . in its internal relationship with the people . . . is passive, that is to say democratic in the fullest sense. In the international relationship with other nations, the best government is dynamic, that is to say democratic in the most limited sense.

—*Sing From the Mountains,* page 311

‡

Sidney's face was drained white with boredom. He might have screamed as us, but instead he cringed away from the match that spurted between his fingers, then ducked his cigarette into the flame. He took one girlish puff and handed it to Lilly.

"Christ, you make me pukey," he said, standing up. "All this dither about the social responsibility of the artist. The artist hasn't any. You don't really think Shaw gives a damn, do you? He just juggles ideas in order to outrage those few people who still believe most people are basically nice. And Dickens! Come along, now! He would have been a revolutionary, quite as you say. Except for one thing. That blacking factory, being stuck in the front window, his father in jail. Dickens was prevented from becoming a radical by his own terror of poverty. He'd scrambled up Gad's Hill, you know. The best he could want was to encourage *others* to lift the poor up. He didn't dare risk going back down to push. What if he heaved—you know?—and got left down there? I'll bet he had nightmares . . . I know he did. Some of them are in his books. Sorry to be a bore, Juan, André, but you have, if I may say so, the Latin susceptibility about art and artists. The only social service the artist performs is that of keeping records for some later time."

"No," I said, and meant it, too, "the artist is not just

some sort of scorekeeper. He is the only person in society that matters, because he is the only person in society who is convinced that things *matter*."

"Ah?" Sidney said, shrugging. "Then why are all artists such ruddy *liars?*"

"Because," André said, his face as congested as a plum, "because the artist alone sees the truth. Society, not art, is the distortion."

"Oh, what a lot of slosh you both talk!" Sidney said wearily. "Slosh, slosh, slosh. Get on with chucking bombs if you think you must, but don't pick on artists. *They* won't help you."

"On the contrary," I said, "they already have. . . ."
—*Place Bastille,* page 481

‡

Each new nation has, at birth, the virus of decadence in the bloodstream, soon to jelly the cartilage and rot the bones. Unless the new nation is quickly and repeatedly injected with other cultures, other creeds, other races and religions, it will soon sicken and die. Racial purity is national poison. The cry "Costa Plata for the Costa Platans" is the death rattle of the national spirit. The Indian peoples have given the later-settling Europeans a myth, a history and a form of decorative art. In return they have been infected with syphilis of the body and of the soul. The concessionaires live now like leeches, sucking the silver blood. The future government of Costa Plata will encourage immigration. Give us lively Greeks, compulsive or tender Jews, clockwork Germans, frugal Saxons, Italians ripe with life like brown grapes, Americans who can see in a mountain three skyscrapers, seven square miles of parking lots for automobiles and no statues, French who can see only the statues resting, slumbering in the same stone. There are not enough Costa Platans with red hair!
—*Sing From the Mountains,* page 249

‡

There is no evil in capitalism that cannot be cured by a just system of taxation. There is nothing but evil in capitalism with an injust system of taxation. Wealth should be the final test of human responsibility, met without flinching, abandoned never. The rich are the servants, not the masters, of the poor.

—Essays, page 12

⸸

A backward nation is always on the verge of revolt, and I include all those nations now chained as colonies. Such retarded national groups enjoy special benefits, a peculiar gift of time, time as gap, as absence, not presence. There is no need for the backward nation to struggle slowly toward material progress; all that has been done by the more enlightened nations, the freer nations. (For no nation that is improperly, inadequately educated in the sciences is free. Consider the Moslem cultures, for example, or the Chinese.) Progress can be snatched up; the savage drops the flint-tipped spear and slides his hand lovingly over the handle of a machine gun. He does not have to progress from the spear to the crossbow, invent gunpowder, study the phenomena of expanding gases. The society that is feudal today may progress a century in a decade. That is progress, but it is not civilization. Ten years hence the man behind the machine gun will still be a savage.

—Sing From the Mountains, page 300

⸸

The rich man has no eyes; the poor man has no tongue. Neither senses life. They must marry each other's sisters.

—Essays, page 41

⸸

God gave us the power to dream. We must give God our dreams. He has always enjoyed the sight of smoke, the odor of sacrifice.

—Essays, page 66

⸸

"No! I don't want a creed, a program, a pattern, a blueprint! Man grows. The only action worth taking is that which makes the heart pang like a bud case in spring. Freedom is not a problem of engineering! No architect can build the love of life. When I hurt, here inside, then I will know what to do, or at least that the time has come to do *something!*"

"That is what is so distasteful about pain. It produces hysteria. You are talking the politics of the scream."

"*So?* Then it is because I hurt all the time."

"Then I pity you."

"Save it for yourself."

"*Salaud!* You are immense. They will rip you to pieces."

"Not until I have made them feel the heartache."

"They will never feel it. The masses feel nothing at all."

"I'm not talking about the masses. I'm talking about this person, this man, that woman, a child."

"And you would trust yourself . . . among the people. They will betray you."

"I will risk it."

"Besides, there is no one else to trust, eh?"

"André, you are dead from the waist up."

"Better than dead all over."

—*Place Bastille,* page 293

In any revolutionary situation the power shifts from right to left, and if the revolution continues, from left to right again in the process of counterrevolution. The party of revolt must watch the pendulum, and carry with them a hammer and a spike to nail the shaft, fixing the plunging shaft until the machinery of the past has been discarded and the new works installed. Then wrench free the spike . . . and beware the force of gravity!

—*Essays,* page 99

The relegation of certain races to certain professions (i.e., the restrictions imposed upon the Indians in Costa Plata) by the national trade union is not only a ruthless abridgement of personal liberty but a national crime and a moral wrong.

—*Sing From the Mountains,* page 324

To speak of land reform to the wealthy is to preach socialism. To speak of land reform to the peasants is to say only what lies in their hearts.

—*Essays,* page 119

Once a shark said to a little fish, "Show me where your fellows swim. I will eat some of them, of course, but that is only because I am big, and therefore hungry."

Said the little fish, "Is it not that you are hungry and therefore big?"

Said the shark, "Which, then, shall I eat, your fellows or you?"

Said the little fish, "But sharks are cannibals!"

"Only when the tide is low," said the shark.

—*Essays,* page 134

⸸

"I am against every law that smothers the human spirit, that empties the soul like a pocket, that taps the heart like a wine keg. I am against every law that is based on the terrifying misconception that Nature abhors a vacuum and all the present emptiness will be filled, somehow, sometime. That implies that one of the Natural Laws is a creed of fair play. I am against all oppression, every act that binds the mind, the hands, the tongue. Yes, I am a revolutionary, partly made but mostly born. Because I was born a human being, a man, not a pocket, not a wine keg!"

"Against this, against that, Juan. What are you *for?*"

"Freedom, equality of all races, a true federated government for my people."

"I hardly think they can be worth the trouble of dying for."

"Only to teach them to want to die themselves, rather than submit to the tyranny of a dictator within and the tyranny of the concessionaires without. It is better to die standing up than to live on your knees."

"It is easier to move away."

"I have moved away. One day I will go back."

"And I will prepare something fitting for your headstone."

"My father has no monument. There will be none for me."

—*Place Bastille,* page 334

⸸

A revolution is permanent. After the upheaval, nothing is the same. Blood may be wiped away, the sense of guilt is eradicable. One can only say, "It had to be." But one will always wonder "Why?" I feel already the sense of shame, the claw of guilt in my heart. What will it be like when the first child dies, because I have given this or that order? I cannot think about it . . . not until it is over. Then I will not be able to think of anything else. . . .

—*Essays,* page 150

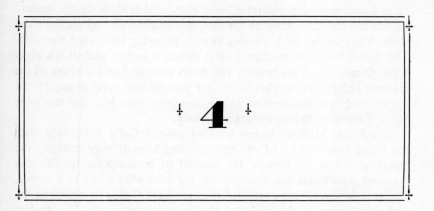

4

"T HERE he is!"

Olmega nodded, his throat too dry to speak. He leaned forward and nudged the taxi driver. The engine sputtered and caught. The driver crossed himself.

"Give us luck."

The yellow light of the streetlamp filled the rear of the taxi like a flood of syrup. Jaime sat on the edge of the seat, holding his pistol in both hands, staring fixedly at the ticking meter. Olmega began to breathe, harsh, dry yanks. The driver clashed the gears and nearly stalled.

The residence of the archbishop was surrounded by a high fence of iron rods, tipped like spears. A puddle of light was spread between the twin stone pillars. The gate swung open. The keeper in tasseled livery and pumps swung the big key in his hand. Olmega drew the revolver from his jacket and pressed back the hammer. Jaime's teeth chittered above the noise of the taxi motor. The automobile slowed.

The slender dark figure stood in the light and nodded once, politely, to the gatekeeper. Olmega stared, astonished. These little, last gestures! How odd it was! How . . . innocent!

The Prime Minister's hair looked golden in the lamplight. He turned and tapped a cigarette on a case, and with a dainty gesture placed the cigarette between his lips. His shadow moved on the sidewalk. The taxi shivered, moving slowly, swinging in toward the curb. The driver began to mutter. Colleo struck a match and lit his cigarette. Olmega held his breath. His heart slammed in his chest like a trapped animal. He curled his finger around the hard prong of the trigger and crowded against Jaime, reaching over him for the door latch. They were twenty meters away now.

The Prime Minister began walking toward Calle Villaverde with the short, light strides of old age, holding himself very straight, the cigarette still in his mouth. He seemed to be cooperating, like the assistant who holds the cigarette for the trick-shot artist at a circus. The taxi driver, Olmega realized, was praying. Colleo approached the first streetlamp to the right of the archbishop's gate. Ten meters away. How skinny the old man was! Five meters. He looked around, his head turning sharply like a night bird's. The taxi drew up beside him. Jaime made a dry, squeaking little cry. Colleo raised his eyebrows. Olmega drove the breath out of his chest in a shout.

"Taxi, señor?"

Colleo turned to face the automobile. Olmega pointed his pistol. The barrel jumped and wobbled uncontrollably. The Prime Minister's face froze in an expression of surprise and terror, his mouth a dark O. Olmega squeezed the trigger four times. The revolver smacked, the butt kicking against his wet palm. The Prime Minister raised his right hand to his cheek, clapping it there as though swatting a fly. Jaime, still holding the pistol in both hands, propped the weapon on the windowsill. Colleo swayed and started to fall backward. Jaime's pistol crashed once, and the slug yowled off the pavement. The pistol fired again, and Colleo spun like a dancer and toppled to the sidewalk. Olmega wrenched at the door handle and shoved. The door swung open, and Jaime fell out into the street.

"Hurry!"

Jaime crawled on all fours, the revolver tocking each time he set down his right hand. He stood up, swaying like a drunkard, and staggered toward the figure sprawled on the sidewalk. Down the street a man began to shout. Jaime bent over the body. Olmega felt purpose and will gush like adrenalin, an injection of brute cruelty. He glided from the taxi, perfectly controlled, lithe and easy. He moved up behind Jaime. The Prime Minister tried to sit up. One hand patted his belly. Jaime twitched his finger and shot Colleo in the face. The Prime Minister's broken dentures clattered out on the sidewalk. Olmega raised his pistol, pointed the barrel behind Jaime's right ear and squeezed the trigger. At the crack of the shot, Jaime dropped like a bundle and rolled over on his left side. His revolver slipped from his fingers. A puddle of blood spread from the Prime Minister's head. Olmega heard running steps. The gatekeeper trotted down the sidewalk, his coattails fluttering, both hands raised as if in surrender. Olmega walked swiftly to the taxi. The driver screeched and let in the clutch, nearly throwing Olmega out into the street.

"The hand grenade!"

Olmega felt the heavy object dropped into his hand. He fumbled with the pin as the taxi hammered for the corner. They rocked, skidding, with shrieking tires. The motor roared.

"Police!"

In a white jacket and helmet, right ahead of them, was the policeman, his right arm raised in the signal to halt. The taxi shot straight at him. Olmega released the lever. The police officer yelled furiously and dodged aside. Olmega dropped the grenade out of the window and ducked his head. The street went bright in the instant of the explosion. The taxi roared on. Olmega straightened and began beating the driver on the head and shoulders.

"Slow down, you idiot! Slow down!"

The driver hunched like a tortoise, cursing wildly. Olmega threw himself forward and shouted into the driver's ear.

"Take the next right! The next right!"

The driver shouted incoherently, but twisted the wheel. The taxi slowed and nosed into a narrow side street alive with children. The driver beat the horn button, and the children scattered, laughing shrilly.

"That's it. Now, don't drive so fast. You'll have them down on us."

The driver shook his head.

"Oh, it's all right for you. But what about my license, eh? What about that? How am I to live? Mother of God, I must be crazy!"

Olmega began to laugh. He slumped back into the rear seat, helpless, the laughter bubbling in his chest. The taxi trundled down the street. Olmega laughed until his sides hurt and the tears streamed down his face. He stopped. They were approaching the Glorieta Colón with the fountains and the statute. The cafés were bright and waltz music floated in the night, sweet, lilting and innocent. Happy faces of men and women turned in the lights like flowers. Olmega wiped his face and sat back. Now his hands were beginning to shake uncontrollably, and he felt terribly chilled. He pressed his shoulders back against the cracked leather of the seat and groaned. A hand touched him, and he started, his hand groping for the useless pistol in his pocket.

"Rotten luck."

"What? What do you mean? We got him all right. Oh, we got him, I tell you!"

"Jaime—"

"Shut up!"

The driver turned his head. He seemed quite calm.

"This place is near the waterfront, you say?"

"Yes. Off Calle San Diego."

"Funny. I've been driving in the city for seven years. Day and night. Night and day. I never heard of it before. A *pensión,* eh?"

"That's right. A blue light over the door. Number seven."

"Never heard of it before. But don't worry. I can find it."

Olmega nodded and closed his eyes. He trembled as if with a fever.

"I'm thirsty. *Jesucristo,* I'm thirsty!"

The taxi rumbled on. Olmega could hear the others whispering, shocked by Jaime's death.

"It must have been part of the plan. From the beginning."

"Why didn't Pepe tell us?"

"No, Sánchez should have told us."

"Idiot, we would have given it away. To Jaime. You see? That's why."

"I never would have believed it. Pepe's cousin—"

"Shhhh. Shhh. He can hear you."

"I don't care. If that's what they made him do, what will they make *us* do?"

"You swore to follow orders. All orders. Damn it, I didn't get a chance to throw my grenade, either."

The taxi halted. Olmega opened his eyes.

"Here we are, boys. Get out. Hurry! I've got to get back to the garage."

Olmega lifted his head. He felt drugged, sluggish, thirsty to the point of frenzy. He dragged himself from the taxi and shuffled to the doorway. The taxi drove away. A woman's head appeared in the slit of the half-opened door.

"What do you want, *chicos?*"

"A room for the night."

"But it's late."

"We are tourists."

The woman opened the door. Olmega stumbled into the narrow vestibule. The others followed him. The woman held a candle up to Olmega's face. He stared at the flame.

"Well? How did it go?"

"It went well. Perfectly."

"Ah! This way, this way . . ."

She turned and climbed a steep flight of stairs. Olmega followed, lifting himself by tugging on the banister and setting his right foot on every step, like a child. He stumbled down a narrow, dark and smelly hall. The woman touched her candle to another. Olmega threw himself on the bed. The woman stared down at him.

"You are very young."

"Ah. Bring me some water, señora. Something to drink."

"Here. Right here."

She filled a wooden cup from a pitcher on the washstand. It was stale and tepid. Olmega drank it at a single gulp.

"More."

He drank again. The water ran down inside him and vanished.

"More. More."

"*Basta!* Enough, you'll be sick."

"More."

"One more."

"Where are the others?"

"In the next room. Don't worry, you are safe here."

"He told me that Jaime was just as important as Colleo—"

"Sssh. Tell me nothing. I don't want to know any more. Go to sleep now."

Olmega groaned and lay back on the bed. The woman took the empty cup from his hand.

"Where is the pistol? I am to get rid of it."

"My jacket—"

"Where? Oh, yes. Sleep, now. You have been very brave."

"I am thirsty."

"Shhhh."

Olmega closed his eyes, and sleep rushed upon him. His right hand twitched. The woman drew a cotton blanket over him and blew out the candle.

⊥

The great fans hanging down from the ceiling churned silently, and the blue-and-silver national flags, the party colors and battalion battle standards stirred sluggishly, the tips rolling out and subsiding. An orchestra played, but without spirit, as though the heat and humidity had softened the violin strings. The banquet hall of the building that housed the headquarters of the Red Beret was a rich scene, the candlelight caught shimmering in the wine goblets, the white tablecloths scored with scarlet runners and explosions of poppies in silver vases. The poppies, Livermore had been told, were the official party flower. The party members were in uniforms studded with medals, orders of merit and loops of braid. The conversation rumbled, subsiding nearly to silence, then inflated again. Waiters in livery, their faces streaming, toiled between the tables. Champagne bottles popped.

There was something not so much wrong as false about the banquet. Livermore could sense it, although it took him more than an hour to study the great hall and the hundreds of guests until he knew. His mind crept this way and that, sensing, testing, listening and watching, responding to the faintest sort of warning, a furtive little series of nudges. There was something of the tension when the lord during the Christmas holidays visited the staff of his house below-stairs. The uniforms, the soft, staccato conversations, the winks, jogging elbows and smiles, the overenthusiastic applause, the careful glances at Vizarra seated on the dais. The analogy came to Livermore from his youth: the headmaster's dinner for seniors and Old Boys, that was it; the same compound of politeness and respect diluted with the acid of envy and salted with contempt. What was pompous and official always struck Livermore as faintly hypocritical.

He could not understand the speeches, long, tedious and rhetorical, full of questions that dragged out a sluggish chorus of *"Sí, sí, sí!"* and damp splatters of applause. Vizarra had seemed at ease and had made a little joke about his bandaged hand. The laughter was perfunctory; the rumor had already started that a sniper had fired on the sedan somewhere in the mountains, the bullet grazing Vizarra's palm. (The headmaster's sprained ankle, twisted on the cricket pitch when he lobbed the first ball to open the match between the seniors and Old Boys. The school rumor was that the "Beak" had got himself squiffed on sherry at luncheon.) Since the rumor was better than the joke, it would survive the banquet and spread everywhere the next day.

Vizarra had provided an English transcript of his own brief address. Livermore had glanced at it . . . the accomplished catchphrases: loyalty, energy, building for the future on the foundations of the past, indoctrination of youth, the sanctity of the home, family and the Church. A titter swept through the stuffy hall when Vizarra read the archbishop's florid apology for his inability to attend. Vizarra had raised one eyebrow, a twitch of irony, as he phrased the company's sense of loss.

Only when the Caudillo responded to the toast tendered him and raised his own glass to give the guests themselves and their historic movement that had secured Costa Plata a place in the sun, did the response seem to have the fervor of honesty. Hundreds of party members surged to their feet, boots battering and spurs clinking. The wine glasses were held aloft, drunk from, passed to the right, then to the left. The singing began at the far end of the hall, and rushed toward the dais like a tidal wave. Uncertainly, Livermore had stood and sipped from his own glass. Dunkel and Herzler pushed back their chairs. The German seemed flushed and somehow pleased. Dunkel grinned and called through the music something about "Rotary."

While it was clearly neither the time nor the place to discuss any sort of official business, Livermore had hoped to sound Vizarra a bit more deeply, to present a few new sketches, as it were, before final shape was given to the blueprints. He and Dunkel had conferred at some length over iced lemon squash in the sweltering cardroom of the ship. Dunkel admitted certain irregularities had taken place over an extended period of time on the railroad. He called it "managerial carelessness," a term that struck Livermore as ingenious. The "carelessness" had brought Dunkel's firm in excess of eight million dollars above legally permitted freight fees. The American was not so certain that the facts were completely damning. After all, Costa Plata depended on the railways, and Costa Platan involvement in the concession was nowhere higher than locomotive engineers, firemen, conductors and porters. All the managerial and executive staff were Americans. How could the trains run without the concession?

The matter of the silver mines themselves was more difficult. Livermore had explained Herzler's position: the German had been told by his government to do the best he could, to make any sort of settlement that would bring hard money to Weimar. Not only the matter of "managerial carelessness," but the fact that the three firms no longer could present a solid front at the bargaining table clearly posed difficulties, even dangers.

Dunkel had thought for a moment. Then he shrugged.

"Then we'll force the krauts out of the mines. Set up . . . well, maybe you wouldn't be interested in a joint firm. I could go it alone."

"On the contrary, I should have to insist on a joint firm. I have contacts in the mining industry in Africa and in Wales. Tin mines in Wales, too."

"Maybe we can work it out. Mining's not my game, but it shouldn't be hard to stir interest back home. I say this. Let's work for a short-term agreement. Two, three years. We'll say we've made a mess of it. I'd go along for increased freight rates. Jump ten, fifteen per cent. That extra amount we just turn over to the government. Act of good faith. How long could the krauts go on paying the new rates?"

"That would depend, of course. New mining equipment is needed now, as I understand it. If they got it—"

"Then there might be some kind of strike."

"Strikes are illegal."

"A walkout, then. Higher wages. The Germans would have to refuse. Either way, we've got them. I'd say eighteen months at the outside before they start to run at a loss. By the end of three years they'll be so busted, they'll have to quit. Have to. We set up a joint firm and underbid anyone who pokes his nose in."

"A low bid, but for a very extended agreement."

"Right. Maybe . . . twenty-five years, fifty, ninety-nine. We'd have to see. I'll drop a word at my end of the table. You talk to him. Sound him out."

But it had proved quite impossible. Vizarra had exchanged politenesses, banalities about the heat, a few bits of information about the

110

Red Beret as an organization (which struck Livermore as an amalgamated veterans' association and the Church militant run by Tories without opposition) and a comment on the rich food. Livermore's uninspired remark that the evening lacked the presence of ladies provoked an odd, disconcerting remark. The Caudillo make a peculiar gesture, a hunched torso twist, as though flinging free of ropes that bound him. His eyes, voice and gestures became animated, and he spoke in his rapid, perfect English about some blind young woman of great beauty he had met in a mountain village. Livermore gathered that the Caudillo saw her as somehow typical of his nation's backwardness, at least in the matter of public health facilities. Yet this blind girl was linked in Vizarra's mind with some objective he hoped to provide for the Red Beret itself, a sort of populist movement of the party and the Church. It was all very puzzling. Livermore made a flattering reference to the young woman who had been his hostess at the Caudillo's villa the previous evening. He had been quite honestly dazzled by her youth and frail beauty, her gay animation. He had been told that Vizarra's mistress was an entertainer and had expected a vulgar female with dyed hair, excessive jewelry, plump hips and no manners. Yet Vizarra had not been pleased. He made a curt, chopping motion with his hand and muttered darkly, something Livermore did not hear clearly. He had smiled wanly and returned to his fillet of *boeuf en gelée* and his study of the hall and the uniformed guests.

The room began to fill with cigar smoke, although the dessert had not been passed. Men now left the table and wandered from one place to another, talking loudly. Areas at the rear of the hall seemed to be given over entirely to drink and laughter. Livermore supposed the party officials were much cheered by the capture of the rebel, Alessandro Martín. Then, too, Latins were given to excesses and social crudity.

Someone brushed rather heavily against Livermore's chair. One of Vizarra's innumerable aides bent over and whispered. The Caudillo could not hear; the room had begun to swell with noise. The aide spoke more loudly. Vizarra's lips thinned. He nodded once.

"*Muerto?*"

"*Sí, Caudillo mío. Muerto. Y un estudiante también. Uno de—*"

The aide moved his finger at the banquet chamber, including all the guests in his gesture. Vizarra nodded in dismissal, turned and spoke to the heavily decorated official to his left. There were gestures of regret, apologies, shrugs and smiles. The Caudillo shook a number of hands. Malata appeared at his side and received instructions. He inclined his sleek, dark head in a bow and glided away. A bell rang for order, and after nearly a minute the crowded hall fell reasonably quiet. An announcement was made. Vizarra stood and made the party salute. The hall stood in a thunder of boots and responded with a grumbling cheer. The orchestra struck up the national anthem, and Livermore dutifully rose to attention. Dunkel, he noticed with dismay, was still seated. Livermore tried to catch his eye but failed. Vizarra left the dais and walked out of the hall, smiling and shaking hands, giving the party salute. Livermore sat down. At once Malata touched his arm.

"His Excellency has been taken away by unexpected business. I will escort you and the other two gentlemen when the dinner is concluded."

"Very good, I'm sure."

The dessert course did not appear. Livermore sat watching the dinner dissolve into groups of gesticulating, shouting swagger. The heat was suffocating. The higher officials abandoned the dais, one by one. Champagne corks popped like fusillades. The singing began, other songs, different songs, the music of past combats and triumphs, strident voices shouting the words to a dozen melodies jumbled and echoing off the roof. There were menace and mockery in the faces that shot out of the cigar smoke and hung there glaring. It was not merely the servants cutting up after the lord has gone back above. These were not Old Boys carousing at the local pub. Boots began to slam in marching cadence on the floor. The orchestra faltered, then swung into the party song again. The brass snarled through the smoke, and the violins stitched and stung. The first glasses and pieces of dinnerware broke. Livermore's interpreter, standing to his right, had gone pale with distress and was calling Malata's name over and over in a bleating voice. Three uniforms stood in a line, braying words of the party song at Dunkel. They kept gesturing for the American to rise and join them. Dunkel grinned, as though watching a circus. He turned to Livermore, then back to the three uniformed men. He stood up and saluted awkwardly. The party members bowed and began chanting.

"Ya-ya-ya-ya!"

Malata appeared, followed by four young party members wearing their red berets. Malata spoke to Herzler and Dunkel. Livermore stood and walked down the table. The slender dark man bowed slightly, his face expressionless.

"The automobiles are waiting."

Livermore walked by him to Dunkel.

"It was very wise of you to stand just then."

"It struck me that they were in a pretty ugly mood. What's up, anyway?"

"I'm not sure."

Herzler was swaying slightly. He seemed intoxicated by the noise as well as the wine. He waved his arm.

"There is much color here tonight."

"Indeed . . ."

Some of the men, perhaps three dozen caught in Livermore's single glance, were now marching, their left arms swinging stiffly from the shoulder. The concussion of the boots shivered the floor. Oddly enough, they carried burning candles in their right fists. Livermore turned away, alarmed.

"Let us get out of here. I don't like this."

‡

"Café, señorita . . ."

Lucía placed the sheet music on the dressing table and cleared a section near the butt-choked ashtray. Her maid set down the pot and the small cup and saucer, then moved to close the window.

"Leave it open. It's hot tonight, even with the fan on."

"Ricardo Belgarito is waiting for you. That is, he begs the honor of being allowed to speak a few moments with you."

"Send him in a moment."

"Sí, señorita."

Lucía poured out the coffee and sipped it, lit a cigarette and began to draw a brush through her thick, black hair. She hummed softly, drawing the brush down with firm, rapid strokes, the cigarette smoke trickling up against her cheek. She squinted at herself in the mirror, dabbed off the creamy mustache on her upper lip and fastened up the front of her thin dressing gown. Someone tapped on the door.

"Yes? Come in?"

The maid entered with a short well-dressed man with pomaded hair.

"Señor Belgarito . . ."

Lucía turned without rising and held out her hand. She felt the brush of his lips. The maid closed the door.

"Señorita, you sang tonight . . . oh, how can I say it, eh? You know when you are in perfect voice. Like a crystal glass touched with a finger. So fine, so pure!"

Lucía laughed shortly and puffed on her cigarette.

"Still the same Rico. Rico Rigoletto."

"Señorita, it is your eyes that wound me, not your words."

"Sit down, Rico. Stop dancing around like that. You make me nervous. You want a drink, I suppose. There's champagne in the corner."

"I am refreshed by the sight of your face, señorita."

"Stop it, Rico. And stop calling me señorita."

"I cannot dare to call you Lucía, my dove, not these days. Champagne. And good stuff, too. I always said you would be lucky, *alma mía*. And so here you are, eh? Your own radio show every week! I heard about the new contract, too. *Dios!* It's a good thing the station is owned by the government. Who else can afford you?"

"Get out, Rico. Just get out."

"Lucía, I didn't mean it that way. You know me. I am never careful enough. Words fly out of me. Oh, if I could only sing."

"You don't have to. Give me some. No, in a big glass filled with ice first."

"So, so. You have changed the way you drink. Someone else drinks champagne in a tall glass filled with ice. Oh, I wouldn't know, of course. But I hear things, you know."

"I'm warning you, Rico. Another insult and—"

"How your eyes flash! You are indeed adorable. The whole nation is at your feet. Soon men will kill themselves because they have not your love."

"I doubt that you will be so dramatic, Rico. Besides, it's Rita now, isn't it?"

"Who? Oh, Rita. Well, she's going to America, you know. To make a few films."

"Ah. Good for her."

"And that is why I am here, of course."

"Now the truth comes. And I thought it was because you loved me."

"I do, I do! I swear it. I am in pain from it."

"Rico, you imbecile. What is it that you want?"

"You *have* changed. But it's to be expected. Very simply, I will tell you. You have not made a film since *Amor y Sangre*. I am producing and directing a new film. Beginning in three months. A sequel to *Amor y Sangre*. It seems that you didn't really die!"

"What a wonderful thought, Rico."

"Exactly. You are so sensitive, my love! Listen, there is a new tenor in the opera, an Italian, handsome as a god and not at all stupid. He will play opposite you, of course, as the doctor in the hospital. You have been brought in, shot, bleeding. He examines you . . . no, don't smile, don't! I will photograph very artistically."

"How? I was shot in the breast, remember?"

"The bullet went through you or something. We photograph only the back."

"Down to the ankles, eh?"

"Of course not! Lucía, don't you trust me?"

"No, Rico. I did once, that was enough."

"That was before . . . ah, I say nothing! . . . The doctor falls in love with you. Unfortunately, he—"

"—is married. But he asks me to be his mistress. I love him, but—"

"Has anyone else been talking with you, Lucía?"

"They don't have to. Go on."

"You love him, but you recall all the misery of your earlier life. We show these scenes."

"Taken right out of the old film. You save—how much?"

"Twenty thousand reales, maybe. You think some more. You are a little girl in church."

"Oh, my God, Rico!"

"Wait! Listen! Also you become great friends with one of the sisters at the hospital, but she is old. An emergency happens, you are there. The sister's heart fails her. She falls to the floor. The patient, a young girl. You nurse her until the doctor arrives. The old sister dies. You take the rosary from her fingers. The patient, the doctor both praise and bless you. You walk away. Entranced. You have the call!"

"Rico, no! You can't be serious!"

"But completely! You take the orders. The doctor is wild with despair. He drinks. He loses his job. His wife, with all his children, she comes to see you. They all beg you to save him. Only you can save him. No, you tell them. God alone can save him. You will pray for him. So you pray. The next day your superiors receive notice that a nurse is badly needed at the hospital. They think of you, naturally. You go. Operating is your doctor. You give him strength. It is his last chance! The operation is very delicate. The girl you saved before, see? Success! The doctor comes to know spiritual love that you embody. How does that sound? *Okay?*"

"What?"

"*Okay.* Americans say it. Rita told me. It means all right."

"And I get the twenty thousand reales you save by using the old shots."

"Plus a percentage of what we make."

"You are a fool, Rico."

"Don't say that, Lucía. You could be a great actress. Great!"

"In the first place, you know very well that Rafa—I mean, His Excellency is no longer willing for me to play on the stage or in films. Only on the radio, once a week. Second, I would never fill in for Rita, just because she's left you for some American."

"She left me? You are joking. I was sick to death of her."

"Third, I make twenty thousand a month now. Five thousand a week."

"Fifty thousand, then, but I couldn't afford any percentage."

"Fourth, after . . . what happened, I would never work for you again. With some Italian tenor. You must be mad. Please go away."

"Look. Here is the contract. I will just leave it here with you. Just *look* at it, that's all! Then perhaps you could call me."

"Ah! Oh, of course!"

"Write a little note. I could come here again—"

"Get out, Rico! Please, just get out!"

"Listen, why not come with me? To my villa. For one drink. A champagne. We will talk a little bit more."

"I have done talking with you and listening to you, Rico. It is impossible. I am going to Paris, anyway."

"Ah? Alone? I have friends there—"

"No. Not alone. I am with him always now."

"Always? You have an innocent side still, eh, Lucía? He won't marry you, though!"

"Imbecile! It is I who will not marry him!"

116

"You are a little fool, then, my sweet one. It is your greatest chance. Why not?"

"There are too many reasons. You would never understand."

"I am a man. I understand. It is said he is impotent. Everyone knows."

"They are wrong. He cannot have children, that's all."

"All? Enough, no?"

"You are very impudent. Now get out, please. I have a headache."

"Ah, my little dove—"

"If you touch me, Rico, I will—"

"No, no, no! I hadn't thought of it, believe me! Señorita, please don't be angry, I beg of you!"

She jerked her head toward the door. He dropped the contract on the chair he had sat on and fled. She drained the glass and tore open her robe. The dressing room was sweltering. She picked up the telephone, suddenly aware of a noise in the street below.

"Please have the automobile brought around to the side, as usual."

The door burst open. Lucía whirled, holding her dressing gown, instantly furious. It was the maid.

"Oh, something terrible has happened, señorita! Something terrible!"

"What is it? Tell me! It is not—"

"They have shot the Prime Minister! He is dead!"

"Oh. Who? Who? Oh, Colleo. Ah, thank God. . . . Get me dressed. I must hurry to the villa. Perhaps I can help. Cancel the rehearsal for tomorrow. They will understand. Tell Vittorio I'm taking the music with me to study. Where are my stockings?"

The bodyguard met her in the lobby. She walked swiftly toward him, adjusting the mantilla around her hair.

"It is true? About Colleo?"

"Unfortunately, señorita."

"Where is His Excellency?"

"At the villa, I believe, señorita."

"We will go there, at once."

The usual crowd waited outside the door. She walked quickly down between the double line of police. Voices cried for her autograph. She shook her head. Then voices of women shouted ugly words at her. One of the policemen cursed and struggled into the crowd in pursuit.

A man bellowed from down the street.

"First Colleo! Then the Old Mule! Then you, *puta de lujo. Hija de puta,* you whore's daughter!"

The sedan door thudded shut. She could see the police heaving against the screaming crowd. A stone bounded off the auto fender. The bodyguard beside her cursed and muttered an apology in the same breath. Lucía fumbled in her purse for a cigarette. She found the packet beneath the film contract left by Ricardo Belgarito.

⸸

The assistant office manager stared across the desk at Fingel. His thin lips wrinkled with contempt. He laughed like someone rapping on a door.

"Your sort doesn't give up. No is not an answer, eh?"

Fingel sighed and played idly with the straps on his briefcase. He shrugged. After all, the cropped-haired man with the cold little eyes was only an assistant.

"I have my superiors to account to. I have been given specific instructions to present my credentials both to the officers of the concession corporation and to the workingmen's organization."

The assistant manager shook his head.

"We have no need of your services. I have told you that. If you wish to make a nuisance of yourself, you may wait until the end of the first shift. Ramos is now in the shaft. You will have to speak with him. He is the head of the 'workingmen's organization.' "

He laughed again, a mirthless rattle of air.

"They must be a pretty set, this company of yours. Who ever heard of insuring the life of an Indian miner? I cannot tell one from another, I assure you."

Fingel leaned forward, pressing at what he thought was a weak spot.

"That, sir, is the beauty of our organization. We offer low-rate insurance to *groups* of workers . . . and officials, too, of course. The larger the group, the lower the rate. For example—"

"I have given you permission to speak with Ramos at the end of the shift. Be good enough to clear out of here by noon at the latest. I don't want to have to send a guard looking for you."

He bent his head and pretended to examine some papers on the desk. Fingel nodded and rose.

"Thank you, sir, for your kindness."

118

The small cold eyes flicked up, searching for irony. Fingel bowed and shuffled from the office. So. Nothing to do but wait. He was used to waiting. Sometimes it seemed to him that most of his life had been spent standing in line or seated on a bench, waiting. Patience was not normally considered a virtue in a business career, but Fingel knew that he did not have a business career. Such a notion implied past successes and future opportunities, and he had neither. He had only the life of Fingel and worked only to live from day to day. For that sort of existence, patience was more than a virtue; it was a necessity, one of the blunt tools of endurance. Over the years, as he moved or was driven from one country to another, from city to city, from town to village, he had gathered nothing in the way of material goods. He had lost interest in money. Who can imagine wealth hunched at a last mending shoes, candling eggs in a poultry market, selling shabby goods from door to door? Money was for food, a place to sleep, secondhand clothes. Money was to keep the life. Money was coins from a newspaper kiosk, shabby bits of paper for collecting bad debts for an agency, for disposing of rickety furniture in half the ghettos of Europe. And so the purpose of life was merely to keep the life. Whatever he saved went for forged papers, working permits, police identification cards. And that was where money and patience came together. Fingel's single skill was in combining small sums with endless patience. Not even a game of wits, which might be amusing. There was nothing comic about the officials, the uniformed ones, the bureaucrats. For them the life was nothing, a thing of no importance one way or the other. Only the papers were important. You could not get a working permit without having proof of employment. But you could not get a job without already having an old working permit. The life was not enough for them; the papers must prove the life. Only the papers were important. That and the small bribes. Small for them, exorbitant for Fingel.

And this job, the result of answering an advertisement in a newspaper. A tiny salary, enough for the life, and a commission, hopefully, to pay the officials. To sell insurance, when he had none himself. It reminded him of an earlier job he had soliciting newspaper subscriptions, newspapers published in a language he himself could not read.

Outside the office building the sun baked the dust. He found a broken chair in the shade of a shed and sat down, patting the dust from his pants. The whole complex of the mine was a mystery to him.

He looked from one building to another, some large, some small, all shimmering in the late morning sun. Machinery churned and rattled, belts flailed and ore crushers pounded. He noticed the aqueduct and the angular constructions of pipes, like some children's game. A locomotive sniffed somewhere. He saw the steel cars on a siding, low, ugly, like wheeled tortoises, the cars that carried the precious ingots from the mine vaults to the Banco Central de Costa Plata. The mine, he knew, was worth millions. The figure was as meaningless to him as the row of zeros after the digits that indicated the assets of his own firm. He wondered briefly if some sort of job might be available at the mine. A night watchman, say; that would suit him. He could stay in one place for a long time. He could guard the life, while he helped to guard the mine.

He thought of the cropped Teutonic head, the chilling eyes. A Jew guard at a silver mine? Laughter like the rattle of pebbles on an iron shutter.

A jet of steam feathered from a stack, and, a few seconds later, the hoot of the whistle sounding the end of the morning shift. Fingel stood up and walked toward the nearest big building.

He wandered from one clanging, water-slushing, metallic-tainted chunk of concrete to the next. The surface workers were white or half-breeds. They tried to ignore him, or gave him only vague directions. After many minutes he stepped into a sort of alley, and was nearly knocked flat by a herd of small brown men trotting all in one direction. He peered at their faces as they darted past. Their cheeks were pasted with dirt and sweat, the whites of their eyes inflamed. Their small hands were hooked like claws, and they ran flat-footed, slapping up the dust, their ropy legs flinging forward their feet to keep their exhausted bodies from sprawling. Their canvas leggings wheeted as they ran, a sound like the cry of many small birds. Straight hair, oiled and glued with dust, snapped against their jaws and shoulders. Fingel expected to see next several men on horseback with long goads, driving them. Instead, one man, an Indian, came walking. His left arm was a tube that ended at the elbow. The foreman? Fingel stepped forward and lifted his derby, holding it tightly and glancing apprehensively over his shoulder. One of the herd that trotted by him was the hat thief; he was sure of it. Perhaps even now he crouched, the wind of desire whistling through his broad nostrils, his eyes shining, ready to pounce and bear Fingel's derby off into one of the prison-like buildings.

120

"Pardon. You speak Spanish?"

The Indian nodded.

"I wish to see Ramos. To speak with him. On a matter of business."

The Indian examined him carefully. Fingel put his derby back on and fluffed the dingy handkerchief in his breast pocket. He felt like clucking sympathetically. The Indian was taller and heavier than others he had seen; his features were regular. But the stumped left arm and the compensating overdevelopment of the right, biceps like a melon, forearm like the shaft of a wagon wired with high, hard veins, the skin like a sheath of polished leather, made him unbalanced, deformed.

"What sort of business? You are not from the company."

"No, no."

"Not from the government. Then what?"

The Indian was not hostile, but cautious, responsible. Fingel liked him at once. He batted his eyes and rushed happily ahead, leaning forward slightly and holding the rim of his derby, as though the words that spilled from his lips were gusts against him as he drove furiously, nearly flying through the air, zooming into the land of milk and honey for all.

"I am very glad you asked me that. Oh, yes, yes, very glad. I represent not so much a corporation but the promise of the future for all the workingmen here at this mine. Now they work long hours, and for many years, but when they *stop* working, there is no more money. But a few centavos, only a very few, paid by each man, now, beginning immediately, in only twenty years—a short time when you think of it—all the money gathers itself and pours out at the end of twenty years, a great sum, in truth. Each workingman may—in fact, ought to—buy now the ease of his body and the repose of his soul in later years. Don't you agree? I can see that you do. Also in case of injury, each workingman will be paid by my people. So much for a foot, so much for a leg, so much for an eye . . . an arm . . ."

He stopped, breathless. The Indian stared at him. Then he turned.

"Come."

↓

Fingel waited. He was uneasy. It was after the noon hour. He opened his briefcase and took out a dry roll. He ate it carefully, catching the crumbs and dropping them back into his briefcase. The Indians squatting on the floor before him stared at him with dark, sober eyes. Fingel took out three small apples, peeled off the wormy skin of one, cut it up and offered it. None of the Indians moved. Fingel sighed and ate the apple. He repeated the offer with the second apple and then gave up.

The place was the dirt-floored outer room of a low, stone dwelling, quite a big place. The room was cool, dim and smelly. He alone sat on a wooden stool. The Indians waited. At first Fingel had counted eleven. One had stood up, although no summons had been given, and walked to the end of the room, pushed aside a faded piece of carpet that hung there and vanished inside. After a while, sometimes only a few minutes, often longer, another Indian would stiffen, rise and walk through the entrance into the inner room. None returned to the waiting chamber. Fingel strained his ears and caught low, crooning noises, like the sound of wind at night blowing through the mountain pines and cedars. Once or twice the high yelp of a dog, often a guttural wet, drenching noise. Fingel shivered and worried about the assistant manager and the mine guards. What would he do if a complaint were lodged against him to the police? Fingel knew Costa Plata, and he had heard of the American gangster, O'Conner, who ran the police. Fingel had once lived in New York City, but his English was poor. He had lived then with a tailor, a single man like himself, who spoke only Yiddish. It seemed so long ago. Another Indian rose. There were only three left.

Fingel tried to hum a little song, but, inexplicably, his tongue suddenly hurt. He thrust his finger into his mouth. A canker from the apples. He dozed, then awoke with a start, remembering his hat. It was still on his head. Without knowing quite why, he stood up, his legs stiff and weak from sitting so long, and walked to the end of the room. He pushed aside the piece of carpet.

He stood on a wooden, filth-encrusted balcony. A flight of steep stone steps dropped to the floor of a large, square room. The floor was strewn with carpets, patches of woven rugs, the hemp sleeping mats of the Indians. The walls of the room were of stone, painted with trees, flowers and birds, all sooted over, only partially visible, the bright blossoms seeping through the smudge like wounds. Two candles thick as pillars with flames broad and bright lit the far end of the room. Fingel saw a dozen Indians crouched and wrenched into rigid postures and scattered against one wall like the dark husks of insects. The Indian with one arm sat cross-legged between the

122

candles, tapping on a wood block with a long, gray piece of bone, his stumped arm hanging like the uppers of an unfinished riding boot. Behind him was a brazier, out of which rose tendrils of pungent smoke. Fingel, to his own amazement, did not hesitate but moved briskly down the steps to the odorous, spongy surface of the floor below. Bits of dry hemp and woven reed flaked off beneath the pressure of his heavy-soled shoes. He swung his briefcase awkwardly, staring at the fixed line of dark bodies tumbled along the wall in positions too twisted to be those of death. Fingel's brain buzzed, an uncomfortable, dazed feeling. His flesh thrilled along his arms as he walked forward. Behind the brazier, sitting in a canvas folding chair, was the man from the railroad station at Casanueva. He was spooning soup from an aluminum pan. The Indian raised the bone and pointed.

"Ramos."

As he said the word, the Indian's face split into a wide grin of spaced teeth like piano keys. He played his bone on the wood block, and his smile slipped away. Fingel tipped his hat.

"Herman Fingel, commercial representative."

The man placed the aluminum pan on the brazier and stood up, carefully sucking his fingers. He swaggered toward Fingel, his long thumbs thrust into his leather belt like pistol butts. On his feet he wore miner's shoes, sections of automobile tire with sandal straps. He inclined his head, his long hair falling forward.

"Don Pedro Ramos, *a su servicio.*"

Fingel swallowed and managed to avoid looking at the figures along the wall. Ramos smiled, a very gentle lift of his lips.

"This is your house. Come, be seated."

The bone on the wood block clocked like Fingel's heart. He shot his hand into his pocket and produced his business card, peeling one free from a sweat-clotted packet, and handed it over the brazier. Ramos dropped the bit of pasteboard into the coals. Fingel watched in dismay as the smoke thickened; a petal of flame bloomed briefly. The card curled and broke to glowing, then gray bits. Ramos smiled again and folded his powerful arms. He stared evenly, expectantly, at Fingel.

"What have you come to give me, please?"

Fingel swallowed, tapped his briefcase and spread his palms.

"What is the best gift one man can give another man? An idea."

The leader of the Indian miners snorted contemptuously. He waved one clawlike hand around the big, daubed room.

"There are ideas here already. Enough for us."

"This is an idea that will make the miners happy."

"Man is never happy. Only when he is . . . so."

He pointed at the rigid bodies along the wall. Fingel swallowed.

"They . . . are they all right?"

"They are happy."

"My idea will give them money. Each worker, if all of them join the plan—"

"Plan? What plan? We want no plans here. Get out! Get out!"

"Please, please, just a moment of your time—"

"You say money. Well, then, hand it over. I will consider it a contribution for the construction."

"What construction?"

"Of Ciudad Feliz. Soon I must take them all away. It has been spoken to me, and so it must be done."

He poked one long finger at the rigid dark forms. His profile was sharp, the nose leaping forward, sharply hooked, his chin pointed, the flesh taut along his jaw.

"They have lost their purity. They are contaminated by the whites. These are all sick."

"My company has a group plan for sickness, too . . ."

Fingel faltered and fell silent. Ramos stared at him thoughtfully, as though considering notes of music, to catch an echo of mockery.

"What company? Not the mine concession. I would have seen you before."

"I represent an insurance company."

"So? What do they do?"

Fingel told him, simply and clearly, his enthusiasm seeping away with every sentence. He wiped his brow, his concentration dithering under Ramos's dark stare. He fumbled to a conclusion that left him feeling ashamed of himself. To be outfaced by this fellow of no education!

". . . and that is the way the workers will be protected. At very little cost per month."

"Protected?"

"Yes."

"Protect them?"

124

Ramos drawled listlessly, then humped his shoulders heavily three times, like a shabby vulture before attempting flight after a glut. He sauntered to the wall and bent, muttering softly, coaxing and wheedling in a monotone. One of the Indian miners there twisted and relaxed, his legs sliding straight, his heels pushing up a roll of carpet. A mouse skittered away to the far end of the room. Fingel pressed his briefcase against his belly and waited. He glanced at the stairs. They looked very far away. Ramos signaled, and the long bone began to tock again against the block of hollow wood. Ramos began to hiss softly and sway, cuffing his hands together in off cadence to the beat of the bone. The small brown miner sat up, swaying slightly. Ramos reached out his index finger and touched the dirty fingernail to the broad, soft little nose.

"Sangre!"

Instantly bright blood burst from the miner's nostrils, pumping over the plump, dark lips and sliding down the hairless chin and chest. Fingel stared, appalled. Ramos snapped his fingers twice.

"Basta, basta!"

He touched the miner's nose again. The blood flow dwindled and ceased. The Indian shivered slightly. The blood spilled down his belly. Ramos passed his hand slowly twice, and the miner's head lolled, as though his neck muscles had been slashed. Fingel began to murmur a chant for the dead beneath his breath. Ramos gestured again, and the Indian stood and walked with slow, dainty steps to the brazier. Ramos carelessly handed him a bundle of dried twigs. He spoke again, and the Indian thrust the faggot into the hot coals. Flames snapped and writhed, racing up the bundle, giving off a cone of thick, pungent smoke. The miner pulled open the front of his canvas pants with one hand, his fingers moving with dreamy deliberation. He plunged the blazing bundle into his groin. Fingel screeched and stumbled forward, dropping his briefcase. His head swam.

The flames, yellow and orange, licked up around the miner's wrist and slack forearm. His canvas trousers ignited, black-splotched first, then popping tongues of yellow flame that wavered and smoked. The burning cloth peeled away in smoldering tatters, touched and set off other patches, until the silent, swaying brown figure was washed in pale flames from the navel to the knees. Fiery bits fell and scorched the rugs. The room filled with smoke and stench. Ramos spoke, and the miner strolled toward Fingel, the remnants of his canvas pants still burning, sliding around his ankles like leg irons. Fingel gazed, frozen in horror. The body was untouched, not a mark, not even the organs, like fragile pods. The Indian halted three paces from Fingel, his unseeing eyes raised toward the ceiling.

"Protect them?"

The terrible, soft mirth in Ramos's voice made Fingel turn his face away. He groped blindly for his briefcase. The clock stroke on the hollow block ticked and knocked, ticked and knocked, tick-ticked, faster, faster, faster still. The gray bone skipped in a nibbling beat; Ramos's hands darted through the smoke like stunned bats. A droning song began to rise and fall; a dirge drifted against the smeared walls and back. Three brown men slowly rose, their limbs slack, their flesh numb. They paused for a moment, as though they waited for the tockering rhythm to speed their hearts. Then they swung in a long, linked, slow, dull-limbed dance, feet stone-shod and shuffling, buttocks churning. Their arms, drooping from their shoulders, sagged and swung like branches in a droning wind. Their fingers touched and tangled, broke apart and touched again. They danced across the room, circled the naked figure still rigid there, and returned in lethargic progress to Ramos.

Fingel saw the thin-bladed dagger stitch through the lower and upper lips, so that the wooden handle hung below the chin like a wood goatee. The second cupped coals and kissed them. The dark fingers touched and turned the brown chest female; round breasts and budded. The fingers drew the skinny blade free, and not a drop of blood fell. The coals tumbled back into the brazier from unscorched palms. Fingel's eyes blittered and blinked, tears stinging on his lids. Ramos bent and blew gently on the bulbed breasts. The Indian chafed his flesh, slid to the floor and slept. The two others squatted and struck up an idle conversation, smiling occasionally and ignoring the others. The bone was silent on the block. Fingel looked about. The one-armed miner was gone. Ramos sighed, yawned and seemed overcome with lassitude. Only his dark eyes showed life and power.

"You see they need no protection from you, commercial representative. I, Ramos, protect them, guard and cure them. I have the power to punish, also. They have no need for you and your company, your pieces of paper. They will soon need nothing, for all will be given to them. It is a question of purification now. Certain rites . . ."

Ramos appeared to doze, standing erect. He shook himself and walked to the brazier, lifted the aluminum pan and drank from it. Black liquid ran down his chin, and he scrubbed at it with the back of his hand. He spoke to the two squatting miners, and they lifted their companion and carried him to the wall. They returned and walked the rigid man up to Ramos, who made a weary pass and mumbled something. The Indian awoke, smiled and laughed, tapping the two others on their cheeks with his thumb, the friendly greeting among the Indians. Ramos washed his mouth out with what smelled to Fingel like brandy, spat some on the floor, some onto the coals, and drank deeply before driving the cork back into the bottle with the heel of his hand. His lank, dark hair whipped as he swung his head from side to side. He seemed to gather new strength. He sprang from behind the brazier and landed lightly on the balls of his feet, his huge arms ready, working, as though to spring on Fingel and crush him to the matted floor.

"You are another who has come to take them away from me, my people! They have all tried! I have told General Vola this, only the other day! You know General Vola?"

Fingel stammered. He had heard of the Army commander, an old crony of Vizarra's. Stories of his drunkenness were Costa Plata legends. "As fat as Vola" was a joke among all the people. He had seen the bloated peasant face in the city newspapers. He nodded.

"So! Now we forget this foolish story of insurance companies. Go to Vola! Tell him that our agreement is binding."

He waved one powerful arm at the pan on the brazier and began to shout, the spittle flying from his dark lips.

"We have drunk of that together! At Casanueva! The defection of the mountain garrisons has been sworn! At the time of the uprising by Alessandro! I will lead my people to their promised city!"

Fingel reeled backward, his heart pounding, mopping the spittle and sweat from his face. Ramos followed him in short, wolflike rushes, shouting incoherently, his fingers clawed. Fingel ducked and dodged, out of breath and feeble. The stairs slammed against his shoulders. He gazed wildly up at the walls, praying, waiting for the nip of steel thrust into his belly. He saw a painted tree, seethed by blue wind, the leaves spread like bayonets. He saw a flower, a tendriled menace, bruise-purple, the stamen fuzzed with tinted goat's hair. He made a sign against the evil eye. The decayed carpets beneath his feet felt like a bog, a mush of sodden fibers about to slit apart, bubble and clutch him down. His bowels oozed, and he shouted, angered and ashamed.

"He's dead, you animal! He's dead! Alessandro is dead!"

Ramos's voice choked off. Fingel clung to the stairs, exhausted. Somehow he still had his briefcase. Nausea surged and subsided in his belly and chest. Liquid gushed into his throat, and he spat it out. Ramos breathed heavily, then began to giggle like a girl. His jaw dropped like a trap, and the stones of his laughter pounded and rebounded from the paint-daubed walls. Fingel closed his eyes in despair, too spent even to pray. Ramos's voice whispered, twisting like a cast thread, a filament of promise and menace, sewing up Fingel's hooded eyes.

"Dead? He's not dead. Look. Look at him. *Look . . . at . . . him!*"

Fingel saw a dark box. Planes shot out and back, quivered and lay still, the top plane studded with bits of light, the side planes swinging in like doors of impossible breadth to form walls. A long cool corridor somewhere. A figure moved in it, a white, wavering shape, like a statue before an unveiling, like a dead man sewn in a sack, sliding through distorting water to the bottom far below. The head nodded, as though butted by sea current. A limping figure, a man somehow spoiled, flawed by birth or later accident. A man in the white uniform of a hospital orderly, with a thin, worn but still-handsome face, carrying an envelope in his hand. A melancholy mustache over a broad, firm mouth, but the eyes vague, blurred, indifferent. The left shoulder hitched as he walked. A sensation of danger filled Fingel. He tried to call a warning. The vision shifted, faded and vanished in horizontal bands of eye-stinging brilliance, streaks of scarlet, cobalt, viridian and molten bronze. The bright reek of hospital antiseptic prickled Fingel's nose. Fingel gave a little helpless cry and his lids popped open. For an instant the finger reappeared, bleached and shivering, then faded to Ramos's slow-stirring fingers, his left hand, the heartside hand, with index and middle fingers dangling down, the thumb and other fingers curled up, hidden.

"I *saw* him! Is that really . . . ?"

"He is alive. The masquerade is over now. Soon the play will begin. Flesh will burst upon flesh, teeth and sinews will strain and crack, diamonds will shatter like glass and the hammer will break the wheel against the stone. Vigo will drink and drink and vomit blood into the gutters."

"I can do nothing. Please, let me go. A poor man, a foreigner. I will tell no one. I promise you. I swear it!"

"You are not of our faith. An oath is worthless. Go. No one needs you here."

Ramos rocked his thong-haired head and gazed around the painted chamber. His dark eyes shimmered with force. He jerked his thumb carelessly at the stairs and sauntered away. Fingel moaned and moved his legs. He had been driven into a foul, dank corner beneath the stairs. He tottered across lumped rugs and the shards of hemp pallets. He heard the pan ring on the brazier. Fingel climbed the stairs, struck aside the fusty slab of rug in the doorway, walked, swaying and holding his eyes through the empty waiting room and out into the dazzling sunlight. Big bodies sprang at him; hard hands seized him. He collapsed, groaning, but did not attempt to resist. He gazed about. Three men in khaki suits dragged him to an automobile and threw him in the back seat. The sedan shot into motion, skidding past concrete buildings, pipes, towers and sheds, out into a field of dust. Fingel beat his hands against his chest.

"Give me my life. That's all. Give me my life. I need it, can't you see that? I meant nothing."

The others did not speak. At the barbed-wire gate the assistant manager, his cropped head shielded by a white pith helmet, swung down from the watchman's booth. One of the others cranked down the window.

"Hier ist."

He turned Fingel's face up, hard fingers driving into Fingel's cheeks, twisting his jaw open. The manager smiled and the hot sun bit into his little chips of eyes.

"Hast du etwas verkauft, Yid? Nein? Oh, tut mir Leid! Zum Bahnhof, Karl!"

"Jawohl, Herr Schmidt!"

The automobile carried Fingel and the guards down the long, smooth dirt road to the railroad station, where the locomotive hissed in the early afternoon sun that slanted through the torn tops of the silver-bearing mountains. On the platform Fingel's legs collapsed, and the guard named Karl dragged him into a third-class car and dumped him on a wooden bench. The train jolted twice and poured away from the mine, like the water-flushed ore driven down into the stamping crushers, a long rattling slide down to the city that lay beside the sea.

When Fingel gathered strength and nerve enough to sit up in answer to the conductor's prods and heat-edged demands for his ticket, he did not at first recognize the young man seated across from him. Then he saw the empty sleeve. The Indian leaned forward.

"I have run away!"

"He is crazy, that one."

The Indian considered this for a moment, his powerful body rocking easily to the motion of the carriage. Then he nodded.

"Truth. But he has powers, too."

"I know, I know . . ."

"What will you do now?"

"I will go to the city. I must sleep. I am very tired. Then I will go away."

"Go away. Where?"

"Anywhere. It makes no difference. It was a mistake to come back to this country. All I want is my life."

The Indian considered this too, chewing his lower lip thoughtfully. His eyes shone with enthusiasm. He clenched his fist, and his great, overdeveloped right forearm threatened to burst the sleeve of his cheap cotton jacket.

"I want my life, too!"

"But . . . you *helped* him. With the bone and the block. I saw you."

A flicker of emotion, a cloud of dread, passed across the dark face. Then the mouth settled, crisp and severe.

"In the city I will find a priest. I will make a confession. After that . . ."

"What?"

"I will go to Alessandro! I will work to make my people free!"

"Shhh. Someone might hear you. From the government, you mean?"

"Yes! And from him, too! Vola . . . Ramos told him—"

"I don't want to hear. I beg you, tell me nothing."

The Indian sat back and flexed his single hand.

"For years I have heard of Alessandro. And all that time I followed Ramos. Like a dog. But I will be a man! Free!"

Fingel twisted his head around in terror. There were only a few peasants in the compartment. They seemed to be sleeping. The train slowed. Fingel started.

"Where are we?"

"Casanueva."

"So soon?"

Fingel looked out of the cracked, sooty window. It was Casanueva. The train panted and sniffed. The sun was hot. Fingel bought a bottle of mineral water from a peddler. The Indian took nothing. He seemed unaffected by the heat. He sat there, powerful and brooding, one arm great, the other an empty, pinned-up sleeve.

"Well, well, but this is very odd! You have completed your business, no doubt. A successful trip?"

A slender young man in a dark suit. The one who had asked all the questions before. Fingel pushed a glance across the compartment at the Indian. He thought he saw the one-armed man nod slightly. Fingel laughed gaily and tapped his briefcase with his frail, slender fingers.

"Oh, why, yes, now that you ask, a very successful trip!"

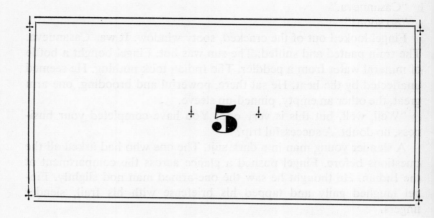

5

GOOD night, Uncle Carlos."

The old man clutched the telephone receiver in both hands and stared out of the window into the garden, where fireflies signaled, their lights pulsing pale and cool, among the flowers. He worked his jaw and tongue, forcing the words past his dry lips.

"Good night, *jovencito. Y suerte, suerte.* Luck, luck."

He dropped the receiver to the cradle and stared at the object for a moment before lowering his face into his hands. Twice now he had telephoned, from a considerable distance, the clear, young voice thin and blurred by static on the line. It was like hearing again the voice of a dead friend at a seance, calling across a void of space and time. The first telephone call had both startled and frightened the old man. Alessandro had said that he and Carlitos were together, working together in hiding. The movement had been "cleaned" and made stronger. He had said not to worry, everything was going well. The old man warned him that the line must be tapped. Alessandro's tenor laugh rang across the night. Comrades in the Compañía Telefónica kept them informed which lines were safe to use. The old man, later, had found himself half relieved, half nettled. The police did not think it worth their time to tap the telephone of old Carlos Sánchez, the last survivor of the triumvirate of the old Movimiento Liberal. It was insulting to be considered politically impotent.

The old man stood and lit his pipe, walked to his favorite chair and sat down, crossing his legs. A slight breeze stirred the curtains, bringing into the dark study the odors of the earth. He shivered slightly.

Why had Alessandro called him? And not once, but twice, both times at night. He had demanded nothing in the way of information. He seemed confident that the uprising would go well, so much so that his first interest had been merely to confirm the exact phrasing of the Costa Platan Constitution, long since violated by Vizarra. Or was that merely a mask, concealing some deeper, more subtle motive? The telephone calls exposed him to possible betrayal. *Betrayal.* The old man's mind, like the delicate horns of a snail, touched the word and shrank. Like a snail, so vulnerable outside the shell, the old man's mind crept away. Why had Alessandro asked about certain phrases used habitually by his father, Felipe?

"Well, I want the proclamation to sound a little bit like him, Uncle Carlos. You know, sort of an echo, or a distant voice calling that you strain to hear. It's no good preaching about the future if the people don't have the past buried in their brains and bellies. Don't you agree?"

He had then, just a few minutes ago. Now he was not so sure. He was getting on, as they said, when they meant he had already grown old; he *was* old. His mind moved slowly, cautiously, avoiding the collisions with words and images that still woke pain in him. Was that Alessandro's secret purpose, to torment him? Did he *know?* Or merely suspect? How could he know certainly, *absolutely?* Only two men knew the truth.

The old man sighed and sucked his pipe. Carlitos, his only son, was still well, still safe. For how much longer, though? A few days only. Since he had fled to Mexico, the boy had a price on his head. Soon the secret police would not want him alive, but dead, a bullet-torn corpse to hang from a streetlamp. And his only son, his Carlitos,

133

despised him, called him a . . . name, refused to see him or answer letters.

His pipe went out, and he relit it. He sat, an old and lonely man, brooding in the darkened study of his small villa in the suburbs of the city. He was astonished at Alessandro's audacity, shocked and grieved at the quick and callous slaughter of his old friend Colleo, and concerned at his own complicity. How easily Alessandro had caught him up again, after all these years. And he thought he had buried the past. How foolish! He *must* be getting senile. As long as Alessandro lived, the past could not be forgotten. Was that what the voice meant to tell him, springing along a wire, flashing through the darkness from some country hiding place, across the arid slopes into the city, the clear, young voice like a barb or lancet, lifting away the slick scar tissue, exposing the wounds again?

Alessandro had allowed him to place himself in danger again . . . if he wished to do so. And he had. He had not reported the first telephone conversation to the Caudillo or to the security police, that Yankee gangster. Nor would he report this one tonight. And not merely because the hoax, the false Alessandro, had been exposed. No, he concealed his knowledge willingly, eagerly. The old urge to scheme, plot, calculate was on him again. The desire for clandestine action crept in his old chest like the last feeble stirrings of lust. It was not fair! His position as Minister of Public Education was little more than a sinecure; he rarely saw Vizarra now. They had nothing left to say to each other, no more crippling confidences to exchange. Since he was unimportant, the Caudillo could and would crush him . . . a boot pulping the shell and soft body of the snail. And Alessandro had put him in a position to choose once again—surely for the last time— security or peril. Danger was like a drug, exposure to it a form of narcosis. Women seemed, by and large, immune. Perhaps simply because they were women, commonsense animals, so confident of what they *were* that they suffered no compulsion to prove themselves. With men it was different, a question of establishing and maintaining manhood, the pride of flesh through the thrill of risk. Alessandro had simply asked: *Are you still a man, a real man? Or have your balls gone dry?* He had answered by his instinctive actions; he had placed himself in danger. Now the threat of arrest, torture and death at the hands of the gringo who ran the secret police hung over him like the sword of Damocles. And he was old, frail, with white hair and bad

134

nerves, feeble digestion, no head for drinking and weak legs. What could he do for Alessandro and the movement? Nothing. The hair that hung the sword could be snipped at any hour, any moment.

The old man cast about, creeping forward, hesitating, receding. There was a new joy in him; the old game of guesswork and calculation played anew. He was handicapped, for there were so many things he had long ago willed himself to forget, so many dark places, so many broken pieces. He thought, creeping like a snail in a ruined dwelling, surrounded by odors of the past, the litter underneath checking his slow progress, aware that the walls, the roof, might fall to smash him to jelly. He had a duty to discover something. If only he could find it! If only he knew what was the object of his slow, uncertain, timid searching. He puffed his pipe and felt the breeze again on his face. The rich, strong tobacco comforted him, quickened his heart.

$$\downarrow$$

He had just taken up smoking, an extravagance on his puny instructor's salary at the university, even considering that his wife, then carrying Carlitos (they had called the unborn infant that almost as soon as Angela knew for certain), received a sum each quarter from the dowry her father had placed in trust. A pipe, good tobacco, they had made him feel older, even wiser. Slightly daring too, since he smoked in the classrooms, which was forbidden by the university authorities. An opportunity had come up. The Cortes (why parliamentarians concerned themselves with such details no one knew; one year they had sponsored a national embroidery contest) had set aside a modest sum to be used for a two-year special program to combat illiteracy. It was interpreted, incorrectly, as an attempt to diminish the achievements of the Church teaching orders. Later, those gentlemen who had supported the bill filled the jails supervised by the Red Beret and many died there before the amnesty granted by Vizarra. Classes were to be held at night: language and literature, history, mathematics, some philosophy (largely a history of the intellectual saints) and a smattering of art. The registration fee was a pittance. It was those students—older, less respectful than the university boys, ignorant of his good connections through marriage—who gave him the nickname: *El Feo,* The Ugly One. He had two sections, one of literature, one of history, something of a plum for a new instructor.

The added reales paid for maternity smocks, the wet nurse, a new horse and several rather expensive suits. And English pipe tobacco in flat, round tins.

Felipe Martín was something of a troublemaker from the very first class, the first evening. He was not insolent but skeptical, a broad-shouldered, bronzed, hard-muscled young man with a harsh *campo* accent, a foreman from a *ganadería,* a ranch where fighting bulls were raised. He had been transferred from the ranch to the city to supervise the unloading of the bulls, to bargain with the *empresarios,* to spread about the name of the ranch and the breed of animal raised. He was, Sánchez soon sensed, not used to listening, but to talking. He muttered scathing or comic remarks under his breath, and the other students laughed, upsetting the class as a whole. Sánchez had considered the matter, spoken of it to his wife, and then, after a particularly annoying session, invited Martín to take a *caña* of beer and some shrimps with him in a tavern. It was unorthodox; the university authorities discouraged excessive contact between the teachers and the students. Sánchez enjoyed flouting these regulations; he meant to make his mark among the student body as a real fellow, progressive, liberal, open. He liked to think that his remarks (that education was a two-way street, that the teacher learned as well as the students) slit through the velvet-robed pomposity of the professors, those twittering academicians, to reach the students' hearts and brains. He liked to think he was gathering a following, a clique, a "school." He was not a snob; his family had been middle-class, no better, proprietors of a ships' chandlery and small rope walk near the harbor. He could befriend a mature student like Martín.

It was not long before they were friends. The first night had been a nearly hilarious binge of beer and pink-and-white grilled shrimp dipped in butter and salt, first the little *cañas* of beer, then big glasses, *dobles,* golden doubles, the glasses beaded and cool to the touch. Martín thought him a good fellow but too bookish. Sánchez found, like flesh beneath work calluses, a quick, daring mind below the *vaquero's* cynicism. They met often, after the evening classes, to drink and talk. Martín seemed to have plenty of money. He admitted, months later, that he embezzled from his employer, a simple matter of falsifying the amounts he received from the sale of the fighting bulls. He had a girl and planned to marry, although he knew several pretty prostitutes. Some of the money was for the marriage. But the rest he kept for some secret purpose.

The baby was born, a boy, as Sánchez and his wife had predicted, after a punishing labor that Angela's parents seemed to feel was exclusively his fault, as though he had bad seed. The instructor and the ranch foreman drifted apart for several months, and then came the summer vacation. Angela remained more or less bedridden, neither better nor worse, under regular treatments from a physician. Sánchez's salary barely covered expenses. The boredom of the hot months was relieved by postcards and notes from his student Martín, who now signed himself simply: *Felipe.* He invited Sánchez to his marriage, and seemed genuinely hurt at the courteous refusal Sánchez mailed off. The instructor felt it beneath his honor to state simply that he could not afford the trip, that he had been driven to rent his horse out to a neighbor; he was afraid Martín might send him the money for the trip. Martín wrote, after a few weeks, enclosing a cheap wedding photograph of himself, very much the dandy, enriched by a thick mustache and a gold watch chain, standing with one hand firmly placed on the shoulder of his bride, a remarkably pretty young girl, slender and quite fair, with large, sad eyes and thick, curly hair. She looked compressed and uncomfortable in her bridal gown, prayer book and beads held self-consciously on her lap. Her pretty mouth was set in a peculiar position. It was Angela who perceived that the girl was trying not to laugh. Angela did not approve of the girl, not even her name, Rosa—Rosalita which was "common." Angela did not approve of his friendship—there was nothing else to call it by now—with young Martín. It was beneath him, as the wisdom of the university officials had long ago comprehended. She did not know what her father would think. Sánchez did. He played with the baby, as much as he was allowed, began an article on the sentence structure in the first book of *Don Quixote,* and took up gardening. Martín wrote him that he had discovered a new "disciple" (how odd that word was in Martín's looping, rather careless handwriting), an Indian named Manón Xaltalpa. Unlike most Indians, this Manón was a real *monosabio,* a wise monkey, and liked to drink beer and eat shrimps. His mother was a Negro woman, and he had worked both in the mines and on the sailing ships. Felipe even called him *"Monosabio."* Sánchez found himself wishing away the August days, the sleepy September afternoons. Martín and the new "disciple" planned to enroll during the first semester, Xaltalpa in the first-year group, Martín with the advanced section. Sánchez chafed at the tediousness of his homelife, his wife a semi-invalid, his in-laws officious, his own parents cautious, standing clear, too impressed by the professional status of their son to treat him as their child. He was alternately bewildered and bored.

The first night of the evening sessions, the three young men met later in a tavern and drank and talked until dawn. Something was up; something new was in the air. Martín had traveled a good deal in the vanished months; Xaltalpa, tall and slender from his Negro mother, had seen more of the world than either of the others. Martín was bitter about conditions not only on the *ganaderías,* but on the *fincas,* the big farms of the latifundia, the landed estates. He brushed aside the university instructor's labored explanations of feudal duties and responsibilities. He wanted change, progress and reform. He had talked to people, getting their views. They had even given him money to solicit members of the Cortes. He relied on Sánchez to make contacts with members of the legislature who were said to entertain liberal views. Xaltalpa breathed on them both like a dark wind, drawing from a charged cloud hanging over the Europe he had seen, a thundercloud called socialism. Sánchez went home with the others, walking unsteadily through the dawn-gray streets, drunk on words, new friendship and too much beer.

Rosalita was more beautiful than her picture. She scolded and laughed at her husband, made coffee and laced the cups with brandy, swirling through the small kitchen of the apartment in a bright, figured dressing gown. Her small feet were bare and quick. She laughed at Manón and was quietly respectful to Sánchez. She called him "Professor," and seemed distressed when he was slightly drunk. Her thick hair was tied in a wonderful loose braid. Sánchez could smell the perfume of it. She had small, round breasts and a narrow waist. She sat with them, drinking coffee, and shocked Sánchez by demanding a cigarette and smoking it like a man. Xaltalpa and the university instructor went out on the still-cool balcony bright with potted flowers and watched the sun rise, smearing gold over the great cupola of the cathedral. Martín and his wife disappeared. Sánchez could hear the unmistakable squeal of the bed and the girl's soft, joyous cry. Xaltalpa's dark, full lips curled lazily. He seemed pleased at the easy pleasure of the young couple. Sánchez was shocked.

They separated, laughing and joking, when the sun was above the city. Rosalita, her hair now torn loose and spilling over her face, her dressing gown gapped and held shut with one small hand, gravely said goodbye with a firm grasp. Sánchez swayed down the stairs, dazzled. He was nearly late to his first morning class, ate alone for lunch and drank so much cooled wine that he took a horse-drawn cab to the beach and sprawled in the shade of a *cabaña* until sunset, sleeping, waking and dreaming. He was infatuated by Martín, his wife and his friend. When he arrived home, Angela was furious, white-lipped and silent; the baby was crying. Sánchez lost his temper. That night he left the house and found Xaltalpa. They drank and visited an expensive brothel.

The following summer Martín's wife gave birth to a boy as easily as a mare drops a foal. She called him an Italian name, Alessandro. She was not at all modest about nursing him, merely turning half aside. Sánchez's wife caught a fever. He lived in an agony, rushing from Martín's apartment to his own house, to the university, then, at night, off to a growing number of obscure taverns near the waterfront. He was censured by one of the university proctors for a lecture during which he had made a number of criticisms of the Minister of Agriculture. Angela improved, left her bed, and made short visits to former school companions, now married and mothers like herself. Sánchez held contact with his family only through occasional meetings with his sickly younger brother, at a café where they took coffee together once a week. He saw his father and mother, his other relatives only on an amputated version of the celebration his father usually concocted for his name day. He avoided his father-in-law. Angela's parent had begun to "hear things."

The university instructor came to spend his free hours at the Martín apartment. He could not tear himself away. The slender, gay girl captivated him; her behavior disgusted him, worried him, finally became a torment he rushed to suffer. He was jealous. Rosalita, even in the presence of Felipe, fondled and teased the tall, taciturn Indian, stroked his glossy, black brow, punched and pinched him, sang to him. And Felipe laughed, as delighted as though seated in some theater. And then he took her away to his bed during the siesta. Xaltalpa dozed and smiled while the woman behind the walls cried with pleasure, and Sánchez ripped the blossoms from the potted plants. Later, disheveled, her smooth neck nape beaded, the bruises of love bites just tincting her shoulders, she gravely brought him coffee and sat, quite dazed, looking out over the tilted slopes of the city roofs, puffing a cigarette with lips still full from kisses. And she still called him "Professor," as serious in her manner as a child. He longed to tear free the front of her robe and feast on the flesh of her breasts, to crush them against his teeth, savoring her like the apples of love. He drank the bitter coffee, avoided looking at her, and praised the color of the geraniums she grew. When she told him that she often poured on them the contents of the chamber pot beneath her bed, he went weak with some inexplicable sensation. Like an injection, it took him days to cast off the effect. The scent and shape of her body made him groan. He stared at his reflection in the mirror when he shaved. He was ugly, *El Feo,* with his misshapen, great jaw and apelike forehead. He longed to be on her, to catch her dark, fine-furred eyebrows between his teeth, while he plunged into her belly.

Angela developed internal pains, queer, shifting pins of distress that nailed her to her bed. Sánchez engaged a new doctor, a gynecologist with dark, tiny hands. Somehow, waiting in the living room for the man to finish his examination, he found himself viewing a blurred double-exposed photograph: the doctor hunched over his sick, spraddled wife, himself tearing at the slicked flesh of his friend's wife, or—and worse—trapped behind the slatted balcony blind while Xaltalpa crooned and stroked her, while from the patio came the terrifying sound of Felipe's harsh laughter, a cuff of sound batting at the potted flowers.

Angela slowly improved, enough to invite the two families to Carlito's second birthday celebration. Sánchez attempted interest, but after the evening meal he put out no brandy, despite his father-in-law's pointed remarks. He got rid of them, brushed his mouth on Angela's sallow cheek and lashed his horse across the city to take bitter coffee from the hands of his beloved. That night Felipe was enraged, his face thickened by the murder of a friend, a young *peón* beaten to death by his master for a theft the *peón* had not committed. The four of them drew up a protest. The next day Sánchez read it aloud in each of his classes. The university seemed to rock on its foundations. An investigation was ordered and abandoned. The crude casket was wrenched from the dry earth and paraded through the streets of the city. Sánchez held the banner pole and made an address. He was arrested in the streets, refused the bail offered by his father, stood trial and was found to be a misguided young intellectual who had disturbed the peace. He was fined heavily and released. He wandered home, dazed, unshaven and crushed, expecting only the bulky reproaches of his father-in-law, crude bribes and threats. His friendship with Martín and Xaltalpa was becoming a scandal. After this incident he might well be finished at the university. He permitted himself the idea of surrender, except that thoughts of her, Rosalita, thickened his determination.

When he rounded the corner of his street, the police were already there. Martín and Manón had gathered students from the night sessions, and their women, university students, prostitutes, beggars and neighbors drawn from their homes by the celebration. Sánchez found himself hailed as a hero. Felipe danced the *jota* with Rosalita, the curly-crowned witch flinging out her legs like a gypsy. Xaltalpa, very drunk, lay in a wheelbarrow, his naked black shanks shining in the streetlight gleam. The students behaved very rudely, and the police, half amused, arrested several. Sánchez was carried on the shoulders of strangers into his own patio. There he faced his wife. Angela, sick, pale, shuddering with fever and rage, rushed up the stairs and closeted herself with her mother. Sánchez tried vainly to break up the party, but all the flowers in the garden were trampled to scraps. He pleaded his wife's illness, but the crowd did not leave until Martín trundled Manón away in the wheelbarrow, Rosalita dancing alongside, her skirt lifted to show her legs, tossing imaginary flowers to the curious on the sidewalks.

Two days later Angela was dead. Sánchez blamed himself, his friends, and the slender, beautiful girl who was Martín's wife. He was prostrate with grief, poured his meager savings into the funeral expenses, lived for days under drugs and was carried by his brother behind the plumed, creaking horse-drawn hearse. He kept indoors for months, only venturing out to his day classes. He found a replacement for himself; another taught the half literates twice weekly. Finally, he lectured incoherently on the role of the Costa Platan female, so violently that the president of the university received a letter from the archbishop, bent to ecclesiastical pressure, and informed the young instructor that he was dismissed from the faculty.

Angela was dead. Once a week Sánchez visited her grave with flowers. The old wet nurse agreed to become housekeeper. Sánchez found it easy in his self-occupation to address a long letter to the

141

archbishop, recanting both his political and social views. He attended church with a zeal unmatched since his childhood. His remorse was tremendous, exaggerated, complete enough to fill his life with penance for nearly four months. At that time he was appointed as a teacher in a parochial school, two sections of language and literature, one of geography, one section of introductory world history.

Angela's death seemed to end everything. He spun Martín's letters into the stove, even destroyed the notes from Rosalita, scented and disturbing, as though she had carried them within her undergarments for days before dropping them into the mailbox. He saw no one from outside the Escuela Santa María. He avoided the city cafés, the haunts of his earlier time, now as lifeless to him as the flattened garments of his dead wife, decaying in wooden boxes at the bottom of the bedroom closet. He stopped drinking and smoking in order to present a model for the students he now taught. He bent himself, like a strand of cable, around the hard shaft of Christian service, all the while attempting a cure, dosing himself like a syphilitic, near toxic with mercury, poisoning away the love for another man's wife. Like a venereal, he was more ill than he believed. His disease had dormant phases but erupted with such virulence that only his clenched prayers and sinful, releasing dreams drenched him with ease.

He surrendered his only son, little Carlitos, to the starched embrace of the nuns. The boy grew up almost unnoticed by the vague, severe zealot who had once aspired to lead men, young men, to a finer life, but who now contented himself with the dry, daily spin of abstinence and endeavor. Each year, the school increased the master's salary by a few reales until he became the highest-paid lay instructor in the city. The principal, a leathery Jesuit, half servant of God, half soul drover, pressed Sánchez to join a seminary for belated vocations, to surrender himself utterly to Jesus Christ. Sánchez found himself pleading for time, begging not his own freedom—for he was not sure that he wanted the privilege of torment, the itch that accompanies the cure—but begging, oddly, wrongly, insincerely even, for his neglected son. The years dragged away like a penal sentence. To stir, at last, his own weakened will and, at the same time, the disgust of his cassocked betters, Sánchez began to drink, deliberately, then with enthusiasm. He stumbled through the months in a belly-warm, numb dream, on half a liter of brandy a day. Each New Year, he wrote a cringing letter to the president of the university, begging for reinstatement. His son was eight years old before his infirmity of passion abated and the academic authorities relented. It seemed to Sánchez quite as though they had somehow studied his affliction, postponing their decision until prolonged examination convinced them that enough scar tissue had slicked the lesion of love.

His reinstatement was of sufficient importance (somewhat to his own surprise) to be printed on the front pages of the three city newspapers, accompanied by photographs. *La Prensa* went so far as to print a photograph of Angela and remind readers of her abrupt death in such a fashion as to subtly suggest that the government was partially responsible. For the next three days, mail poured into Sánchez's lap, some anonymous scrawls filled with threats and obscenities but mostly congratulatory, encouraging and flattering. Sánchez struggled to remain unmoved, but within a week he was overcome. The flood tide of enthusiasm and flattery tugged him, drew him away, tumbled him into the wash of intellectual and social storms. His first day on the campus was a near fiesta. His hand was numb from the fervent clasps. He was dazed and delighted. He had managed to forget his colleagues and students, but they had not forgotten him.

The heightened pitch of enthusiasm could not and did not last long. The Costa Platans, quickly kindled, flared and soon burned out. Sánchez accepted this, recalling his own youthful view of himself as a piece of pyrotechnics, soaring and exploding, then spent and falling. He sensed that the national character, the family blood of the country, matched his earlier view of himself. He was identical with them, because he was one of them. He had been quite correct in his previous estimate: sound, color and excitement soon forgotten, the triple shock fading in the brain, dwindling dim moments after the stun and splash. He wrote a series of articles for *La Prensa,* the point of them all being that no reform could be successfully accomplished by the glare of rockets; progress was not a public amusement. The image stuck in his mind, and he bound to it the image of the charcoal burner, the slow-smoldering transformation, and the votive candle of the Church, calm, steady illumination. Everyone agreed, but declared that the situation then was quite hopeless. All the articles produced was a middle-class cult of despair, briefly fashionable but forgotten with the discovery of a sensational new matador and a seductive dance imported from Brazil. The lecture halls were now never more than half filled. Sánchez turned to Catholic youth groups, but his position was difficult. He was forced to talk down to them, to modify his own views. They were cautious, neither ready nor willing to commit themselves. They had their families and their priests and knew that he really had neither. Sánchez eventually abandoned attempts to reach them; they could do each other no good. He published a volume of mediocre short stories critical of the parish priests, their conservatism, their moral lethargy. Where, he demanded, were the warriors of the Faith? The book was condemned from the pulpits. He was rebuked by the archbishop. The second printing was remaindered. In two years' time everything seemed over, done with; again he was isolated. He settled into a routine of teaching and writing articles that no one printed. He was thwarted, but not given to despair. He had won a victory over himself once before; he would struggle on and, somehow, win again.

As he suspected, his dead wife's family began negotiations for Carlitos. Letters arrived, invitations to birthday parties of female cousins, little packages, presents, games and toys. Sánchez controlled his anger, answered the notes, refused the invitations, but allowed the boy to keep the presents. The physical effort began to tell on him: he was like a commander in the field, leader of a tiny force, gallantly besieging a vast fortress of indifference, only to find himself gradually encircled, besieged in turn. In his preoccupation he did not hear the third band of pioneers beneath the earth, picking there, mining the defenses. When the sappers had done their work and the mine was sprung, Sánchez was caught by surprise. His housekeeper toiled into his study one evening and announced, between wheezes and lamentations, that a black man had rung at the gate and wished to speak with him. It was Manón Xaltalpa.

They sat together in the garden over brandy and coffee. Sánchez felt a kind of numb shock, as though the flash of the mine had burned away his eyebrows and seared his face but had left him otherwise untouched, standing on some shattered parapet, staring into the breech. Instead of being the victor, he felt as though he had surrendered his sword. A curious sensation filled him: that he was the guest, and Xaltalpa had offered him coffee and brandy. Twice he glanced at his watch, quite as if he did not wish to overstay his time. If Xaltalpa had led him to the gate and bidden him good night, he would have stepped out into the street without a thought.

Xaltalpa was dressed in worker's corduroys with a wide-brimmed

144

hat and brand-new, elegant, shimmering patent-leather shoes of exaggerated length. He looked older, worn, as though pumiced by the years. He was a high, glittering figure, a dark, ill-feathered night bird. Sánchez found himself staring at this chieftain of pioneers who had tunneled through the dry years to take him prisoner once again.

They exchanged banalities: the coffee, the quality of the brandy, the beauty of the star-filled sky. Xaltalpa had been out of the country again, but he had kept in touch with the others. There were many more, now, it seemed. And they had felt, all the time, the influence of his writings. Yes, it all seemed so long ago. They were well, quite well, Felipe and Rosalita. No, curiously enough, no other children. Just Alessandro.

Xaltalpa tasted his coffee, a second cup, barely touching his full, violet lips to the bitter liquid. Sánchez fumbled with his pipe, nervous, even abashed, before the silent strength of his visitor. The thought began to race in his mind: Here, here is one of us, yet a man so different that he can remake us. The color of his skin, the stringy power of the muscles gliding on the bones, the dogged perseverance of the glow-lit figure at night in the cold mountains . . . the charcoal burner. Sánchez's voice shook.

—What do you want, Manón?

—I want nothing, Professor.

—I mean all of you.

—Oh. Well . . .

Xaltalpa's thick lips split; he showed his teeth, but it was not a smile.

—Felipe wants you to educate the boy, the son.

—Alessandro? Why? There are schools.

—Not for him. No one will take the boy.

—Why? Is he incorrigible?

—No, not in the usual way. But he is so different, you know. Ah, I forget. You have not seen him. He is eight years old now.

—Why will no one take him? Because of his father?

—And you. And me, too. He has never attended school. No one will admit him.

—Then I will speak with the Mother Superior at—

—It will do no good.

—Don't be foolish. She is an excellent woman.

—This has nothing to do with teachers or nuns. It is a political matter.

—The education of an eight-year-old boy is a political affair? He plans to run for the Cortes, this boy?

—The government has taken careful steps to see that the son of Felipe Martín will never receive an education. Neither in the sister schools, private academies or the university.

—That is contrary to the Constitution. I will write an article denouncing this whole affair. But I must have proof, Manón. Facts!

—There you go. Facts. I say this is a political situation. But not of the present. Of the future.

—And I am to give some solution, eh? Why?

—They respect you, Professor. The boy is clever, very clever.

—Professor. She used to call me that.

—You have not seen them?

—No. Never.

—I think I know the reason.

Sánchez stiffened. The dark man's remark, so casual, struck him as impudent beyond endurance. He slammed out his pipe on the chair leg, dropped it on the gravel and fumbled for it, grunting. He recovered the pipe and his composure. Xaltalpa sat leaning back, staring at the sky.

—For years I loved her. Now it is over, thank God.

Xaltalpa rolled his read to look at Sánchez.

—You never told her?

—I imagine she knew.

—Of course. But you should have told her.

—*Mono,* how could I? Felipe's wife? It would have been . . . dishonorable. Yes, an act of dishonor.

—Dishonorable. Not for her, of course.

—For her? No, for *me!*

—Eh. Eh.

Xaltalpa lunged forward, swooping down on his brandy. His arm shot out like a tendril and dumped the contents of the glass into his throat. He swallowed noisily and sat back.

—How little you have learned, *amigo.* Was it because you knew so little at the beginning, I wonder? Do not be angry. I don't mean to insult you.

—I knew . . . enough. Or I thought I did. I was certain that

146

you . . . I cannot say it, even after all these years. You and she. *Dios,* Manón, but I was jealous!

—That I slept with her? Oh, yes.

Fury smoldered in Sánchez. This insolent black took her like a glass of brandy, while he . . .

Xaltalpa stroked his chin. His face was puzzled in the candlelight, his dark brow ridged.

—But why did you not tell her, my friend? The others—

—You were not alone?

Sánchez twisted his pipe in his hands. The stem snapped.

—Others? Oh, yes. A number. Of course, Felipe knew. He knows. There are others now. It is her way.

—Her way! The juicy little bitch!

Manón tilted his head back and laughed, a gentle burbling noise. He sat up again, wiping his nose with the back of his hand, a gesture that had always disgusted Sánchez.

—I am sorry, Professor, but it is both sad and funny that you should have had pain. From her of all women. Of course she knew that you loved her. She used to say, *"Mono,* why does he stay away? Why does he not come to me? *El pobre."* You see, you had only to *ask* . . .

It was unbearable. Sánchez thrashed out of his chair and strode down the gravel path. He calmed himself with great effort, dried his sweating face and walked back to where Manón sprawled, lean and gleaming beside the pale table.

—What a mockery! To love a whore. What a cheap romance!

Xaltalpa's face twisted like a cramped muscle. His hand snaked up into the air as though he meant to strike a blow. Instead he pulled off his hat and scrubbed his short, kinky hair.

—Eh, what nonsense. You are a fool, *amigo.* Too many books, not enough people. A whore? But I have told you, it was just her way. A woman who gives freely to men.

—She practices charity, then? In Felipe's bed?

—I think it must take much education to learn disgust.

—I cannot help it. It *is* disgusting!

—But you are only humiliated. A lost opportunity.

—Because of her I lost . . . everything. *Everything!* And you say she gives freely. It is I who have paid. Only me!

—You don't understand her. For Rosalita the body is nothing, a

147

thing, only. A thing of no importance. Someone wants it, let him have it. That is pleasure. It is enough. And good. I have only known two other women like her.

—How lucky you have been!

—Bitter herbs, *amigo,* do not sweeten when dried. Irony is the last indulgence of the intellectual. To the very end he believes it has power to move or give pain. Felipe knew all this long before he married her. When she was a girl, she gave herself. Eleven or twelve years old. To the village boys. Felipe told me he wore horns on his wedding day.

—And now he has the longest horns in all Costa Plata. He walks through the door of his house sideways.

—Listen. She sees a man. She likes him.

—No, you will tell me that she does it only with her friends. And has no enemies in all the world.

—Will you listen? Sit down. She sees this man. She senses the ache of desire. It is her way, that's all. What is so terrible about it all, anyway? Up in the mountains the men often take the bride. Out into the *campo* or up into the hills to some cave. They build a fire and drink. She drinks, too, the bride. She dances. The men play with her white body like on a guitar. When they are done, it is dawn. The girl is half dead from lovemaking. It is the custom, that's all. You are too, too civilized. For her, Felipe's woman, well, she feels the man *simpático* . . . a few minutes to ease him of a spoonful of—

—Shut up, will you? You make apologies for animals.

—An animal? No, Professor, she is much woman.

—And I am a fool, then, as you say. I wear the horns, not Felipe.

—All you had to do was ask . . . not even that. Just to *be* there at this or that time.

—Only that—

Sánchez was struck by the comedy of his past love-illness. He laughed helplessly. He could not stop laughing. He choked down some brandy, and it burned in his lungs. He gasped and wiped his streaming eyes. The stars spun overhead. He felt like a man released from prison, told by the warder that he was innocent, that some little mistake had been made. That he was the wrong man. Fate and error, the twin jest makers who never smile, for their faces are made of stone, never weep, for their eyes are stone. How much of human agony is due to a lack of a sense of humor? Sánchez poured more coffee and refilled the glasses. He felt a sudden desire to get drunk.

148

—So. So. All right. What about the boy?

—They wish to send him to you. To have him live here. You will be his tutor.

—I have my classes. I could give him three hours each afternoon. No more. Carlitos comes home from the sisters at five-thirty. They could play together, I suppose. They might become great friends. We have an extra room.

—How much do you wish?

—What?

—Well, Felipe is now part owner of the *ganadería*. Four times last year he shipped bulls to the plazas of Mexico and Peru. He will pay, but he wishes to pay all at once, in full, before the boy comes.

—So that if I find him stupid, I will have him for a year anyway. That sounds like Felipe. I will take nothing.

—Nothing? But—

—It seems a fair price. Call it the bargain struck between his mother and myself years ago.

—But you cheat yourself, Professor.

—That is my intention, Manón. Only this time by choice, you understand.

—Clearly. But you could go to her now.

—I feel nothing for her now.

—No?

—Did you . . . love her, Manón?

—Love her? What for?

Again Sánchez laughed. When he stopped he was leaden with fatigue. His hand shook as he raised the bottle.

—Come. A drink.

—No more, *amigo*.

—You have stopped?

—I must go back to Felipe. He is leaving the country.

—On business? No? The police?

—Yes. Our whole group is breaking up for a while. It is too dangerous here. Only you are safe, you see?

—They will find out about the boy, Manón. Is there a record of his birth? Confirmation? Anything like that?

—No. He was born at home. No doctor. He has never been confirmed.

—Then I shall call him mine. He is two years younger than Carlitos. So, I seduced a girl and took the child. I was drunk during the fiesta of Santa Rosa. We were both in costumes, masked. We came here together and made love all night. I never knew her name. These things happen, of course. It will be so simple that it will be believed.

—Let's hope so.

—How can it be proved otherwise? I sent the child to a woman in the country. Because of my old job, you understand. Now that I have been reinstated at the university, I can afford to keep the child. Besides, I can afford the scandal now, too. And one condition.

—Yes?

—I do not wish to see her. Not ever.

—You are afraid. Or have regrets. You envy me.

—All those things. Truth. I prefer my memories, let us say. I do not want to find myself rolling on her upstairs while our sons play in the garden below.

—If you did that, Professor, in three weeks it would be all over, finished.

—Or it would never end.

—Eh!

—That is my way.

—A man who never learns to swim will surely drown.

—Only if he goes in the water. I will stay on the beach.

—No, *amigo*. No, you will not. You have agreed to take the boy. You were one of us then. You have joined us again.

—Felipe has planned this!

—All of us have planned this, *amigo*. You will hold the movement together for us. Felipe goes to join with the others already in Mexico. You have the boy, a hostage of the heart. The movement is growing now. In a few years—

—Always a few years.

—Until the day.

—If it comes.

—It will come.

—Yes. Yes!

When they parted, Sánchez nearly wept. He sat long over the bottle of brandy. How it was that he lived, like all men, in three times. The present instant shaped and pressed, each instant's senses conditioned by every instant existed through before, and time stretched out like Manón's black arm through the night of the future groping for a wish. And those three time units contained within the unfathomable flow,

150

the glacial slide of history, always growing, always creeping, always dumping the titanic refuse of life into the blank, cold sea.

His past pain, his future dreams, caught in an instant of drunkenness. He was fated now; he had agreed to hold the boy . . . the hostage of the heart. *In a few years.* Time's slow flowing. A man cannot surrender if he has never been free. He cannot protest his ignorance when he can never be wise enough to know. He can only remember, live, hope and wait. Always waiting . . .

The bottle was empty. He fell asleep. Before dawn the gate bell rang. Standing outside was a small, slender boy with long hair, carrying a cardboard suitcase and a wicker cage imprisoning a sleeping bird. Sánchez stared through the grill, unlocked the gate and beckoned the boy inside.

The boy hesitated, sensing and smelling the brandy. Sánchez was very unsteady. He clung to the gate, his head throbbing, his eyes raw-feeling, each tooth in his head gluey. He beckoned again.

—Come in, *jovencito.*

The boy stepped precisely, delicately, three paces forward, passing through the opened gate, and set down his cardboard suitcase. He held out one slender hand.

—*Muy buenas,* Señor Sánchez. Alessandro Martín.

—*Muy buenas,* Alessandro. *Estás en tu casa.*

The boy looked swiftly around the dawn-damp garden, yawned slightly and shivered. He glanced up at Sánchez.

—Tío Manón said you would be waiting. Are you very drunk?

Sánchez blinked slowly and shook his head carefully.

—No. Did "Uncle" Manón say that I would be?

The boy shrugged and swung the cage with the bird. He smiled shyly.

—No. He said you *might* be.

—Ah. I see. He is a clever one, Tío Manón.

—They say that you are the clever one, señor.

Sánchez took the boy's hand, picked up the suitcase and led him to the table and chairs. The boy sat down, holding the cage on his lap. Sánchez examined him; he looked like both his parents, as well as he could recall them, and like neither. They had fused in him. The boy was really very handsome.

—First, you must not call me *señor.*

—I was told that. I forgot.

—Not *Tío* Carlos, either. Papa. You must call me Papa.

—Yes . . . Papa. Where is Carlitos? I want to see him.

—He is asleep. Are you sleepy?

The boy shook his head. He bent down and looked into the cage.

—Hey, *guapo*. Hey, hey! No. We members of the movement take sleep when we can. Carlitos will have to learn. But that's all right. I can teach him.

Sánchez smiled and reached for his pipe, stared stupidly at the two pieces of it and dropped them back to the table. He nodded cautiously. His head felt enormous, as though stuffed with wool.

—That's right. I will teach you. And you can teach him. We will learn together.

The boy did not seem particularly interested. He gazed around the garden and held out one hand, his fingers spread, trying to feel the mist rise from the gravel walk.

Manón Xaltalpa had not been wrong. Alessandro was a clever and eager student. Sánchez located the textbooks he had used at the Escuela Santa María and purchased others. The boy was clever with figures; his father had taught him basic mathematics and he progressed at once into simple word problems, regarding them as a game, even making them up for himself. He read easily and wrote a clear hand. Since grammar bored Sánchez as well as the boy, they studied language by reading works of history, stories and tales. They began the elements of Latin and Greek, using Carlitos' new book. When Sánchez left in the morning for his classes at the university, he left a slip of paper with Alessandro's assignments written on it. They ate lunch together, often in the garden, then rested. For three hours they reviewed and corrected the work the boy had done, read and talked. At five-thirty Carlitos, breathless and sweaty, clanged the bell at the gate. Sánchez surrendered his pupil to his son and left them to play until dark. Always it was Alessandro who invented the games; always it was Carlitos who won them. This puzzled and displeased Sánchez.

The movement lay dormant for two years. The boys grew and became the greatest of friends, although it was soon obvious that Alessandro surpassed Carlitos in every field. But the younger boy's modesty prevented friction or jealousy. Sánchez did not ever notice that Alessandro's modesty was a useful technique for the manipulation of others. Instead he found himself drawn to the intensity of the

152

boy. He answered the letters from Felipe, always including a summary of the boy's activities and achievements, his clever sayings, his first, stolen cigar shared with Carlitos, his delight in the bulls at the *plaza de toros.*

When the movement became active, the rush of events fell too swiftly on Sánchez. Once again he was unprepared. He had been lulled. He had waited a long time, too long. The letters and directives poured in. He obeyed, but with reluctance. A new political journal had been founded. The editors demanded his articles. Members of the organization, his ex-students, circulated a petition, and Sánchez found himself running for a seat in the Cortes. The thought frightened him, particularly when it became obvious that he would easily win. His routine of life was disrupted, his office hours disturbed. His housekeeper died. The boys ran loose in the city; instead of attending school, Carlitos joined Alessandro down at the harbor. Sánchez campaigned and made speeches. The President General shortened the campaign to prevent the spread of the movement. The elections were set ahead three months, but Sánchez won easily. The city began to stutter with violence. Sánchez drafted both the list of public grievances and the manifesto of the Movimiento Liberal. The day he was invested at the Cortes and rose to deliver the speech—instantly famous with its opening sentence: *"It is not enough for the government to promise, not enough for the governed to yearn!"*—the illegal press stamped out the first edition of the newspaper *Arriba,* and Xaltalpa's fighters slashed into the *campo* looting and burning. Felipe Martín led the attack on the provincial army garrison near Boca Perro, broke into the police prison and freed twenty men. A gang of mercenaries recruited in Mexico robbed three banks of nearly a quarter-million reales. Sánchez never spoke in the Cortes again. A group of anarchists dynamited the Opera at the hour he took the two boys in a peasant's wagon out of the city. Warrants were issued for the arrest of all members of the movement. It was a futile gesture, too weak, too legal, too late. The flames of revolt sprang up in the *campo,* like the dread fire in dry grass. Sánchez brought the boys to a mountain pueblo to join with the others. It seemed the goal, the end of his waiting, the instant in time he had thought of, the fusion of past, present and future.

He was needed, as two sides of a triangle need the third to form a coherent figure, to enclose or delineate space. Xaltalpa and Felipe directed the quick, brutal thrusts out of the *campo* toward the sea. Their forces swelled with the *peones,* turncoat soldiers and *vaqueros.* The bandit army ripped like a bull at the cape of society. Violent strikes broke out in the capital, screaming mobs against the sticks, pistols and plunging, walleyed horses of the police. Captured presses slammed out issue after issue of *Arriba.* Sánchez issued new paper money to confound the economy. The army wavered, then split in half. The loyal troops were led by a young officer: Rafael Vizarra.

The struggle dragged on, one day's success followed by a week of flight across the scorched countryside. The insurgents smashed and fled, wheeled and struck at their relentless pursuers, but they never penetrated close enough to the sea; they never seized the capital city. When Felipe Martín learned that the Church opposed the M.L., that priests surrendered their parishioners to the nationalist troops, he ordered the churches to be burned. The ancient missions sagged into the booming flames, and bell metal boiled and ran in the cobbled courtyards, searing the torn bodies, consuming the black robes.

Vizarra became not a name, not a man, but a great fear to Sánchez. Martín and Xaltalpa were like children, grown versions of the two boys. They were incapable of grasping the terrible significance of the Red Beret, the fused shafts of the loyal army, the existing government of the President General, the Church and the wealthy. When at last Sánchez convinced them, it was too late.

During the weary months of the winter, that last rainy season on the Costa Plata highlands, Sánchez's fear of Vizarra altered to grudging respect. The commander of the nationalist forces was cautious. He had no real sense of tactics, but he occupied territory. The slow advance of the army was always preceded by heavy bombardments; each column was backed by regiments of newly recruited youths in red berets. Vizarra did not take a town; he punished it. The central villages were thrashed with shellfire, whipped with machine guns and left broken and smoldering beneath a wheeling scatter of ravens and dusty vultures.

Against the ominous mediocrity of Vizarra's army, the dull sledging advance, the insurgents stabbed with the broken lances of faith and genius. Sánchez scraped together the bullets, the horses and the food. Felipe, thinner now, gray and drawn, gestured over the crude maps, his hand the magnet drawing the iron filings together, assembling the enfeebled troops, the worn guns, the galled horses. Manón

154

Xaltalpa, his skin dusty with fatigue, led always the left wing. Again and again, every resource of men and equipment was flung like a hammer from the right to clang on the dark anvil of the left. And still they came on, the blue-uniformed gunners stacking the new, clean brass shells, feeding the howitzers, the lanyards snapping, howling destruction into the desolate hills.

Sánchez struggled with logistics: ammunition for thirty-seven different makes of small arms, a thousand kilograms of rice purchased on credit with worthless currency, the campaign for bandages that came at last to corn husks smeared with glue boiled from cattle hoofs. He wrote protests to the nations of the world, each letter a shrill plea for nonintervention. His notes went unanswered. In the capital the steamers bunted against the piles and the cranes screeled, unloading the foodstuffs, the crates of hand grenades, the saddles, the dull boxes of Belgian munitions, the blankets from England, the new, crested helmets of steel from France. The interests of the nation, new-bundled by Vizarra, tipped by the hatchet head of crude successes, swung against the movement. Sánchez sensed, long before the sudden death of Xaltalpa, the doom of the revolt. He told himself that it was only wise to arrange for the salvation of some remnants of the insurgent force. To fight on into the spring and summer as Felipe demanded was only to fling weary carcasses into the slow hopper of Vizarra's crushing machinery.

Sánchez's conception of time vanished. There was only this day, the next and the one after that. The rebel force degenerated after Xaltalpa was shot by his own soldiers. The hammer was left with no black anvil; each blow mushed through flesh, but fell weaker and weaker. Night attacks were by bayonet alone; the enemy trenches were the sole source of food and munitions. What had been resistance became scavenging. No harvest had been planted in the *campo*. The battered insurgents fell on ruined acres beneath the mowing machinery, the whistling sickles of German Mausers.

Sánchez did not remember the day. He no longer even possessed the ability to call this period Monday, the next Tuesday. He saw the horses go out, haunches down and stiff-legged against the dry pitch of the mountain pass. With the troopers, a twilight patrol of twenty men, rode the two boys, Carlitos with a captured rifle, Alessandro's fist enormous with a pistol, a shark-toothed bandoleer of cartridges slung across his skinny chest. They waved, happy, exalted, underfed, exhausted. It was the moment of surrender for Sánchez. He resolved to save them at any price. The sunset gilding their fair faces, touching Alessandro's hair, burning on the cheek crest of Carlitos, seemed like an omen. Once he would see it and then no more. He sat on a stone, overwhelmed with a sense of ruin, utter desolation, the present devouring without appetite the promised morsels of tomorrow. He felt that to permit youth to perish would be a sin; he would fall before God, his soul black as Manón's lead-ripped flesh.

She stood near a stand of scrub pine, her arm raised, the ripped sleeve falling back to her elbow, her tanned hand clenched in salute. She wore pants, like a man, and riding boots. Her hair fell over her shoulders, streaked with gray now, dulled by bad food. Her body was slender, her hips slung forward. She held an officer's cap by the leather bill and slapped it once against her flank. The patrol, with her son and Carlitos, crawled down the stone-cackling path to the valley floor, where already the shadows lay long. From behind the far ridge came the deep, dull *pongs* of nationalist shells falling into the thinly manned trenches. The sunset flamed on her face. She was young still, unquenched, caught in a slouched posture of salute. Sánchez felt his heart roll like a bobbin in his chest. Up at the stone hut that served as headquarters he could hear Felipe bellow like a bull behind the *toril*. Twenty minutes out on the sand, the sad brass of trumpets, the *faena*. Always the dull mules waiting to haul away the bloody-nostriled lump of bone and muscle. And she there, beneath the trees, had suckled the wicked power of the calf. And now saluted it, her whole body twisted dark, like dissolving smoke in the furnace of the dying day.

Her hand bade farewell to the scrambling horses and plucked back a banner of brassy light from her slim son's bandoleer. Sánchez drew the sight of her into his chest, the last suck of pain. His ears rang with Felipe's thwarted rage and the far fall of heavy shells beyond the purple wrinkle of the hills. He turned, his brain dead, to his table beside the mouth of the cave. The telephone, a gleaming tube, the long yards of wire, the diaphragm plate waiting to buckle with the shock of his words. He picked it up, the receiver cool in his hand. He stared at the mouth of the cave before him and felt his soul fall, shrieking without sound into the total darkness. He who had dreamed once of salvation, white and gold, fell, eager only for safety, his whole life debauched, into the gloom. *It is for them,* his brain drawled, *only to save them.* He closed his eyes, totally ashamed. The receiver buzzed in the blackness.

↓

Too long, too much time. It had sapped him, stripped his manhood, corroded his pride down to fear and final numb acceptance. He had never been worthy of the trust they had placed in him, but if it had only happened, all of it, to ALL of them, if it had only happened *quickly.* Yes, quickly, all at once, when he was young, before the years had taught him caution, before time had wasted him. He must do something. It was not too late, no, not even now!

He turned on the lights and toiled to his desk, found paper, and envelope and a pen. His thin, white hair fell over his brow. His long jaw jutted, that freak of genetics that had made him seem strong in his ugliness. He began to write, first the address on the envelope: the woman who ran the *pensión* off the Calle San Diego. Number seven. Then he dipped the steel nib into the well.

Alessandro, jovencito, hijo mío.

God will only grant your dreams if you are strong enough to suspect your friends and never trust them. A stranger never knows you well enough to confuse love with a dishonorable act. Only a friend can be poisoned with hatred. Trust no one and triumph. But you must free yourself before you can free others. What ever became of your bird, the one you brought with you to my house? Carlitos has waited too long. It was good to hear your voice tonight. I will pray for you, my son. Do not falter. Be terrible, like an angel. That is what she would have wished. We will endure what you will do to us. It is the only way. I know that Colleo was necessary. He had to die. I await my turn, rejoicing. I hand you the flint knife of sacrifice. May your hand never shiver and fail as mine did, so long ago.

—CARLOS SÁNCHEZ ("Papa")

157

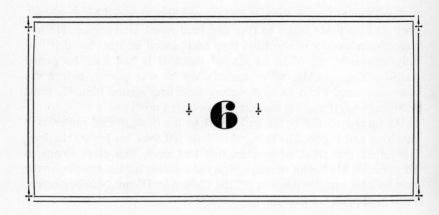

6

THE Caudillo watched the foreigners very closely but without moving his head or body. He sat at the head of the green-baize-covered table in full uniform despite the lateness of the hour and the punishing humidity. He had deliberately chosen the smallest antechamber in the palace for the negotiations. Neither the American nor the Englishman was used to the damp, sultry Costa Platan nights. Now they were actually struggling against it, a physical battle to remain alert, attentive. The Caudillo was grimly pleased. Dunkel and Livermore were breaking down.

Vizarra reflected on the number of times he had pointed out to his head of secret police, O'Conner, the usefulness of boredom, the power of fatigue. Herzler, weakened from the start by the demands of his inflation-bloated government, was now helpless. He wallowed in his seat, sweat-soaked and beaten, impatient to sign anything. The other two were weakening, Dunkel first. They had been together in the cramped, stuffy chamber for nearly nine hours. No liquid of any kind had been provided, not even a carafe of lukewarm water. Malata had made it known that the Caudillo did not tolerate smoking in his presence, ever since he himself had renounced tobacco. Livermore had toyed fretfully with his silver cigarette case. Once he had excused himself from the room to pace up and down the polished corridor. Malata had foreseen this and had removed the urns and vases. The Englishman had tapped the ashes into his pocket, stubbed his cigarette on his shoe and placed the butt in his pocket along with the ashes. A small annoyance, to be sure, but a man can be killed by pinpricks as surely as with a saber slash. Livermore's long face was wet; he mopped his brow repeatedly. Dunkel had stripped off his jacket and loosened his necktie. Where his bared arms touched the baize, two damp spots darkened the cloth. The American's voice had become hoarse.

The Minister of the Interior was a perfect confederate: a small, bloodless, juiceless man, his patience practiced over the years in senseless negotiations with the Unión de Trabajadores, his voice an instrument carefully tuned to a brain-numbing monotone. He repeated himself endlessly, waited for the translator, and droned on, never lifting his eyes from the papers piled neatly before him. He prolonged an answer to Dunkel's last, impatient question nearly five minutes and skillfully avoided any commitment. Vizarra was delighted. The Minister's salary deserved reconsideration. The ability to produce in others such enervating boredom was worthy of reward. The Minister stopped talking. Dunkel swabbed his flushed face and shook his head.

"I just don't see how we can agree to that, Your Excellency."

Vizarra raised his brows. His bulky body was pinched by his corset. He was terribly thirsty. His neck had been rubbed raw by the stiff collar of his tunic. Since he had spoken little, his voice was strong.

"And for my part, as representative of the peoples of Costa Plata, I see no alternative that can be honorably proposed and accepted. You gentlemen have had a great deal of experience with corporate structures. Far more experience than I. I believe I am correct in saying that interlocking corporations—or cartels, if you like—are a normal part of the financial structure of your respective countries. As the proposed agreement clearly states, this government would neither direct the formation of such an interlocking corporation nor interfere in any way with its operations, once established."

"Farben. And the Krupps . . ."

Herzler was now eager to consider this section of the agreement. The German was shrewd and experienced. He understood what Vizarra was offering; if the three foreign firms now running the concessions were forced to merge, the position of the German mining firm would be guaranteed; there would be no way for the English and American corporations to squeeze the Germans out. Livermore sighed. His voice was very light now, almost fluting. He had sensed that the meeting had become an endurance contest. He concealed his irritation. Hardly sporting. He was trying to save his voice.

"What Your Excellency says is quite true. However, one foresees very considerable obstacles, quite conceivably insurmountable barricades to such a proposed merger. Banking interests being as they are, cautious in the extreme, particularly in the matter of overseas investments. The whole problem of stock shares, for example. Without desiring to cast aspersions on any corporation here represented, a triad would be less appealing as an investment than the three corporations listed separately. One firm, after all, has such limited assets that the interlocking corporation suggested would obviously be somewhat weakened."

Vizarra nodded. The hope in Herzler's face began to fail.

"Then, Mr. Livermore, no doubt the two stronger firms could arrange a loan or series of loans to the lesser firm. Thus, on paper, in a brochure or prospectus, each firm thus reorganized would appear equally solvent, equally strong, equally attractive."

Herzler grinned and nodded, muttering to himself. His eyes shone with gratitude. He felt that his loyalty to the government of Costa Plata was being repaid. The Caudillo was protecting him from the English and American sharks. Livermore waved his hand languidly and smiled.

"I can speak only for my own firm, you understand. Our interests, as you know, I'm sure, are broad. Our liquid capital is already spread rather thinly among our subsidiary firms. I cannot see that we would be able, much as we might approve Your Excellency's suggestion, to endorse it by any transfer of funds."

"No? Surely you could buy German mining stock on the Paris Bourse. Such purchases—I believe the shares are listed now at thirty-

160

eight and one-half—would automatically cause the value of the stock to rise. The stock itself, thus strengthened, could be turned over to Herr Herzler's corporation. Or, alternately, a bank loan of sufficient size could then be negotiated. The increase in the value of the German mining stock would quickly increase that firm's assets. A personal loan of a few million would do the rest. At least, that is the way it seems to me. Of course, I am not so experienced in these matters as yourself."

The Englishman forced a smile and fiddled with his cigarette case.

"You are extremely modest, Your Excellency. I wish you were a board member of my corporation, if I may say that without offense."

Vizarra nodded politely. If I were a member of the board in your London office, I'd gut the corporation like a fish and toss the stinking carcass aside. We do not fool each other, Englishman.

"In addition, it strikes me that a fresh issue of stock for the interlocked corporation might best be presented in America. The stock market there is astonishingly strong, going higher every week. Such an issue of cartel stock would propel the individual stock of your firm, Mr. Dunkel, even higher. It would ride on the cartel's coattails, so to speak."

Dunkel shook his head wearily. His broad face was flushed. He wrung his hands nervously. Vizarra could hear the even breath of Malata beating in the heat-thickened air. Malata, too, was unaffected by the humidity that sapped the foreigners.

"Now, wait a minute, Your Excellency, there's a hell of a risk involved. I'm not accredited to make this sort of a deal. Even if I wanted to, my hands are tied. I'm responsible to my board of directors. Guess I'm not as lucky as you are, sir, not in that way. I can't just say do this and that and it's done, you see."

"Really? Yet your board has approved the last twenty-three proposals you personally have placed before them. I would gather from such figures that you enjoy *carte blanche*. Even your credentials handed to the Minister of the Interior state quite clearly that you are prepared for—how is it phrased?—'full, extensive and permanent, if that is possible, renegotiation of the concession with the Costa Platan government.' Perhaps we had best hear those credentials."

As though prodded with a stick, the immobile figure of the Minister sprang to life. He snatched up Dunkel's credentials and read the page through, deliberately mispronouncing the English, retracking to read a whole sentence over again. Vizarra leaned back and relaxed, watching Dunkel. The American thrashed in his seat. The Minister droned on and finally stopped. He sat there, staring at the paper. Dunkel waved one heavy arm.

"That's just a general statement. What we hoped for. But this is all different. If I can say so, I didn't come here to get pushed into signing anything that's going to lose my firm a lot of money. We don't lay out capital on any say-so but our own. Besides, the present agreement has another year to run, no matter if it does say that the future arrangements must be negotiated for twelve months before the original agreement lapses."

The American was angry now. He glared at Livermore, who remained unperturbed. Dunkel jerked his thumb at Herzler.

"His gang gets the break, as I see it. How can I go home and say to my board that we're in for ten or fifteen million dollars to put starch in some kraut outfit just so we don't get dragged down on the big board or stuck with worthless stock?"

"Worthless! Herr Dunkel, with all apologies, the value of the enterprise undertaken years ago by my firm is currently valued at—"

"I know all that. And I know you've been scratching for a loan to replace your equipment, too. And you can't get up but half what you need. Don't tell me, Manfred. I wasn't born yesterday."

Livermore shot his cuffs and leaned forward. Dunkel had turned toward the German, his face truculent, one big fist clenched. The Englishman spread his hands and smiled at Vizarra.

"You see what I mean, Your Excellency. The liquid assets of my firm are already committed, and the combination of probable board restrictions, in view of the risk on the part of Mr. Dunkel's firm, would prevent any effective steps toward refinancing an interlocked corporation such as you propose. Unless, of course, the government of Costa Plata would consider a substantial investment in the project. A purchase of bonds, perhaps, or a straight loan."

Very clever, Englishman, very clever.

"The Ministry of Finance is authorized to loan money by the Cortes, as you know. The interest figure is ten per cent."

"Ten per cent! Your Excellency, we are businessmen. We could not operate with interest payments double those of any bank."

"Then go to the banks, Mr. Livermore, as I have already suggested so many times."

162

Dunkel muttered something that ended in "goddam."

"Also, Mr. Livermore, perhaps you are not aware of this. The Cortes has granted the Ministry of Finance the power to issue both municipal and federal bonds at certain fixed numbers and rates. The Ministry has no power to *purchase* bonds. I assure you that the Cortes would never approve any measure taken to increase the dependency of Costa Plata as a nation on the whims of foreign enterprises."

"Whims, Your Excellency? A most unusual word. I'm afraid I do not quite understand."

"You understand, I am certain, that a firm capitalized outside Costa Plata could manipulate the value of stock shares or the final value of bonds issued, and the government of this country would be powerless to prevent it. It could all be explained away by economists. I do not understand economists and I do not trust them."

Dunkel leaned forward, struggling to remain polite but failing. He growled, and Livermore's face flickered with distress for the first time in the long, dull, sweltering evening.

"I just wonder, Your Excellency, if you aren't asking us to trust your government while you don't trust us at all. How are we to know if any agreement we sign is going to be worth the paper it's written on? I can smell trouble around here, right now. What the hell, your police hasn't even caught this Alessandro fella. The other bird was a fake. I saw it in the papers today."

Vizarra waited. The stifling antechamber was silent. Herzler was obviously holding his breath, waiting for the explosion. Livermore looked shocked. Dunkel was hinting, in a crude fashion, that he had begun to consider Alessandro as an alternate with whom to negotiate. The Caudillo's anger lay beneath his stiff tunic like a grenade. It was not quite the time to permit the detonation. He spoke gently but firmly, as Malata slipped the case, already open, onto the green table near his elbow.

"I respect your concern, Mr. Dunkel, and I trust you will be able to provide satisfactory answers or explanations for the very incidents of irregular operation of the railroad concession that have caused, as you suggest, a lack of complete confidence in the concession system as it now exists."

"There aren't any irregularities, Your Excellency."

"No? These freight rates and schedules, Mr. Dunkel—"

"Every firm makes mistakes, Your Excellency. Honest errors, miscalculations."

Vizarra waited, letting the room swell with expectation. He stared at the American. Dunkel stared back, bluffing, an American poker player. But in the metal box lay the trump cards, proof of systematic exploitation and dishonesty, the contrived swindling of millions. The air hung heavy, hot and dead. When the Caudillo drew his glasses from his tunic pocket, the braid on his epaulet squeaked.

"I inform you that I am not in the habit of tolerating interruptions. I will now read the contents of this box. Then we will talk about who trusts whom and why. Or why there is no trust."

He drew out the papers, slowly and deliberately, laid them on the green baize, placed his glasses on his nose and began reading.

He read for more than an hour, his voice falling into the room like stones dropped into a sponge. At every pause he could feel a squish of apprehension, could see the spreading pool of dismay. When he was done, he tossed the papers back in the dispatch box with a flip of contempt, his hand and braided forearm angled on his elbow, his index finger pointing down the table at the American like a pistol barrel.

"You have heard. Now listen. As listed in Section Three of the agreement, the three firms will merge into a single interlocked corporation. That single corporation will receive a single percentage. There will not be three concessions, three percentages. *Only one.* If you wish to practice these irregularities among yourselves, that is your own affair. Setting up the cartel is your own affair. The government of Costa Plata will tolerate no other form of agreement. Moreover, the sums listed, the result of these dishonest and deliberate manipulations, will be repaid to the Banco Central de Costa Plata within a five-year period, as stated in the rider now being distributed by the Minister of the Interior. These sums are to be paid in full, with five per cent interest. The scale of concession percentages has been worked out and are included in the rider in the form of a graph. No exceptions will be made."

He waited for the last flurry. It came from Livermore, who drew sheets of paper from a briefcase.

"Yes?"

"Your Excellency. If we suspend for a moment further consideration of the interlocked corporation—"

164

"Then you may consider the operations of Livermore Lines Limited also suspended, sir! I will be happy to show you certain documents forwarded to me by the Compagnie Générale de Transport."

"I beg your pardon, Excellency, you mistake my meaning. I suggest rather an expansion of my firm's operations. Not only high-seas freight and passenger service to New York, Liverpool, Hamburg and Naples as before, but also a coastwise service."

"The coastwise service is adequate. I have studied it."

"Then no doubt you are aware of the illegally transported merchandise entering Costa Plata, specifically via the fishing fleet operating out of Boca Perro. I believe smuggling is a crime, Your Excellency?"

"There is no smuggling in Costa Plata."

"The operations of these fishing vessels, Your Excellency, is in violation of the agreement dealing with the high-seas freight concession, both as it now stands and as it has been proposed. Now, quite candidly, I would term these activities *irregularities*. I can see no method by which this smuggling can have persisted without the complicity of the *Guardia Costa,* and the Coast Guard is a federal force. What I am saying, therefore, is that the government of Costa Plata itself, by granting tacit permission to the fishing vessels to operate in such a manner, is guilty of breach of contract. Setting aside the difficulties of accounting you have so thoroughly elucidated for us in reference to the railroad and mining concessions, I discover minimum—mind you, *minimum*—losses in revenue to *my* firm."

The sharks have turned against themselves. One cannibal against another. Livermore abandons the pack, let them flop and bleed, to wrench again at Costa Plata.

Vizarra leaned forward.

"You have a monopoly, sir. I do not discuss minimum losses with the representative of a foreign monopoly. I will not hear unsubstantiated charges against the loyal citizens and government officials of this nation. I will not hear estimated minimum losses that cannot be proven in any way whatsoever."

"I have here figures, calculations—"

"Submit them to the Minister of the Marine, sir."

"I beg to remind you that Your Excellency's government is in breach of contract."

"I beg to remind you, sir, that your monopoly terminates within twelve months! If you do not care to continue with the negotiations—"

"I have not indicated, I think, any intention of withdrawal, Your Excellency, only—"

"Very good, then. Let us proceed to an examination of Section Four of the new agreement."

Livermore took out a fountain pen and wrote the address of the Costa Platan Minister of the Marine on a manila envelope. He rustled the papers noisily as he placed them in the envelope. He asked in a polite but rather loud voice for a messenger to forward the documents to the proper bureau. A page took them away. Vizarra noticed the stiff little frenzy. Livermore would continue to gnaw wherever he could. The Minister would know his duty without being told. The smuggling would cease temporarily, long enough for the Englishman's proposed coastwise freight service to be forgotten.

Vizarra cleared his throat. Nearly two o'clock. Time to press on, force the agreement to a conclusion, if it took until noon the next day. The foreigners were not to be allowed from the room to gather their weakened forces. These sharks grew teeth too fast.

"Section Four. The length of the agreement herein agreed to in full, and signed by the representatives of the interlocked corporation and the respective, responsible officers of the government of Costa Plata, shall be a single, unbroken term of ninety-nine years without renewal. Yes, Mr. Dunkel?"

"Why so long? Why not ten years or twenty, Your Excellency?"

Vizarra drew a breath. So. They had accepted the interlocked corporation with a single percentage. Very good.

"Allow me to explain. A matter of security. I think we can both agree that a business enterprise needs the assurance of stability, or at least as much as can be arranged, leaving open always misfortunes and acts of God."

The American grimaced, but nodded.

"I notice, Your Excellency, the percentage payments are scaled."

"Yes. The largest percentages paid to the interlocked corporation will be during the first five-year period. To repay swiftly the capital investment and to ease the repayments with interest due the people of Costa Plata as the result of past irregularities. Thus, in the middle period, the profits shared from the mines are equally divided between the government of Costa Plata and the corporation. In the final

166

years—the last five years, to be precise—no percentage will be paid the corporation. During that five-year period our government will be purchasing, at cost, the assets of the corporation: machinery, building, vehicles and so on. Plus the railroad equipment, aircraft, steamships and so on."

"In effect, then, the corporation will be liquidated. Completely."

"My dear Mr. Livermore, at the end of ninety-nine years I very much doubt whether such affairs will concern either of us."

The Englishman smiled for the first time in more than seven hours.

"Very true. Of course, the value of the stock will gradually diminish to nothing, long before the corporation is liquidated."

"Frankly, Mr. Livermore, I do not see why the exact conditions of the agreement need be made public, do you? Your investment prospectus might merely carry the terms of the agreement to the forty-fifth-year period, the period of equally shared profits. The corporation, then, might gradually divest itself of its preferred stock."

"That is a manipulation of doubtful honesty, Your Excellency."

"No more and no less than any other. Much less than watering—is that the proper term?—watering stock, for instance. You are speaking, perhaps, of the general public. There will be no manipulation among ourselves. Only stability."

"But the investors in the corporation, the shareholders, will not be Costa Platans but Americans and Europeans. In the end they will be subject to fraud."

"I do not see how the misguided enthusiasms of American and European speculators a half century hence is of much concern to me. Or any of us, for that matter."

Dunkel suddenly laughed.

"By God, that's right! At the end of forty-five years we can start to unload and get out with whole skins. None of us will be alive and kicking. Let somebody else get nicked. Too bad for them, that's all!"

The American seemed delighted at the simplicity of the percentage agreements. Vizarra rubbed his jowls in the stiff collar of his uniform. Let their enthusiasm carry them on. He had already printed instructions placed with the Ministries of Finance and the Interior and the Unión de Trabajadores. After the fiftieth year, labor slowdowns were to deliberately sabotage the corporation. The money earned was to be invested in the purchase of gold, the gold let out for loans abroad.

Costa Plata, mining silver and buying gold, would become the banking nation of Latin America. And its first foreclosure would be on the foreign corporation that had made the new wealth possible. True, none of them would be alive to see it, but perhaps the soul could dream in the dust of the tiny nation, one vault, one bank, against which the nations of Latin America could draw. The Caudillo's final gift to his people, a legacy of fabulous prosperity, the silver coast exchanged for gold, the dream at the rainbow's end come true. And the school of foreign sharks slaughtered, their future generations of spawn crushed forever. Vizarra straightened.

"It's very late, gentlemen. The Minister of the Interior will now read Section Four in full. Then, if we are agreed as we seem to be, we will progress to Section Five."

⸸

She lay in a chaise longue beside the swimming pool. Already the midmorning sun was uncomfortably hot, but beneath the trees lay a patch of shade. She had washed her hair, and a damp towel lay across her bare legs. On the table by the chaise longue was an untidy stack of sheet music, a pack of cigarettes, and an empty coffee cup. She lay staring idly at the transparent water of the pool. Birds fluttered and sang in the gardens.

She heard the sound of automobiles on the long gravel driveway, then the thud of doors. Had he come home, finally? The speaking tube beside the diving board whistled, and she swung off the chaise and walked to it.

"Yes?"

"El Caudillo, señorita."

"Muy bien."

She plugged the tube, walked back into the shade and straightened the music sheets, found her hair band and slipped it over her still-damp hair. She could hear his voice. He was on the balcony, talking loudly and rapidly to someone. She caught the name "Julio." He was with Malata still. She grimaced. Why did he insist on keeping the ex-café waiter as his aide? There was something repellent, unhuman, about Malata. He never perspired; even on the hottest days his skin was as dry and cool as a snake's.

Two servants rushed down the garden path, awkwardly carrying a large champagne cooler packed with bottles and ice. They bowed to

168

her clumsily, dragged the cooler into the shade, bowed again, and vanished. She could hear him in the garden, singing hoarsely. He appeared through the arbor at the far end of the pool, striding quickly, his hands tearing at the buttons of his tunic.

"Lucía!"

"Here!"

He sprang toward her, holding out his arms, his lips smiling, his face eager as a boy's. She waited for him. She had an instant's glance at his weary, red-lidded eyes before he crushed her against his chest, butted her chin up gently with his knuckles and kissed her, as a thirsty man might drink a glass of water. He held her tightly and kissed her face and eyes. His voice was hoarse, enthusiastic.

"So? Here you are. I'm late for dinner, eh? And breakfast, too. Well, I'm home now. And thank God. How have you been, *guapita?*"

"Oh, well enough. Fine."

"Ah, champagne! God, I've been waiting for this. I'm dying of thirst!"

"I'll get it, Rafael. Sit down. You must be exhausted."

He tore off his tunic and flung it over the ladder to the high board. The sun glinted on the grizzled hair on his naked chest. He raised his hands and massaged his neck, blinking his eyes. He looked like a sleepy little boy. She bent over the bucket, stripping away the foil from the cork of a bottle, hiding her smile.

"Tired? No, not really. They can't wear out an old mule like me. But the others! Huh! Dead on their feet, absolutely. They're all worn out. Even Julio dozed coming out in the car."

"Him? I don't believe it."

The cork popped. She lifted the bottle, filled a large highball glass with champagne and dropped in a handful of ice. The bubbling wine ran over her fingers. He sprawled on the chaise, wiggling his bare feet. He sat up, took the glass from her and drank it off, gasped and flopped back, grinning.

"Mother of God, that's good! Get me another. Have some, Lucía."

"It's too early for me, Rafael."

"What foolishness! Too early. Why, we're celebrating!"

"Ah, that's different."

She poured two more glasses, added ice and carried them to the chaise. He shifted his legs to make room for her, took the glass and touched it to hers.

169

"What do we drink to?"

"I don't know, Rafael. Tell me!"

"Ah, you're curious? Well, you should have seen the crowd outside the palace. The Plaza Mayor was half filled. Here, to your beautiful dark eyes. Kiss me."

She bent over him. As her lips touched his mouth, she felt his hand on her breast. She drew away slowly. His hand dropped to her hip. He looked up at her, his eyes shining. She rubbed his cheek.

"You have a beard like . . . like a wild pig."

He gulped his drink, gasping as the cold wine plunged into his belly. He rumpled his hair, still grinning, and clapped her on the thigh.

"And like a wild pig I got them!"

He bared his teeth ferociously, laughed and emptied his glass.

"Another!"

"Not so fast, Rafael. In this heat. Have you eaten?"

"Coffee and roll. Enough."

He sat up and hugged her. She pressed her face against his neck, her eyes closed, inhaling the hard, rank smell of his body. The stubble on his jaw scraped her cheek. She rolled her head slowly from side to side, making a noise in her throat. His arms loosened, and she kissed his face and ears, tickling him with the tip of her tongue.

"Don't leave me alone so long, Rafael. I don't like it. No one here but the servants."

"Lucía, don't worry. I'm here, I'm here. It's all settled, finished!"

"They signed?"

"They signed! We all signed. At eight o'clock this morning. After thirteen straight hours. As written, too, just as it was written! Not one change. I wore them down, all right. You should have seen them! I didn't even give them water. They were dry as turds at harvest time! And the American! 'Oh, *goddam, goddam, goddam!*' He would have sold his mother for a glass of beer by the time I was done with him!"

He released her and lay back on the chaise, shaking with laughter, tears running out of his eyes. She took the glass from his hand and refilled it, adding more ice. He sat up, cross-legged, grinning proudly.

"Ninety-nine years . . . so they think. I called the Cortes into special session to ratify it. They should just finish before the fiesta.

Ah, this time we've got something to tell Santa Rosa! Now, now, I can make this country rich and strong!"

He sipped his drink and nodded his head, then laughed again.

"How polite these Englishmen are! You know? The worse things get for them, the more polite they grow. But cold? Brrr! You could ice-skate on his thank-yous. And Manfred Herzler—you know him, the German from the mine concession with no hair—I thought he would cry. He thinks I'm doing him a favor. He even thinks we haven't found out that the last shipment of machinery—new stuff, his company said—was secondhand. Yes, secondhand, the pumps and the crushing equipment. It came from South Africa, not Germany. Just wait! Another one like that and O'Conner will take him to the harbor and throw him in, the bastard! We're done with that now, I tell you. It was worth the wait to catch them. *Madre de Dios,* but the Americans are the worst of all. What thieves! Bandits! You wouldn't believe it! Not only the freight rates, Lucía, but the spare parts, every ton of coal, every rail, every damned spike! That new line to the mines? My God, they could have built a railroad from New York to the moon for what it cost. And we, we, supplied the labor! That red-faced *ladrón* and his 'irregularities!' "

He rocked from side to side, clutching his glass. He had forgotten her, really. He was talking out loud.

"Never again, though. No, *Jesús,* no. They've signed and they'll have to stick to it. So we'll show them the fiesta and send them home. No trouble, though, there can be no trouble. Nothing. Julio will see to it that the buildings are cleaned off. That O'Conner! That Yankee turd! Another one. After the fiesta, I'll kick him out. Yes. One day we'll throw them all out of here, the Germans, the English and the damned Americans. Thank God, we don't grow bananas in this country! Ahh, I feel dirty from being with them. Foreign bloodsuckers!"

He drained his glass, stood up and struggled out of his trousers. He stood there, pale and muttering, his belly encased in his corset. He plucked at the laces, groaning. She began to giggle, her teeth clicking on the rim of her glass. He freed himself, stamped naked to the edge of the pool and flung himself into the water. It shattered like a mirror; a thousand glints danced and rippled as he exploded back to the surface, huffing, the water streaming down his distorted face.

"Ahhh! That's good! Come on in, Lucía!"

"Not now. Besides, I haven't got a suit."

171

He wallowed and rolled, snorting and kicking, flinging his arms in white crashes of spray.

"A suit? What's that? Come, show me your pretty white rump, girl!"

"Qué malo, tu!"

"Open another bottle, then!"

She went to the cooler and tore the foil off a cork. He swam steadily, strongly, three lengths of the pool, then hung on the ladder at the deep end, his heavy chest heaving.

"Bring me a towel, eh?"

She walked over to him carrying the towel. His powerful body gleamed white, distorted by the stirred water. He flung back his head and squinted at the blue sky.

"What a day! Splendid! Magnificent!"

His hand shot out and clamped around her ankle. She shrieked and grabbed the ladder. He growled like an animal, tugging at her.

"No, Rafael, no! Come on, please! Oh, don't!"

"You're a witch, that's what! Witches are afraid of water!"

"Bruto, let me go!

He released her and surged up the ladder, the clear water streaming off him. He scrubbed his paunch and dug his fingers into the dark fur on his groin, then picked up the towel and dried his face.

"Is that bottle open?"

"Yes. Come have a drink."

He knotted the towel around his waist and took the glass from her. He drank and smacked his lips.

"Good. Maybe I'll throw the others out and bring some Frenchmen here. They can show us how to make champagne. Drink, girl, drink! You can feel it sparkle in the blood, no?"

"You look tired, Rafael. Come, I'll rub your back."

"Good."

He stretched out on the chaise. She sipped her drink, then clapped her slender hands at the base of his neck and began to knead the heavy meat of his shoulder muscles. He groaned, delighted.

"Oh, that's stupendous. *Dios,* you have claws! Oh, oh. Aaaah! Ow!"

"Don't be such a baby. I'm not hurting you."

"No? Then why do I feel blood?"

"That's the water running off."

She kissed his shoulder and drew her hands down along the twin straps of muscle along his spine. She pinched his sides.

"Feel that. You're getting fat."

"Ah, that's what we wild pigs need. Keeps us warm."

He raised his head and brought the glass to his mouth. Champagne spilled down his bristled chin, and he choked.

"Not so much of that. Your stomach will bother you again. The doctor said—"

"A damned Swiss. What does he know? All he can treat is edelweiss poisoning. You want to learn how to ski? We'll go there, too. First to Paris, then to Switzerland. I want to get away for a while."

"What about—"

"Alessandro? We'll get him. Any day now. I will crush him like a fly, a fly. Then we'll take a trip. I want to show you off. These foreigners think that the only thing Costa Plata produces is silver. They don't know about our pretty girls yet. Who knows? I may start exporting them too."

"Ah, you. You're in a good mood today."

"Wrong! I am in a magnificent mood today!"

"Stupendous!"

"Right. Stupendous!"

He rolled over on his back. His damp hair curled crisply over his brow. Some of the fatigue had washed away. He looked younger, even with the deep lines drawn in his face like knife wounds. She bent down and kissed him. He touched her breasts and fumbled with the buttons of her blouse. His heavy arm encircled her, drawing her down on top of him. They lay quietly for a moment, kissing. She opened her blouse for him, then pulled away.

"Come to the villa. Someone will see us."

"*Tonterías.* I gave orders that I would see no one. Not until tonight. We're having the three of them here for a later dinner. Lots of champagne. To take the sting out of their wounds. You must be very beautiful."

"Let's go up to the villa."

"How can I? I can't go around like this. Look at me, eh?"

"What? Oh."

"Oh? Is that all you can say?"

She slipped her hand under the towel and lay down beside him.

"Ai-ya! And I'm just a little girl . . ."

"Kiss me, Lucía."

"Rafael, someone will see us!"

"Then take your hand away."

"I don't care, I don't care."

He pulled up her skirt.

"Wait, I'll take it off."

"No, never mind."

"Ai-yah, Rafael . . ."

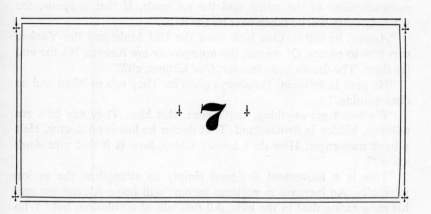

7

THEY peeled the petal-tinted shells from the shrimps and tossed them on the floor. Behind the bars the waiters rushed to fill the glasses with cool, amber beer or the nearly transparent white wine chilled in stone pipes packed with ice.

Pigeons wheeled and flapped above the banks and office buildings. Tar bled on the streets, and the shutters thundered down, sealing out the heat. In the parks, they sipped *gaseosa* and fanned themselves with the thin, shoddy newspapers. They glanced impatiently at the meaningless headlines and calculated the hours until the evening editions came off the presses.

Telegraph keys chattered in the offices of brokers and bankers. What were mining shares worth on Wall Street, the Paris Bourse? Buy Livermore Lines Ltd. or sell? North American Foundry, Inc., up three-eighths. Did it mean anything?

"He's done it this time. *Hombre,* he has sold us all. You and me, my children, your grandchildren. For a handful of green stuff."

175

"The railroads and mines will be nationalized. My cousin's friend knows this girl who works at the U.T. We're taking over next month."

"Naturally, the *last* thing we can afford to have happen is the nationalization of the mines and the railroads. If that happens, the whole country will be taken over by the Reds."

"*Amigo,* he did it. One kick from the Old Mule and the Yankee cart flew to pieces. Of course, the *bourgeoisie* are furious. It's the end for them. The dream gone forever. *Qué lástima,* eh?"

"He gave in to them. He always gives in. They rob us blind and he does nothing."

"We won't get anything, that's sure. But him. They say he's got millions, hidden in Switzerland. That doctor he has is no doctor. He's a bank messenger. How do I know? *Chico,* how is it that you *don't* know?"

"This is a movement designed simply to strengthen the nation internally. An increase in national income will leave Alessandro and his gang eating dust in the hills. All this talk of revolution, bah! Who can throw bricks with both hands full of bread?"

"It was a near thing. They tried to put something in his coffee, but he didn't taste it. Yes, some narcotic. Of course I'm serious. I had my hair cut this morning, no? Is not my barber the same one who cuts the hair of the *médico* who cares for the Minister's children?"

"If it's one thing he is good at, it's handling these gringos. They got nothing from him this time."

"It all depends on the ingot price, I tell you! We're not making bracelets like a bunch of Mexicans. I'm talking about silver, *hombre,* and at twenty kilos an ingot!"

"An entirely new conception of percentages. Absolutely! Do you know García? Ah, you see visions, perhaps? No? Miraculous that your information is more accurate than García's who helped draft Section Four with his own hands! No, no, not another word from me. Such ignorance as yours is divine, no question of it. You will be a saint, believe me."

"It will make no difference, brother. He is coming, our Alessandro. He is here now. Truth. In a month, what will it matter what the Old Mule has signed? It is what Alessandro will sign that will matter!"

"Let him talk to the foreigners. Just give me twenty minutes with that Bosola bitch. That's my idea of negotiations."

"It is his constant interference that hinders our natural progress.

176

Whether the agreement is good or bad, you may rest assured that the Minister of Interior would have done better."

"He is, of course, notoriously bad at dealing with foreigners. But you can't fool him on money matters. Malata did all the talking, while he waited outside."

"Agreement? That word stinks. Swindle, that's what I say."

"If this goes through, the U.T. is going right to the Minister of Finance. Three reales an hour. That's a raise that means something."

"Already they are printing more paper money. In a year you'll wipe yourself with a week's pay."

"Sell. Sell everything except your clothes. This agreement will touch it off. When Alessandro hears of it . . . *pooom!* Sell everything. They say Mexico is nice once you get used to the altitude."

"He is a genius. Nothing less. We have never had a greater leader. History is selective; the forces of national destiny select one man in every century ideally suited to govern. Politics is no more than knowing when to step aside."

"Finish up. Let's have lunch. To hell with the agreement. What's it mean to me? *Mierda,* that's what."

"What ever happened to that priest they caught?"

"What priest?"

"Let's have another *caña.* Too hot today to think about politics."

"He's coming, brother. He's coming. Alessandro's in the hills. Colleo's in his grave. Next one is the Old Mule."

"Beer or *vino blanco?*"

"In strictest confidence, you understand. So. You've read the *Essays?* Good. And *Sing From the Mountains?* So. It's all there. Every bit of it. Remember where he's talking about dictatorships? The part where he calls dictatorships machines with too many parts? *Claro.* The state is overly bureaucratic, by nature inefficient. Since the state runs on a deficit, it must either expand by military conquest of weak neighbors to balance the budget or by trade. Oh, the Old Mule's clever, all right. He trades, that one. But he cuts his throat. If anything goes wrong, the Americans will be down here in two days. The principle of overreliance, you recall, and the dwindling sense of national sovereignty. Fiscal puppets. That will all be done away with. He's coming, brother, and damned soon. No? Then why did they bury Colleo at night? Eh? The Prime Minister and they stick him underground after dark? Don't make me laugh. Read Alessandro on terror, real and imagined. The Old Mule's got his tail up and the brown stuff is streaming out."

"Drink up. In a year this stuff will cost a thousand reales a glass."

"Gentlemen, I give you the Caudillo."

"Beer or *vino blanco?*"

"*Camarero!* Psst! Another dozen shrimps."

⸸

"Ferguson, this is Mr. Dunkel. From America. North American Foundry. The railroad concession."

"How do you do, sir?"

"Mr. Dunkel, Ferguson, our manager here."

"A real pleasure, sir."

"We should like to use your office for a bit, Ferguson. It's so much cooler there. Sorry to have to put you out. We shan't be long, I think."

"Certainly, sir. Right this way. Will you be needing anything?"

"Some telegraph blanks, Ferguson. Oh, and proper address for the home office of Amalgamated Fruit and Produce Corporation."

"It's in New Orleans, Louisiana, Mr. Ferguson. But we want the cable address for their Guatemala and Mexico City offices, too."

Ferguson nodded and left them at the door. Dunkel sat down and stared gloomily at the floor. Livermore slipped behind the desk and lighted a cigarette.

"Very good of you to come."

"What else can we do? He's not going to pull any long-term arrangement on us. Not on those terms. What the hell, if it wasn't for us, these people would still be living in mud huts. Herzler can't make it, but he'll play along."

"You told him?"

"Enough. He thinks a million will do it. If he'll take it."

"If he'll take it? I should think he would. We are assuring the success of his movement. By the by, will you take pounds as our share?"

"Sure. We can work it out later. The thing to do first is to make a delivery to wherever this Alessandro bird wants the stuff dumped. I'm not much up on that end of it, but I know Eddie at the Guatemala office of Amalgamated Fruit. We'll either buy from them or have them buy out of Mexico and give them five per cent for handling the details."

178

"How much will a million dollars buy, do you suppose?"

"Figure twenty-five dollars a rifle, ammunition at ten cents a round."

"Ten thousand rifles would run a quarter of a million."

"More or less. Another quarter for ammunition. That leaves us a half million in reserve. We'll set up a drawing account for a quarter million. The rest will have to go for shipping charges and hush money."

"What?"

"Hush money. You know, to cover up."

"Yes, of course. Ah, Ferguson, here you are. Good enough. Just have a boy stand by outside, will you? We shall want to be sending these cables off right away. Oh, have you any iced tea? Excellent. And arrange for a car to take Mr. Dunkel back to the ship. I shall want to speak to you privately, Ferguson, but later, later."

‡

"Impossible!"

The director of the sanatorium set down the piece of paper and glared at Sánchez, who shrugged, his shoulders hunched in his maroon bathrobe. The director's liver-spotted wattles shook with indignation.

"Impossible. This is inhuman!"

"Don Alonso, there is no other way. You have seen how they've been pouring in here. We need the space."

"I have given you all the space available!"

"They are sleeping in the basements now."

"Let them sleep on the lawn! I will not move my patients out! Never! Not for you, not for Alessandro himself! These people are *tuberculars*, can't you understand that?"

"Of course, Don Alonso."

"There are two hundred and fifty patients here! More than one-half of them will die if they are taken down off this mountain. I have given everything to the movement I can. But you ask me to dishonor my name, my reputation! I will not be party to mass murder!"

"Alessandro has given the order. The patients are to be moved out. This afternoon."

"That is quite impossible, Sánchez. Please go away and do not bring such pieces of madness to my attention again. The members of the movement can sleep in the corridors."

"They are already."

"I know it. There are the lawns."

"They'll freeze at night. Then you'll have more pneumonia patients."

"I have my sacred duty."

"Don Alonso, these tuberculars will all die soon anyway."

"That is not so! More than half will be rehabilitated."

"That's not what your own doctors tell me. Get them out."

The old man was white with rage. He gasped for air and flapped his hand on the desk. He shook his head.

"You will kill them . . . kill them."

"There is no other way. We have five trucks waiting outside loaded with munitions. They go in the cellar. Where do those seventy-five men sleep then?"

"On top of the ammunition."

"Have your secretary type up the directive and send it around to all the wards."

"No! Don't you see? It is not only that I will not. I *cannot* obey him! I cannot kill my patients."

"If you refuse, we'll take them out ourselves."

"If you do, you will make yourself a murderer."

Sánchez shrugged again. He was tired of arguing. He wanted a cigarette and a drink of brandy.

"I'm not trying to frighten you, Don Alonso. I'm just telling you."

The old man jumped to his feet. His hand shook as he pointed to the door.

"Get out, you . . . butcher!"

Sánchez walked to the door and stepped out into the corridor. Olmega stood there, wearing a pistol. He raised his brows.

"He refuses. Lock him in his office, both doors. Get your boys to start getting them out of the wards. Is that ammunition unloaded yet?"

"Yes. The trucks are empty. Where do we take them?"

"How would I know? Alessandro just ordered them out. He didn't say where they were to go."

"To the railroad station?"

"Beautiful! In two hours the whole country will know something is up. Two hundred patients at the railroad station? Come on, *chico,* don't be stupid."

180

"Well, there isn't room at the pueblo, either. The last batch of delegates from the *campo* moved in there. And there's another group of miners recruited by that one-armed Indian. They're due to stay here, right?"

"Right."

"Then I don't see how or where—"

Sánchez scrubbed his face wearily and shrugged.

"Don't bother me with such things. I've been with those damned Belgians for half the day. Artillery, artillery, artillery. Ya, ya, ya. I'm half crazy. Just find a field someplace, not too far away, but far enough so they won't come back. I don't know how many can walk or how far. Find some field about ten or fifteen kilometers from here. Don't waste a lot of gasoline."

"What about food and water?"

"What about it? Let them find their own. Alessandro said nothing about food and water. Now get going. And remember, all of the staff members stay right here. Just dump them and come back for another load. Be back by 1800 hours. You have a meeting with the other students and teachers, the whole business of seizing the university buildings. You'll present your plan at midnight."

Olmega turned the corner, the pistol thumping against his thigh. The weapon increased his confidence; he wore it all the time. It was the sign of his profession. The newcomers to the sanatorium stared at him, awed and respectful. *Yes, that's him. The one who shot Colleo.* And the old-timers, men like Rota, now looked up to him, feared him. The U.T. chief crossed himself when they passed in the corridors.

At the end of the corridor, near the stairwell, Olmega saw a familiar figure, a man he saw twenty or fifty times a day, although he didn't know his name. The thin sunlight streamed through the thick, green glass of the skylight. Olmega saw a figure, a white, wavering shape, like a statue before an unveiling, like a dead man sewn in a sack, sliding through distorting water to the bottom far below. The head nodded, as though butted by sea current. A limping figure, a man somehow spoiled, flawed by birth or later accident. A man in the white uniform of a hospital orderly, with a thin, worn, but still handsome face, carrying an envelope in his left hand. A melancholy mustache over a broad, firm mouth, the eyes vague, blurred, indifferent. The left shoulder hitched when he walked.

181

He could help direct the loading. Olmega raised his arm and shouted.

"Hey, you! You, there! Come here!"

The head turned, one dark, stabbing glance, a flash of white teeth. He slid down the stairs, quick, without a sound. Olmega knew he was too far away to be caught. He shook his head angrily.

"Lazy little bastard!"

By the time Olmega reached the stairwell, the orderly had vanished below into the labyrinth of narrow service corridors and storerooms. Somewhere a door shut with a soft, teasing hiss.

‡

Pablo drove the goats up the dry, stone-littered ravine. The ones in front disappeared into the thick, chill mist that lay over the ground. The goats ran easily, lightly, their small hoofs scraping stones loose, kicking them down the slope. Pablo swung his stick and heard it burr in the cold morning air. His belly was still warm from hot milk and bread. He had more bread, a piece of cheese and a *bota* of water with him. It was always hard to wait until the sun stood high. He always wanted to eat earlier. Driving the strays back to the herd made him hot and hungry. They could eat all the time, any time, the goats could.

He was still proud. His father trusted him. He was seven years old and tended the goats. Every day. Twenty-one of them, driving them up into the hills every morning before sunrise, watching them all day, then bringing them back down to the pueblo in the late afternoon for his mother and father to milk. Then he helped drive the goats through the streets. The women came out with pans and pitchers. His father milked the goats, while his mother gossiped and took the centavos.

Pablo ran forward to find the Judas goats, but they had started down the path that skirted the fields. Pablo ran on. Sometimes the goats broke from the herd and got into the fields. The beans and squash that grew there belonged to a rich farmer in the next village. Once his brother had let the goats get into the fields. The farmer had come with a policeman, and Pablo's father had been made to pay ten reales, a huge sum.

He looked for the goat with the white spot on the left shoulder. He saw her sliding down the hill, scrambling for the squash and the rough green vines. He ran after her, whistling between his gapped front teeth. The goat reached the valley floor and began to trot, her slack udder bouncing. Pablo rushed down the slope, angry and reckless, not even bothering to check his plunge. Wiry bushes whipped against his legs, stinging him. The goat had disappeared into the cloaking mist. He whistled brokenly, gasping for breath. He ran on until he reached the edge of the fields, a slight mound, a low wall of earth and stones grown over with herbs and small, brittle ferns.

He saw something move and ran between the long bean rows, jumped over a few and headed toward the squash patch. If the goat hadn't reached there, he could find her by walking back through the bean rows. He could take a few beans, too, to eat, hard and juicy, for his meal. It was wrong to steal, but he didn't think God could see through the mist very well. God might think it was the goats.

It lurched up out of the mist, thrashing in the vines, calling something in a thick, wet voice. A tall thing and terrible with a white, billowing body and naked hairy legs. Pablo screamed in terror and ran away, crashing through the bean rows, blind with fright, until he reached the second path. He flung himself down, his eyes fixed on the field below. He cursed the goat with every bad name he could call her. She was evil and had led him to where the spirits lay hidden in the mist. He could not go get her out until the mist lifted. By that time she would have eaten a full belly of squash and beans and cut the vines to pieces with her sharp little hoofs. He cursed hopelessly and began to cry.

It seemed a long time until the sun came out, and the sun and the wind sucked up the mists where the dead souls walked. He stared, looking for the dark, horned shape of the goat, until his eyes ached. His heart pounded again, and he clung to the earth, digging his fingers into the stony ground. They were still there!

He did not dare to count them. They lay, some in neat rows, head to foot between the bean rows. Others walked slowly about, sat and squatted, then stood again. They gathered in groups, all alike, white flapping bodies and naked legs. Some had long hair, too. And there was the goat, eating beans, pulling up whole plants with sharp, strong jerks of her head, grinding the leaves and beans together. Pablo pounded his fists on the ground, wept and stared at the field, then at the west, where the herd had thinned, now no bigger than ants, a long way away.

He made careful preparations. First he knelt and said his Pater

Noster, then three Ave Marias, one for his father, one for his mother and one for himself. His brother could pray for himself. He wasn't cursed by these goats and dead spirits, too. Then he took out his little knife and made a holy cross of two dry, stiff spears of grass. He kissed it and prayed, then took up his stick and carried that and the knife in his right hand and held the cross in his left fist against his heart. He walked slowly, almost creeping down into the valley, watching them and watching the goat, too.

He stepped into the beans. He dodged along one row, keeping low, dragging his stick. He could hear them talking and coughing. He could hear the goat, damn her, tearing up the plants. He began to weep again, hot, silent tears of anger and fear. His father would beat him, or the spirits would suck his soul out through his nostrils or his ear holes. He had to get the goat. He could hear his father shouting and cursing him as a liar, his mother wailing and biting her fingers. He began to shake all over.

He raised his head and blinked. Ah, *Jesús y María!* They had seen the goat, too, and were after her! But they were driving her toward him. She ambled a dozen steps, then snatched at a plant and came on again. He kissed his little grass cross and moaned. He could hear them calling in the field.

"Where is the boy? Where is he?"

The dark little legs flickered between the bean plants. He waited until the last instant. He could hear their terrible white, flabby bodies dragging against the leaves and how they gasped and sucked, trying to draw the soul from him. He flung himself through the row and fell with a wash of torn leaves and snagging vines on the hard, bony body of the goat. The animal thrashed in terror, bleating. He clung to the fur and her hard foreleg, his face pressed tight. The goat began to drag him, staggering back through the ripping plants. They bellowed and came for him.

"There he is! He's got the goat! Get them! Get them!"

Somehow he remembered the knife, raised his fist, let go, and drove the blade into the goat's haunch. It shot out from under him and bounded over the next row. He scrambled to his feet, ran to the right, whirled, howling with fright, and ran to the left. He had dropped his stick. A pale body burst through the green leaves. He saw a man in a white, short robe and naked legs, a fearful face, carrying a cup made of paper. The man spat into the cup and walked, slowly, heavily, toward him. He had glued the cup with his spit. That's where he was going to put his soul when he sucked it out. He turned and ran, bashed through row after row, crawled over the mound and ran again. He could see the goat ahead of him. Behind him they called and called.

"Niño! Niño! Little boy, come back! Come help us, little boy! Help!"

He ran, crossing himself, until he fell exhausted on the second path. The little goat danced down the hoof-cut track, her udder flopping. He could see the bright splotch of blood on her haunch. She stopped and tried to lick it, all the while staring at him with golden, cruel eyes. He shook his fist at her, too tired, too out of breath, to curse. He staggered to his feet and followed her. They called to him. He looked back. They stood in the field, waving their white, clutching arms and hooting. He gasped for breath and praised the name of Mary for saving him. He was shocked and giddy and had to stop. The world rocked and tilted before him. In a few moments he could breathe normally and repeat his prayers and thanks. The goat ran on ahead. He ran after her, afraid all over again.

It did not occur to him until much later in the afternoon, when his terror had dulled like a wound, that he would have to go back with the goats by the same path, by the same field, and that this time, since they did not vanish with the morning sun, they would be waiting for him, each with a little cup, surely, for each wanted a sip of his soul to eat with his flesh. He sat on the ground and wept.

✝

"Two hundred eighty-four, eighty-five, and five is two-ninety. Where are the other ten?"

"Here. We were just looking at them."

"If you've seen one pistol, you've seen them all. Hand them over. Are they clean?"

"Of course they're clean! What in hell do you think we've been doing down here for the last five hours, diddling ourselves?"

"All right. Don't get angry, brother. It's the light. The light down here is lousy."

"Let's go outside, then. The others are cleaning the rifles out on the lawn."

"It's raining, stupid. They came in hours ago."

"I've been busy. Stupid, yourself."

"Come on, you two, get me a total on the ammunition. There should be a hundred rounds for every pistol. Get counting. Remember, the big boxes are hand grenades. Don't get mixed up. We've got to have this stuff ready by tonight. It's being distributed to the student cadres."

"Lucky bastards. They won't leave a classroom standing with these grenades. Who's the leader?"

"Alessandro hasn't appointed brigade leaders yet. But it'll be Pepe Olmega all right. That kid's got no nerves at all."

"Uh. I'm glad I'm not his friend, that's all."

"Afraid he'd blow your head off?"

"Ah, he's a stuck-up little craphead, that one."

"Like hell! He's tough—all balls, that kid."

"Come on, will you? Count the boxes. You count the ammunition and I'll count the grenades."

"I think those Belgians are right. We need artillery and machine guns."

"What do you think we're going to do with all this stuff? We're going to capture guns and . . . lots of other stuff, too."

"You and your friend Olmega. Big talk."

"I never said he was my friend."

"In the movement a man has no friends, but a thousand comrades, a million compatriots."

"Listen to him. He's been reading again."

"At least he knows how, *hombre*."

"Shut up and start counting."

"One, two, three, four, five. And five is ten. And five is fifteen and fifteen is twenty . . ."

"What!"

"Sorry, thirty. Thirty-one, two, three, four. Thirty-five . . ."

✢

The manager of the Guatemala office of the Amalgamated Fruit and Produce Company read the telegrams over once again before he broke the seal on the packet marked CONFIDENTIAL. The mail plane from Mexico was still at the landing field being refueled. Fortunately, the pilot scheduled to fly the next leg, down to Costa Plata, was late arriving. The telegrams had insisted that the transaction be carried into effect immediately, but the details had been left open for local decision. The manager glanced at his watch. He had about thirty minutes. He drew the papers from the packet and began to read. He nodded from time to time, impressed. Both Mexico City and the home office were well-informed. He himself had heard of Alessandro Martín, but the home office had discovered earlier shipments of "farm machinery" and "insecticide" from a Belgian firm, routed through Mexico into Costa Plata. The most recent shipment had been made only two weeks earlier. The manager turned to the next few sheets. He shook his head and tilted back in his chair. He drew out his watch and placed it on his desk. He stared at it. He was on the spot. Twenty minutes before the plane left.

It was like a game of "Button, button, who's got the button?" North American Foundry had decided to back Alessandro Martín, but they didn't want to get stuck with the button. Dunkel had recommended him, and the home office, after checking with Mexico City on the availability of "farm machinery," had approved. But the home office didn't want the button and didn't want the Guatemala office to end up with it either, if it could be avoided. He was to bring in still another company, now operating in Costa Plata, not connected with the big concessions, and preferably a firm that owed Amalgamated a few favors. After all, they had only to deliver a message to Alessandro. Amalgamated Fruit would deliver the "machinery."

The manager drew an address book from his desk and flipped the pages, at the same time mentally discarding the names of companies and individuals. He studied one name, shook his head. His finger slipped down the page and stopped again. He thought carefully for several minutes, then picked up the telephone.

"Six-five-three."

He waited, listening to the static crackle on the line. The mail plane would get off just before the rain started. Twenty minutes.

"Hello? Mr. Bressoud, please. Paul? *Muy buenas*. Eddie here. You busy now? Good. How's Martha? Gee, that's a shame. What's she taking for it? No, but Alice and the kids were laid up last spring for a couple of weeks. Not too bad. We had a blowdown on one of the plantations last week. Lost about a thousand trees. One of these fluke windstorms. Listen, I've been put on the spot by New Orleans. Yep. No, nothing local. Costa Plata. That's the problem, see? We don't have an office down there. No, Livermore has the freight and passenger concession. They're involved, too; otherwise I'd bother them. It's a question of a letter. I need a courier. No, this is a very personal business. They open the mail. Besides, I don't know the address, and even if I did, I couldn't use the regular mail. No, it's all written up, ready to go on the plane. But you have an agent down there, don't you? Sure, a salesman would be fine. Nothing to it. I'll just shoot a little note along with—right. Right. All he has to do is deliver it and mail us an answer. I don't like to bother you, Paul, but as I said, we don't have anybody down there. . . . What's the name again? Pringle? Maybe you'd better spell—F-i-n-g-l-e. Oh, g-e-l. Got it. Fingel. And the address? Just care of Cook's, eh? You hear regularly from him? Just got there a week ago. Okay, well, that's swell, Paul. Really, this is a big help. Right. Listen, what about getting in a little fishing one of these weekends? When Martha feels better. Sure, sure. Thanks again. Right."

He set down the receiver, wrote a note and fastened it to a single, typed sheet, resealed the envelope and wrote "Herman Fingel, c/o Thomas Cook Ltd., Costa Plata." He pressed a button on his desk. A young man entered.

"Mario, weigh this and put on the right postage. Get your bicycle and ride out to the airfield. Put it on the plane. And hurry. He takes off in fifteen minutes."

"*Sí,* Señor."

The office boy left. The manager leaned back and lit a cigar. Now somebody named Fingel had the button. He glanced at the telephone. It was a funny thing that Paul's company hired Jewish boys. Maybe down in Costa Plata it didn't make any difference. He pushed another button, calling his secretary. He could dictate a letter to the home office and a standby note to Mexico City and get them off on the Panama plane when it came in after lunch. How long would it take to get an answer from Costa Plata? Maybe five days. That would be fast, too. Anything that was urgent took a week to do in Costa Plata.

He walked to the window and looked up at the sky. Thunderheads stood off to the west. The plane would get off before the storm hit. The door opened. He turned and walked back to his desk.

"Personal letter to the president and copy to Mexico City. Ready?"

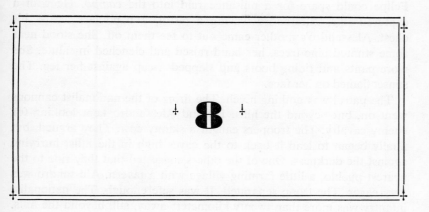

8

CARLITOS SÁNCHEZ was drunk, but his mind was still steady. He walked very carefully, but his progress was uncertain and slow. His shoulder bumped again and again on the cool sanatorium wall. He fumbled for the doorknob and pushed open the door. There was somebody in his bed. A girl. He tiptoed over and looked at her. She sprawled on her back, the blankets down to her waist. Her breasts spread, soft and oddly uninteresting, the nipples two tan studs. Her white nurse's uniform, crumpled and stained, lay on the floor. Sánchez pulled the blanket up over her. The girl muttered and rolled over. He recognized her, but could not recall her name.

He pushed open the glass door and stepped out onto the balcony. The air was clear and very cold. He went back into the room and took a heavy blanket from the chest. He picked up a cigar and a box of matches.

Mist, thick and white, hung over the stiff pine trees on the slope of the hill below him. The sun was not up, but the clouds to the east were washed pale gold. Sánchez huddled on a chair, wrapped in the blanket, smoking and remembering. . . .

One afternoon, out on a patrol with twenty or so roughnecks that Felipe could spare for a nuisance raid into the *campo*. He with a captured rifle, Alessandro waving a pistol, a bandoleer across his chest. Alessandro's mother came out to see them off. She stood near some stunted pine trees, her hand raised and clenched in salute. She wore pants and riding boots and slapped a cap against her leg. The sunset flamed on her face.

The patrol was nothing much. The firing of the nationalist cannons went on, but beyond the hills. He and Alessandro kept looking for enemy cavalry. The troopers caught a skinny cow. They argued, but finally began to lead it back to the caves high in the hills, hurrying against the darkness. One of the others suggested that they ride to the nearest pueblo, a little farming village with a tavern. Alessandro was very eager. The troop separated. It was safe enough. The nationalist infantry was more than twenty kilometers away, still beyond the hills. Six of them rode into the pueblo.

The people there were loyal and friendly. They accepted the worthless scrip for *cordero asado* and harsh red wine. They ate the lamb with their knives and fingers. It was rich, juicy meat, slightly underdone and tasting of the thyme that grew wild in the hills. One of the troopers called for a guitar. There was more wine to drink in the low, hot room, filled with the smells of food, stale wine and tobacco smoke. The older men talked together and laughed a great deal. There were two girls, the kind one found in such a place. Dark-skinned, silent, with Indian eyes and long, straight, dirty hair. They brought wine and food and dodged away from the hands that tried to grab them. After a while, the drinking went on, but this time raw brandy. The men were rough with the girls, smacking their bottoms and running their hands under their skirts. The *patrón* of the place was drunk, and the guitar rang and shivered. The *vaquero* sang well, the sad songs of lost love, poverty and vengeance. Alessandro got quite tipsy and danced. He danced in the center of the room, his eyes fixed on one of the girls. In all the time she had served them, she had not said a word. She stood against the wall. Her feet were bare. She stared at Alessandro as though hypnotized. He danced closer and closer to her. The other men leaned forward, nudging each other,

190

watching and waiting. Carlitos felt himself grow excited. The girl, a firm-bodied, silent animal, stared steadily with her dark eyes. The guitar sang on, and Alessandro danced, lean and perfect, his heels pounding the rough plank floor, his fingers clicking. He was dominating her. His dance, his body, told her what he meant to have. The front of his tight trousers bulged. The guitar stopped, and Alessandro swayed and mopped his streaming face. He reached for her, and the girl struck him once with all her strength in the face. Her nails ripped his cheek. The men all breathed out at once, a groan. Alessandro did not flinch. He drew out his knife and rammed the girl back against the wall with his other hand. She stared into his face, her eyes gleaming. He lowered the point of the knife down into the front of her blouse, between her young, firm little breasts. He jerked the knife, slitting the blouse open to the waist. The girl made no attempt to run away or to cover herself. The men whispered and craned to see. Alessandro clasped her to him, crushing her against him, kissing her neck. Her face was a mask. He released her. She began to tremble violently. Alessandro moaned like a calf and the men laughed, a peculiar, knowing sound. Alessandro drew the girl down to the floor. They sank down together, embracing. Sánchez could see the girl's hand moving slowly, steadily. Alessandro thrust the girl's dress up and knelt between her thighs. The men laughed again, a soft, cruel sound, and muttered obscenities. Carlitos watched Alessandro on the girl. They strained together, frantically, silently. Then the girl moaned and Alessandro cried out. The men shouted *"Olé! Olé!"* Wine splashed into wooden cups and the guitar began to play again. Alessandro lay on the girl. Her arms stroked his back and shoulders. One of the *vaqueros* grabbed Sánchez.

"Your turn, *chico*. Go ahead!"

He stood, frantic with desire, half drunk. It seemed a dream. Alessandro stood up, leaving the girl. He thrust past Alessandro. The girl lay with her eyes closed. She did not help him at all, and it was over in a minute. Then the others took their turn with her. Alessandro was sick to his stomach and crawled on the floor like a dog. The men roared with laughter and staggered through the smoky room, singing and cursing. The *patrón* snored with his head on a table. The men wanted the other girl, but she had run off. They finally let the first girl up. She walked out of the room, her breasts bare, her face hidden in her hands. An old crone brought bitter chicory coffee in a tin bucket. It was nearly dawn.

They rode back as the sun came up. The men were quiet now, most of them half sick from the wine and brandy. Now they longed for a drink of cool water and sleep. The horses stumbled on the stony track. They walked the horses the last few kilometers.

The first sense of disaster touched them at the sentry post, a high boulder with a peculiar notch eroded on the top. There was no challenge, and one of the troopers found three expended cartridges at the base of the stone. They ran, stumbling and falling, up to the slot between great stones, the entrance to the refuge, the big caves and the wooden huts. They found a dead comrade wedged in the slot, and had to drag him away before they could get the horses through. Carlitos saw the dark shape swinging in the wind. Felipe Martín hung naked by one leg from a stunted pine, his hair brushing the dry needles. His barrel chest was spotted with small bluish holes.

Vizarra's soldiers had done to Alessandro's mother what the troopers had done to the tavern girl. They had used a knife, too, but to rip open her belly. Blood-smeared stones had been packed into her body. Flies buzzed. Her hair, tangled with twigs, lay stiff in a caked puddle of blood. When they had finished with her, one of them had put a pistol to her head. Her mouth hung open, and her dull eyes stared up at the sky. Sánchez could not bear to look. The troopers turned away, cursing horribly in stunned, whispering voices.

A few bodies lay scattered in the mouth of the first cave. But where were the others? More than three hundred men lived with their women and children, dogs and animals in the dry little valley along the face of the mountain. The single men lived together in the caves. Carlitos called his father's name over and over. They found only a smashed table, a drift of scattered papers tumbling in the breeze, and the brass telephone with the wire cut. The men had gone. Had they been captured or taken somewhere and shot? There was not much to show that there had been resistance. Only five dead comrades in all. The ground was covered with spent cartridges, new ones, used by the nationalist raiders.

The men sat down in the shade, murmuring, shaking their heads, still whispering curses. It could not be believed. Some one had betrayed them, and Felipe Martín was dead and his wife, too. *El Feo* was gone, and his son Carlitos sat with them and wept. The men offered no comfort. They had none to give. Everything was over for them. They had survived the ambush, but they were dazed still.

Alessandro walked with jerky steps, took out his knife and slashed the rope. His father fell, his head striking the pine needles, wrenching his dead neck. His legs thumped with a terrible loose sound, and the body rolled face down. Alessandro turned and tore off his shirt. He wrapped his mother in it and tied the sleeves carefully around her ripped, stone-stuffed belly. He bent and lifted her. The men shuddered. They saw and heard the bloody stones slide out from under the shirt and strike the ground. Alessandro carried her, walking slowly, to the first wooden house. He dropped the body on the floor just inside the doorway. The men watched him, fascinated by his calmness. Alessandro walked past them, not seeing or sensing them huddled in the shade. Two of the *vaqueros* began to weep and lament, but the others shut them up. Alessandro could not carry the body of his father. He dragged it, holding onto the dead man's wrists. Felipe Martín's bare feet rutted the needles and the sun-dried dust. Alessandro placed the body beside that of his mother, just inside the open door of the wooden house. Then he slowly stripped off his bloody trousers and stood naked. He took up his pistol and his knife. He walked out into the sunlight, stood still for an instant, and then walked to the first house on the left. He kicked open the door and went inside.

A woman screamed and a little girl raced out through the doorway and crouched in the center of the horse track that served as a street. She covered her head with her arms. The pistol spat once, then again. Alessandro came to the doorway, holding a crucifix in his hand. He smashed it against the doorjamb and flung it into the street. A dog squirmed out from beneath the house. Alessandro ran and grabbed the mangy animal by the neck. It snarled and wrenched, clicking its teeth. The knife whipped, and the dog floundered in the dust, blood bursting from its throat. Alessandro seized the twitching creature up by the tail, carried it to the nearest well and dropped it in. The water plushed. Alessandro walked to the second house. A cow stood tethered there. Alessandro put the pistol to the cow's left eye and squeezed the trigger. The animal dropped to its knees and rolled over. Smoke streamed out of the windows of the first house, and flames roared in the roof of woven river grass and thistles. An old man knelt in the doorway of the second house, his hands clasped. Alessandro

193

plunged the knife into the old man's chest and leaned down, pressing the blade through the ribs. Blood spurted from the old man's nose. He clung to Alessandro's naked legs. Alessandro stepped over him. He raised the pistol and shot the old man's wife. She crawled out of the doorway and died on the steps. Alessandro took an ax and broke open the clay stove. Fingers of fire ran over the rush sleeping mats.

The troopers followed him at a distance. They did not speak, but watched and listened. The sheep bleated and rolled their eyes. He stalked them in their pens, his knife, wrist and arm to the elbow bright with blood. He tore their throats, ripped the heads off the squawling chickens and shot the rest of the cattle. He flung the dogs and sheep into the other wells. When he ran out of ammunition, he walked slowly back to his parents' house and took five cartridges from a wooden box on the table, fitted them in the chamber of the blood-sticky pistol and walked back down the street. He drifted in slow, gliding steps through the smoke of the burning houses. Five children huddled in terror in the center of the street. The flames roared, blown by the wind that sucked the thick white smoke up into the blue, shining sky. The pistol smacked. A cow rolled in a dung patch, its four legs jerking. A woman screamed. The pistol spat twice. Alessandro stalked slowly through the smoke and whirling ashes, carrying a shrieking infant by one arm. He dropped it down among the huddled children and turned back.

A fat woman dressed in black ran to him, sobbing, and knelt, twisting a rosary in her shaking fingers. Alessandro took the beads and broke them, flung the crucifix in the dirt and stamped on it. The woman screamed. Alessandro shot her through the throat. He walked away. The woman rose after a minute, holding her throat. She ran after Alessandro. The pistol cracked again. The woman sat down in the street and then fell back. A clay stove flew into fragments, and coals tumbled on the wooden floor. Alessandro snatched a brand and stuffed it into a corn-husk mattress. The fat woman's house filled with smoke.

Nobody in the village tried to get away. The troopers crept back away from the flaming houses and watched. Alessandro came back through the smoke. His knife was gone, but he had a bottle of brandy in the crook of his arms. He sat down in the street, smeared with blood and ashes, his penis lolling in the dust. The children crouched a dozen paces away, too frightened to weep. Alessandro drank what was in the bottle. He stared at the children. Then he rose and staggered to the nearest burning house. He flung the bottle, then his pistol, into the roaring wreck. The cartridges popped like Chinese crackers at a fiesta. Alessandro walked to his parents' house and slammed the door.

The troopers stirred out of their trance. He had released them. They could move about and talk now. They chattered wildly, gathered up the children and skinned a lamb. One kicked up a cooking fire at the mouth of the cave; another found three *botas* of wine. They passed the leather bottles around, squirting the wine into their throats. The sheep turned on the spit. They sat in the shade, passing the wine back and forth, watching the houses burn down to rectangles of ash, with the air shimmering above the fire-stumped walls. When the sheep was cooked, they fed the children and ate themselves. The infant screamed, but none of the men knew what to do. They waited for Alessandro.

At dusk Alessandro began to sing. This disturbed the men very much, and they began to argue that Felipe's son had lost his mind. At first he sang lullabies and children's nonsense songs. The children with the troopers began to sing, too. One by one, they walked back down into the ash-strewn street and squatted there, clapping their hands, their thin, treble voices ringing off the rocks. Alessandro sang the same song over and over. Carlitos imagined him squatting naked on the bare wooden floor of the hut, beside the glaring, stiffened bodies of his mother and father, clapping his hands in time to his songs. The *vaqueros* shook their heads and tapped their temples, but did nothing. When it got dark, Carlitos went down for the children. He cut the udder of a dead cow and caught the milk in a charred gourd for the baby.

Just at dawn, Alessandro set fire to the last house. Carlitos and the others awoke to the rough sound of the flames tearing through the rush roof, wind-whipped orange banners that lashed at the darkness and the thick, spilling smoke that rolled away down the dry valley. The children clapped their hands and crowed with delight. The men cursed and tried to go back to sleep. Sánchez wrapped himself in a blanket and waited.

The sun rose. When it stood above the mountains, Alessandro appeared, dressed in his best suit of heavy black stuff, his good boots and a wide-brimmed, flat-crowned hat. His face was white and the

195

flesh around his eyes looked puffy and bruised, as though he had been beaten. He said nothing. He mounted his horse. The others mounted, too, seating the children before them. The infant they left behind, screaming on a discarded bit of blanket. Dusty vultures flapped down on the sun-warmed rocks as they rode away. Three troopers turned back to bury their five dead comrades; they had forgotten about them. Alessandro, Sánchez and another rode on in silence. At noon they had crossed the spine of the mountains. Carlitos found a guide, an Indian, and they crossed the border at twilight. They rode to the nearest village on the railroad line, where they sold Alessandro's horse for half the animal's value. Alessandro bought a ticket. When the train came in, he boarded the last car and was drawn away. Four months later Sánchez received a postcard from Havana. There was no message, just the name: *Alessandro.*

☩

Sánchez flung away his cigar. The sun was up. He needed coffee. He groped and found the bottle and swallowed a mouthful. The brandy warmed him again. He did not feel too drunk. He wondered how long he had been out on the balcony. His feet were chilled. He walked back into the room, his blanket trailing on the floor. He brought his hand down hard on the sleeping girl's rear.

"Come on, *guapita.* Get up and get out of here. I've got work to do."

☩

The priest's hand, raised in benediction, fell slowly to his side. The organist cuffed his assistant, and the boy began to jam the handle up and down on the bicycle pump. The priest smiled stiffly at the wedding party as the first notes squeezed and fluted out of the organ. The miner and his young bride rose, then the thirty or so Indian men and women who half filled the little stone church. The groom, wearing a rented long-tailed coat over his canvas trousers, marched down the center aisle, his hands stuffed into his pockets, his bare feet slapping the floor. The bride followed, her head meekly bowed, the bouquet of wildflowers already wilted in her small, brown hands. The others waited for her to walk out onto the broad steps. Then they burst into excited talk and jostled each other, almost fighting to get out of the church. The priest sighed and signaled for the organist to cease. The music wheezed off in a long, weary-sounding drone. The priest yawned with his mouth closed and waited. These Indians' weddings were all the same. In a moment the one selected would come back. He would be in a great hurry, for the second part of the ceremony might begin in his absence.

It could not be said, of course, that the Indians who worked in the silver mines were pagans. On the contrary, they were very devout. But their very devotion was a cause for concern. The archbishop wrote regularly on the subject, those odd pastoral letters that warned of the grave danger of mistaking politeness for comprehension. The Indians would and did agree with all teaching, or at least said they did. At the same time, the priest knew from experience that if he asked one of the miners if such and such a pueblo lay five kilometers away, the answer would be yes, although the pueblo might really be two kilometers distant or two hundred. It was their habit. If another believed that the village was five kilometers away, not an Indian would contradict him, for that would not be polite. One had to be careful about the type of question one asked and then make certain corrections and allowances for that type of politeness known as flattery. If the priest asked the distance to a village, he had discovered, he usually received an answer in the form of approximate hours it would take him to reach the place. Then the answer must be tripled, for the Indians, recognizing that the priest was a white man and a man of God and thus doubly strengthened, proportionally shortened the time of the journey. The priest smiled again and shook his head. Could it be that these small, expressionless people possessed a sense of humor? Were they subtly mocking him? No, it wasn't likely. But how could you tell? If an Indian agreed with you about a matter of false distance or time, how could you tell what he really thought or believed about God?

It was certain that such people as the miner and his new wife were badly muddled, from an outsider's point of view. But they were very clear in their own minds. The archbishop never failed to stress this point and had actually written a monograph on the subject. The priest had studied his copy with great care: "Automatic Transference and Accretion of Belief Among the Indigenous Tribes." A long, awkward title, but then, His Grace was both very thorough and very interested in scientific studies. Such a man was given by nature to long titles. Another of the archbishop's pamphlets was called "Some Cursory

Notes on Skulls, Jawbones and Baked Pottery Shards Recently Unearthed in the Excavations for the Municipal Football Stadium."

The priest heard the sound of bare feet in the church and looked up. An Indian trotted down the aisle, ducked before the altar and gently handed the priest five reales. The priest thanked him in dialect, but the Indian had already turned. He trotted out of the church. Could such a man, hurrying out to watch the old rituals, be a true Christian? His Grace insisted that it was most likely so, despite the fact that the Indians showed no interest in distinguishing Satan from Vigo or Axoloqui from the Saviour. They had accepted Christianity out of politeness, since it so nearly matched their old myth. They accepted the sacraments of the church, gave alms, regularly confessed. The young groom, however, was out on the dusty plaza being sprinkled with herbs to keep away harmful influences (symbolic fumigation, the archbishop termed it, actually a crude medical technique not to be confused with superstitious belief in local evil spirits). In a few minutes, after a chant of some sort, the groom would drink off some nauseating concoction out of a gourd and beat his wife. His Grace dryly remarked, when such ceremonies were deplored, that many pure Catholic marriages that he knew of would have been better regulated by the addition of such a ritual.

The priest counted two reales into the damp, plump palm of the organist, who, in turn, handed a centavo to the boy still waiting by the bicycle pump. The priest and the boy walked together down the left aisle to the door.

The wedding party walked up the narrow footpath to the place where the wedding ritual was held, a shallow depression surrounded by a ring of boulders. One flat stone stood in the center of the ring. The women in the party stood at the east of the ring, the men at the west. In that way, the women could observe the size of the new bride's breasts and make the traditional comments on the number of sons she would suckle, while the men were reassured that the beating was done in the proper manner, neither too hard nor too light. The bride walked slowly into the center of the ring, unfastened the front of her white cotton dress and knelt at the stone. She shrugged off the dress and, bare to the waist, stretched out, face down on the stone. Her father handed the groom a stick the thickness of his thumb and as long as his arm from the shoulder to the tip of his index finger. The girl gripped the edge of the stone. The women called

198

encouragement in low, soothing voices. The groom stood beside his wife, two paces from her left hip. He held the stick in his right hand and threw it up into the air. It turned over and over. He caught it near the end, raised it, and brought it down firmly on his new wife's back. The girl squirmed, but made no cry. The men nodded approvingly. The stick was thrown high, well caught and correctly swung. To drop the stick was bad luck. No one in the wedding party noticed that Ramos stood up on the hill, watching the ritual.

Twice more the young Indian tossed the stick, caught it and cracked it across his wife's bared back. He waited until the three welts began to rise, then clicked his tongue. The girl rose, modestly buttoned her wedding gown, and thrust her hand into her husband's palm. The men and women standing around the ring clapped their hands and laughed. One of the women saw Ramos and moaned. The laughter died at once.

He walked down the path, his curved arms swinging, his taloned hands bumping together. The men bared their heads, all but the young groom. Long, straight hair lashed over Ramos' face as he scrambled stiffly down the path and stepped into the ring. His eyes glittered, and his face was flushed with drink. He walked through the party and stopped before the groom.

"You are One-arm's cousin. I know this. He has gone. I know this. Where is he? This I do not know. This you will tell me."

The young Indian said nothing. Ramos fixed his gaze on the girl. She turned her face away, white with fear.

"No children will grow in your belly. Your womb is a dry gourd. You have no husband. You will have no husband. You will grow sick and die."

The women moaned, but the men said nothing. Ramos turned again to the groom.

"Where is your cousin? Two times I have asked you. He served me. Now he is gone. *Where is he?*"

The groom said nothing. He, too, turned his face away, unable to bear those eyes. He shook with fear. His stick slipped from his hand and fell to the ground. Ramos leaned forward until his twisting lips nearly touched the young miner's cheek.

"Down in the earth is the Dark One. This you know. He has called to me. He has said to me that you know where One-arm is. You will

199

tell me this. Or I will take you there and give you to the Dark One."

Spittle dampened the groom's cheek. His head sank on his breast. Ramos moved his hand and wrenched the boy's jaw, lifting his face. He stared at the boy's squeezed lids.

"You do not answer. Three times I have asked. Three times you have said nothing. Now come. Now come. The Dark One awaits you. Down in the earth the great stone is rocking, shifting. He lifts it with one tip of his wing. For now he must fly. Only you can keep him silent, hidden under the stone. You must go to him. The Dark One is waiting! Now come!"

Ramos stretched out his hand. The bride clung to her husband's hand, weeping in a harsh, groaning voice. Ramos touched her on the brow with his finger, and she fell to the ground. Her young husband walked forward. The wedding party shrank away. The young miner walked rapidly, stiffly. Ramos followed. The wedding party scattered swiftly, many of the women crossing themselves. The men were silent. Ramos climbed up the narrow, winding path, the young miner a few paces ahead of him. The girl lay sprawled in the dirt, still weeping. No one looked back at her or went to her aid. She was barren. She had no husband. Soon she would grow sick and die.

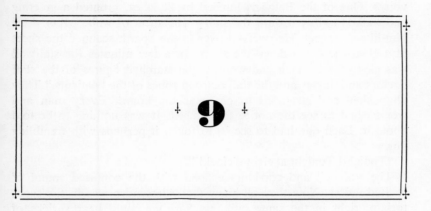

9

SÁNCHEZ tore down all the notes and bulletins thumb-tacked to the board. He stepped back, surprised. The bulletin board at the head of the central stairwell was bigger than it looked. Now it seemed naked without a covering of schedules, duty sheets and notices. A big, bare, tan slab at the top of the stairs. He drew the piece of stiff paper from under his maroon bathrobe and pinned it in the exact center of the board. Only he was familiar with the handwriting, the bold, tall strokes of black ink on the white sheet and the nearly illegible signature he had seen so often.

GENERAL MEETING AT 2000 HOURS
IN
AMPHITHEATER
ALESSANDRO MARTÍN

201

Sánchez walked away and stood leaning against a wall. He heard the sound of women's voices. Two nurses in white dresses and caps came up the stairs. They did not pause, but walked directly to the bulletin board, stared at the notice and began talking again in shrill, excited voices. One of the Belgians hurried by Sánchez, grunted a greeting and walked swiftly toward the stairs. The sheet of white paper drew him like a magnet. He swerved over to the board, scanned the sheet at a glance and ran down the stairs. In a few minutes the stairwell was clogged with men and women, the starched figures of the staff doctors and nurses and the dull maroon robes of the "patients." They all pushed and struggled to get near the board. Every man and woman had to see the notice for himself. It was nothing to be told about it. Each one had to see it, to touch it perhaps with trembling fingers.

"Tonight! Tonight at eight o'clock!"

The stairwell and corridors echoed with the confused sound of excited voices. Now they all knew that Alessandro was in the sanatorium, right in the same building. Sánchez could hear shrieks of laughter. Some of the men had caught one of the nurses.

"Off with the wig! Come on, we know you're him. Up with the skirt. Come on, come on! The secret's out now. Show us!"

The nurse broke away, still laughing, and tucked her disheveled hair under her cap. She ran by Sánchez, her face flushed.

"Have you seen it? Have you? On the board? The notice. Tonight at eight o'clock!"

He shrugged and drew out his cigar case.

"Have I seen it? *Guapa*, who do you think put it there?"

"Then you've seen him! What does he look like?"

"Who?"

"Oh, come, please tell me! Please! Is he handsome? What does he look like?"

"He looks like . . . his pictures."

Sánchez struck a match and walked away. The nurse pouted, her fists on her hips, then dashed away, calling to her friends. Sánchez grunted and sucked on his cigar. All this female hysteria. He pushed open the door of his room. Pepe Olmega was waiting for him, sitting on a chair with his pistol on his lap. One of the workmen, an ex-patient now employed as an electrician, sat near the window. He seemed relieved to see Sánchez.

202

"There is something you both should see. On the bulletin board."

They left, Olmega running. Sánchez poured himself a drink of brandy and sat on the edge of the high bed, smoking and swinging his legs. In a few minutes Olmega and the workman were back. The notice had taken effect on them, too. Olmega's eyes shone, and he could not stop smiling. The workman's hands twitched and two spots of color stood on his cheeks. They babbled together like children until Sánchez finished his drink and cleared his throat. They stared at him expectantly.

"First, the amphitheater is to be locked. It will be opened again at 1930 hours, not before. Second, the overhead lights are to be turned off at 1945 hours precisely. The lights over the table must be turned off at 1955, so that the entire room is in darkness. At 2000 hours exactly, you will turn on the lights over the table. He will be standing there. Keep the overhead lights off until he calls for them to be turned on. Got that?"

"Overheads off at 1945 and kept off until he calls for them. Table lights off at 1955, on again at 2000. Right!"

"Olmega, get your boys in three groups, one in the center, the others at each end about halfway up. When the overhead lights go off, have them begin to clap, together. Keep it up as long as you can. Then have them begin to shout his name, in unison. Also, find out who has the flag. The one that is usually out front."

"That? What do we need that for?"

"Just find it and take it there. You, what's the name of the old woman who takes care of the laundry? The little fat woman."

"Ah? Oh, that's Tía Anna, old Aunty."

"All right. You both know what to do. Now get out of here."

Olmega frowned, disappointed.

"Nothing else? Aren't we going to issue equipment? Hand out the guns?"

"And have them waste half the ammunition this afternoon? Get going."

Sánchez yawned deliberately and puffed on his cigar. When he was alone, he pulled a carton out from under his bed and found a photograph. Six men sat at a table in a room somewhere in Brussels in 1903. In the center was the Russian, Plekhanov. At his left sat a young, slender man staring fixedly at the camera. Sánchez stared at the young man's face, then closed his eyes. He muttered, dropped the picture in the carton and thrust it under his bed again. It was no use. He couldn't connect that face with the face of anyone in the sanatorium. He poured himself another brandy and gulped it down. The bottle tempted him. How he would like to drink, to slide into peace, to lie on his bed warm and numb, indifferent to the excitement that single sheet tacked to the board had raised. The gong for lunch rang in the corridor. He dragged himself out of the room and turned toward the east wing so he wouldn't have to shove through the crowd at the main stairs. Lunch. He wasn't hungry, but he would eat and talk. Then, after lunch, a nap. No brandy, though, no matter how much he wanted it. After the siesta, another meeting with that damned Belgian Voget. The Communists were demanding an open line through the switchboard. Voget insisted on it as an "act of good faith." Too bad for him. Then a meeting with the miners, with young One-arm translating. You could never tell if the Indians understood you or not. How could you? There was no word in their tongue for "agitation," none for "propaganda," none even for "revolution." Instead it was "quiet talk," "big talk," and "long fight." It was like talking to children. After that he had to inspect the arms and munitions and make sure that each batch was clearly labeled and the men there were certain of shipping instructions. The *peones* with the burro carts had to be yelled at for a half hour until they got it into their thick heads just where they were supposed to take the bundles of arms for distribution in their various pueblos. They were not to talk with anyone, not to stop at a tavern and drink. There, that was something. Their best dark suits would be confiscated, and they would be forced to hand over all their money. That way they would stay away from the taverns; no one would sell them drink on credit. What a tangle of petty details! The others never knew, never even guessed, at the work he did, the obstacles he cleared away, the little traps he avoided. They just ran around like a bunch of women. *Have you seen him? What does he look like?* As if he had time to play guessing games!

He stalked into the dining room. The place was in an uproar. He looked around from his chair at his usual table, his brows drawn together in a scowl. He sucked on his dead cigar. The others chattered loudly, waved their hands and arms in quick gestures, laughed and called to each other. Except the Belgians. They crouched over their plates, once in every few minutes straightening to nod respectfully at some grunted comment from their leader, Voget. That was party discipline for you. They were all serious, the Communists, even when they ate together.

Rota, that fat, sweaty bore from the U.T., swaggered up and bumped his thigh against the table.

"Well, *amigo,* where are you keeping him, eh? Got him locked up?"

Sánchez raised his head and glared across the room. The orderly limped between tables carrying a tray. Sánchez snapped his fingers.

"Camarero! Bring me something to eat."

Rota fidgeted for a moment, shrugged and walked away. Sánchez heard his angry voice.

"He thinks he's better than the rest of us. Big with secrets like a pregnant farm girl."

Sánchez picked up his fork and began eating the sardines set before him. He chewed mechanically, without appetite. The noisy men irritated him. He raised his head again.

"Hey! Shut up, can't you? How can a man eat with such a racket? Save your voices for tonight!"

They stared at him. He could feel their eyes fixed on him. To hell with them. Gabbling like a bunch of ducks. The dining room was quiet for a few minutes. But by the time the orderly brought Sánchez a veal steak with *patatas fritas,* the conversations roared again. He pushed the food away and walked from the dining room, the dead cigar jammed in his mouth.

All afternoon the excitement mounted slowly like an incoming tide. Even the plump little crone in the laundry was half delirious when Sánchez showed her a sketch for the revolutionary banner. She offered to tear up her best blue dress to make the four stars, one for each province, four blue stars on a background of pure white sheeting. The men in the arms storerooms kept running up to see if something new had been stuck up on the board. Everyone seemed convinced that only shouting could be understood and that even the mildest suggestion called for someone to run, not walk, into the next room. Sánchez shuffled from one place to another, unhurried, speaking slowly, smoking a cigar with great deliberation. He calmed them, gave them small jobs to accomplish, ignored their endless questions. He argued patiently with the Belgians about the telephone, broke up a meeting of U.T. delegates without infuriating Rota, explained for the twentieth time to the miners the role they would play. Over and over he found himself repeating the same few sentences to the Indians, the *peones,* the students and teachers, the *vaqueros,* even the nurses.

"A revolution has, in fact, occurred when the existing government is prevented from governing. If the central government cannot deliver the mail according to regular schedules because activists prevent all deliveries, then there is revolution. If the trains don't run, if no silver is mined, that is revolution. If the government orders the streets emptied at nine o'clock and they are still crowded at eleven, that is revolution. It is not shooting in the streets and blowing up buildings and fighting with the police. Our first steps will be to prolong the fiesta of Santa Rosa by means of a general strike. If the general strike is successful, then we have a revolution. The shooting and the excitement come later, not before. First we must know who to shoot at, no? Think of it that way. Stop worrying about rifles and hand grenades and get back to work. That's what revolution is: ideas turned into hard work. Get busy, now."

Over and over, like a litany, damping down the energy, the enthusiastic splurging of strength. He settled petty squabbles with his words, turned arguments into discussions of tactics. The tide still flowed in, still mounted, but it was a slow force building. He watched it, gauged it all the long afternoon. He went into every room, down every corridor, spoke until his voice grew hoarse.

"Uniforms? You have a uniform. Bathrobe and pajamas. Slippers on your feet. What do you want, a field marshal's baton?"

"I see no reason why the dinner hour should be advanced. We will eat at seven, as usual."

"If some of the patients have reached the pueblo, just take them to the nearest barn and lock them in. Keep them away from the railroad. Ah. Well, then, take a shovel and bury them."

"Before we make the long fight, we do no work. Tell them that. No work is part of the long fight."

"Start in your carts after dark. Take your women and children home, then leave for the city. Decorate the carts when you get there. Have your women come down on the train. That way, you will get the guns into the university and other places and will have your fiesta, too. Your women will bring your good suits and your money to you. You must get the guns into the city first. Then the fiesta."

"Each one of you comes from a big farm. You have listed the

206

cattle and poultry. We have the lists. When we call for food, *va-queros,* cut out the fat steers and drive them where you are told. Your first revolutionary act will be to say 'Go to hell' to your landlords. Your second act will be to bring us food. Only then will you be issued arms and formed into cavalry units."

"The details of the funeral parade I leave up to you. The cadre selected will dig up Jaime's coffin. Another will find a wagon and horses. Another will paint the signs. Still another must form a unit at the barricades, to force through and clear a path for the wagon. Then you have only to watch for the police and to run like hell when they come for you. Forget about the coffin. Let the police bury it again."

"Distribute the pistols and the cartridges separately. No one is to be handed a loaded weapon. Someone will get hurt. We've got to make those bullets count."

"An act of good faith, Comrade Voget, such as you suggest, would merely antagonize other members of the movement. Is it the Comintern's position that proletarian movements depend on private telephone lines? Comrade, the switchboard is open to all. Use that. No charge."

"No, señoritas, I do not think that a reception committee with flowers would be appropriate. It is charming, indeed, of you to think of it. But why not put the flowers on the tables at dinner? A special touch, eh?"

"The cantina is to remain closed. No, not even beer. Well, let them borrow cigarettes. No, not even wine."

"Put the trucks in the garage and bring me the keys. We must conserve the gasoline."

At six o'clock Sánchez went to his room, stripped to his pajama pants and poured himself a large brandy. He was very tired. His legs ached from climbing up and down the stairs. His throat was slightly sore, but he lit another cigar anyway. He had poured a lot of oil on the waters. Now it was up to Alessandro to do the rest. They had been brought together, initiated into some conception of the coming struggle, carefully selected and divided into cadres, tentatively joined into shock brigades. Each man had certain first steps to take and now had been convinced of the importance of taking those steps automatically. Tonight they would receive the call to rise. By tomorrow they would have formed an insurgent government and a fighting force. Alessandro had stolen in among them, had fired all their

207

hearts. Now he must turn their hands and brains to action. At eight o'clock. Eight o'clock.

Sánchez finished his brandy. He felt lonely, depressed. He flung his cigar away half smoked, and fell into a fitful sleep. The dinner gong woke him. He swallowed a great amount of water, glass after glass until he felt bloated. He did not want to go into the dining hall, but knew he should. It was seven o'clock. Already they would be crowding the corridor outside the amphitheater. He must continue to set an example of self-discipline. He knotted his bathrobe and shuffled from the room, carefully closing the door.

‡

Sánchez looked at his watch. Quarter of eight. 1945 hours. He snapped the cover shut and mopped his face. The amphitheater was stifling. The overhead lights went off, and the crowd murmured restlessly. The tiers were jammed. The amphitheater had been designed to accommodate about a hundred people; nearly three times that number sat crushed shoulder to shoulder, squatted in the aisles, and more pressed into the exits leading out into the main corridor. Voices beat steadily, like the turning of an engine, an even, dull, deliberate noise.

The operating table was bare; the stirrups and straps had been removed. The clean slab shone white and cool. The voices of the men rose and fell. Everyone stared at the table. Sánchez longed for a cigar, but he had posted a sign NO SMOKING. He touched his cigar case again and again, tapping it with his fingers and running the lapels of his bathrobe between the damp palms of his hands. He looked around. The other men, all dressed in bathrobes and pajamas, stared down into the spotless arena pit. Then the students began to clap in unison.

The others took it up. José Petarna and his gang of dock workers, all anarchists, all Negroes. Their teeth shone, and the sweat glittered on their black faces. They waved pink palms like fans, smacking, smacking, smacking. Sánchez saw Pepe Olmega, overanxious, too conspicuous, half standing on his seat, jerking his arm and looking across the dim room to see that the cadence was kept by the student group to the right. One-arm, the Indian, pounded his fist on the arm of his seat. He sat with a group of stumpy, short-legged men with long straight hair and compressed, bony faces like walnuts. They swayed from side to side, but did not join in the clapping that beat on and on. Sánchez sniffed, just short of laughter; he saw one of the Indian miners kicking his legs like a child, his hard little heels clear of the floor, his hands folded tidily in his lap. A nurse stood beside him in the aisle, her face rapt, slapping her hands. Sánchez saw the professors and instructors from the university shifting in their seats, butting each other with elbows, sucking on pencils, some staring up at the ceiling as though bewildered by the simple fact that the lights had been turned off. Slowly they too began to clap. Sismondi, the cadre chief of the *vaqueros,* his face as dark and drawn as leather, beat his hands together, but on every other crash of sound. His cadre members took it up, an off beat that intensified the flacking rhythm of flesh on flesh, every other beat a stinging, flat concussion that echoed off the walls. The *vaqueros* wore their bathrobes like capes; they had refused to discard their everyday clothing. They stamped their feet, and their spurs began to ring. A doctor slammed a clipboard on his knee.

1950. The cadenced applause began to weaken. Sismondi folded his arms. Petarna rolled his violet lips and whistled between his teeth. The sweat trickled down Sánchez's side. He waved to the nurse and fixed his mouth in a stupid smile. Olmega gave up leading his group and slumped, disheartened, in his seat. Sánchez tried to show him his smile, but the boy did not raise his head.

Bodies poured up and down the aisles; men rushed out of the amphitheater for a drink of water, a cigarette, a visit to the toilets. Every minute there were false alarms, sudden silences when "an angel flew through the room." Everyone leaned forward, their eyeballs bursting, seeing only the cool white slab below the lights. Here and there people bobbed up for a better view of nothing. Hands snatched at their robes.

Five minutes to go. The breath, the air, felt stuffed behind his teeth. Sánchez stretched his arms and cracked his knuckles. For some reason, a half-dozen people giggled. Then Petarna clicked his fingers, lifted the tails of his robe and farted. The crowd laughed uproariously, and the clapping began again. Each minute seemed stretched like rubber; elastic seconds sagged around Sánchez. Then, without warning, the lights over the table went out. 1955 hours.

The crowd was shocked into silence. Sánchez leaned forward, as they all did, his hands grasping the back of the seat before him. He

209

heard cloth rustle and knew what it was: the national banner run up on the back wall by the electrician. The expectancy was thicker than the muggy air, tighter than the dark hide drawn over Sismondi's cheekbones, as solid as the stumped arm of the leader of the miners. The sweat drops skidded down Sánchez's ribs. His genitals felt as if they floated in a pot of warm water. His dry throat clogged, and his heart began to jerk. He stared into the darkness, lost like the rest of them, his reserve blotted in the black tension, his bare heels shivering in his slippers. He could not see the face of his watch. Olmega started his students. They clapped; the whole, dense-packed, sweating slope of flesh began to beat their hands together.

Then the students began the chant. At once the dark room rocked; it seemed to Sánchez that the amphitheater would be broached like a wine keg, burst with noise.

"Alessandro! Alessandro! Alessandro! Alessandro! Alessandro!"

The chant lost cadence. Wave on wave of voices smashed and fell, one over the other, lifting and dropping like the sea on a beach. The amphitheater was a wet, roaring cove of noise, hissing and booming with his name.

"Aless—Aldrosanessdroalsanalessandroandalesdroessandroessand!"

The light above the table popped like a fat spark. The men and women in the ranked seats lunged upright, shrieking. A slender young man with dark hair stood behind the operating table. A gasp of surprise whistled through the darkness, then the rumble of astonished laughter. The nurse screamed, the Sunday shriek of the *plaza de toros* when the matador was flung by the bloody bull. It was the little orderly! He, he was Alessandro!

Sánchez, jarred and buffeted, felt his face stiffen. His chest went liquid with shame, as though his ribs had melted. His heart seared and steamed with rage. *Why* had he not been told? The little white-coated *cabronazo,* sneaking into his room every morning, every afternoon, with his messages, wearing that sad smear of mustache! The laughter shumbled and ragged around Sánchez. The darkness spun, and the lighted table skidded like a flipped coin. *Alessandro*—that drag-footed orderly with the lusterless eyes? There he stood down there beneath the lights, his slack face firm, both arms raised in salute, his slender body clothed in a uniform. Where had the uniform come from?

Sánchez stared, racked with grudging admiration and boiling rage.

He had been betrayed, made a fool of, right up to the last instant! He, of all men, who had faithfully carried out every order, pushed pistols into the hands of reluctant killers, threatened, cursed, struggled untold hours to hammer the movement into shape, to make men ready and able to accept a leader—he had not been allowed the simplest secret of all, the identity of Alessandro! His eyes stung, and a curse ripped out of his chest, damning the slender figure swaying there beneath the lights. The breath rushed from Sánchez's lips like liquid fire. His bellow of rage and anguish was lost in the roar that plunged from the darkness toward the light. He felt as though Alessandro had spat in his mouth. Alessandro! The name was a curse! Alessandro! They howled at him like dogs! That bloodless lump of arrogance! That stone! That close-mouthed, skulking, limping little sad-eyed mother-lover!

"Alessandro! Alessandro! Alessandro! Alessandro!"

The dull eyes shone now like bits of obsidian. The full mouth curled with scorn. He rolled his head loosely with the stuttering, dying laughter. Then he jerked his head up, and the lank hair snapped on his skull. The crowd dulled, hushed, strained forward, open-mouthed, their hands still stretched toward him in welcome and yearning. He had tricked them, true, but so effectively, so cleverly, that they forgave him at once and only marveled at his daring. The sloping shelf of eager flesh bent toward him; every breath was suspended, lungs emptied, waiting for the breath he must now pour out; his disciples of destruction, so long frustrated, strained to catch the lanyard snap of his first order to action.

He spun one hand on his wrist and cleared his throat.

"You call yourselves a movement, a political party? You are nothing. Nothing, do you understand? No, of course not. For months I've lived among you, brought you food to gobble, drink to swill. What have you done? Nothing. What can you do? Nothing. Because you are nothing. *Nothing!"*

They sat stunned. Seats creaked and rattled as they slowly settled back, still open-mouthed but shocked now. Was this their leader?

Alessandro was transformed. He was not the skinny, dull-eyed orderly limping down a corridor but a slender, quirt-voiced director, laying the lash on them without passion, without anger, without pity.

"What can you do? Nothing! A sloppy street murder and a handful of guns. This is revolution? No. The Old Mule will kick you to death.

When his hoof breaks in your faces, all you will do is lick the dung up like ice cream. And why not? You're used to the taste, aren't you?"

The bodies around Sánchez shrank, as though Alessandro's words pressed them back in their seats; instead of filling their lungs, he punched them empty. The amphitheater, dark and shocked, was silent. Pepe Olmega's head dropped forward as though a blade had whipped across his naked neck.

Alessandro crossed his legs, his right ankle against his left shin. Sánchez heard one of the nurses whimper. Alessandro frowned, the pale flesh of his brow furrowed. When his lips opened, his words bit at them, nipping and tearing at their self-esteem.

"I look at you and what do I see? Men? No. A gang of cowards sucking on their lips, sitting there and stinking with fear in the darkness. If the lights were on, you couldn't bear to look at each other."

He moved, a sudden shift, and the front rows shrank back as though he had tossed a viper into their laps. He crouched beneath the lights, his right fist clenched.

"Thirteen years. And I've come back. Who made me run like a dog over the mountains, to sweat and starve in Europe, to freeze in Russia? The Old Mule Vizarra? No. No! It was *you!* Every night I dreamed of coming home. Who wouldn't let me? Vizarra? No. No! It was *you* who condemned me to exile, you who tore my birthright to ribbons and said 'Here, suck on this and grow strong.' "

The dark rows of bodies bent and swayed. Sánchez saw men hide their faces. But they could not escape the voice.

"You call yourselves men. Listen, I've seen French soldiers squat in the mud and piss in their helmets, ready to throw it in the faces of officers who ordered them up out of the trenches to get their guts blown out. And the officers stayed away. They gave no orders, and the soldiers won. They ruled the trenches, because they were men. I've seen German workers, bare-handed, fight with the police in the streets of Hamburg . . . and *win!* I've seen women with screwdrivers in their hands gut a horse and beat the rider to death with stones. But you . . . you people, what do you do? Nothing! Nothing! *Nothing!*"

Sánchez squinted. His anger had subsided to a sodden pang in his breast. He squirmed in his seat. These words were not meant for him. He had been loyal; he had worked, yes, all those years. Why, he had carried out a purge of the old-timers himself. His hands were wet with blood to the elbows. The others, they were nothing, true. But he, he was—

"In the winter, in St. Petersburg, I saw the women march. From Vyborg they came, by the thousands. And the Cossacks, the horsemen, were in the streets with their rifles, pistols and sabers. You could hear the snow squeak when the horses shifted weight. Did the Cossacks fire on the women? No. No! Why? Because they felt it, like spring sunlight in the winter air, the breath of the people. Look at you! Look! You're strangled now. You can't breathe. There isn't a lungful of air in this whole room. You're not a party, not a movement. You're nothing. Nothing. A gang of sick-hearts with no balls. Vizarra will kick you to pieces. For thirteen years I broke my back, and this is what I have raised. *Nothing!*

"Frenchmen would have torn up the streets. Germans would have taken half the city. Russians would have emptied the jails, burned the secret police barracks to the ground and stamped on the ashes. The fighting workers of any other nation would have risen years ago and torn the shackles that bound them like so much thread! What have you done? Nothing! Other men rise when the boot beats down on their necks. They become leg breakers! What do you do? You roll over and shine the boots, at two centavos a pair.

"You make my guts weep. My father bled for you when you were kids. They hung my father by his heels from a tree and packed my mother's belly full of stones. Manón Xaltalpa killed forty-eight oppressors of the poor with his knife, with his own hands! In those days kids bent nails and threw them on the roads to slow down the infantry. In the city, university students dropped marbles under the police horses and used the Plaza Mayor as a drill field. Mothers and wives threw their sons and husbands into the streets and said 'Fight! Fight and make us free!' What do you do? You sit in the dining room and order fried potatoes.

"Is this what you want? Do you want this life to go on forever? Is this what you'll give your sons, this half-death? How many newspapers do you have? Three. Do they print the truth? I ask you."

The darkness blasted back at him.

"No!"

"Has there been a free election in thirteen years?"

"No!"

"Do you vote for the members of the Cortes?"

"No!"

"Do you want the Yankee businessmen to suck your children's blood?"

213

"No!"

"Can you read, speak, think what you want?"

"No!"

"You! *Peón!*"

The man shot to his feet as though touched by an electric wire: an old man, wrinkle-necked, mustached and burned by the sun, bowed by labor.

"How many generations have your men worked the land?"

"From the time of my great-great-grandfather."

"Do you own it, the land?"

"No."

"Will you ever own under this government?"

"No!"

"No! No! No!"

"Rota. Stand up."

He rose, podgy and discomforted, scrubbing his face on the sleeve of his robe.

"Can you strike?"

"No."

"Can you express grievances to the newspapers?"

"No."

"Petarna!"

"Here!"

"How many of your fellow workers have been arrested?"

"Twenty-three."

"Have they been released?"

"No."

"Have formal charges been brought against them?"

"No."

"Do you expect them to be released?"

"No."

"Do you think they are alive now?"

"No!"

"I ask you all. Is this justice for the working classes?"

"No! No! No!"

Alessandro spread his hands and smiled gently. His voice was soft, a feather of insult that flicked against all their faces.

"Well, what do you want, eh? You want to be told what you can do, what you can think, what you can read, what you can earn, what you can eat, what you can tell your children? You want this forever?"

214

"No! No!"

"Well, what will you do? What *can* you do? You have done *nothing* for *thirteen years!*"

Olmega jumped up, his fists raised.

"We'll fight!"

The amphitheater shook with the roar of voices. Alessandro raised his hand, patting down the frenzy, and shrugged.

"Fight? What for? What do you want?"

"Freedom!"

"Petarna!"

The Negro dock worker rose, his head bowed.

"Here."

"Where can you live?"

"In the barrio near the docks."

"There you live. You can't vote. You can't strike. The police watch you all the time. Is this what you want?"

"Alessandro, I want to be free."

"Do *you* want to be free?"

Alessandro had flung out his arms, embracing the blackness, sweeping the unseen ranks toward him, men and women, professionals, *vaqueros,* students and *peones.*

"Yes!"

"Do you want to elect honest men, not court toadies, to the Cortes?"

"Yes!"

"Do you want to own your land, farmers and workers on farms?"

"Yes!"

"Do you want to reap the honest rewards of your toil, city workers?"

"Yes!"

"Will you fight to be free, so that you may freely learn and freely, truly, teach, young men of Costa Plata?"

"Yes!"

"You—the rich ones—will you empty your pockets so that all men in this land may fight to resist tyranny and foreign exploitation?"

"Yes!"

"If it makes you beggars and your children walk in rags like the children of workers now?"

"Yes! Yes!"

"Then will you be men?"

"Yes! Yes! Yes!"

"How? What will you do? Will you strike in the streets? Will you disobey every proclamation of the government? Will you lie, steal, cheat? Will you kill your best friend?"

Olmega climbed on his seat, his head thrown back, his arms shivering.

"Yes! Yes!"

"A muzzled pack of journalist hirelings!"

"Kill them!"

"A Cortes packed with hyenas and bloodsuckers!"

"Kill them!"

"A corrupt dotard and his whore!"

"Kill them!"

"Traitors to the movement!"

"Kill them, kill them all!"

Alessandro shook his head in pity. He smiled gently again. His lips looked pale, like strips of silver beneath the lights.

"Kill, kill, kill. That's the simple way, the only way you can imagine. I want to know if you are willing to be bored, if you are willing to go hungry, if you will sacrifice your wealth, if you are willing just to stand all day in the hot sun without a drink of water or wine. That is revolution, too, you know."

"Yes! Yes!"

"Will no one say no? Are there no honest men here who will say, 'None of that for me'? Who will say, 'Yes, I will fight, I will be poor, I will die if need be, but I won't be ordered around, I won't do anything my heart kicks at, I won't do anything that makes my belly turn'?"

Alessandro waited. No one answered him. He clenched his fist. This time his smile was bright, without malice or irony, the pure curved smile of a child.

"Well, then, maybe we can do something about this, eh?"

"Yes!"

"Maybe we can make Costa Plata free, take back the mines, kick the foreigners out. Maybe we can own our land, raise our children, live and love without some Yankee gangster leaning over us with a club, some foreigner hired by a traitor to his nation, his people, a tyrant crushing us all. Maybe if we work! If we sacrifice! If we love our land as we say we do! If we love each other, man to man, black,

216

brown and white, student, peasant and worker! Shall we try this? Shall we try to make our movement, now a spark, a flame that will burn and purify the whole nation and cleanse every heart?"

"Yes! Yes! Yes!"

"So. So then, we will try. We will do what seems necessary for what will one day seem good, and be good. We will try to be men, so that our children will be men. This we will try, with God's aid!"

"With God's aid!"

He stood below them, down in the lighted pit. He was slender, alone and strong. They hunched in the darkness, many and weak. He raised his arms in salute to them. He welcomed them to him with his stiff, solemn gesture. The echoes of the last cry rattled off the bare walls of the amphitheater. The crowd then began to applaud. Alessandro held the same posture of salute until the men and women above and around him dropped their stinging hands into their laps.

Sánchez grunted, his mind already moving ahead, busy with practical considerations. What was to be done first? Would Alessandro proclaim a provisional government of the insurgent forces? Would he order a general strike or armed attacks against the government military outposts? Sánchez writhed uncomfortably, shifting from buttock to buttock. His mind kept circling back to the same question. Again and again he asked himself: *What will I be? What will my position be? What will my rank be?* What about the miners, still under the thumb of that madman Ramos? *What will I be?* The Belgian Voget is no doubt right about machine guns and artillery. They would need them at once. *Will I have a rank in the fighting force? Already we are short of gasoline. Will I be a member of the Central Committee?* Nearly one-third of the U.T. delegates are Reds. Rota is a Communist. Alessandro, I have done everything for you. *What will you do for me?*

Alessandro dropped his arms and turned to the national banner hung on the wall behind him. He pointed to it.

"This flag is defiled. It is the flag of Vizarra, the man who murdered my father and mother, the man who murdered your fathers, brothers and sons, the man who murders every day to keep himself in power. I do not salute this flag."

His lips puckered and a gobbet of saliva slipped down the broad blue stripe.

217

"I spit on this flag! This is not my flag. This is not your flag. This is not the flag of the free people of Costa Plata!"

He seized the fabric in one hand and tore it off the wall. There, revealed, was the banner stitched by the old laundress, a pure sheet of white with four bold, blue stars. Alessandro waited until the crowd quieted, then stroked the banner. His eyes shone as he touched the stars.

"This is my flag. This is your flag. This, this is *ours!* This is beautiful. *Ah, qué bonita bandera! La bandera de Costa Plata, eh?"*

The audience sat rapt, impressed, but unable to discover any method of showing their unanimous approval. Some were shocked by Alessandro's spitting. They were used to seeing the blue and silver stripes of the national colors. All their lives they had known nothing else. They were not yet capable of matching Alessandro's contempt.

Sánchez waited another instant. Then, before the silence became embarrassing or choked completely any more demonstrations, he rose to his feet. He felt clumsy and foolish with his bathrobe clutched against his belly. But he had to do something. He had always been ready to follow commands. Now he could act alone, could aid Alessandro at a critical moment. He swallowed nervously and then shouted at the top of his lungs.

"Insurgent comrades! On the day Felipe Martín was betrayed and murdered, he wrote a song. Do you know it? Let them hear it in the mountains, in the *campo,* in the city! Sing, brothers! Sing for freedom!"

The chairs thundered all around as the crowd rose. Sánchez began the song. Women began to weep, but their voices were drowned in the simple powerful chorus of singing men.

> Men from fields and streets and mountains,
> How the future brightly gleams!
> Forward, brothers! Federation!
> Bring to life our people's dreams!
>
> Drive the tyrant from his stronghold,
> Give our nation liberty!
> Break the strangers' bloody shackles!
> Raise the banner! Make us free!
>
> Let us join our hands together,
> All our races interdrawn,

218

> Sons of Costa Plata, courage!
> See now freedom's shining dawn!

Sánchez felt the small, horny fingers of an Indian miner steal into his own damp clasp. His other hand was crushed by a roaring mestizo. The crowd rocked from side to side as they sang the last verse.

> Men of courage, men of valor,
> Men united for the fight!
> Forward all, for liberation,
> Strike for God and human right!

The men and women cheered and applauded. Alessandro waved his hands and smiled. The audience collapsed back into their seats, swatting each other on the shoulders, embracing and talking, many openly weeping. Sánchez sat down slowly, sliding into his seat, his head turning from side to side as he peered into the darkness, trying to gauge the mood of the crowd. Once again he had acted to help Alessandro. *But what was the reward?*

Alessandro sat down on the operating table and crossed his legs. He squinted up at the crowd. An excited student whispered in a hoarse voice that echoed off the walls.

"What a moment! What an historic moment! The greatest moment in our history!"

The crowd applauded his words, and the student stood up and repeated what he had said. Applause dashed in the darkness again. Sánchez relaxed. They were focused now. All their attention was devoted to Alessandro. He could make them stand on their heads or cut off their left arms if he wanted. They were one body, and he was the heart and the brain. Alessandro grinned, a good, open, comrade's smile.

"Does anybody here have a good South Province cigar?"

Sánchez tore open his robe and scaled his cigar case toward the operating table. The air was filled with brown missiles. Alessandro covered his head with his arms and shrank in mock terror as the cigars pelted his body. He snatched one from the air, struck a match on his heel and puffed for a few seconds, the thick, blue smoke curling around his shoulders. Then he leaned forward and a loose lock of hair slipped down over his forehead. Sánchez groaned, half pleasure, half envy. The men and women in the darkness knew that pose; one of the few pictures ever taken of Alessandro in exile was just that: legs crossed, hair trailing, eyes fixed, determined, mouth twisted slightly on one side, the whole body in a jaunty slouch, relaxed and confident. *Come on, you little bastard, what am I to be? Let me know my worth. Let the others know me. Give me something!*

Alessandro placed the cigar on the table edge and drew a sheet of paper from his pocket. The amphitheater was absolutely silent. Alessandro looked into the darkness. He gave a little nod, as though sufficiently convinced that he could speak for all of them, that he was the tongue to utter their thoughts.

"We will now begin to construct the future order of the People's Republic of Costa Plata."

Just like that. As though nothing could be more obvious, more simple! Alessandro glanced at the piece of paper.

"Until the movement spreads—and we will delay the discussion of tactics until later—the disposing and directing center will remain here at the sanatorium. Decisions will be deliberated on in open session. More of that later, too. I will appoint the chairman of the Central Revolutionary Committee. Five other members will be nominated and elected in a few hours. I will vote with the Central Committee in case of a tie. All decisions so voted and approved or disapproved will be issued in writing and transmitted directly to the leaders of the various cadres now formed and those formed in the future. All such written directives will be final, subject neither to veto, appeal or further discussion. The essential strength of an insurgent movement is absolute unity, the devotion of men and women bound by a blood oath."

The audience growled approval. Sánchez wiped his hands on his robe again and again. Alessandro looked at the piece of paper.

"You know the chairman. He has set a standard of devotion that all must match. My old comrade. Carlos Sánchez!"

The blood bubbled in Sánchez's ears. He hardly felt the hands thumping his shoulders, wringing his fingers and scrubbing his hair. Voices rushed and roared around him. He covered his face with his hands. He was too weak to stand; joy and relief crippled him. Chairman of the Central Committee! It was much more than he had hoped for. He had never dreamed that Alessandro would so honor him. He sat still, his face hidden, until Alessandro spoke again.

"Fellow members, you will find a scheme of organization pinned to the central bulletin board. Each cadre has been assigned a room. In each room you will find typed sheets dealing with the proposed general strike. These proposals must be transformed into general orders and submitted to the Central Committee. Any objections or amendments must be voted on by all cadre members, carried by majority approval and submitted in written form to the Central Committee before midnight. We will assemble here again at one o'clock to draft together a declaration of the aims and purposes of our movement, an appeal to our countrymen to join us in the coming struggle. All right. Let's get to work!"

The corridors and stairs were jammed with shouting men in maroon bathrobes, doctors and orderlies in white uniforms and nurses in their starched, flaring skirts and crisp caps. Tobacco smoke swirled and drifted above the bobbing heads. The crowd parted to let Sánchez pass. He climbed the stairs and stopped before the board. Two hard-faced men, sailors or fishermen, saluted. Sánchez read the cadre lists. Very few changes had been made in his original recommendations. He walked down the hall. The others shrank out of his way. He suppressed a giggle. Here they were, all united at last to topple Vizarra's government, and every man of them was forced to shuffle along like an invalid for fear of losing his slippers.

The office of the Central Committee was located in the two rooms formerly occupied by Don Alonso, the director of the sanatorium. What had happened to the old man? Pepe Olmega must have taken him down into the fields with the last truckload of patients. Sánchez pushed open the door, eager, yet dreading the next moment.

Alessandro was waiting for him. He sprang out of a chair and ran across the room, his fine, dark eyes shining with pleasure.

"Carlos!"

"Hello, little one!"

The two men crushed each other in a bear-hug *abrazo*. They shoved each other out at arm's length and circled in a clumsy dance, grinning and laughing. A sliver of something like fear pricked Sánchez. Alessandro's upper lip was pale. He had found time, somehow, to shave off the melancholy mustache that had been part of his disguise.

"Carlitos!"

"*Jovencito!*"

"Ai, Carlitos, you didn't tell me you were *ill!"*

Sánchez laughed and shook his head.

"The chairman of the Central Committee is never ill! Never! That will be my first order. No one in the movement is to be ill at any time!"

Alessandro nodded and chewed his lip. He shrugged and stepped out of Sánchez's embrace.

"We're a long way yet from giving orders, Carlos. First we must see that the discussions in the general assembly are properly directed."

"Ah, always so serious. Come, we have the rest of our lives to be serious. Let's have a smoke and a chat first, eh?"

Sánchez saw the cigar mashed out in an ashtray.

"Maybe you're sick, *jovencito?* Or is it too strong for you? A good South Province cigar can make your teeth fall out."

"I don't smoke, actually. I never have."

Sánchez felt himself flush.

"A circus trick, eh? To make them feel they are your friends. Half the men out in the corridor now tell each other that you are smoking the cigar they threw you."

Alessandro nodded soberly.

"A little thing, Carlos. It does no harm. Promotes a strong feeling of brotherhood."

Sánchez forced himself to nod. A trick, and he had been as gullible as the dullest *vaquero.* Christ, he had even thrown his cigar case, a whole case of the finest Coronas. How stupid he had been to forget that Alessandro did not like tobacco.

"You're not angry, Carlos?"

"Me? What for? Why should I be angry?"

"I don't know . . ."

"What's a cigar, eh? Tonight of all nights."

Alessandro frowned and ran his finger over his upper lip.

"Yes, tonight. How long I have waited for this night!"

"Jovencito, all the time I worked, I thought of this night."

"I recognized your voice. The singing. That was good, very good."

"So? You smoke a cigar, I sing a song. We're even. There is more than a single way to move a crowd. We've been in this business a long time, you and me."

"Your work is just beginning, Carlos."

"Oh, I know, but it's my life. Since we were children. Since the old days. Since . . ."

Alessandro broke the seal on a wad of papers and spread them over a desk.

"Exactly. That's why I appointed you chairman. I'll head the political committee and see if I can't take some of the load off your shoulders."

"Political committee? What for? Hell, load on the work! You direct the military. I'll handle the rest of it."

"A political committee is essential to promote unity."

"Why can't the Central Committee do that?"

Alessandro looked over the papers he had spread out. He spoke without looking at Sánchez.

"You weren't in Russia, Carlos. The Bolsheviks used the political committees to recruit. And to get rid of undesirables. We've got plenty of those. Rota and the Red U.T. delegates. You gave the list to me. Here it is. A political committee, well, it's like in the church. To formulate dogma, you might say. And to prevent heresies."

"Well, if you want it—"

"I *insist* on it."

"All right, all right. I suppose you'll be the only one on *both* committees, eh?"

"*Claro.* And the military committee, too."

"And the military committee, too."

Sánchez shrugged. Alessandro stopped looking for whatever it was and glanced up, then half turned toward the windows.

"It must have been a strain on you. To know that I was disguised like that. Never able to tell anyone. Not even able to talk to me as a comrade, even alone in your room."

Sánchez swallowed. He could not tell whether Alessandro was joking or not.

"I'm used to keeping my mouth shut."

"How long ago did you guess?"

"Oh, quite a while. I've forgotten actually."

"Yes, that can happen. Every morning I had to remind myself not to get lost as an orderly, not to abandon my own personality. I got so I walked with a limp automatically. That bothered me. I thought I was losing my mind. I was afraid I'd become just José the orderly. What a joke that would have been, eh?"

"Ha-ha-ha! As if you could ever forget that you were Alessandro Martín!"

"Eh? Well, it's hard to keep a secret that long. I admire you, Carlitos."

Sánchez swallowed again. His saliva tasted bitter. He was certain that Alessandro knew that he had never guessed at the orderly's real identity. Alessandro was being generous, making it possible for him to save face. What were they—old friends, revolutionary comrades, nearly brothers? Or were they two bowing Orientals? Sánchez was furious at his own stupidity. He should have known at once that the orderly was Alessandro, even despite the long years of exile and the sad mustache. He could not endure the thought that he should be grateful to Alessandro for making them both liars.

"It was a beautiful disguise, Alessandro. You'll have a great career as an actor. The man of a thousand faces. In America, making films, sleeping with all the pretty blond actresses—"

Alessandro shook his head and drove the hair up away from his brow.

"You sound like we might fail in this. We will *not* fail! An actor? That disguise saved my life. That and your silence. And now you talk as if Vizarra is going to chase us to America."

"Jovencito, I never meant—"

"Listen, I spent nearly half my life working on ships and along the docks, in factories and mills and on farms. I stole what I couldn't earn or borrow. I lied and forged and pimped for the police in a dozen cities, just so that I could meet the leaders of other parties. I haven't come back to my homeland to chew clay or to be driven out again by Vizarra! *We won't fail!"*

"Alessandro, I was joking!"

"Then *don't* make jokes, Carlos!"

Two bright spots colored Alessandro's cheeks. He drove his fingers through his lank hair and shrugged.

"Preparations for the general strike must begin at once."

"At once? But there is no strike fund. There have been no collections of food and clothing."

"So? If they're hungry, they'll steal. When the workers steal food, that is a problem for the government, not for the revolutionary party."

"The Unión de Trabajadores will not accept—"

"The U.T. will do exactly as it is told. When they send in reports and recommendations, throw them into the wastebasket."

"Right. But Rota."

"The political committee will take care of Rota."

"That's what those Belgian Communists want, Alessandro. They want Rota out."

"Correct. And we'll get him out. And when the Belgians have outlived their usefulness . . ."

"I understand, little one. But what about the army?"

"I'm going to see General Vola."

"How? When?"

"As soon as the fiesta of Santa Rosa begins, I'm going into the city. I have to meet some men. Vizarra is declaring a partial political amnesty. To impress his foreign visitors."

"An amnesty? Why wasn't I told about this?"

Alessandro shrugged and handed Sánchez a list of names.

"This is the responsibility of the political committee. As you see, they are radicals, some moderates, a few Christian Democrats and some old Socialists. No Reds, though. I've got to get to them and bring them in with us. Then I see fat General Vola. That will leave Vizarra with nothing but the National Guard."

"The city is full of police. O'Conner has taken on a lot of new men. The members of the Red Beret are on the watch, too."

"During the fiesta half the police will be drunk. The city will be safer than any other place. Remember how they caught my father? The mountains, he used to say, that's the place to go. The rocks will hide you. Well, they hide him now, all right. He and my mother. If they had stayed in the city, they'd both be alive."

Sánchez said nothing. Alessandro had obviously made up his mind. He was stubborn, like his father Felipe. In physical form he resembled his mother, at least as Sánchez remembered her, slender and strong, a narrow handsome face, large eyes and thick, soft hair.

"But, little one, don't you think—"

"Carlos, no more questions. I'll have to answer a thousand questions tonight. I've only got so much energy and not enough time. Are the cadres properly organized?"

"Of course. I did that work myself."

"Have they got enough to keep them busy?"

"What do you mean? They have fulfilled the orders that were given to them."

"Then make up new orders. Keep them separated from the nurses."

"Keep them from the nurses? But the women are party members!"

"Post a curfew. The women are to be in their quarters by ten o'clock every night. If they are party members in good standing, let them demonstrate their loyalty by obedience. Tomorrow every drop of liquor in this place goes. Have a group take the stuff out to the rubbish heap and pour it out. Save the bottles. They'll do for gasoline bombs. We're going to be short of hand grenades as it is."

"No women, no liquor. These are the wrong kind of robes, little one. You should have chosen a monastery instead of a sanatorium."

Alessandro did not smile. He nodded once.

"I thought of it, but they are all too small or too remote."

"Even monks have wine with their meals."

"Monks do not make revolutions."

"They won't like it. The fiesta of Santa Rosa?"

"Let Vizarra and his gang celebrate. We're here to work."

"We have no more money. How are we going to get more guns?"

"Very simple. We're going to borrow them from the army against a promise of silver taken from the mine. General Vola and Ramos have reached some sort of agreement already. I don't know what it is, but I'm going to find out. The soldiers and the miners must be brought into the movement. Loyal army units must be cut off, isolated, until the soldiers mutiny. Enough questions and answers. Everyone wants to know when the meat will be cooked. First we have to chop the wood and build the fire. Then we have to catch the cow."

Slippers scuffed in the corridor outside the office. Three members of a liaison cadre reported, grinning and eager for work. Alessandro flicked his hand around the room.

"What will you need in here, Carlos?"

Alessandro's voice was edged. Sánchez sensed that the question was really a command. He spoke without looking up from the list of prisoners soon to be released. He recognized most of the names.

"Two big tables, three typewriters and comrades to run them. Another telephone to make calls within the building. We can't have messengers running up and down the stairs with slippers on. Someone will break a leg. The casualties start in the city, not out here."

The men left. Alessandro clapped Sánchez on the shoulder. A messenger arrived with a letter for Alessandro, forwarded from a loyal woman who ran a *pensión* in the city. Alessandro stuffed it into his pocket and smiled.

"You see, Carlos? I shave off my mustache and already I receive love letters."

"Read it. We'll have a laugh."

"Ah, later. This reminds me. Every cadre captain is to be fully responsible for reports submitted, suggestions, everything. Return every document that is not signed by *every* member of the cadre. They are to put their names down in two columns, *in favor* and *opposed*. The political committee will want to isolate obstructionists as soon as possible."

"You mean the committee is going to spy on members of the movement?"

Alessandro shrugged and turned away.

"Put it that way, if you like. Surveillance, that's all."

Obstructionists. Sánchez puckered his mouth, annoyed. All these fancy Moscow terms, Bolshevik jargon to conceal tyranny. The words themselves were tyrannical; men acted on them without thought, blindly. A firing squad would shoot an obstructionist, but they wouldn't execute a comrade who was merely confused or of independent mind. Sánchez seized Alessandro's arm and spun him around.

"Listen, *jovencito,* if you're going to clean out the cadres, understand now that your splendid political committee will have to do the dirty work. I purged the party for you once and—"

Alessandro's dark eyes glittered, and his mouth thinned.

"What are you talking about? No one's done anything."

"Not yet, you mean."

"All right, not yet. All the members of the movement must march in step. There can be no breaks in the ranks. Those who waver will be removed. No matter how high their rank."

Sánchez could feel his face chill. He clenched his fists.

"How can you reconcile your democratic writings with the practices you've picked up in St. Petersburg? This is two-faced, Alessandro! You talk about free elections and now you say that opponents will be purged."

The two men stared at each other. Alessandro shook his head slowly, and his hair slid down over his brow.

"We must *win* the revolution, Carlos. *Then* we install democracy. The insurgent movement must have discipline like steel, total unity of thought and action."

"A dictatorship, you mean."

"A temporary, voluntary reduction of individual rights for the benefit of the movement as a whole. Believe me, on this matter the Bolsheviks are right. The people need a group around which they can rally. Ulyanov thinks the workers are by nature revolutionary. I don't. They need a group, a vanguard to follow."

"Who is Ulyanov, for the love of God?"

"Lenin, *hombre,* Lenin."

"Oh, yes, of course."

"Trust me, Carlitos. There are things I know—"

"Of course. There are many things you know that we are ignorant of here. But we are not fools, Alessandro."

"*Amigo,* your nerves are bad. Trust me. If you don't like the activities of the political committee, bring it up in the Central Committee. Remember? That group has the final word."

"That's true."

"Of course. Don't be so suspicious. If we overcontrol the movement, it is to prevent anarchy. We want a controlled revolt, not a mindless, undirected blood bath. Believe me, it is better to liquidate five disaffected party members than to tolerate breaches of discipline that may develop into mutiny and cause the death of hundreds. Or the failure of the revolt. You can't make an omelet without breaking eggs."

"You're right. Yes, you're right."

Alessandro placed his hands on Sánchez's shoulders and shook him gently.

"My old warhorse. The nervous liberal. Always loyal, despite your good Catholic conscience. How I have relied on you these years!"

"Ah, *jovencito,* you have been my life, you know. We have been apart so long, too long. We're not kids, you and me. We're men."

"And so we must disagree! It's natural. All right, let's get over the next bad spot in the road. You must organize a gang of strikebreakers. Pick out the leaders tomorrow, deal with them in absolute secrecy."

228

"We make a general strike, then we break our own strike?"

"Exactly. And a few heads, too."

"I know."

"It might be fatal to the movement if the capital remains paralyzed after we take over, just because some types start to play for power themselves. We'll have to watch the timing on this business. I think the Belgians would be good men to use. Voget's really very experienced. He's a foreigner, you see? It would throw blame on him, not on us."

"He breaks the strike, and we break him. I'll take care of it, don't worry."

"Good."

"Then we'll have a pattern to work from. The Reds will pull the revolution to the left. What do you call it? I've forgotten."

"The power shift. I saw it happen in St. Petersburg. The revolution nearly got away from the Bolsheviks. They dragged their feet. The men in the Soviet were more radical than the Bolsheviks themselves. It just seems to work that way. A revolution of moderates shifts left, faster and faster, until the moderates discover, too late, that the people now think of them as reactionaries. We can't let that happen for two reasons. First, we must keep moving *left,* ahead of the Reds. We'll frighten the hell out of everybody. Including most of the people here right now. Second, we've got to watch the landowners. We'll need them. They'll get frightened first, because of the promised land reforms. They've got money and they'll act."

"What are we going to do with a bunch of capitalist counterrevolutionaries?"

"Well, they'll be terrified of a Reign of Terror. We'll take steps to see that doesn't happen. There will be no Robespierres in Costa Plata. We'll have to ride *with* the forces of counterrevolution. First we are more radical than anybody. We smash the Communists and drift back toward the center, just left of center. The landowners will have lost their fear during this time when we cooperate with them in bringing the revolution to a halt. But it stops when and where *we* want it to. Nobody else."

"What if the landowners get too strong? We'll get too much reactionary feeling."

"Perhaps. But insufficient reactionary activity. There aren't enough of them, Carlos. The *peones* will be with us. We will promise them land and give it to them. The government land first, though. When things settle down and business is back to normal, we will start to break up the latifundia. But with compensation to the owners. We can't afford to drive out capital. Just the foreigners."

"Have you talked with any of the landowners?"

"About thirty. In Mexico. All of them young men. Reasonably liberal. At least you can talk with them."

"Can we trust them?"

"Carlitos, revolution is the favorite recreation of cannibals. The eaters get eaten if they linger too long at the table. The last thing we can afford, the last thing we can endure, is a civil war between the left and the right. Only the army wins a civil war, *amigo*. That means General Vola or somebody worse. Can we trust them? Carlitos, believe me, the only person I trust is *you*. Only you. You I trust absolutely."

"You can't make an omelet without breaking eggs, but it is also very important not to kill off the hens."

"Or get pecked to death by them."

Someone knocked on the door. Alessandro sighed and stepped away from Sánchez. "There's a uniform, army fatigues, in the closet, Carlos. It should fit. You'll look more official than in that bathrobe. Boots, too. Let the intellectuals scuff around in their slippers. Get the women in the laundry to cut armbands for the members of the Central Committee. You're the boss now. Well, have we forgotten anything?"

"Yes, little one, my cigars. I tossed my case at you."

Alessandro frowned and walked toward the door.

"Go get it yourself. These people are comrades, not house servants."

‡

It was five minutes after one o'clock in the morning. Sánchez hurried down the stairs to the amphitheater. He passed a group of students and young instructors from the university, intellectuals assigned to a propaganda unit. One of them was speaking in a high, nervous voice.

"What we need is a new revolutionary anthem, brothers. To be frank, Alessandro's father was neither a poet or a musician. The song we have could be termed a traditional piece, or rewritten to fit a march tempo. More spirited, don't you see? But we really need an anthem, conceived of as a piece for organ and male choir."

230

"No, we need a simple slogan. The fighting workers will create their own revolutionary music. A good slogan will focus their minds continually on the struggle. What about that? *Siempre la lucha.* 'Always the struggle.' "

"Struggle for what? *Lucha y libertad.* 'Struggle and liberty.' That's better."

Sánchez nodded absently in response to the students' greetings. In the main foyer he could see the members of his office unit, now dressed in denim overalls with crimson armbands. Their work was to see that all the men were seated in cadres at assigned rows in the amphitheater so that they might be more easily identified. The Belgian Voget was there, arguing as usual in his crude Spanish. He turned as Sánchez descended the stairs.

"Comrade Sánchez. A word with you."

"What is it, Voget?"

"These persons demand of us that we sit on the far right side. Why is this? We sit on the far *left*. *Always* the far left."

"There are no seats there. They have already been assigned."

The other Belgians gathered around. They all wore the sleeves of their bathrobes rolled above the elbows, as if to signify their eagerness for work. One of them gestured and scowled fiercely.

"*El frente rojo a la izquierda!* Red front to the left!"

"Voget, the meeting is already late."

"But we have not come all the way from Brussels to encounter deviationist assembly techniques!"

"The seats are all the same. Right, center, left. Please take your places. You are delaying the meeting."

"Voget shook his head stubbornly.

"I am deaf in my left ear. I can hear well only when seated on the far left side of the hall."

The Belgian turned and twisted, tapping the side of his head. Sánchez laughed shortly and walked away, pounding his boot heels smartly on the parquet floor. Voget tore off his slippers and flung them across the foyer. He shook his fist at Sánchez.

"We foreign delegates demand an equal clothing ration! Give us boots like yours! Where is your sense of democratic behavior? Are we convicts to walk in bare feet?"

Sánchez pushed open the door and stalked quickly into the lighted pit. Alessandro was already there, waiting. A spatter of applause greeted Sánchez. He spread his papers on the operating table and lit a cigar, then rapped the glass ashtray on the table to call the meeting to order. He was slightly nervous. He and Alessandro had prepared a system to speed up the meeting and to avoid all situations which might lead to argument and rejection of Alessandro's strategy for the general strike. Sánchez stood up.

"The following reports and amendments have been rejected by the Central Committee and returned to the cadre captains for revision or correction. No such document will be accepted unless signed by all members of the cadre, in two columns, for and against."

"What Central Committee? There is no Central Committee."

"The matter of the Central Committee election is first on the agenda. The rejected reports and amendments: from the U.T. that present methods of arms distributions cease and . . . "

Sánchez read swiftly, ticking off each rejected suggestion with a red pencil. He repeated, his voice very earnest, that the proposals had been rejected only because of improper form. He had been careful to reject documents from all the cadres that had submitted them. When Rota of the U.T. protested that his group had been discriminated against, Sánchez ruled him out of order. He proceeded in a calm, businesslike fashion, called for nominations, seconds, brief discussion and voice votes. One of the Belgians nominated Voget; another harangued until Sánchez cut him short. The assembly rejected Voget. Alessandro leaned over to Sánchez.

"Carlos, I'll send a messenger up to him now. Offering him a seat on the political committee. Also an invitation to your secret meeting of the strikebreakers. We can't afford to lose the support of the Belgians. Not at this point."

"Right. The chair expresses sincere disappointment at the rejection of delegate Voget. Comrade, knowing your skill in political action and as a director of shock brigades, let me say that you have narrowly escaped suffering from acute boredom."

The crowd laughed politely.

"Next nomination? Yes."

"Pepe Olmega, first youth hero of the movement! Righteous avenger of the people's sufferings at the hands of the senile and corrupt Prime Minister Colleo!"

The leader of the student's cadre was accepted immediately. The U.T. nominated Rota, and the fat union leader was promptly elected.

Sánchez nodded and smiled. This had been foreseen. Rota was

232

probably the best-known of all the delegates. He was a national figure of some importance and trusted by the workers, who had not discovered his membership in the Communist party. Even if they knew, few would care.

"The chair notes with great pleasure the election of such a skilled and energetic organizer of the fighting workers. Next nomination?"

"One-arm. We want One-arm."

The strange, maimed Indian was elected, too. Sánchez raised his eyebrows at Alessandro: *What will we do with that one?* The elections ended swiftly with a standing round of applause for the new committee.

"If the assembly approves by voice vote, the Central Committee will meet after this and appoint a political committee to serve as advisers on matters of party policy and internal security. Is this acceptable?"

"*Sí!*"

"Very well. Members of the political committee will be posted on the main board. I now turn this meeting over to our leader for consideration of the proposed general strike."

Alessandro read the first draft of his proposal. The strike was to begin at midnight on the first day of the fiesta of Santa Rosa. All public utilities and public transportation were to cease operations. In the gay confusion of the street dancing, parades and parties, the failure of lights and telephone service would not be immediately noticed. Under cover of darkness the university buildings were to be occupied, the main electric building and telephone building seized, but without recourse to shooting.

He paused. There were no objections.

"Very well. To the activity of the railroad workers. Yes?"

Joachím Lara, the cadre captain of the railroad engineers and firemen, an elderly man with a kind face and stiff short hair, stood up, grasping the back of the seat in front of him.

"I regret to say this, but I'm afraid that even if we order it, many of our boys won't strike. You know, the old excuses—wife and kids . . ."

There were hoots of derision from the U.T. delegates. Alessandro raised his hand for silence. Voget stood up.

"My cadre, among other duties, will occupy the Estación Central at 2100 hours and take over the switches in the marshaling yards at sunrise. If your band of class weaklings won't come out, they still will not be able to move anything in or out of the city!"

Voget sat down. Lara shook his head slowly.

"I don't see that as a solution. What about the army or the National Guard? They can take the station and the yards back right away. The problem is to get the trains out of the city back up to the mines without showing our hand. Isn't that right?"

"Central Committee member Pepe Olmega?"

"Here!"

"Ever run a locomotive?"

"Not yet."

"Well, you're a student. Do you find learning difficult?"

"It's easy, except for one thing."

"What is that?"

"The professors!"

The remark drew a small laugh. His fellow students applauded ironically. Alessandro grinned easily.

"Well, how would you like to begin lessons at the Estación Central at 2200 hours? If you get them as far as Molinos, we can arrange to have you and those with you brought back near the university by truck. You can still direct the occupation of the university buildings."

"Muy bien. How many of us, though?"

Sánchez knew that Alessandro had the answer. The railroad workers were a mixed lot, with no strong political affiliation as yet. Sánchez and Alessandro had drawn up lists for fresh locomotive crews. But Alessandro turned to Lara, nodding respectfully to the old man.

"Well, if I can count on three engineers and take one myself, these young fellows can fire the boilers, I suppose. Say a dozen who don't mind getting their hands dirty."

Olmega nodded.

"Count on us. We've had plenty of experience with *pistón.*"

His fellows laughed again, louder than the professors or instructors who sat around them. *Pistón* was student slang for "pull" or influence with a teacher. Sánchez noticed a group of *vaqueros* repeating the word, puzzled. Alessandro nodded.

"Perhaps fourteen would be better. I think there are seven trains scheduled?"

Lara thought for a moment.

"Sí, seven trains. As far as Molinos. I'll get regular crews on there. And we can get the trains up to the mines."

234

"All right. Olmega, your group must stay on the locomotives until you are relieved. Is that quite clear? Can you guarantee crews at Molinos?"

"Yes. You see, those fellows live out of the city, away from the trouble. They won't know anything. I'll just give orders for special duty. It's the city boys who are afraid of the police. Their families will get taken in by O'Conner. They won't risk it."

The old man sat down, obviously troubled. The amphitheater rang with whistles and catcalls.

"Call yourself a revolutionary? Are you a man or a dry-balls? Coward! Throw him out!"

Alessandro raised his hand and glared up at the packed rows of seats.

"Silence. Respect is necessary, as well as obedience. It is quite proper to express thoughtful concern for the natural weakness of workers who have not yet been politically oriented. The willingness to sacrifice is based on the knowledge that suffering gives strength. And who among you has suffered himself? Answer me that. No one. Not one of you. Let us have respect, then."

Lara looked at Alessandro. Tears stood in the old man's eyes. He smiled gratefully. Alessandro walked back to the table and whispered to Sánchez.

"Put Lara on the political list. If he fails us at Molinos . . ."

Sánchez nodded and wrote the name. Alessandro moved to the next point.

"The demonstration in the middle of the parade has been partially organized. The coffin containing the body of the young martyr will be exhumed and placed on a wagon. When the figure of Santa Rosa passes the corner of Calle Rivera, the barricade must be torn down and . . ."

Step by step, Alessandro drew them all forward. As they accepted each succeeding strategic movement, they more readily accepted the next proposal. The U.T. protested only feebly over the lack of a strike fund. The delegates from the Southern Province eagerly submitted their full plans for a triple bank robbery. They promised fifty thousand reales ready in two days to be distributed among the workers' families. Alessandro fired them with quiet confidence. He repeatedly praised the organization for the distribution of weapons, without mention of how few pieces would be available. At last he threw the program sheets on the table and Sánchez initialed them after calling for the approval of the Central Committee members. He looked at his watch. Three-thirty. Where had the time gone? Alessandro looked fresh and eager, but men here and there nodded and yawned.

"One more thing. All members of the student and professor cadres report at 700 hours for practice at the rubbish heap. Throwing gasoline bombs. Comrade Voget will run the demonstration and supervise the training period. All right. Let's go to bed. We've got a full day tomorrow. Check the bulletin boards *before* breakfast. Every cadre will have an assignment."

The room rumbled as the men and women stood up and began to file out into the corridor. Alessandro walked back to the table and gathered the papers.

"It went well, Carlos."

"Very well. You'll have Voget kissing you if you keep that up."

"Huh. Well, we can have the kids get some practice in on those empty bottles. Listen, *amigo,* before you give the order to dump the liquor, get us a bottle of good brandy, eh? We've worked hard tonight. We'll have a drink for the old times, eh?"

"All right, little one. Where?"

"Your office."

"Always my office."

"Thursday, Friday, Saturday. By Saturday night you'll have a new office. In the national palace."

"Right!"

The two men left the amphitheater and climbed the stairs. The guard posted outside the door straightened to attention and saluted. Sánchez sent him for a bottle of brandy. Alessandro flung himself into a chair and groaned, holding his head.

"Mother of God, but I'm tired, Carlos! My head aches. And I used to think my feet hurt running up and down from one ward to another as an orderly. Open the window, eh? Give us some fresh air. Are you tired?"

"Yes. But I'm always tired. I'm used to it. There. A breeze, not much. But this mountain air is cold."

Sánchez stood at the window. From one wing of the sanatorium came sounds of shouting, singing and the laughter of women. Alessandro straighted.

"What's that?"

"Oh, the students, I suppose. After the nurses. Or the nurses after the *vaqueros*. What eyes they have for the *vaqueros!* Hoo!"

"Close the window. I don't want to hear it. Didn't you post the curfew?"

"Of course. That's why they're at it. What's the sense in posting a ten o'clock curfew at midnight? Starting tomorrow."

"Tomorrow. I should have thought of it earlier. Yesterday."

"Why get upset? One night of fun."

"Almost four o'clock, though. What kind of shape will they be in tomorrow morning?"

"The students or the nurses?"

"The students. To hell with the women."

"I'd say to hell with the students, myself."

Alessandro frowned wearily, rubbing his eyes.

"You can't be serious, Carlos."

"Yes and no. I'm joking. There's still time for jokes, no?"

"One day, maybe two. Then there'll be nothing to smile at."

"Oh, one must laugh to live. And love to live. And live to love."

"You sound like some Parisian dandy, Carlos. Women, women. A bunch of rubbish, all that talk. I'm always too busy for that sort of thing."

"Too busy for women? Not always, though, eh?"

Alessandro hesitated. He seemed to be reflecting on the past. He smiled briefly, then scowled. He brought his fists down on the arms of his chair and jumped erect.

Sánchez started and gaped at him.

"What's so surprising about that? All these years. I lived like a hermit, a monk! Why? Because I knew that I had to spend every ounce of my strength working! Sundays, holidays, day and night! Working for the movement. Every ounce of strength had to be twisted into francs, marks, lire and rubles. Would you rather I spewed it all away in a Hamburg gutter or spent it on *vin rouge* and whores from the Boulevard Sebastopol?"

"No, *amigo*."

"Then you think it's queer?"

"I didn't say that. I only know a man is a man. Women like handsome young men like yourself."

Alessandro's face was pale, as though all the muscles bunched beneath the smooth skin had squeezed the blood away. He swung his fist into his left hand and paced up and down.

"They nearly cost me my life. A dozen times, damn them. Their false promises of silence. Then they babble to some pimp and the police come down like a pack of dogs. And for what? A few minutes, that's all. There was a countess, Hungarian, a perverted woman of forty years. She gave me money—remember the bank draft I sent you from Buda? That was her. They shot her other lovers, two Serbians. She informed on me, too, but I got away."

"So there *have* been women! Not such a monk after all."

Alessandro shrugged and dragged his lank hair away from his brow. He stared out of the window and opened it. A woman shrieked in protest and then laughed. Alessandro slammed the window shut and grimaced. Sánchez smiled. A look of longing hung in Alessandro's fine, dark eyes. His lashes, too, were like a woman's—"bedroom eyes."

"No love affair? No grand passion?"

Alessandro spoke softly, so seriously that Sánchez nearly laughed, before he realized that Alessandro was utterly in earnest.

"Love affair? Yes, I have been in love. I am in love. With ideas. Ideas for the people. Of this country and other countries, too. The future of Latin America. Our time will come. Soon. Freedom, democracy, will spread. The people will get the land. The rich will be fairly taxed. I love those thoughts. Unlike women, one's own ideas are faithful. They cost something to acquire, true, but only courage to keep. An idea is never jealous."

"Eh-eh. And an idea never gets pregnant at the wrong time, either."

"That's very interesting. I remember a discussion of free love with some Scandinavian women once. In Copenhagen. They are ungodly people. I could not make them agree to the obvious fact that love is a gift from the Divine Spirit, from God. That alone is how we know Him."

"Well, I've had half the nurses here and I don't know Him any better. I guess maybe He knows more about me than He used to, though."

"That is wrong of you to say that. Even to think it. I love the idea of love. That is correct thinking, because it is universal. All other thoughts of love are selfish, if not sinful."

"Tell the nurses that. They'll have your pants off before you finish."

Alessandro frowned.

"You think you are teasing me, making fun of me. I think this is disgusting talk."

"Such lofty ideals you have now, little one! You're hard to get along with. You'll have to come down to our level, you know."

"So? Consider moving to a higher plane, Carlos. It is always less crowded, the higher you climb."

"And colder, too. No, thanks. I'll stay down with the nurses in the valley. In the tall grass."

Alessandro stiffened as though he had been struck. His voice shook with emotion. He chopped the air with his hand.

"Carlos, I give you warning! If I find that you have violated your own curfew law, I will order the political committee to—"

"To what?"

"Don't interrupt me!"

"To do what? If I want to bed some girl, that's my business, see?"

"Not if it endangers the movement!"

"You are absurd!"

"Very well. I am absurd. I exaggerate. But there are some things a man does well to exaggerate. Glorification of the senses is a sin! Cynicism is likewise very dangerous. Men are not pigs."

"Better to say pigs are not men."

"That's what I mean!"

"Oh, come on, you make *my* head ache now."

"I warn you, Carlos."

"Warn away. I don't have to listen to nonsense about women. If I want a woman, and she's willing, that's the end of it."

"Make sure it is not the end of you. I'll have no glutted fornicator heading the Central Committee!"

"Eh-eh-eh. And I'll have no monks on the political committee, either. Then where will we be? Both out of a job. You should have spent more time in Italy, man. Those Northern women are all frigid anyway."

Alessandro stared at Sánchez for a long moment. Sánchez shifted and looked away.

"You consider chastity an impossible virtue, Carlos. Try it sometime. Just once. For a week."

"I'd go crazy."

"No. You are crazy now."

"Alessandro, please shut up. All you're doing is warming my balls."

"All those letters you sent me. All those broken hearts."

Alessandro's voice thickened in disgust.

"And all your false, damning confessions and contritions. How you wasted your time, the priests' patience and the flesh of all those stupid girls."

"I haven't been to confession in years. One day it came to me that a man kneels to enter a woman and to confess to a priest. It seemed quite a coincidence. Guess which I gave up."

"You are mocking me. Go ahead."

"I wouldn't think of it, monk."

Suddenly Alessandro smiled; his whole face shone with good humor. He spun around on his heels, grinning, and flung out his arms.

"A monk? No, I am the abbot, and this is my monastery. Soon comes the fiesta and the crusade!"

The guard knocked on the door. Sánchez shook his head.

"Here comes the brandy, anyway. And just in time. Another minute and I'd have kicked your bottom."

"Go ahead! Here, take a shot at me!"

"So you can turn the other cheek? I'd rather drink."

Sánchez opened the door, but Alessandro darted forward and took the bottle.

"Many thanks, *amigo!*"

"*De nada, señores.* It's nothing."

"Señores? You mean comrades."

"Yes, sir. I mean comrades."

"Go to bed, boy, you look tired."

"Not me."

"Do as you are told. At once."

The guard saluted. Alessandro butted his rear against the door. It slammed in the guard's sleepy face.

"Now then, Carlos, two glasses. Why, this really is the best stuff.

240

Carlos Primero. Very appropriate, too. You're the first Carlos around here, no? By the way, how is your father?"

Sánchez walked into the lavatory and found two small glasses on a shelf. He had been expecting Alessandro to ask about his father, but he was surprised to notice that his hands shook. He set the glasses down on a table and thrust his hands into his pockets.

"I don't know, really. I haven't seen him, of course, in a long time. Years, now. I visited him then on his name day."

Alessandro peeled the lead foil away from the cork and took a knife from his pocket.

"He is still the Minister of Education, though."

"He wants to retire. As I understand it, no one else wants the job. The pay is nothing, see? Well, not enough to make people fight for it."

"How was he when you saw him last?"

"Oh, about the same. Puffing on his pipe. Very quiet."

"Quiet? He used to talk all the time. But that was in the old days."

"Yes. I can remember him like that, too. Up in the mountains, around the fire at night."

"That's right. 'The Professor.' You're much like him, Carlos."

"Me? Say, man, don't tell me that! A few years in prison, then he crawls out to lick Vizarra's boots."

Sánchez flushed. Any mention of his father made him half sick with shame. One of the old triumvirate, a leader of the Movimiento Liberal, a national hero. Now what was he? A toady, a husk of a man, morose and silent, his job a mere sinecure. *El Feo,* an old, dry man, with his ugly jaw, despised by everyone.

Sánchez watched Alessandro draw the cork. He spoke, and his voice was bitter.

"How I wish he had died, little one! With Manón and your father. He would have meant something to me. But to crawl back on his belly. When they didn't shoot him—after his trial, you know—I had a crazy idea that I would shoot him myself. I spent months trying to find out how to get at him."

"You were in Panama then?"

"Yes. The best I could do was to get a sketch of the prison. He wrote to me. I never answered his letters. All he kept doing was trying to justify himself. About saving me. Saving you, too. He really

241

meant himself. But that's what he lost. Like in the Bible. What does it profit a man if he gains the whole world and loses his soul? Something like that. He was a revolutionary and then went over to Vizarra. He lost his soul, all right. How I hated him! Now he just makes me sick. It is a terrible thing to have a father who is a coward, a weakling. He claimed they drugged him at his trial, but that's no excuse."

"I remember the story. They put stuff in his food."

"That's what he claimed. There was something bad in his heart, *jovencito,* something weak, rotten. Just to think about him brings a bad taste to my mouth."

"Carlos, that was a long time ago. Let's talk about something else."

"No, no. You talk a lot of foolishness about women. Now it's my turn. My father. A man of no honor. No honor. A father with no honor dishonors his sons. The others went to the wall shouting party slogans and singing, with no blindfolds on their eyes, their hands raised in the old salute. I heard they shouted and sang so that you could hear them beyond the prison walls. The people stopped in the streets to listen, and the women crossed themselves and prayed while the tears ran down their faces. And what was my father doing? In a courtroom, babbling like a child, confessing, recanting, taking back every word he wrote or spoke. What does he do now? He checks the lists the secret police give him. Schoolteachers who will be loyal to the regime. The *sinverguenza!* The shameless one!"

Alessandro carried his glass to a chair and sat down, carefully, so as not to spill the brandy. He chewed his lip thoughtfully.

"My old man was a fanatic, Carlos. Yours wasn't. He had a breaking point. Only the fanatic is safe from himself and from others. He doesn't care if he lives or not. Maybe he'd even prefer to die. But the average man, well, he can be afraid, that's all. He doesn't want to die. Life is more important to him than any idea."

"I suppose that's right. When I think of your old man, I think of him laughing. He laughed all the time. Laughing or shouting. My father talked. God, how he talked. Always with his pipe in his mouth, a dry, quick voice and puff-puff on his pipe. I envied you so. I wished all the time that Felipe was my father, not yours."

"Children think many things, mostly wrong or foolish."

"It's not wrong or foolish to admire strength. He was a real man. But *my* father!"

"He couldn't make himself a fanatic."

"You mean he had no real will. No balls."

"He wasn't like Felipe. My father had to have danger in his life. Always more and more danger. It was like a drug. He too terrible chances. Always proving to himself that he had courage. That's why he laughed a lot. A nervous reaction, I think. And he had to have my mother there, too. To make love to. After a raid he'd come back, laughing and joking, always joking about death. Then he'd eat and drink and take her. He had to do that, too. All to prove he was alive, that he had nearly been killed again but not quite. Then the next day he was washed out. He'd just lie around while your old man talked to him. Some pair, eh? Drink, man."

"To what? The sins of the father visited on the son?"

"That's no toast. That's a curse or a warning."

"Maybe it's because I'm afraid I'm too much like him."

"Don't be stupid, *amigo*. You're a worker, you are. I'm the talker. You see? Things have turned themselves around. Who else has worked as hard as you have? Only you could have done this. Any other man would have given up a long time ago."

"You mean I'm a fanatic, too."

Alessandro smiled sorrowfully and shook his head. He still held his glass, untasted, in his fingers.

"Forget what I said. I've talked a lot of nonsense tonight. You must be sick of me already."

"*Chico,* there is only one Alessandro. There are a thousand people like me. We can help you or we can hurt you, but we can't be like you."

Alessandro laughed, and the brandy spilled from his glass. Sánchez filled and drank again. Was it his third or fourth or fifth? He had no idea and didn't care.

"So much the better for both of us, I guess. We're like an old married couple. We know our differences, eh?"

"Your father used to say *Salud y reales,* remember?"

"Yes. 'Health and wealth.' And never had either. That last year in the mountains, why, he must have been wounded four or five times. How my mother endured it I don't know. She suffered, but it only seemed to make her more beautiful. At least I thought so."

"She *was* beautiful, *jovencito.* Dressed like a *vaquero,* too."

"Please, Carlos, I don't want to talk about her."

"I'm sorry. She was a saint, a real saint."

"To the Movement!"

"To the Movement."

"She was no saint, Carlos, believe me. I knew it and so did my father. It never bothered him, the horns she gave him to wear. I hated her for a while. A man looked at her, and she went into the bushes with him. Right up to the end. And you call her a saint. She was the best sort of woman for men like us, too. She didn't care, didn't give a damn. Only for my father. How she used to hang on him. Always touching him, fondling him, talking to him like a baby. And she was no girl, either. How old was she when they caught her? Thirty-seven, thirty-eight. She was an animal, always happy, always healthy. And always in heat."

Alessandro emptied his glass and made a face.

"Huh! I'll never get used to this stuff. A little wine is all right, but brandy—I take two and my face gets numb. You do all right, though."

Sánchez felt the words as a reproach. He snatched up the bottle and poured his glass full again. He filled Alessandro's glass, drank his own empty and filled it again. Alessandro cupped his face in his hand.

"Well, God forgives us. Men find it hard to forgive, but that is what God is. Love. Forgiveness and mercy. Man is a scrap of filth in an endless, pure ocean. Nothing a man does can pollute that sea of grace. And if it weren't for that, what would we have? All our actions would make no more sense than the activity of ants. Instinct, and nothing more. Without God, life would be the tireless scamper of ants in a dung heap. All energy but no dreams. That's no way for man to live. Look at my father."

"Look at mine."

"It's not quite the same, Carlos."

"You mean that mine is still alive. Yes, you're lucky that way."

"Man, let it go. Don't drink bad milk. You get used to the taste. Try to forgive. That's God's way."

"I gave that up. God means nothing to me. Just an empty word. If there's an ocean, like you say, well, it's an ocean. Science, evolution, natural development. Maybe the ants are better off than man. They don't know anything, so they can't be disappointed or ashamed."

"No, you must forgive. And trust, too. Trust is a form of forgiveness. You forgive in advance when you trust. Someone betrayed my father, told somebody in Vizarra's army where the hideout was. I have learned to forgive him, too. It's the only way."

"Do you forgive Vizarra, then, too?"

"It's not a question of that. Vizarra is a tyrant, a usurper. And he is not stupid. Far from it. Therefore he knows the consequences of his actions. He is aware that he has acted in an evil manner. He is a criminal, Carlos. Society is harmed by him, by his existence. He is that scrap of filth we shall throw into the ocean of God's grace. I feel nothing against him. Not as a man. But as an idea."

"But you will shoot him."

"Yes. Because that is logical. If he is left alive, he will continue to be evil. He has had thirteen years to change, to reform himself. He has merely hardened. He is like a crustacean; he lives in a shell. We must break the shell, kill what is inside and discard the creature. And those like him, too. That is our purpose. We are doing God's work. The good life, Carlos, is simply that. To work always for the control of evil. It can't be stamped out, but it must be struggled against. In this time and place I am a revolutionary, because that happens to be God's work in this time and place. In fifty years' time, in another country, I might be a priest, a teacher, a doctor struggling to find a cure for a disease—who knows? Fifty years ago I would have been a farmer, say. God's work is there, always there. It exists, like His mercy. Men are blind and so see neither. Half of life is growing up and learning this. The rest of life is living in accord with that awareness. You know, I think a little brandy helps, too. It loosens the imagination. Or the tongue, anyway."

Sánchez drank and filled his glass. He could feel the brandy in his blood. The sense of shame was dulled now. He felt happy, listening to Alessandro talk.

"My father never grew up, Carlos. Not really. Nor my mother. They never understood. Think about what I have said of them, and it's very clear. A man who loved danger and lived by it, and his wife who never thought, only felt. Two purely sensual beings. And in a way, I think they were pure. Uncorrupted, even innocent. But you and me. We are the sinners. We do God's work, but we sin. Always we sin. And that's why we must forgive. For we need the forgiveness of others."

"Ai-yah, that's true. So many people will suffer, little one, because of us."

Alessandro stood up. A false dawn was breaking above the snagged mountain peaks. The sanatorium was silent. A breeze rattled the window. Alessandro looked out into the half night, half dawn of the new day. He looked old, weary. He set down his empty glass. His voice was calm, matter-of-fact.

"Yes. And I will suffer, because of them. For them. That, too, is God's way. His Son, in that time and place, was a revolutionary too. That has strengthened me. What gave you the strength, Carlos, all these years?"

"Brandy. And the shame I felt because of my father. And you."

Alessandro shook his head. Tears stood in his eyes. He looked at Sánchez as though his heart was breaking. His voice was a whisper of dismay.

"That's not enough, Carlos, *not enough.*"

"It's all I have, little one."

"It's never too late to change. Never. The ocean, the pure sea."

"Alessandro, our fishermen, the men who sail out of Boca Perro, they never learn to swim. You know why? Because if they swim, it prolongs the agony of drowning. It gives a man false hope, the belief that he can save himself. Better to fall in the ocean and sink quickly into the depths. That's mercy, too."

"That is despair."

"No. Common sense. Another glass?"

"No. Not for me."

"Listen, Alessandro, it's too late for us. We won't have time to change. We are different. Let it be so. But we're in this together, to the end."

"Yes. To the end. Give me a little more. I will drink to that. To the end."

"To the end."

Alessandro rested his brow against the cool pane of glass. His eyes closed. His lips moved.

"May God forgive us all. We play at controlling our fate, but what are we to do? When we turn loose the force of revolt, it controls us. We only dream that we guide events. We sit on a glacier with an ice pick. The glacier slides because of the slope of the mountain. And it slides all the way to the sea."

Sánchez picked up the bottle and walked to the door. He looked back and then stepped out into the dim corridor and closed the door quietly.

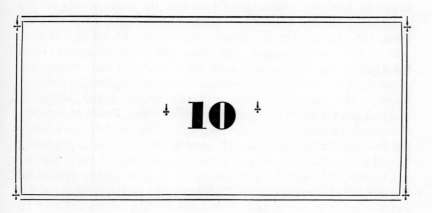

OFFICIALLY, the traditional fiesta in honor of Santa Rosa began at sunrise on Thursday with the celebration of Mass in the cathedral dedicated to her name and ended at midnight on Sunday with the celebration of Mass in the tiny, ancient church dedicated to the Virgin and built by Manuel Huelta the *conquistador*. Actually, the fiesta commenced with the parade which passed from the slum suburb of Miraflores through the market district, then along the waterfront and up the long, broad, palm-shaded boulevard to the Plaza Mayor. There, within the high grille which surrounded the palace, was the reviewing stand built every year by the carpenters of the Jacata district. The parade started shortly after three in the afternoon, when the heat of the day began to diminish, and dragged on until dusk. Then the Plaza Mayor became a vast dance hall, with music supplied by more than fifty bands and orchestras, each playing in turn until midnight, when the first rocket slithered up into the sky and cracked out a shower of sailing silver stars.

The archbishop arrived early, riding in the open carriage built for the first archbishop of the country one hundred and seventy-eight years earlier, a vast, creaking, uncomfortable boat shape with painted panels and fixtures, studs, medallions and figurines of gold and silver, drawn by four glossy bays. His Grace used the carriage only twice a year, at Easter and the fiesta in honor of the patron saint of Costa Plata. He climbed from the vehicle and sighed with relief. The footmen in blue livery frogged with silver folded the collapsible stairs quickly and shut the carriage door, then sprang to their places. The driver lifted his whip, and the bays moved off, leaning into the slathered harness. His Grace, sweating profusely in his heavy vestments, climbed quickly up to the shaded reviewing stand. Beads of perspiration stood on his long, lifeless upper lip. He mopped his face with a silk handkerchief and extended his hand to the first security guard who bowed to kiss the ring. As usual, the Caudillo and his party had not yet arrived. The archbishop extended his hand to all the guards and the uniformed members of the Red Beret. His Grace greeted the Red Beret officials by name, politely but coldly. The uniformed men responded in similar fashion. The archbishop's political views were well known. Tens of thousands of reales donated to his charities had not softened his opinion of the party. His Grace drew back his hand when the greetings were completed and turned his back to the guards. He waved slowly, steadily, to the crowd.

The Plaza Mayor was a great quadrangle surrounded on all four sides by the stiff, gray, grandiose buildings constructed by the Spanish government at ruinous expense during the eighteenth century and never fully occupied. The top floors of all the buildings were dusty, airless. Cobwebs netted the cracked and peeling walls, and rats flitted in the gloom, lashing up the dust and droppings. Each corner of the quadrangle was pierced by a great arch, sculptured and inscribed, second-rate stonework that had long ago fixed the pride of the constructors for all to look upon and envy.

The crowd was held back from the high iron grille by a barricade of sawhorses left by the Jacata carpenters and ropes contributed annually by the city cordwainers. The parade entered through the southwest arch, marched along that side of the quadrangle, turned left to pass before the palace and the reviewing stand, then straight on out through the northeast arch to end at last at the *plaza de toros*. Blue-and-silver bunting and pennons stirred languidly in the still-sultry air. Water sellers and vendors of paper fans and sunshades pushed through the crowd. Boys sold lemonade, *gaseosa* and beer. The crowd was quieter than usual; the archbishop had been greeted by only a patter of applause when he stepped from his carriage. He could hear the distant braying of a brass band, still far down the boulevard; the bearers of the great papier-mâché figure of Santa Rosa were toiling up the sloping street, setting their burden down every fifty feet or so, conserving their strength for the final triumphant circuit of the Plaza Mayor. The archbishop stopped waving. A guard showed him to his seat. His Grace thrust out his long, slack upper lip and sat pouting, a nervous habit he was unaware of, as he studied the crowd.

The sound of the band grew louder. He could distinguish the trumpets from the trombones, and the muggy breeze carried the high crish of the cymbals. The crowd stirred and then flowed like a wave toward the barricades facing the palace. The single, dense voice of the waiting throng grew stronger, richer, no longer a murmur but a low, sustained roar, neither approving nor angry, the carnival sound. The reviewing platform shook from the tread of heavy boots. The Caudillo's bodyguards had arrived. The archbishop stiffened his spine and stared straight ahead at the bunting-decked façade of the Ministry of Culture across the plaza. He knew too well the kind of men who surrounded Vizarra. They were not even citizens of the nation for the most part, but foreigners, hirelings and thugs from the slums of Buenos Aires, Rio and Mexico City, imported by that *Yanqui* O'Conner.

His Grace noticed a beautiful, slender coffee-colored girl with rich lips and splendid teeth. She stood at the barricade, staring boldly at a policeman who tried to flirt with her. Her hair, dressed with oil, shone like a helmet. Her breasts strained the flimsy, bright material of her blouse, and her hips swung to the music. The archbishop clucked, mildly scandalized. Such a tight dress. Still, she was young. And she was lovely, so lovely.

"Your Grace . . ."

The archbishop turned his head slightly, still watching the girl. It was the dark, sleek, ferret-faced aide, Malata. The archbishop extended his hand and felt dry lips brush his knuckles.

"No doubt Your Grace would grant the courtesy of receiving our foreign guests?"

249

The archbishop nodded. He had been informed daily, by various sources, of the activities of the American and the Englishman. Manfred Herzler was an old friend; His Grace frequently invited the humorless, precise German to dine and discuss archeology over brandy and cigars in the residence. But the American and the Englishman struck a sort of cold curiosity in his chest. Dunkel was a countryman of that gangster O'Conner, the brutal jailmaster. Somehow, illogically (for he knew very well that the act had been performed by a gang of young terrorists), he held both of these Yankees responsible for the assassination of another old friend, white-haired, scholarly Don Diego Colleo. When foreigners were not a nuisance, they were often dangerous. Moreover, very few were members of the Faith. The Englishman, although a perfect gentleman by all reports, was flawed to the archbishop's mind by the fact that he was an admitted Anglican, an inheritor of Henry the glutton's sect. His grace had not yet forgiven the English for their cruelty to Catherine of Aragon. On the other hand, he held that the Armada was a fool's conception from the first and that the English had been quite within their national rights to shatter the huge galleons in the sea battle long ago.

"Mr. Dunkel from America, Your Grace."

A big man in a white suit, smoking a cigar and trying to hide it behind his back like a schoolboy. A red, wet face. Thin brown hair shot with gray, a broad, good-humored smile and piercing blue eyes. He wore a diamond ring on the little finger of his left hand.

"Mr. Dunkel says that he has greatly admired the cathedral of Santa Rosa and looks forward to viewing the fiesta in her honor."

"Give him my thanks. Ask him if it is not true that the largest religious edifice in America is being constructed by a sect of polygamists."

Malata spoke in his dry, swift voice. The archbishop listened intently. He was considering taking up a course of study in English by means of exchanging letters in that language with his younger brother, a wine merchant in Lisbon. A strange, gasping tongue, indeed, no doubt suitable for shouting in the marketplace.

"He begs to correct Your Grace. The Cathedral of St. Patrick in New York is the largest he knows of."

"St. Patrick? Oh, yes, the Irishman with all the snakes."

Malata translated, and Dunkel boomed a laugh that startled the bodyguards. They looked around nervously, their fingers tapping their pistol holsters. The archbishop smiled, an odd flexing of his upper lip.

"What else does he say?"

"He says that his firm would like to make a donation for the maintenance of the orphanage he visited yesterday. If it would be acceptable to Your Grace."

"Tell him it is most acceptable and I give him my sincere thanks. The children will be instructed to remember him in their prayers."

Malata spoke, and the big American bowed and stepped back.

The English gentleman. Not tall, but seeming so. Very slender, in a beautiful pearl-gray suit, carrying a light silver-knobbed walking stick. Very fair, very youthful-looking, considering his age. A little strip of mustache. Perfectly at ease, no doubt from years of experience in pouring whiskey into florid, gaitered clerics after a morning of harrying foxes and watching them torn to death by rabid dogs.

"Mr. Livermore expresses his pleasure at making your acquaintance and is moved to extend his condolences."

"For what? Ah, Colleo, of course. Say that I thank him. His concern for our internal affairs is most gracious. Tell him that I have often climbed to my tower to observe his splendid ocean vessels entering and leaving the harbor."

While Malata translated, the archbishop studied the elegant figure before him, from the neat, small shoes with gray spats to the tips of his pink ears. The Englishman smiled and spoke slowly in a fluting tenor voice. An aristocrat, all good manners and fine clothes. Underneath a cold, implacable hatred of the Church. The English could be admired, even imitated, but never trusted.

"Mr. Livermore wonders if you would enjoy inspecting the vessel now in the harbor and then take a short trip out to sea. He places the vessel at your service and hopes that ecclesiastical duties will not prevent such a voyage tomorrow morning. He regrets deeply not having thought of this before and hastens to make amends. He hopes Your Grace can forgive his rudeness."

The archbishop wavered inwardly. The thought of visiting the liner *Silver Princess* and actually putting to sea aboard her was delightful and could, moreover, become the subject of his next letter to his brother. However, the threat of kidnaping, the Tower of London, the block and the ax, all shot across his mind. Like a flock of dark birds,

251

those thoughts vanished, leaving behind a sensation of faint discomfort. He was getting foolish in his old age. He nodded and smiled.

"I would be pleased to accept his invitation. I will arrive with my secretary, Monseñor Blanco, at nine o'clock tomorrow morning."

"If it is your wish, why not bring along the children? He, too, visited the orphanage yesterday."

"No, no. Oh, no. They will spoil the trip by falling overboard. I can promise that Monseñor Blanco and I will not so disgrace ourselves and inconvenience him by any such doings."

The Englishman smiled and looked frankly relieved. He stepped back, bowed deeply and smiled.

"Until tomorrow, he says."

"Fine. Excellent! Ah, Manfred! Come, sit down beside me here."

The German bent and kissed the archbishop's ring, then dropped into the chair to his right.

"It's hot, Your Grace."

"God gives the sun so that the crops may grow and the farmers prosper."

"God is too generous. His bounty is baking me alive."

Herzler squinted out at the crowd and fanned himself with one hand.

"I feel . . . something, Your Grace. Something is not right today. In the streets, coming here, I noticed it. A nervousness, but not of good feeling."

"Ah? You think so?"

"I feel it, really. A tension, like in the sky before a sudden storm. Last night they painted out those letters. This morning there are more of them than ever. The letter A."

"So I have been told. And the Cortes yesterday. Even though Vizarra himself addressed them in special session, they did not ratify the new agreement but delayed until after the fiesta. They gave very plausible excuses, but still . . ."

"Ja. Always they have acted at once when in special session. And the police. I have not seen so many since when I was last in Berlin and Munich. In 1919."

"But there have been no acts, Manfred."

"None that we have been told of. Since . . . you know . . . Colleo."

"I do not think that the person now in charge of the police will retain his position much longer."

The archbishop spoke in an even whisper; his upper lip did not move. He appeared to be watching the restless crowd and listening attentively to the approaching band. Malata bent to speak in his ear.

"His Excellency is coming."

The noise of the crowd swelled again, much louder. National flags appeared and jerked madly back and forth. The throng applauded and yelled. Herzler stood up, and the central part of the reviewing stand was cleared. The archbishop remained seated, watching a frantic little man brandish a red beret with one hand and give the party salute with the other.

The Caudillo, dressed in a splendid uniform, stalked quickly to the front of the reviewing stand and stood there in the wash of noise from the crowded plaza. He smiled, his heavy, handsome face turning from side to side. He raised both arms in salute. The sunlight sparkled on the decorations pinned to his breast. The archbishop observed him, the most interesting specimen of the military type in the entire country. His Grace felt a certain respect for Vizarra, although he hated to admit it. The man was stocky, sturdy, used to power and the applause of thousands. He had improved the country, too; it was only fair to admit it. He was more honest than any ruler the people had known and he had made work for them. These foreigners had yielded to his demands. Yes, it was really he who had dictated the terms of the new trade agreement. Somehow the Old Mule had found a way to break the grip the concessionaires had too long enjoyed. His shining riding boots bulged with his heavy, strong calves. His back was straight, his broad shoulders wide beneath the encrusted silver epaulets with the shining stars of a general. He grinned and saluted the party faithful again. He was Authority. He ruled them, taxed the rich as much as he dared and fed the poor. He had never once interfered with the Church.

He stood with his legs spread apart, one hand on his hip, the fist clenched, a posture now famous, even imitated by urchins arguing in the streets. He had admirers, but no friends and thousands of enemies. His chest swelled regularly; he seemed to suck in the applause, to feast on the cheers and blowing banners and the crash of the cavalry band as they came trotting through the archway, the sun

253

slashing off their silver breastplates and plumed helmets. He dropped his strong, stiff arms, and the kettledrummers whirled their painted sticks and thundered out a marching cadence. He executed an about-face and marched to his raised, plain wooden chair.

The mounted band on their splendid horses passed steadily through the high arch. A whistle shrilled, and the music blasted off the gray façades of the official buildings. Behind them rode the color guards. The national banner streamed above the lowered standards of old Spain, the regimental flag and the pure white pennon spotted with blood-red roses, the pennon of the patron saint. The band wheeled at the northwest corner. A stamping column of Red Beret youth spun silver cornets and blew the opening notes of the party marching song. Their blue flag with the scarlet cross rolled in the hot, muggy air. Behind them swarmed the masked figures, huge heads worn by staggering men. More banners and flags of youth groups sponsored by the national labor union, a band in army uniforms and a detachment in white from the *Guardacostas*. The cavalry clattered past, the riders frozen at salute. Then the Red Beret youth, their young spines stiffened, stamping their boots in exaggerated cadence, cornets held hard on their hips, their right arms trained like lances in the party salute, all the young faces serious, eyes shining with pride. The archbishop slowly shook his head. He looked across the plaza.

Clowns and maskers, smeared and costumed, capered and rushed at the crowd, flinging buckets of sawdust and confetti. Streamers shot and spiraled, flimsy tangles of color. Another band and then the Organización de la Juventud Católica in their white uniforms with blue piping and blue sashes, young boys carrying golden crucifixes, pictures and tableaux of the life of the saint. Then, out at the arch, the ponderous figure of Santa Rosa, white, scarlet and gold, twenty meters high with staring blue eyes, death-pale face, clumsy fingers clutching shut the blood-smeared robe, hiding the mutilated maiden's breasts, a crude, ugly, awe-inspiring monster of papier-mâché. The archbishop could see the famous "two hundred legs" flicker under the wooden platform on which the saint stood. A singing choir in purple robes and hoods urged on the bearers. They lifted their huge, rigid burden. The figure swayed and jerked forward, turning so that the fat, bloodless round face, smiling and capped with a crown of gold and twisted roses and thorns, faced the reviewing platform.

The crowd took up the anthem, composed more than a hundred

years before by Giraldini, choirmaster of the cathedral and the nation's most renowned artist. The figure thundered forward, the rumble of two hundred boots lost in the soaring harmony of the hymn. Then the great effigy stopped as the bearers rested, gasping, their shoulders aching from the cruel lifting-poles slung beneath the platform. They stood pressed together, shoulder to sweating shoulder in the gloom and heat. Perspiration ran into their eyes and they mopped their faces with sodden kerchiefs. The chief bearer (always one of the banking families in the city) coughed a command. The bearers bent and set their shoulders beneath the lifting-poles. At the next command they straightened, staggering beneath the weight. The figure jerked forward again as the bearers struggled to keep cadence to a drum. As the figure of the saint passed, the ranked police knelt and crossed themselves. As though the figure loosed a massive, invisible bolt, or swung a crystal scythe, the crowd fell as it passed; hundreds at a time fought and grappled to force room so they might kneel and make the sign of the cross. Behind the figure, like the tossed wake trailing a great ship, the crowd rushed and butted wildly. An ugly noise rumbled up, drowning the anthem. Maskers, bicycle riders and clowns tangled with running police. Some sort of drunken brawl had started. The archbishop frowned. Nearly every parade was marred by this sort of brandy-fumed disgrace. The figure lurched forward again. The crowd gasped and whistled and fights broke out. The police were seized from behind and pinned to their own barricade. Shouts and the sounds of colliding bodies reached the archbishop's ears. His long lip pouted sourly.

But now the police were actually battling the maskers and clowns. A milling group of some sort of demonstrators dodged and punched, then cringed away from the flailing clubs of the police. Whistles shrilled. The Red Beret youth about-faced and tried to march back along the parade route. The army band dropped their instruments and mashed into the young, white-clad O.J.C. Banners and pictures of the saint jerked and swung back and forth like metronomes, faster and faster. The voice of the crowd was a snarl, a belly roar that boomed off the buildings. The great, gaudy figure lurched forward like a juggernaut, butting the disorganized marchers out of the way, dashing them against the buildings and the barricade. The archbishop flinched when he saw two men disappear beneath the float. It slipped over them and they writhed and screamed in the sweating, straining darkness beneath the platform. Vizarra snapped an order, and his body-guards bounded over the railing, down into the crowd. The Red Beret youth tried to swarm over the barricade. The crowd refused to let them pass and hurled them back to the pavement. The boys began to use their silver cornets as clubs, swinging wildly into the ducking, shouting crowd. Malata stepped in front of Livermore, blocking the Englishman's view, and asked politely and at length if he cared for either lemonade or iced tea. Vizarra attempted a joke with the American, who obviously was not listening. A muscle in the Caudillo's cheek jerked.

The police made a sudden thrust into the marchers and scattered them for a moment. The archbishop and Herzler both leaned forward, the former unconsciously gripping the German's arm. Herzler pointed, sputtering. The archbishop's jaw dropped.

A group of kicking, wild-slugging young men battled the police on all four sides of a farm wagon. On the wagon stood a cheap pine coffin, strewn with black crêpe ribbons, resting on two sawhorses. To the sides of the wagon were nailed crude signs in black and scarlet: MARTYR OF POLICE BRUTALITY!, IS THIS THE FUTURE OF COSTA PLATAN YOUTH?, MUERTO POR LA PATRIA! JAIME GÓMEZ, SOLDIER OF FREEDOM'S ARMY! The wagon was drawn by a gray, knob-headed, ancient mule. To the animal's harness was pinned another sign: JEFE DE ESTADO, Chief of State. A policeman tore the sign off, the mule dropped its head and kicked, slamming the wagon shafts. Two students swarmed on the policeman and dragged him to the ground, but they were immediately set upon by a half-dozen club-swinging police.

The brief, brutal struggle went on in silence while the crowd roared like a storm at sea. Police reinforcements ran through the southwest arch, swinging clubs and lead-weighted capes to deflect knife thrusts. Four students on the tailgate of the wagon flung stones at them, and beer bottles sailed out of the crowd. The archbishop could see the fragments fly. Before the reviewing stand the parade collapsed into chaos, the members of the army band tangled hopelessly with the shrill, vicious little gangs of Red Beret youth and the O.J.C. The ponderous figure of Santa Rosa jerked forward a few feet and halted. An army unit poured through the southwest arch on the dead run, their bayonets shining. The clowns and maskers fled. Huge papier-mâché heads, abandoned by their wearers, rolled on the pavement, grotesque decapitations. The mule lunged from side to side, terrified by the police snatching at the harness. The wagon wheels scraped and sparked and the sawhorses trembled. The mule bolted forward, scattering the police, biting at them blindly. The rear sawhorse toppled, and the coffin slid toward the tailgate, rolled sideways, hung teetering on the corner of the wagon over the left rear wheel and crashed down into the street. The crowd shrieked as the lid snapped off and sailed a dozen feet, felling a policeman. The stiff, black-clad corpse rolled out of the shattered coffin and lay, hands folded, the ruined face covered with a gauze mask. Two figures tumbled off the wagon. Something bright spun in the air, then another. A double flash of flame on the pavement and sudden runnels of liquid fire shot across the street toward the barricade and under the wagon. The flames boomed into the sultry air. The frantic mule plunged into the barricade. The police staggered back, shielding their faces. The flaming gasoline, fluttering, almost colorless, flowed toward the great float of Santa Rosa.

The archbishop sat rigid with horror, unable to speak, his fingers crushing Herzler's arm. The flames, now in a long reptile's tongue, flicked beneath the platform, licking the feet of the bearers. The melting pavement bubbled, and pillows of dense, black, choking smoke rolled into the crowd. His Grace saw the tongue of flame slip out from under the front of the platform. The screaming mob surged back and forth. The soldiers battered with their gun butts. The southwest corner of the barricade broke, and the fighting, screaming mob spilled into the parade passage and began a trampling flight for the arch. A man, his shirt and trousers flaming, rolled out from under the platform, threshing and clawing at his back. Running figures hurtled in and out of the roiling smoke clouds. Vizarra bounded from his seat, roared and swung his arm. The foreigners were grabbed and half carried away. Flaming figures, dancing horribly, darted and staggered about the float. A wallop of flame burst through the blood-smeared robe, spraying fragments of papier-mâché into the crowd. Yellowish smoke poured out through the hole, and flames shot up. The fresh paint on the aged papier-mâché blistered and ran. The great, broad, death-pale face with its round fixed glare vanished behind a curtain of smoke and flame. The huge figure lurched once and settled to the left, hung there an instant and fell slowly, streaming fire and flaming bits, the clumsy, clutching hands dissolving, yellow smoke rippling out through the lattice of the inner structure. The ponderous, roaring mass crashed down into the screaming, scattering mob. Whirling hunks rebounded and soared like fiery bats, tumbled and jerked through the smoke and settled in searing plummets on the terror-stricken crowd. The flames reached the face of the figure; the cheeks charred, the smiling lips collapsed into a black hole spouting a tongue of fire, and the whole face vanished in a yellow hissing ball. The archbishop slid off his chair to his knees. Voices shouted, and the platform shook. He closed his eyes and prayed for the innocents trapped out there. A blast of oily smoke and scorched flesh swept around him. He gagged. Someone hauled him to his feet. He stumbled blindly, clasping and unclasping his hands. He could hear now the howl of the sirens, as the fire engines ground into the Plaza Mayor. The archbishop groaned and fumbled with his vestments. He jerked free and turned, staring into hell. He walked toward the closed gate, tears streaming down his face. He must get out there somehow! Surely there were priests in the crowd, but not enough of them to administer the last rites and conditional absolution. He broke into a clumsy run and bellowed in a croaking voice for the guards to open the gate. The grille yawned as the frightened guards yanked it open. The archbishop marched into the plaza, holding high before him the wooden crucifix that normally hung from his waist. His bright vestments vanished in the black, acrid smoke. The shrieks of the tormented rang in his ears above the seething rustle of the flaming effigy of Santa Rosa.

↓

The petal of flame bloomed on the fat cotton wick and the water bubbled in the pot, a cheerful, soft noise. The room, a bare wooden rectangle uncarpeted and sparsely furnished with crude chairs about a low, worn table, was cool, for the house stood in a grove of firs. Outside the wind soughed softly and drove through the open window the rich scent of resin. Fingel took up his glass and sipped the sweet tea. He smiled. This was good, as it should be, the three men drinking tea in such a room, while outside a soft wind blew, the air was cool, and all calm. He nodded; his voice was softened with pleasure so that it hardly seemed that he was speaking. The sight of long beards and dark caftans stirred memories he had thought lost forever. He spoke in Spanish—the modern idiom, not the antique Latinized tongue these men had inherited from their fugitive forebears, those Jews driven from Spain during the Inquisition. Only once before had he met such a sect, in a village in Bosnia before the Great War.

"One can live well here. Why is it that tea tastes better now?"

Bergman, the rabbi, bearded to the eyes, nibbled a bit of sugar. The others waited politely for him to speak.

"Friendship is sweeter than honey."

The others nodded and sighed. Fingel's eyes watered as he gazed around the simple room. A woman passed across the open doorway carrying a plucked, pale chicken for the evening meal. He waved one hand.

"And here is peace, too. Or do the others, the Christians—"

"Usually there is peace outside. Always there is peace inside."

The others did not seem so sure.

Fingel looked from face to face.

"Can one, you know, live? Here, I mean, just in the village."

Bergman shook his head and wiped his hands.

"No. You have seen our homes, our fields and flocks, the market. It is not enough. We are too few. We must trade outside. Woolen cloth that the women weave. Leather goods. Shoes. It has always been so. On market days some of us go by cart to the next pueblos. And for us there is a special license fee."

One of the others leaned forward and tapped Fingel's knee.

"An old regulation. An old injustice, but we endure it. Where others earn reales, we must be content with centavos. You, no doubt, have experienced this yourself."

Fingel felt himself flush. He sipped his tea and shook his head.

"No. I have, you see, a French passport."

"So? There are no Jews in France?"

"Of course, but . . . well, in business, in the cities, I don't . . . it's hard for me to say . . . I don't draw attention to myself. I don't point a finger at myself. You see me. I shave my face. I eat their food. I try to hide myself. But it has never worked. Never."

The others looked shocked. The rabbi clucked disapprovingly. Fingel stared at the floor. No one spoke for many minutes. The water bubbled softly, and the piny wind streamed through the window. Fingel could hear the voices of children playing between the houses.

The village was not on any map of Costa Plata. Fingel had found it with difficulty. On his first trip to Costa Plata he had heard of it, but learned only that there was a town of Jews on the southwestern frontier, somewhere in the pine forests. Finally he had located a ramshackle turpentine distillery, and a worker there had sent him by farmer's cart deep into the cool shelter of the woods. Near a small, clear river was the village, no more than forty wooden houses, raised on stilts because of the spring floods that dropped silt on the narrow fields torn from the undergrowth. Sheep grazed, and chickens scratched and bobbed. The village was surrounded by a palisade of pine logs set upright in the earth and chinked with clay-soaked moss. Blue smoke drifted up from the clay chimneys, and pigeons cooed and gurgled in coops. Children dressed in homespun cotton broke off their game of hide-and-seek to stare at him. Behind him the river rushed and foamed over black, shining rocks, and a watercart drawn by a burro creaked up the path toward the gate.

The rabbi gestured, encouraging Fingel to speak.

"You have come from the city. What happens of note there? What is the news?"

"There is trouble. A group of men wish to change the government. I think there will be fighting, killing, soon. Perhaps it has already begun."

The rabbi shrugged and nibbled another cube of sugar. Fingel cleared his throat. These men were not interested in the government.

"Well, trade is good and may get better."

"Ah? This is good, perhaps. What is the price of leather now?"

"I don't know."

"Of woolen cloth, handwoven, especially dyed?"

"I could find out and come back."

"Yet you have traveled, you say?"

"Yes, but in business, different business. I am not a merchant."

"Ah. Not a merchant."

"I have been one, but not now. I could be one again. It seems to me that direct sales in the city . . . the government encourages folk crafts, pottery, the making of jewelry and so on. Such goods are sold in special shops for good prices."

"Good prices? But there is the license fee."

"Perhaps not. I could find out. You see, folk crafts are special. You have been selling your woolen cloth and leather just for what they are."

"There is another way?"

"I think so. Perhaps. I will find out. I could arrange trade, take some samples with me."

The others exchanged wary glances and waited for the rabbi to speak. Bergman stirred at last.

260

"Another glass of tea?"

"Thank you, Rabbi, no."

"A piece of sugar?"

"No, thank you."

"It costs money to travel. The city is a great distance. I have never been there, of course. None of us have ever been there. Only to the nearest pueblos."

"Perhaps the buyers at the pueblos ship your goods to the city and receive more money. Perhaps they sell your goods at these special shops."

One of the others pulled his beard. His voice was scandalized.

"This could be done? Without the paying of the special fee?"

"I say that I think so. Perhaps. I could find out."

"I think that—"

Bergman looked steadily at Fingel and picked bits of sugar from his beard.

"How many days does it take to reach the city?"

"Two and one-half. Three days. By train, bus and cart."

"I have seen pictures of the steam engines. Surely such a machine is very dear to ride upon. Even a *peón* demands a centavo for each three kilometers. What is the price of such a journey?"

Fingel thought and finally counted on his fingers, slowly, so that the others would be more convinced by his answer.

"Nine reales, fifty."

"Huh!"

They all shook their heads. Such an expense was unheard of.

"And that is the cheapest. However, a man may take a certain amount of goods with him free of charge. If the goods take up too much room or weigh too much, then he must pay extra. How much are you paid by the meter for cloth?"

"Oh, fifty to sixty centavos."

"So little? For fine, handwoven wool? In the city you would get— oh . . . one real, seventy-five. Maybe a little more, depending on the quality."

The others stared politely at the bubbling teapot. Fingel sensed that they did not believe him.

"Of course, the less you make, the higher the price."

"Eh? How is this so?"

"Well, what costs more? Gold or sugar?"

261

"Gold, of course. Ah, I see, I see!"

"This cloth. Could I see some?"

"Why not? There is a loom house very near."

The men rose and left the room. Fingel followed, calculating in his head. They went to a low but airy building. Fingel nearly gasped with pleasure. Three women sat working a wooden loom the size of a motorcar. He had not seen such a loom since his childhood in a Polish village. The shuttle slipped back and forth, back and forth. The women stepped aside to permit Fingel to examine their work. He nearly whistled. The cloth was beautiful stuff, smooth, soft and glossy, tightly woven, a rich russet color. As he handled the cloth, he asked questions, eagerly but politely.

Yes, the wool was sheared, soaked in human urine in big earthenware pots, combed, carded and spun all by hand, then dyed by various infusions of herbs and berries, the color fixed so that it would not run when wet, then finally woven into bolts of fabric, either one or two meters wide and as long as the raw material permitted. There were two looms in the village. This was the two-meter loom.

"And the leather goods. Shoes, you said?"

They took him across the village to a square workshop that stank of the tanning vats. No one was there; the supply of leather had been exhausted, but thirty-one pairs of shoes—low-cuffed boots, really—stood on a shelf. The scraps had been fashioned into belts with a wooden toggle device instead of the traditional Costa Plata silver buckle. The rabbi showed him two dozen hand-tooled knife scabbards for machetes, popular with the foremen and gang leaders on the sugarcane plantations. Fingel asked about prices. Very low, hardly worth making when one considered the work involved.

Fingel began to talk earnestly, but slowly. He did not wish to frighten them. But something glowed in him like a lamp. The men returned to the house. Others were waiting there for them; they, too, wanted to see and hear this man from the city. Fingel soon found himself seated on a stool. The men squatted along the walls, smoking and sipping tea. Fingel told them what they wanted to know. How many people lived in the city? What were their houses like? Was it true that all people could ride on the steam trains? How much did a half kilo of sugar cost? A barrel of flour?

Fingel, stimulated by three more glasses of tea, saw before him, like a dream, his life, the life that he wanted at last. Why, the loom house stood close to the river. If they built a waterwheel, they could power the loom. He knew nothing of how such things were done, but somewhere he would find a carpenter on a big *finca,* offer him wages and travel expenses. It could be done. Yes, it could be done!

He felt like a merchant of the old days. The tinkle of mule bells, a caravan of burros to the railroad line or to the bus. He would take the goods, apply for a handicraft permit and sell to the specialty shops. What splendid capes the wool would make! Deep russet, a green deep as the living needles of the trees that sang in the cool dusk, a black glossy as polished ebony and nearly waterproof as well. The low boots and wooden-toggled belts. If the heels were raised slightly on the boots, the *vaqueros* out in the *campo,* vain dandies every one of them, why, they would snap them up! More leather could be bought from the nearest pueblos. Was the license fee for selling only, the old law? Or for purchases, too? Only for selling. Good, good! Fingel raised his finger.

"I will pay, myself, right now, seventy-five centavos a meter for the wool."

"Seventy-five. But before you said one real, seventy-five."

"True, friend. But that is in the city. When the wool is off the sheep's back, it cannot walk there. It must be carried. This takes money. And time. And it takes someone who knows the way. Someone who can find the right sort of buyers."

He had them there, and all knew it. They turned their heads to the rabbi. Bergman flung a handful of twigs into the fire that now burned, filling the room with an orange, flickering light.

"One real, seventy-five? But only seventy-five for the wool. One real for the carrying and the knowledge. But the burros and the trains carry. One real is a great deal to pay for a few names."

"Eighty centavos, then. Not one more. I would be ruined."

"If, on the next market day, the wool was taken to the pueblos and the buyers then told that another buyer offered eighty, and the goods were sold there for eighty, then, less the fee, the price to us would be seventy-five. I do not say this would be done. But it could happen. People will talk, especially on market days."

"Eighty-five."

"The same thing might happen. Who can tell?"

Fingel bargained carefully, shaving back the price on leather for every centavo he went up on the woolens. At last he struck hands with the rabbi three times, pen and paper were brought and a box of sand. Bergman drew up the agreement. The papers in Hebrew and Spanish were read aloud in both languages, and the men of the village voted to accept ninety centavos a square meter for one-meter goods, one real for a meter length of the two-meter fabric. The leather goods were fixed by a sliding scale, with a minimum price and higher prices if Fingel disposed of all the boots, belts and scabbards. Fingel guaranteed to present written receipts of all sales, to pay cash in advance and assume all responsibilities of shipment, damage and loss. The villagers were cautious; they turned over to Fingel only one-half of the leather goods and one-third of the fabric. If he failed them in any way, they had the rest to sell in the pueblos, as they had done for years. Sweet cakes and wine were served to seal the agreement. Fingel nearly danced with delight. He paid out the money. The rabbi convinced the others, after much discussion, that the paper bills were worth the same as the silver coins. The money lay in a heap on the table. The men and women of the village stole up to look at it, their faces rapt. They had never seen so much money in one place at one time. Fingel had increased the average year's revenue of the village by nearly thirty per cent . . . and in a single day and night of bargaining! The men drew lots for the honor of carrying the goods twenty kilometers to the village where the battered, charcoal-powered bus made its last stop.

Fingel lay in the bed in the rabbi's loft. He was exhausted, but happier than he had been in years, truly happy. He had what he wanted now, his life. Just his life. He would travel back and forth, buying and selling. The agreement was good for a whole year; that meant he would handle two separate shipments. With any kind of luck he would realize a fifty per cent profit on both trips. After the first year he would bargain for the entire output of the village and offer a higher price. It was true, it would be quite a few years before he became even moderately wealthy, but he would be comfortable. And he would live here in this simple wooden village beneath the sweet, singing pines. He would again eat according to the laws, worship and study with Bergman. And he would marry. In one year's time he would take a wife. He giggled happily, delight like froth in his nose. What a bargaining session that would be! So many goats, sheep, meters of wool. Not a silly young girl, of course, but not a woman too old either. Of childbearing age by necessity, for both the villagers and he himself would need the son of Herman Fingel to carry on the business. God had been good to him, far beyond his worth. His life, his life.

From where he lay, he could see a single star through the open slot that served as a window at the far end of the loft. He looked at it, drowsy now, his lids flickering. The star was where it was, so still, so bright and cold, yet it was really a flaming mass whirling along through space. How could a man find his little life in such a world where great things like stars were not what they seemed to be? The star seemed to twinkle, as though laughing at him. Could he really find himself among a village of exiled Jews clinging stubbornly to the old ways? Was not his place within the cities of the world instead of a single walled village hidden in a pine forest? But he could go back and forth. He could live in two worlds, with a city apartment and a motorcar, with a wooden house like this and a burro cart. He could be like the star, two things at once, because God willed it, and he himself had worked it. How odd to suddenly know that his life was not a single unit but composed of parts and places and people all mixed together! But he had found the pattern of it at last. God had granted him the good fortune to see at last the pattern. And how long he had waited! It went to show that a man must be patient, for all went together—the Polish police, the Bavarian soldiers he had fought with in France, the senseless, frightened women and children milling in the streets of Berlin and Munich, the bored, pockmarked bureaucrats in France and Belgium, border guards and merchants in Bosnia, which later, somehow—a miracle like the star—had become Yugoslavia, the smelly ships, plunging trains and slow oxcarts, the worthless marks, the francs, lire, pounds sterling that had passed through his hands in many cities, even the feeling that he must run, that he had to run before they started to chase him—all went together, all had served to bring him to this small troubled country, to this tiny, tranquil village, to this bed. The star spun and shivered, then dwindled into darkness. Fingel's head rolled on the mattress, and he began to snore.

⸸

The telephone began to ring at the sanatorium before the firemen had extinguished the flames in the Plaza Mayor. Seventeen times the telephone rang, and Sánchez and Alessandro listened and spoke, both jotting notes on bits of paper. Finally Alessandro ordered the switchboard to accept no more calls, and he and Sánchez locked the office doors. Alessandro walked up and down, stopping each time at the desk to rap his knuckles on it. At first he had been alarmed, then furious. Now he seemed calm, deliberate. He turned to Sánchez, who had been waiting patiently, smoking a cigar.

"Well, they've done it."

"*Claro*. We must make a new plan of action."

"Not a new plan. We must accelerate the old one. Gasoline bombs. What gave Olmega the idea to take them on the wagon, inside the coffin?"

"He killed Colleo. I suppose now he thinks he can do anything and get away with it. He must be called before the Central Committee, of course. He had no authority to provoke a full-scale riot, merely to create an incident and then escape."

"Well, he did get away. Or at least they haven't caught him yet."

"I'll catch him, little one, and by God, I'll twist his ears! What if they had caught him? What if O'Conner worked him over? He'd talk. Christ, he'd *talk!* He'd tell everything . . . the trains, the occupation of the university, the power plants, the carts coming into the city with the guns, everything!"

"No. I don't think so. Not that one. I've seen it happen before. They'd kill him, but he wouldn't say a word."

"Maybe not Pepe. But there are others."

"Yes, and several are going to get caught. And beaten. And they *will* talk. The brave ones will lie, of course, and that will cloud the whole business. Then O'Conner will have to decide which story to believe. I think he will try to figure it out by himself. After all, he must be about one step away from being thrown out on his rear. He's been looking for the two of us for months. Yes, rather than send two or three stories to Vizarra at once, he'll puzzle out one that is consistent. That gives us hours, maybe a whole day, before they act. But we can't count on it, Carlos. He may be so worried that he'll turn whatever he finds out over to Vizarra at once. Then he can't be held responsible for any mistakes. And Vizarra will act at once. It's too bad—"

"What's *too bad?* My God, the whole business has fallen on our heads and you stand there and say it's too bad."

Alessandro picked up a piece of paper and stared at it, then shook his head.

266

"No, it can't be done. We'll need them. No, I was just thinking that it would be better for us all, for the movement, if Olmega could find and liquidate the rest of Black Cadre before they get caught."

"You mean just shoot them?"

"Of course. It would be a pity, but we'd be safe for another day."

"They're only kids, Alessandro. Jaime Gómez was bad enough."

"The age of a revolutionary means nothing. You can be a revolutionary at the age of eight. The point is that we are going to need those kids. They're going to help get the trains out to Miraflores and then take the university."

"Tomorrow?"

"We accelerate. They take the trains out tonight. And occupy the university tonight."

"What about the general strike?"

"Cancel it. Cancel all previous orders. The capital is in a turmoil, but for some reason Vizarra has ordered the fireworks display as usual—you heard them say that. As soon as the Plaza Mayor was cleaned up, they began preparations. That's very good."

"I suppose the Old Mule is still stuck with those foreigners. He has to do something. To explain away what happened. Excessive enthusiasm, religious fervor or something."

"Yes, also the fiesta has to proceed as planned. He'd only make matters worse if he canceled anything. The kids said they ran the bulls this afternoon, and the plaza was jammed."

"And the crowd whistled at the matadors, the bulls, and picked fights with each other. They're in the mood for it."

"And so we accelerate. All plans and orders effective at 1200 hours tomorrow must be rewritten for 2400 hours."

"What about Rota? What about that fat little bastard and his boys from the U.T.?"

"We have no choice. We don't have the time to hold a general strike. That's not until Monday. We'll lose the city mob if we wait that long. They'll all be too drunk, too tired, too hung-over. We're going to distribute arms to the U.T. and put them in the streets. Let them shoot the city up."

"But you said only this morning that the U.T. was to be used only to force the strike!"

"Carlos, don't be stupid. That was this morning. Everything has changed."

"So we accelerate. Accelerate, accelerate. Christ, who's going to lead the U.T? Not Rota. Voget and the Belgians?"

"Why not? They'll get on. Rota is frightened of Voget. You know, a petty bourgeois face to face with a thug under direct orders from the Comintern? Voget will run the show while Rota signs the papers."

"It's dangerous, *jovencito*. Christ, it makes my pants wet to think of it. Voget with all those workers!"

"For one day only. I'm going in tomorrow. Give Voget orders to begin street fighting with three cadres and take the other two to the power plant. At midnight the lights go out. We've got nearly two hundred people to get into the city, and they've got to go in before daybreak tomorrow."

"Why so fast? They'll get confused."

"Because Vizarra will seal off the city to prevent reinforcements. A city mob is one thing; armed shock brigades are another. Tomorrow they'll start stringing the barbed wire. So that's it."

Sánchez puffed on his cigar and frowned. He was worried.

"That damned Belgian. He'll grab power from Rota."

"He'll try, naturally. I think he'll succeed. Even in one day, twenty-four hours, he'll have the Reds in the U.T. behind him. He must know who they are, anyway. Rota is stupid enough to tell him if he doesn't."

"So now we play with the Bolsheviks. I suppose there's no other way."

"Leave Voget to me. His orders will give him authority for twenty-four hours. Then I replace him. We accelerate Saturday's planned attack on the ordnance depot to tomorrow night. Voget will lead that."

"Not with the U.T.! You're not going to give them artillery!"

"No. He'll lead the three cadres from the waterfront, the sailors and longshoremen. I'll take the U.T. brigade with me."

"And where will you be? Dining with the archbishop?"

"No. With General Vola. I've got to find out what he and Ramos are up to. They must have agreed to something. I can find out from Vola."

"*Claro*. And so easy, too. You just walk into army headquarters and say 'Excuse me, please, General, but I'm Alessandro and I think you ought to bring the army in with us because, you see, we're going to overthrow the government.' Just like that. You'll get killed by the sentries outside the gates, little one."

"I don't think so."

"You don't think so."

"It has to be done. We can't hold the city with the men we've got, recruit and arm the people all at the same time. We don't have the weapons. We've *got* to bring in the army. Even if they do nothing against us, they will help. Voget takes and I invite, both at the same time."

"Ah, Christ, what a mess! And all because that little bastard Olmega takes two gasoline bombs to the parade of Santa Rosa."

"You'll stay here, of course."

"It looks like I'll have to. Three—no, four—members of the Central Committee will be in the city. Ah, well, I always wanted a nice, quiet office job, answering the telephone and feeling up the secretaries. Don't look at me like that. I was just joking."

"Save the jokes. Call the Central Committee right now, what's left of it. Accelerate all orders. And suspend Olmega."

"With pleasure! With love!"

"We'll promote him to shock brigade commander. Set him over the Green, Blue and White Cadres as well as the Black. He can recruit in the west end of the city. We'll use him as a wheelhorse tomorrow. Somebody's got to pull the wagon when the driver gets off to take a piss."

"That's true. With Voget in the suburbs and you visiting Vola. Do you suppose Olmega will have the strength tomorrow about 1800 hours for an attack?"

"More likely a counterattack. He'll have to hit police stations all day tomorrow. It all depends on what he's got left and what his cadres have recruited. Which is the best one for recruiting?"

"Green. Definitely the Green. Intellectuals, a few professors."

"You distinguish between the two?"

Sánchez stubbed out his cigar and stood up, his thumbs hooked in his belt.

"Ever since my old man took over the Ministry of Education. But the professors will bring in the students. And we'll need them."

"Carlos, order me a truck. I'll go down to the southwest somewhere and come into the city on that little bus line. They won't be watching that end of the city. I can cut through the San Pablo district to the university and join with Olmega, then switch with Voget at the U.T. building."

"How? That's nearly three kilometers right through the center of the city."

"There's a main sewer, *amigo*. I looked it up yesterday on a map of the city. That little man with the beard you saw me talking to is a sanitation engineer."

"Splendid! Let's put him on the Central Committee. I'll need someone who's used to getting rid of tons of shit."

↓

By nightfall a wooden platform for dancing had been built over the melted pavement to hide the effects of the fire. The Plaza Mayor had been washed down with hoses, scrubbed and sprinkled with sand, but the smell of charred wood, ashes and petroleum smoke still clung to the pavement and the buildings. Near the arches the guitars bummed and skittered, and the flamenco dancers whirled, their heels pounding, castanets churring, arms, hair and ruffled costumes tossing in the light from the streetlamps. Up on the bandstand an orchestra blared a tango. Searchlights mounted on the trucks of the city fire department swept across the building façades. A blackened piece of bunting rose and fell. A snake column of men and women coiled through the shifting crowd, chanting, the dancers drunk and howling incoherently. One victim of a knife fight had already been carried away, clutching his belly, his face shock-white. Children ran and screamed, waving tiny national flags. Gay balloons lifted slowly, hung in the searchlight shafts and drifted up and off into the darkness. Grim-faced police stalked back and forth, back and forth, watching. A gang of boys began to torment a dog with a broken leg, pelting it with stones. A woman turned around, hissing like a snake, and struck the man standing behind her in the face. Seven men in red berets, with arms linked, slammed through the crowd, roaring their party song, daring anyone to stop them. Dozens of whores idled under the archways. Costumed figures whirled and dipped on the dance floor. A triple rank of police surrounded the area where the fireworks were stored. Two little girls whirled themselves giddy and collapsed, shrieking with laughter. A gang of students in their medieval robes marched with a banner, swinging it slowly from side to side as they moved with long gliding steps to the tune of an old serenade.

The first rocket whished up and boomed. Stars gushed across the sky and the crowd ohed. A triple aerial salute, three rockets at once, each exploding three times, deafening cracks that shivered the windows on the official buildings. A dozen bands played at once, and the crowd boiled and swirled, laughing, singing, dancing. Pickpockets slipped here and there, watching for an upturned face and an open jacket.

A limousine, one of the official black Daimlers, crept through the police cordon and halted before the grilled gate of the palace. The two guards in dress uniform, standing at parade rest, stiffened and saluted across their rifles. A short, powerfully built man stepped from the sedan.

Colonel Lucca snapped two bits of ash from his tunic before returning the salute. The sedan drove through the gate and halted, the lights off, but the engine still running softly. Colonel Lucca plucked a cigarette from his breast pocket, fussed with it for a few seconds and struck a match. He stared out at the crowd, squinting slightly. The rockets slithered up and slammed out stars. Raw, brassy music echoed off the buildings. Colonel Lucca could feel in his chest the concussion of the big rockets. He noticed the guard nearest him shift and sway.

"Wish you were out there getting drunk and chasing the girls, Corporal?"

"My duty is here, Colonel."

"But you will be off duty soon, no?"

The man grinned and his loose helmet, too big for his head, tilted forward until the brim nearly touched his wide Negroid nose.

"Yes, sir!"

"A good night for the fiesta. Clear sky."

"Yes, sir."

"How is the crowd behaving?"

"Just starting to get rough, sir."

"And you can hardly wait to join them, eh?"

"Yes, sir!"

Lucca puffed on his cigarette and scowled.

"You're an idiot, Corporal, do you know that?"

"Yes, sir."

"No, you don't. You're such an idiot that you don't know you are one. A soldier, and yet you can think of nothing better than running with a mob made up of idiots just like yourself. The twin products of Costa Plata: silver and idiots. In equal amounts. Too bad no one wants to buy our idiots."

"Yes, sir."

271

"Do you understand me?"

"No, sir."

"That's what I thought. Take off your helmet and adjust the lining. Who do you think you are, Don Quixote with a barber's basin?"

"I don't even know him, sir."

Lucca turned on his heel and strode up the gravel drive to where the officer of the day waited in the guard hut. They exchanged salutes; Lucca gave his name and was checked in on the security list.

"What is the hour, *Teniente?*"

"2340, sir."

"I did not believe that I was late."

"The display was begun a half hour earlier than usual, sir."

"Mmm."

Colonel Lucca nodded and left the guard hut, strode up the gravel drive, then climbed the wide, stone stairs to the promenade. He sat on the balustrade, smoking, swinging his right foot and muttering disgustedly. Great Roman candles blew spinning globes of colored fire up into the night. Catherine wheels hissed and whirled like pieces of machinery out of control. Rockets smashed off the dark canopy of the night, and the crowd screamed and applauded.

"Look at them. Drinking themselves blind and playing in the streets like children. The expense of it—thousands gone up in smoke and noise. Why not just take the money out and burn it? What a waste! And already half of them have forgotten what happened this afternoon. This is sacrilege, nothing less. In honor of Santa Rosa music splits your ears, children are burned up by fireworks and trampled underfoot, café owners swindle their drunken customers, and married women act like—"

Footsteps scraped behind him. Lucca spun, his hand tearing open his holster flap as a curse snapped through his mind for talking out loud.

"Who's there?"

A man in uniform, smoking a cigar and carrying a bottle and glasses, leaped out of the darkness as two rockets detonated overhead. He was younger than Lucca, bigger, and swayed in the glare unsteadily. Lucca grunted and pretended to be making some small but necessary adjustment to his holster.

"*Hola,* Colonel! Major Luis Zamal, just down from the mine. I struck it rich . . . in the palace wine cellar."

He sniggered at his own joke and edged forward, then sat down carefully on the balustrade. Lucca frowned. Zamal was by no means even an acquaintance. Although a Regular line officer, he had not graduated from the military college but had risen up from the ranks, much too fast. An investigation had proved certain irregularities, gifts of money for the most part, and Zamal had been posted to the mines, the most tedious duty in the army. Lucca's voice reminded him that neither friendship nor respect existed between them.

"What do you mean, sneaking about like this, eh? Didn't you read the orders issued this afternoon on maximum security?"

"Oh, yes. But *I'm* not nervous."

Zamal's voice was lazy, almost insolent.

A reprimand burned on Lucca's lips as the rocket glare again lit the bottle and the glasses. He checked himself. Zamal had stolen from the palace wine cellar . . . a nice scrap of bitter gossip to toss across the table at headquarters mess.

"I trust you are off duty, Zamal?"

"Finally. I came in on the late train to see the fun. You're escorting the foreigners to the ship, I hear."

"Yes."

"After this afternoon's business, it might turn out to be a delicate and responsible job."

Zamal was flattering him. How typical. Lucca lit a second cigarette from the stub of the first.

"I do not expect any difficulty whatever."

"I don't know. I don't like the way this crowd looks. I was at the railroad station. So much free *vino tinto* spilled that the place looks like a slaughterhouse."

"Perhaps so. That is the responsibility of the police. Not my affair at all."

"Tell me, Colonel, why is it that these foreign millionaires don't feel safe unless they've got an escort in full-dress uniform?"

The question seemed so senseless to Lucca that he said nothing. Zamal cleared his throat and held out the bottle.

"Here, Colonel, have some of this."

"No, thank you."

"The best champagne. I stole it myself."

"Hardly a thing to boast of, Major."

"Good stuff."

"Frankly, it makes me dizzy."

Zamal chuckled and shrugged, then blew out a fat cloud of smoke.

"But it's *supposed* to! Speaking of being dizzy, I heard General Vola put on a nice show. He came in on the first train with his staff. They've been on some sort of field exercise—"

"Mapping the terrain for the winter maneuvers, to be precise."

"As you say. But ordered back after the fire during the parade. You've heard about it?"

"No."

"He was drunk, of course, and fell out of the car, down the steps and rolled across the platform. Medals flying this way and that. Drunk as a pig, they said."

"Junior officers, I find, have a tendency to exaggerate wildly. I never listen to such tales and discourage them at mess."

"But everyone knows that Vola has been living on brandy ever since his troops were ordered to lay the tracks for the new southern line. You were there when the Caudillo put the hammer in his hand and said, 'General Vola, you have the high honor of being the first citizen of Costa Plata to drive a spike for the new railroad.' Ha! Vola heaved up the hammer and dropped it right on his foot! Remember?"

Lucca permitted himself a thin smile, recalling the roar of laughter from the crowd and the flush of shame that had flowed across the general's sweaty, peasant face. It had, indeed, been a comical sight. Zamal sniggered and poured himself a glass of champagne.

"I thought I'd piss in my pants. General Vola and his army of day laborers. Twenty thousand men sweating like niggers to lay railroad track. At the express command of the Caudillo. Between you and me, Vola holds a grudge. Seriously. You know how he is. I talked to . . . well, one of his staff last week. They were up at Casanueva, you know. When Vola gets drunker than usual, he rants about the shame of it, the dishonor. He's got it in his head that the army was made to lay the tracks to weaken their prestige among the people."

"He is quite wrong. It is obvious that the army has the only engineering corps. To employ civilian engineers would have been a foolish waste of money. It was a matter of economics, nothing more."

"Try to get Vola to see that. He hates you people in the National Guard, anyway. And with some reason, to be fair about it. Here I am, a garrison major, but I make seventy reales a month more than Vola, who's a full general."

"That is simply because the general is paying back loans from the government to settle his affairs."

"To pay his brandy bill, you mean."

"His affairs are his own. The railroad incident aside, Vola should devote his time to improving the army. Last year's maneuvers were a disgrace. Discipline is so poor that only half the men are fit for more than manual labor. This is strictly between ourselves, Major. I do not wish to be misquoted. There is more than enough friction between the Guards and the Regulars as it is."

Zamal sucked at his glass noisily.

"I was up on the roof earlier. Brand-new, aren't they?"

"The machine guns? Yes. Belgian manufacture. Thirty-caliber. Water-cooled."

"How are they integrated in your division? May I ask that?"

"Each company has been increased. Two machine guns per company, three men per weapon. One loader, one carries the tripod and water cans, the gunner carries the barrel. I have requisitioned burros, but haven't received them yet. I am considering mobile mounts, perhaps pony carts with light bicycle wheels."

Zamal whistled softly. His voice was envious.

"The best of everything. You expect to use these weapons?"

"During the winter maneuvers."

"Perhaps before then?"

"Why do you ask that?"

"Oh, it just strikes me as odd that your Guards division should receive the newest machine guns, while we Regulars are still equipped with those Hotchkiss machines."

"You forget that my division is the regular city garrison. Of the *Guards,* I mean."

"The Guards' city garrison was always light infantry, just like our Regulars garrison. It's an odd change, I must say."

"That does not concern you, Major."

"No? Well, one hears things."

"In the mountains one hears many things. Owls, rabbits, wild dogs."

"And the voices of men."

"No doubt."

"It's the voices of men that interest me most."

"And what do these voices say?"

"That Alessandro will lead the rising during the fiesta."

"This has been foreseen, Major. Believe me, there is no cause for alarm."

"But there is cause to place eight machine guns on the roof of the palace."

"The men need experience. No matter what the mountains whisper to you, Major, keep in mind that Alessandro is a young man with big ideas, a big mouth and no followers. Do you plan to swig all of that stuff?"

"Eh? No, no. Of course not, Colonel. Here."

Zamal carefully filled the second glass and handed it to Lucca, who nodded his thanks. Zamal puffed his cigar.

"He's a dirty little Red."

"He has been in Russia."

"Is it true that the French gave him a *Croix de Guerre?*"

"No. He was in France with false papers. Such a clever forgery that his regimental number was included. His regiment was called up. He was wounded at the Battle of the Marne. A second time somewhere else, near the end of the war. There is some talk that he helped start a mutiny that only General Pétain could quell. Concessions were made to the soldiers. The last time I visited France, I found the officers very reluctant to discuss the whole affair."

"I can imagine. A mutiny . . . that would be dangerous—terrible, in fact. Lack of discipline, of course. A mutiny could happen anywhere, couldn't it?"

"Theoretically, yes. Alessandro's battalion received a group citation for a successful assault, that's all. You see how stories are spread, distorted."

Lucca sipped his wine, savoring the sense of his superiority. Zamal was not much better than the guard at the gate. He believed what the mob believed, and even thought himself clever. A real idiot. Lucca tossed his cigarette away.

"One burst from my machine guns, and Alessandro will run back to his hole and hide."

"But then you'll have to find him. And young Carlos Sánchez, too. Like the old days. Martín and Sánchez. Do you suppose they've got a third man with them? O'Conner can't—"

"O'Conner is a civilian. Of course he failed. What has been needed is the application of military intelligence units. At college this was stressed. Insisted upon, I might say."

276

"It seems to me that any man with brains—"

"Regular military intelligence, trained in the academy and experienced. They would have found Alessandro months ago."

"Of course, O'Conner's a renegade Yankee. What can you expect?"

"I never expect efficiency from amateurs. Only a trained elite can—"

"But they need machine guns, your trained elite."

Lucca pointed down at the crowd in the Plaza Mayor. Music smeared through the tossing, flare-lit bodies. Rockets cracked blue and silver stars.

"That is why we have machine guns, Major. That down there. The mob. They always follow a young man with big ideas and a big mouth. They are incapable of understanding the automatic benefits of supervision by a self-disciplined, aristocratic inner circle that moves with quiet strength as a guardian force upholding the honor of the nation. If they cannot understand, then they must be shown. They can understand a machine gun."

"If you ask me—"

"I'm not. Alessandro is raising revolt and will surely attempt it. Very well. His father, to some misguided so-called liberals, was a martyr to the cause of mob anarchy. Therefore, pursuing the corrupted logic of the mob, the son is a hero. While General Vola's army was cracking rock and laying railroad ties, Vola himself ignorant of why he was so ordered, the mob, matching blockhead for blockhead, begins to laugh in the cafés. A public figure loses power or influence with every *chiste,* every joke. Vola's influence has shrunk like an orange left too long in the sun."

"Therefore the machine guns to the National Guard."

"We in the Guard, Major, represent permanence, stability, order, and self-discipline wrought on the anvil of superior, specific education by the hammer of will. Such a force naturally will check and overwhelm mob tendencies."

"Provided there are enough machine guns. . . . The old movement had a third man."

"A cheap imitation of a triumvirate. Debased Roman traditions, quite foreign to the natural process of evolution and selection that propels the gifted to the top and permits the second-rate to fall like water to their proper level. Manón Xaltalpa was an illiterate Indian with a Negro for a mother. He stole money and was shot by his disgusted followers. There's your Roman triumvirate for you. No, natural forces creating a natural aristocracy; that's the only way. I suggest that you read Darwin, Major. Although it is prohibited by the Church, I'm sure if you inquire at our headquarters mess, one of the junior officers will lend you a copy."

"Well, I see a good deal of this Ramos. The one up at the mines. If he joined with Alessandro . . . all those miners. They would match in numbers the northern garrison. We'd rip them to pieces, of course. My men are real fighters."

"Any civilized nation, Major, would have exterminated the mountain tribes years ago. They are all debased physical types with no social potential. The natural process is eliminating them slowly, so that it would be quite correct to aid nature. Moreover, their removal from the scene would solve the city problem of unemployment. The gutter rats that fill the slums down here would be provided with vigorous work at a pay rate commensurate with their abilities and group worth. I confess that I find myself distressed when I recall that General Vola was one of that type. Raised on a trash heap in the San Pablo section by some old sow of a woman who sold cucumbers in the marketplace."

"Curious that you should move, by such a natural process of logic, from Ramos to General Vola, Colonel."

"What do you mean by that? Ramos and Vola?"

"The general spent three days with Ramos. In a pueblo in the mountains. Officially, it was a combination of maneuvers and an expedition to discuss the construction of a dam. The mine, you know, uses a tremendous amount of water, and now there's talk of opening three new shafts."

"The government has an aqueduct now in the planning stages. Go on."

"Three days is a long time to talk about water, Colonel. Especially when everything is merely in the planning stage. A long time."

"The truth."

Lucca bit his lip. This was something he had not known. What did Zamal want?

"Have you reported this, Major?"

"Not yet. I haven't had the time. Of course, it may be nothing. Ramos and Vola. Better than Ramos and Alessandro. If that had been the case, I would have reported immediately."

"You see what I mean? The natural rise and fall. A drunkard and an ex-priest."

"Well, at least Ramos can read and write. That's more than General Vola can do."

Lucca silently accepted another glass of wine. His mind spun smoothly. Zamal wanted to bargain now. He was an opportunist, of course, endowed with some few abilities, perhaps, but essentially a follower. Incautious, too. If a handful of silver was slipped to the keeper of the wine cellar, a paper signed, another witness or two gathered and properly instructed, why, Zamal might be made to appear a thief on a grand scale, openly raiding the cellar and selling liquor illegally. Perhaps he already had done something like that. Where did a man like Zamal get the large sums that had figured so prominently in the investigation of his sudden promotion? Lucca drained his glass.

"Another little sip, Luis, please. I don't have to report for another half hour."

"Of course, of course. Here."

Lucca touched his lips to the cool, fizzing wine and accepted a light for a fresh cigarette. He no longer heard the noise that filled the plaza. He was blind to the rockets and the Catherine wheels. He nodded and half closed his eyes. His mind plunged smoothly along an accustomed track.

"The mob always chooses such admirable types to worship! A slum-bred drunkard, an unfrocked priest, or a cotton-witted reformer with a name like a king. What a country this has become, Luis! Half the wealth stolen from us by foreigners, the rest squandered on the thankless poor, the national army laboring like slaves and the mountains crawling with little, brown, dirty vermin. And the people, the mob, dance in the streets, on the very spot where anarchists and atheists wreck sacred objects and burn innocent civilians and escape, laughing, from the powerless police force mismanaged by a foreign criminal!"

Zamal nodded. He was half drunk and impressed by the clarity and vigor with which Colonel Lucca explained himself. To share in such a conversation man to man, on terms of brotherly equality, was, in a way, a tribute. Of course he had no evidence about the meeting between Ramos and Vola, but accusation by innuendo had brought

279

forth this burst of warm confidence. Although his voice was slightly slurred, Zamal spoke with firmness and dignity.

"Shameful, indeed! And it is obvious, as well, that the new trade agreement will perpetuate all these evils. Clearly it is the National Guard alone that keeps the country on its feet. Like a sick man, the nation needs strong friends. Sober friends. Friends who will strike down anarchy. I believe it will come to that. Do you, Colonel?"

"Yes. The people have been infected with the disease of socialism, that repugnant pseudo philosophy of college professors, rabble-rousers and dreamers. It chokes me to think of it. As if one could not see through their shallow schemes. Redistribution of wealth, indeed! An artificial policy running directly contrary to all the natural economic laws. Wealth is—"

"Yes, yes. But what's going to happen?"

"As I see it, everything depends on the National Guard. The Red Beret, just between ourselves, has atrophied. The glories of the old campaign have faded. Like . . . well, like roses, I suppose."

"Roses, yes. The perfect comparison."

"The national party has become a mere collection of bureaucrats, dry husks, wasting time and money. After a whiff of gunpowder disposes of these would-be revolutionaries—keeping always in mind the central role that will be played on the stage of history by the National Guard—we will be in a position to strongly recommend certain fundamental reforms to His Excellency, who, in turn, can hardly be expected to turn a deaf ear. Personally, I believe that a natural extension of those most efficient units of order and stability should be carried out at once. Since smaller units, elite groups, are more efficient, it would be within the natural tendency of selective superiority to reduce the national army to a militia force."

Zamal nearly gagged on his cigar. His face stiffened, and he nodded woodenly.

"By the same natural process, the duties and manfully supported responsibilities of the Guard would expand. Nature abhors a vacuum. I can hardly express to you the readiness—no, the eagerness—of the junior officers to seize up heavy burdens for the benefit of the people."

Zamal croaked, coughed, cleared his throat and nodded. My God! Reduce the army to a militia force! He might be thrown out on his rear, cashiered at half pay or put on permanent mountain patrol!

"That would be the best thing for the country. Clearly."

280

"Whatever happens, our group will work toward that end."

"But if the army is reduced and the Guard expands, capable and trustworthy army officers—"

"Will be considered as candidates for new openings. Most likely at slightly reduced rank."

"I see."

"A centralized administration would mean immense savings. The money might well be spent in developing the truly national, patriotic spirit of the young men of Costa Plata. New youth movements, extended military service, an expansion of the air force. Interceptors and bombing planes."

"Bombers? Yes, that would be . . . nice."

"An extension of the naval services. As a wing of the Guard. The Sea Guards, they might be called. Such a pity that the Germans are forbidden to manufacture submarines. Field guns, siege cannon. Well, these are our dreams, our long-range plans. I really must go. But still . . ."

"But still . . . ?"

Zamal, even though seated, swayed slowly from side to side. He tried to rise, thought better of it, and flung away his dead cigar.

"What a fortunate thing this has been, Colonel! Our little chat, I mean. You are absolutely correct. A rebirth of ideals! Projects for the future. The growth of national destiny! Expansion of the frontiers! New plans! For example, I have a wife and three daughters. Can you imagine it?"

Lucca could imagine it without any difficulty, a wife fat as a cattle tick with black down on her upper lip, and three blubber-rumped daughters with nappy hair and squinting eyes. He shook his head. Zamal was distressed, nearly weeping.

"Frankly, Colonel, a natural change such as you have so powerfully described would make things very difficult for me. Three daughters to marry off. Three dowries. I might be ruined."

"Well, perhaps these little financial problems will be taken care of by this business. Certainly the Regular forces will be unable to hold the *campo,* let's say. The Guard will be called upon to secure the area. Accidents happen. Property suddenly becomes available. If the *peones* rise, the landowners will suffer. This is natural, if regrettable. A year passes, perhaps two. A *finca*—a beef ranch, for example—could be picked up for the unpaid taxes. A fraction of the cost."

"But without capital—"

"Officers are more than leaders. They are brothers. In my own youth I had occasion to turn to my brothers for personal loans from time to time. How grateful I was, I could not express it. They pressed money on me. An agreement between brothers. You take my meaning?"

"Clearly, clearly! Listen, Colonel, we must drink to this! Ah, *mierda,* it's empty! Wait here. I'll get another bottle. I know right where it's kept."

"Perhaps some cigars, too?"

"Of course, of course, cigars!"

"If I'm not here, Major, you'll understand that the Caudillo has called for me."

"I'll wait for you!"

"A good idea, Luis."

Zamal rose, tottered backward, then plunged off across the flash-lit promenade, bent forward and swaying like a man caught out in a summer storm, battling a stiff wind and threatened by thunder and lightning bolts.

Lucca set down his glass and walked briskly down the steps, down the sloping drive to the wooden guard hut. The officer of the day touched his cap in salute.

"Teniente, call the military escort at once. What are your thoughts on the crowd outside?"

The young officer frowned.

"They're all drunk. I think there's going to be trouble. The riot vans were called out twenty minutes ago. They're parked southwest and southeast. Some sort of disturbance down near the university, too. It looks worse than I ever remember it, sir."

"Call Guard headquarters. Two trucks, twenty men each, northeast and northwest. Have them check with the Policía Armada, using my name, and offer support. At once."

"Yes, sir."

Lucca thought for an instant. The university. The students followed Alessandro, of course. So it had started already!

"Have you a radio set here, *Teniente?* Sending and receiving?"

"No, sir. But I could requisition one."

"An excellent idea. Do that. Carry on."

Lucca started to walk away, clicked his fingers as though he had just remembered something and strolled back to the hut. He smiled in comradely fashion at the young officer.

"One little thing, my boy. There seems to be a senior officer from the Regulars up on the promenade. He's been celebrating, shall we say? You know what champagne can do to a man's legs. It would not be pleasant were the Caudillo or his guests to see—"

"I'll take care of it immediately, sir!"

"But with discretion, my boy. Suggest another diversion for him. A gay nightclub, for instance, eh?"

"The Rex is nearby."

"You have an automobile and a driver?"

"I could put them at his disposal. A gesture of amity between the two national units."

Lucca smiled and slapped the young man on the shoulder.

"Precisely! You're quite the diplomat, my boy."

"I'll get him away, sir, don't you worry."

"I knew that I could count on you, *Teniente* . . . ah . . . ummm?"

"Romero, sir."

"Romero. Very good. To your duties, my boy."

Lucca returned the salute. *Romero, Third Battalion.* Smart as a whip. Useful someday. Perhaps soon.

Colonel Lucca turned left at the fork in the gravel drive and hurried to the side entrance of the palace. He could hear that fool Zamal singing, *singing,* up on the promenade. That was the Regular Army for you. No discipline whatever. And Zamal would talk. He was the kind that couldn't keep a secret. Anyone who came up from the ranks believed he owed some sort of debt to friendship and so fraternized with the junior officers instead of treating them with polite contempt. Without realizing it, Zamal would demoralize his own battalion. The rumor that the Regular Army was to be reduced in size would paralyze the anxious, feeble opportunists, the vulgar, corrupt flunkies who surrounded the drunken general. So much the better. The Regulars would bungle the job of suppressing the revolt. The Guard would be called up. Everything would depend on the Guard. The whole future of the nation! It was a matter of making this state of affairs unmistakably clear to His Excellency. An awkward business, since the Caudillo was the commandant of the National Guard as well as Supreme Commander of the Regular Army. On the other hand, the natural course of history, selective destiny, would allow Vizarra no choice. He would have to use the Guard or face a civil war. After the revolt had been crushed, His Excellency would discover that certain adjustments were in order.

Lucca touched the epaulet on his left shoulder. The single star of a brigadier general would replace his broad colonel's stripe. The natural process of selective superiority.

┼

The Caudillo was not a superstitious man, but he felt something, an uneasiness, a malaise. The terrible business of the fire in the plaza, the running tongues of gasoline, the screams of the burned men trapped beneath the ponderous effigy—the memory of those moments crept in his blood like a virus. He had ruled for thirteen years, and only today had he any reason to doubt his own ability, his own authority. But when those bombs had been thrown, and the gasoline had spread, licking runnels of pale fire, flowing with the irregular slope of the ancient paving in the Plaza Mayor—neither common sense nor power could halt that liquid horror. Stamp on it, and you only spread it. Stamp again and your leg caught fire. In the effort to extinguish it, it consumed you, searing the clothing, skin and hair, charring the flesh until it fell from the bones in blackened lumps. The thought of such a death made the Caudillo's scalp crawl.

Threats and promises, shifting and conflicting, filled Vizarra's mind. The students must be apprehended and publicly tried, then executed. He must attend the Requiem Mass for the victims of the outrage. Additional trucks must be added to the municipal fire department, sand trucks. The idiots had pumped water, and the white, stiff streams had merely propelled the flames deeper into the panicky crowd. The university must be closed indefinitely. A special fund would be needed to build another figure of the saint. But it was the gasoline, not the students, that had turned the plaza into a crematorium. Who could legislate against liquid fire, the slope of pavement?

Vizarra could feel the muscles in his cheeks. He had been smiling all day long. He shifted in his chair, tormented. His corset pinched the gathered flesh along his spine, and his gout had begun to pang, as though a nail were being tapped very slowly through the joints of the great toe of his right foot. Damn these formalities, damn the rich food, damn the foreigners, damn O'Conner, the students, damn Alessandro, gasoline, and damn the saint and her fiesta! Vizarra smiled and nodded to Malata, who gestured for the waiters to refill the glasses. Vizarra smiled and stared around the room, feeling ill, ill at ease, disgusted with everything and afraid of something all at once.

He hated the Grand Salon of the palace. Three years after taking power he had made a brief visit, incognito, to France. He had visited Versailles. The Hall of Mirrors there was the original, this Grand Salon a reduced, cheap and tasteless copy. The paintings, the gilt and glass, the furnishings were an insult. It was as though the Madrid government had said: *There, that's good enough for the Costa Platans. They will think it splendid, those backward provincials.* The whole room should be gutted, repainted and redecorated in the very latest, most expensive fashion. The Caudillo squinted, trying to visualize it. Pale, billowing flames spread before his eyes; dragon tongues of fire licked the walls. He jerked in shock and nearly spilled his glass of champagne.

Even though the bands still played in the plaza, the noise that penetrated into the palace was not the usual happy racket of uninhibited drunken fun. The crowd sounded like surf on a beach of boulders, steady, strong and menacing. At regular intervals, like the seventh (or was it the ninth?) wave, the noise swelled to a roar. Vizarra crossed his right leg over his left knee. His toe panged. He had heard many crowds, but never had they made such a strange, unsettling sound. Livermore seemed quite at ease . . . a pose, of course. Dunkel kept glancing at the windows as though he expected the tall sashes to implode from the pressure. Colored lights flickered on the dark panels of glass as the rockets and Roman candles rushed up from the plaza. The detonations of the rockets were damped, soft cuffs of sound, barely audible above the surf voice of the crowd standing out there, their shoes scraping the very pavement where some man or woman had fallen, insane with agony from the pallid kiss of fire tongues. They danced on scorched bits of clothing, black splinters of wood, ash flecks.

His hand trembled. He set the glass on a table and strode across the room, forcing himself not to limp, his teeth clamped against the pain that now seemed to burn his right foot. As though he had stepped in that damned gasoline!

"Mr. Dunkel. Mr. Livermore. Are you enjoying the pyrotechnic display? I think it is very good this year. The fireworks are a traditional part of the fiesta. There, you see? A fixed display. The national flag."

Dunkel rolled his glass between his palms and peered out of the window.

"Well, the folks out there are really whoopin' it up. Eat, drink and be merry."

"Whooping it? . . . Yes, exactly. The fiesta of Santa Rosa is something like your Mardi Gras in New Orleans, I believe."

"I couldn't say. We don't have anything like this in Chicago, though, that's for sure."

The American glanced out through the window again and drew a short, sniffing breath through his nose. Vizarra turned to the Englishman.

"Mr. Livermore, we in Costa Plata have a saying at a time of farewell. Not only *adiós,* but we say *'Go with God, and when will you return?'* "

The Englishman smiled politely.

"That depends, Your Excellency. I feared that my rather abrupt decision to depart would create such inconvenience that I would be a rather unwelcome visitor another time."

"Not at all. On the contrary, I assure you. Let us be quite open. Essentially we are men of business, no? In business certain things must be done at certain times. If one waits, delays, the opportunity is lost. I understand perfectly. I only wish that you could have stayed to witness the entire fiesta, but business before pleasure. We Costa Platans have still this to learn. Please consider that you are setting us here a good example."

"Your Excellency is the perfect host. I am grateful, believe me. This has been an informative as well as a relaxing visit. I have taken the liberty to extend my sincere apologies to His Grace, with my earnest wishes for a speedy recovery."

"The last reports were quite encouraging. Second-degree burns on the legs and feet."

"A lamentable accident. Unavoidable, surely."

Livermore's voice was bland, detached, quite as though gasoline normally ran through the streets, as though it happened regularly in Trafalgar Square. Vizarra shook his head slightly.

"On Monday the Cortes will approve the trade agreement. The Minister of the Interior will cable your London office."

286

"That is completely acceptable, Your Excellency."

"You are fond of sport, I know. We have a species of duck, blue teal. They cannot compare to your grouse, of course, but the season is quite long and the shooting generally good. In the salt marshes to the south. Perhaps this coming autumn you would honor us by a visit? Very informal, you know, just for the sport."

"You are extremely kind, Your Excellency. I hardly know, however, the state of affairs back in London. Usually the fall is a crowded time."

"I will write to you, if you like. Better to have things in writing, even an invitation to shoot ducks, no?"

"Very good of you, I'm sure."

"One thing I must insist upon."

"Your Excellency?"

"Why, Mr. Livermore, you actually looked concerned just then! No, only to take another glass of champagne with me."

"I should be delighted."

"Herr Herzler. Mr. Dunkel. Come, another glass. I deplore toasts, but tonight I will make a very little speech. Let us drink, as colleagues in a great and progressive enterprise, to the future. To the future!"

"Hear! Hear!"

Vizarra studied his hand as he raised his glass. Steady again. Good.

"You know, that is quite an untypical toast. For a Latin like myself, you understand. I have the greatest admiration for the vision, may I call it, of the America that lies to the north. Such a faith in the future. And England, too, of course. England occupies the present perfect, like a grammarian's tense. The balance between the past history of the nation and a concept of continued greatness. We here have a tendency to dwell in the past. Always we look back. The Spanish *conquistadores,* the viceroys, all still exist as though it were yesterday. We here think too much of the past, of sorrow and death. So how can this attitude be changed? By a stroke, a dramatic, bold movement. The government must pick the people up and fling them forward. Ninety-nine years, gentlemen! A century. But for the first time in the history of this nation a century that is to come, not one hundred years lost forever to be mourned. That is the real strength of our agreement. My people are so dazzled by the very boldness, the confidence expressed, that they hesitate. But only momentarily. The

Cortes will honor the agreement in full. This I can promise you. Believe me. I know them. Show me one child in the world who does not look forward to Christmas. Do you think of yourself as Santa Claus, Mr. Dunkel?"

"I'm afraid not, Your Excellency."

Livermore tasted his champagne.

"Children only believe in Saint Nicholas when they are young, Your Excellency."

"Saint Nicholas? Exactly. A saint, you see? My people are Catholics. They do not lose faith as they grow older, I assure you. They will soon believe that our trade agreement includes God as chairman of the board. Ah, the archbishop would be very annoyed with me for saying that. I shall have to confess it."

The others smiled politely. Livermore drained his glass.

"I find your words very reassuring, Your Excellency."

Vizarra nodded, no longer smiling. He set down his glass and rapped his fist against his left palm.

"And you will find the actions of this government very reassuring as well."

"I sincerely hope so."

"There will be absolute political stability in Costa Plata. Absolute!"

Something was wrong. The Caudillo jerked his head toward the window. The others turned with him. The crowd was silent. Why? Vizarra gazed out into the darkness. Thousands of them, all so quiet? What had happened?

A lurid glow spread through the Plaza Mayor. The huge fixed display fastened to the façade of the Ministry of Marine burst into white and scarlet fire. Ten meters tall, the figure of Santa Rosa hissed and smoked, bleeding flames. The crowd shrank away from her, moaning. The great paw raised in benediction puffed and died, leaving the arm stumped. The crown of gold and roses glared, fiercely burning. Sparks shot out of her eyes, and her smiling lips trembled, ember-scarlet. Vizarra stared in shock. Livermore sucked in a breath, and Dunkel cursed softly. Herzler crossed himself and closed his eyes. The figure burned on. The flaming traceries were extinguished irregularly, first the hand, then the lower robe, the left arm, until nothing was left but the round, scalding face, flaming eyes and smoking, smiling lips. The next instant the plaza blotted black, and red squiggles jerked on Vizarra's retinas. He crossed himself and turned away, wetting his lips.

"Julio! Who was responsible for this outrage?"

"Your Excellency, the displays were ordered months and months ago. No one could have foreseen . . . the parade . . . the figure of the saint. The fire in the plaza . . ."

Vizarra lunged forward, his right fist clenched, his whole body shaking with anger.

"You fool! You fool! All afternoon you had to take that damned thing down! It burned out there before everyone! Everyone! You let them build and burn a blasphemy!"

"Your Excellency . . . your guests!"

Vizarra caught himself. Malata sidled away, his face impassive. Vizarra turned just as Livermore finished murmuring to Dunkel.

". . . grotesque . . . barbarity . . ."

"Gentlemen, I beg your pardon."

For what? He could think of nothing to say. Livermore stepped forward, his hand extended. Vizarra grasped it, dumb, his face flushing. He hardly heard the Englishman's polite farewell. His pulses thudded in his ears as he shook the American's hand. Malata slipped between two chairs, followed by an officer of the National Guard in dress uniform.

The Caudillo took a limping step forward.

"Lucca! Colonel Lucca. Just in time!"

The officer's broad, flat face twitched once in surprise. He saluted and glanced at the foreigners.

"Now, Colonel, a glass of champagne before accompanying these gentlemen to their ship."

"No, thank you, Excellency. I never touch alcohol."

Vizarra jerked his head at the windows: *How is the crowd?* Lucca frowned: *Bad.* Vizarra nodded at the three foreigners: *Get them out of here at once.* He leaned forward slightly and muttered through clenched teeth.

"If anything happens to them, Colonel, I promise you . . ."

Lucca nodded once.

"Well, gentlemen, Colonel Lucca tells me that the sedans are waiting. I regret that this delightful evening has come to a close. But time and tide wait for no man, not even the president of a steamship company. I wish you a pleasant voyage, Mr. Livermore, Mr. Dunkel.

Do you shoot? No? A pity. Mr. Livermore and I have made tentative arrangements for a private little shooting party this fall. It would be a great pleasure . . ."

Vizarra propelled the three men toward the door, where Colonel Lucca stood waiting. With a smile again fixed on his lips, the Caudillo endured the prolonged farewells. The door finally closed, then opened again. Colonel Lucca exchanged a few sentences with Malata. Vizarra limped across the room to the windows and sat down heavily in a chair. The door slammed, and the Caudillo cursed. He leaned back and closed his eyes. That face, that burning face! Twice in a single day he had stared at eyes of flame!

He stood up and peered down at the gravel drive. Two limousines crept down the slope toward the gate. Motorcycle motors started up. Colonel Lucca ducked into the black Daimler. The sedans passed through the gates into the plaza and turned right. Vizarra groaned with relief as the red taillights vanished. The gate swung shut.

"Thank God! What did Lucca say, Julio?"

"There is some sort of disturbance out at the university. Also, he believes that General Vola is no longer loyal."

"How does he know?"

"The general spent three days with that man Ramos. The leader of the miners."

"What has O'Conner been doing? Nothing! He should have foreseen difficulties with that madman. Must I be forced to make every decision concerning the security of the nation? This Ramos person must be done away with. Some kind of accident. Soon. Better late than never. As for O'Conner . . . Lucca will arrest him and get rid of him. He is worthless."

Malata waited and said nothing. The Caudillo limped back to his chair, threw his right leg up on an embroidered stool and beckoned. Malata drew off Vizarra's gleaming boot. The Caudillo cracked his knuckles, glancing from time to time at the windows.

"First, Vola will spend three days anywhere with anyone who will drink with him. Second, he was on regularly scheduled maneuvers near the mines. Third, he was accompanied by a detachment of engineers. One, two, three. And fourth, Lucca is in the Guards. Fifth, Lucca is Lucca. What else did he say?"

"There seems to be a demonstration of some sort over at the university. The proper steps have been taken. Police, a group of Guards, will join them. Colonel Lucca will supervise."

"Colonel Lucca is very trustworthy, Julio."

"Yes, Excellency."

"He is very loyal, Julio."

"Yes, Excellency."

"He is *too* loyal, Julio."

"Yes, Excellency."

Vizarra sat up stiffly and stared at the wall. His mouth jerked at the right corner. Malata glided across the carpet and returned with a notebook and pen. Vizarra cleared his throat.

"The political prisoners released this afternoon are to be rearrested on charges of conspiracy. Direct order to O'Conner. Got that? Next, direct order to General Vola. The entire army is to be mobilized at once and put on emergency standby readiness. Light field dress, doubled ammunition, side arms for noncommissioned and commissioned officers. Heavy cavalry to patrol the city streets in units of ten. First and Fifth Divisions march into the *campo* and bivouac at the site of last winter's maneuvers. To maintain radio contact at all times and lay telephone wire. Got that?"

Malata's pen raced across the page. He nodded his sleek head without looking up.

"Direct order to Colonel Lucca at National Guard headquarters. The city is to be sealed off. Emergency procedure Number Two, but with doubled barbed wire. Personal letter to the provost of the university. Due to the recent provocations etc., etc.—put in undesirable elements, atmosphere directly opposed to that conducive to learning, you know how to say it—the university is to be closed until further notice. Any students or faculty members discovered participating in any way . . . be dismissed at once from the university."

"If the provost refuses, Excellency?"

"Good point. Have O'Conner make up a warrant for his arrest and hold it, just in case. Copy of the letter to old Sánchez at the Ministry of Education. Prepare an edict declaring martial law, but do not issue it to the newspapers. Issue nothing to the newspapers unless I give you direct orders."

"They're holding back the evening editions, Excellency, because of . . . what happened. They have submitted copy for approval."

"Call each in turn and simply say that the government will make a statement tomorrow morning, in time for the morning editions. No authority granted for the printing of an evening edition. What time is it?"

"Shortly after midnight, Excellency."

"All newspaper offices are to close at one o'clock, all workers to be sent home. The printing plants may open at eight tomorrow morning. I will receive a delegation from each of the three newspapers at nine. Downstairs in the Blue Room."

"Very good."

"Bring the documents back when you have them ready for my signature."

Malata rose and left the room. Vizarra tried to flex his toe and winced. He unbuttoned his tunic and loosened the lacing of his corset. Malata opened the door and walked quickly over to him.

"Both O'Conner and National Guard headquarters have telephoned. There is open fighting at the university. The students and teachers are armed with small arms and fragmentation grenades."

"Well, what's the situation?"

"The buildings have been occupied by the students and teachers. Seven police have been killed. It is not possible to seal the buildings off with the number of men already out there."

"Send fifty police and two hundred Guards. The university is to be surrounded. No attempt to seize the buildings until morning."

"O'Conner reports that the citizens have erected barricades in the principal streets leading to the university and that his men are being harassed by bricks, scalding water and live coals being dumped out windows. They can't get close to the university."

"Barricades?"

"Yes, Excellency. Apparently they were constructed shortly after dark."

"In other words, orders were given sometime this afternoon that they be built. Huh! We've had troubles before, Julio. But they were puffs of wind. A little dust stirred up, nothing more. Now Alessandro is going to bring a hurricane upon us. Tell O'Conner to take the searchlight trucks from the fire department. Light up the barricades and start shooting. Those streets must be cleared tonight! Not tomorrow, tonight!"

Malata bowed and slipped away.

Vizarra rose and hobbled over to the window. He could not stay away. The dark panes of glass drew him. He stared down. The last of the Roman candles and Catherine wheels were going off, but the bands were no longer playing and the crowd was oddly quiet, still shocked from the sight of Santa Rosa again in flames. The palace guards had turned the floodlights on. The gravel drive and wide, stone steps gleamed pale yellow. A truck stood outside the main gate. The Caudillo could see the tops of helmets and rifle muzzles.

Somewhere in the plaza a band began to play, raggedly, uncertainly, the national anthem. Directly across from the palace the last fixed display fizzed and then caught. A low, angry hooting sound started. Vizarra blinked. The display was a portrait in three colors of himself. The beams of the searchlights swung and probed. The crowd bellowed. The lights swung wildly, then focused on the flaming display. Vizarra squinted, then drew his glasses from the case in his tunic pocket and slipped them on his nose. Confused, ugly noises sounded through the window. He fumbled with the catch and heaved the tall sash open. The racket of the crowd struck him like a blow. Figures dashed around the base of the burning display. Knots of men tangled and broke apart, knocking each other to the ground. The motors on the fire engines thundered, and a long, pale plume gushed into the struggling, shouting mob. The truck outside the gate started up; the lights snapped on and it bucked away across the plaza. Dark bodies scattered and turned back to shake their fists and howl. The band stopped abruptly, in mid-phrase. Vizarra watched as a group of men swung a ladder against the frame of the still-sputtering display. They battered whole sections loose, disfiguring the portrait. The fire hoses knocked them sprawling. One of the searchlights exploded, spraying hot glass. More dark figures crawled over the thundering fire engines. The helmeted firemen swung hatchets and jabbed with long wrecking hooks. Hands snatched the hooks and dragged the firemen down into the pummeling, shrieking mass of men and women. The hose was turned against the portrait. The powerful jet of water smashed the framework to stinking, hissing kindling, at once seized as clubs. The windshield and headlights of two engines dissolved into shards, and the crowd jolted and heaved, rocking the engines. The National Guard truck snapped on the siren; the soldiers tore back the canvas sides and dropped off the tailgate, their rifles held at ready. Their officer, his pistol on a lanyard hung around his neck, fired the weapon straight up into the night, blew his whistle and swung his arm. The Guards moved forward in an arc toward the fire engines. The crowd melted away before them. Vizarra heard the sound of horses. Mounted police, with long, lead-tipped sticks, trotted into the plaza and fanned out. The crowd began to scream now and crush toward the archways, shoving and trampling. The soldiers reached the firemen and then dashed after the crowd, swinging their gun butts.

Now there was no mob, perhaps thirty sprawled bodies, some obviously injured, lying in twisted postures, others crawling feebly over the soaked pavement. Sirens moaned, and three blue-and-silver riot vans shot through the southeast archway and halted, plugging the escape route. Everywhere men and women were running, running wildly to get away. Vizarra nodded grimly and slammed the window shut. He turned. Malata was standing there.

"Yes?"

"The Estación Central was raided. The Policía Armada reports four of their men killed outright, seven wounded. The rebels escaped with seven locomotives and approximately forty cars of various types, freight and passenger. The raid was apparently very well organized. In less than a half hour the trains were gone. There is fighting now in the marshaling yards. The police have been able to make no progress. They believe that they are outnumbered and request assistance from either the Guards or the Regular Army garrison."

"*Mierda!* Very well. Seven locomotives? Mother of God! Send a hundred Guards. Didn't anybody go after them?"

"The police seized a yard engine and coupled a gondola car in front of it. It was derailed in the marshaling yards."

"All right. Notify the Estación to cancel all service, both passenger and freight. Effective at once. All operations are to be directed out of the engineering office attached to the Regular Army garrison. Call the barracks and wake them up. Tell them they're in the railroad business. Also, I want detonation teams out with O'Conner's police at the university. They are to dynamite the barricades only if there is no other way to clear the streets. Make sure they understand that."

The lights went out. A soft drone filled the dark room.

"What's that?"

"The ship, Excellency, clearing the outer harbor."

Vizarra blundered through the darkness to the window again. Yes, there was the ship, lights glimmering from bow to stern, her deep screws threshing the dark water a kilometer off the outer jetty. Another long drone floated across the city on the tropic breeze.

"Safe. They're safe."

Vizarra stared at the ship. How beautiful, how serene it looked, gliding smoothly, safely, out of the harbor!

"We got them away just in time, Excellency."

"What's that? Yes, yes . . . just in time."

"Colonel Lucca has returned. He says the waterfront is comparatively quiet, but he could hear the gunfire over at the university."

"Ummm. I'll . . . I'll speak with him in a moment."

Vizarra stood at the window, holding by one hand to the thick velvet drapes. The Plaza Mayor was empty now. The soldiers had been posted at the archways. Their abandoned truck stood in the center of the square. A mounted patrol clopped by the palace. The fire engines were gone to the university. The riot vans had moved on, chasing the crowd down the boulevards, scattering the last of them, making a few arrests whenever somebody fell down. Some soldiers had begun to string barbed wire up against the grilled fence before the palace. The Caudillo clawed open his collar. The sight of the wire made him feel as though he were being locked in, not the mob out.

"Julio?"

"Yes, Excellency?"

That dry, respectful, detestable voice in the darkness. Always there, ready, waiting, the damnable patience of a cabaret wine steward!

"Have old Carlos Sánchez arrested tomorrow when he goes to the Ministry of Education. Unspecified crimes against the state."

"But he and his son are enemies, Excellency. I don't see how that would—"

"Have him arrested."

"Yes, Excellency."

"And brought here."

"Here?"

"Yes, God damn it, here! Perhaps I want to enjoy a little intelligent conversation for a change! You? Christ, you can't even make certain that the fireworks display goes off right!"

"Yes, Excellency."

"Have you given instructions that the generator is to be turned on?"

"Not yet, Excellency."

"Why not? What do we have the thing for? Do you imagine I plan to sit here in the darkness like this? Find out if the telephone works! Contact the power stations! Don't just stand there saying 'Yes, Excellency, yes, Excellency,' like some damned puppet! You like to play at being a statesman, Julio. Now let's see you work! Roll up your sleeves. Get your hands dirty! You haven't worked since you left that

295

nightclub. Well, now you'll be cleaning up the garbage—Vola, Ramos, O'Conner and Alessandro and his bunch of swine!"

Vizarra clung to the drapes, his face streaming. He stared with longing at the brilliant ship, like a splash of diamonds on the dark sea.

"Shall I call the villa, Excellency?"

"I don't want her here tonight. It's too dangerous. Just send over some police. A dozen or so. Tell her to stay indoors. Say that the lights will be on again in a little while."

"Very good."

"And . . . give her, you know, my love."

"I will."

"Oh, and, Julio, see if you can wake up that Swiss doctor. My gout is very bad again. I want an injection. Something for the pain."

The door clicked shut. Vizarra looked out over the dark, silent city. Not a light anywhere. The buildings looked snipped out of sooty tin and propped against the sky. In those buildings, in the dark rooms, the men and women whispered together, wondering, filled with fear and hatred. Why did it have to be this way? Why was he here, alone in the darkness, behind an iron fence and barbed wire? How quiet it was! Not a sound.

The ship called again, a last, sad moan of farewell, as it turned between the dark, donging buoys for the open ocean and Europe. Vizarra stared at it, his throat tight. He dropped the drapes and shuffled back, limping badly now, until he bumped against a table, banging his hip. He pulled open a drawer and fumbled inside. The lights flickered and came on. He found the button and pushed it. The door opened.

"Yes, Your Excellency?"

"I want the airplane, Julio. The big Ford trimotor. Have them take it out to the landing field near the villa."

"Very well."

"Telegraph my bank in Switzerland. You know the one. Have them change everything to Swiss francs. All the paper money and securities. Change everything to gold."

"Everything to gold."

Malata bowed and softly shut the door.

296

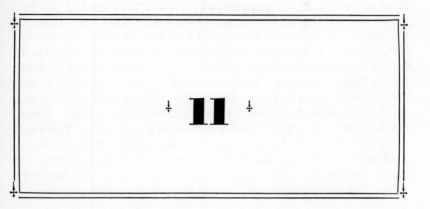

11

IT was a hot morning, and most of the off-duty men loitered inside the police station, drinking coffee, playing cards and talking in low, sour voices. They were all annoyed about the new orders which forbade them to go to their homes, even when not actively on duty.

The sergeant walked out of the charge room and down the hall to the front of the building. He stepped out into the sunshine and lit a cigarette. Across the street the iron shutters of the shops were still down. The street was empty except for a small, yellow dog nosing around an overturned garbage can. It was quiet; a sinister silence lay over the San Pablo district, as though the citizens had smothered beneath their blankets during the night. Every so often a faint spatter of gunfire came from the university district. A single cloud of dark smoke rose from a burning building down on the docks. The sergeant flipped away his cigarette, looked at his watch and walked back into the station. Two of the riot vans were due back, but the two Dodge patrol cars were scheduled to stay out until noon. He looked at his watch again. Time to go on duty at the desk.

The cells in the basement were already full—twenty-four people, three of them women, seven needed medical attention—but the lieutenant had received no instructions either to send for a local doctor or to remove the injured to the nearest hospital. The sergeant climbed up to the desk and glanced through the charge book. The names were hardly legible; whoever had the desk from midnight on had scrawled by the light of an electric lantern, writing as fast as he could so that the prisoners could be dragged down the stairs to the cells. The man at the desk yawned and muttered his thanks as the sergeant climbed into the chair. He yawned again and asked about coffee. There was still plenty. He walked across the room, pushed open the low, wooden gate and walked from the charge room, his boots knocking on the worn, wooden floor. The sergeant swatted at a fly, missed and tried again. The insect escaped and circled through the room. The sergeant twiddled a pencil and stared at the brass telephone. He hoped it wouldn't ring until the lieutenant came back on duty. The sergeant was afraid that reinforcements were going to be called out to the university. The dawn attack had been beaten back by the students, and one of his friends, a patrolman from this very station, had been shot through the throat. What was the army hanging around for? The fellows in the outside room kept blaming the army. Why hadn't the city garrison been mobilized two or three days ago?

He heard the sound of a motor and the grinding of gears, then another motor. He pressed an alert bell that rang in the duty room, calling out six men there to receive however many broken heads would come crawling out of the vans. He heard the sound of footsteps in the hall, a guttural voice calling something in a rude tone, and the door to the duty room slam. Four patrolmen came into the charge room, herding a half-dozen kids in street clothes who stood gaping around with their hands locked on top of their heads. The sergeant opened the charge book and dipped a pen in the inkstand. When he looked up, the officers and police were inside the barricade. Something was wrong!

"What is this? You're not from this station."

One of them pointed a pistol.

"Call the warder."

"What is this?"

"Call the warder. Open the cells."

"Open the cells? You're crazy!"

The officer jerked his head. The prisoners dropped their hands and drew pistols from their jackets.

"Make sure those two rooms are closed back there. Get the armory. Clean it out. Make sure you get the tear gas."

The sergeant slowly raised his hands and edged his right elbow toward the alert button. More men, some in street clothes, others in uniforms, streamed into the charge room and down the corridors leading to the cells. The warder and his assistant began to shout. A pistol popped three times. A wild hubbub of voices rattled off the corridor walls. Footsteps pounded in the front of the building. The sergeant slid off his seat, dragging the telephone with him.

"Hello, hello! A raid! This is San Pablo! Precinct Twelve! We are raided by rebels. Raided by rebels!"

He fumbled for his revolver, changed his mind and stood up, his hands held high. Three of the rebels shot him, at point-blank range, in the chest and stomach. He fell across the desk, swatting the charge book to the floor.

Olmega tore off the dead sergeant's belt and holster and thew them at one of his cadre members. The freed prisoners, nearly all of them hysterical, poured into the charge room. They were certain that they were being taken somewhere to be shot. Olmega bellowed above the uproar.

"Get them out into the vans! First van takes the wounded to San Pablo clinic! Hurry up. You, there, wreck the inside office, dump the files and get ready to set it on fire!"

Olmega hurried from the charge room. Christ, they had only twenty minutes. He beat his followers about the head and shoulders as they stumbled down the corridor and out into the sun, their arms laden with seized weapons and ammunition. He thrust open a door. Two students were smashing file cabinets, wrecking the switchboard and flinging papers about. Out in the corridor another student fired a pistol every thirty seconds through the door of the duty room. The trapped officers inside bellowed insanely.

"The armory is empty, Pepe!"

"What about the prisoners?"

"In the trucks."

"Where's the kerosene?"

"Behind you. Look."

Two men in police uniforms slopped kerosene over the papers that blew ankle-deep down the corridor. Others poured the reeking stuff over the seats and benches in the charge room. They flung a can against the desk and it bounded back, gulking slowly, a puddle spreading across the floor.

"Everybody out! Come on! I'll set it off!"

The others brushed by Olmega, hurrying for the vans. Faces stood at the second- and third-story windows of the dwellings across the street. Olmega rolled a fistful of papers into a torch, lit it and flung it through the office door. He waited a moment until the broken furniture and rubbish burned well, then clumped down into the charge room and touched off the kerosene. It caught at once, with a soft *whump*. Smoke poured out of the office door. Olmega cursed. The fools had forgotten to break open the windows. He plunged into the office, snatched up a table lamp, and hurled it with all his strength against the glass. It shattered, and the draft began to suck the smoke out. He ran for the door, whirled and raced down the corridor. A bullet sizzed and panged off the front of the station. He ducked low and scuttled for the nearest van, scrambled up beside the driver.

"Who's shooting? Who's shooting?"

"Two of the bastards on bicycles. The next corner."

"Let's get them!"

The van bucked forward and shot out into the street. Olmega saw the bicycle leaning against a lamppost. A blue figure crouched. Smoke puffed from his pistol and his slug creased the hood of the van. The other one was flat against the wall, reloading.

"Stop!"

Olmega flung open the door and dropped down to the running board. The driver lay down on the seat, holding his hands over his head. The rear door of the van clanked open. A half-dozen shots echoed in the street. Olmega crawled to the front of the van and peered around. He pointed his revolver and squeezed the trigger three times. The officer reloading dropped his weapon and held his stomach. He fell forward to the sidewalk. His hat tumbled away, rolling, and stopped in the gutter. His partner stood up and began to run. The boys at the back of the van opened up. Bullets sang off the cobbled street. The blue figure jerked once, twice, and then sprawled on his face. Olmega ran to the back of the van. Two students bent over another. Blood streamed from the injured boy's face. Olmega tore them away and shoved them toward the van.

"Back inside! Back inside! Hurry up!"

"But he's hit!"

"I know. Who's got the damned flag? Hand it out, Jorge!"

The crude banner tacked to a mop handle was thrust at Olmega from the dim interior of the van. He stepped over the body on the street and ran back to the cab. As he climbed in, he glanced back at the station. Smoke poured out of the open door and the office window, black clouds of it. He could hear the trapped police screaming.

"Let's go!"

"Where now? Back to the university?"

"No, the municipal garage two blocks from U.T. headquarters. We've got to deliver this stuff first."

The driver nodded and shifted gears. Olmega looked back, then up the street. No sign of the first van. Good, they were on their way back to the university after dropping the wounded at the clinic. He unrolled the banner, cranked down the window and set the mop handle in the double socket welded to the hood of the van. The revolutionary banner fluttered in the wind. The boys in the back of the van were shouting and singing. Olmega noticed the star in the windshield directly before him. If he hadn't got out of the cab, he would have been hit. He whistled softly and crossed himself. The van swung heavily around a corner.

A dozen men with rifles crouched behind a string of overturned café tables. They began firing. Olmega cursed. He had a glimpse of a red flag with letters painted on it. He grabbed the blue-and-white banner from the socket and waved it as the truck slowed. The men behind the café tables stopped firing.

Olmega stuck his head out the window.

"Hey, *camaradas! Aquí el Cuadro Negro!*"

"*Mierda!*"

"*Sois vosotros de la U.T.?*"

"*Sí! La Guardia Roja!*"

"Christ, they've got a Red Guard in the streets already! . . . Listen, *chico,* let us pass! We've got arms for you!"

"Dump them in the street and go back!"

"I'll piss in your mouth! Get that junk off the street! We're going through!"

The Red Guards clustered together, then kicked apart their flimsy barricade. They waved the van forward. Olmega swung down from the cab and walked up to a skinny man with bad teeth who seemed to be the leader.

"Listen, *amigo*. I am Brigade Commander Olmega. Black Cadre has two of these trucks. We'll get them painted today. But the next time you block us, I'll report you to Voget and you'll end up eating your own balls for dinner!"

"I take orders from the U.T., that's all. I'm to hold this street."

"Can you understand or not? I am the brigade commander from the university. Voget and I share military jurisdiction. You obey my orders if they don't conflict with Voget's. The other van has a flag, too. Save your bullets for the stuff that still belongs to the police."

"All right, all right! Where did you get them?"

"Ambush, this morning, near the science building.. Out of the way, we're in a hurry. *Suerte, amigos!*"

The leader of the Red Guards clenched his fist in salute.

"Viva la revolución!"

Olmega climbed back into the cab. He fixed the banner in the socket. It would be easier just to paint flags on the vans.

"Let's go. We haven't got all day."

"You've got guts, kid, I'll say that. Why, those idiots could have shot you! In that uniform? Christ, don't take such chances."

"Next time I'll wear a smoking jacket. Come on, move this thing."

⸸

The Edificio de la Compañía Telefónica (called by the city wits Our Lady of the Bad Connections) was attacked across the open square by U.T. fighters who rode to the assault in commandeered streetcars. The building was well defended by police and National Guards. Two machine guns had been placed behind sandbags, one on either side of the main entrance. The streetcars were well within range. Slugs lashed broken glass from the windows and sprayed the rear platforms. The men from the U.T lay flat, pinned down. The machine gunners swept the plaza twice, then waited. Then they heard the sound of fighting from the rear of the building, scattered rifle shots and the thud of a grenade, the answering volley from the company of Guards stationed on the second floor. The machine gun placed there lashed twice and stopped. Out in the open plaza the wounded crawled away. The attack was over. A lieutenant from the Guards counted the bodies left tumbled around the battered streetcars, grunted with satisfaction and went off to report the successful action to headquarters.

‡

The university, located on the border between the San Pablo district and the narrow, twisted section of streets called Ciudad Vieja, the Old City, was a dense mass of buildings in the architectural styles of two centuries, all crammed behind a high brick wall pierced at only two places by iron grates. The six streets leading to the walled quadrangle had been plugged by barricades: mounds of brick, broken furniture, scrap metal and rubble heaped over ruined automobiles that had been seized and turned over. Each of the barricades had been built approximately half a kilometer from the walls of the university proper. The buildings, shops and cafés behind the barricades flew crude revolutionary flags. Some of the shops, particularly the wine caves, were open for business.

Inside the walls the Green Cadre had set up their recruiting center in the administration offices. The corridors were jammed with students and men from the Ciudad Vieja who had come to volunteer. They were told off into "decades," instructed to elect a leader and to report to the auditorium (a bedlam of nervousness and shouting) to join their "century." Each century had been numbered from the first A.D., assigned specific buildings to defend and marched off—without weapons. Their first tasks were to purchase, requisition or simply seize food and bring it back to the student canteen for redistribution. The ground-floor shops thus gutted were sealed and dumped full of whatever sort of rubbish could be found, to prevent the occupation of the shops by the attacking force, since that would close off the floors above. The narrow streets were clogged with men and boys wearing various-colored armbands. They carried sacks and boxes, string bags crammed with vegetables and fruit, crates of squawking poultry. Every four hours the "century" leaders reported to the science buildings, the most central, best-sheltered area, where they received instructions on the defense of the university and surrounding area. The six barricades had to be defended, and losses were beginning to mount. Each "century"—reduced, usually by ignorance or confusion, to about seventy men—manned one barricade for four hours, taking over the weapons of the "century" they relieved. It was a very awkward system but the only one capable of keeping most of the volunteers occupied at some sort of useful task. After their duty on the barricades, the survivors removed the wounded, ate, and were marched away to the classroom buildings to sleep, rolled in blankets between the desks. In midafternoon the water in the San Pablo district and in Ciudad Vieja was turned off. The hydrants trickled and the faucets dripped, useless. In twenty minutes everyone was possessed by a raging thirst. Beer and wine were locked up in the faculty library and lounge, and ration chits were issued to the "century" leaders. A meeting was called for 1800 hours to discuss the problems of continued defense. A distillation apparatus was set up in the biology lab to purify water from the canteen that had been used for boiling vegetables, washing dishes and cleaning the floor. "Decades" drilled with clumsy ferocity up and down the concrete paths between the buildings. There was talk of constructing something called "sally ports," so that attacks could be launched beyond the barricades.

The first aircraft flew over the university in midafternoon, dropping leaflets demanding immediate surrender. The leaflets were collected for use as toilet paper, a joke but also a necessity. The planes returned forty minutes later. There were five of them. They flew in a line, low, their motors hammering, small bombs slung under their silver wings. They attacked what the rebels called the "front" barricades that led most directly to the center of the city. Since the attacks on four stations had driven the police from the San Pablo district, the "rear" barricades—three of them there—were only lightly defended. The sixth barricade sealed off Calle San Jerónimo, the long, steep slot that ran through the Old City down to the waterfront, and the longshoremen there had been standing off a rather cautious army group since early morning. Three Coast Guard vessels lay in the harbor near the docks, but had taken no part in the fighting on either side. Reports had it that the sailors were doing their washing and swimming inside shark nets rigged from their ships.

The first bombs whistled down a hundred meters outside the barricades, blasting the front off one building. The rubble wrenched free and fell with a shattering roar on a police van parked there, killing three men. The black plumes boomed up from the pavement, twenty meters apart, spraying broken stone off the iron shop-shutters. The "centuries" fired wildly into the air at the planes. A direct hit tore a gap in "Front" Barricade No. 2, killed six and wounded four, two of them girls. More bombs fell inside the university quadrangle, damaging the chapel and one wing of the library slightly. There were no casualties. The aircraft returned, flying lower, to machine-gun the reinforcements crowded behind the breached rampart of Barricade No. 2. Again there were five planes, but, by luck or the expert advice of the mathematics professors charged with the duty, one of the craft flew into a storm of bullets that sleeted into the wings and fuselage. Smoke burst from the engine nacelle and the plane slid sideways, the propeller whickering slowly. It rolled over, drifting southeast, smoke streaming in a long feather, and fell through the corrugated roof of the market on the lower end of Calle San Jerónimo. It burned for an hour, a crumpled wreck of wrenched aluminum tubing, melting rubber and popping ammunition. The planes bombed the university again, and strafed Barricade No. 1. Olmega got a message through to U.T. headquarters and received a promise that an attack would be launched at the police and Guards from the rear. Rumors of artillery being assembled on the Plaza Mayor created more fear than the aircraft, although the raids had taken nearly twenty lives.

↓

The old man had debated all morning. At length, unable to consider eating lunch, curious and only slightly apprehensive, he told his chauffeur to bring around the car. The streets were nearly empty. They were stopped five times by patrolling police and Guards. He saw a few companies of soldiers in field dress marching across the empty squares and stringing barbed wire. They passed through the normally crowded section of stores and theaters. There was no one out. Even the newspaper kiosks were shut up. A few cafés, manned by nervous waiters, were open on the main boulevard leading to the Plaza Mayor, but the inhabitants of the luxury apartments were keeping inside. They were permitted to pass through the wire at the southwest arch. The old man climbed stiffly from the sedan and told his driver to return at five. He walked up the steps of the Ministry of Education. In the foyer four men in uniform were waiting.

"Señor Carlos Sánchez?"

"Yes."

"You are under arrest. Please come along with us. You've kept us waiting, so quick-march!"

The old man nodded docilely and walked out of the building. He was not alarmed. He had expected to be arrested, but at home. A police sedan was waiting.

"To the palace!"

The old man blinked. What in heaven could the Caudillo want? He turned politely to the officer beside him.

"Are you sure that it's me you want and not my son Carlitos?"

"We know who we want."

The Minister of Education looked out of the window. A gang of soldiers swept refuse and pieces of charred wood into neat piles. Oddly enough, the dance floor and bandstand were still standing. The palace was heavily guarded. The automobile started to move.

"We could have walked. It's just across the plaza."

"I have my orders."

"Pity to waste the gasoline."

The officer looked at him contemptuously. The Minister nodded.

"You may need it."

"Need it? What for?"

The old man gazed at him mildly.

"Why, to escape. To escape!"

⸸

At dusk the battered green Hispano-Suiza bus jolted over the cobblestones, turned left and stalled twenty paces from the police barricade. The driver squirmed out of his seat, opened the door and walked away quickly into the crowd, as though the vehicle alone was his affair and the passengers would have to take care of themselves. The driver asked a few quick questions. Yes, the San Pablo quarter had been open all day. The police had arrived only an hour or so earlier. There had been some bombings and after that artillery fire. The police had come in trucks. A young man drew a diagram in the dirt. The rebels were here, so, and now the police were here, so, like a ring outside a ring. And the U.T.? They were in the streets, fighting and demonstrating. About one-third of the city was in rebel hands, but there was no water, no electricity. The driver nodded and stared thoughtfully at the bus. Should he leave it where it was and walk to the nearest U.T. office? Should he go home? Should he drive the bus away and wait for orders? He did not know. The young man scuffed out the diagram and strolled off before the driver could ask him any more questions.

The passengers untangled their belongings and climbed slowly from the bus. A *peón* carried two trussed-up chickens. A feeble old woman with a cane, her face hidden by a shawl, was helped down the steps by two Indians in cheap cotton suits and paper collars. A very fat young woman with three skinny children and a baby held against her bosom squeezed through the door, followed by three laborers who laughed and made rude remarks, offering to bring levers, to fix a block-and-tackle, to grease the doorway. The woman flounced away from the bus, driving her children before her. One of the laborers leaned against the fender of the bus and drank from a half-empty bottle of *aguardiente*.

Fingel, his small, podgy body soaked with perspiration and caked with dust, struggled down the steps with a fat bolt of cloth tied neatly with twine. He placed it carefully on the fender and climbed back into the bus, returning a moment later with a bulky carton and his briefcase. He sat down on the carton and fanned himself with his derby, gazed around and smiled faintly, puzzled. It was nearly dark, but the sawhorse and barbed-wire barricade were lighted by hissing gasoline lanterns that hung from the dead streetlamp stanchions. He could hear a sound like someone breaking twigs: rifle fire in the center of the city. He sighed. How was he to do business now? If only they had waited a few days, he could have sold his goods and gone back to the village. Still, if none of the stores were open, the owners and buyers would be at home. He could see them there. But if they were at home, they probably wouldn't come to the door because of the police. He sighed again and sniffed.

He was hungry. A street stall was open. Baked sweet potatoes. Grilled veal sprinkled with red pepper and basted with olive oil. Coffee. He gathered his bundles, the bolt of cloth under his left arm, with his briefcase dangling from his crooked index finger, the heavy carton under his right arm. He shuffled over to the stall, studying the men behind the wire: four young thugs in street clothes, with police caps and armbands. O'Conner's *bravos,* not regular police. Fingel clucked his tongue. Young men like that ought to be learning a useful trade or exercising at some sport, not standing around bothering people. What were their fathers thinking of? He looked at them again and decided that they might very well not have fathers.

Fingel bought a sweet potato and a cup of black coffee. The veal tempted him, but a portion cost two centavos. He munched the potato and looked at the crowd. About fifty people, mostly men. They would have no proper papers, of course. Lost them or sold them or never had them. The men were poorly dressed, almost in rags, and carried hoes and sickles. Each morning they walked out of the city through the suburbs to the truck gardens, where they worked for a few centavos a day, just enough to live on. The police would keep them outside now, as much for the hoes and sickles as anything else.

The police were joking with the *peón*. They told him that his chickens could enter the city, but that he could not. The poor fellow, probably a bit simple-minded, took them seriously and handed over the trussed birds. Then he squatted outside the wire to wait. For what? For how long? Soon he would pester the police, and they would drive him away. The old woman crept through the wire, her tattered but valid documents clenched in her wrinkled, brown fingers. The police had nothing to fear from an old woman.

So. It was still possible to get through. That was the main thing. Fingel drank his coffee slowly. The crowd waited, talking a little in low, uneasy voices. The three laborers who had come in on the bus with Fingel squatted against the fender, their cloth caps pulled low over their faces. The lanterns hissed, giving off a harsh, white light and making shadows dark and thick as tar. Beyond the barricade the street vanished. The cluttered, smelly tenements that shouldered together were silent. Usually the San Pablo quarter was a tangle of carts, herds of sheep and goats, peddlers, porters and laborers, women in cheap, flashy dresses and bands of restless, dirty, noisy children. San Pablo was Fingel's favorite district. He was used to the hard faces, the petty thefts, the cheap vice, the vermin and filth. The sagging blocks of old buildings seemed to burst with life. The silence and darkness disturbed him. He thought of a ghetto, the shuttered tenements, the smell of cooking cabbage, the furtive life behind boarded windows after the curfew. The silence brought back something of the old terrors, the gliding street gangs with clubs and lengths of chain. This was San Pablo, not Warsaw, Berlin, Munich. Still, police were police anywhere. He sat and sipped his coffee, now cold.

They would demand that he tell them his destination. He thought about it. Seven blocks up and two to the left was the massive stone warehouse that had been converted years ago to an army barracks. Directly across the street was the school for girls run by the nuns. Once he had sold one of the sisters forty pairs of shoelaces, black ones. There the street forked. To the right was the low iron-roofed shed of the market. At one time he had had a stall there: socks, underwear, razor blades, wax, cheap perfume, costume jewelry and soap. Even though his license had been valid, the police had kicked him out. Now it was different. He smiled to himself as he bent and picked up his briefcase. If there were no buyers for wool and leather, he had another card to play. Could there be a better time to sell insurance than during a revolution? Well, he might as well get it over with. He drew out his French passport and placed his license inside it. There. All ready. No police officer could ever say that Herman Fingel was uncooperative. He gathered up his packages and scuffed up to the wire. He could feel the crowd watching him. Beetles burred and blundered against the gasoline lanterns. Fingel looked back. To his surprise, the three laborers who had come in with him on the bus were standing only a few paces behind him, watching intently. Fingel smiled cheerfully at them, then turned and bowed at the police.

"*Buenas tardes, señores.* May one enter the city?"

One of them slouched up to the wire, his hand resting on the butt of his revolver. Fingel swallowed. Irregular police. They were always the worst.

"Let's see your papers."

"Right here, sir!"

His passport and license were snatched away. Another man joined the first. They studied the passport with a pocket electric torch, although there was plenty of light from the lanterns. The first one flapped the passport against his palm.

"You're a foreigner."

"That's right."

The police looked at each other. No one said anything for a moment. Fingel's arms began to ache, but he didn't dare set down his bundles.

"Are you a tourist?"

"No. You have my license right there. Perhaps you didn't see it? The pink piece of paper? I am . . . a merchant."

They looked at the license, then again at the passport. Finally the first one jerked his head.

"Come in here."

He opened a little wooden gate, and Fingel edged cautiously into a small, open square in the center of the tangled coils of wire. He sucked in his breath. The bolt of wool had nearly snagged on one of

309

the iron thorns. He blinked at the police and tried to smile. The police officer pointed at his briefcase.

"Hand it over."

Fingel set down the carton, shifted the bolt of fabric from his left arm to his right and steadied it, one end resting on the carton. He held out the briefcase. The officer snapped it open and turned the case upside down. Fingel cringed in embarrassment. His soiled underwear and one torn sock spilled out with a shower of insurance brochures, pamphlets and policies, company stationery, bright bits of stamps, the agreement he had signed with Rabbi Bergman and a battered Hebrew prayer book. The officer stirred the scattered stuff with the toe of his boot. He bent and picked up a fire-and-theft policy and the prayer book. He scowled and stepped close to Fingel, stopped and studied the book.

"What's your game? Answer me!"

"There's no game. I'm a businessman."

"What sort of answer is that? What game is this, eh?"

He slapped the stiff, blank policy against Fingel's chest.

"A game? That's a policy. Selling insurance is a game?"

"Where have you come from?"

"On the bus."

"Where did the bus come from?"

"I got on at Rota."

"So."

He walked back to the loose heap on the ground, squatted and picked over the papers. He found a railroad ticket, examined it and brought it to Fingel.

"You used this?"

"Last week."

"From the city to the mines. *Ida y vuelta*. Round trip, eh? What for?"

"I went to the mines."

"To the mines."

The other police gathered around the briefcase. Fingel wet his lips. They pawed slowly through the papers. One picked up the sock and tossed it into the tangled wire. Another ground Fingel's toothbrush into the dirt. They handed around a batch of papers. Fingel blinked at the gold lettering: PARADISE LIFE INSURANCE CO., INC.

"That's all written in English. You see, I work for an American

310

company, even though I have a French passport. That's why I went to the mines. To talk to Ramos there, perhaps you know of him? A simple group insurance plan, but he—"

"Shut up, will you?"

"Dangerous work and no insurance? I ask you."

"Ramos, you say. At the mines. He says Ramos."

"Oh, he does, eh?"

Fingel watched them pass the prayer book from hand to hand. They found the agreement Bergman had written and grew very excited.

"Code. Secret code!"

"Clearly."

"Clearly."

"What is this thing?"

"That is a book of prayers."

"You are not telling the truth. What are these letters?"

"Read the one in Spanish, sir. Perfectly harmless. An agreement with some villagers in the south. To sell some of their goods. I have the samples right here. Perhaps you'd like to see them? Some very fine wool and boots. Best-quality boots. Nothing like them. That's what it is, an agreement—a contract, if you like. The copy is in Hebrew."

"Hebrew? Never heard of it. Have you?"

"No."

"Never."

The first man suddenly grabbed Fingel by the dusty lapels of his coat and shook him savagely. Fingel's eyelids fluttered. The snout of a pistol, big as a water pipe, wavered in front of his face.

"You're a spy for the rebels! That's what! Confess it!"

"No! No, I'm just—"

"Well, we've got you now, so you might as well talk."

"You and Ramos, eh? We've got our orders about that one."

"But he chased me away!"

"He's a spy, all right."

"No! May God never forgive me if I'm lying!"

"You admit to seeing Ramos. Provoking riots and disturbances in the mines."

"What riots? I don't know anything."

"You mean to say you don't know that they refused to work to-

311

day? That's why you were hiding down near Rota, eh? Didn't think we'd catch you! And now you try to enter the city with secret code papers for the rebels!"

Fingel began to laugh. It was all such a foolish mistake. Such ignorant young men. Then the police officer swatted the bolt of wool from his hand. It rolled in the dust and snagged against the wire. Fingel lost his temper. He raised himself on tiptoe, jammed his derby on his head and shook his finger in the policeman's face.

"If you weren't a *mal educado,* you would know that those papers are in English, and the book and the letter are written in Hebrew!"

The policeman drew back the pistol and slapped it into Fingel's face. He dropped like a stone and rolled in the dirt, howling with pain. Tears and blood gushed into his cupped hands. His nose was broken. They kicked him twice, but he hardly felt it. They jerked him to his feet, but he fell down again. They held him up. His trousers ripped in the wire. He swayed from side to side, blind and weeping, shaking uncontrollably. Hot blood ran over his lips, and he sputtered and blew droplets into the dust.

"Don't talk that way to me, *sin cojones!* We know it's secret code, you dirty spy!"

Fingel tried to shake his head but couldn't. His neck ached, and the whole front of his face felt swollen, broken open. He tried to talk, but only got out a juicy blubber.

"What's he say?"

"Give it to him again!"

"A . . . mis-mish . . . mistake . . ."

"Ya-ya-ya! Your mistake, spy!"

The crowd watched in silence, some of them gazing steadily at Fingel, others noticing that the laborer with the bottle handed it to the youngest of the three. The young one passed a pair of wirecutters behind his back. They disappeared into the drinker's trousers. The young laborer staggered up to the wire, brandished the bottle and began to bawl in a drunken voice to the police.

"Throw him out here, the dirty bastard! We'll take care of him! We're loyal, we are! Throw him out and let's beat him up! Let's hang him. Hang him right now!"

"You! Stupid, get away from the wire!"

The young laborer stumbled and pitched into the barbed wire. He yelped and floundered. The crowd laughed suddenly and surged forward to see him. One of the police opened the gate and held on to it, steadying himself, while he kicked clumsily at the laborer who sprawled just out of reach. He lay on his back and tipped up the bottle. The liquor ran down his chin.

"Ah, *Madre de Dios,* the agony! Give me more to drink!"

The police grinned at his foolishness. The crowd laughed and applauded. Fingel snuffled and groaned into a blood-soaked handkerchief. The laborer heaved out of the wire. His shirt and trousers ripped and his bare back was studded with oozing holes. He swayed there under the bright lantern light. The third of his companions snatched a woman's red scarf and shook it. The drunken young man lunged for it, snorting like a bull. The other danced away. The crowd called and clapped.

"Olé! Olé!"

The police grinned and shook their heads, then turned back to Fingel.

"All right, Frenchman. You're under arrest. Suspicion of antigovernment activity."

Fingel gasped. His nose felt as big as a gourd. He spoke in a thick, choked voice.

"Antigovernment? I sell insurance. Let me go. I haven't done anything. I'll never come back. I promise."

A vision of dark pines, neat wooden houses, children, the light of candles on friendly, bearded faces and the white, rushing water dashed through his mind.

"Too late. Too late."

Fingel fumbled out a roll of banknotes, the last of his money. His hands shook so that he dropped the packet. He bent over; tears and blood pattered to the ground. He wiped his eyes with trembling fingers. He straightened up, clutching the little wad of bills, his mouth open. Two of the laborers were now behind the police, sliding forward on their bellies, cutting the wire with a pair of pincers! Fingel swayed, stricken with temptation. His thudding heart shook his entire body, like a piece of machinery running uncontrolled. He could hear the *pink* as the pronged wire parted, and the laughter of the crowd as the young, drunken worker rolled like a dog, still chasing the red scarf. Fingel turned slowly, blinking. Yes, another man, one of the crowd, now jerked the scarlet scrap of cloth this way and that, his feet kicking up a great deal of dust that drifted into the wire. Fingel

313

kneaded the roll of bills and shivered. Temptation had stricken him like a fever. All he had to do was shout and point. The police would shoot the two men crawling through the wire. He would seem a friend to the government. They would give him a better chance to explain himself, to some better-educated superior. Then he would be released. He would have his life again. He would be safe.

"*Achtung, alle Juden!*"

Fingel started. The blood was wrung from his belly by the harsh shout. He raised his hands in the air. The young worker slued out of a dust cloud, waved the bottle and grinned fiercely.

"*Machst du d' Maul zu!*"

Fingel gaped, his hands still in the air. The man whirled, snatching his pale, contorted face away into the sifting dust. His leg dipped in a limping stride as he dashed again at the fluttering scarf. He skidded on his face again. The bottle rolled away into the shadows. The crowd laughed and shouted.

"*Olé! Olé!*"

Fingel lowered his arms slowly. The two others were nearly through the wire. No more than a meter to crawl. Fingel pretended to fall forward. He clutched at the policeman and muttered rapidly, dabbing the roll of bills against the officer's hand.

"*Señoritos* like yourselves must know lots of pretty girls, no? Girls like presents, silk stockings, flowers . . ."

The hand tore the bills away. Fingel was jolted upright. The policeman leered at him.

"Attempted bribe!"

"But . . . I meant it as a gift, only—"

"Get out of the way, Joselito. I'll shoot him."

"No, no!"

"Wait a minute. You have to have a permit to shoot a civilian. Besides, he's a foreigner. Go up to army headquarters and get a permit signed."

"Alone? Nothing doing. You go."

"Go ahead. Someone will sign the permit for you."

A look of cunning passed across the second officer's face. He tapped the barrel of his revolver in his hand.

"We could say he tried to escape . . ."

Fingel swayed, waving his hands in front of his chest.

"Me? Escape? At my age? I can't even run!"

Someone punched Fingel in the stomach and he toppled back into the dust and wire. He sat there, sickened, the wind knocked out of him. The two were through the wire. The third one, the young one who had pretended to be drunk, was just sliding under the last strands. He ran off into the darkness. A policeman whirled and fired blindly into the darkness. The slug sang off the pavement, and the sound of running feet died away.

"Who was that?"

"I don't know. Someone was standing there. He started to run back. I shot at him."

"I didn't see anyone."

"He was there, I tell you!"

"What difference does it make?"

"Look, let's take this one up to the barracks and let them decide what to do with him. I can't read this stuff. Maybe it's what he says it is."

Mierda, he's a spy!"

"A foreign agent. We should shoot him, anyway."

"Clearly. But we're here to guard. Let them do it."

Fingel was dragged to his feet again, shaken ferociously, and stunned with furious threats. He held his broken nose and watched while the police stuffed the spilled papers back into his briefcase. They snapped a handcuff on his right wrist and yanked him up the dark street. He looked back at the wire, the flaring lanterns and the two men still standing there, holding back the crowd.

Fingel spoke in English, his voice tremoring with contempt and fear at the narrowness of his escape.

"You stupids. They cut the wire and got through, and you didn't even see. He wasn't drunk at all. You stupids!"

"La boca, Tío!"

Fingel grunted and shut up. His carton of fine boots and the bolt of wool were still back at the wire. He shrugged in resignation and fingered his broken nose with his free hand. It had all been too good to be true. Now everything was over for him.

⊥

Voget marked the positions occupied by the police and the army groups that had supportd them in the afternoon assault and shook his head. Barricade No. 2 had been dynamited and the students thrown back nearly the whole length of the street, leaving at least one "century" scattered along the retreat, dead or dying. A desperate counterattack with hand grenades had checked the advance long enough for Olmega's Black Cadre to plant charges and blow two tenements into the street. The counterattacking force, cut off completely, had died fighting in the doorways and cellars. Voget sniffed. He had no illusions. Unless the night attack on the ordnance depot was successful and the army somehow brought to a halt, the university would be overrun, the walls breached, and the students left to fight as long as they could.

Voget drew in the positions held by the forces of the U.T. with a red pencil. Henri and Coco were down on the docks; what Rota called the "Red Guard" spread between the waterfront and the San Pablo district, including the Ciudad Vieja, a shape like a fat funnel from the harbor up to the university. Very dangerous. Directly south was one corner of the San Pablo district, the old warehouse where General Vola had his headquarters and garrison. North, beyond the harbor, lay the airfield, and two kilometers west the fortified armory. The only benefit of the situation was precisely that the depot was so far removed, nearly twelve kilometers north and two west, lying in a little pocket formed by three hills. Vizarra's forces could hardly expect a strike that deep into their territory. It would take them by surprise.

Voget lifted his head when the knock came at the door. That pest Rota again.

"Come in."

The sentry, with a clenched-fist salute.

"Comrade. He's here. Alessandro."

"About time. Let him come in."

Voget snapped the string around the folder which held his plans for the assault on the ordnance depot. He sat back and waited.

Alessandro walked into the low room, kicked the door shut in the sentry's face and thrust out his hand.

"Good to see you again, Voget. You are well off here."

Voget shrugged and took Alessandro's hand.

"Ça va?"

"That's for me to ask you, no? I've just come from Olmega. They're working all night, of course. They'll counterattack if you can support them."

"Support them? We did that this afternoon and look what happened!"

"You can't expect kids to stand up against field guns, Voget."

"That's what I mean. Support movements are worthless. They spun two 75s around and let off a half-dozen rounds. Poof! Our boys couldn't stand up, either."

"Rota tells me that the Red Guard distinguished themselves. Covered themselves with glory."

"He means we had heavy casualties. We've got the men. It's a question of artillery."

"We agreed on that. Let's talk about tactics later. Now we must come to a political understanding."

Voget leaned back in his chair.

"Political understanding? What do you mean, Alessandro? This is the time to fight."

"Exactly, but with a coordinated command. Olmega told me of three incidents between his group and the Red Guards. One this morning, two this afternoon. He lost five men this afternoon. This must cease at once."

"Ah, the boys were nervous. They want to fight, too. So they shoot at anyone who moves."

"That is not a truthful summation of the two incidents."

"You accuse me of lying, Alessandro?"

"I accuse you of giving instructions designed to frustrate the coordination of the insurgent forces!"

"That's not so. I merely gave written instructions for the Red Guards to allow no one to pass through their lines."

"But you knew that the Black Cadre was hitting the police stations in those districts!"

"They could have gone around."

Alessandro leaned across the table. His dark eyes burned.

The Belgian waited, impassive, sucking his cheek.

"We are reorganizing, Voget, politically and militarily. No further obstructionist activities will be tolerated!"

"Precautions are now obstructions?"

"Shut up. I give the orders here. You don't have a headquarters here now. This is mine."

Voget blinked slowly.

"Sentry! Guard!"

317

A laborer with a pistol belt around his waist stepped into the room and glanced expectantly at Alessandro.

"Gamarche, where are the U.T. men who were here?"

"Out in the trucks, ready to be taken to the docks."

The blood beat in Voget's temples. Alessandro smiled blandly.

"You see, Voget? There has been a change in command."

He drew a paper from his pocket and passed it across the table.

"The Central Committee has made certain alterations. Read it. Go ahead."

"Why should I bother?"

"Rota is out. The Central Committee holds him responsible for the actions of the Red Guards this afternoon. He has been expelled from the Committee. In fact, he was arrested when he left here an hour ago. No, arrested is too strong. Detained. He is to be detained to answer charges of counterrevolutionary activity. He is still head of the U.T., however."

"Oh? Good for him."

"The Guards have been placed under direct commands from headquarters, as have all the student cadres and new recruits in the University-San Jerónimo-San Pablo districts."

"You command the united force?"

"Correct."

Voget shoved the folder across the table and stood up.

"Here, you'll need this stuff, then."

"Sit down, Voget."

"I'm not—"

Alessandro pointed a pistol at him. Voget sat down.

"I haven't finished, Voget."

The Belgian growled and shook his head.

"I guess not. Well?"

"I need your signature on a few papers here. Here, this one. You acknowledge and accept promotion to the rank of brigadier commanding the Second Army of Liberation."

"I do, eh? And what is this army?"

"The shock brigades you're taking to the depot tonight and the two brigades on the waterfront. You must name either Henri or Coco as second-in-command. You will use the Hotel Miramar in the—you have a map there, eh?—Playa Plata section. See? Here. This point of land. The boats will take you there and return to us, bringing whatever artillery you capture. Howitzers and 75s. Split them up, understand? Keep about forty per cent for yourself. Send the rest to Coco or Henri. They'll get them unloaded at dawn and up into the city."

The Belgian shifted in his seat uncomfortably. He forced a grin.

"They will, eh?"

"Absolutely. I have just come from the docks. I spoke with both of them. In fact, that's why I am rather late. They have agreed to cooperate. I left a few of my people there, of course . . . just to help out."

Voget swallowed. His palms had begun to sweat.

"Listen, they are good boys."

"Of course they are, Voget, of course. Of course. Why, they have been promoted to the rank of colonel by the Central Committee! You have only to name one as your second-in-command and the Second Army of Liberation is an accomplished fact. By the way, everything is waiting for you at the Hotel Miramar. A group of partisans have seized the crossroads. There are about a thousand of them, but poorly organized. A man called Trop. Ask for him. He leads the biggest group. An old fighter with my father."

"Trop. Hotel Miramar. Second Army of . . . Henri will be second to me."

"Sign this, then."

"What's that?"

"You promote him to full colonel."

"All right, Alessandro. There. Now, tell me, as comrade to comrade, what in the name of stinking hell is all this? Eh?"

"Sign the other paper and I'll tell you."

"I will sign nothing!"

"Then Olmega will take over the Second Army, Sánchez the First."

"And me?"

Alessandro looked at the Belgian and smiled.

"And you? Why, you'll be dead, poor fellow. Because if you don't sign, the Central Committee will find you untrustworthy and the political committee will demand your arrest and execution."

"You are so positive—"

Alessandro leaned forward, yanked the hair off his brow and slapped two documents on the table.

"Yes, Voget. Because the papers have already been drawn up.

Sánchez has signed for the Central Committee and all I have to do is sign for the political committee. You are trapped, Voget."

"So . . . so it seems. I either take the Second Army or—"

"Or else. You won't get out of this room. Oh, you could sign and then betray us. Bungle the attack. But there is Trop, of course. I wouldn't bungle it, Voget. It's a perfect setup. No, that's all right. I don't need to study the plans. I've already seen them. Olmega showed me a copy."

"How did he—"

"Three of your clerk typists are members of the Black Cadre. They joined the Communist party last year. We thought they'd come in useful. And they have. The plan is good, Voget. Carry it through."

The Belgian leaned back, picked up a pen and bent over the paper. He placed the pen on the desk. Alessandro crossed his legs and nodded encouragingly.

"Go on. It's all right now. You see where you are."

"Yes. But where will I be?"

"Why, I would have thought that the Comintern would have told you that. Haven't you read the texts? Why, by the arrest of Rota, you have risen to be the Party first secretary here in Costa Plata. A few days ago there was only one party—the Red Beret. Now there are three. Them, us, and you Communists."

"I don't trust you."

"But it's very clear, Voget. We need each other. I need a striking force north of the city. I am prepared to simplify the structure of the local Communist party by my own actions in order to accelerate the development of the revolution. You can't expect us in the M.L. to wait for you Reds to cut each other's throats. That would take too long. So I eliminate Rota. Now you have the Party. You have four brigades. You have Henri, Coco and the others. You will have full autonomy—I mean as regards political activity—in the north. You will obey all orders either from military headquarters here or from the Central Committee. Come, are you a gambler or not?"

Voget grunted. The fall of Rota had caught him off balance. He began to see the possibilities before him. His own command, a free hand politically, the opportunity to build up his force with further seizures of artillery. Henri would keep in constant contact with him. He would know Alessandro's actions in the city. But . . .

"Some gamble. You send me off to be slaughtered."

"Don't be foolish. We need those guns. More than anything. If we don't get them, the university will fall by tomorrow night."

"That's true."

"Then get them."

"But the army . . . General What's-his-name?"

"I'll take care of him. That's what I'm here for. Why should I betray you to Vizarra? Then I won't have the fieldpieces. You are thinking, Why don't I take the brigades myself on the raid? First, I have not studied the problem fully. Second, the brigades are used to you now. They have followed you for thirty-six hours, eh? Third, your key men are Party members. I wouldn't be safe with them. But fourth, I must see General Vola. If the army moves en masse tomorrow, we'll be crushed, guns or no guns. We must have both, Voget! Now do you understand?"

Voget nodded.

"Sure. I understand. I understand plenty. I look at you and what do I see? A man who calls himself a liberal . . . with a pistol in his paw. You call this a political understanding? I call it fascism, nothing less!"

Alessandro grinned and thrust the pistol back inside his tattered laborer's pants. Voget scowled and thumped the table, trying to stir within himself enough indignation to smother his feeling of helplessness.

"I remember once talking with Lunacharsky. He told me never to trust men like you. You have no sense of Party duty!"

"No."

"You employ fascist techniques of intimidation, threats and force."

"The end justifies the means? You Bolsheviks believe that, not me. Or haven't you read your Lenin lately?"

"You have no faith in your co-workers! The actions you have taken tonight . . . why, the Central Committee is a joke! A rubber stamp! Your actions betray you, Alessandro!"

"On the contrary—by the way, I cannot believe that Lunacharsky ever bothered to speak to you at all—I have a great deal of faith in my co-workers, as you call them. It is simply that I no longer have faith in Bolsheviks. This is Costa Plata, *mon ami,* not Petrograd. I learned a great deal from the Bolsheviks. I saw a People's Revolution twisted into Party dictatorship. I have no intention of letting that happen here."

321

"No? But you are a dictator right now! You know Rota is not guilty of anything!"

"Exactly. You are guilty. However, the revolution needs you. No one needs Rota. Therefore he has been removed. Why, just think how happy your superiors will be! And you have to admit that our new political understanding is better. Much simpler. Much clearer."

"Yes, it's clearer——"

"Then what are you yelling about, *hein?* You Reds are all the same . . . and that's your weakness. And your strength. But you all make so much noise. The same words, accusations, charges, slogans spouted over and over. It makes an honest man laugh. A bunch of parochials with megaphones. Secretly you're delighted. Your nose is twitching. You can smell it. An opportunity. I say, all right. I'll set you up. But you must follow orders and work honestly with the people. The people trust me, Voget. You must make them trust you. We will support you with propaganda. *The Belgian Bolívar!* How does that sound? Remember, you're a foreigner. You've got to win them, Voget, and you've got very little time. If you can make them trust you as they trust me, then we will win."

"Maybe . . ."

"Are you a gambler or not? I'm offering you on a plate what it would take you weeks to achieve!"

"Some offer. At pistol point. After you've knocked over my headquarters."

Alessandro glanced around the room and raked his limp hair away from his brow.

"Stop fussing over trifles. What do you think this place is, the Hotel Negresco? All I've done is shift your staff. Make up your mind, Voget. We don't have much time. The night is running away from us. Your men are waiting. So are mine. We must strike together. What we do tonight will mean success or failure. Tomorrow the people must rise with us. We will guide them, you from the north, me from here. Vizarra lies between us like a rotten walnut between the jaws of a cracker. When the jaws press together . . . we will destroy his dictatorship."

"And afterwards? Then is the time for a new political understanding."

Alessandro stood up and wandered across the room. He spoke in an idle, offhand manner.

322

"Oh, we will come to some agreement, you and I. We'll work it out. I don't doubt it for a minute. We're old hands, Voget. We'll get on."

"What will the position of the Party be? You cannot expect us to fight with you, then to be thrown aside?"

"We will discuss this later. Now is the time for action."

"I demand a promise that the Party will be granted every right, every freedom."

"You are talking nonsense, Voget, and you know it very well. What if I give you a promise? Tonight I say yes. Tomorrow I say no. Typical Bolshevik nonsense. The future of the Communist party in Costa Plata will be decided by the people themselves."

"You will manipulate public opinion."

"Of course. But I give you an opportunity to do the same. I make no promises, written or verbal, Voget. I expect none. I give none. The will of the people. You Party boys don't like that much. It's the will of the Party for you. Well, here things are different. Make up your mind. Take it or not. Sign or . . . don't sign."

The Belgian smiled grimly. He was ignorant, he knew. The Comintern had supplied him with only sketchy information about Alessandro Martín, and he knew too little about the history of Costa Plata. But his experience as a revolutionary, his instincts, his ambition, urged him to risk everything . . . *now*. Afterwards—that was another story. If there was no *now,* there would be no *afterwards.* They had stolen a day, kept the government forces checked and had shown the people how they could fight. Everything hung in the balance. The guns, the still-sluggish army, the city cut in two pieces without light or water in the rebel sector, no word yet from the *campo* or the mines. These were the crucial hours, the dark time of risks, of stunning action before the drugged populace thrashed and, out of that convulsion, took sides. And Alessandro knew what he was doing. He might be young, but he maneuvered swiftly and surely. He was not ignorant. He couldn't be. He offered a chance—a long chance, to be sure. *Afterwards.* Alessandro offered the Party, offered him the opportunity to plunge the country into civil war. Together, with the people's backing, they could overthrow Vizarra. Then would come the time to form the new government. Alessandro was deliberately, coolly, setting up the conditions for a possible coup, another March rising, another attack on the Winter Palace!

323

Voget groaned softly and held his head in his hands. Of course, he knew . . . of course Alessandro had calculated on the Comintern, was even now relying on the power of the international Communist party. If he failed to snatch up Alessandro's offer, Voget knew his life would be worth nothing. His superiors would find him a coward, a traitor to the Party. Some day or night they would come for him, no matter where he went, no matter where he tried to hide. He would be kidnaped and taken to Russia. Lubyanka Prison. Or, more likely, simply murdered as a blundering coward who had been offered the chance to bring in Costa Plata (Christ, the mines! The silver mines!) as the first Communist nation outside the boundaries of Russia itself. He couldn't refuse.

Voget sat frozen, his mind tumbling. How neatly he had been trapped! By this Spanish *kid!* Why, it was absurd . . . yet perfect. Perfect. He, Voget, who had fought in Petrograd, Hamburg and Berlin, caught like a melon seed between two fingers—Alessandro and the Comintern. He could only squirt forward, propelled by powers that could crush him flat, either now or later. Forward. There was the chance, the possibility, of plunging Costa Plata into civil war, of spreading the true revolution of the working class. Even if he failed, the Party would honor his attempt. Like a damned melon seed! So . . .

Voget picked up the pen and signed both copies of the document, accepting the command of the Second Army of Liberation and pledging himself as loyal to the people of Costa Plata and the Central Committee of the Movimiento Liberal. He flung down the pen, filled with disgust at his own blindness and grudging admiration for the young man who sauntered up to the table and pocketed the carbon copy. He had a right to grin, the little bastard!

"It's too bad you're still politically contaminated, Alessandro. If you came with us, you'd have a brilliant future in the Party."

"Thank you, Brigadier. I'm flattered. But I am more interested in the brilliant future of the people here in Costa Plata. I'm sorry to say that I find myself quite unable to imagine myself an associate to the drab contamination of mind and spirit the Party has come to be. I am in favor of human beings, not a bunch of theories. I am in favor of human beings, not against them. But these are subjects you and I will discuss . . . *afterwards.*"

324

Voget laughed and shook his head. He stood up and shook hands. He stared into Alessandro's dark eyes.

"We know where we stand with each other."

"We are both willing to take a chance. We are both aware that we have very little choice. But within that narrow range, Voget, there is failure or success."

"True enough. We do what we must so that we can do what we will. *Bonne chance,* you Spanish Trotsky!"

"*Buena suerte,* Belgian Bolívar!"

Voget ducked out into the corridor and climbed up the stairs. In the street the trucks were waiting. He climbed into the first one.

"To the docks, comrade. And fast!"

Down in the room, Alessandro hung over the map of the city. It compared favorably with Olmega's. Communications had been remarkably good. Voget had done a fine job. Alessandro sat down in the chair still warm from Voget's solid behind. Something rattled in his pants pocket. He drew it out. A letter. He had forgotten it. And the handwriting was familiar. He glanced at his watch. Half an hour before they hit Vola's headquarters. He nodded once as the trucks roared away into the night.

Alessandro drew out the crumpled letter. Yes, the handwriting was familiar. He knew it, now. Why had he not noticed it earlier, at the sanatorium? He had passed it off as a love letter. How stupid! He tore open the envelope and began to read.

> *Alessandro, jovencito, hijo mío—little one, my son—*
> *God will only grant your dreams if you are strong enough*
> *to suspect your friends and never trust them.*

True enough in the case of Voget. When had this been written? There was no date. The night after the last telephone call? Most likely.

> *A stranger never knows you well enough to confuse love*
> *with a dishonorable act. Only a friend can be poisoned*
> *with hatred. Trust no one and triumph.*

Like Rafael Vizarra? Never. And how could a friend be poisoned with hatred? A friend knew no hatred. The essence of friendship, of love, was forgiveness. Why, he had explained all that to Carlitos. And here the old fellow was turning things all around. The telephone call must have upset him terribly.

But you must free yourself before you can free others.

True enough. And he was free. No family, no property, no past that mattered or inhibited action. Only the present and the future.

What ever became of your bird, the one you brought with you to my house?

What bird? The old man's mind was wandering. Oh, yes, a canary or something. Mother had given it to me on my name day.

Carlitos has waited too long.

Too long for what?

It was good to hear your voice tonight. I will pray for you, my son.

Yes, the telephone call had upset Uncle Carlos. The old man had scribbled off a letter, an incoherent, sentimental note. What a good man he was!

Alessandro skimmed over the remaining lines: *Do not falter. . . . We will endure. . . . It is the only way. . . . Was necessary. . . . I await . . . rejoicing . . . the flint knife of sacrifice . . .*

He glanced at the signature but did not read the last line. He did not see there the answer to the question he had lived with since that morning in the mountains when he had found his mother dishonored and disemboweled, his father hanging by one heel from a tree. He stuffed the letter back into his pocket, changed his mind, rolled it into a ball and dropped it into the wastebasket.

⊹

Shortly after midnight a cool, heavy wind breathed across the city. Clouds filmed the star-pricked sky. A soft, delicious rain drifted down, the type of rain called *dedos de los ángeles,* "angels' fingers." The seven trawlers, running without lights, rolled in the greasy swells,

326

butting bow waves that hissed and bubbled. The engines, underneath blanket-padded hatches, beat steadily, spinning the shafts. The propellers bored in the black sea, screwing the rolling trawlers north. Each vessel carried fifty men, crammed down into the brutal stench and slipperiness of the fish holds, huddled in the forecastles, miserable in vomit-smeared blankets. A high wave sliding under the hull thrust the stern out of water, and the propeller raced, racking the bearings. Shovels clanked and ash buckets rattled. Reeking smoke spilled off into the night. Voget lay on the great, tarred trawl, the huge, lumpy net spread over the stern of the trawler *Christina*. In three hours they would be on the beach before the Hotel Miramar. Now there was nothing to do but listen to the thresh and hammer of the propeller, the steady hiss of the sea and the muffled sounds of voices from the wheelhouse. The trawler wallowed on, first in line, heading for the rendezvous with a man named Trop in the beach *cabaña* of a second-class resort hotel.

‡

The patrol stamped down the rain-slick, glassy pavement, their boots slugging in cadence. Alessandro flattened back in the doorway. The sergeant passed within six feet of him, trailing an odor of wet wool and stale brandy. The patrol marched steadily, their left arms swinging. A canteen clacked against a bayonet scabbard. The boots beat away down the street, echoing dully off the shuttered house fronts. Alessandro hefted the short iron bar and crept across the sidewalk. A pale point of light jigged at the street corner. The others followed him. One nudged his arm and pointed. Police patrol. Alessandro pulled away and knelt on the slippery asphalt. He wedged the tip of the bar under the edge of the sewer cover and leaned on it. The cover grated, the noise terrifyingly loud. The light came dancing closer, like a honey drop suspended in the cool fingers of the angels. Alessandro gestured, and the others flattened on the street, silent, all facing one way, watching the light, the acetylene torch mounted on the handlebars of the policeman's bicycle. Alessandro pried again, and the cover lifted, but with both hands on the bar he could not slide the heavy steel disc. Two of the others crawled over him, crushing the breath from his chest. The sweet rain lay cool in his hair. The cover clanked.

"Quick!"

The two men at the end of the line opened fire with pistols. Hands seized Alessandro and dragged him forward across the hole. He swung his legs down. The police fired back. A bullet bit through the loose cloth of his sleeve as his feet found the gritty ladder rungs. He dropped down, quickly but carefully. A distorted voice wowed up the shaft, and the smell of the sewers rammed into his nose like plugs of fecal paste. A shoe ground on the fingers of his right hand. The voice wowed again, a senseless gout of noise blown up the vertical pipe. Alessandro climbed down. The cover clanged as the two men left above dropped it into place. Now there was nothing but blackness, the filthy ladder and the voice screwing up with the smell, a spiral of stench and bubbling, shrill warnings. Then light shot up between his legs, and a hand grabbed his ankle.

"You have to let go and drop."

"All right. Get out of the way."

He fell, jarring hard, on a dry shelf of stone. An electric torch played about. He saw a heavy stone arch, a grate tangled with refuse, and the vast maw of a pipe.

"They saw us, all right. Jesus, what can you do? A patrol every four minutes, with police scattered in between."

"That's fine. We made it this far."

"Ya-ya-ya. But we've got to come back."

"You said we can go to the university."

"True, but this is a junction. Right here."

"General Vola will take us back in his car."

Someone else slammed down on the shelf and cursed softly, then laughed.

"Why didn't he come pick us up?"

The others came down the ladder. Alessandro called their names. The sound of his voice echoed weirdly, caroming and rebounding off the stone walls.

"Torches on. Go ahead. Lead us."

They crept along the ledge. A thin sludge oozed along the floor of the sewer. A rat sprang away from the torch beams, a bit of bright eye, scruff of fur and naked, whipping tail. Every sound pounded back off the curved walls, the scrape of a boot like a landslide, a muffled cough like someone starting up a diesel engine. The ledge ended at the archway; a rusted, flimsy-looking catwalk stretched over rushing water. Alessandro urged them on.

Somebody muttered in the darkness.

"What if they turn the water back on? Right now?"

Alessandro grinned.

"You hold your nose and pretend you're out on the *playa,* swimming with your best girl."

They trotted on, split into two groups, each running on the slopes of the great pipe, a two-meter belt of soft muck separating them. Another sewer drooled out of the left wall. Alessandro saw a glow. He halted, bracing himself, as the others stumbled against him.

"Lights out!"

The second group crept across the sucking filth. They waited and listened, trying to quiet their breathing. Foul water purled over the lip of the pipe to their left. Distant voices yelped and echoed incoherently. A point of light flicked on and off, as though someone signaled.

"Police?"

"Maybe not. Let's go. Two of you stay here. If it's the police, shoot and then go back the way we came. Don't worry about us. We'll get back somehow."

"In Vola's sedan, eh?"

"That's right."

The voices called again, slightly closer, wowing down the pipe. Alessandro drew in a chestful of air and ran ahead. The great pipe began to slope at last, very gradually, and he could hear the sound of falling water. The air was clearer, too.

"The central cistern?"

"That's right, like an underground lake. We go around the rim, the second tunnel as far as the ladder and we're there."

"All right."

They walked forward, turning their torches on and off, just enough light to see a half-dozen paces, the light off, quick cautious steps in the echoing darkness and the light snapped on again for another instant. They reached a parapet. To the left was a huge, clogged grate. Water gushed over the dam of refuse and fell with a roar to a deep, seething channel of brown water that foamed away swiftly, four meters wide, plunging down into the darkness. Alessandro played his torch over the grate. It was at least ten meters high and as many wide, a great strainer set in the concrete cloaca that ran from the belly of the city to the purifying sea. Branches, baskets, plugs of cloth and nameless lumps of smelly rot jammed the gaps, packed by the power of the stream. Rats clawed and climbed, rear legs kicking. One slipped and vanished into the dark, roaring torrent.

Alessandro turned.

"Fine. Here we are. How do we get to the other side?"

"There's a sort of drawbridge that hits up there on the other side. See the hole there? No, higher. That's it."

Two of the group tripped the mechanism, freeing a long iron spar fitted with a handrail. Gears chattered above the din of dropping dark water boiling in the gloom. The tip of the spar gnashed into place. Alessandro sprang forward, set his feet carefully and crossed. He heaved himself up through the hole and wiggled out on a wide, gentle slope of stone, the beach of the underground lake. He waited until two others joined him, then stood up.

"*Tía Ajo!*"

He whirled, his chest wrung with alarm, clawing at his revolver. The echoes slipped away and sprang back as he cocked the pistol and snapped on the torch, holding it far out from his body to draw a shot wide.

"*Tía Ajo! Tía Ajo!*"

The beam swept back and forth, then caught and held a figure crouching on the slanting stone. The man behind Alessandro jerked out a dry sob of laughter.

"Who is it?"

"Old Aunty Garlic from the San Pablo market."

"What's she doing down here?"

The figure rose, gathered some garments in odd, hooking motions and rushed down the slope, straight into the beam of the torch. Alessandro rose, his finger still touching the trigger. He stared intently and saw a face, dark and filthy, wrinkled as a monkey's paw, toothless, with great eyes, the dilated pupils closing against the glare of the torch. Purple garlic bulbs twisted around the dry, corded throat like a necklace. The creature dropped a stiff curtsey and nearly fell.

"I'm *Tía Ajo*. Are you the cleaners?"

Alessandro smiled and nodded.

"You live down here, Aunty?"

"Better here than there."

"Where is there?"

The old woman stopped beating her chest and pointed vaguely

around, at the hole above the grate, at the dark pool of water, the walls and finally the ceiling.

"And what do you do here, Aunty?"

"I bleach things, see?"

She waved a skinny arm into the darkness. Alessandro pointed his light beam. The torch picked out what looked like a fungus heap. The old woman scuttled over the stone slope and snatched up a pale, putrid garment, flopped it on the stones and began kneading it frantically.

"It takes the color out, see? You find them and put them back. The pool does it. It takes the colors out. Then I take them up and bleach them. Here's a fine shirt. Three centavos."

Alessandro turned. "It is so? This poor creature lives here in the sewer?"

"Only in the warm months. The rest of the year the sisters take her in. She does the wash for them and sells her garlic in the market. She's been crazy for years."

"Two centavos. Cheap, very cheap."

"Where do you get these things, Aunty?"

"Get them? Why, from the floaters. I have a long stick with a nail in it and another with a loop of rope. Sometimes I get them here. Sometimes down at my net. My floater net."

She pointed at the grate, her toothless mouth curled in a soundless crow. She stole up to Alessandro and laid her dry little claw on his arm.

"She was such a beauty. Such skin and long, fine dark hair. On her arm was a little gold bracelet, too. I sold it. You mustn't tell. The prettiest floater ever. A party dress of silk in the newish fashion. Chiffon, it was, thin as a shift, pale blue. What a beauty. And her little throat ripped open. They all looked for her, but *Tía Ajo* found her. I bleached. We did it, the water and I."

She spoke in a breathless, catchy croaking voice, her fingers gripping Alessandro's arm. She smirked at him, bobbing her head in and out of the torchlight.

"Who is *she?*"

"She must mean Carlota Brinzia, the banker's girl. It was last year. She disappeared. Never found the body. I guess Aunty did."

"Oh, yes. I found her. Then through the net with her. But I never do that with the little ones. So sweet they are, the little floaters. I save things for them and wrap them up and say a prayer for them before I let them go on down."

"Do you ever tell the police, Aunty? About what you find down here? Where you get the clothes you sell?"

"Police!"

The old woman gave a strangled yip of fear. She tried to break away, but Alessandro seized her. The old woman's jaws butted in terror. She jerked feebly, her fusty clothes stirring the garlic bulbs until they rustled dryly like the wings of insects.

"Listen, we're not the police. We're the cleaners, Aunty."

At once she quieted. Alessandro released her and she smoothed her bodice. Her eyes glittered.

"No, you're not. I know them all, and they know me. You're from the trouble up above. You've sent me three floaters today already. I know. *Tía Ajo* knows. Sent me some more, eh? There's a sweet little man. Send me pretty ones and big ones, too, eh?"

"Can we trust her, Alessandro?"

"Who would believe the poor soul? Let's go on. We can't keep the captain waiting."

They walked on around the gently sloping beach of stone that ringed the dark lake. She scuttled along beside Alessandro, picking like a rat at his sleeve.

"Everything comes here, comes through here, you know. It goes in the mouth, down to the belly and then to here. Or it comes from the brain to the hands, then on the back, but at last . . . I get it! We take the color out, we do. You and him. You'll both come to me, down here. Everything drops down, loses color and goes away. The thing to do is just to sit here and wait. That's all. If you wait long enough, all the cats and dogs and birds . . . the tiny floaters and the big ones. Be sure you wear your best suit, *Señorito* . . . I wouldn't get much for what you've got on now. Poof! You should make it, not *walk* in it. But I'll wait. For both of you. For all of you . . ."

"Get away, *Tía Ajo!* Leave us alone."

She fell back into the darkness, twittering. Alessandro could hear her sop the heap of garments on the stone beach and behind her the dull roar of the cascade through the grate.

One of the group brushed by him, hurrying away from her.

"Jesús y María!"

Alessandro caught his arm.

"Don't think that. We're fighting for the ones like her. When we win, no one will live in a hole like this."

"Ya-ya-ya. But where there is carrion, there are also flies, no?"

"Hssst! Here's the tunnel."

Alessandro shook his head and waded up the stream of water that spewed into the lake. Ahead he saw the ladder, the stiff rusty shafts leading up to the little courtyard behind the *taberna* where Captain Chinchón waited to take him to General Vola. His right foot came down on something soft and elastic rolling beneath the water. Something for *Tía Ajo.*

⸸

"She is here, Your Excellency."

Vizarra opened his eyes and lay staring up at the painted ceiling. His Swiss physician had given him several injections. The inside of his mouth tasted of copper, and his head throbbed. He blinked at Malata and sat up, shivering.

"Eh? What's that? Oh. Send her away. Tell her I'm busy. Take her back to the villa."

Malata shook his sleek, dark head. Vizarra glowered at him in a dull rage. Did he never get tired? Did he ever sleep?

"You heard me. Take her back."

"But this is the girl from the pueblo, Your Excellency. Remember? The flat tire? The blind girl with the baby? You gave orders that she was to be brought into the city. For the nuns to take her."

"Then why is she here?"

"The streets are still closed."

"Is there no Red Cross? Put her in an ambulance. Take her someplace and make the others take care of her for a while."

"Take care of her?"

"You know what I mean. Get her across the lines to the sisters. You can still telephone, can't you?"

"They've tapped the wires—"

"*Claro,* they've tapped the wires! For six hours we've been coding everything, and you say they've tapped the wires. Just call and tell them to be ready to receive a blind young woman with a child. Is that so difficult?"

"No, Your Excellency. Except that it might be mistaken as a code signal."

Vizarra groaned and swung off the hard couch. He thrust his feet into his slippers and scrubbed his jowls.

"I will call the convent and speak with the Holy Mother myself. Will that satisfy this rabble who have torn up the streets?"

"No doubt, Excellency."

"And you? Will you be quite satisfied?"

"I have nothing to say or do—"

"Exactly. Exactly! I . . . I do everything here. Everything. There is nothing so small but I must make a decision. Do you suppose you can locate some hot water, soap and a razor, or must I find them for myself?"

"At once, Excellency."

"Has she called? The other? Lucía?"

"Twice. She sounds alarmed. She doesn't know what to do."

"Eh? Well, you told her I'd be out today, didn't you?"

"Yes, of course. But she doesn't know what to do."

"Do? She has her weekly broadcast, hasn't she? Tell her to rehearse her songs. This business will be over by then. What about that damned Vola?"

"The lines are down."

"I know that! Has anyone made an attempt to reach him?"

"Two companies have gone down into the municipal sewers!"

"Regulars, from the garrison?"

"Yes."

"A good place for them. When the sun comes up, release the pigeons from the roof. Three or four. Code the messages. Vola must try to break out. If he stays there too long, he'll have to fight every man, woman and child between there and the Plaza Mayor. He is to strike south to the waterfront, relieve the commanders of the Coast Guard vessels there and arrest them. He is to place three artillery officers, one on each vessel, and begin bombardment of the university. Can you remember all that?"

"Of course, Excellency."

"Amazing. Amazing. But then I keep forgetting. You used to be able to serve a party of twelve from appetizers to dessert without a mistake, eh?"

Malata bowed stiffly, his face impassive. Vizarra buttoned his tunic, glanced at the map of the city spread across the table and grunted. He ran a blunt finger down the map.

"Get Zamal. He is to lead an assault column to take the pressure off Vola. What's the news from the mine?"

"Still quiet. The workers walked out yesterday, but they've done nothing since. They seem to be just talking about things."

"Have the locomotives been found?"

"Ten kilometers north of Casanueva. The last report was that they seemed to be taking on material from trucks. There's a small village there to the east, obviously held by the rebels. Near the sanatorium, you know."

"Send up the aircraft. Get the trucks first. We'll see about the trains later."

"There is a rumor that Rota has been arrested."

"Good. Good and bad. That means a centralized command. Anything else?"

"Scattered street fighting. Some female prisoners were taken. Factory workers. They upholster furniture."

"With rifles and pistols, eh?"

"It would seem so."

"Women! Blind ones, fearful ones, furniture workers and those dressed in uniforms of the garrison. Have them sent to the women's prison."

"I am sorry, Excellency, but that won't be possible. The rebels under the student Olmega captured the prison about three hours ago. O'Conner feels that Olmega's unit may be shifting their headquarters away from the university, to get away from the assault scheduled in a few hours. He requests permission to attack and recapture the women's prison."

"No. The university first. We must crush the place where the snakes nest. Send the female prisoners to the Convent of Saint Anna. Lucca's Guards are still holding the center?"

"They have advanced slightly, some four blocks. I took the liberty of marking the new positions."

"You did. Well, in the future, wake me up, understand?"

Malata's eyes flicked a glance at the Caudillo. He nodded his sleek head.

"I understand you perfectly, Excellency."

335

"Fine. Soap, hot water and a razor. I can't telephone the Holy Mother looking like this."

↓

Captain Chinchón, tiny and neat as a wasp, perched on a stool, his stiff cuffs pressed against his chest. He spoke in a thin, treble voice, gazing all the while with disgust at the sticky tabletop. The back room reeked with the sodden clothing cast off by Alessandro and his men. Alessandro nodded as he dressed himself in the uniform of a first lieutenant. He shrugged into the jacket. The sleeves were too short. Chinchón drew a breath.

"I felt it was important to communicate certain basic facts of psychology, if you understand my meaning."

"I do. Please continue."

"The recital of scientific data in the rear room of a café is merely the expression of one's scientific interests, no?"

"*Claro*. A conversation, so to speak. Not to be mistaken for anything more. It is quite natural for a junior officer to study at length the personality of his superiors. After all, he must get on with them as perfectly as possible. It is a duty, really."

Chinchón nodded, his nose wrinkled against the odors. The room seemed jammed with stinking, silent men, their hands like hooks ready to shred his immaculate person.

"To proceed. The general is entirely self-educated. That is to say that what he knows or thinks he knows—the two are not entirely separated in his mind—he has learned from experience only. He has had no formal education whatever. I cannot consider that his years in the army constitute any sort of sophisticating influence. Basically he is a primitive. What he does not understand he fears. What he does understand he either respects or dominates. Now, as a primitive man, he understands and respects force. What he does not, cannot, understand is the force of forces. He does not understand the force of the . . . uh, insurgent movement. He has experienced such a force before, of course, during the previous rebellion, since he served with the national troops. But he does not understand *why* such a force exists. Men in the streets, shooting, yes. Why they are shooting, no. He cannot understand this. He is not capable of comprehension."

"Go on."

"It is the sign of the psychologically primitive—if we grant that his personality is well integrated before—to be deeply troubled when faced with incomprehensible forces. Anxieties are produced. The effort to raise the personality to a higher level and to reintegrate with the external environment is simply too difficult. This in turn produces a fracturing of the integration of the *internal* environment—"

"That means he's drunk all the time, Alessandro—"

"Quiet, please. I must hear this."

"He is therefore doubly anxious. Now, the primitive or the child resorts to imagination, superstition and magic."

"Magic?"

"The belief that some unknown power will aid him. He remains now inert, but secure inside. His superstitious beliefs counter his dread of incomprehensible external forces; he has reverted to a simple, integrated level. He is waiting, quite literally, for a sign. You must remember, he most certainly has some Indian blood."

"This is all very interesting, Captain. Do you believe that is why the general sought the company of Ramos?"

"I do. He does not understand you or your movement. I have heard him admit that he believes you to be your father, at least at times. You pass back and forth between two persons, because that is the way he thinks of you. Because this tells him you have some special powers, he is afraid. But he also fears the Caudillo, for quite different reasons, concrete reasons, comprehensible to him. He went to Ramos for magic, something to check the unknown."

"Were you there?"

"Yes."

"What did they say, did you hear?"

"The two met in secret."

"Were there written agreements?"

"Between them?"

"That wouldn't be possible, would it? Then you have no idea what he agreed to do or not to do?"

"No more than yourself. He received orders to mobilize the army. He sent out instructions to that effect. He mobilized the garrison. But gave no further orders. He was to have moved yesterday, but did nothing. I am told he was indifferent. Completely indifferent. He seemed to be waiting. For what, I do not know."

"Can you guess?"

"For the sign, I think."

"I wish that I had known this yesterday . . ."

Chinchón shrugged and sniffed. He drew out his watch.

"Come, it is now time. I have my receipt for one uniform left with the *patrón* here to be cleaned and pressed. I have encountered a lieutenant slightly the worse for drink. Now I will accompany him to the barracks with his orderly. I will wait at the front door."

The captain stood and walked swiftly from the room. The others gathered around Alessandro, their faces strained with anxiety. A guttering candle swabbed their faces with shadows.

"Don't go, Alessandro!"

"I don't trust—"

"Little sneaking bastard—"

"If he'll turn his coat now, he'll do it again."

Alessandro thrust his revolver into his holster and drew on his cape.

"How do I look?"

"Fine. You'll pass. Remember the watchword?"

"Fundador."

"Don't trust him."

"Listen, why not just let him stay there? Waiting for this sign."

"I must see him! Tomorrow depends on it. Everything depends on it."

"No, Alessandro, everything depends on you!"

He pulled away from them, then stopped in the doorway and stared at them somberly.

"Listen, the government depends on one man. Our movement is that of the people. I am here to bring the army together with the people."

"But if he refuses, you'll be trapped!"

Alessandro tapped his fingers on his holster.

"Not for long. You will have to get along without either Vola or me. Supreme command will then be the Central Committee. You can trust Carlos Sánchez absolutely. Now, *adiós.*"

"Adiós, Alessandro . . . go with God."

He stepped through the door and was gone, followed by his "orderly." The *patrón* of the café bent and blew out the candle.

Outside the *taberna,* Alessandro adjusted his cape. Down the street a sentry called a challenge. The great block of stone that was the garrison headquarters was invisible. Captain Chinchón waited patiently. Alessandro walked up to him. The officer nodded approvingly.

"You wear the uniform well."

"I have had some practice."

"Indeed. Well, let us go. You will oblige me, of course, by pretending to be rather drunk when we reach the sentries."

"Of course. You will direct me to the general's office?"

"And immediately after that, I go off duty."

Alessandro smiled ironically.

"Yes, it would be rather dangerous to stay around."

"Exactly. I devote my free time to my work. I, like yourself, am an author."

"Really?"

"Not poetry and novels, however. Although I must say that I have enjoyed your work immensely. Particularly the insights into the character of the revolutionary. Your analysis by types: the frustrated liberal, the intellectual, the lower-middle-class failure in business or professional work, the worker with his mixture of sentimentalism and defiance, the malcontent—I found that essay on the malcontent character in the plays of Shakespeare entrancing."

The man accompanying Alessandro sniggered. Alessandro sighed. How strange it was to be strolling in the rain in a stolen uniform, while this little man buzzed on like a fly.

"I'm afraid that my analysis by type, as you call it, was hardly constructed from scientific principles. I simply wrote down what I had observed."

Chinchón waved his hand nonchalantly.

"So much the better! You observe facts and draw them into a coherent order, scattered truths drawn by the magnet, like iron filings, to make a new, artistic truth. There is the truth of raw facts and the truth of art. The poet can be most useful to the scientist. The artist may dare more. The single flash of lightning from the soul, eh? The brilliance, the power, the destructive slash across the darkness. The worthy scientist observes the artistic lightning bolt—"

"And estimates the kilowatt hours of electricity expended?"

"Something like that. You see, the scientist must err on the side of caution, the artist must err on the side of risk. The reckless scientist is a fool; the cautious artist is, *ipso facto,* a traitor to himself."

"Very interesting."

Chinchón nodded. They were fifty paces from the sentry boxes. The captain's voice dropped to an odd, treble, whistling whisper.

"I should especially enjoy talking with you at some later date. My work could not be considered complete without some serious attention given to the psychology of command in irregular and guerrilla groups. Also terror as a form of command. I could promise you full acknowledgment in the preface. Here, here is my card."

Alessandro accepted the bit of pasteboard and thrust it into his pocket. He was dumbfounded. Laughter tickled in his chest. Chinchón stepped out like a bantam, pecking his way across the street to the sentries. He whirled and trotted back. Alessandro bent to hear his words.

"Please remember that you are drunk. Perhaps you know a bawdy song you might sing?"

" *'Juan en la casa de Putas'?*"

"Yes, that will do. You there, sort of hold him up, eh? But with respect, delicacy. He is your superior!"

Chinchón darted ahead. Alessandro dragged his officer's hat down over his brow and flung his arm around his companion. He began to bawl out the words in a thick baritone.

"Una noche a la taberna . . ."

"Quién?"

"Capitán Chinchón. Tercera compañía."

"Juan bebe la cerveza . . ."

"La palabra?"

"Fundador!"

"Pase, Capitán. Y los otros?"

"Di', 'Voy a la casa de putas . . .' "

"Pues, un amigo . . . un poco—"

"Di', 'Voy a la casa de putas, Voy a ver mi mamá!' "

Ten paces from the sentry. Five.

"Un' hora mas tarde, borracho . . ."

The sentry was grinning, but Chinchón was watching attentively.

"Who is there?"

"Eh? Oh, *Teniente* Milami."

"What unit?"

"Second cavalry. Fourth company."

"The password?"

"Fundador, hombre! Best cognac there is!"

He slumped forward. Chinchón and his "orderly" carried him through the gate and along the cement walk to the inner courtyard.

Alessandro made a fussy attempt to appear dignified, thrusting himself free and wavering a few paces forward, clutching his cape. Behind him the sentries guffawed.

"Tocando con su carajo . . ."

Chinchón touched his arm.

"Very good. Now, straight on through that door. I'll go with you to the top of the stairs.'

⸸

General Vola poured his glass full of brandy. The office was stifling hot, the windows sealed. Bugs swirled around the lantern set in the center of his desk. Outside it was raining and dark, unhealthy, the whole night crawling with disease, a wash of fevers. Vola patted his stubbled cheek with a dirty kerchief, then prodded the soaked bit of cloth down under the paunch that fell over his belt. He mopped his hand on his stained tunic and groaned. His little bloodshot eyes blinked as he fumbled for a cigar.

"Not good enough for them. Build their stinking railway. But not good enough to drink champagne with the gringos. General of the Army. The sons of whores. Now I am to kill children. Ai-ya, *qué pena . . ."*

He shook his bushy head at the shame and injustice and drank from his glass, pouting his full lips to sip the brandy. The chair squealed beneath him as he heaved back and waved his cigar and sang:

> I'm a little army burro;
> I carry heavy loads
> Of food and guns for soldiers
> On a thousand dusty roads.

He groaned again, and tears leaked from his lids.

"Vola, do this. Vola, do that. Never a minute's peace. Me. The bravest man in all Costa Plata makes a railroad for gringos. *Jesús y María.* Cheaper, he says. I am cheaper for him, eh? He'll learn. They'll all learn."

Vola belched juicily and puffed his cigar. He hummed for a few moments, blew out smoke and sang again:

> I'm a little army burro
> That always worked so well;

He bobbed his head, and his fat, wet lips stretched into a grin of guile. Vola was a cunning one. You had to watch out for him. No one knew how deep he was. Oh, yes.

"Vola has a little plan. Oh, yes, yes, yes, yes, yes, yes. Drink to that. Aaah. *Muy bien.* General, you're a smart one. That's what he said. *Jesús,* those eyes of his! Like a snake. *La plata.* The silver. Oh, the silver."

He swayed from side to side. The chair cracked and squealed. The insects swirled and fluttered around the lantern. He pawed at them clumsily and nearly overturned the lantern. He filled his glass again.

I'm a little army burro;
I've been beaten, cursed and kicked,
And when my days are over,
I know that I'll be tricked.

He moaned and puffed his cigar. *Jesús,* what a sad little song. *Qué pena.* But Vola won't be tricked. No, no. He rolled his head from side to side, grinning happily as he watched the whole room cant and swoop. His face was numb as bacon.

I'm a little army burro;
I'll grow too old to run.
I'll be led behind the barn
By a soldier with a gun.

He squinted at the lantern until the light danced like a bead of gold.

"Twenty thousand reales. Ramos has promised. What a lot of money! And just for a favor. Just for doing nothing. He's a terrible thief, that Ramos. So? I am a man of honor. I sit here, do nothing. Vola gets his money and—hup!—across the border. Huh! Let them kick me out. I'll be rich. Yes, rich."

He would buy an automobile first. An American auto. Bright red. With a loud horn and lights on the front. And a motor of great power. Then a hacienda. With women. Fat women with red lips and thighs soft as cream. He would die the little death three times a day, each time with a different one. God, what a life he would lead! And all for doing nothing, while Ramos took the silver from the mine.

> I'm a little army burro,
> But soon I will be dead.
> My reward for years of duty?
> A bullet in the head!

A shadow fell across the desk. Vola squinted at it. The tears blurred his eyes. Why was there a shadow? It moved. . . .

He looked up. He tried to focus his eyes.

"What do you want here, you two shits? Get out!"

"Two? Look again, General."

Vola felt a nameless dread grip him, as though the fat on his body thickened to suet. He tried to move. He blinked. One man. Two men. One. No, two. No, just one. Who was he? He stared stupidly across the office at the coat rack. His holster was there, but the pistol was gone. The tongue seemed to swell in his mouth.

"Who . . . are you?"

"Look at me. Don't you know?"

"No. Go away. I'm busy."

"You sing well, little burro."

"Don't call me that, you shit."

"Look at me. Have you seen this face before?"

Vola stared, his flesh crawling. The figure before him did not move.

"No, I—"

"Hanging upside down. From a pine tree. In the sierra."

"No, no!"

"Staring up. Stones rammed in the belly."

"No, *Jesús y María,* I did nothing! I swear it!"

"I have come to see you. Now you know me. I am Alessandro Martín."

Vola opened and shut his gummy mouth. His heart thudded and sweat gushed from his armpits. He tried to shout, but his words seemed to clot in his chest.

"Guard . . . call the—"

"What for? I walked by them. They know me here. They let me come to you. They know it's necessary for you to see me."

"Where . . . where did you come from?"

The slender figure did not stir, but stared at him with great, luminous dark eyes.

"I come from Ramos."

"From . . . him?"

"He has joined us."

"That can't be."

"I can't be here, either. But here I am. Touch my hand."

Vola leaned back and swallowed. It was the brandy. He was drunk. The room was too hot. Something he ate. He was dreaming.

"No, I . . . don't want—"

"The miners have come with us. Against the government."

"But that's not the plan!"

"The plan has been changed."

Vola nodded. The words fell from the figure's lips like stones dropped into a dark pool. It was the truth he spoke.

"We no longer march against the rebels?"

"That is for you to decide."

Vola covered his face with his hands and groaned.

"But what about my money? I was to take the troops out, and then seize the mine. Ramos was to load the silver, give me my money. Then blow up the mine. Take a horse and a few men over the mountains. He has betrayed me, that swine who calls himself a priest!"

"No. He has joined his miners with us, with the people."

"But . . . but he was to go off and build a big city for his miners, with the silver. That was it. He has silver, and I have to dynamite the mine to keep the others away."

"Everything has changed now. God has spoken to Ramos. And now Ramos speaks to you."

Vola swung away. He stared at the window. Black night and the cool, strangling cobwebs of rain, like a dripping tomb. He shuddered and closed his eyes. High in the mountains Ramos crouched like a snake with broad wings and black, boring eyes, invisible beams eating like streams of acid through the night. How could it be? This one and Ramos? Vola swung back and stared at the lamp. Here there was the steady shadow. Even inside it was not safe from them. They were everywhere. The room was cold now, not hot. Vola gagged on his fear.

"What does he say? What does he say, Ramos?"

"He will lead his people down the railroad north and west of the city. A new force will advance from the northeast. We hold the west part of the city. The dock workers are with us. We will close the port. That leaves only the south."

"But . . . that's away from the mountains!"

"Your place, as a patriot, is here. You can be the liberator of the south."

"But that's the wrong way . . . wrong, all wrong."

"Deny the support of the army to Vizarra. That leaves only the police and the National Guard. We'll take care of them. The people will be with us. The government will fall."

Vola squinted and grinned. Suddenly he felt warm, as though the cold suet had melted and ran like heated oil. Why, of course the government would fall! The two forces had become one. Nothing could stand against such power! How simple, how clear and safe it was! Vola chuckled delightedly and puffed on his cigar. Now it would be his turn. The Caudillo would be made to do this and that. Finally, he would run for his life, off with his gringo friends. Vola slumped in his chair, his belly bubbling with amusement but one eye fixed on the black, pattered glass of the window that shielded him still from some of the nameless things he feared. It might be done still, getting the money and getting away. He drew himself up, sucked in his paunch and tried to strike a businesslike pose. The cigar slipped from his fingers and fell on the floor. He tried to crush it out with his heel, but his leg was too short. He thumped the floor four times, then shrugged and allowed the cigar to smolder in a bubble of melted varnish.

"So. Very well. How much?"

"What do you mean, how much?"

"Ramos promised me twenty thousand reales."

"Naturally, you refused. A man of your standards could spend that much in six months."

Vola swallowed and relaxed His shoulders settled. He reached for the brandy bottle and flicked his finger against it.

"I refused. Naturally, I refused."

"What is silver after all? Does a man sell his honor as a soldier and patriot for thirty pieces of silver?"

"No, not thirty. Twenty *thousand*. Oh, I see. Yes. Well, of course not. Just what I told him, the swine."

"The admiration of the nation. That is worth twenty thousand silver *ingots!* Ramos, of course, knowing your power, encouraged you to think only of exile. But as commander of the Third Army of Liberation only your opponents would be in exile, from the moment you took command!"

Vola nodded, his head spinning. He could barely follow the words that fell on him like drops of rain. But he was cunning, shrewd; you had to watch out for him. Let the other one talk. He would listen and nod, and perhaps everything would work out well in the end.

"How you must have laughed at him."

"Oh, I did. I did. I laughed right out loud. Two or three times."

"To think that he, a leader of miners, could suggest such dishonorable action to one of the great patriots of the country."

Vola sighed. It was true. He loved his country. He could feel it within him. His voice trembled with a sincerity that shocked him. He snatched up the bottle.

"I should never have listened to that Ramos. I nearly sold myself for next to nothing. He's crazy, anyway. It's all right if you don't look into his eyes. Now, you can trust me. Everyone knows that Vola's word is worth . . . whatever he says it is. We are patriots, both of us. We are brothers. But Ramos is a cattle snake. You just can't trust him. Have a drink?"

"Not now."

"You will excuse me? I have been ill lately. I think . . . I am nearly certain that he cast a spell on me. Well, not that exactly, but he has influenced the air or something. I have had bad dreams. Of being trapped in the mines, looking for him. I wake up all cold. Terrible. Very bad. I find a little of this helps. Are you sure? Come on."

"Not now."

Vola drank and belched again. If only he would take off his cape, sit down, have a glass. Why did he stand there motionless, his lips barely moving when he spoke, like some . . . some spirit of the dead?

"Ramos has poisoned them, the miners. He has taken them back so that they believe in Vigo. Maybe you know this?"

"In Vigo? You can't be serious. They are good people, the Indians. Good Catholics."

At the word *Catholic,* Vola crossed himself and belched.

"You don't know, see? He's got them in his hand. I saw it. Be careful with him. He's not a good fellow like me. I don't even think he's a patriot. You know what?"

Vola glanced cautiously around his office and leaned forward.

"What?"

Vola tapped his fat lips with his extended forefinger and whispered hoarsely.

"I think he's just out for himself!"

"No. You can't mean that."

"I never meant anything more. Just out for himself."

"I will be careful. I promise you."

"Oh, that's all right. Just a word of warning. We are brothers, no?"

"Are we? Ramos and I want to know."

Vola rolled his eyes from the slick, shining, gilded cape to the black, dripping rectangle of glass. Behind each stood a presence. He was caught between them.

"Well, I have my official responsibilities . . ."

"Exactly. You retain command here."

"*Claro.* Command. Responsibilities. My men. Loyalty and service."

"An officer's first responsibility is to his troops."

"Right!"

Vola thumped the desk with his fist. Brandy splashed from his glass. He tilted up the bottle.

"Are you sure?"

"Not now."

"And if the troops reflect the will of the people . . ."

Vola sank back into his chair, sucking his fingers and grinning.

"Impossible. My troops reflect *my* will."

"But you are a man of the people."

"Right!"

Vola pounded the desk again, carefully snatching up the glass in his left hand as his right struck the surface. The lantern light wavered.

"Then the troops reflect the will of the people as expressed through their commanding officer!"

Vola sipped his drink and reflected, his small eyes blinking slowly. He sighed at last and set the glass down empty.

"That depends."

"On what, General?"

"The will of the people . . . call it the affection of the people?"

"Affection? Why?"

"I would be more certain of the will of the people if I had some sign of their affection."

"They will love you if you act in their name."

"Ah? But how can I be sure of this *before* I act?"

"A gift might—"

"Yes, a gift might—"

"Fifty thousand?"

"No, you said twenty thousand ingots. If a gift were made—in the name of the people, of course—I could be certain in my own mind. Once a man is certain, he can act! How I will act when I am certain! Why, you won't believe it until you see me. Surely the value of twenty thousand ingots is a small sum for such action?"

"I could promise you the money within five days."

"Ah? And I could promise action beginning in five days."

"You have my word."

"And you have mine. In five days . . . very well, in five days."

"Vizarra will remove you if you don't act against us. How can you last five days?"

"Ah. If I *do* move against you, how can *you* last five days?"

"There is the army on the northeast—"

"Never heard of them."

"You will."

"Umm."

"And there is Ramos—"

Vola glanced once at the window, once at the gleaming cape, and fumbled with his glass. His mouth had gone dry again. He shivered.

"If you are with us, General, you will triumph and receive a gift of the value of twenty thousand silver ingots."

"I am under direct orders from the Caudillo—"

"Who depends on you almost completely."

"Of course, of course."

"If you withdraw your support . . ."

"Run away? Abandon my troops? Never!"

"Just by staying here. Do nothing. Allow the garrison to make up its own mind."

"That would be mutiny. Nobody mutinies against Vola."

"But you are not afraid to deny the support of your troops to Vizarra when the motherland cries out to you?"

"Afraid? Vola afraid? Never in my life!"

348

"Then you'll—"

"It's simply a question of being practical. I could be arrested. Even shot."

"How can they get to you if you are with us? That leaves only the Guards and the police."

"And Vizarra."

"One man."

"Eh? Wait and see. You'll find out what sort he is."

"General . . ."

Vola poured himself another glass of brandy. He fumbled for a cigar, remembered the one that had fallen to the floor and looked about for it. It lay dead in the center of a blistered pool of gummy varnish.

"Vola demands the confidence of the people . . . first."

"I can give you a written pledge."

"I prefer cash to pieces of paper."

"But if you accept the promise now?"

"Then I feel sure that I will find it very difficult to act. In any way."

"What if they replace you?"

"What if they try, you mean?"

"If they try, yes."

"Accidents happen. Every accident now can be blamed on the rebels, especially where someone gets killed."

"Have you received any orders?"

"No."

"Do you know that Major Zamal is going to attack south of the university tomorrow . . . today, really, in a matter of hours?"

Vola yawned and belched, then scratched his bushy head.

"Yes? I wish him luck. Without orders, I will not lift a finger."

"Good."

"And no one is going to replace me. If that's what the Caudillo wants, he will have to come here himself."

"He may try that."

"Eh? So did you. But he'll have to get out. And so will you."

"A good point. I'll need an automobile. Do you have a staff car with a radio transmitter?"

"Yes. Four."

"I want one. I have given you a promise of the people's gratitude and affection. In return, I need a sedan with radio equipment."

"You will have need of such equipment?"

"*Claro*. And soon."

"You expect difficulties with the Telefónica?"

"The wires are being cut all over the city. Right now."

"But the national radio transmitter?"

"We will use it to proclaim the People's Republic of Costa Plata. I hope you will have a speech prepared?"

"I have never spoken over the radio . . . yet."

"The sedan, General?"

"Go ahead. Ask the clerk downstairs for the requisition form."

"In four or five days, General . . ."

"The situation will be much clearer in four or five days. Many things will have happened."

"Will the troops of the garrison be restricted?"

"I have received no orders."

"I do not think you are reflecting the will of the people, General."

"I have not heard their voice yet. Have a drink?"

"Yes. Fine, enough. What will we drink to?"

Vola looked at the dark window and the shining cape.

"To the patriots of Costa Plata?"

"*Salud!*"

"*Salud!*"

"Liberty or death, General!"

Vola leaned back and slapped his paunch. His flesh felt as though it slipped and skidded underneath his skin. The figure before him blurred. The room leaned and whirled slowly counterclockwise.

"Twenty thousand ingots . . . eh?"

"You have my word."

"We are brothers. Brothers, yes, yes."

Vola leaned forward until his face rested on his arms. He began to weep again. He stared numbly at the top of his desk, a stained slab of brown. He heard an automobile start down in the courtyard and the clash of the outside gate. He fumbled with his holster.

"He took my pistol, the little shit. But what a bargain I drove, what a bargain!"

⸸

Diego swept the beach. Each morning at daybreak, even during the rainy season, he walked from his plank-and-tar-paper shack to the

350

Hotel Miramar. The head porter asked after his health and gave him a rake and a broom made of bound twigs. Diego walked through the misty gardens, down the path. At the concrete wall he stopped, took off his sandals and rolled a cigarette. For a few minutes he sat there, even in the rain, his cigarette sheltered, smoking and gazing at the sea. Then he carefully shredded the stub of his cigarette and placed the unburned fragments of tobacco back into his pouch. He stood up and stretched his old, stiff frame and padded down to the sand. The beach ran for more than a kilometer. Every dawn Diego swept it clean of sea wrack, bits of board and tarred rope, net floats, scraps of sodden paper, an occasional bottle and the dismembered bits of crabs. The summer storms brought a wash of seaweed, brown scarves of kelp, and thousands of jellyfish. Diego began at the seawall and raked south until the beach ended in a tumbled mound of barnacled boulders. He turned and raked back, gathering the refuse of the sea into neat piles every fifty paces. The end of his morning harvest brought him to the water's edge, where he stood watching the gulls soar and tilt and the sandpipers skitter and poke for food. Then he walked back to the wall for the steel drum, rolled it across the sand and set it upright. He picked up each small pile and carried it to the drum. When all the piles had been dumped in, the barrel was nearly full, too heavy for Diego to lift. That was the job of two busboys, who came out before breakfast and carried the drum away, while Diego moved back and forth over the coarse, white sand brushing patiently, smoothing out the hills and covering the few stones, effacing even his own footprints, until at last the job was done and the whole beach lay smooth and unmarked, ready for the rich clients of the hotel. Then he returned the rake and broom to the head porter and took *café con leche* and a *churro* in the hotel kitchen. He dipped the fried dough in the coffee and ate it, finished the coffee, wiped his mustache and left quietly to walk back to his shack.

When he sat down at the seawall and unstrapped his sandals, he saw the fishing trawlers a few kilometers offshore. He stared at them a moment, trying to remember when he had seen steam-powered fishing vessels. His own sons, three of them, owned and sailed a lateen-rigged open boat six meters long, painted bright yellow with blue eyes on the prow to see the rocks. He finished his cigarette, gathered his tools and walked down to the sand. By the time he had reached the boulders, he could hear the slow thresh of the engines driving the trawlers toward the beach. He leaned on his rake, puzzled. What did they want in so close? There were no fish worth catching in over the shoals.

Diego dropped his rake and thrust his hands into his pockets. Should he tell the head porter? The manager would not yet be awake. But could the head porter do anything? Perhaps it was an error, some sort of mistake. But so many trawlers, all with men on the decks! Diego hurried toward the pier. Normally he stayed away, content merely to admire the fine yachts. But these men had set them all adrift, and now three trawlers were tied up at the dock. Diego winced as he saw a heavy cabin cruiser butt against a yawl and sheer the sailing craft's bowsprit off like a twig. A smaller powerboat rolled wildly, the new sun flashing off the windows. It slued into the surf and careened drunkenly toward the beach. The next sea foamed into the cockpit and drove the craft sideways. Dark, dirty-smelling smoke streamed away from a trawler as its propeller lashed the water under the stern. It backed away from the pier, and another swung in slowly to take its place. The cabin cruiser tumbled under a hissing roller and crunched on its side, swamped. Diego was appalled. Between the pier and beach a dozen yachts bobbed and butted, drifting free toward the high, punishing surf and the beach beyond. And the men had guns. There were hundreds of men with guns!

Diego broke into a jerky trot, away from the beach, up the slope toward the hotel. Something buzzed over his head. A spout of sand lashed up to his left. He heard the shots, the flat snap of rifles, and men shouting. Diego flung away his rake, stopped and raised his hands in the air and turned into the second volley of riflefire. Two bullets struck him in the chest. He fell backward, kicking and tearing at his shirt. His shriek bubbled out in blood, staining the unswept sand.

✢

Major Zamal nodded once. The lieutenant called, and the gunners snapped the lanyards. The field guns slammed and rolled back along the street. The loaders tossed the new shells from the caissons. The breechblocks opened and the smoking brass shell casings clattered on the pavement. Zamal watched through his field glasses as the high explosives pounded the barricade. Thirty rounds were to be fired at nearly point-blank range. Another shell hit near the side of the barricade and wrenched off a hunk of masonry. Fragments scattered like shrapnel. Return fire from the rooftops snapped harmlessly down the street, the rifle bullets ricocheting off the pavement a full block away from the gunners. The fieldpieces slammed again, and the shells tore at the barricade. Zamal looked around. The infantry waited in the side streets, sheltered and ready to go. The barrage stopped, and the sudden silence rang in Zamal's ears. He turned to his aide.

"Send them in! Attack! Attack!"

The soldiers rose and streamed sluggishly out of the streets. Zamal shook his fist and bellowed.

"Attack! Attack! Run! Run, you animals!"

The troops moved forward, keeping close to the house fronts. The men in the lead stopped to fire at the barricade. The soldiers weren't running to seize the barricade in a single, splendid assault. They were walking! Zamal stared through his glasses. He could see men at the broken barricade and figures on the rooftops and at the windows down the street. The firing quickened and the attack slowed and stopped. The soldiers pressed against the sides of the houses and fired wildly up at the roofs. The street echoed with the crackle of rifle fire.

"Another twenty rounds on the barricade!"

The gunners sprang to the fieldpieces, and the light cannons slammed. The shells howled down the street and blasted into the barricade. Zamal screamed with rage. The troops were panicking! They dropped to the ground and began crawling back. The attack was broken before it fairly began! Zamal shook both fists, his face crimson, and shouted in a strangled voice.

"You cowards! You traitors! You dogs!"

The soldiers slunk back along the walls, dragging their wounded. A dozen bodies lay in the street. Zamal wrote a report with shaking hands, stating that he had met unexpectedly heavy resistance and demanding reinforcements. He insisted on being informed why the city garrison had not launched their attempt to break out of the rebel-held San Pablo district. Was he expected to capture the university single-handed?

The field guns fired until the ammunition caissons were empty, and the street was littered with spent shell casings. The barricade had been bashed to a heap of rubble no more than waist-high. A second sluggish attack was repelled, the soldiers breaking and running before

353

they had come within a block of the ruined position. Zamal slumped in his command car, his face white and twitching. He asked permission to execute twenty men as an example. The garrison lay silent. Three aircraft hammered over the city, flying low, heading for Casanueva. The gunners sat down and drank coffee, turning every now and then to bellow obscene insults at the infantry who huddled back into the shelter of the side streets.

A sudden short fusillade sent the gunners scrambling on their bellies. A bullet punched through the windshield of Zamal's command car, making a spider web of jagged cracks. He bellowed at the driver, and the open car bucked back fifty paces, the motor roaring. An officer without a hat ran out of an alley holding his left arm. His legs buckled and he fell forward and lay still. Zamal's aide jumped from the car and ran to him. A few more shots rang out, then silence. The aide came back.

"Third Company has mutinied, Major! Two officers killed, this one wounded. They've run off, taking their weapons with them."

"Mutiny? Order these pigs back to Plaza San Marco. Place them under the military police stationed there. Draw lots for two firing squads. At once!"

The aide walked away, shouting for the company commanders to assemble their sullen troops. A motorcycle rider brought Zamal a message from the palace. No reinforcements were available at this time. The attempt by the garrison to break out of the rebel encirclement had been unavoidably delayed. Two machine-gun units from the National Guard had been attached to his command. The automatic weapons were to be placed *behind* his troops. Those soldiers who failed to attack with the spirit expected of loyal and enthusiastic defenders of the nation were to be fired upon. Zamal bit his lip. It was working out the way Colonel Lucca had said it would; the army was feeble . . . the Guards would take over the task of crushing the rebellion. The best thing to do would be to cooperate fully, in every way. Some shreds of honor and reputation might be salvaged yet. Five men from each of the remaining four companies would be shot as an example for the others. Hopefully, the machine guns could be used against the rebels, and the third assault prove a successful combined action of loyal army units and the Guards.

By the time Zamal had reached the gasoline station in the Plaza San Marco that served as headquarters for the military police, it was known for certain that the company of mutineers had gone over to join the rebels. Zamal ordered the remaining troops to fall in to witness the executions. He could hear the sounds of heavy fighting over at the railroad station and marshaling yards.

↓

Herzler walked slowly down the corridor, stepping over and around the men, women and children who had overflowed from the emergency ward into the foyer of the hospital. Many had already been treated hastily. They talked in low, moaning voices, praying and cursing. They did not seem to Herzler dangerous in any way, but, he reflected, the injured never did. Who ever saw a savage survivor? The sisters in their starched aprons and big, winged caps moved swiftly and surely; their faces and hands calmed the adults and drew smiles of gratitude from the children. Most of the injured, Herzler had been told, had been passed across the lines by the rebels. Only a few were bullet-wound cases; the majority had suffered gashes from flying glass and masonry, broken bones and burns.

A stout sister manned the elevator. Herzler removed his hat and stepped into the iron cage. An intern with a bloodstained jacket sucked on a cigarette. The door crashed shut, the nun heaved on the cable, the weights clicked and dropped down their tracks, hauling the elevator up the shaft.

"How is His Grace this morning?"

The nun smiled, her broad, pale mouth parting to reveal fine, even teeth.

"Much improved. He has made us all very merry, you know. His poor legs all burned and he says it's all his fault . . . for smoking cigars in bed! He has been wonderful. He wanted to come down to see the people this morning, but of course the doctors won't let him."

"Ah."

"It will be at least two weeks before he can get out of bed, poor man. But you'd think nothing had happened. He still gets quite a bit of morphine."

The intern scowled and threw his cigarette to the floor of the elevator.

"Morphine! How much longer can the supply hold out? Two hundred people downstairs and not another bed!"

The elevator stopped, and the nun opened the door.

"God will provide us with what we need."

"Ya-ya-ya. Since when does God run a dispensary?"

The intern hurried off. The elevator moved up again. The nun coughed gently.

"He has been on duty all yesterday, all last night. He has more than forty children. The poor fellow is frantic for them. They seem to cry all the time. Nothing can stop them. He has to get the older ones to sing at the top of their voices while he changes the dressings on the little ones."

"Is this it?"

"Yes. Down the hall to the left, the last door on the right."

The hall was lined with cots. Many of the patients had no covering, but lay in their dirty street clothes. One man, his face covered with gauze, stretched out an arm toward Herzler and mumbled. Herzler walked on, averting his gaze. At the end of the hall he saw the archbishop's secretary, Monseñor Blanco. The dark Jesuit looked up.

"Stretching your legs, Monseñor?"

"I have some office to read. His Grace is waiting to see you."

"How is he this morning?"

"Better, praise be to the Almighty God. We have prayed for his recovery incessantly."

Monseñor Blanco spoke in his hollow, doomsday voice. Herzler recalled the intern sucking on a cigarette, drawing some sort of strength from tobacco smoke and nicotine.

"Presumably the physicians did a little something here and there."

Herzler passed through the open door. A pale green screen shielded the foot of the archbishop's bed. Herzler advanced on tiptoe, his shoes squeaking.

"Your Grace?"

The archbishop lifted his head. Herzler winced inwardly at the great, white, clouted hands lying on the smooth blanket. The room smelled strongly of ointments and sweet salves. He hardly recognized his friend. His Grace wore no vestments; he seemed small and frail in his hospital gown. His thin neck, circled by a gold chain, protruded like a scalded stalk. The archbishop had lost his eyebrows and most of his hair. A fine white stubble grew over his blistered cheeks. His eyes were bright, but he spoke in a soft, muddled voice.

"Ah, Manfred . . . good of you. I am not allowed visitors, so I had to send for you."

"And here I am."

"Sit down, please. Take that chair."

356

His Grace lay back on the pillows. He could feel his heart beat like a finger snapped slowly, steadily, against a damp drumhead. The pulse ticked in his ears. He breathed softly for a moment, while Herzler studied him. The Church officials had obviously concealed from the faithful how badly burned the archbishop had been.

His Grace smiled slightly.

"I hope you will forgive me, my friend. I find that I stink."

"Not a bit. Well, a little."

"Yes, a little. The flesh is not only weak, Manfred, but it smells badly when it is half toasted."

"Well, at least you're *au point* and not *bien cuit,* eh?"

The archbishop laughed softly.

"Leave it to you to think of food. I have been meditating. Perhaps God is giving me a foretaste of my future torments. If so, it has been sufficient. I am an extremely repentant sinner, I assure you. It was a foolish thing to have done. I could reach no more than a half-dozen poor souls. And now look at me. I am a burden to everyone. It will be weeks before they let me out of here."

"The doctors know what they are doing, Your Grace. You must trust them. They are specialists in the body, after all."

"True. Well, what's happening? Outside."

"Who knows? No one."

"You mean that you don't know, so you can't tell me. You must not be selfish with ignorance, Manfred. There are times when it is a valuable commodity."

"I mean that no one really seems to know. The authorized newspapers have not published, and I have not come across a copy of the rebel sheet. *Arriba,* it's called, as one might expect. Full of lies and hysteria, I'm sure."

"It was feared that the light and water would be turned off in this section, too. That would be terrible for the doctors, the sisters and the patients."

"Only the western sectors are without utilities. Though there's no saying what will happen if the rebels gain. Right now they seem to be holding on. Something has happened to the army. Except for scattered groups, they have not come out for the government."

"You see? You know more than we do. Go on. What else?"

"Well, the rebels seem to have won some sort of skirmish at one of the barricades."

"I heard the cannons. Every shot . . . new souls in torment. Pain and bleeding. The innocents. The people are soft, Manfred, they are not used to suffering like this."

"No one is used to revolution, Your Grace. I've seen this sort of thing before. Now is the time when all the careful plans go wrong, on both sides—when equipment and men and ideas get misplaced, or lost, or broken, and those who are left have to work with what is left. Soon there will be no plans, just people, two groups or more butchering each other. The first side that quits loses."

"The government . . . will it fall, Manfred?"

"I don't know."

"You sound as if you don't care, my friend."

"But I do. It would be a disaster if the rebels won! I speak selfishly, of course. I speak for my corporation, the Weimar government at home."

"And for yourself?"

"I would rather not say."

"A Teuton and a democrat, Manfred? You are a walking contradiction."

"Alessandro made a name for himself in Hamburg and in Berlin. Right after the war. 1919. He was with the socialists, a radical group, allied briefly with the Reds. The thought of Germans led in street fighting by a youth from Costa Plata—who had heard of Costa Plata, after all?—well, I was impressed."

"He is a good man with noble ends. Too young perhaps to avoid cruel means to attain those ends."

"Against this government he has no choice."

"Will he win?"

"It is too early to tell. No one knows enough. A bit here, another bit there, but you can't put anything together. The National Guard will finish taking over the city today, I expect. By nightfall His Excellency will probably speak to the people. The rebels will do everything they can to prevent this. If they can get the mobs into the streets . . . well, the Guards have machine guns. You see how it is. It won't be over for a while yet. There will be a good deal more fighting."

"More killing. Soldiers and civilians."

"Yes. Vizarra has ordered that any civilian in possession of firearms is to be executed without trial. General Olmega, naturally, ordered his so-called army to take no prisoners. You say these people are soft. I think not."

"Who is General Olmega? My word, I never heard of him."

"One of the students from the university. A nice boy, to be sure. The rumors name him the assassin of Colleo. You had better start praying for the boy's soul, Your Grace. I think he's going to need it. Barely twenty, and he's got blood on his soul as well as his hands."

"How sad it is, when young people turn to savages. Killing and burning."

"Well, the young haven't far to turn, Your Grace."

"And our people at the mine?"

"I arrived by automobile this morning. We had to go way out into the *campo*. The rebels hold the railroads, most of Casanueva, though there's still some fighting going on there. It was quiet when I left. We have armed the guards, of course. Too quiet, though. Something has happened. A young Indian disappeared. On his wedding day. The others are very excited. I think Ramos is finally losing his hold over them."

"Thank God for that! Their minds and souls will be free again."

"*Ja?* Perhaps. Anyway, they won't work, the miners. They won't do anything. Just stay in the barracks and talk."

The archbishop lifted his swaddled hands. They looked like white fruit growing on the ends of his thin, pale arms.

"How helpless, how useless I feel, Manfred!"

"You must get well. When this throat cutting stops, the people will need you, you know. They must have a center of authority. Someone blameless to whom they can turn."

"Something must be done, Manfred. That's why I summoned you. The Church must take a position."

"I beg your pardon, Your Grace, but it is too soon."

The archbishop rolled his head on the pillow. His bright eyes stared at the ceiling. His long, stiff upper lip twitched once.

"I only hope it is not too late. The ecclesiastical authorities have a duty to the laity, Manfred. I am not like certain other members of the Church . . . I name no names, cite no bad examples. I have never concealed my opinions of Vizarra's regime. Coward that I am, I know perfectly well that what happened to me in the Plaza Mayor is a blessing in rather uncomfortable disguise. The Caudillo can hardly arrest and imprison a bedridden old nuisance like myself. Therefore I feel it is time that I began to meddle wholeheartedly in the present situation. Don't sit there with your mouth open, waiting for a chance to interrupt. I won't be interrupted. Vizarra has acted in the past to separate the Church and the state. Very well. But he has not separated the Church from the people. Let us consider that I represent the Church and you the people. Rather presumptuous on both sides, but God will understand."

"He is a politician, then?"

"God? Of course. He is an expert on chaos and anarchy. If you call yourself a democrat, you must at least admit that the Lord is a mild monarch indeed."

"I am not so certain, Your Grace."

"This is no time for metaphysics, even the cheap and easy sort. I am talking about politics. I think that I shall issue a statement."

"There are no newspapers."

"Then by pastoral letter or, failing that, posters."

"Posters!"

"I have no intention of calling the laity to take arms. The Church cannot encourage or support any movement that multiplies sin. This is obvious. What I want is for you, personally, to direct a movement of the laity, in my name, and with my full blessing. The hospitals everywhere are now crowded. First the victims of the fire in the Plaza Mayor, now the wounded and dying from the street fighting. In a matter of hours there will be fresh casualties streaming in. Go to the leaders in each parish. I will have Monseñor Blanco prepare a statement. Raise money, clothing, assemble food, clear bed space. See if you cannot obtain aid—impartial, disinterested aid from the foreign concessions. Appeal to their hearts, not their pocketbooks. If you succeed, Manfred, you will have done a splendid thing. Try always, steadily, to draw as many of the faithful away from the fighting, off on the sidelines, as it were, working to bring comfort to the suffering of both sides. You can do it, Manfred! I know you can. Come, we are friends, no?"

"*Ja,* Your Grace."

"You are a good Catholic, too. Don't you feel in your heart that we must do this . . . that *you* must do this?"

"My employers—"

"In a case like this, you owe allegiance to God, Manfred, not a mining company!"

360

"I am sorry, Your Grace. I will do my best."

"Good. That is all I ask, in Christ's name. Blanco will draw up a letter of credit for you. He will see that the churches are open. Use them as field stations. Encourage the people to leave the western sectors. Shelter and care for them. Work with the Red Cross. See if you can gather private automobiles for transportation."

"This will put us squarely between the Caudillo and Alessandro's rebels, Your Grace. We shall be hampered, even attacked, by both sides."

"Perhaps at first. Between them, you say? But there is no other place for us to be. Perhaps we can make them stop fighting. Perhaps we can—"

A light whuffling noise came through the open window, then the deep crump of a detonating shell. A corner of a building three blocks from the hospital slid into the street with a prolonged roar of toppling stones. A plume of smoke and dust rose above the rooftops. Herzler sprang to the window and tore back the curtains. Another shell passed over the hospital and wrenched up asphalt and paving stones. A third smashed into an apartment, blew out the façade of the building and flung broken bodies into the street below. At once the building began to burn. Herzler spun around, his face drained of color.

"But that's from the *north!* Why should Vizarra shell this? It's them! The rebels! They must have captured some artillery. Those are howitzers. Heavy ones! They're firing at the palace but falling short. In Calle Velázquez."

"Velázquez? So, not only the poor of San Pablo suffer but the rich as well. Go call Blanco. We've got to get busy."

Herzler hurried into the hall. Another battery fired off in the north. Four shells plunged down into the city, battering stones and glass, furniture and crockery into the streets. A siren began to wail like a lost soul. Smoke spewed up from the burning apartment house. The hospital shook with every dull, thudding fall of high explosive. A low-flying aircraft snarled over the rooftops, the sun gleaming on its wings. The smell of burning leaked into the archbishop's room. He closed his eyes, shuddering with compassion. Behind his lids swam a vision of the Plaza Mayor just before he had sagged senseless in agony, his heavy vestments flaming. Bodies with bursting faces, twisting like snakes in a vast lake of seething fire, a view of the Pit. His long, stiff upper lip jerked as he began to pray. Herzler was shouting in the corridor. In his excitement he had lapsed into German, and Monseñor Blanco was bewildered. Another shell fell from the sky, another and another dull *pong, pong, pong,* and the sirens screamed helplessly and the ground shivered.

⸸

The guard flung open the door without knocking and rushed to the desk.

"He's here! He just came through the village in a captured command car!"

Sánchez looked up from the proof sheets of *Arriba* that he had been editing. He dropped his blue pencil.

"Stand at attention. Salute. Present your information in such fashion that it can be transcribed into the official records of the day. Very good. Steno? Take this down."

"The Commander has passed through the pueblo. One man is with him, identity unknown. Both dressed in captured uniforms. The vehicle is an army command car. No more information at this time."

"Dismissed."

Sánchez stood up, struck a match and lit a fresh cigar. He felt as though a great weight had been lifted from his shoulders. He was back at last! Sánchez wanted to shout and dance. Instead he glared around the office, champing his cigar.

"There is no cause to declare a holiday, comrades. Continue to prepare the text on the Rota story, according to the corrections I have made. You, finish up with that report from General Voget. He will want a full list of captured weapons. Messenger, carry the information to the other members of the Central Committee. We will receive him in the main foyer and meet immediately afterward in the game room."

Sánchez blew out a violent swirl of smoke and hurried out into the hall, past the bulletin board and down the stairs. He waited, listening to the racket spread through the sanatorium. A nurse, pretty and flushed, sped down the stairway toward him, smiling. Sánchez fixed her with a stern gaze.

"Where are you going, señorita?"

"To see—"

"Back to your duties! A general meeting will be called in the cafeteria at lunchtime. I understand you had two truckloads of wounded come in an hour ago?"

362

"Yes, we—"

"Go back to them. At once!"

The girl curtseyed and fled up the stairs, screaming something in a wild, happy voice. Sánchez grinned and stuffed his hands into his pockets. He could hear the car grinding up the gravel drive and the voices shouting a welcome from the front windows. He was unable to bear the suspense. He flung open the front door, brushed by the cheering guards and ran down the steps. The brown command car swung in before the building. Alessandro stood in the open tonneau, his arms raised in salute and embrace. The sun beat on his joyful face and the wind drove his hair in his eyes. A belt of cartridges was slung over his shoulders and his lap filled with scarlet poppies and golden dahlias. He was smoking a large, brown cigar and laughing, his white teeth shining.

The car slid to a stop, spraying gravel. The driver began to beat on the horn. Guards, nurses, workers from the propaganda section, armaments and the motor pool surrounded the vehicle, all shouting, asking questions, slapping each other on the back and laughing. The car rocked and tilted as they swarmed over it to say a word to Alessandro, to look into his face, to touch him. Sánchez stood back alone, pleased and envious, trying to keep some sort of dignity. He chewed his cigar and blinked away the tears that glittered on his lashes. He noticed that Alessandro was wearing a Regular Army uniform, as was the driver. Alessandro pulled free of the hands that tapped and plucked at him. He smiled, tried to answer a dozen questions at once, struck the hair away from his brow and swung lightly over the side of the open tonneau. He landed, quick and graceful, poised like a prizefighter. Two guards surrounded him and held away the laughing, cheering crowd. Alessandro walked rapidly to Sánchez who opened his arms, and they crushed together in an *abrazo*.

"*Jovencito!*"

"Carlitos! Look at me! I've been promoted. See? A lieutenant in the cavalry!"

"Comrade Alessandro, I shall have to report you to the Central Committee. You have been stealing automobiles!"

The crowd laughed. Alessandro slipped off the heavy bandolier of cartridges and hung it around Sánchez's neck like a garland of flowers. He laughed and handed Sánchez the cigar he had been smoking. Sánchez stood there, his head bowed by the cartridge belt, a cigar in each hand. The crowd applauded. The two men walked to the steps. Voices called, imploring Alessandro to speak. He turned and propped himself against a column. His eyelids twitched. Sánchez saw the lines of fatigue drawn in his face, a tic flicker in his right cheek. He gave a little huffing sigh, as though uncertain how to begin. The crowd laughed softly and fell silent. Sánchez could hear the wind hissing in the great dark pines and the bright call of birds. Alessandro spoke in a taut voice that quivered with emotion and fatigue. He turned his face slowly from side to side, searching the crowd until he found a face and then speaking directly to that man or woman. The crowd listened with an attentiveness that was almost painful. Their faces stiffened, stretched to seize every syllable, as though he fed them with his words.

"Comrades! You have worked and waited. You have had little news of your friends and fellow fighters. What they have done! I know that you will rejoice with me at their success. For we have met with success. We are *winning!*"

The pretty young nurse jumped up and down like a child, clapping her hands together. The crowd cheered wildly. Someone threw a cap into the air.

"The student cadres have seized and still hold the university! The San Pablo district is ours. Our flag flies over Calle San Jerónimo! You all remember Pepe Olmega, our first student hero? Well, he is now Brigadier General Olmega, commander of the victorious First Army of Liberation. He has captured the hearts of the people as well as seven police stations. He has driven terror from the streets like a steel broom. His troops have been shelled and bombed by aircraft. They have not retreated so much as a centimeter. Even now his force is joining our other comrades who have driven the tyrant's mercenaries from the waterfront. Long live Olmega and the First Army!"

The crowd yelled and battered their hands together. Some began to sing. The pretty nurse jumped up and down, up and down, her face radiant.

"More than this! A shock brigade led by one of our gallant foreign comrades has made a landing at a place northeast of the city. There he joined with our allies, the gallant underground. Right at this moment—Quiet! Listen! Listen! Can you hear them? They are marching, comrades, marching. The force swells. A hundred new fighters join them every kilometer. They march on the city, sweeping the oppressor before them. Our new flag ripples in the breeze above every liberated pueblo. It is the Second Army of Liberation marching down the peninsula. Already the shells from captured cannons fall on the city, each a hammer blow, nailing fast the dictator's coffin. *Viva Voget, the Belgian Bolívar!*"

"*Viva! Viva! Viva!*"

"Now, comrades, now is the hour. We are loading fresh troops at Casanueva. I have ordered a locomotive and eight cars to come up to the station here. We will detail a small force of drivers and assistants to remain. I know that you all want to go. But we have wounded comrades, men who have already given their blood . . . yes, and women, too! They will need aid, doctors and medicine. But for the rest of you—come and fight with us! The battle for the railroad begins!"

The crowd roared. Sánchez dropped the cigar that Alessandro had given him and slowly, deliberately, crushed it flat, grinding it with his heel until only scattered flakes of tobacco remained. His ears rang with the frenzied shouting. Alessandro raised one hand.

"Good! Very good. The train will arrive in two hours. That gives us plenty of time. And, comrades, my stomach tells me that I am hungry. A juicy steak with *patatas fritas* and red wine. Where in hell is that lazy little waiter, anyway?"

The crowd laughed, nearly delirious, laughing beyond all measure of the humor of Alessandro's reminder that he had served them secretly in the now half-forgotten days before the fiesta of Santa Rosa. He waved to them, seized Sánchez by the arm and hurried through the door into the foyer.

"Can you get me something to eat, Carlos? And coffee. I'm rather tired."

"Come to my room. We can talk and eat there. I'll have food sent up. Tell me. How does it go? Really."

"Fair. Only fair. You heard from Voget?"

"Yes. He called in at 0930. His bunch wrecked the Hotel Miramar, but he got them fed and to the rendezvous. Trop had everything ready. They hit the depot from two sides, just at morning muster. There was some ground mist. That helped. They cut them up, *jovencito,* more than a hundred dead, nearly three hundred prisoners. Caught them all half asleep. He had already sent the trucks ahead with Trop's men and half of his own. The prisoners loaded ammunition and hitched the howitzers to the horses. They were going in at eight kilometers. Within range of the city. Listen, were they really shelling?"

"Yes. We could hear and see everything from the hills to the west there, you know. But—"

"What's the matter?"

"The *Guardacostas* didn't come over."

"How do you know?"

"I watched through my glasses. They put out to sea, all three gunboats. They can hit Voget's guns. He's got no spotters on the seacoast. Also, they'll pick up the trawlers coming back."

"*Mierda!* Here, inside. Want a drink?"

"Yes, a small one."

"Here. *Salud.*"

"*Salud.*"

"And Vola?"

Alessandro sank into a chair, spread his hands and sipped his drink. He coughed slightly and shook his head.

"I found out what it was. He and Ramos agreed to loot the mine. For twenty thousand reales. They both knew we were going to strike, but they planned to just wait for the right moment. Vola expected the movement to strike first into the *campo*. He would march out, then swing to the mine. And keep going. Right across the border."

"Very neat, the fat toad!"

"That's it. He sits there at headquarters, drunk and grunting."

"Then he didn't come in with us."

"No. Not yet. He wants the equivalent of twenty thousand ingots. In advance. Within five days."

"You agreed, of course."

"Carlitos, I had no choice. I promised him. I gave my word."

"You know we don't have more than a hundred thousand reales."

"Yes."

"But if he does nothing—"

"There's not a great deal he can do. Olmega's got him surrounded. The U.T. Red Guards hold the entire section. He sits like a toad in a pool of mud."

"It could be worse. What are the plans now?"

"Two. Olmega is going to attack at dusk. Try to cut off the Telefónica. Go around it on both sides, so. That will bring him to the

Glorieta Colón. The U.T. are going to come up off the waterfront in buses. Now, wait . . . empty ones first. To plug the southeast and southwest arches of the Plaza Mayor. We know that Vizarra is going to hit the Estación and the freight yards. You see? We'll have them flanked! With Voget still shelling the city from the north."

"But Vola, *Chico,* if he moves out, then—"

"Then we'll be cut to ribbons. We'll be on Vizarra's flank, but Vola will be behind us."

"*Jesús,* that's bad, *jovencito.* Let's think it over."

"Get some food, eh?"

Sánchez picked up the telephone and ordered two meals and a bottle of wine from the cafeteria. Over the line he could hear the cooks and their assistants singing and shouting.

Alessandro slumped in his chair, batting dust from his cavalry boots. He looked up at Sánchez.

"I arrested Rota, Carlos."

"Why? *Hombre,* why?"

"The U.T. wouldn't have cooperated with us. Olmega had trouble. Rota's locked up in a squash court at the university."

"Ai-ya! What next?"

"We're taking the train in. Both of us. We're going to lose a lot of them, too."

"The people, Alessandro?"

"They are coming in with us. Olmega expects demonstrations between the barricades and the Glorieta Colón all afternoon. Have you heard anything about troop movements? Vizarra's got four divisions scattered around. We can forget about the southern forces for a day or two—"

"A day or two! Alessandro, you cannot work miracles!"

"We must try."

"Ya-ya-ya. Well, I confess I was wrong about Voget. He did magnificently."

Alessandro gnawed his thumb. He gazed out of the window, blinking slowly.

"He's going to get cut up, too. Those gunboats."

"Oh."

"What's the matter?"

"Alessandro, Trop was killed."

"How? Where?"

"At the depot. I don't know how. You don't suppose Voget—"

"No, of course not. He needed Trop. You never met him."

"No."

"A friend of my father's. They worked on a *ganadería* together. He must have been the last of my father's friends."

"Next to last."

"Ah, yes. Next to last. I wanted to ask him . . . about what happened. Up in the mountains. I didn't want to go to him. I was afraid I'd compromise the old fellow. He was only released from prison eighteen months ago. I wrote letters to his son. Well, maybe Trop didn't know anything, anyway."

"Maybe not."

"I . . . I got a letter from your father."

"And what did he have to say? Did he offer you a job teaching children in the provinces? Offer to use his enormous influence with Vizarra so that you could skip the country? Maybe he recommended a good tailor, ordered you a jacket, a coat already turned yellow on both sides, eh?"

"I meant to bring the letter, but my clothes got soaked in the sewer."

"I couldn't bring myself to read it. He used to scribble stuff to me when I was up in Mexico. I threw them into the fire."

"He sounded very lonely."

"He should have stayed in the mountains and died with his friends. Instead he took an inspection trip to the trenches and got captured. Alive."

"Well, he's still alive."

"Not . . . morally. Morally he is a cadaver."

"Ah, here's the food. No more, Carlos, you'll spoil my appetite."

↓

Malata glided across the carpet and set down the cup of *café con leche* sweetened with wild honey. He pushed it across the cluttered desk to the Caudillo's elbow. He stared down an instant at the thinning, rumpled hair twisted on Vizarra's crown. He backed silently away and waited. Sweat stains discolored the Caudillo's shirt. A dead cigar jerked as he spoke into the field telephone. He had not slept at all, and his eyes were swollen and scarlet-rimmed. He nodded his thanks.

"What do you mean, you lost half a company in the sewer? Eh?

No one issued orders for the pursuit of anyone. Those men were to get to Vola, arrest and shoot him! Who blew it up? They did. So it's sealed, eh? Well, where is Zamal? You don't know. Listen, I give you exactly ten minutes to locate him. He left Plaza San Marco two hours ago for the railway station. Two hours! If you have not found him and brought him in to a field telephone position within ten minutes, consider yourself under arrest and report at once to O'Conner at police headquarters!"

Vizarra crouched over his desk, driving his words into the telephone, packing the wires with energy like a generator. Malata walked over to the sandbagged windows and stared out over the smoldering city. The shelling had stopped on both sides, but distant rifle fire crackled. An airplane swooped down beyond the dome of the cathedral. A feather of smoke rose, then the *plump* of the exploding bomb.

"Brigadier Lucca. No, not Colonel Lucca. Don't you people at Staff even read your own documents and orders? Yes, of course he has been promoted. What happened to that cavalry squadron that went out? Never mind all that. I want the truth. I see, I see. Yes. Send more men. Half of what you have in reserve. You'll have enough men when Lucca breaks through. I want that station cleared! Have you been in contact with—you have. Go on. Excellent. Excellent. Are they pursuing? Good! Drive them into the sea. Two wounded whats? Belgians. So what? No, there's no point in that. What were you thinking of, lodging an official protest to Brussels? Don't you know a mercenary when you see one? In civilian clothes? Shoot them both, at once. Call back whenever the situation changes."

Vizarra hung up the receiver, struck a match and sucked on his cigar. His pulses had been jumping again. Maybe the Swiss doctor was right; maybe he shouldn't smoke. But he had to do something with his hands. He leaned back and scratched his armpits. The anteroom beyond the closed door echoed with the noise of typewriters, jangling telephones and the excited voices of division liaison officers.

"Good and bad, Julio. They wrecked the cavalry we sent to the station. Gasoline bombs dropped from the roofs. The horses bolted. But they formed up and joined with the others. They've got the iron bridge south of the station and all the freight buildings. We're going to have to use artillery to get them out of there. That means taking it from Lucca's unit."

"Perhaps Major Zamal is engaged in transferring the fieldpieces."

Vizarra drew the map of the city to him and flicked ashes off the penciled surface.

"Why are railroad stations always built right in the center of a city? Look at this. There's no way we can get the people out of the way. Their only hope is the cellars. There's an orphanage, too. I wonder . . . get the Red Cross, Julio. Get someone out there to arrange for some trucks. There must be two hundred children in there."

"Perhaps they've been evacuated."

"How? Right into the line of fire? If you can't be intelligent, keep your mouth shut."

"There was some good news, Your Excellency?"

"Yes. The Sixth Infantry hit those rebel guns in the woods. They were only a kilometer from the villa. She must be terrified. They made contact with guerrillas first, cleared the pueblo and drove into the woods. There was some hard fighting. They took one battery. The rebels have pulled back along the peninsula, but the Sixth struck up along the north road, picked up their trucks and expect to swing in behind them. Right at the salt marshes. No word from the Coast Guard?"

"None. They have a heliograph station at Miramar, but no word yet."

"And the southern garrison has boarded the trains for Casanueva?"

"At 800 hours, Your Excellency. One derailment, about fifty men injured. Blown-up track. The rest will reach Casanueva tonight."

Vizarra rose, pushed away the papers that covered his desk and limped across the room. He bent and tapped his leg.

"That Swiss is a quack. These shots do nothing for me. Nothing at all. Suspend his license to practice. Can you remember to do that? Of course. You never forget anything, do you, Julio?"

"I have had a splendid instructor in the significance of small details, Your Excellency."

Vizarra shrugged and squinted against the smoke that curled up into his reddened eyes. He paced across the carpet and back, muttering to himself.

"As long as they have those damned gasoline bombs, we can forget about the horses. What we need is armored cars. By the time they think of throwing nails on the streets, we'll have the suburbs clear and the station and university cut off. How many machine guns still on the roof? Eight?"

"Six. Two were sent to Zamal this morning."

"Right. Order three taken down. Tell the man outside. Lieutenant Romero. Hmmm, an ordinary truck, not too big, with a steel dumping body. Sloping sides of wood with sheets of metal nailed over. They'll shoot for the tires. Iron plates buckled over the fenders. Set a hundred-liter drum upright through the roof."

Malata reached for a pad of paper.

"How many carpenters and mechanics does O'Conner have in jail?"

"I'll find out."

"Yes. Two companies of infantry. Three trucks from the motor pool. First to the nearest lumberyard. Then a boiler works or metal fabricating shop of some sort."

"The lumberyards are near the waterfront, Excellency."

"I know, I know. That's why two companies. One to provide covering fire, the other to load lumber. Which way is the wind blowing?"

"South, Your Excellency."

"South? Fine. We could smoke them out of the university, eh? If Lucca took the library and set it on fire . . . yes, I'll tell him that. Now, then . . ."

Vizarra limped back to his desk and sketched rapidly on a block of paper.

"So. Lumber three meters long by one meter high, sloping in and braced. A flat roof, with the drum set upright for the gunner, just behind the cab. Sheathe with galvanized iron, nailed on. Not much protection, but some. Two holes drilled in the fenders, metal skirts over the tires. Where is the gasoline tank on those Dodge trucks? In the back, right? Then a plate across the rear, so. Paint them gray, if there's time, If not, forget it. Here, take this to the ordnance people, have them make a half-dozen copies. Use my figures where they are accurate. Where not, tell them to use their heads. Notify the motor pool and detail two companies, as I said."

Malata gathered the sketch. The drawing was executed with bold, simple, clear strokes, a crude turtleback fitted on a Dodge truck. A rather detailed figure crouched inside the shelter of the steel drum. The legs of the machine gun were indicated as tied by ropes to the top of the truck cab. The sides of the turtleback were slotted for three riflemen. The Caudillo's neat, accountant's figures covered the second sheet, so many meters of three-centimeter lumber planking, eight kilograms of nails, sixty nuts, bolts and washers, three steel drums, acetylene torches and tanks of gas, even an estimated construction schedule.

The telephone chittered. Vizarra snatched it up.

"Yes? Good. Good. How many? Four. Fired on from the land. No damage. Continue to patrol and to return fire. Sink all surface vessels within the three-mile limit. Request other vessels, foreign vessels, to stand off outside the limit. Release one gunboat to return to the harbor, reload ammunition and begin bombardment of the university."

The Caudillo hung up and closed his stubby fingers around the cold cup of coffee.

"They got them. Four trawlers. In close to shore, landing ammunition. The rebels have nearly reached the salt marshes. I think we've got them. I wonder how many trawlers there were originally? That may be important."

The telephone rang again.

"Yes? This is the Caudillo. Ah, Zamal! Come to the palace at once. You have a new command. Yes, at once!"

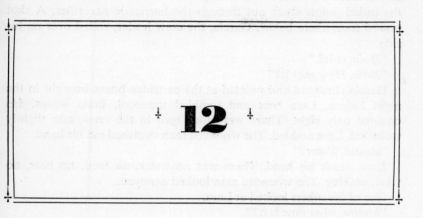

12

JOAQUÍN LARA left the assistant director's office on his hands and knees. Beneath his palms he could feel the grit gnawed from the walls by small-arms fire. The upper windows were gone; only glass fangs remained in the frames. Pale yellow sunlight, the last warmth of the day, streamed into the third story. Lara could hear men shouting out in the freight yards and the staccato rapping of rifles. He crawled down the corridor, past the bulky body flung on its back outside the bursar's office. Flies crawled on the dead man's face. A slug smacked into the wall, and Lara scuttled out of the sniper's view. He stood up and dusted his wrinkled trousers. They were still holding out; that was the main thing. The ground-floor waiting rooms were gone and the artillery had bashed the second floor to a ruin of gaping walls, weak ceilings and sagging floors. Since the Guards had occupied the orphanage, the second floor was not safe. Seven men had died attempting to defend the corner baggage room against point-blank machine-gun fire.

At the head of the stairs a crew rested. One of them lay on his back, smoking. The others huddled behind the wall of suitcases, trunks, boxes and packages they had dragged from the Lost and Found Bureau. Lara saw that they had fixed three umbrellas so that the furled points stuck out through the barricade like rifles. A shot powed somewhere below. García, the crew leader, rolled over on his side.

"*Hola,* chief."

"*Hola.* How goes it?"

García shrugged and pointed at the cartridge boxes brought in the night before. Lara bent and tumbled the cool, brass wasps. He counted only eight. There were four men in the crew, one slightly wounded. Lara nodded. The wounded man stretched out his hand.

"*Agua?* Water?"

Lara shook his head. There was no water, no food, no beer, no wine, nothing. The wounded man looked annoyed.

One of the others looked at Lara.

"*Madre,* what time is it?"

"A little after five. Two hours until dark."

García grinned and ran his finger across his throat.

"*Kkkkkt!* Two hours to dark is right. No news, heh?"

"No news."

"*Hay agua?*"

"No."

"*Tengo sed.*"

Lara shook his head. More shots rang out on the second floor. He nudged García.

"Who's down there?"

"How should I know, chief? Alessandro himself, maybe."

The others laughed. Lara counted the cartridges again. Eight. Three more in the rifle chambers. Another shot came up the stairwell and screwed off a spray of plaster. It was still hot. Lara lay down behind the trunks and looked up at the ceiling.

"I don't know what's happened. I just don't know . . ."

He felt it was his fault. Ever since the meeting at the sanatorium, when the others had jeered at him, he had felt himself a weakling. The others were so sure! But where *were* they? For two days and one night the crews had held the station and the freight yards: one engineer, one fireman, three conductors and three workers from the yards. Only eight men to a crew with only four rifles between them.

Lara knew from the beginning what the crews had only discovered the second day—that they could win nothing, that their function was simply to hold on as long as possible, in a riddled building, with no food or drink, cut off from the rest of the city and the ammunition running out. Here, on the third-floor landing, was the end. The wounded man closed his eyes and appeared to be sleeping. Lara rolled his head and gazed back down the corridor. A honey-colored light streamed in through the shattered windows. Dust motes drifted on the hot, heavy air. A truck groaned up. A spatter of shots from the roof and the stiff, lashing sound of the machine gun from the orphanage. More reinforcements for the Guards on the first and second floors. García blinked and blinked. His grainy lids fluttered over his weary eyes. He touched the cartridge box.

"How long, chief?"

"They will come for us. We have only to hold this until it gets dark."

"With these?"

"García, I can't make them."

"Have you seen the other boys?"

Lara nodded, the ceiling sliding back and forth as he moved his head. The station had three flights of stairs, north, south and the main spiral. The main landing was still held by more than twenty men. But the last assault would not come there and everyone knew it. The third floor of the building was a double rack of small offices on either side of a broad central corridor. If the Guards came up the north or south stairs and set up a gun, they could sweep the top floor. Eight cartridges and three in the rifles. Two hours until darkness.

"Well, what do they say?"

"What do they say? Why . . ."

Lara tried to remember. He licked his cracked lips and stared up at the ceiling. They must have said something. He had crawled down there only a few hours earlier.

"They say freedom or death."

"*Mierda!* I don't believe it."

García flopped over on his back, too, and screwed his knuckles in his eyes. Somebody murmured, directly below them, on the stairwell at the second-story level. Lara felt his scalp creep. He drew a revolver from his pants and cocked it. There was still one shell left in the chamber. García laughed softly.

"Christ, I'll say this. When I started heaving coal, I never thought

I'd end up like this. Yay-ya-ya. Shot in the ass. Well, I wonder what my woman's been doing. 'Where is Tonio? I want him to look after the baby. Where is he? Where is Tonio?' Where is . . . what a pain."

A shot thucked into the suitcase over García's head. The noise of the rifle report echoed up the stairwell. García puffed out his cheeks and turned over on his belly.

"All right, you bastards. Here they come again. Let them shoot. When you can see somebody above the belt, over the edge of the landing, let him have it."

The wounded man and Lara lay on their backs. Boots knocked on the stairs below. Something rattled against the rails. García slapped out with his hand, and the men screamed. A flat, sharp smack spun smoke, powdered plaster and a burned smell up the stairwell. García sucked his fingers. From the floor below came a sound of a man sobbing.

"Grenade, chief. The dumb bastards try to throw them up."

Lara nodded again. He was thinking of the city outside the station. If he left, he could take the *tranvía,* the Number 16 car, directly to the Glorieta Colón, change there for the university, get off at Plaza San Marco and walk five blocks to his apartment in Calle San Jerónimo. The boy who brought the ammunition said an airplane had crashed there, right through the market roof. It would be something to see.

"Tengo sed."

Lara turned his head and tried to smile. His lips were dry and stiff.

"Everyone's thirsty, comrade. But there's no water. They'll bring water when they come."

García laughed and went off into a coughing fit. One of the crew patted him on the back. Lara felt that he couldn't move, that he was pinned to the dusty floor behind the heaped, forgotten luggage. His arms and legs felt like lead. García laughed again.

"When they come. You should be on the stage, chief. They'll never come."

Lara stared at the wounded man. A boy, really, no older than his daughter's husband. The boy began to cry softly.

"García, you never know. I have absolute trust."

"Shit. You don't even *know* them, chief."

"You don't have to *know* people, García. Not always. You just feel things."

One of the crew, to the left of García, sat up and grinned.

"Right. You just feel things. Like me."

He stood up and unbuttoned the front of his pants. Lara rolled over on his stomach to watch. García braced the man's leg, holding him on top of the heaped suitcases. The pale yellow stream arched out, fell through the dusty, lemon-colored air, blended, disappeared and spattered on the landing below.

"Lick it up, you mother-lovers!"

García stuck his finger in his mouth and popped his cheek. The other finished urinating and dropped back behind the shelter. García laughed.

"*Cordon Rouge,* you milk-lickers! Come up and get served!"

Lara lay and listened to the cannons firing. The artillery had been taken away after the guns had broken up the second floor and the Guards had overrun the street-level waiting rooms.

"Back at the university . . ."

"They'll never get out."

The other man of the crew buttoned up his pants.

"You mean no one will ever get in."

"In, out. Out, in. What difference does it make? It's all over for us, anyway."

The wounded man began to cry louder.

García drove his heel into the wounded man's ribs.

"Shut up. Stop that noise. Go and die someplace else if you can't be quiet about it!"

"I'm . . . so thirsty."

Lara rolled over and looked up at the ceiling.

Boots clattered on the stairs. The crew leaned against the barricade, and García worked the bolt of his rifle. He spat on his fingers, crossed himself and touched the front sight.

"Me and María here got four downstairs, chief."

"That's good."

"Never used one of these things in my life. Never thought when I started heaving coal that I'd end up with a bullet in the guts outside the director's office. That's something, huh?"

"They've gone down to the other end!"

García raised himself and leaned on a green footlocker. He slammed the top of it with his fist.

"*Aquí! Aquí!* You milk-lickers! Come up here and suck on my fat one!"

A deep bass voice muttered down on the second floor. A pair of boots squeaked as someone stole along the wall, away from the stairwell. Another voice shouted a command, and footsteps beat on the floor below and died out. The wounded man sighed.

"How long? How long?"

García dropped on him, grabbed his shirt and began shaking him.

"*Una hora! Media hora! Diez minutos. Cinco. Un' momentito! La boca, cabronazo!*"

He slumped back exhausted and wiped the spittle from his lips. His protruding eyes rolled at Lara.

"*Jefe?*"

"*Qué quieres?*"

"*Alessandro, jefe! Donde está Alessandro?*"

Lara shook his head slowly.

"*No sé, chico*—I don't know."

García grabbed Lara's wrist, rolled him on his side and snatched the watch from his pocket. He tapped the face with a dirty, trembling finger. Rifle shots panged and howled, and the crew at the main staircase fired back. A grenade smacked. García tapped on the face of the watch.

"*Dos horas, jefe! No puede ser!*"

Lara drew away and scowled. García dumped the cartridge box into his lap. Lara brushed the dull brass cartridges away.

"*Ocho, jefe! Solamente ocho!*"

A slug sizzled down the corridor and puffed into the wall. Lara looked to his right. The corridor was clogged with men. He could see the dark shapes, their legs, necks and shoulders, as they knelt and sprawled to fire back. Another shot, then a solid crash of noise. One of the men fell down. Bullets sizzed. The corridor was empty except for the dark lump. Footsteps hammered over the floor beneath. García began to gather the cartridges. He shrugged.

"*Pues . . . aquí tenemos. . . .*"

He tapped his buttocks and shrugged.

"*Aquí, jefe! En el culo.*"

The wounded man sat up. His eyes jerked from side to side. He touched García's face, very tenderly, with the tips of his fingers.

"*Tengo sed . . .*"

A rush of men filled the stairwell. García snarled and rose to his knees. Slugs slapped into the green footlocker. García squinted and squeezed the trigger. A grenade exploded at the north end of the corridor, then another. Lara spread his hands. García turned and fumbled for a cartridge.

"*Siete. Solamente siete!*"

Lara began to crawl away. The men stationed at the head of the main flight of stairs were shooting and yelling. The sounds jumbled off the walls. A rifle crashed, and Lara heard the titter of the spent casing on the floor.

"*Seis! Y cinco!*"

Lara crawled down the corridor. Slugs whistled over him. He lay there and felt his bladder betray him. His pants soaked and clung to his thighs. Voices gobbled up the stairwell. A grenade whomped, and someone began to scream. García's rifle banged.

"*Y quatro, María!*"

Lara squirmed over the plaster-strewn floor. The dead man lay outside the bursar's office, the flies crawling on his face. Gunfire whacked and echoed. Lara hunched forward, cringing, waiting for the sniper. The bullet socked into the wall. Another snapped off a fang of glass from the broken window and sprayed glass dust over Lara's neck. The top floor of the building shook with the detonations of grenades. Lara dragged himself past the dead man. He heard García shout again.

"*Tres!*"

Lara scrambled to his feet, looked back to glimpse a dark mass of tangled forms corking the north end of the corridor. A blade shimmered in the weak, yellow light and a door exploded out, spinning like a chip. The concussion punched Lara in the belly. Boots beat up the south stairwell and solid flesh thudded against the barricade of lost luggage. Lara carefully shut the door of the assistant director's office. Two rifles crashed, and someone—it could only be the wounded man—was buried beneath a long, sliding fall of piled suitcases, packages, bundles and trunks. In the silence that followed, the luggage flopped slowly to the gritty floor. A man yelled something, and footsteps ran toward Lara. He walked slowly, wavering like a drunkard, over to the desk and sat down in the assistant director's leather-cushioned chair. A little girl in pigtails smiled out of a silver frame at Lara. A sniper's bullet shattered the ashtray. Lara grunted and drew the telephone off the desk. He sat down on the floor, holding the receiver in his hands. Glass broke over his shoulders. He lifted the receiver.

"*Oiga! Oiga! Aquí Estación! Estamos . . .*"

The line hissed. Lara pressed the instrument to his face. A pistol popped, and García yelled as he fired back.

"*Dos! Uno mas, coño!*"

Lara jiggled the receiver prongs.

"*Oiga? Oiga, senorita? Aquí Lara. La Policía Armada, por favor. Quiero . . .*"

"*Venga, coño!*"

The line ticked twice and a blurt of static deafened Lara. An incomprehensible stream of foreign words poured into his ear. He clung to the receiver and stared at the closed door. Bullets sleeted down the corridor. García worked the bolt of his rifle and laughed grimly. The distant voice crackled over the line.

"Ferguson? Are you there? Yes, Livermore here. Can you hear me? The connection's very faint, I'm afraid—"

Lara huddled over the telephone. Suddenly he wanted García in the office with him.

"*García! Veng' aquí!*"

"*No. Voy a matar un otro!*"

"What's that? Oh, the connection is so poor. Someone is on the line, I expect. No. In Panama. Listen to me carefully. We've been trying to contact an agent. It's very much worse? That's what we assumed. We've had no word from him. We tried to make contact by letter, but I gather that nothing has gotten through to you people. You are safe and well, I trust? Excellent. Can you hear me?"

García fired his last cartridge. The English voice drawled faintly in Lara's ear.

"We had hoped to be able to do this indirectly. Make contact with the leader of the insurgent movement. Yes, that's right. Can you hear me?"

Lara jiggled the receiver hook. His dry lips moved soundlessly. He coughed once. García's feet scraped out in the corridor.

"You must get to him, Ferguson. Offer him unlimited credit locally. Tell him we'll ship in arms and ammunition, beginning immediately. As much as he wants or needs. Can you hear me?"

Lara pressed his mouth to the telephone.

"*Es el final para nosotros . . . el final.*"

"What's that? Oh. Someone on the line, then. The shipments will be made as soon as you contact him, Ferguson. By Panamanian freighter. Three miles off Boca Perro. Have you got that? Five thousand rifles and twenty thousand rounds of ammunition . . ."

Men ran down the hall, the last rush, closer and closer. García snarled and rose to meet them. Lara pointed his revolver at the door. The handle rattled, and García backed into the room, holding his rifle by the barrel like a club. Lara dropped the telephone. Thin little sounds continued to come from it. A pistol cracked and García dropped his rifle, fell against the doorjamb and slid down to the floor. Lara crouched behind the desk. He could hear them whispering out in the corridor. A dark shape slipped through the door. Lara squeezed the trigger and the gun butt jogged once. He closed his eyes and flung the revolver into the darkness.

↓

Voget lay in the dune grass staring out at the sea. The sun bled through the low clouds in the west. Long rollers swept in, the crests breaking into pinkish froth as they curled and slammed on the beach. The gunboat was gone. Every few minutes someone fired a rifle, a flat, dry crack. Voget had scattered what was left of his brigade among the dunes, spacing the men far apart so it would appear that the group was bigger than it was. The dunes were reasonably good cover, but if the troops across the marsh made an attack before darkness . . .

Sand hissed from someone's boots. Voget sat up but did not turn. He stared at the broad, gray sea. A gull soared away to the west, gliding on wind-rippled wings. Voget crossed his arms on his knees and rested his head. He was exhausted.

"Here you are."

"Yes, Henri."

"Do you think they know?"

Voget shrugged.

"Will they come for us?"

"Maybe. Maybe not."

"The gunboat's gone. You think we hit it?"

"Yes. At least twice."

"Well, that's good. I mean, that's something anyway. We're holding them. They don't seem to be trying to come straight on us through the marsh."

"Then they'll just go around it."

"I told them to dig pits in the sand. For protection."

"Good."

"There's plenty of ammunition. I don't think they'll attack at night, do you?"

"No. Either soon or they'll wait until morning."

"Ummm."

Voget watched the sea lift, sweep in, crest and curl forward, smash and sluice up the sand and draw back in a sucking roar of tumbled stones. Wave after wave after wave. The sun touched the horizon.

"What are you thinking about?"

"Got a light?"

A shot rang out off to the right. Henri lit a cigarette and crumpled the empty packet. He sat smoking for a minute. The damp breeze snatched the smoke from his lips and dispersed it instantly.

"I was thinking that once a few years ago I took my vacation in Holland. Not a vacation, really. I stayed with some comrades who had a cottage by the sea. I went swimming every day. With the wife of one of the comrades."

"That must have been—"

"The beach looked a lot like this. The same big waves."

"Is the tide coming in?"

"Yes. I think so."

"That's good. They can bring the boats right in to the beach."

"If they send boats."

"We don't need many. They could send one or two."

Voget shrugged. The gull came soaring back, sliding on the wind. The sun dropped, and the air grew cool. The twilight in Costa Plaza was short, only a few minutes of dusk before the night closed in and the stars sprang out of the sky. He sat and listened to the steady pound and wash of the waves.

"We could attack. As soon as it gets dark. Break right through them, got those trucks we saw this afternoon and—"

"And what? Drive back into the city? Just like that, eh?"

"We could do something."

"These men can't attack at night. They'd shoot each other. It's getting dark. Tell them to pull in tighter, closer together. About three or four paces apart. No fires. No smoking. Keep twenty in reserve. We'll rotate them so everybody can get at least a little sleep. I'll come with you."

Voget stood up and stretched. He ached all over.

He climbed stiffly over the crest of the dune. He could see the line stretching right and left, each man sprawled on his belly in a shallow pit. A group of men sat on the sand near the two howitzers. They stared at Voget. The damp wind stirred the dune grass. The sand dragged at Voget's feet. He gave a few orders in a flat, mechanical voice. There were seven wounded. The men had gathered a pile of driftwood. Voget kicked it apart. No one protested. They simply stared at him with dulled eyes. Voget turned away.

"Get some sleep, now. We'll be fighting again in the morning. We'll have reinforcements. Plenty of men and guns and food. Everything."

No one spoke. The sand hissed against the grass. The long waves curled and boomed. The darkness came down like a blanket. Voget could hear the men talking and moving as they drew closer together and dug new pits. He turned and walked away.

The stars low on the horizon shifted slowly. Voget blinked and rubbed his eyes. He stared out over the water. He breathed cautiously, short sniffs, turning his face right and left. The stars were moving. He smelled coal smoke. No, he was imagining things. A dark shape, low in the water, broke across the strip of moonlight. Voget scrambled to his feet. Another one, following the first. The stars were the running lights on the rigging. The damp wind smelled of coal smoke.

Voget ran up the beach. Every dozen strides, he stopped and looked back. It was true. There were three of them out there. He floundered through the sand. One of the men shouted something.

"Les bateaux!"

"Cómo?"

"Los barcos!"

A feeble cheer drifted to him. He struggled through the heavy sand and flung himself down.

"Quick. Make a fire. They don't know where we are. A fire!"

The fire flickered and caught. Twigs and dried bits of board snapped and twisted. Voget found a good-sized tree limb and thrust it into the fire. The men gathered around the blaze.

"The cannons! Fire a couple of rounds. They'll be able to hear that."

The men moved slowly. The sight of the fire seemed to have drugged them. They stumbled across the sand, hesitated, stood staring at the blaze and finally trudged off to the guns. The breechblock clicked and the shell was slipped in. Voget cupped his hands over his ears. The howitzer slammed and the shell screamed away into the darkness.

"Again!"

Voget picked up the flaming branch. The damp wind tore at it. Voget began walking backward toward the beach, sheltering the torch with his body. Hands steadied him, half carrying him over the dunes. The howitzer fired. Voget walked backward. The torch fluttered; the heat from it stiffened his face. The sea boomed and hissed. Voget felt the firmer sand of the beach beneath his boots. He turned and waved the torch.

"Can they see us? Can they hear us?"

"Sure they can."

"See? They're turning around. See the lights?"

Voget waved the torch. The wind blew it out. But the trawlers had turned.

"You. Go back to the others. Tell them to keep firing. Start at the left end of the line. Take every other man out and send him down here. Bring the wounded, too."

He gave the man the glowing stump of wood. A bead of light flickered on the first trawler. Voget watched it come closer, a low, dark shape butting the sea, trailing a scarf of torn wake. The man brought back the torch. Others followed him. They gathered around Voget as he waved the glowing brand back and forth above his head. The men began to shout. A few fired their rifles.

"Stop that. They can't hear you."

The trawlers crept closer. Voget breathed in the coal smoke. He stared at the surf.

"They'll never get a boat through there. We'll have to swim for it."

The trawler rolled heavily, out beyond the surf. The signal lamp flickered. The men swarmed down across the beach, yelling. Voget lashed out with the torch. The glowing tip shattered, spraying ruby bits onto the sand.

"Get back! Get back! Back to the guns! You've got to hold them off!"

Rifle fire spattered from the dunes. Voget dropped the broken torch to the sand. The line had broken. The men had simply left their pits to run to the beach. They milled about in little groups waving

384

their arms and shouting. Voget grabbed the man nearest him and drove him down on his knees.

"Start digging, comrade. And shoot at anything that moves!"

He got fifteen men in a rough line and ordered the others to strip and throw their rifles into the surf. No one obeyed him. The line broke. The men waded into the smashing surf fully clad. The wounded rolled on the sand and begged to be carried. They grabbed at Voget's legs, hooked their fingers into the tops of his boots. Here and there a man knelt and fired into the darkness. Voget tore off his shirt and trousers. Men floundered in the shallows, knocked off balance by the waves. Bullets began to sing in the darkness. Voget ran naked down the beach. The sea washed up to his knees, then sucked sand out from beneath his bare feet. He lurched forward into a wall of seething foam, steadying himself with his rifle. The next wave tore it from his grasp. Roaring water sluiced around his legs. He looked ahead and up. The black mound heaved high, the crest sizzling. He lowered his head as the great wave loomed and curled. He plunged into a cool, solid, rolling wall of water. It tugged at him, a single powerful yank. Then it was gone, and he was swimming blindly. The next wave rose before him. He took a deep, strangling breath and let it slam over him. He came up gasping. Someone splashed in front of him. He swam slowly, digging his arms into the dark water. Another wave lifted him, buoyed him an instant and rolled on, breaking behind him. He was through the surf. The waves blotted out the horizon. He swam fifty strokes and floated. There! The trawler wallowed in the sea. He tried to shout, and water slopped into his mouth. He choked and began swimming. A light played over the water. He swam toward it. A voice called to him, and he could hear the sound of oars grinding in the thole pins. A dory slid down a wave toward him. He yelled and started to tread water. Voices called to him and then he touched the narrow stern. Hard hands grabbed him under the arms and dragged him in and dumped him against a thwart. He tried to say something, but the breath merely poured in and out of his heaving, scraped chest. Somebody patted him on the shoulder and then covered him with a sheet of damp canvas. He clutched it and lay in the slopped bilges of the tossing dory, staring up at the wheeling stars.

⸸

Olmega set the cheap, nickel-plated watch on the table beside the scrawled message: *Delay action one hour*. How was that possible?

There had been action since dawn. "Centuries" battled the National Guard, seized two machine guns and drove forward as far as Plaza San Marco. U.T. activists had been demonstrating and rioting against the police all along the waterfront. Swarms of young men and women shrieked and sang, poured through San Jerónimo and out into the fashionable boulevards. Dozens were killed and wounded by mounted police. A carnival of hysteria had sprung up. Men danced in the streets and howled revolutionary hymns, the *Marseillaise,* the *Internationale* and the Movimiento song. Any kind of song. The tunes and words jumbled all together. Blue-and-silver banners rolled in the breeze beside the scarlet flags of the U.T. Gangs of workers, students and women rushed through the side streets and back out to the boulevards. The plazas were strewn with rocks and broken bottles. The houses of Red Beret members had been stoned, set afire and looted. Overturned automobiles smoldered, filling the sky with black, foul smoke.

Olmega put his watch in his pocket, buckled the heavy revolver belt around his waist and stood up. He gathered his map of the city. He walked from the room. A dozen men and young women, all in uniforms taken from the garrison headquarters, stood up and stared at him. Olmega spoke in his quick, rapping voice.

"We attack at once. Notify the U.T. units and the Second Army headquarters. A decade from each century out into the streets. Mingle with the people and lead them. A decade in reserve on the barricades. The rest follow the crowds in close formation according to previous orders. Ammunition supplies in four trucks, two in reserve. Demand artillery support from Second headquarters."

He swept his eyes over the group. Once they had despised him. Now he was their leader. Energy rolled in him, flooding his arms and legs. He hitched up his belt and drew on his steel helmet.

"On to the Plaza Mayor! To the palace itself. No prisoners. None! Shoot anyone who resists the people's army!"

"It's a matter of time, that's all. Of course they will win."
"How?"
"Because they are winning now."
"I was in Calle Velázquez. Right after the shelling. *Hombre,* we gave it to the bastards. A girl—pretty one, too—walked right by me,

holding her face where her eyes had been. The blast blew her blouse off. Nice little bubbies . . ."

"Why did they stop? Another half hour and the Old Mule would have run up the white flag."

"His brown shorts, you mean."

"He is standing firm. Repressive measures have already been taken. Tomorrow morning this mob will be swept off the streets. What's left of them."

"You know what he asked me, my old man? Where was I all day. Oh, I said, playing football. In your street clothes, he says. The changing room is closed at the university, I told him. *Jesús,* I nearly laughed right in his face! Of course he is pretty hard of hearing, my old man. Half deaf, really."

"They tore open Fiorelli's meat shop. That Italian fascist. Broke the place up, handed out the knives. They left Fiorelli and his wife hanging from the hooks in the cold room."

"Nothing has changed. It is all cyclical, like the wheel of a game of chance. The shill gives it a shove, and it goes around and around. Who will win? The shill has his foot on the brake beneath the counter. He rakes in the cash. You can't tell me that this business, terrible as it is, is any more than a cheap carnival swindle. Vizarra will pay him off."

"There is nothing like it. I wouldn't have believed my eyes. We are blind, all the members of our class are stone-blind! The sincerity of the lower classes, their very simplicity, is terrifying. All their lives they have been treated like domestic animals. No, don't interrupt me, please. Like animals. Now, like animals, they have turned against us, their *soi-disant* masters. We will die, I tell you, bitten by our lapdogs, clawed to ribbons by our cats, our flesh mumbled up by sweet-eyed lambs in a herd panic. I myself am quite prepared to be mooed to death by our little Julieta who has spent two days polishing rifle barrels instead of the demitasse spoons."

"It's in the blood, like an infection. Revolution is a virus for which there is but a single antidote. If Alessandro had been caught and killed a year ago, a month, even last week, this never would have happened. One mad dog in the streets. He bites and the populace is infected. Take a rifle, stand your ground, and *pam!*"

"I have prayed all day. For both sides. I have never been political. I am a Christian. I cannot join or accept the existence of any group that wantonly kills men, women and children and then labels the corpses rebels or fascists afterwards, quite as though they expect God to bend down to examine every bleeding package before He makes His judgment. They are wrong, evil, all of them."

"It's all the fault of the army. Where have they been? Where are they now? What do they do? Nothing! Nothing at all!"

"The Party will provide the final solution. The burning and looting, wives and children killed. This will be taken into account and interest wrung out of the mob and set down on the pages in blood."

"Ran off? Like hell. I told him today, 'Get your hairy ass out of bed and get out in the streets and fight. Be a man! Fight for the poor against the rich. Or I'll snip off your balls with the kitchen scissors. And bring back something decent. A nice dress for me to wear.' He moved, I'll tell you. I'd have done it, too."

"I'm getting out. Hell, I'm not going to have this scum touch what's mine! I've got three daughters, man, the youngest only fourteen."

"Four million. That's all. Enough, eh? My life's work. Gone. You see my eyes? Red? A man weeps when his fortune goes up in smoke."

"They will win tomorrow."

"They will not win if they fight for a hundred years."

"He's had a plane waiting for days. Out at the villa. He's going to skip."

"Millions in Swiss banks. Millions . . ."

"Look at my hands. I ask you. I've been holding a scalpel all day. All last night. Seven leg amputations this morning. I've lost count of the probings for fragments. We're just dusting with sulphur. Half of them are dying by the time they arrive. No morphine, of course. Give me another cup. My eyes will be ruined. Operating with gasoline lanterns. That idiot wanted me to use ether. Whoof, the whole place would go up."

"Santa Rita, saint of the afflicted, bring him back to me. I'll light a candle every day. I'll pay for Masses . . ."

"Holy Santa Teresa of Avila, don't let them get us . . ."

"Father, I have sinned. Today I have killed two men, strangers to me, in the streets. One with a knife, the other with a club . . ."

"Holy Mary, mother of God . . ."

"God is with us. God is with the poor."

"God will protect us. Vizarra and the army. And the Guards. Everyone who is good is with us."

"It's too well organized. Too compact. What is needed is scattered acts of terror. Terrorism. Everywhere. The baker's boy with a bomb. The man who stops you on the street to ask for a light and shoots you in the belly. The enemy must be totally unnerved. But this is a war. It's all wrong . . . of course, I am with the movement, you understand. It's just the tactics that I object to."

"Crush them like so many lice. What is Vizarra waiting for?"

"The divisions from the southern frontier . . ."

"Wiped out at Casanueva . . ."

"They caught them at Casanueva. The Red scum ran like sheep."

"What time is it?"

"Too late. The government will fall."

"Too early. You can't think of going out. You have to wait until dawn, until they can see your uniform. Otherwise they just shoot."

"Time will tell. Both sides will soon become exhausted."

"Comrades! We shall never give up fighting! We shall beat them to their knees, then beat them to their bellies . . ."

"You are Guards. The elite fighting men of the nation. The only men who know what courage is! You will prove your manhood by raising a heap of corpses that blots out the sun! Your courage will create the chaos out of which the new Costa Plata will be born . . ."

"Abajo Vizarra! Arriba Alessandro!"

"Arriba yourself, *coño!"*

"It's the children. You know where they were? This afternoon? Up on the roof. *On the roof!* They wanted to watch, they said. Can you imagine!"

"Dead. My son . . . my only son. One of his friends brought a note. And his cap. Here, his little student's cap. *Aiii . . . hijo mío . . ."*

"We're winning."

"They're winning."

"They can't win."

"They can't hold out much longer."

"Time will tell."

"It's a matter of time, that's all."

⊹ **13** ⊹

THE needle tracked in the grooves, and a soft rasp came out of the morning-glory horn. Lucía frowned and dropped the little brush with which she had been lacquering her nails. She started to rise from the chaise longue, then lay back and clapped her hands. A moment passed. She stared across the room at the phonograph, hating it. She clapped her hands again. Her maid appeared.

"Señorita?"

"La máquina. Turn it off."

The maid lifted the needle and took up the record.

"La Paloma. If I may say so, you sing so wonderfully, señorita."

"It's a stupid song."

"Ya-ya."

"Don't say that!"

"Don't say what?"

"Ya-ya. Ya-ya. Like a baby. When you can't think of anything to say, you make a stupid noise."

She flung out her hand and overturned the lacquer bottle. The shiny liquid ran across the marble tabletop, soaking the scattered cards of an incompleted game of patience.

"Now look what you made me do! Hurry. Get a cloth and clean it up!"

The maid ran forward, then darted back to the machine, still holding the record in her hands. She set the disc on the edge of the open cabinet. It slipped and shattered on the floor. Lucía lay back and picked up a package of cigarettes. She took out three and mashed them into the pool of sticky lacquer. She threw the empty packet on the floor.

"Can't you see that I'm out of cigarettes? Go get me some."

"Ya-ya. Oh, how clumsy of me!"

"Yes. Yes, you're clumsy and you're stupid. Look at your white face. Come here."

She sat up as the maid approached her.

"Closer. Closer still."

She drew back her arm and struck wildly. The maid shrieked and dodged away, clutching her cheek. Lucía laughed shrilly.

"There! Now you have pretty pink cheeks. Go and clean up all this filth."

The maid ran from the room, sobbing. Lucía sniffed in disgust, knotted her dressing gown and found her slippers. There were cigarettes in the pocket of the robe. She lit one and tossed the match on the carpet. The mirror caught her, and she stared briefly at her reflection. Her hair was uncombed; she had too much lipstick on. Her eyes were red from sleeplessness. She snatched up a brown bottle and swallowed a pill. She dropped the bottle back into a litter of jars, powder boxes, brushes and cosmetic tubes. She walked, slouching carelessly, from the room, ignoring the maid who hurried past her carrying a cloth and followed by a fat, wheezing woman with a mop and pail.

The tapestries that hung along the hall muffled the sounds of gunfire from the city. She opened the door and walked in, the cigarette dangling from her lips. A narrow iron bed, a cheap pine bureau. She pulled open the closet door. Four uniforms, two business suits, three pairs of slacks. On the floor a pair of riding boots, a pair of dress pumps and scuffed tennis shoes. Over the bed hung an inexpensive wooden crucifix, the kind sold to tourists at shrines. She reached out to stub her cigarette in the bare, clean center of the bureau. She grimaced and drew her hand back. The window was wide open. She heard the distant concussion of a shell. She left the room and strolled down the hall. Two footmen in livery were whispering. They broke apart as she approached and stared at nothing. One of them was young, rather good-looking.

"Any news?"

"It is said that the railroad station will soon surrender. The Guards have already taken part of the building, señorita. Victory is assured."

"Ah. Do you know how to play honeymoon bridge?"

"I beg your pardon, señorita?"

He didn't even look at her. His eyes stared at nothing. She turned away.

"Never mind."

She started down the long, curved flight of stairs. The great foyer was gloomy. It filled the center of the north side of the building. She paused in the center of the huge Persian carpet. The villa surrounded her, ornate and silent. She turned back to the stairs.

"You! Hey, tell them to saddle my horse."

"Señorita, forgive me, but His Excellency has forbidden—"

"I tell you that I want my horse!"

"His Excellency has forbidden it. The danger of assassins."

She made a disgusted sound and strode swiftly across the foyer to the music room. Her heels snapped on the glossy parquet floor. The last golden flood of sunlight streamed through the French windows. She threw them open. The cannons were firing. Four, five, six times, as fast as her pulsebeat. She tossed her cigarette out on the balcony and sat down at the piano. She played scales for a moment, thinking of nothing. Her hands lifted and dropped. The Beethoven piano concerto that was his favorite. She played five measures, made a mistake, and slammed a discord with her fist. Tears glittered on her lids. She swept back her hair, lit a cigarette and played the American vamp that the orchestra had played when she began her act. She remembered the stuffy, dark room filled with smoke, the candles on the tables, the rattle of ice and glasses. The sounds stopped as she walked out, while the manager introduced her. He made her pad the bosom of her cheap gowns. Once a week she slept with him. He liked to do it in the bathroom. In the corner was the table with two or three young army officers, drinking champagne. The other girls sat around at the tables, envying her, pretending to be bored because their men hissed them silent and leaned forward to listen to her sing. Across the room, sleek and silent as a ferret, Julio slipped, a wine card under his arm.

She began to play *Burrito Mío,* "My Little Burro." Every line had a double meaning. She smiled languidly, as if she had come from making love. They applauded wildly. The manager bowed and smirked at her, patting his palms together. For twenty reales a week, plus two per-cent of the tips. And once a week doing it in the bathroom. The young officer bought her some flowers. The manager nodded. When her act was over, she would wait a discreet few minutes and join him at the corner table.

" 'And when I ride my little burro . . .' "

She jumped up, her heart pounding, her hands clutching the front of her robe. A man's laughter came from the balcony.

"Ah, I'm sorry. I frightened you, my little bird."

"Rico! What the hell? What are you doing here? How did you get in? How you frightened me."

He brushed aside the light drapes that billowed in the golden sunlight. He smiled at her and took off his dark glasses.

"You're crazy to come here! Someone will see!"

"But Lucía, this is the safest place to be, no? You wouldn't want me to stay in the city? Why, a man could get killed there."

"A man, yes. Not the famous Rico Belgarito, though, eh?"

"I don't believe in taking chances. Only in love."

"Love."

"You are very beautiful. How the sunlight touches your cheek!"

"Beautiful. I look terrible. I haven't slept."

"Alone?"

"How did you get in here?"

He shrugged and rubbed two fingers on his thumb.

"So much for the men at the rear gate, so much for the gardener, so much for the one with the two pistols who wanders around by the swimming pool looking tough. It cost me a couple of thousand, but, you know, I can't keep money in my pocket anyway. It comes, it goes. What better way to spend it? And here I am."

"He'll find out. Or Julio will. He'll tell him."

"Ah, but then they'll have to catch me, no? And that won't be easy. Besides, a strictly business discussion, my heart. Strictly business."

"Business! You?"

She began to laugh.

"Play something for me."

"No . . . I . . . oh, it feels good to laugh again. My God, I've been locked up in here like a novice. I've been so *bored,* Rico!"

"Poor little one. Say, we might have a drink, eh? It's warm in the sun."

"Yes, Rico! A gin sling. You used to love them."

"I still do . . . Lucía, my tastes never change."

"Come. In the little parlor. Right here, see?"

"Ah. Very cozy. And here you sit at night, while he snores and you do the sewing. Mending his socks."

"Oh, shut up. Sit down. Stop pacing around like that. I'm nervous enough. Ring that bell."

"And what happens? The floor opens up! A trapdoor! God, I'm falling down, down into the dungeon. Forty niggers with whips and clubs jump on me. But I reach down so! Zap! I show them my magic weapon. They are amazed. Terrified. I wave it at them. They scream with fright. They have never seen anything like it. Watch out, they yell, it's a bull! No, an elephant!"

He bounded from the sofa to the fireplace and back, his face twisted into comic expressions of fear. The door opened and a footman stood there. Belgarito jerked down the tails of his jacket and turned to her, his face expressionless except for his glittering eyes.

"You understand, señorita, that these jungle films are becoming quite popular . . ."

She covered her face with her hands, unable to look at him. Her shoulders shook with laughter. The footman waited. Belgarito lit a cigarette and tiptoed across the room to drop the match in an ashtray.

"Yes, señorita?"

"Make us a tray of gin slings and bring a bucket of ice. Or perhaps you would prefer champagne, señor?"

"No, many thanks."

The footman bowed and closed the door. Belgarito grinned and shrugged. She laughed delightedly.

"Oh, Rico, you are impossible!"

"Me? No, everything I do is quite possible. That's why people trust me. I can help them. Why, a few people even like me."

394

"How does it go in the city, Rico?"

He stuck out his lower lip and pretended to be shooting a rifle. "Like this. All day long. I don't really know. I've been staying at the studio."

"Breaking in a new actress, eh?"

"Lucía, such vulgarity from the first lady of our nation! I'm shocked, really. You must have fallen into bad company lately."

"Now, Rico, I'm warning you. It's bad enough that you're here."

"But I must watch myself, eh? Very well. I will begin by watching my magic weapon."

He frowned and stared at his groin, then blew a smoke ring.

"Ooops. Missed."

She giggled.

"Stop it, you fool."

"Well, that depends, my dear, on what makes a fool. Ah?"

The footman brought in a tray and a silver ice bucket, bowed and left the room. Belgarito handed her a glass.

"Hmm. How do they manage it? Walking backward like that. Must take years of practice. Ya-ya. Well, to the loveliest girl in Costa Plata."

"To the biggest liar in Costa Plata."

"You want to know how it's going? I'll tell you. This gang of Reds is going to win."

"You're joking. Rafael would never permit it."

"Never permit it. You have no idea how odd that sounds."

"The railroad station has been taken . . . or very nearly. Then the university. What's left?"

"Just the rest of the country, Lucía. And that is why I am taking a little vacation."

"You're running out? Well, that's like you, I must say."

"I am taking a vacation. I have been working very hard."

"With your magic weapon. Is she pretty, your new one?"

"Only you are pretty, Lucía. Pretty? Beautiful. Ravishing. My little nun, locked up here in your convent. I've always wanted to see this place. But somehow, I've never been invited. Who makes the best films south of Hollywood, eh? No, I'm not boasting and you know it."

"He doesn't like films."

"You mean he doesn't like to see his Lucía in her skin kissing another man. That scene in *Amor y Sangre*. It offended absolutely *everyone!* We have made a fortune on it."

"I was stupid enough not to demand a percentage. Put some ice in another for me."

"Thirsty, eh? Well, it's warm out. Lucía, I regret to say that if you had demanded a percentage, I would have looked around for some other girl."

"At least you're frank, if not honest."

"Better to be frank. That's why I'm telling you. Get out of the country. He's going down, Lucía, and he'll take all of his people with him. You know that."

"But he can't lose! It's impossible! He's a great general! Why, the people love him! All he's done for them . . . the new trade agreement!"

"Then why do the people steal locomotives? Turn off the electricity? Kill the police? Why does the army still refuse to fight? Why is the garrison now shared with the rebels? Why did they shell the city this morning? Must have been delightful for you. Every shell right over the roof, eh?"

"*Jesús,* Rico, I was so scared! I hid with the servants down in the wine cellars. It was awful."

"Awful. Yes. But better than being in the city. What will you do if they drop a few right here, eh? They could do it any time. They could be aiming the guns right now."

"Stop it! I forbid you to frighten me."

He shrugged and dropped on the sofa beside her and sipped his drink. She drank thirstily and held out her glass to him. He handed her another.

"Pretty girls shouldn't drink too much. It will ruin your figure and your complexion."

"I want to feel gay. Just shut up, will you?"

"You want to know how it goes? There are no government troops west of the Glorieta Colón. That's exactly half the city that the rebels hold. So they lose the railroad station? Means nothing. I left the studio lot and drove north. I have a press pass. I was stopped a couple of times. But the rebels hold the rest of the highway. But I could see Casanueva. His brand-new city. His first gift to the people. It is burning, Lucía, from one end to the other. The entire city is in flames. You can see the smoke from your bedroom windows. But I suppose you haven't looked. They shot down three aircraft. The division ordered up from the south is stuck in the riverbed outside Casanueva, pinned down. Alessandro himself is there. When a bunch of guerrillas can tie up the southern force . . . well, you'd better think again, *paloma mía*. They're going to get him. But they aren't going to get me. I have an airplane. A De Havilland. Seats three plus the pilot. My car is outside the rear gate. Ring the bell, have it driven up beyond the swimming pool. I'll finish my drink while you change. Just one suitcase. I've got plenty of money. And the contract, *querida,* bring along the contract. It's your only chance, I'm warning you. Can you imagine what they'll do to you? When the men are through, they'll turn the old women on you and stand around and watch. Just watch and listen. They'll make it last, too. You want that?"

"No! No!"

"Well, then. Hurry up. Just ring the bell."

She rose and blundered across the room, then stopped and turned. "I'm afraid . . . of him."

"In three hours you won't have to be afraid of anybody."

"But if you can get away, so can he. I know him. He'll come after me! No matter where I go. I'd never be able to get away from him. He'll send O'Conner!"

Suddenly she burst into tears. She felt his arm around her shoulders.

"Ah, don't cry, *guapita*. Come, come. That won't help."

"Go away, Rico. Don't . . . tempt me!"

"This is foolishness, Lucía. Come right now. You'll be safe with me."

"With you? Don't be a fool! I'm not such a fool as that. No! Get out! Get out now!"

"Lucía . . ."

"Get out or I'll scream and ring the bell. I'll tell them you tried to rape me. They'll shoot you! And it would serve you right, too!"

"Lucía, you're hysterical, my love."

"Get out of here . . . you *traitor!*"

She fell from his arms to the floor and knelt there sobbing. The door opened and shut. She remained weeping for a long time, then wiped her streaming face and crawled to the tray of drinks and picked

397

up a glass and drank half of it. The glass slipped from her fingers and rolled on the floor. She stared stupidly at the dark stain that spread across the figured carpet.

↓

Malata walked softly down the corridor and through the open door. The chief cipher clerk handed him a batch of flimsies and cleared his throat. He permitted himself a faint smile. Malata glanced up.

"Yes?"

"It's ready. The transcript and a translation."

"Very good."

The clerk crossed the room and drew a folder from a file cabinet.

"It was taken down in shorthand by one of our best boys. Just the phonemes. Then we turned the phonemes into English . . . not hard, if you know what you're doing."

"Who did it?"

"Why, I did, actually."

"These are all the copies?"

"One for our records. We keep one copy of everything that goes in or out, you know."

"I want that copy, too."

"But . . . yes, if you wish."

The clerk rummaged through a wire basket, found the flimsy and handed it across the desk. Malata nodded.

"The copy will be returned."

"We have to keep our records straight."

Malata stared at the clerk.

"Of course. An irregularity would be unforgivable."

The clerk wet his lips and stared at the record copy in Malata's hand.

"You will return it?"

"That depends on His Excellency."

"Claro, claro . . ."

Malata opened the folder and glanced at the sheets of paper. He could read a certain amount of English, enough to be convinced that the translation was accurate.

Ferguson? Are you there? Yes, Livermore here. . . . We've been trying to contact an agent. . . . Make con-

tact with the leader of the insurgent movement. . . .
We'll ship in arms and ammunition, beginning immedi-
ately. . . . By Panamanian freighter. Three miles off
Boca Perro. . . . Five thousand rifles and twenty thou-
sand rounds of ammunition.

Malata rubbed his trembling hands on his trousers. He must get
hold of himself. The Caudillo was in conference with Lucca and
Zamal. Soon he would demand the newest flimsies from the code
room. Malata alone had free access to the ciphers. His Excellency did
not trust even an officer from the army intelligence department to
handle the decoded documents. Malata held his future, perhaps his
life, in his hands.

Was it the right time? Would it be worth it to burn the papers? A
telephone call to O'Conner, and Ferguson would be placed under
house arrest. Then the problem would be to take the folder to Alessandro. Obviously he was still at Casanueva. But he certainly would
not remain there. This night or in the morning, he would undoubtedly
come into the city. It could be done, not without difficulty and danger, but a contact could be made. Once out of the palace, Malata
knew, he could never return. He would be at the mercy of the rebels.
He would ask for a safe-conduct pass and an escort over the border.
Alessandro was a man of honor. They were both men of honor. But
not Carlitos Sánchez. Like father, like son. And the old man, *El Feo,*
was locked up and under heavy guard in the janitor's quarters in the
basement beneath the west wing. No, Carlitos Sánchez would take the
information and call for a firing squad. Five thousand rifles. Twenty
thousand rounds. That would be merely the first shipment. If the
rebels could hold out until the freighter lay outside the three-mile
limit off Boca Perro, they would win. The new weapons would turn
the battle for the city in their favor. The government would fall.
Vizarra might flee, he might not. In either case Julio Malata would be
abandoned, captured and shot.

Malata smoothed his palms on his trousers. He had no illusions.
Vizarra had lifted him out of a cheap nightclub. He could drop him
just as easily, like turning a dog out of doors. He could run, but how
far? They would shoot him. But if the freighter from Panama were
intercepted, forced to turn back, an act of piracy, perhaps—Livermore would hardly be in a position to protest, not with a transcript of

his conversation with his representative Ferguson in Vizarra's hands —why not *seize* the ship and cargo, after all? Proof would be needed. With the army hanging somewhere between torpor and treachery, the Guards would be strengthened. The gratitude of Lucca might be more valuable than the protection of the Caudillo. Lucca was ambitious. With more weapons, the destruction of the rebels would be a certainty. Lucca would be the most powerful man in the country, the savior, the man on horseback who had broken the Red menace. A realignment of internal power would no doubt follow the victory. Like all ambitious men, Lucca talked too much. Malata had heard scraps and bits—enough, enough. Lucca right now, unaware, was in Malata's power. A word to the Caudillo, and Lucca could be promoted into a harmless sinecure, something to do with state security. O'Conner could watch him and when the moment came . . .

Malata smiled faintly. All these lives caught and tangled, a mesh of snarled cords or wires. You pluck one, and all the others vibrate. Lucca, Alessandro, Vizarra, Carlitos Sánchez and his father, all the men who believed that they controlled the fate of the nation. It was he, Malata! With one movement of his finger, the web shivered. Perhaps each of the others felt or knew the intersection where his strand crossed with another. Like an insect, assuming that he crouched in the center, that he was predator, not prey. Only Julio Malata saw it all. He could . . .

A bell rang. Malata rose and placed the cardboard folder under his left arm like a menu. He glided soundlessly to the door, unlocked it and snapped off the light. He slipped swiftly down the corridor, a faint smile still on his thin lips. The chief clerk was standing in the center of the code room.

"Great news! Great news!"

Malata took the flimsy and ran his eyes along the single line: *Miramar peninsula cleared of rebels. 67 dead. 23 prisoners. Gómez.*

Malata placed the flimsy on top of the stack he held in his hand. He drew the record copy from the folder and handed it to the chief clerk.

"Here. Please put this in your daily file, as usual. We must not have any irregularities."

The clerk gasped and nodded, clutching the sheet. He did not meet Malata's steady glance. Malata nodded and left. The bell rang again. The Caudillo wanted him. The chief clerk had translated the telephone conversation himself. He knew. He knew. He would have to be removed. Perhaps the game was not quite played out.

Malata walked into the anteroom to the table where O'Conner's man sat. He straightened respectfully as Malata stopped before him.

"Yes, señor?"

"Please inform your superior that Ferguson of Livermore Lines Limited is to be placed under house arrest at once."

"Ferguson. House arrest."

"His entire family. No one in or out. No letters or packages. Remove the telephone."

"Very good, señor."

"One other thing. A loyalty check on the chief clerk in the code room."

The policeman raised his eyebrows and glanced briefly at Malata.

"He has been cleared before. Two days ago, señor."

"A man's conception of loyalty may change in two days, no? Two hours. Two minutes, even."

"Yes, señor. If we find anything?"

"It may be convenient to find something."

"You want papers drawn for his arrest, señor?"

"Yes. Just hold them until you receive further instructions."

"Very good, señor."

Malata passed through the other door of the anteroom into the small chamber where the Caudillo's bodyguards idled and smoked. They stood up hastily, like guilty schoolboys. One of them scowled out into the darkness, demonstrating ferocious alertness. Malata opened the door. Vizarra limped across the room. Zamal and Lucca muttered over the map, moving bits of colored wood.

"Where have you been? I rang twice."

"In the code room, Your Excellency. The new ciphers are in."

"Well?"

"The Belgian, Voget, has driven into the sea."

"Good! Did they get him?"

"The message did not say. No doubt Gómez has no method of making such an identification right away. I will have O'Conner's office forward a description."

"Good."

"One other thing, Your Excellency."

"What's that?"

"This, Your Excellency."

Malata drew the folder out from beneath his arm, deftly opened it and extended it, like a menu, bowing slightly from the waist as he did so.

The telephone rang. Malata picked it up.

"Yes. Very good."

Vizarra read the transcript and the translation. His jowls quivered. He slapped the folder shut and thrust it at Malata.

"Put this in the small safe. Notify the Coast Guard. Seize the Livermore office. Arrest this Ferguson as a spy."

"I took the liberty of notifying O'Conner. I think, Excellency, that house arrest would be more satisfactory. If he attempted to leave his dwelling or make some sort of contact . . ."

"Very well. Who is that?"

"Staff."

"I'm busy. What do they say?"

"The three armored trucks have been completed."

"One at the northwest, one at the northeast of the Plaza Mayor. Keep the other in reserve at the motor pool. Anything else?"

"Yes. The first reports are coming in from the observation posts. Olmega is bringing his troops out. The movements have just begun."

"All right. Keep the line open. Get a stenographer in here."

"At once, Excellency."

Malata held the telephone while Vizarra limped slowly back to the map. The Caudillo's powerful shoulders sagged. His bulky body rocked clumsily as he dragged himself across the room.

"Switchboard? Keep this line open. Give me another in the ante-room. Commodore Mejías at Coast Guard headquarters, please."

Malata left the room silently. Mejías. A long record of crude graft and payoffs from the Boca Perro smugglers. He had made himself wealthy by pretending to be stupid. Would he follow orders and seize the freighter from Panama? Was he loyal? Another strand, another snarled strand to twitch. The pressure of a fingertip, and every strand trembled.

↓

Ungrateful. They were all guilty of the sin of ingratitude. And look what things had come to. Ingratitude was the father of anarchy. And the more the giver gave, the less thanks he got. It was a paradox, but a criminal paradox.

There were criminals everywhere. Not only the rebels outside, but Vola and Ramos, too. The government had tolerated Ramos. He kept the miners peaceful and working. And what happened? At the first disturbance, the miners stopped working. A grateful labor leader, properly appreciative, would have compelled the miners to go down into the shafts and would have punished those who refused in the manner of a bailiff wielding the master's quirt.

Lucca and Zamal. Neither of them had the brains or initiative to think of converting trucks to armored cars. And the result of that? Lucca was infuriated because he had been deprived of three of his machine guns—*his* machine guns—and Zamal was sour-faced because there were only three of the new trucks and not thirty or a hundred and three. Put on a uniform on a man and it automatically brought out his worst points. Lucca and Zamal were as selfish and jealous as two hags begging in the markets.

Malata. From a cheap nightclub to the national palace. His petty ambitions accomplished in a single stride. Grateful? Never. Malata had a headwaiter's mind. Gratuities were not freely given, but were due, expected. Was any headwaiter overtipped? Impossible to do so. Behind that dark, frozen face was a lump of vanity, not a brain. His perfect manners were not perfect manners at all, but rather insolence barely checked by efficiency. Checked, but for how long?

Lucía had everything. Clothes, jewels, servants, a career. She had been pretty, but now she was transformed. What she wore was immediately imitated. What she sang on the radio became instantly popular, the tune on everyone's lips. Schoolgirls copied her hair styles when their mothers weren't watching. The new films she had made played all over Latin America. Lucía Bosola. She was famous. But still, she was what she was. Only the outside, the surface, had changed. But inside, instead of gratitude and love—yes, love—what? A secret ambition, no doubt, to marry some lisping little aristocrat, from one of the first families of Costa Plata, some droop-lipped weakling with bad blood. Their lovemaking would be all tweaks and flutters, like two feeble birds, eventually to produce some pallid *Conde* of This or *Marqués* of That. An alliance, a respectable alliance . . . and in the meantime she might be giving him horns. If she dared. Some servant, one of the footmen, an undergardener. Women paid back trust with treachery. Ingratitude came naturally to them. Men had to learn to be unfaithful.

Eyes that should have shone with joy turned inward until only the blank whites stared. The future they cast away for what? The meningitis of liberty. Liberty to do what? Murder each other, burn and pillage, wreck the city, smash transportation, waste the countryside, the fields and grazing lands. Liberty was killing personal enemies in the name of politics, stealing in the name of equal distribution, lies in the name of influencing the masses to do their worst. It all lay in ingratitude, selfishness, envy and hatred. Sins piled on top of sins, a heap of slime. Liberty was a mass of blind, wriggling maggots feeding on the corpse of the state.

There was no loyalty, not even to a dream. It would be pathetic if it were not so stupid. One could have no sympathy for the ungrateful. Like maggots, they deserved only to be crushed. A failure to destroy such criminal activity was a sign of moral cowardice. God granted to the strong and wise the right to rule the weak and foolish in His holy name. The work demanded by God was that of purification by extermination. Scientifically the virus of anarchy, the fever of radicalism, must be isolated and destroyed. When that occurred, the directed society could move forward bathed in the light of gold and silver, the smile of God, to a future without limits.

"Here they come, the Red bastards!"

Vizarra opened his stinging eyes and stifled a groan. His gout panged; his empty belly rolled and ached—his ulcer again. He sat up and lit a forbidden cigar. His hands trembled slightly as he fastened the top button of the wrinkled tunic slung around his heavy shoulders. He stood up and limped over to the sandbags piled before the tall windows. He sat down on a dainty embroidered chair and peered out through a slot, like a sportsman waiting for the first flight of birds. He could hear the rattle of rifles and the thud of exploding grenades.

"Where are they?"

"Across the Glorieta Colón. Coming up the boulevards, right toward the Plaza Mayor. Right at us. And fast. They're in buses and trucks."

"Uh. Lucca?"

"Yes, Excellency?"

"The Guards will fall back before the pressure? You have insisted on it? No foolhardy stands in the middle of the streets."

"We should see them in a moment. Each section has a separate section of an official building to defend, establishing fields of fire. Any attempt to penetrate the Plaza Mayor will be crushed."

"Ah. Zamal?"

"Yes, Excellency."

"You have ordered Gómez to bring all the artillery into the city?"

"He telephoned into Staff, Excellency. The fieldpieces are already deployed for the counterattack. The howitzers, of course, will be of no use to us, since they cannot be depressed enough for street fighting."

"I have seen a howitzer before, Zamal."

"Yes, of course, Excellency."

"Malata."

"I am here."

"The guards on the roof have been notified? The gunners?"

"Two bursts over, the third right into them. I have a copy of the official apology already typed and ready to release whenever you approve the printing of newspapers. A cup of coffee?"

"No."

Vizarra sat and listened to the distant roar of battle. Strange orange lights glowed in the darkened streets, then the crisp, scarlet flash of an exploding shell. Down in the Plaza Mayor, Zamal's soldiers, the palace guards, and Lucca's National Guards waited behind sandbags. The armored trucks, like ponderous beetles, crouched under the northern archways. The rebels beat through the dark slots of streets. Buses with no lights butted blindly through barbed wire and smashed sentry boxes. A loudspeaker rasped, and another detachment of Guards fell back, firing steadily down the long slope of a boulevard. Vizarra sucked on his dead cigar.

"A light, Excellency?"

"No. My throat is as dry as a hayfield in August."

Zamal moved a chip of wood on the map, shook his head and replaced it. Lucca took the telephone call from staff headquarters.

"A number of units from Vola's garrison have joined the rebels. They have distributed arms and ammunition. They seem to be split, some with the U.T., others with the M.L."

Vizarra nodded. Malata stood near him. Vizarra looked up.

"I have taken the liberty of writing the official apology, Excellency. A Captain Cefalato is held officially responsible for the totally unwarranted killing of—I have left a space blank for the number—peacefully demonstrating citizens. He is court-martialed and executed. You call him a lamentably overzealous defender of the state, whose actions, while well-intentioned, unhappily wrought tragedy."

"You make me sick, Julio. Who was Captain Cefalato, anyway?"

"An obscure artillery officer. He died from a fall in the mountains during maneuvers six years ago. No known relatives."

"Tear it up."

"I beg your pardon, Excellency, but—"

"I said tear it up. There will be no official apology this time. Peacefully demonstrating citizens. Listen to them . . ."

"Here they come!"

"But, Excellency, there is always an official apology."

"I do not apologize for tonight . . . or for what will follow. Is that clear? Let them count the bodies. That is my answer to them."

Malata bowed and stepped away. Vizarra peered out through the slot. The Plaza Mayor was dark. Motors thundered. A whistle blew, and the southeast arch flickered with rifle fire. The Guards ran toward the sandbagged emplacements. Glass smashed and fell from the façades into the square. Lucca looked over the Caudillo's shoulder.

"That's the third brigade up there, Excellency. About seven minutes early. They've been pushed hard, I suppose."

Vizarra grunted and gnawed his cigar. Lucca's presence was irritating. He could almost feel the man's breath on his neck.

"If they can't fight, they can run."

"They are obviously outnumbered, Excellency."

"Ya-ya. And this boy Olmega has got guts. He must have iron balls to order a full attack in the middle of the night. And his men . . ."

"The majority are Vola's troops, of course."

"The majority are university students, workers and dock niggers. And look at them!"

A dark shape flowed through the southeastern archway and spread across the Plaza Mayor. Lucca swallowed nervously.

"Why don't they shoot? They have their orders!"

Vizarra grinned and chewed his cigar. Lucca whirled and ran to the telephone.

"Third brigade! Get me the third brigade!"

A municipal bus roared into the square, followed by another mass of running men. The Guards behind the sandbags fired by volley three times. Two more buses appeared and a truck. The south end of the plaza was covered with moving, shouting figures. The Guards in the buildings fired down into the mob. A light machine gun stuttered. Vizarra nodded.

"Vola's men. That's a Lewis gun . . ."

A long, shrill scream floated up to the tall windows. Some of the palace guards had been hit. The rebel Lewis gun fired again, and the window over Vizarra's head broke into flying fragments. The Caudillo covered his head with his hands. Bits of glass pattered down on his arms.

"All right, that's enough. Give it to them."

The machine guns mounted on the palace roof fired two short, warning bursts. The plaza seemed to explode with return fire from a thousand rifles. Spots of light flicked from the windows around the square.

"Come on. Come on. Get the trucks out."

The armored vehicles lurched into motion and rolled across the square. The machine gun on the roof fired again, a vicious, prolonged hammering. Slugs spewed out into the darkness and howled off the pavement. Shouts and screams echoed off the stiff, stone façades. A chuff of yellow flames lit the southwest arch, outlining the gunner on the first truck, crouched in his iron drum, turning his leaping gun from side to side. Then the dull *whomp* of the exploding gasoline. One of the buses had been hit. A tiny, flaming figure sprinted out into the center of the square, whirled and clawed, then fell forward. Vizarra winced and chewed his cigar.

"What a way to die. Burned to death. The poor devil!"

The two trucks stopped, but the gunners fired three more bursts. A long, yaahing cry went up from the palace guards. A grenade exploded ten paces short of one of the armored trucks. Whistles shrilled and equipment clanked as the guards ran forward to their new positions along the iron fence. Some voice bellowed for an attack. Vizarra shook his head automatically. The rebels were stunned, but they had not broken. Already they had smashed in the doors of the official buildings and were fighting on the first floors. More buses and trucks appeared. One bus ground in a slow circle and headed for the nearest armored truck. The gunner fired and stopped. Vizarra saw him grapple feverishly with a new ammunition belt. The bus engine roared. It slammed into the truck and jolted back. The truck slewed sideways. The bus turned slightly to ram again. Vizarra's fingers twitched.

"The pin, *hombre!* Pull back on the pin!"

The gunner was hit. He clutched his left shoulder. The bus rolled ahead. The gunner swung the barrel and fired a long burst into the bus windshield. The bus coasted up and gently nudged the right front fender of the truck. The gunner slipped down into the steel drum and the truck reversed, drawing back. The crowd of rebels rushed forward. Vizarra pounded his fist on his knee.

"Now! Now!"

Orders were shouted down on the parapet. The great gates swung open and the palace guards streamed out into the square, covered by machine-gun fire from the roof. The rebels milled uncertainly around the bus, firing at the two armored trucks. Lucca leaned over Vizarra.

"Look at that column drive!"

The palace guards swung to the right, past the east end of sandbagged emplacements held by Lucca's troops. The men there shouted and swung over the heaped sacks. Vizarra grunted. Lucca sucked in his breath.

"Too much to the right. He's left his flank exposed."

"But he's close to the buildings. See? He's getting covering fire from the Ministry . . ."

The stones and plaster spouted into the room, a deafening shatter. Vizarra rolled on the floor, stunned, his ears aching. He crawled forward blindly until his fingers touched Lucca's boot. Someone helped him to his feet. He stared, dazed, into the white, twisted face of Zamal. Zamal was saying something. Vizarra stared at the hole punched in the wall.

"*Dios,* they've got a gun out there . . ."

The center of the room was a wreck of shattered chairs and tables. Plaster dust hung in the air. The chandelier, still lighted, hung at a drunken angle. The door opened, and Malata stepped into the room, an expression of mild concern on his dark face. Vizarra burst into shaky laughter. He shoved Zamal away. Another shell struck the palace up near the roof and wrenched off stone and tiles that fell shattering on the parapet below. Vizarra picked up the telephone. A voice gibbered in his ear.

"Staff? The Caudillo. Send every field gun General Gómez has to the northeast arch of the Plaza Mayor immediately."

Lucca was sitting up. His face was coated with plaster dust like a circus clown's. The room shook, and the concussion squeezed Vizarra's head and chest. He ran to the shelter of the sandbags and sat down hard. He looked up at the chandelier and fumbled out a match.

408

He turned over and knelt, looking out through the slot. The fighting splattered along a line of parked buses and trucks. The rebels struck out at the advancing column, but the machine guns on the armored trucks slashed into them. The column drove along the building front, a man dropping out of line, another slapped against a pilaster by the force of the bullets that ripped him. Bayonets flashed in the glare of the burning gasoline. The column flanked the rebels and drove them away from the southeast arch. There was the fieldpiece. A tongue of flame shot from the muzzle. The palace guards swarmed over the cannon, shooting and jabbing with their bayonets. One armored truck ground over a scatter of bodies and hung there, one wheel spinning. Lucca's Guards drew in near it and began lobbing grenades. The fragments panged off the Ministry façades. The palace troops began firing by volley, kneeling to shoot, then running forward a dozen paces. All at once the rebel force broke. Hundreds of men struggled in the southwest arch. The steady fire tore at them. The armored trucks lumbered forward, the machine guns lashing. Vizarra stood up and dusted off his pants. The carpet was covered with bits of broken glass. The machine guns on the roof stopped firing, and the men there cheered, a thin yelping in the night. Malata dusted off the map of the city with his pocket handkerchief.

"Julio."

"Excellency. You're quite all right?"

"I'm all right. Find out the name of the officer who led the attack. He is to be promoted one full grade and decorated. That is, if he's still alive."

Malata nodded. Lucca turned away from the shattered window. He had mopped his face, but his brows were still white with plaster dust.

"The guns have arrived from Gómez, Excellency. Six of them. Zamal has gone down to deploy them at the arches. Reserve infantry units have taken positions in the center of the plaza. The column has gone out into the streets."

"Very good. You're all right?"

"Yes, Excellency. But yourself?"

"It will take more than a 75 to get rid of Vizarra."

Lucca smiled stiffly and nodded. Plaster dust spilled from his brows. Vizarra chuckled and turned away to gaze at the hole punched in the wall. The night wind blew in through the jagged opening.

"Five meters to the right and—"

A shell whistled and fell into the plaza. Vizarra started away from the hole, half crouching. Another shell blasted into the Ministry of Marine.

"Zamal! Zamal!"

"Here! Right here, Excellency! Staff has . . ."

"What?"

"Staff has called through. Very heavy fighting. Gómez has sent in all his troops. They are pushing them back, but—"

"Tell Gómez to unlimber his howitzers and begin firing. At once!"

"But, Excellency, what are they to fire at?"

"The city. From the Glorieta Colón west to the university. They are to destroy the university and reduce all rebel positions between it and the Glorieta Colón."

"But . . ."

"But what?"

"But that is a residential section. Filled with families. Women and children."

"And Olmega's rebels. And the anarchist criminals! And Alessandro's gangster-murderers! If they love them, then let them die with them!"

"Excellency—"

"That is an order, Zamal! Direct order to you and to Gómez."

"Yes, Excellency."

"Lucca. You take over here. The Guards are to advance with the infantry sent in by Gómez. Have them stop at the Glorieta Colón, if they get that far . . ."

Another rebel shell dropped into the plaza. The chandelier swung gently. Vizarra dropped his cigar and stepped on it. The others looked at him. He bent forward, hugging himself, his face twisted as he rocked from side to side. He seemed to be struggling in a net, thrashing to free himself. He groaned and straightened, thrusting Malata away. His eyes fixed on Malata, a steady glare of hatred. His voice was hoarse.

"We're going to arm the Red Beret . . ."

The telephone jingled. Lucca picked it up, still staring at Vizarra.

"Yes. Yes. Very good! Casanueva has fallen to us, Excellency. The railroad is now clear from the city to the mines!"

"Zamal. Take your brigade up there. To the mines."

410

"Yes, Excellency."

"This must be done at once, Zamal. The railroad is ours. But for how long? We don't ask questions now. We act. No act of insurrection is to be tolerated. The miners have not the right to cease work."

Vizarra swung around and stabbed his forefinger at Zamal. His weary eyes twitched as he flagged his hand up and down in cadence with his rasping words.

"The mines are to be reopened at once. The government tolerates no interference, either from this creature Ramos or from the military—and you can expect efforts from both parties. I don't have to tell you how to handle any exponents of Alessandroism. Or the U.T. The U.T. is totally discredited. I will abolish the U.T. I have created the system for the settlement of all labor problems. Anyone who does not use the system is a criminal and will be treated as such. Do you understand your orders, Zamal?"

"Perfectly, Your Excellency."

"Well, you'd better."

"Sir?"

"You know what I mean. Now is not the time for second chances. Now is the time for loyalty, total loyalty. Lucca?"

"Yes, Your Excellency."

"The government will proceed to arm volunteers from the party."

"There is no . . ."

"No what? Then make it. Or I will make whatever is needed. Without you . . . or your kind, understand? I don't need you. Your kind needs me. Don't forget that. Party volunteers are to report to party headquarters. Have your people draw up a transportation system and order trucks from the motor pool. You will speak on the radio."

"Really, Your Excellency, I have never spoken on the radio in my life . . ."

Vizarra's heavy brows lifted. He dragged his nails across his brow.

"So? Then it's time you did. Once, anyway. It's a bad habit, Brigadier, speaking to the nation. A man confuses his will with what the people wish too easily. I will try to keep you from contamination."

Vizarra turned again, his loose tunic whipping around his heavy shoulders, his thick face stiff, turned like a bludgeon against the men who sidled through the sifting clouds of dry dust. His hand fell limp; he locked his fingers, then pulled them apart, spreading them in a

411

beggar's gesture of futility. His coarse voice thinned to a metallic drone.

"Thirteen years. Thirteen. You know what that means? No. An unlucky number, eh? But what about those years that get taken out of a man's life—and for what? I'll tell you. Nothing. That's for what. To begin with a civil war started by discontented intellectuals and thirteen years later to have the same sort raising hell again. Well, I will have five thousand more men in the street tomorrow. How many will he have? The Red Beret. They'll have messy jobs. And how they'll enjoy it! These years to sharpen their teeth . . . like a kennel of hungry dogs. How to stop them from biting: that's the problem. I . . . I never wanted it like this. I didn't think it would come to this. That little Red bastard . . ."

The Caudillo's voice quavered off into a moist, incoherent croak. He thumped his hand into his palm and shook his head blindly. Malata offered him a cigarette. The Caudillo snatched the packet and bent over a match. He straightened and exhaled a cloud of blue smoke.

"Julio, get me a drink. Whiskey. In the cabinet over there."

Malata moved across the figured carpet. The shattered glass crackled under his heels. He brought back a bottle and a glass.

"Get others, Julio. You know I don't like to drink alone."

"Yes, sir."

"Some more glasses and the city telephone directory."

"The telephone directory?"

"You heard me, no?"

Lucca and Zamal stood near the map table, watching, listening, Lucca in a Napoleonic posture, his fingers thrust into his tunic above the belt. Vizarra grimaced and waved at the plaster-snowed armchairs.

"Sit down. Please. Here. Take a whiskey."

Vizarra swallowed his drink, fiddled with his cigarette and limped up to Lucca. He brought his face close to Lucca's.

"Did you study the classics at war college?"

"Caesar, Your Excellency. I was very poor in Latin."

"And Greek?"

"No better. Worse. Thucydides in translation, as I remember."

"I suppose you are more modern. Now you read the German philosophers . . ."

"Some of them."

"Also in translation."

"As you say, Your Excellency."

"Give me another, Julio."

Vizarra walked a dozen paces away from Lucca, carrying his glass, then pivoted slowly on his good leg and dropped his cigarette to the carpet.

"Then you do not know what the word *hecatomb* means."

"I'm afraid not."

Lucca touched his lips to the whiskey in his glass and stroked the left side of his nose.

"Something to do with graves, Excellency, no?"

"In a sense. Yes. From the ancient Greek."

Lucca squeezed a smile on his face. The Caudillo prided himself on his ability in the study of languages. Lucca glanced at Malata, hoping for a nod, a grimace, a gesture of support or encouragement. Malata stared down at the section of torn carpet between his feet. Vizarra cleared his throat. Lucca straightened, but did not look at the Caudillo. The harsh voice rasped in his ear like a file on a splintered plank.

"The word *hecatomb,* from the Greek, means one hundred oxen. A ritual sacrifice, so to speak. Tonight we will practice this old custom, and tomorrow and the day after that. As long as it is necessary. Orders to this effect will supersede any regular orders now standing. Failure to comply will mean the firing squad without benefit of court-martial. Understand?"

"Yes, Excellency."

Vizarra's voice cracked. He caught himself, spat on the floor and continued.

"We will arm the members of the Red Beret. They have been proving their loyalty in the streets already. We will turn them loose to aid the police and your Guards. There will be wholesale arrests, beginning at once. The troops under Gómez will seize the docks at the north end of the harbor. You will set up a radio transmitter there. Hostages, one hundred of them at a time, will be taken to the docks and shot. Men. And women. Yes, Christ! And children too! In groups of one hundred! Every hour. Every hour beginning at noon!"

Vizarra turned and limped over to the map table and sat down. He scribbled furiously on sheets of paper. The other three men did not watch him. The Caudillo's fingers scurried like rats, scuffling the crumpled sheets. Lucca looked up at the dangling chandelier.

"What people for hostages, Excellency? The wharf niggers?"

"Anybody! Anybody who is not a party member. We will broadcast the executions over the radio. Every hour! Every hour! We will meet terror with absolute terror! Alessandro must know it, feel it in his heart. He is responsible for this hecatomb, not Vizarra! It is all his fault, not mine! He will be guilty. The blood will be on his hands, soak into his soul!"

Lucca turned around. Tears shimmered in the Caudillo's eyes. His voice was a cracked, ragged whisper. His shoulders sagged, and his bulky body shuddered. His jowls were gray with stubble and his mouth drooped. He looked like an exhausted shipping clerk sneaking a drink on the job, up to his wrists in dirty pieces of papers. He rolled his head from side to side, dazed.

"They will hate me for this. Mother of God, I will be named in their curses forever. But it will work . . . it cannot fail. . . . There is a weak spot in Alessandro . . . somewhere. But he is breaking me to pieces. . . . He makes me kill children from the slums . . . and they will hate me. Me! God, it isn't fair! We will make him . . . I will make him surrender. And they . . . will love him. Love him? Yes. When we hang him by his heels from a lamppost, they'll come running to kiss his bloody hands. . . . Ah, Christ!"

Vizarra lurched to his feet. Lucca stepped back. The Caudillo seemed quite drunk. His face was a terrible mottled shade, like the skin of a sick snake. His red eyes slid beneath his puffy lids. His mouth quirked into a wretched smile. He tore open the throat of his shirt and drew out a crucifix. His voice dwindled as he bent to kiss the silver emblem.

"Christ and the Holy Virgin forgive me . . ."

He held his lips to the crucifix, then opened his fingers. The cross and chain fell into the crumpled papers and slid out onto the map of the city. Vizarra straightened and pointed his finger, first at Lucca, then at Zamal and Malata.

"You are with me. All of you against him. You are with me to the end. To the last drop of blood. Until the last body stiffens in the streets."

Lucca stared into the red eyes of Vigo. He could not move. He could not turn his face away. He looked at a mouth that chewed and swallowed, not out of hunger but out of habit, even when gorged. The mouth smiled, a bitter spasm of the lips. Vizarra nodded.

"Sánchez . . . old Sánchez. *El Feo*. We will make him announce the hecatomb over the national radio. After all, he is Minister of Public Education, no?"

Down in the dark plaza the guns of General Gómez boomed slowly. Each muzzle flash smeared the fang points of the broken palace windows. The shells whooped up into the night sky and stabbed down on the city. Vizarra crept closer, his finger curling, beckoning, drawing Lucca, Zamal and Malata to him. He reached out and pressed their hands in turn. His own palm was hard and dry, his fingers strong and cold. The bitter twist lifted one corner of his mouth.

"So. We are brothers now. All of us are brothers, each to each."

His lips twitched, and disgust rippled across Vizarra's face. He dragged his tunic tight around his throat and limped across the ruined carpet to the door.

"Call me an auto, Julio. I'm going home to the villa. To rest. Lucca, you are in charge here until I return. Your orders are on the table."

Vizarra raised his hand in salute. His face was expressionless.

"Long live death."

The door opened and closed behind him.

‡

The shelling stopped at dawn. In the white, cool light, the smoke rose in straight plumes up from the burning city, mingled and made a cloud, slim, long and dark, like a coffin lid. The new day smelled of scorched stones and charred timber, powdered brick, spoiled food and dead flesh. Alessandro left the barricade and walked out into the stricken capital.

A tenement had been ripped open by the bombardment, exposing an apartment. Splintered sticks of furniture, a smoldering blanket, a smashed picture of the Holy Family askew on a cracked wall. Beneath the picture was a ripped armchair. In the chair was a dirty bundle of clothes and bones, what was left of a man.

Three bodies lay near the blackened metal skeleton of an automobile. Across the street was a shop, windowless, the display shelves puddled with jam oozing from shattered jars. Next door the iron shutter had been laced by bullets. A crushed dog, brown and white, stiff in the gutter near a baby carriage with one ruined wheel and a rust-stained blanket hanging over the side.

A house, an idiot face, with two blank windows and an open, lolling door. A sergeant of the National Guard, dead in the street, his eyes staring at a cartridge clip just beyond his fingertips. A boy lay near him, still holding the bloody knife, stiff hair pasted on his broken brow.

Smoke leaked up through the rubble, fine, bluish tendrils. Two women scraped at the smashed bricks and plaster chunks, clearing the fallen wall off the bodies buried there. One of the women worked with a silver spoon.

A barricade of lumber and wire, packing crates, paving stones, broken bottles, ammunition boxes. Near it a dusty loaf of bread and three mashed pears. Spent cartridges littered the street, gleaming brass bits. The scarlet banner of the U.T. hung on a pole like a sated leech. Beyond the barricade, the bodies lay dumped in the empty silent street.

Men and women, with five children, plodded across an open square. An old man with a white mustache tottered at the head of the little column, tenderly waving a handkerchief knotted on the end of his cane. The others bent under bundles, sacks, suitcases and grimy blankets. They walked in single file, staring straight ahead. A little girl in bare feet clutched a legless doll.

A girl dressed in a shapeless army uniform knelt by the dry bowl of a fountain. Her thick, dusty hair was bound in a red kerchief. Scuffed tennis shoes on her small feet. A rifle lay in her lap. Between her shoulder blades, two dry red blotches.

Smoke, fine as a lace mantilla, tipped the soft flames that coiled and lashed through the split stones of a gasoline station. A heap of bodies flung against a wall, all in brown uniforms, all weaponless, their hands tied with butcher's twine. Blue-and-scarlet shoulder patches. Mutineers from Zamal's brigade, shot by their comrades.

A cat squirted through a cellar window. On the sidewalk a priest bent over a woman. Her son held her up and smoothed the curls away from her pale forehead. The priest gestured, and the wafer slipped from his fingers and dropped to the pavement. He picked it up and blew on it.

A man in a worker's coverall and sandals cut from an auto tire crouched in the center of an alley, leaning on his rifle, chewing a chocolate bar, his dirty face runneled with dried tears.

Like a dying bull, broken to the knees in the stained sand of the arena, the truck, slued sideways, blocked the narrow street. The front tires were punctured. Three men huddled as they had been hit. The driver lay half out of the cab, propped against the riddled door.

Smoke gushed from the upper stories of a tenement, gray, smooth smoke pouring up into the dawn. Men and women with faces dry and wrinkled, gritty hair and dull, red eyes stood around six bodies—four women, an old man and an infant—ranked neatly in the gutter, foot to head.

An empty plaza, a vast, gray plate of concrete, covered with paving blocks. In the center the pigeon-slutted statue of Huelta the *Conquistador*. The stone fist still gripped the sword and held it high, but the left hand, extending the Bible, had been stumped by flying shrapnel.

A café, a heap of twisted rattan chairs draped with the slashed tatters of the awning. A student from the Black Cadre stood in the open door, stroking the dawn dew from the barrel of a revolver. Stale beer and bitter coffee.

Two men yoked to a rubber-tired cart heaped with clothing and furniture. Behind the cart a goat minced, tied fast in a halter of knotted neckties.

Smoke above the rooftops. Toy-small figures waited between the chimney pots, ready to flinch back into the shelter of a dovecote. On a top-floor balcony a steel insect spraddled. Three men hunched near, ready to feed it belts of bullets.

A row of expensive *boutiques*. A wax mannequin in a lime-green satin gown seated gracefully in a drift of shattered glass, headless. Sweetness of spilled perfumes like anesthetic.

Brick dust, powdered stone and plaster pounded to talcum. Burdened figures reeling over the rubble. Dirty children stared at a stripped body sprawled in a doorway.

A wounded burro with buckling legs lunged forward, towing a wagon filled with children, little girls in blue smocks. A nun ground the rope halter tight, the burro staggered and fell, dark liquid bubbling and smearing its chest.

Smoke filled an alley, the bitter fumes of burning cloth. Stretcher-bearers, staggering with exhaustion, drove with their burden through the choking clouds toward the open maw of an ambulance, where an intern in smeared whites waited.

A man in a neat blue suit, with oiled and shining hair, balanced deftly on a jumble of wood, concrete and scraps of furniture. In his left hand he held a wooden fork and a chipped demitasse saucer.

A blind beggar, his jacket gay with the scarlet and yellow lottery tickets pinned to his lapels, stood on the crumbled rim of a shell hole torn in the street, waving his white cane down into the mystery of new nothingness.

A crowd, crones with broken shoes and dark shawls and dresses, toiled toward safety beside white-faced boys, mothers with a hasty bundle of clothes and the best cooking pot, fathers carrying babies and briefcases, stunned faces, deafened, slack-lipped, staring. A Negro carried an empty, flopping violin case.

Smoke spewed from a flaming warehouse. A man sat beside a twisted bicycle, tapping his clenched fists gently against his face. A young woman, her red lips brilliant, led a small boy by the hand. She showed the man a photograph of a girl in Communion dress. The man stared and shook his head. The woman walked away.

Great shell pocks in the sweet grass of the park. A unit of soldiers with rebel armbands squatted beneath the topless trees, waiting.

In the center of a fashionable boulevard, a dentist's chair.

A bloated horse across a sidewalk. Dull eyes and wrecked teeth, shiny intestines, jeweled with flies, tangled in the stiff hind legs.

Smoke and the flat reek of ashes lifting up from a block of gutted, roofless buildings, the shattered stones still shimmering in the cool dawn.

A rebel patrol, seven students, an older man wearing a Panama hat, two soldiers in shoddy field dress and a gaudy whore, barefoot and stumbling, a wooden box of ammunition held like an infant in her arms. Each member of the patrol with a green armband.

A first-aid station at a covered bus stop. A woman dressed in a beige satin suit and a neckpiece of fox fur ladled cocoa into enameled cups and tin cans. A half-filled truck waited at the curb. Two men swung a young woman up onto the tailgate. Her head a bulb of bone-white gauze, she fumbled blindly to pull her skirt down over her naked thighs.

The end of a street, the mouth clotted with rubble. A milling crowd of people stared across the open plaza at an office building. Six women clustered around a child, a mestizo boy, his face paled with shock and loss of blood. He held his right arm tight against his chest, his left arm against his flat belly. The women looked up at Alessandro, their faces clawed with horror. They had just found him, on the floor of the butcher's shop across the street. Both his hands were still in there, in the shop, on the greasy chopping block. The stumps of the boy's arms were bound with kerchiefs. During the night some men had taken shelter from the bombardment in the shop. They had shot the butcher and raped his wife. At dawn they left, but they found the boy hiding in the front of the shop. Soldiers, students, Guards, U.T. militiamen . . . who could say? Only five minutes ago.

Across the plaza, in the office building, the German's place, a clinic or hospital, with some nursing sisters and at least one doctor. But on the rooftops, on two sides of the plaza, National Guards, with rifles.

The boy's face was cold; his large, dark eyes rolled up in his head. A blade of ice slipped into Alessandro's chest, delicately probing for the heart. He picked up the light, slack, smooth-limbed body and scrambled clumsily over the rubble. He walked out into the empty plaza, striding steadily, the moist stumps bunting against his chest. The boy's head rolled with every step. Bits of cobblestone, flicked up by a bullet, snapped against Alessandro's legs. His heels beat on the uneven stones. The rectangle of the open doorway to the building slid closer. A bullet burned the taut muscles of his right shoulder, and he stumbled to his knees, a teeth-cracking jolt. His eyes blurred as he heaved erect again. He strode forward steadily, the sticky wrist stumps beating on his breast. Dust puffs sprang around him. The corners of his mouth tasted of salt. The black slot of the door was right before him. Another ten paces. Bullets starred the wall, an instant's spray of slugs. Hot liquid leaked down his back. The body in his arms was weightless. Salt poured into Alessandro's mouth. Five paces. They glided over the sidewalk, through a stinging shower of glass, into the dim, cool foyer. Figures in white sprang forward, gesticulating, their mouths yanking. They floated the boy away, down a hall into a sun-touched patio.

Alessandro swayed, blinking his blurred eyes. He plucked at his sticky shirt, then ground the sleeve across his eyes. He could see again. He stared at the wonder of his hands, the marvels of his fingers and thumbs, tinted on the tips with the boy's blood. He clasped his hands together, his head and chest ringing with joy at the perfect knit and flex of muscle, tendon, bone and flesh. He sank to his knees on a hemp mat. His teeth chattered together, and a groan of agony bored, awling up from his chest, prying his jaws open till they cracked. The shout of pain sprayed the salt from his lips. Out in the plaza, rifle fire cracked, a machine gun lashed and flames beat through the broken stones of the smoke-palled city. Someone, a man, spoke to him in a voice rough with a German accent. Alessandro shook his head, mute from the effort of his offering and the savor of his tears.

⊹ **14** ⊹

THE room was square, seventeen paces each way, with white-and-gilt wainscoted walls and a high ceiling. From the ceiling hung the crystal chandelier. On the floor lay a Persian carpet, frets and blocks, a frozen frenzy of colors and connected shapes, dyed and knotted, thick, resilient. Against the west wall the great canopied bed, like a gilded barge. The morning sun streamed through the high east window and touched the tangled sheets; the rumpled satin shone like a cerecloth of silver. His breakfast, untouched, stood on the delicate table, the steam still rising from the *café con leche*. Outside, the guards muttered and paced, restless with boredom.

Old Sánchez sat staring hopelessly down at the carpet. He was bored with the soft slab of colors and shapes, bored with pretending that the patterns revealed a total design, bored with denying that the thing was no more than threads knotted by some little Persian slavey. It made no difference one way or the other. In the same way, it no longer seemed ironic, poetically just, that he was imprisoned in the chamber once reserved for the mistress of the last Spanish viceroy to rule Costa Plata. They probably had no other place to put him, that was all. It was senseless to twist coincident into design. A carpet, a bed, the glitter of the chandelier that smashed against the wincing eyes, the armoire with his clothes neatly hung, his shirts laid out on the top shelf, the humidor of excellent cigars.

The city was quiet. Only the far, faint snap of a rifle broke the morning hush. He was not hungry, not tired, not anything. He felt merely old, feeble, unwilling to move, to judge, even to think. The colored carpet blurred before his eyes. He felt no outrage, no relief; he was neither a martyr nor quite a fool. He was nothing. Not a man, but a husk, empty in the belly, heart and brains. He felt filled with dust. One could not be disgusted, even with dust.

"Your breakfast, Señor Sánchez? You don't want to eat?"

He was there in the room, unaware of posture or pang, staring at the figured carpet, waiting to fall on the surface and to be ground down between the colored threads, sometime to be shaken free to float forever in a dim void.

"That's five meals in a row. Tell them upstairs that he's not eating. Have them send that Swiss doctor down. He'll have to be given some kind of shots if they're going to use him to make the radio broadcasts when the killing starts."

⇂

The truck rolled into the courtyard and stopped. Voget climbed down out of the cab and stretched his cramped arms and legs. A few soldiers watched him. The garrison was quiet.

"All right. Set up the howitzer near the main entrance. Henri?"

"Yes?"

"Have them take the transmitter inside. Use the flagpole for an aerial."

"Right."

Voget stood for a moment, watching the men unload the radio equipment. Some students with black armbands sewed to army blouses came out of the building and walked across the courtyard toward the truck. Voget tapped Henri on the shoulder.

"How long have they been here?"

"A day, I guess. A lot more came in last night. Olmega told us he was forced to shift his headquarters here. Half the university was on fire. That's what he said, anyway."

"How many of them?"

"A thousand, more or less. Most of them have rifles. They took over a barracks. That's the big building to the left, there."

The students waited politely until the radio was removed from the truck. Then one of them walked up to Voget and saluted.

"General Voget? We've been expecting you."

"Comrade General Voget. We brought what we could. There's another truck and one more howitzer."

"That's all?"

"And the radio, as you see."

"But your men?"

"I will discuss this with your leader."

"General Olmega is waiting for you."

"And General Vola?"

"He has been relieved of command here."

"I see. Well, let's go."

Voget followed the young man into the great, squat, stone building. The air was cool and sour. The offices were filled with young men and women dressed in borrowed uniforms. Voget noted soldiers and non-commissioned officers, and one small captain wearing a cape.

"Who's that one?"

"Captain Chinchón. Intelligence. Interrogating prisoners."

"Oh."

Voget grunted with shock when the aide, a girl in uniform, opened the office door and gestured for him to enter. Olmega sat behind a bare wooden table, trying to smoke a cigarette. He blinked slowly at Voget. His eyes seemed set in bruises, as though he had been punched. The lids flickered and twitched. His dirty face was gray-yellow, his lead-colored lips plastered with bits of cigarette paper. He guided the cigarette across his cheek, using both hands, until his shaking fingers touched his nose, then dragged down over his mouth. His lips writhed convulsively and bits of tobacco spilled down the front of his tunic. The effort seemed to exhaust him. His hands thudded slackly on the bare table. He stared at them. His voice was a dry whisper.

"Welcome back, comrade. We're glad to see you. Forgive me if I don't try to take your hand. We'd waste a half hour. You see?"

Olmega raised his right hand above the table. His whole arm shook, and the nicotine-stained fingers waggled like puppet legs. Olmega pushed his mouth into a smile.

"Fever. Bad time to come down with it, eh? I've lost nearly ten kilograms. It takes away your appetite."

"If you have someone explain what the situation is, I'll take over so you can sleep."

"Sleep. I can't."

"But you'll break down, man!"

"Maybe I already have. Maybe this is what it's like. I look pretty bad, don't I?"

"You look sick. And exhausted."

"But you . . ."

"I slept coming back on the fishing boat. As soon as we reached the harbor mouth we got hit. The *Guardacostas*. So we walked in. Not too far. Just in time to help Henri's group evacuate the warehouses."

"He told us he couldn't hold out there."

"There was no point in losing the men. We have two fieldpieces and nearly a hundred rounds of ammuniton."

"Good."

"The university?"

Olmega shivered. He clamped his elbows against his ribs and fought against the spasm. Sweat gleamed on his dirty brow.

"We still have what's left. Actually, the main trench is in Calle San Jerónimo now. They'll show you on the map. After the shelling last night, they just walked around us. There was nothing we could do to stop them. We filled the houses in Jerónimo, split the U.T. troops in two, one group west, the other southeast. And here we are. This is headquarters and barracks for reserve troops. But there's plenty of room for your people."

"Who's leading the U.T.? Rota again?"

Olmega shook his head slowly. His eyelids shivered, hooding his eyes. He shook himself like a wet dog. Voget picked up the cigarette and held it to Olmega's lips.

"*Gracias*. I had forgotten all about Rota. He's dead."

"Dead?"

"We locked him in the men's toilet in the administration building. Until he came up for trial, you know."

"Trial? On what charges?"

"I don't remember. What difference does it make? He and six others were killed yesterday. A bomb. Direct hit."

"Where is Alessandro?"

"I don't really know. He was in Calle San Jerónimo. But that was a couple of hours ago."

"And his second-in-command? Sánchez?"

"The chairman of the Central Committee is with him."

"You mean they've cleared out. The two of them. And left us with—"

"No. No! Alessandro would never abandon us. Never!"

"Then where is he? Why isn't he here?"

"Inspecting the lines."

"Comrade Olmega, I don't believe you."

"It isn't necessary to believe me. Just believe in Alessandro."

"I might as well believe in God. What is Alessandro doing out in the city? Performing miracles? I have nearly four hundred men coming in. We need food, blankets, ammunition. What arrangements have been made about gasoline? What orders have you concerning the two howitzers? What is to be done with General Vola? Where is this Ramos person with his miners?"

Olmega fumbled with his cigarette. His whole body trembled. He whispered and stared at his dancing hands.

"I have done all I could. But we're all back together now. It will be better . . . we will fight and win today."

Voget grunted and turned away.

"I'll report later."

"I'll . . . be here. He's . . . counting on us, Voget. We must not fail him . . ."

Voget slammed the door and seized the uniformed girl by the arm. She glared at him with weary eyes and pulled free.

"Keep your hands off me."

"Listen, *guapa,* you go to the dispensary and get him some quinine and some aspirin. You don't want him to die, do you? Can't you tell how sick he is?"

"He refuses to take quinine. It makes him see things. He just takes coffee."

"No more coffee. Water. Fruit juice. And the medicine. Put him to bed. And keep him there, if you have to crawl in with him."

"What right have you to give orders like this?"

"You know who I am, señorita?"

"Of course. You're the foreigner, Voget."

"I am Comrade General Voget. Until Alessandro returns, I am in command here, understand?"

"Who says so? Where's the order?"

"I say so. And I will issue an order to that effect. Now do as you're told!"

Voget drew back his hand. The girl ran out of the office. Voget followed her, stopped another student and demanded to be taken to where the radio was being assembled. The room was filled with men talking and watching the work.

"Henri!"

"Yes."

"In here."

Voget sat down at a cluttered desk, rummaged under the papers until he found a pencil, and began writing rapidly on a block of lined paper.

"We're taking over here."

"What?"

"You heard me. Alessandro and Sánchez aren't here. Olmega, the kid, is sick. Worn-out, and he's got some kind of fever. Here, have this typed at once. A statement that he is to be removed to the dispensary at once. We'll need a typing pool. We'll take over Olmega's office. Here, have *this* typed. Until further notice, all student cadres and our people are considered a single, unified command. The First Army of Liberation. General Vola is under house arrest. Some bastard's killed Rota. I'm writing a general notice about it. Copies to be distributed to the U.T. militia. I'll speak to them this afternoon."

"You'll want an election, right?"

"Yes."

"How many candidates?"

"Just one. Me. With Rota finally gone, the U.T. will fall into our pocket. Now, all students, plus our people, to assemble in the courtyard in exactly one hour. I'm making a speech. I'll give it to you in about twenty minutes. Copies to all units. Now, listen. Set up a group of ten. Six of us, including yourself and Coco. Four students, one of them a girl. We're very democratic, you understand. They will select commissars from our people and assign them to each of the remaining 'centuries.' Understand? The remaining soldiers are to be taken from the student cadres and put with our people. Promote each soldier one full grade. Promise them a new pay rate beginning at once. Give them, oh, say twenty reales each. But not until they sign up with us."

"Right. What about the radio?"

"As soon as it's operating, call Mexico City. Have the comrades there arrange for arms shipments. And men, too. All they can send."

"The Englishman, Ferguson, is under arrest."

"Who arrested him? Alessandro?"

"No, no. Vizarra."

"We'll have to try to get him out. Can you organize a raid? Is he in jail?"

"No. At his house. That's what they say here. The government has started arresting people. Even the foreigners, see?"

"Good. If we get Ferguson, we'll be able to get our hands on some more money. All right, that's enough for now."

"What if Alessandro comes back?"

"We'll have to risk it. Olmega's sick. We're reorganizing. Take over the mess hall, too. Feed our people first. No, feed them with the soldiers. And by the way . . . find an officer. A little fellow with a cape. I want to see him."

"Right now?"

"At once."

☩

Voget sat behind the desk. His face felt raw and sensitive, but he was shaved and clean and dressed in a fresh officer's uniform. On the table stood a field telephone, a wire basket of dispatches, a new duty roster and a glass of lukewarm sweet tea. The windows were open, and the sound of sporadic rifle fire drifted on the burned breeze blowing across the city. The only fighting seemed to be at the university. Voget had given orders to hold the buildings there to the last man. The reports from command outposts were puzzling. The National Guard and the Policía Armada were using a great many trucks, but no large units were actually fighting. Only an occasional nuisance barrage fell in the San Jerónimo sector. What was Vizarra up to? And where was Alessandro?

The telephone rang.

"Comrade General Voget here. Henri? You've got him. And his wife. Good. Very good. She's wounded? Then get rid of her. At a hospital somewhere, anywhere. Bring him here. How do you spell his name? F-e-r-g—all right, all right. No, but there must be someone here who can speak English."

Voget hung up and scribbled a report for the radio room: The rebel forces were courageously making every effort to protect foreign nationals against the gangster tactics of the discredited, tottering regime of the bandit Vizarra and his henchmen.

The door opened, and the girl stood there.

"Yes?"

"He's still waiting, Comrade General."

"Send him in. How is General Olmega?"

"He's asleep."

"Good! I mean, he needs the rest. You agree, of course."

"Yes, Comrade General."

She stood aside, and Captain Chinchón entered and saluted.

"Captain Chinchón reporting as requested to—"

"Yes, yes. Never mind all that. Sit down."

"I prefer to stand."

"As you wish. Why are you still here? Your fellow officers cleared out, didn't they? Except for that drunken pig upstairs. You are especially fond of General Vola?"

"I have remained at my post out of personal convictions. My opinion of General Vola is of no consequence."

"Exactly. None of your personal opinions and convictions are of consequence. Only your political beliefs mean anything here. I've looked at your service record. Graduate of the War College. Intelligence officer. Your ex-superiors felt that you were not completely to be trusted, Chinchón, you know that?"

"Yes."

"You're going to the opera, perhaps?"

"No. I mean, of course not. Why do you ask?"

"Then get rid of that cape. You'll have new duties from now on. That is, if you wish to stay, and we wish to keep you."

"I do not believe I have any choice."

"Very astute. No wonder they put you in intelligence. You speak English, I see."

"Some."

"The manager of Livermore Lines Limited has been freed. You will interpret for me. He is to turn over all company funds to us immediately. He is not to refuse this, understand."

"I understand."

"I have read this bunch of rubbish you call a report. These secret documents. What is this idiocy, anyway?"

"The man is—"

"I can read. Herman Fingel. A representative of an American company. I have ordered him released."

"But that book! Those documents may be code!"

"I shared a stateroom with him on the boat coming to this country. Can't you read Hebrew? I guess not. Well, you can read Spanish, can't you? After we get through with this Englishman, you will take over the operation of the mess hall as commissary officer. Dismissed."

"But, Comrade General—"

"Dismissed. Wait in the outer office until I send for you again."

Voget picked up his pencil and began writing. The girl let Chinchón out and stood there.

"Yes?"

"Comrade General, a messenger has just arrived. From him."

"From what him?"

"From our leader."

"I am your leader."

"From Alessandro."

"So what?"

"He wants to see you."

"Very well. Let him come here."

"He is in the San Jerónimo district."

"And I am here. I'm busy. If he wants to see me, let him come. Sánchez, too. We might as well get this over with right now. Tell him that."

"Very good."

"And, señorita? Another glass of tea, please. No sugar."

⸸

Vizarra reached out to touch a blossom of the bougainvillaea that made a thick, green pelt on the wall of the villa and trailed between the columns of the balcony. His fingers closed around the flower to wrench it free. The first bright notes of piano music startled him, and he jerked his hand away. Behind him the French windows stood open, and the pale curtains tossed like scarves in the warm morning breeze. He turned slightly and looked down into the garden, at the low-growing roses and beyond them the clipped lemon trees. The swimming pool was a brilliant rectangle mirroring the cloudless blue of the sky. In the distance, smoke still rose over the city.

Beyond the pruned perfection of the park, flame lashed from the muzzle of the cannon. The deep buff of the explosion made the Caudillo start again. The flower fell from his hand. He muttered and hunched his shoulders. He felt chilled, all at once, as though touched by fever. Behind him the music trickled slower and stopped. Vizarra turned and strode toward the French windows. He glanced at his watch. Eleven o'clock. Just an hour before the rifles and the machine guns started their work, just an hour before Alessandro began to die.

She sat at the piano. Her long hair was dressed very simply, drawn back from her brow and tied with a blue ribbon like a schoolgirl's. Her large, dark eyes glanced at him. She was afraid. Her face was pale, and her lips unnaturally red. She tried to smile.

"Please don't stop. Play some more, Lucía."

"Was that one of our guns?"

"Yes. One of ours."

She pressed her hands together and stared down at the keyboard.

"It was so quiet this morning. After last night . . ."

"Yes. It was very bad last night."

"I . . . I sat up. Waiting, you know. Then I went to the window and watched. I could see the shells when they hit. And the fires. It looked like the whole city was burning. The sky was so bright you could even see the mountains."

"That wasn't such a good thing to do. No wonder you couldn't sleep. You should have closed the windows and pretended that you were listening to a summer storm, thunder in the hills."

She closed the cover of the piano and smoothed her skirt with nervous fingers. She turned her face away from him. He felt annoyed. She cleared her throat and muttered something.

"What?"

"I say that I am not a child. I can't tell myself pretty stories. I saw where the shells were falling. Right in the center of the city."

430

"It was a strategic necessity. You don't understand military matters, Lucía. Please calm yourself and play for me."

"It's always a strategic necessity to drop bombs on innocent people . . ."

"Ya-ya. Do you really think everyone is innocent? I was nearly killed yesterday by some of Alessandro's innocents . . . with their cannon. We are fighting to win. What do you expect? Am I to give orders that the loyal troops arm themselves with fly whisks?"

"I'm sorry. I am just being stupid. What do you want me to do today? I know you'll be busy."

"No. Not until this afternoon or later in the evening. I don't expect them to hold out very much longer."

"It's so quiet."

"A new plan goes into effect at noon. The plan that will bring victory."

"Just as long as the shooting stops."

"It won't last much longer, I assure you. Come, would you like to go riding? Swim in the pool? If I'm busy tonight for a few hours, you can watch a film. There are some new ones from America. One of the footmen will run the projector for you."

"Watch a film with this going on? While people are dying? That's impossible."

"No, it's not, Lucía. The day my own mother died I spent the whole afternoon at a cinema. Watching Chaplin films. I laughed. My mother was dead. But I laughed. It was a very funny film. A man is a genius who can make a mourner laugh. I escaped, you see, to another world. We need another world, right here. Heaven can wait."

"I'm not sure that I believe you. You are always telling me stories, just to cheer me up, make me feel better. Do I behave like such a child?"

"Sometimes. But then you are very sweet, you see?"

"Huh! You should have known me when I *was* a little girl. You wouldn't have thought I was very sweet then. I used to be very good at killing rats, better than the boys even. That was because I hated them so. And I was afraid of them. My little sister died because of the rats."

"Well, that's what we are doing now. Getting rid of the vermin."

She turned to look at him. She stared into his face for a long moment.

"Is it so difficult for you? I don't think it can be. You're not afraid, are you?"

"No, Lucía. Not of them."

"That must be wonderful. Not to be afraid."

"Well, the stupid man isn't afraid. He doesn't know enough to fear. Courage is only a virtue when it has become a habit."

"And you don't hate them, either."

Vizarra tapped his stubby fingers on the polished piano top.

"No."

"But they hate you."

"Yes."

"Then it must be terrible."

"No, that's another habit of mine. I am used to being hated. But . . ."

"But what?"

"Well, if he hadn't hated me, perhaps Alessandro would have come to me. Just to speak with me. I would have listened to him."

"Ah?"

She grinned and shook her head slightly. Vizarra shrugged.

"Well, all right. I would have *tried* to listen to him, Lucía. I'm not a monster. But he, *he* has made me into one. What would you have me do? Just let everything go? Have I not worked hard, eh? For the people, I mean. Tell me the truth."

"Well . . . I don't really understand the new trade agreements, Rafael, but . . . I mean, it sounds very good."

"I have worked hard for the people."

"In your own way, yes."

"But that's the only way I know to work."

"I suppose so. But is the only way *you* know the only way?"

"I am a limited man, Lucía, a soldier. I have never had big dreams for myself. I have had only the simple desire to govern what was left to me by default."

"Then why do they hate you?"

The girl rose suddenly and walked across the room until she stood in the sunlight. She stroked her bare arms and shivered.

"I feel cold."

"So do I. Maybe a little fever, that's all."

"A little fever? Is the only way to live to live by killing rats?"

"You said yourself . . . your little sister . . ."

432

"I grew up. I discovered there were worse things. Bigger, stronger animals. With teeth just as sharp."

"And I took you away from them."

"I have tried to be grateful, Rafael, you know that."

"Grateful?"

"Why didn't you just . . . let it go? What is so grand about ruling this country that you must always keep it in your grip? You forget that we have been together so long. I know all about O'Conner and what his security police do to the people. And I know that you have old Sánchez again, caught between your paws. What are you going to do to him this time?"

Vizarra thrust his fists in his pockets and walked over to her. She stared at him defiantly.

"What do you mean, *this time?*"

"I know what happened. He told you where Felipe Martín was hiding. You gave him his life, the life of his son, too, and a sinecure as Minister of Education."

"He was afraid to die, like Iscariot. But much more expensive, I assure you. You forget that a Judas wishes to profit from his fear."

"Does that explain the bank accounts in Switzerland?"

"Aaah."

"Yes. I know that, too. You have taken too much. You gave a life here, another there. And then you have the guns fire on the city."

"I can explain about the money in Switzerland. Investments in land, through some friends."

"Confiscated land. Impounded bank accounts. You just took what you wanted."

"And do you know where the money comes from that I give to His Grace the archbishop every year for his private charities? Eh? The interest on those accounts. Those people are dead. I keep their money alive and working."

"How can he take the money? I don't understand."

"Because he needs it for the people."

"Then give it all to him."

"But there would be nothing left for me . . . for **us!**"

"Let me sit down. You make my head spin."

She sat on a small chair and crossed her ankles. A cannon boomed again. Vizarra glanced at his watch. He knew she was staring at him. He shifted uncomfortably.

"All right. There's the money. I wanted some, yes. I was poor, like you. We didn't have rats in the house, but we were poor. My parents died. I invested what they left me. I did well, made more money."

"Another habit."

"If you like. Not a bad one, I think. Well, that's in the past. Now is now. Naturally, I didn't want it this way. I did my duty as a soldier. I defeated Felipe Martín. There was no one else. I took over the government."

"But you never gave it back. You never meant to give it back."

"How do you know? How do you know, eh?"

"Malata told me. Malata, your friend."

"Malata."

"Yes. We worked in the same cheap nightclub, remember?"

"Don't worry, Lucía. It's hardly likely that we will ever forget that."

"You didn't have to take me. You could have made an honorable marriage. Not at once, perhaps."

"I didn't want a honorable marriage. I wanted you."

"Malata first, though."

"Well, I wanted to be admired, to have friends about me, real friends. And I got him instead."

"Another habit."

"Lucía . . ."

"But you can break away, Rafael! You don't have to stay here forever! You don't have to stay because of Julio or anybody else. If you don't want to. Why not give it up?"

Vizarra groaned and kicked at the floor. He turned to her.

"Because it's too late. I have given orders . . ."

She stood and drew close to him. He put his arms around her, embracing her gently. He brushed his lips against her shining, scented hair. She raised her face.

"Let's go away. The plane . . ."

"The plane is the last resort. I am the Caudillo. I have given orders to the police, what's left of the army and the National Guard. I have ordered weapons distributed to the Red Beret. I cannot leave them now. It would be cowardice, dishonorable. It would wreck the country. Believe me. In a matter of hours they would plunge the county into anarchy. O'Conner's police against Lucca's Guards, against the party, against the U.T., against the Bolsheviks. No. No. We are trapped on

434

both sides. Alessandro with his followers, I with mine. He has their allegiance still. And those on our side obey me out of fear. Just out of fear. But it's better than nothing. If I leave, there will be a civil war that will drag on for months, maybe years. The foreigners will come back. Like wolves. Already they have attempted to contact Alessandro, to give him weapons and ammunition. If I leave, the American Navy will come down here. With the Marines. Just like in Nicaragua. Believe me, I know. You are young, Lucía. You don't know. You say I don't have the right to rule. I say I don't have the right *not* to rule. I don't have the right to leave."

"I want to live. I want you to live. I want us to be at peace. Let it go. Let them have it. I love you."

"This is politics. This is revolution. Love will have to wait. I must put my feelings for my country first. The new trade agreements—"

"To hell with the new trade agreements! I am sick to death of hearing about them! What about us?"

"We don't count. This is my country. My homeland."

"But it's not yours alone!"

"Today it's all mine."

"And what are you going to do with it?"

"Never . . . never mind."

"You won't tell me?"

"I don't want you to know."

"Why?"

"Because you, too, will hate me. And then there will be nothing left . . . except my bad habits. Someday I will make a confession. And spend the rest of my life doing penance."

"Ah, Rafael. I cannot hate you. I love you."

"Ah, you know so much and still love me. That proves you are a woman. If you were a man, you'd cut my throat. Or try to."

"Do you love me?"

Vizarra smiled sadly and nodded. He turned her and walked with her back to the piano.

"Yes, Lucía, I love you."

"In your way."

"If you like. In my way. The only way I know."

She freed herself and sat down on the piano bench and looked up at him.

"Would it be different if you had a family? If I were your wife and you had sons? One son, even. You could leave all this to him."

"Different? Well, I would simply send you away. I would remain here, of course. But Vizarra with sons? I didn't know you were such a good Catholic, Lucía. You believe in miracles still?"

"Please, Rafael."

"Vizarra the Mule."

"Don't—"

"Or would you give me horns as well as sons? They'd have to find a new nickname for me then, eh?"

"Stop! We could have adopted a son. And still have our love."

"Huh! Sterile, yes. Impotent, no. Sixty-two years old and I can still make you groan, eh?"

"There is no need for you to talk like this."

"Forgive me. I feel like a prisoner in a cell. Allowed to babble. Today is my last day, Lucía. I have sentenced myself to death. I will have to get rid of O'Conner. I will need a better bodyguard. More secret police. I will never be able to visit the theater or the racetrack again. I will have to have the Guards on every housetop when I ride through the streets in my bulletproof sedan. I will be very patient. I may have to wait for him for a long time. But he will find me at last."

"Who?"

"My executioner. My assassin. You talk about the airplane waiting out there in the field. There is no aircraft made that can fly me to safety after today. There is no country to fly to, Lucía. Today I pass beyond the grace of God. There is no going back. Only waiting, until at last my executioner finds me. And ends it. All I can pray for is that he will be a good shot. Ah, you see? You make me begin to pity myself. I have no right even to do that."

"No one is ever beyond the touch of Mary's finger."

"No? I think differently. If God's mercy is infinite, there would be no Hell. But there is. I know. I have damned myself and for what? To drag on through the years in terror, to learn how to be afraid. I can spend the last years piling up good works for God to laugh at. Vizarra the Mule, busy right up to the last minute. The sterile one."

"There are doctors in Switzerland. In America."

"I have a doctor, Lucía. He can't even cure my gout."

"But maybe, maybe, we could have a son. Your own son."

"No, Lucía."

"Then adopt one now. Take him with us."

"You still think I can leave. *Pobrecita*—poor little one. I have a son. Only he adopted me, it seems."

"What? Who?"

"Why, Alessandro. He is my son. And he wants to get rid of me. I am old. I am in his way. He wants to dominate the herd now. He will kill me if he must. And he will have to. But perhaps he thinks that to do so would be an act of mercy. And you know something? He has been a good son, Alessandro. Yes, I am very proud of him. A terrible child, a nuisance, a troublemaker. Worse, he's dangerous. But. But he has brains, and courage. And youth. He writes excellent poetry . . . well, you've seen the volumes upstairs. And his novels, too. In France, one critic compared his last book to a symphony by Beethoven. That is praise! Yes, I am proud of him. Well, today is our day together—my son and I. We have a present to give each other . . . death. Quick and clean. I know him well enough. He won't waste time with me. And if he fails, I will not force him to surrender. I will shoot him and make him a martyr. He has earned that much. And if he wins, he must drag me through the city, then throw me on the heap to rot."

The girl cupped her hands over her ears. Vizarra pulled her fingers away and held them. He bent over her, speaking gently, reassuringly.

"There. That is the truth. The reality of our two fates, mine and his. Oh, I exaggerate. All papas like to boast, no? You think I'm after pity? No. We have none for each other, Alessandro and I. What will happen to us both will turn on how much pity we have for the others, for the people of Costa Plata. There, one of must must break. His hand must fall first or mine. One or the other. But pity for our victims, not for ourselves. Oh, we need pity . . . especially since the curses will ring so loud in our ears. So what will we do? Why, all this butchery must be more than pitiful. The slaughter must stop with an act, some act that is more than mere reflex, some act of the will that raises us from beasts. The sacrifice must be a ritual that lifts, that hurls us high, that makes us more than men. But not too high, of course. We are neither saints nor devils, he and I. Antagonists to the end, but still just two men. To the end. Then one of us will cringe and say 'No, no more,' and fall. Now do you see why I cannot run away? I owe it to Alessandro, my son."

Vizarra released her and stepped back, still smiling. The girl bowed her head and brushed at her eyes.

"You . . . you always did like to make a lot of noise. Just like a schoolboy. The grand gesture . . . when all you've been is naughty."

Vizarra sighed. His heavy shoulders sagged. He shook his head wearily.

"I tried to explain, Lucía . . ."

"I don't understand."

Vizarra stared at her hopelessly. She sat up, but did not look at him.

"Perhaps . . . I will practice for a little while. Do you mind? Today is Thursday, after all. My program is tonight. I suppose the city will be quiet. It will be safe enough."

"Yes. It will be very quiet, I think."

"Then let Vizarra's little whore sing to them, eh? Wonderful!"

"Lucía."

"Please, don't touch me."

"If the rebels win, I will send you away."

"No!"

"Listen, my girl. In my house I make the grand gestures and the loud noises. You will fly away in the trimotor to Mexico. By boat to Europe. The money in Switzerland has been left to you. A copy of my will is there, too. Julio will give you the information. You will take the money and marry a blond ski instructor and breed little ones. Just like an alley cat. Understand? That is an order. Do you know what they'll do to you if they catch you? The mistress of the dead dictator? Think about it for a minute."

"Stop, please stop!"

"And if we win? Well, then, I think you should go to Paris for a little. As long as you like. Paris is a good city to be young and pretty in, a city for love. Not like here."

"No. I won't leave you."

"Will you sing a song for me tonight? On the radio?"

"Of course, Rafael."

"A love song."

"Naturally. You must have some last little bit of cruelty to practice on me."

"Cruelty? To send you away from here at last? To make you

438

happy? You don't want an old mule like me. Besides—oh, the song. Make it the last number. *'Adiós, Alma Mía.'* Do you know it?"

"Of course. But it's forbidden. Alessandro himself wrote it. You banned it years ago."

"Exactly. It will be very appropriate."

"What are you talking about? Why do you look that way at me, Rafael?"

"After the program, go to your apartment in the city. You'll be very carefully guarded. If you try to come here, they will close the gate in your face."

"Rafael, no! Please! I beg you! Don't do this! If you do . . . I'll —I'll kill myself!"

"Don't be absurd. And stop shouting. You look ugly when you shout."

"I will. I will kill myself. I'll cut my wrists!"

"Lucía, I forbid you to talk this way."

"You'll have me on your soul."

His powerful arms shot out and seized her, his strong fingers clamping around her head. He bent over her and touched his lips to her forehead.

"Now, for the love of God, have some manners and be kind to an old man. I will still love you. But you must go away from me. Stop this mad talk of suicide. I have enough sins to damn me already. Don't waste yourself. You are young and pretty. I only want to set you free so that you may live and be happy. You can't be happy with me here, not after today. Today is the end of many things, and the beginning of many others. Trust me, Lucía, this once. I am trying to be a good man, to you, at least. It is not easy to be cruel—just the opposite—that is, if you're sane. And I'm sane. I'm not mad. That's just the trouble. But you must go away. No more talk of suicide. There will be enough blood spilled today to sicken even Vigo. There must be an end to the rage in the blood. Do you want to make God puke, girl? Play the piano."

"I . . ."

"Play the piano! Very loudly. A Chopin polonaise. Play it over and over until one o'clock. Then mix some *sangría* and meet me out at the swimming pool."

"Where are you going?"

"I'm going to listen to the radio. A special broadcast."

"I want to come, too. I want to hear."

"Stay there. Play the piano. *Play!*"

Vizarra stamped across the room and slammed the door. The girl sat very erect on the piano bench. Tears slipped down her cheeks. She snapped open the cover of the piano. Her fingers pronged down on the keys, and the first ten notes of the Polish anthem rang through the sun-washed room.

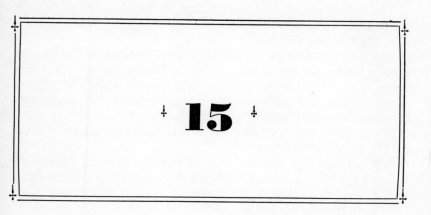

✦ 15 ✦

SÁNCHEZ dragged the match over the worn surface of
the table and touched the flame to the tip of his cigar. He sucked
greedily, rolling the cigar slowly. He puffed out smoke and gazed
across the table at Voget.

"General Vola bought good cigars but cheap razors, eh?"

The Belgian touched his raw-looking cheeks and shrugged slightly,
then took up his glass of tea and sipped it like a man swallowing
medicine. Sánchez wanted a brandy. But the brandy would have to
wait. Henri, the other Belgian, fiddled with a pencil, drawing five-
pointed stars on a block of white paper. Alessandro slumped in a
chair, holding his face in his thin, strong hands. A pile of flimsy
papers lay on the table before him, transcriptions and translations of
the interview with Ferguson, the agent for Livermore Lines Ltd., and
recent radio contact with Voget's Comintern associates in Mexico
City. Voget set down his glass. He looked fresh, alert. Sánchez smiled
politely.

"What did you do with our fat friend, Voget?"

"He's upstairs in his room."

"Under guard?"

"What for? He's got his brandy."

The smile stiffened on Sánchez's lips. A knock sounded through the bare room like the blow of a mallet.

"Here's General Olmega."

The door opened and three soldiers stumbled awkwardly into the room, carrying the leader of the students. Olmega was swaddled in a cheap woolen blanket that stank of disinfectant. Alessandro slipped from his chair and moved swiftly across the room, his hands outstretched, his voice hoarse with concern.

"Easy. Easy, now. Put him here, where the pillow is. Don't drop the blanket, *hombre!* There."

Sánchez saw the two Belgians exchange a glance. Alessandro snugged the blanket around Olmega's shoulder and placed his hand on the young man's brow.

"There. How do you feel, *chico?*"

"Fine . . . reporting for duty . . ."

Olmega shivered violently, his arms and legs twitching beneath the blanket. His eyes glittered with fever. Voget muttered to Henri.

"Stupid to bring him into this. Look at him. He can't sit up straight."

Sánchez drew on his cigar and blew a cloud of smoke at the Belgian.

"General Olmega is commandant of the First Army. It is a tribute to his loyalty, his devotion, that he is with us at this time."

Alessandro walked back to the table and sat down. Sánchez waited a moment. Olmega breathed slowly, harshly, as though his lungs had stiffened. He kept jerking his head up, trying to hold himself erect. Sánchez tapped ashes on the floor.

"I declare this conference officially ready for business. You will be recording secretary. First, we must consider the strength of our fighting forces. General Voget?"

"Seven hundred men, formed into seven shock brigades of one hundred men each. All armed with rifles and bayonets. Approximately one hundred pistols. Three machine guns, one with no tripod. Two howitzers with sixty-two rounds of ammunition. Small arms ammunition is fifty rounds per man."

"Then you've had about sixty per cent losses."

"Correct."

"General Olmega?"

He seemed to be asleep. Alessandro nudged him.

"How many men do you have left, *chico?*"

Olmega stared fixedly at his trembling hands. His mouth moved. He shuddered and clamped his elbows against his ribs.

"Five hundred. And eighty-four women. All are armed now. But we have no more hand grenades."

Alessandro nodded.

"Not as bad as it might be. You did a fine job holding your cadres together. That gives us a little over twelve hundred men."

Voget shook his head and poked his finger into his glass of tea, stirring the chunk of lemon that floated on the surface.

"That gives us seven hundred men and five hundred kids. And no general for the kids. He can't command. Just look at him. The students have been cut to pieces. I recommend that they be re-formed and incorporated with us."

Sánchez smoked and studied the Belgian. He knew the answer to his question, but wanted Voget's reply down in writing. It might be useful later, if there was a later.

"Who is *us,* Voget?"

"Why, what we've got left. The U.T. militia and those soldiers from Vola's army group aware of the necessity of proletarian solidarity."

"Who leads your seven shock brigades?"

"Worker patriots."

"From the U.T.?"

"Of course. But don't misunderstand me. The students fought well. They were magnificent at the barricades. But the barricades are gone. The university is lost. The railroad station is lost. We don't have the docks any more. And we have only two field guns. Therefore, the shock brigades must be reinforced at once."

Alessandro raised his head and pushed the lank hair away from his brow.

"The student cadres will remain intact. Under no circumstances are they to be parceled out. Despite what's happened to them, their morale is excellent."

"And their numbers are few."

"I'm surprised at you, Voget. We were both in Munich in 1919. It doesn't take a full army corps to make a revolution. You've forgotten your reading in Lenin."

The Belgian flushed angrily and jabbed the lemon down into the tea.

"I've forgotten nothing! But then our fellows were soldiers back from the front. And there was a single central organization."

"There is a single central organization. Seated right here at this table."

"We must re-form into a single unit!"

"And I'm telling you, Voget, you will not create a soviet here in Costa Plata. Our forces will remain as they are."

"But that's madness! We have only twelve hundred men."

"Here in the city, you mean. That will be quite enough. Especially since they are all equally loyal to this committee, eh?"

"Our boys are loyal. That's the point. We must have complete openness, free discussion, exchange of opinion."

Alessandro stirred languidly and stared across the table at the Belgian.

"Very true. And we've just had it. And I have given a direct order. The discussion is closed."

"We insist on democratic procedures! Let the workers and soldiers and the students vote."

"The discussion is closed."

Alessandro's voice was very soft, as though he meant to soothe a hectic child on the verge of a tantrum. Voget snatched up his glass of tea and drained it. He scowled and grimaced. Henri drew a line across his notepad and waited, his face stiff with anger. Sánchez threw back his shoulders. Alessandro had scored the first victory. Sánchez gathered up the filmy sheets and gazed at them, without reading the typed lines. He chewed his cigar.

"Next we must consider the offers from our respective friends. From Ferguson . . . from the British and Americans, let's not deceive ourselves there. And from . . . an export-import company in Mexico City."

Henri scribbled on the pad and spoke without raising his head.

"Clearly we cannot betray the revolution by accepting arms from capitalist imperialists who wish to seize this country and make it a colony of Wall Street."

Alessandro smiled and slumped in his chair.

"And clearly we cannot betray the revolution by accepting arms from the Comintern who wish to make Costa Plata a colony for the Kremlin. No, our position is quite clear. We accept no arms at all. We accept nothing from either group."

Sánchez could not keep the alarm out of his voice. He waved his cigar and slapped his hand on the table.

"But we need arms! Either side will supply us with all we need."

"True. For a price. So many obsolete rifles and defective ammunition for the sovereignty of Costa Plata."

Voget spread his hands and tipped over his glass. The piece of lemon rolled across the table.

"Where are the men to use these weapons? If the civilian patriots knew we were to be supplied, they would rush to join us. Look what happened in Petrograd. When the city was threatened by Kornilov, the Provisional Government supplied arms to the workers; they opened the arsenals. At once there was a new army created. We could do that here!"

Alessandro drew the hair away from his brow and sat up, throwing his body into the bright sunlight that streamed into the room through the open window. His face and throat gleamed and the bloodstains on his shirt became badges, emblems of struggle. His voice bit into the air and pounded back off the bare walls. His right fist clenched as though he held fast a banner that rolled high, invisible above his head.

"Yes! We have them. We have men by the thousands. Workers and fighters. In the mines. Nearly ten thousand Indians work the silver mines in the mountains, tearing from the earth the wealth that is due to all the people. They will rise and fight with us until the final victory!"

Voget pouted his lower lip and shook his head.

"In the mines. And they are still *there*. Where is this Ramos? Why isn't he fighting? Where is your other man, the one with only one arm? Why isn't *he* fighting? This is nothing but words, empty gestures, a case of revolutionary infantilism. My God, who can believe this sort of insanity? One minute you talk about the Communist coup in Munich, the next you want us to believe that some undisciplined mob of Indians can help us win. It's crazy."

"No! Not crazy. Correct. They are the true indigenous people of Costa Plata. They are the soul of the nation."

"Those little brown animals? This is bourgeois idealism."

"They live and work in the earth, in the bowels of the mountains. We will go to them, bring them here. The forces we have here can hold out until tomorrow, easily. There is food, water, ammunition here. And the men have faith in the movement. Nothing has been lost that cannot be regained. Thousands everywhere stand in the darkness straining toward the light they know will come soon. We will give them this light, burning like a torch high in the sierras. When the miners rise, do you think Casanueva can be held against them? Never! They'll swarm over the defenses, scatter the troops and retake the city. With captured weapons, with the terrible press of their numbers, they will march down the railroad line. Directly for the city, a resistless force. Vizarra will have to divide his troops. Once he faces north, he turns his flank to you, Voget. Then you strike. One blow across the city, like a fist, to smash the walls of the national palace into dust. I tell you, we don't need help! We can win alone. We must win alone. And we will because we must. Tomorrow!"

Sánchez struck another match and lit his dead cigar. He spoke slowly, watching Voget, estimating the Belgian's capacity for compromise. Alessandro sat stiffly, his body tense, as though ready to spring to the attack.

"Well, *jovencito,* tomorrow is tomorrow. We Costa Platans believe too much in tomorrow, not enough in yesterday or today. But it is precisely today that is important. Until we do what we have to do today, we won't be able to do much tomorrow. Because tomorrow we'll still have today's work still undone. We must be reasonable, eh?"

"Revolutions are won by faith, Carlos, not reason, by passion not prudence. I know this. And so does Voget. We have both seen it happen. It will happen here. It will!"

He sat stiffly, his hand clenched on the invisible lance shaft. He turned his piercing dark gaze on Voget; on Sánchez, who looked away, nodding slowly; and then on Olmega. The body in the blanket thrashed, tearing the acrid folds away from the face. The pale mask, slick with sweat, lolled forward, as though bent beneath a blade that slithered down, down, through the air. Olmega's hand worked slowly, writhing into the salute of the Movimiento Liberal. The head, pale and wasted, sank forward and the stiff fingers snatched at the air, reaching out to touch once more the invisible banner rolling on the soft wind. Olmega's voice, quivering, slipped from his lips and trickled across the room:

"Yes! We will win! God, let me live to be a hundred so I may fight for one hundred years. *Arriba Costa Plata! Viva la revolución!"*

Sánchez felt his scalp crawl. Only the young held such murder in their hearts, had so little pity. He longed to press Olmega's face back into the blanket, to cram the reeking cloth between the teeth, to smother and still that voice. He turned away, snatched at Alessandro's sleeve and poured out words.

"As chairman of the Central Committee, I hereby urge the acceptance of the earlier proposal of a joint force, but under single command. General Olmega is a magnificent, true son of the revolutionary movement. But he is clearly unfit to continue his work. If he is allowed to retain his post, five hundred men will be rendered as incapable as he is. We must have those five hundred men in action. There is no other way. No other way at all. To surrender to the impossible is neither cowardice nor compromise. Olmega has revolutionary passion. But he also has a terrible fever. He cannot be allowed to murder others and himself as well! Reason will not accept this. Let a new commander be appointed at once. Those in favor of a single command—with the student cadres to remain intact—raise their hands."

Voget and Henri raised their hands. Sánchez lifted his own. Alessandro drummed on the table, his face expressionless. Olmega's arm sank slowly, until the shaking fingers were horizontal, pointed accusingly at Sánchez.

"So. That is settled. Now. Alessandro, as supreme commander—"

"Henri. Henri will lead the students."

The Belgian nodded his head once and wrote in his notebook.

"I accept the promotion."

Alessandro slouched back in his chair and scowled. He flicked one slender finger against the edge of the table. The sunlight still touched his blood-splotched shirt.

"Sánchez and I will leave at once for the mines. Voget will have command here. But understand me, all of you. This is not a village market. I haven't come here to bargain. We are talking of men, not vegetables. This new solution is acceptable to me only as a temporary arrangement. Is this understood?"

Voget nodded.

"We understand."

"You are to take no offensive action whatever. Patrol the streets in the sector, defend the new barricades. Don't use the heavy guns. Keep a route open to the south, to Boca Perro."

Sánchez felt his heart leap. He leaned forward, biting his lips.

"Then you'll accept the arms shipments after all! Delivery to the fishermen out of Boca Perro?"

"Did I say that?"

"No, but naturally I thought—"

"I have stated that there is no necessity to accept arms, money or aid from foreigners. The revolution is a national action and must maintain national purity. You and I will bring the miners down. When Vizarra turns to face us, Voget will hit his flank. We will win. Alone, and perhaps at great cost, but alone!"

"How am I to strike this blow on the flank? We haven't the troops. It can't be done."

"It must and will be done! We will win if we have to fight with clubs, with stones, with our bare and bleeding hands!"

Voget's face turned slowly to a mottled crimson shade. His jowls shook as he stood, thrusting back his chair which fell over with a crash.

"Then I request transportation from the city. I resign command. Fight this fool's war by yourselves, damn you! You people are crazy, I tell you. The arms shipments are not merely a set of possibilities to be discussed like some ideological quibble to be settled at some café. The arms are an absolute necessity!"

Alessandro remained slouched in his chair, idly tapping his fingernail against the table edge, an even, dry ticking like a slow pulsebeat. His eyes were half closed. He seemed to drowse, half smiling in the sunlight. His voice was a thick, soft drawl, mild and mocking.

"Sit down, Voget, don't knock the chairs about like that. You're damaging property that really belongs to the people, no? You can't get out of here and you know it very well. I wouldn't let you leave the room. Oh, there's transportation, to be sure. You'll even have your own command car from the motor pool. You haven't let me finish. Certainly, radio to your comrades in Mexico City. Have them send as much materiel as they can. We will make no effort to conceal this. Simply inform Ferguson that we have declined his offer in favor of a better arrangement. Send him back to Vizarra. It will be important, really, only if Vizarra knows our decision."

Voget pounded on the table. The piece of lemon jumped and skittered when his fist crashed down.

"Then he hits us right here!"

"He would if he knew about it in time. But he won't. When he finds out, we shall have retaken Casanueva. You have only to hold Ferguson until tomorrow afternoon. Now, if you were Vizarra, what would you do, street-fight against a thousand men on the rumor of an arms shipment or turn to fight a column advancing in open territory down the railroad lines?"

"Fine tactics! You know Vizarra has enough men to do both at once!"

"Does he? Where are they? Why has he broken off pursuit? What sort of tactical sense does it make to break off contact with a force in retreat?"

"Perhaps because he's in no hurry. Perhaps because he knows he has us outnumbered by five to one. He can wait, gather his strength and crush us like *that!*"

Voget's fist smashed the lemon flat on the tabletop in a puddle of juice and pulp. Bits of fruit and drops of liquid flew, striking Alessandro's face and clinging there like tears.

"No, Voget, no. The Old Mule knows what it would take to drive a thousand of us from this sector of the city. He has bombed and burned the university, wrecked the center section with artillery barrages. Even Vizarra must stop turning stones to dust. As it is, it will take us years to repair and rebuild the city. No, he will not try to drive you out. But with the information about a shipment of arms, he will not be able to run the risks of a long siege. Besides, each day your force holds out, the more impotent the army will seem, the more the people will swing to our side. No, Vizarra is setting a trap. What it is, we don't know yet. But Chinchón will find out."

Voget turned and stalked over to the open window and leaned both hands on the ledge, like a man about to be sick.

"Chinchón. That little ballet teacher in the fancy uniform. So. He's a spy, eh? I should have guessed."

"Yes, he's a spy. Among other things."

"I gave orders for him to take over direction of the mess halls. Why isn't he in the kitchen tasting the soup?"

"Because he follows my orders and no one else's."

"Can he be trusted?"

"Can you ever trust a spy completely? He has given us some information you should know. Zamal's troops have been seen leaving the city in full field dress, by train. With machine guns."

"Machine guns? Is this true? That would help us, if only . . . but there's Gómez and his artillery."

"I have explained that I don't think Vizarra will use the guns. He'll turn them north when we strike out of Casanueva anyway."

"Then Zamal must be moving in a circle. Out of the city north, then swing around to hit us from the south . . . Boca Perro! They'll close off the road to Boca Perro. Ah, Christ, then if we hit across the city, as you say . . ."

"Then Zamal will be behind you and cut you to ribbons with his guns."

"Then we're trapped!"

The words broke from Sánchez. He felt chilled to the bone. The taste of the cigar gagged him. He flung it to the floor and wiped his face. Alessandro shrugged.

"It takes five men to serve one machine gun. They have to be carried in pieces, mounted on a tripod, the water cans and ammunition belt attached before they can be fired. You've seen the kids in the streets running before the bulls on the way to the *plaza de toros* during the fiesta of Santa Rosa. A man runs very fast when he's chased by a bull. That's what your attack will be like, Voget, a man running before a bull."

Voget grinned bitterly and shrugged.

"I've seen photographs taken at Pamplona. The same thing, eh? Some attack that will be. *Attaque à l'outrance.* Run like hell into bullets so you don't get hit by bullets in your ass. Your little friend Chinchón brings great news."

"It's certain that Zamal has left the city. As Sánchez tells us, we must try to be reasonable. It's reasonable to think that Zamal will swing south. Why would he go north? The miners haven't moved, and Casanueva is held by part of Gómez's army. Our troops, what's left of them in the *campo,* can't do much damage around Casanueva. But when the miners . . . You see?"

"Yes. I see. It can work. We'll need luck."

Alessandro smiled and stood up. He held out his hand and Voget took it.

"Comrade Voget, in Costa Plata we have a proverb for nearly everything. To us, luck is a whore, not a lady. She does not give; she

450

sells. So we say: *When you meet her, be wealthy.* We are going by car. We'll contact Ramos and then get into the mines somehow. We'll get a message to you from the *campo,* then again when we hit the trenches at Casanueva. You know what to do here. So. *Be wealthy.* God and all of Costa Plata know you are brave."

Voget nodded glumly.

"That's me. The Belgian Bolívar. Well, good-by again. Come on, Henri, let's go show the students their new professsor."

The two Belgians hurried from the room. Alessandro walked back to the table.

"There's some brandy in the desk there, Carlitos."

"There is? Oh, I don't want any."

"Take some. You'll need it."

Sánchez found the bottle and a dirty glass. He carried it to the table.

"There. Have some, *jovencito.*"

"After you. There are other things. Chinchón says they're taking hostages—men, women and children. By truck. To the bullring. The Red Beret has been given arms."

"What?"

"Yes. They started shooting the wounded kids captured at the university."

"Mierda . . ."

Sánchez filled the glass and drank it.

"Christ, we're done for. Here, let's have a drink to death. There is nothing left to drink to, is there?"

"I'd never drink to that. We're going to meet her and be wealthy, Carlitos."

"How, Alessandro, *how?*"

"We still have nearly two hundred men in the city. Behind Vizarra's lines. Voget isn't the only one who's going to be running before a bull tomorrow."

"Two hundred? But who commands them?"

Alessandro smiled lazily and picked a lemon tear off his cheek and sucked the fleck of bitter pulp.

"Who commands them? Why, Chinchón, of course."

"Chinchón!"

"Yes, an exercise in the psychology of command. That's his specialty, don't you see?"

"Where are they?"

451

"Down in the sewers with *Tía Ajo*. The main sewer and the one that leads to the radio station. We're going to need that, you know. To proclaim the People's Republic tomorrow night. It must be tomorrow night. The hostages . . ."

Sánchez shrugged and picked up another full glass.

"They accepted Vizarra as chief of state for thirteen years. Now some of them will have to pay for it. If some of them had balls enough to stand a fight with us two days ago, we'd be drinking brandy from Vizarra's private stock at the National Palace right now. To hell with them, I say. You spend your life working to make them free men and they don't lift a finger. Some men like to drink piss better than champagne, especially if someone tells them that piss *is* champagne. They don't have the balls to fight and they don't have any political sense. Let them drink piss, then. They're not like you and me. Not like us. Not like Olmega here. Right, Pepe? To hell with them all."

"If we aren't wealthy when we meet *la puta Suerte,* those people will be drinking blood, not piss, Carlos. Their own blood. They'll drown in it."

"Vizarra wouldn't have those people shot. Not at random. Ah, Christ, but if he lets them shoot wounded students, a bunch of kids . . ."

Alessandro stared at him. Sánchez took a fresh cigar and rolled it in his mouth. The brandy burned in his belly. He felt strong and sure again.

"And they arrested your father, Carlos."

"So. What for? Who cares about him these days? Nobody."

"Vizarra cares about him. And so do you."

"Not for years."

"He's your father."

"It doesn't matter."

"You're his son. His only son. He loves you, Carlitos, I know it. And you must love him too. Even if you deny it. Even if you say you hate him. Maybe especially so."

"I don't believe in love. I don't believe in hatred."

The figure swaddled in the blanket lurched erect. The shuddering sweat-slicked face twisted. The eyes bright with pain fixed on Sánchez a pitiless glare. The voice licked out like a silk whip.

"If you don't believe, then why did you make me kill my friend? Why did you make me kill Jaime? Who are you going to kill next? Who are you going to kill next?"

452

Sánchez backed away from the table and stuffed his trembling hands into his pockets. He blew out a cloud of blue smoke and muttered around the butt of his cigar.

"We'd better get the guards to take him back to the dispensary. He doesn't know what he's saying. Just look at him. He's soaked right through the blanket. Then we can go to meet Ramos and the miners. Everything's settled here now."

⸸

Fingel sat on his bunk, holding his briefcase on his lap, waiting for lunch. The door to his cell was unlocked and stood open. He could hear steps in the stone corridor, boots knocking closer and closer. He placed his briefcase on the bunk so that he could hold his tin tray on his knees. But the uniformed figure paced by the open door and on down the echoing corridor, hurrying to complete some important task.

Fingel was first dismayed and then angry. He was being cheated. What kind of a jail was this, anyway? At dawn the warder had given him a tin can half filled with cold, greasy coffee, unsweetened, returned his briefcase filled with his papers, all in order, and said simply that he was no longer under arrest. He had left the door open. No longer under arrest. Did that mean he was free? No one had said he could or had to leave. So maybe he should stay. What kind of a jail was it that broke both the rules of jails: first, to tell the prisoner exactly what he could and could not do and when, and second, to feed the prisoner?

It was a trick. Fingel snuffed through his swollen, still-tender nose disdainfully. They expected him to creep out into the corridor, look both ways and then make a run for it. Of course the corridor would be empty. They would all be empty. And the door leading to the courtyard would be half open. And out in the sun, the squad of soldiers with their rifles, waiting. An officer with a pistol for the *coup de grâce*. Fingel's lips curled with scorn. They thought Herman Fingel had never been in jail before? Herman Fingel had been in detention camps, behind miles of barbed wire, locked up in ruined churches, bolted in the basements of shell-smashed schools, manacled to the leg of a kitchen table and fed *choucroute garnie* by a gendarme's wife. Herman Fingel had been not merely in jails, but in famous prisons. In all those places, in Poland, Germany, France, Mexico, Brazil, he had obeyed the rules and eaten the food. They couldn't fool an old hand. He knew his rights.

The open door was a terrible temptation. He tried not looking at it. He faced the other way and read all the inscriptions scratched onto the walls, the names, initials inside bleeding hearts, threats of suicide, and numberless obscene pictures, poems and phrases in a half-dozen languages. But it was no good. Even if he couldn't see the open cell door, he could feel it. He even imagined a draft tickling the back of his neck. He thought of the food they would bring him, that they *had* to bring him. Two small boiled potatoes, cold, a hunk of black bread and three thick slices of *chorizo,* the cheap reddish sausage that tasted like soap. It was due him, and he expected, demanded, to get it. The open door was a torment. He got up and drew it shut.

But that was no better. Even if it was shut, he knew it was unlocked. He waited until steps rang down the corridor. He giggled until the laughter made his nose sting. Oh, that was one in the eye for them! He had shut his own door. He was still a prisoner. Now they would have to bring him his food. The steps went on down the corridor and faded. Fingel hugged his briefcase and grinned, imagining the consternation sweeping through the official offices located somewhere high above in the great, gray, stone pile. Men in spotless uniforms hurled themselves erect, their faces stunned white. They gnawed their mustaches, cursed and stamped, tore papers to shreds in a frenzy, and stared at each other with wonder-filled eyes. New standby orders were hastily written for the firing squad and the kitchen cooks. Out of a pot of boiling water a hand fetched two small potatoes, carefully, oh, carefully. A knife blade wavered over a brown loaf, then reckless, inspired to duty, hewed off a one-hundred-gram hunk. Fingel sat on his bunk and smacked his lips, savoring the soapy sausage. He waited and waited. But nothing happened. In all the vast box of stone, no one moved. He stood and stared out into the courtyard. Four soldiers sat beside a howitzer drinking wine from a leather bottle. Fingel urged the wine to become vinegar and worse. In a rage he spat through the bars at them until his mouth went dry. Maybe he had a terrible disease that would spread—a plague, perhaps, harmless to the carrier but deadly to those who drank wine and refused to provide cold potatoes. He sank back on his bunk exhausted, and began a hunger strike.

In a half hour, his mind was swimming with images of steaming, buttered noodles, tender, crusty breasts of chicken, salads bright as jewelry, bursting with succulence when just touched with the tongue, stuffed fish, a whole roast leg of lamb sprinkled with herbs, a cold, teeth-aching cold golden glass of Pilsener, a beer capped with white, tangy foam, the very glass itself sparkling, beaded. His stomach roiled uncontrollably. He bit off his fingernails, chewed and swallowed them, then sucked on the end of his belt. Creamy soups, roast goose, pancakes with soured cream, a wooden platter spread with cheeses, powdery-rind Camembert, stiff, oily Gruyère, crumbling goat cheese sprinkled with minute sugar gems. He rolled on his bunk, moaning. The whisper of the straw beneath him sounded exactly like the deft hands of a waiter spinning a magnum of Pol Roger in a bucket of fine-smashed ice. He could smell the starch of linen napery, the perfume of *sauce hollandaise*. He fell off his bunk, and the jolt of the fall drove him erect, brandishing his briefcase, shaking his fist. He marched to the door and kicked it open. He rushed into the corridor, his mind drenched in mayonnaise and lemon juice, saliva gushing out under his tongue. He threw back his head and bellowed until the corridor boomed.

"Give me my potatoes!"

Nothing. The echoes batted back on him. He turned and marched up the corridor, slapping his feet down hard to let them know he was coming. Not out through the half-open door into the courtyard. Oh, no. Straight to the kitchen. He would know his tin tray among hundreds, thousands, every dent and scratch. He would insist on that one and no other, his bread, *chorizo* and potatoes. Not hot potatoes, either. Cold, as was right. And a tin can half filled with tepid water. He wanted no special privileges. He wanted his due, nothing more. He would take his tin tray back down to his cell, slam the door in their astonished, respectful faces and munch away, while they muttered in awe out in the corridor. When he was done, he would write a formal petition to the head of the prison, requesting, politely but not servilely, whether or not he was actually free. He refused to leave until they granted permission. He would obey all the rules, but they must be made to understand that he insisted on there being rules and those rules strictly enforced. He walked on, his whole face stiff with anger, his lips set.

He climbed a flight of stairs, then another flight. He stopped at the landing, panting and mopping his face. He heard voices, low-pitched and anxious, and slow, shuffling steps. He raised his briefcase to deflect a sleet of flying bullets. They would not find him running from them, but advancing toward them. He began climbing a winding stone staircase.

Halfway up he stopped and edged respectfully over against the wall. Three soldiers were carrying a body wrapped in a blanket. They did not speak, but made little grunting noises of warning to each other. Fingel took off his derby, out of respect. But the boy—it was a boy of perhaps twenty years—was not dead. He moaned and twitched with fever, staring with mad eyes. His lips were dry and cracked. Fingel clucked his tongue and shook his head; his heart twinged with sympathy. The soldiers brushed against him as they bore their burden down the stairs. Fingel put on his derby again and called after them, softly, so as not to give offense.

"Fruit juices. Try fresh fruit juices."

At the landing, a glass-paned door yawned open. Fingel hesitated. He could hear the rapid rattle of a typewriter and the fritzing static of a radio set. Somehow, it didn't sound right. A girl in brown trousers and a soldier's blouse with a scarlet armband walked past him, glanced at him without curiosity and walked on, her hips swaying neatly. No, surely this was not the right office. He climbed another flight of stairs. The corridor there was empty, stifling and dark. A dim bulb burned, casting a weak lemon light. Someone, a man, was singing softly. Fingel adjusted his clothes, dusted off his derby and took a firm grip on his briefcase. He marched down the hall toward the voice, found the door, opened it, and stepped inside, remembered with a pang of terror that he had not knocked for permission to enter, and swung his right fist wildly across his chest and struck a blow against the door that instantly made his knuckles flame.

An immensely fat man in the soiled uniform of a Regular Army officer sat behind a desk littered with glasses, ashtrays, cigars and bottles. The man's face was shrouded up to the eyes with gray whiskers, as though he had walked into a very thick spider web. The room stank of smoke, sweat, urine and stale liquor. The man looked at him out of bloody eyes and belched.

"Who are you?"

"I am, or rather I was, that is, I think I am—"

"If you don't know, shut up. What's in that thing you've got?"

Trembling, Fingel tore at the straps of his briefcase. His passport, prayer book, glossy advertising pamphlets, his agreement with the rabbi and varicolored insurance policies splashed onto the desk, scattering sticky glasses and foul cigar stumps. The fat officer reared back in a screaming chair and gazed at the scatter of printed sheets with dread. Fingel, embarrassed but unable to bring himself to snatch back his property once it lay on an official's desk, waved his hands helplessly.

"You see, they arrested me because they thought I was a spy from Ramos—"

"Ah! Hah! Ramos!"

"Yes, but it's a mistake."

"To get arrested. *Claro,* that's a mistake. A secret agent, too."

"No, I'm an agent for an—"

The fat man bent, wheezing brutally, the blood coloring his boar jowls. He rummaged in a drawer of his desk, snatched out a bottle of brandy and slammed it on the desk with a crash that made Fingel's face twitch.

"So. You are from Ramos. At last!"

"As God is my witness, sir, I—"

"With all these secret documents, too."

Fingel groaned and bit his lips. This, then, was the trick. They were going to arrest him all over again!

"I am General Vola, revolutionary patriot and commandant here. Don't let those others fool you. Been hiding here. Saving my strength. And thinking, too."

Vola snatched up an insurance policy and squinted at it. Fingel flapped his arms, his voice rising to a thin squeak.

"I have tried to explain that those are only—"

"Explain? Explain what?"

Vola spun the policy and held it sideways to study the margin and the three little staples. He nodded his round, flushed face and belched juicily.

"Alessandro sent you from Ramos. That is enough."

"Please don't let them shoot me, sir, General, sir . . ."

Vola wallowed up out of his chair, blundered around the desk and crushed Fingel in a bristled, slobber-mouthed embrace.

"Shoot you? *Amigo,* we are brother patriots!"

The blood jigged in Fingel's eyes, and he screwed his head from side to side to protect his broken nose. Vola released him and blew brandy-foul breath in his face.

"Courage, *amigo*. You are safe here with Vola. Here, drink some brandy. You look sick."

"Sick? Oh, only my nose. *Mil gracias,* but I seldom drink. A little wine . . ."

Vola blew into Fingel's face again like a freezing man starting a fire. Fingel's lids fluttered. Vola's face settled into a truculent, suspicious scowl.

"You *refuse* to drink with Vola?"

"Refuse? Oh, no, sir. General, you misunderstand. I mean, I don't explain myself well. These misunderstandings."

Vola tore the foil off the bottle, wrenched off the cap and thrust it at Fingel.

"Drink to the success of the Movement!"

Fingel looked at the bottle, then at the gross, whiskered man in the soiled uniform. He tried not to be frightened, but his voice was still shrill.

"Of course, of course, General."

He put the bottle to his lips and sipped cautiously. Vola glared at him with fiery eyes. Fingel tried to watch him around the upturned bottle. Liquor trickled into his mouth until his cheeks bulged. He closed his eyes, moaned softly and swallowed. Molten metal spilled down his throat. The fumes shot into his swollen nose, and tears flowed down his cheeks.

"Hoo-hah! That's very pleasant . . . very nice."

Vola snatched the bottle away.

"To the Movement!"

Fingel watched, open-mouthed, feeling his belly begin to glow, while Vola's throat jerked four times. The general's knuckles were covered with thick, soft fur. The brandy exploded like a bomb of gold in Fingel's empty stomach. Vola handed him the bottle. Fingel swallowed a little more, but fingers like caterpillars twisted the bottle against his teeth. He choked and spluttered, then swallowed once, twice, a third time. Vola clouted him between the shoulders with a roar of laughter. Fingel sprawled half over the desk, his ears pinging slowly.

"What's your name, agent? I like you."

"Fingel. Herman Fingel."

"But you speak well, *amigo.*"

"In my business, you have to. Last time it was door-to-door."

"Ah, *sí!* Recruiting, eh? What's the news from the mines?"

"Business was slow there. You know, slow. Besides, Ramos is the worst—"

"*Claro,* but he is ready now, no? Listen, I saw him."

"Who?"

"Who? Why, him. *Him!* Alessandro!"

"When I was at the mines with Ramos I saw . . . Alessandro, eh? Oh. That's good?"

"He stood right there. Where you stand now!"

Fingel glanced over his shoulder and stepped hastily to one side. Vola drank again from the bottle. Fingel wondered what he used all the glasses for. The desk was covered with them, stubby, sticky glasses with dead flies in the bottoms. Vola stumbled around the desk and fell into his shrieking chair. He waggled his head.

"Alessandro is my friend. Yes. My friend all my life. We are brothers. Ramos is my brother, too. Hell, you are my brother, Bingel. Have a drink. I will sign all these papers for you. But first, first, you drink. To the Movement!"

"Just a little one. You see, I haven't eaten because—"

"Of the revolution. No one eats during a revolution. Drink. I'll sign."

"You'll sign that, that one . . . right in your hands?"

"What are you staring at, eh? You have been told by someone downstairs, eh? Some lying son of a whore that Vola can't read and write, eh? Well, that's not so, my brother. I can sign my name very well, and no damned priest taught me how, either. I can sign my name. As well as Vizarra himself. *Better* than Vizarra. Almost as good as Alessandro. But his name is longer, so he gets more practice every time he writes it. That's important. Where do I sign? Huh! Such little words at the bottom of the pages."

Fingel cuddled the bottle and tittered nervously. Vola was pawing a life insurance policy for one hundred thousand dollars. The general glared at Fingel.

"Drink!"

The blood was booming through Fingel's belly and chest. His arms went silly and flapped around. He nearly dropped the bottle. His face felt hot and rather stiff. He drank, gasped and wiped his mouth. The stuff didn't seem to be so strong, for some reason. He swaggered away in a little circle, tipping his derby and fingering his broken nose. He could hardly feel it. Maybe it was going to drop off. The thought made him laugh. He rushed back to the desk.

"Ah, yes, well . . . hah, yes, ha-ha, that's right. They *are* little words, aren't they? Right, right there, at the bottom of the page. And there, too, no . . . wait, here. Right here."

Vola's thick tongue, discolored like a lemon rind, stuck out between his fat lips. He groaned with the effort as he slowly drew blotchy letters, the pen nib spattering the printed sheet. His plump, fuzzed fingers held the pen like a toothpick. He swatted his belly, laughed triumphantly and waved the policy.

"See? See?"

"Yes, indeed. Beautiful. Bravo! Well done. Now I sign."

Vola snatched the policy away and pressed it to his soiled tunic.

"You do? What for?"

"Well, I'm the agent and—"

"*Claro*. Ramos isn't here to sign and neither is my brother Alessandro. So sign. Look, here's another one. *Muy bien*. Hurry up with the pen."

"You want to sign that, too? That's two hundred thousand dollars worth of—"

"Absolutely! No one says I can't write. I'll sign everything!"

He scrawled his name on the second policy. Fingel's hands scampered through the sheets. Vola signed the bottom of the hurricane-damage brochure. Fingel slipped a fire-and-theft policy in front of the general, remembered the revolution and snatched it away, his heart thudding.

"Oh, that's fine, General. May God bless you. Really, I assure you, you'll never regret it. Never, General! You can trust our organization absolutely. We pay in dollars. We back every statement here with—"

"Good! Now you sign, no?"

"No! I mean, yes! Yes! There. We can worry about the medical examination later."

"Medical examination? But I haven't had a case since I was a boy."

"Never mind. Now to name the beneficiary."

"The what?"

"The beneficiary—who will get the money when you die, God forbid."

Vola crossed himself and nodded. Two tears leaked down his fat, stubbled cheeks, and he hummed a little tune about an army burro. He sighed, a greasy gush that fluttered the papers tumbled over the desk.

"*Pues,* all men must die, no? And these are dangerous times. But we have courage."

"*Claro,* General . . . courage."

"Have a drink. To courage."

"To courage."

The brandy seemed as mild as rainwater. Fingel felt very warm and wanted to dance. He beamed at Vola, who shrugged.

"So. Give me the bottle."

"Right here, General."

"Call me José, I beg you."

Fingel blushed and took off his derby. He watched Vola drink, hesitated, then picked up the two policies.

"General . . . José . . . you really must make up your mind. Who gets the money?"

"Who gets the money? Vola gets the money! Forty thousand reales, was it? Can't remember. Maybe it was a hundred thousand."

"But this is two hundred thousand dollars!"

"What? In dollars? Give me that pen. I'll sign! I'll sign! The more you sign, the more you get, is that it? *Magnífico!*"

"Well, more or less."

"Eh?"

"Don't you have parents?"

Fingel bit his lips, rather shocked at his own question. He squinted and tried to imagine a woman giving birth to General Vola. A forty-pound baby with red eyes and whiskers. He clucked his tongue sadly. Vola burst into tears. He rolled his head and roared like a bull. Fingel held out his own soiled handkerchief, but Vola mopped his face with his sleeve.

"They are dead, God save their souls . . ."

Vola crossed himself and sniffed, then blew his nose into his fingers and wiped them on an auto insurance application. He stared at the bottle and picked it up.

"*Perdón* . . . but all this writing has made me very tired and thirsty."

"No, you forgive me. Please, for making you sad."

"Sad? Who's sad?"

"General—"

"José."

"José, are you . . . are you married?"

"No. All the women in this country are whores, anyway."

"Oh. Well, someone else. A friend?"

Vola slammed the bottle on the table and tried to get out of his chair. His legs buckled and he fell across the desk, his furry fingers knotted around Fingel's necktie.

"A friend? *Exactamente!* You. You're my friend! Eh? *Amigo?*"

"Me?"

"You. That's an order."

"This is very irregular. I'm very flattered, but I'm not sure that the home office would—"

"If you drink with Vola, you're his friend. Forever!"

Bright fire flecks whirled before Fingel's eyes. He clawed at his collar, gasping and nodding his head. Vola collapsed back into his chair, dragging Fingel belly down onto the desk. Fingel's left shoe slipped slowly off. He curled his toes, but it thudded to the floor. Vola released him and scrambled the papers.

"Eh. Off my desk. Where's that pen? Here. Sign. When I die, all my money goes to you, *amigo*. Sign!"

"Momentito. My shoe . . ."

Fingel bent down to pick up his shoe. He swooped gracefully down and up, missing the shoe by six inches. He smiled. It was the most graceful bending he had ever done. He did it again and giggled with delight. It was so easy, so pretty, like a bird. He hopped back to the desk, took the pen and wrote his name. His arms and hands had become very graceful, too, and the pen ran right off the edge of the sheet onto the blotter and raked up a lump of inky fuzz. Fingel crowed and hugged himself. Two hundred thousand dollars! He had his life, his little life, at last! He took off his derby and danced a polka to the coat rack and back to the desk.

"But just to think that a few days ago! A few hours! Minutes, even. My life! And I'll be rich, rich! Two hundred thousand dollars! Wait until I tell the rabbi this!"

"Rico. Right. Rich. Drink!"

"Wait until they hear about this at the office! Gladly, José, my friend. *Salud!"*

Vola folded his fat arms and scowled. Fingel quickly put the bottle down on the desk and backed away. Vola stared at him. Fingel fixed his necktie and glanced down at the front of his pants.

"I do this for Ramos and Alessandro, no? An act of patriotism and honor."

462

"For yourself, General . . . José. With the coverage you've got, you can wish for trouble."

Vola flung out his arm and knocked over the bottle. Fingel bobbed down, tied his shoe and bobbed up again.

"Trouble? Trouble is nothing to me. I have courage. Trouble is nothing. *Nada.* As long as there's money in it."

"Truth. Now . . . yes, money. Let's see."

Fingel sailed up to the desk, found a pencil, figured his commission, whistled and clapped his hands together, then totaled the premium payments made out quarterly and converted the figures to Costa Plata currency. His mind was graceful.

"Two thousand, one hundred and fifty-seven reales. And twenty centavos."

"Not bad. Not bad at all. Hand it over. You can give me the rest later."

"No, no, José. You don't understand . . . I mean, I haven't made myself clear. You give that to me. You. Give. To me. That money. Two thousand, one hundred and fifty-seven reales. Forget the centavos."

Vola stared at Fingel and shook his head, slowly.

"To you? *Madre de Dios,* there isn't an honest man left in the country. Even you, my best friend. Well, I'll give it to you."

Fingel discovered he had been holding his breath. He smiled and wiped his face.

"Think of it as a loan, José."

"A loan? *Mierda! I give* it to you!"

Vola yanked a key ring from his pocket and bent over, wheezing and sniffing. Fingel wanted to offer to open the drawer. He could bend so gracefully. But Latins were so sensitive. Perhaps the general would be angry if he saw a foreigner bending more beautifully than himself. Vola heaved up and slapped a wad of blue banknotes on the desk.

"Help yourself, *amigo.* Take it all."

"Oh, no. Thank you, but I couldn't. Just what you . . . what's due."

Fingel freed some bills. They were cold and greasy and stuck together. He discovered he could see them better if he closed one eye. He wrote out a receipt in pencil, then drew over the pencil marks with the fuzz-clotted pen nib. Vola picked up the Hebrew prayer book and reached for the pen.

"I sign this, too, right?"

"No, no, José!"

"A secret language. You're a clever one, *amigo*. When does Ramos rise to join us? Tomorrow?"

"I guess so. It's supposed to be a nice day. Why not, eh?"

"You go back to him with these."

"Not all. These are your copies here. And mine are . . . I'll just put them back in my briefcase, so we don't get them mixed up."

"I keep these? All right. It takes courage, big *cojones,* but for Vola that is nothing. Now, you'll need a car and a driver."

"What for?"

Vola suddenly heaved himself out of his chair and tiptoed over to the door, then back to his desk. Fingel blinked, impressed. The general was very graceful, too.

"Ssst. Listen. Alessandro is going to meet with Ramos. No, don't ask me how I found out. But I'm clever."

"Truth. Very clever."

"So you go to meet with them. Before, you were Ramos' agent. Now you're mine. I gave you the money, didn't I?"

"That's true. You have a point."

Fingel nodded. After all, this Alessandro was the leader of the rebel forces. He needed a life insurance policy more than anyone Fingel could think of. He tiptoed over to the door and back, just to try it. It was amazing. His heels floated, and he hit the coat rack. He tiptoed back to the desk and put his finger to his lips.

"Sssst! José, I'll do it."

"Muy bien. Tell them I'm still holding out. I'll never surrender."

"Good for you, José."

"Have a drink, *amigo.*"

Vola opened another drawer, took out a pad, breathed on a rubber stamp and thumped it on the pad. He handed Fingel the stamped sheet.

"Requisition to the motor pool. Sedan and driver."

Fingel took the requisition and stuffed his papers and prayer book back into the briefcase. He shook his head when Vola held out the bottle.

"No more for me, José. Business before pleasure."

"Truth. *Viva la revolución!* Farewell, my brother!"

464

Fingel felt himself lifted from the floor. Vola kissed the rim of Fingel's derby and set him down.

"*Adiós,* José. May you live a long, long time. Don't worry about anything. The next payment is a long time off. Next year."

"Next year? If you're not back in two days, I'll have you shot."

"Exactly. Tomorrow afternoon. *Adiós!*"

Fingel hoisted his briefcase, tacked carefully around the coat rack and shot out into the corridor. He paused and fell gently against the wall. He had forgotten something. What was it? He straightened up and shook his head firmly. This was disgraceful, a man of business, worth two hundred thousand dollars, and he could not remember what it was. Something about food? Yes, that was it, the potatoes!

He shot back into the office, smiled and tipped his hat.

"Please give my compliments to the chef!"

↓

The sun-drugged shapes shifted and slowly stirred across the hot disc of sand in the *plaza de toros.* Dark bodies bumped and butted in torpid collisions, muttered and thrust on to see and touch the shoulder-high, horn-splintered barrier, the circle of wood within the circle of stone. The sun flamed, squeezing down like a piston on the foot-scuffed plate of sand. The guards up in the broad funnel of stone circled on the tiers, hurrying out from beneath the pressure of the sun into the slender moon-rind of shadow, picked at their shirts, mopped their faces, thrust their thumbs under the sweat-slick rifle slings and stepped out again into the heat. A burning breeze licked at the blue-and-silver banner high in the official's box. The boot heels of the guards pocked, and a child cried. The bodies herded against the splintered ring of wood, waiting for the shade to slide down and ease them. The guards circled on the stone rings that rose up and out and ended like a cylinder or a bucket open to the pale, hot sky.

"*Cabrón!* Push again and I'll bend your horns! María, bring her over here. There, see? I'll stand like this. It's cooler, no?"

"Look at those bastards up there. Drinking beer. *Gaseosa,* too. Why don't they give us water?"

"Look, if we got together in a group and made a rush for it. No, listen. Twenty of us, say. *Hombre,* we could make it. Over the barrier. There aren't enough of them. They'd have to come down, see, come down. By the time they made it, most of us could be out through the passage there."

"Chico, I'll be 'most of us.' And what's outside, eh? Eh? More of them with their red berets and their guns. It's nearly two hundred meters to the nearest building. Don't be stupid."

"Why don't they give us water? Just some water?"

"Madre María, qué calor! I'll faint from the heat. The sand burns right through my shoes."

"Yes, may God never forgive them. They took him out of the place. In a truck with the others. Out of their beds they took them, down the mountains, and left them in a field, dumped there to die. A whole field of them in their hospital gowns white as crosses, spitting and drowning in the dirt. My Antonio. It's true, I tell you. But that's not enough. No, they arrest me. Me, a woman my age."

"Spit? Who can spit? I'm frying like a *churro."*

"So it's this. When they open the gate. But then the *plaza de toros* is full, every seat up there filled. Filled with us, watching and waiting for the trumpet to blow."

"Chico, I admire your grace. Three times you have stepped on me, each time from a different direction."

"When we get out, I'll call for you. Your father seems to like me. I mean, we've met, no? We could go dancing. At the Rex. Ever been there? Never? Oh, *elegante.* And you'll be the prettiest girl there. I think your aunt would like it, too."

"Psst. Hey, *hombre.* Look down here. Me. Listen. Who's your boss? I want to see him. There's been a mistake. You don't want me. It's absurd. You tell him Belgarito. Belgarito. Go to the cinema? Remember *Amor y Sangre?* With her? *Her.* You know. I made that. Producer and director. Psst, listen. You've got a good face. I remember faces. That's my business. I haven't done anything wrong. I could use you. No, I mean it. Why, I'm casting now for a new film. With her. How would you like that? In a film with her? Remember the scene in *Amor y Sangre,* when she's dying and he wants to make love and she lets him? And he gets on her, eh? And I show her face when it's her time of the little death, then cut to the blood on the mattress? Eh? A thousand reales a month. I swear it. Belgarito. *Hombre,* get me out of here. There's been a mistake. Hey, don't go away. Hey! Psst! Come back! Two thousand a month!"

"A thousand, easily. I know. In the bank you develop a head for figures. You can estimate. Come in any day at closing time and I can tell you within ten people how many have come to my window. A thousand of us and exactly thirty-four of them. In percentages, about what you get from a savings account."

"Save us? How? I ask you. Tell me. I should have listened to Mama. A weak face, she said. Well, here we are. You, me and the two little ones. You like to see María Dolores faint and fall into the mess someone did on the sand? Then do something! Anything! Get us out of here!"

"I just was setting out the tables. The boss said we should open up again. It was quiet, you know. The shooting had stopped. Well, I was setting out the tables and this truck came up. Empty. I was the first, you see, so I didn't know. Identification card. Work permit. I showed them. One had a list of names. He drew a line through my name and they grabbed me. 'What for?' I asked them. They didn't say a word."

"*Cerveza.* A tall, cool bottle of beer. Brown, with little cold beads of water and the label all slippery. Just to hold it in my hand would be enough."

"That one. Over there. See him? No, in the brown suit with the briefcase. He tried to give money to the Guards when we came in. We were in the same truck. He's got enough, I tell you. I saw it. Maybe a dozen, twenty, hundred reales, the big blues, *chico,* a fistful. In his jacket pocket, inside on the left side. So, easy now. I'll bump into him from behind. You get next to him and when he turns, make the dip."

"Make sense? Of course. Everything makes sense. God is logic, even if He does make the sun too hot. We're not arrested. We're in custody. *Amigo,* for many years I worked out in the *campo.* Selling harness. You know what they fear out in the latifundia, the rich ones? Fire. Grass fire. When it happens, you can see the smoke ten, twenty kilometers away. And smell the cattle that get caught. It roasts them, see? Well, when a fire starts, they go out and light another one. But small. They control it. It burns a section out, absolutely black. Then when the big fire comes, there's nothing for it to burn. So it goes out. That's us. They make a little fire of us, that's all. So the big fire burns out."

"I'm burning up. My face. Look at my face. My dress. It feels like it's burning."

"Agua fría! Agua fría! Cold water! Come have a drink! One centavo. Ah, how good that tastes!"

"Shut your mouth, you crazy bastard. The sun's got you."

"The sun? *Hombre,* I'm freezing! Hey, give me your coat. It's going to snow, I tell you."

"Watch him. See? He turns his back. Now, if twenty of us made a rush for it, we'd be over the barrier by the time he turned around. In ten seconds we'd be in the passage. Then, under the stands, we separate. They couldn't get us all. We'd get out, into the city. Tell the people, warn them. They can't do this to us. They can't!"

"The mules drag the dead bulls *out* of the ring. But our Old Mule drags us *in!*"

"For myself, I don't mind. But the women and children. It's indecent, that's what it is. There's no place for them."

"They could close the entrances and let us under the stands. But out here. *Dios,* man, it's inhuman."

"I don't understand it. I've never been the least interested in politics. Live and let live, I say. Live and let live."

The square strong gate swung open, the jaw of the *toril.* Heads turned to see into the dark slot, to see the dark body rush hooking into the scalding light while the trumpet blare still shivered and the stiff magenta capes were shaken loose for the doubling. The muttering swelled up and hushed. The Guards unslung the rifles and stared down at the hot, scuffed pit. The gate creaked and banged once. Four men—two in the uniforms of the National Guards, two in red berets—walked out of the *toril.* In each right fist a shining pistol. The bodies butted and jostled away, pressing, stunned and shrinking from the four figures that stepped stiffly across the sand. One with a red beret strode to the quailing mass and tore a body free. He stood separate, arms hanging loose. An old woman, her lips twisting in prayer, was thrown against him. Another man, two boys, a man in a brown suit with a briefcase. The National Guards thrust them into a line, two abreast, until there were twenty. One with a red beret gave an order. The double file scuffed across the sand and into the dark gullet. The *toril* gate slammed shut, the bolt rattled and a truck motor coughed and roared. A sigh swirled up from the hot sand, sifted against the stones and died.

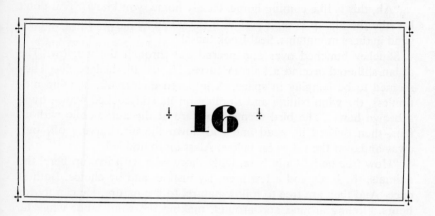

16

THE command car ground up the rutted road that twisted up the barren, wind-worn mountain. The driver cursed steadily in a soft, imploring whisper and yanked the gearshift lever into low. He let in the clutch, and the sedan shuddered. Behind the automobile a plume of dust lifted and blew away, off in the air over the valley below. Sánchez moved his elbow and jerked his head back.

"See that? I don't like that."

"The wind blows it away, Carlitos."

"But it can be seen. If they've got an airplane up. It would be natural for them to fly out here."

"Yes. Or patrol the border. Or fly over the city. Besides, this is an army vehicle. Why should they fire at us? The airplanes have no radios. They must fly all the way back. By that time, we'll be there."

Alessandro smiled and leaned back in the seat. He unbuttoned the throat of his shirt and struggled into a clean army tunic. He breathed deeply, greedily sucking the cool air into his chest. He looked over the jagged range, the blocky hunks of stone that ran off to the horizon. The far peaks were tipped with snow. He stretched and yawned, then held his jaw open so the cool wind beat down his throat.

"Ah, this is like coming home. Really home, you know? You don't breathe the air up here. You feel it. You can suck freedom from the wind in these mountains. See! Look there!"

Sánchez hunched over and peered out through the window. The sedan slithered around a hairpin curve. He felt his belly draw. They seemed to be hanging in space. A hundred meters off, hanging motionless, the wind frilling and rippling on its stiff-cocked wings, hung a brown hawk. The bird seemed to stare at the automobile without fear, then twisted its head and slid down the air, curving off, out, away and over the valley far below. Alessandro nodded.

"How free he is! Only here. Only those who wish live up here, the animals, the birds and a few men. By instinct and by choice. Both at once. And they are free to follow nature, to use nature. He can fly for hours, circling around and around, making the wind labor while he rides it. That's the trick we've lost. We forget that nature needs us to use her."

Sánchez snorted and flung himself back in the seat. The sedan slammed over ruts and stones and slued into another curve.

"Tell the driver that, eh? He'll have us over the side."

"It's so beautiful up here. Clean. Pure and perfect."

Sánchez watched the wind tear at Alessandro's shirt and whip the dark hair across his brow.

"Well, it's safer, anyway. Not safe, but safer. That's my idea of perfection. Besides, what's up here? Your hawk. A few goats. Some shepherds . . . and they spend their time buggering each other. But I suppose that's freedom, too, eh? Well, give me a decent apartment with a woman in it, some cigars and a glass of brandy. Freedom is down in the dust, *chico*. Up here there's nothing but the rocks and the wind. Let's stop and eat. I'm getting hungry."

Alessandro nodded absently. Sánchez tried to light a cigar, but the cool wash of wind blew out his matches. The sedan lurched up the road, doubled back, turned and climbed again. The driver whispered curses and rammed the shift down into low. Despite the cool wind, the man was sweating. The road lifted at last and ran straight up to a stone marker, a broken hut and a stand of distorted trees. Alessandro leaned forward and touched the driver's shoulder. The command car rumbled over the rocky shoulder, jolted beneath the clump of stunted pines and stopped. Dust seethed around the sedan. Alessandro and Sánchez climbed out of the car. The driver opened the hood and stared fearfully at the radiator. A feather of steam rose in the air. Alessandro nodded.

"Don't touch it. It's the altitude. It will cool while we eat."

The driver nodded and went to the rear for the food and wine. Alessandro walked away toward the herder's hut. Sánchez ran after him, fumbling with his pistol holster.

"Hey! Don't!"

He grabbed Alessandro by the shoulder and dragged him back.

"Are you crazy? You don't know if anybody's in there. What if they shoot? Even if they're ours they might shoot."

Alessandro pulled free and shook his head.

"There was an old man who lived here all alone. A road mender who kept a few goats. He planted the tree, too. He was once a priest, he told me. He used to call this place his monastery. He tried to feed the few people who passed this way. I stayed with him once. With my father. Before . . . you know. Before the end. Or the beginning."

"I don't see any goats. No smoke from a fire. Look, the roof has fallen in. Keep away from there."

"There's no one here, Carlos. He must have died."

"Alone. Some freedom. Free to be dead a week before anyone passes. Come away."

"I want to see."

The two men walked toward the hut. The leather hinges, long ungreased, had dried and broken, and the door tilted over the sill. Sánchez thrust it aside and poked his pistol into the room. The ceiling poles had broken, spilling the roof of flattened cans and slate sheets over a low table and a bunk. The clay stove was shattered. Sánchez kicked at a sandal cut from an old rubber tire.

"Maybe the hawk got him."

Alessandro lifted a few pitted sheets of tin off the bunk and sat down.

"He was a good old man. He fed us well. A stew with rabbit and dried beans. Some onions. A cup of wine. He talked with my father. The old man was with the Movement. He could see the new road from up here. He counted the trucks carrying Vizarra's troops. We

471

rode out one afternoon to get his regular report. I wonder if he really was a priest."

"Maybe the soldiers got him."

"What for?"

"For nothing."

"For being free. They might have taken him for that."

"If he was a priest, then maybe the priests got him."

Sánchez shivered slightly. The interior of the hut was cool, almost cold, and smelled of wood rot and damp stones. He walked outside. In a few seconds Alessandro joined him. They stood looking at the arid valley that ran north and south. The new highway to the mines lay on the valley floor like a glossy ribbon on a dusty counter. Beyond the valley, across a low gap in the stony hills, a railroad bridge spanned a riverbed. Alessandro pointed to it.

"When the miners come down, we've got to get some men out of the sanatorium over there, Carlos. There are two bridges. One here, the other twenty-three kilometers to the south. But this one leads into a tunnel. We must have the tunnel and the bridge. Otherwise the miners will have to turn west, come over the hills right out into the valley. Vizarra could bring soldiers up the highway."

"Let him. We could split the miners. Some down the railroad line. Some down the highway."

Alessandro shook his head slowly, feeling the clear, cool wind on his face.

"No. That's the problem. They think and act as a group, a tribe. What they will do, they will do together—"

"Or not at all?"

"They are used to being led. That's why this Ramos—"

"I tell you he's crazy, *jovencito*. Instead of sending young Olmega and his cadre to get rid of Colleo, we should have sent him against Ramos."

"Umm. But we had no one to replace him. We didn't know about that boy with only one arm. He came to us too late. We should have gone looking for him."

"How?"

"Anyway, it's too late."

"Where is he? The one with only one arm?"

"Up ahead somewhere. Waiting for us."

"You're sure?"

Sánchez sat down on the running board of the sedan and let his head drop into his hands. His voice was hoarse and shaky.

"They've got the highway. They can shoot up the railroad lines. That leaves only this mule track. How long will it take them to remember it? They may have posted roadblocks already. We'll be trapped here, Alessandro!"

Alessandro twisted the dials and slipped the earphones on his head. He hunched over the receiver, his face immobile, intent.

"Chinchón is going to have to take the radio station for us. With his gang of sewer rats. We'll need it. Even if we only hold it one day—this is it. . . . No, nothing, just static. I want the archbishop to speak to the people, too."

"You have gone crazy! Here we are trapped like two goats up here, and you talk about the archbishop!"

Alessandro turned the dial back and forth very slowly. Sánchez wanted to spin the knob one way and the other, to know at once. His hands shook. He snatched the cork from the bottle and gulped wine, choked and the cool liquid ran down over his chin.

"He supports the Movement, Carlos. Did I tell you that he wrote to me when I was in Europe? Unofficially, of course. He went to Rome, too. I met him there. It was not easy. I was doing six months at hard labor for antigovernment agitation in France. Mending roads. This road needs work up here. Since the old man died it has gone . . . here! Here it is. Now listen!'"

Alessandro jerked the jack free and dropped the earphones on the seat. He flipped a switch. The speaker crackled and whined. The voice was faint at first, then suddenly louder:

"Therefore, by order of His Excellency, extreme measures are now being taken to shatter forever the hyena pack of Bolshevik-inspired and Bolshevik-led insurgents and traitors who have perpetrated every unspeakable crime against the people of Costa Plata . . ."

"Who's that, Carlos?"

"Malata. Julio Malata."

"His Excellency . . . with the utmost sorrow is compelled to announce that hostile and dangerous elements . . . in very large numbers . . . as examples . . . solidarity of the party, the state, the people and their Caudillo . . . one hundred traitors . . . each hour from . . . until the unconditional surrender of the terrorist bands . . . authorized by Decree 457 . . . bloody paws to snatch

477

for Bolshevik power . . . loosed upon Costa Plata . . . campaign of anarchistic . . . murder, arson and rapine . . . violating the sanctity of the parish churches . . . twelve priests shot and mutilated . . . wanton slaughter of innocents whose sole crime was steadfast support of the regime and their children, unwavering in their love for His Excellency . . . crush these pitiless beasts . . . without mercy . . . public executions. Arriba Costa Plata! Viva Vizarra!"

The radio fizzed and then the blare of the national anthem dinned in Alessandro's face. He blinked twice and turned down the volume.

"Tonight everyone will be listening to our words . . . the truth . . . and hear our song . . . Wait, there's something—"

The music stopped with a crash of cymbals, and a voice, high-pitched and strained, shrilled. Alessandro blinked once.

"Mobile unit 14 . . . on Dock C. Fifty meters long the line stretches . . . drawn up on the very edge of the dock. Three machine-gun squads are at their posts. Ammunition has just been delivered. The whole area is a field of red berets. The loyal party members face this stern task, their hearts filled with savage joy . . . enthusiasm and merciless energy of loyal citizens . . . against banditry and terror, so long will the Red Berets punish . . . swiftness of absolute justice and divine will."

Sánchez shook Alessandro, who pulled away. The driver stood beside the sedan, his mouth hanging open.

"It's a fake, little one. Just Malata's propaganda. Let's get moving. We can't just stay here and get caught!"

"Tsssst!"

". . . to describe the scene of execution . . . the Minister of Public Education . . ."

"Ah, *Jesús y María!*"

". . . patriot . . . unflinching duty . . . Don Carlos Sánchez."

Alessandro turned in the seat. The mountain wind fluttered the open throat of his shirt. The twisted pine trees bent and seethed. Alessandro stared at Sánchez for a few seconds, then slowly shook his head.

"This is no fake, Carlos."

The radio spluttered. Thin voices shouted unintelligibly, shrill, fizzy shrieks. Then clumping sounds, the rattle of metal on metal. A

478

voice thick with anger blurted something. Alessandro reached out to adjust the dial.

"Get up there. Start to talk."

Alessandro tilted his head, frowning.

"O'Conner? The head of Vizarra's police?"

Sánchez nodded, his eyes fixed on the speaker panel of the radio. He started and dropped the bottle when the voice wheeted at him.

"Carlitos! Carlitos! Listen to me. If you can't hear me, listen to what the others will tell you soon. Dios, this is terrible! They have them out on the dock in the sun. Many have fainted. They are tied together. I can see two women holding in their arms little naked babies. Little black babies . . . I cannot—"

The radio speaker spurted a confused animal sound of anger and terror. A distant voice rapped orders, each word like a whip pop. The old man's wavering voice began again:

". . . taken the cartridge belts and feeding them into the machine guns . . . pointed right at them. She holds up her baby . . . no one takes it . . . on the dock, crawling and crying for her . . . they are praying now . . . no priest here. . . . His hand is in the air . . . one hundred of them, one hundred souls, Carlitos! Hundreds more waiting in the plaza de toros *. . . they are ready . . ."*

The voice was drowned by the long, lashing fire of the machine guns. The driver wet his lips and crossed himself. Alessandro's face was drained of color. He stared at the radio. Sánchez moved his mouth, but no sounds came. He reached to the dashboard and flipped the switch. The wind droned through the trees and curled the edge of the blanket spread on the bare ground. Sánchez choked and coughed.

"He was right, the Belgian. . . . It is insanity!"

Alessandro's slender fingers twitched. He seemed to watch his hand with curiosity as it crept down to his knee, hesitated, curled and sprang to the switch. The dry, scraping voice rose and fell.

". . . knocked over. . . . Oh, Jesús . . . tied together . . . the first ones pulled the others after . . . edge of the dock all blood . . . some still sit there, their eyes watching . . . pulled over the edge into the harbor . . . not all of them hit . . . splashing in the water like stones . . . the baby still crawling . . . no one moves. . . . One of the gunners is vomiting. . . . He's got a knife! Running for him . . . they catch him . . . knocked down . . . clubs . . . Carlitos, hear me! One hundred, and they mean to go on all

day! The order has been given. There will be no mercy, none. None!
God, don't let this go on! Carlitos, they mean to make me watch it all
and tell you what I see. You can't believe it . . . the faces when the
bullets . . . like cattle . . . bleeding, bleeding . . ."

Sánchez beat his fist on the back of the seat. His face was crimson
and the words clotted in his throat. He cursed and shouted.

"Don't do it! Don't talk for them! Those swine! Don't watch it!
Get out in front of those guns, like a man! Be a man or God will piss
on you!"

". . . Carlitos, hijo mío . . . Carlitos, my son . . . hear them,
if you won't hear me . . ."

"I am deaf, you filthy coward! *Deaf!*"

". . . was Don Carlos Sánchez, Minister of Public Educa-
tion . . ."

"O'Conner again."

The driver touched Sánchez's sleeve. Tears glistened in the man's
eyes.

"Where did they get them from, señor? Please, where did they take
them from? What part of the city?"

"Shut up. We don't know. Shut up, will you?"

"Attention, Alessandro Martín. Attention, Carlos Sánchez, el jo-
ven."

"You *Yanqui* pig!"

"Tsst, Carlos!"

"Martín and Sánchez. This is the Director of the Security Police of
Costa Plata. You have heard the first broadcast. Already the dock
area is being prepared for the next executions. Every hour we will
take one hundred persons and shoot them. By this time tomorrow,
two thousand four hundred citizens will be dead. As long as terrorist
revolutionary action persists, we will meet terror with terror. We will
shoot and we will keep shooting. If it is necessary to kill every citizen
of the city who is not a member of the party, it will be done. The
executions will cease when you, Alessandro Martín, and you, Carlos
Sánchez, surrender yourselves to either myself or Brigadier General
Lucca of the National Guard. All insurgent troops must lay down
their arms. The student Olmega, the Bolshevik Voget and General
Vola of the Regular Army must be surrendered to us, alive. The
telephone lines will be kept open to receive your surrender without
conditions. Carlos Sánchez, Carlos Sánchez, at some time within the

480

next twelve hours, your father will be led out to die with the others. On your heads, yours alone, betrayers of the people, this blood spills. Surrender at once, and the shootings will stop. This is the Director of the Security Police of Costa Plata. You have heard the first broadcast. Already the dock area . . ."

"*Mierda!*"

Sánchez snapped off the radio. Alessandro sat motionless, staring at his hand. Sánchez shook him gently.

"Little one . . . what in the name of God are we going to do?"

Alessandro turned and stared at Sánchez. He seemed dazed. He lifted his right arm.

"Do? See my arm, Carlos? See my arm? They have cut off my hand. Yes, they've cut off my right hand."

The driver moaned and sat down on the running board. Alessandro shivered and fumbled with his left hand at the open throat of his shirt. His voice was firm.

"We must contact the barracks. Have them shell the docks."

"But we'll be killing—"

"The Red Berets. The machine gunners."

"Shell, shell. How much ammunition is left? What about the attack across the city? What about—"

"Carlos, we must stop them."

"So we stop them. They move the guns. And begin again."

"Your father, Carlos—"

"To hell with him. Forget him. He's worthless."

"We will shell the docks. Make them stop, even if it's only an hour or two. They must stop."

"What do we do now? Us, I mean. We can't stay here."

"Driver!"

"*Sí!*"

"Start this thing. We've got to get to Ramos and the miners. Quick!"

Sánchez stumbled into the back seat. Alessandro jumped in beside him. The engine churned and caught, and the sedan jolted into motion. Sánchez tipped up the bottle and emptied it. He flung it out the window. It shattered on the rocky ground, spraying glittering fragments. Above the roar of the motor, a thin, wheeting voice called to Sánchez: the voice of his father, imploring, begging understanding and forgiveness. The blood beat in his wine-numbed cheeks. Alessandro was dragging them all to death. Tears of pity leaked from his

481

lids and streamed down his flushed face. He felt Alessandro touch his arm, a reassuring pat. He nearly shrieked with rage and fear, but the cry bubbled in his throat like a sob.

↓

General Vola moved slowly down the corridor. The floor shivered beneath him. He pushed open the door of the communications room and stood there, scrubbing his jowls with the back of his hand. He peered into the room, stupefied. A young boy wrapped in a blanket sat in a chair near a radio. Another man sat in front of a microphone. A sending-and-receiving set, a field model, stood on the floor. The boy spoke, his voice weak and strangled, as though he held his teeth together. Vola blinked.

"Get Chinchón."

"*Allô, allô? Ici Bureau Central. Général Voget. Allô, sous-marin? Répondez. Répondez. Allô? C'est vous, Chinchón? Comment? Pas de cartouches? Impossible. Nous avons envoyé des . . .*"

"Is that Chinchón?"

"Yes. But he says he has no cartridges. The runner must have— *Allô? Combien en avez-vous? Ah. Deux cent soixante-cinq? Bien. Et de grenades? Vingt. Bombes d'essence? Pas plus? Un moment.*"

"The runner left an hour ago."

"He admits he has two hundred sixty-five rounds. Twenty grenades but no gasoline bombs. Hell, he's an army, no? *Chinchón? Tranquille, amigo. Il reviendra, Allessandro. Oui, je suis positif! À cinq heures . . . cinq et demie. À bientôt, Chinchón.*"

"Good enough. Get the howitzer."

"He wants to know his orders. Let him wait. I told him Alessandro will be back at five-thirty. Right?"

"*Muy bien.* The howitzer."

"*Allô? Allô? Coco? Bon gar'! Ça va? Bien. Écoute. Il faut que vous bombardez les quais. Oui, avec l'obus! Pas avec caca, amigo. Le groupe . . . vous avez munitions? Combien? Dix-huit? Pas plus? Merde!*"

"Only eighteen shells?"

"*Coco, écoute bien, eh? Alessandro a téléphoné. Ses commandes: Bombardez les quais. À trois heures. Oui, je le sais . . . des ôtages. Tant pis. . . .* He's worried about the hostages."

"He's killing fascists."

"*Bombardez les quais, Coco. Combien de blessés? Ah. Non, non.*"

"What's the matter?"

"They've been fired on. He has four badly wounded. They've moved the gun."

"Too bad. Tell him we're not the Red Cross. My students, the girls, are out in the streets fighting."

"*Nous n'avons pas de Croix Rouge ici, Coco. Tu penses c'est comme Paris. Pas d'eau? . . .* They have no water."

"To hell with the water. Get them firing at three o'clock. A little before."

"*Coco? Pissez dans les casques et buvez bien frais. C'est comme vin blanc. À trois heures. Et bombardez bien.*"

"They must fire well. Accurately. No mistakes. Right on the docks. They've got the quadrants and a forward observer in the church tower."

"*Coco? Bombardez bien. Pas de bombardement bâclé. Écoute. Nous avons dynamite. C'est pour attaquer le poste de radiodiffusion ce soir. Bon. Comment?*"

"What does he want?"

"He wants to know if the Indians are going to attack the radio station with the dynamite."

"Why should he know about Chinchón? Just tell him they haven't reached the city yet, but they'll be here soon. Trust to Alessandro."

"*Coco? Pas des indigènes. Il reviendra, Alessandro. Vive le Brigade Rouge! Au 'voir, copain.*"

Vola lurched into the room and thumped against a table. He glared at the two men.

"Soldier? Have you called the mines?"

"No answer, sir."

The soldier spoke with a strange accent. Vola shook his head and nearly fell. The soldier grinned. The boy in the blanket showed his teeth and tried to rise.

"Where is Ramos?"

"Don't know."

"Where is Alessandro?"

"Don't know."

"Where is Fingel?"

"*Quién?*"

"Fingel. The agent."

"Don't know him."

"Imbecile! Who is in command here?"

"General Voget."

"Shut your mouth. Who are you, sick one?"

"General Olmega. Shut your own mouth."

"General? *Mierda.* You are all crazy. I must inspect the lines. Get me a car. At once. We are winning, of course."

"A car? What for?"

"Shut your face, you foreign pig!"

"Get him a car, Henri. Voget wants him out of here. Alessandro won't care, and O'Conner can have him."

"Call the motor pool, *cabronazo!*"

"*Allô? Charlot? Une voiture. Vite. Pour le général. Non, pas Général Voget. Vola, le lourdaud. Il fait une promenade. Dans la ville? Oh, tohu-bohu, comme toujours.* . . . You wish a driver . . . sir?"

"*Claro!*"

"*Charlot? Gros Papa ne veut pas sortir tout seul. Bon débarras, eh?* The car will come right away, General."

"*Muy bien!* Have this kid arrested and shot. That's an order!"

Vola scowled and slammed the door. He walked heavily up the stairs and paused, the breath groaning in his chest, at the landing. His office door stood open. He wrestled a large suitcase from his locker and packed a dress uniform and two bottles of brandy in it. He hesitated, listening, swaying from side to side. From the floor below came the sound of voices and laughter. He thought he heard steps on the stairs and walked softly to the door, closed and locked it. He sighed heavily and shook his head. No one was to be trusted.

He turned the dial on the office safe, left, then right, and left again. He tugged the door and cursed. He reset the dial at zero and spun it again. This time the safe opened. He lifted out four stacks of bank notes and scattered empty, unused pay envelopes on the floor. He placed the notes in the suitcase, took a small automatic pistol from a tray in the second shelf of the safe and put it in his pocket. He lowered himself into his chair and tumbled the papers that lay strewn over his desk. He sat staring at them, the tip of his tongue protruding between his thick lips. They all looked the same. Which were the ones he had signed, the ones that would make him rich? He drew them into a heap and pawed over the sheets. The sweat broke out on his forehead. The little Jew had taken them! The swindler! Vola crushed the papers together in a loose mass and crammed them into the suitcase, lurched to his feet and stumbled to the coat rack. He drew his cap on and threw back his shoulders.

484

At the entryway a small group of men and women in dirty uniforms sat on the steps, sharing cigarettes, cleaning rifles and watching a plume of smoke rise over the city. Vola saluted clumsily. The command car was parked out in the courtyard. No one answered his salute.

"I am making an inspection tour of the front lines. Somebody else is in charge here now. Obey orders. Be brave. *Viva la revolución!*"

Ironic applause patted behind him as Vola stumbled out to the waiting sedan. A high, slithering sound passed overhead. Vola ducked and tore open the door of the automobile. The shell burst in the barracks area, a plume of dust, fragments of wood and tile and whining splinters of shattered glass flung by a slam of high explosive. Vola and the driver fumbled and punched in the front seat. Vola kicked open the far door and heaved his bulk against the driver, slowly forcing him across the seat and out through the door. The driver punched and cursed. Vola snatched the shift lever into low, released the brake and let in the clutch. The sedan lunged forward, and the driver rolled on the gravel. The door banged shut as Vola roared out through the gate.

Vola drove rapidly through the rubble-strewn streets of the western suburbs. He saw nothing but the holes torn in the streets, the heaped rubbish and carcasses of animals. The buildings flashed by; faces whirled like petals on a dark breeze. He wrenched the wheel, stamped on the brake and crashed the gears. The heavy sedan rocked and squealed over trolley tracks, around roadblocks, down narrow streets, across empty squares. The kilometer stones beyond the city flicked past: 1, 5, 9, 13, 20. Vola relaxed and began to hum the song of the army burro. He wanted a drink. He slowed and pulled to the side of the road. Two kilometers ahead was the turnoff for the new highway that led to the mines. He set the brake and twisted to stare into the back seat. He looked on the floor, then beside his fat thigh. It wasn't in the back seat or the front. He had left the suitcase back in the gravel courtyard. He dropped his head on the steering wheel. Fat tears squeezed out between his lids and trickled down his cheeks. Behind him howitzer shells were falling on the docks.

☦

"How far is the tavern now?"

Alessandro looked out of the window and stared at the tumbled blocks of broken granite and the weedy rubble and sand.

"Not far. Over this next hill, down the other side. There's a dry river there, with a bridge over it. Perhaps three kilometers beyond the bridge. Only a few more minutes."

"Are we late?"

"A few minutes, no more."

Sánchez could think of nothing to say, nothing to do. He leaned back in the seat, exhausted. He had argued until his throat ached, but Alessandro shook his head. There was no turning back. They must meet with Ramos, come to a quick agreement and allow Ramos to lead the miners against the trenches at Casanueva. Alessandro was certain, now, that Zamal and his machine gunners had been sent out to protect the mines against sabotage. The railroad tracks would be clear to Casanueva. All Ramos had to do was get the miners on board the cars. The locomotives could run through whatever barricades Gómez had ordered out to block the tracks. With luck the trains might smash through far enough so that the miners could attack the trenches from the rear, from inside the town limits of Casanueva, instead of across the open fields.

He was so sure, so certain. Sánchez closed his eyes and groaned. He had no mercy, Alessandro. He never stopped, never gave up. There was never time to relax, laugh, eat or drink or sleep. He was not fair to those who worked with him, who tried to give themselves completely to the Movement. Sánchez felt the map he held on his lap slide loose. Alessandro folded it, turned it and bent forward, muttering softly to himself.

The driver shouted and slammed on the brakes. The car skidded, turned sideways and plunged down the slope, the tires fubbling and dust pouring through the windows. For an instant the sedan balanced on two wheels, then slammed down, slued the other way, flinging him into Alessandro, then splintered through a barricade surrounded by burned, bearded men shouting and waving rifles. Sánchez dragged Alessandro down off the seat as the bullets smashed through the windshield, spraying glass and thucking into the seat. The driver made a cawing noise, like a bird.

Sánchez lay stunned, his face pushed into the dusty plush of the floor mat. Something hot and wet trickled down his neck. He pawed at himself and stared at his bloody fingers. The door opened and someone beat him on the shoulders. Sánchez snarled and punched with his free hand. Alessandro said something in a quiet, even voice.

There was silence, then a babble of voices. Sánchez crawled out of the car, shaken and furious. How he hated the voices, all shouting at once, a whole gang of militiamen, fawning on Alessandro, cheering and touching him, embracing each other, nuzzling their hairy faces together like animals. Sánchez walked away from the sedan, his legs trembling. His belly felt cold. He stared at the militiamen, hating them. He longed for a machine gun so he could rip them into pieces, then pack the guts and bones into the command car and drive it off a cliff.

The sedan stood in a wrecked mass of dead trees, stones, and gasoline drums filled with sand and broken wire. Beyond the barricade some fifty meters was the bridge, a stumpy prong that ended in space. Sánchez crossed himself. On the other side was a truck, some men in uniform and the far fragments of the span. He stared at it dumbly. When the leader of the mountain militia came up to him with Alessandro, Sánchez took his hand without looking at him. He was staring at the other men, tenderly lifting the dead driver out from behind the wheel, sweeping the shattered glass off the seat with their caps. They took the driver to a pile of sand beside the road and dropped him there, face down. Sánchez put his head down between his knees and breathed slowly. He sat up and accepted a cigarette. Alessandro was squatting behind the barricade with the leader of the militia.

"When did they blow it?"

"This morning. There was no way to get word. We had horses, but we ate them."

"No importa. Have they fired on you?"

"No, Alessandro. They came with the truck and sent men down under the bridge. We went over with a white flag, as were our orders."

"Yes. Go on."

"They are foreigners. They do not speak our tongue."

"Yes, they can. They are guards from the mine."

"Yes, I know it now. But I could not understand them."

"Brother, why didn't you shoot at them?"

"I had no orders to shoot at foreigners who do not speak our tongue. Soldiers, *sí.* The Guards, *sí.* But foreigners . . ."

"They had weapons."

"But they did not shoot at us."

"But you could see what they were doing! Stringing the wires!"

"Alessandro, forgive me, I beg of you. I am an ignorant man. I thought they were making a telephone."

"A telephone?"

"Only once have I seen a telephone and heard it march. In Casanueva on the last fiesta of Santa Rosa. I do not know how such a thing is made. But it is a foreign thing, the telephone, no? I thought they were making one here."

"And when they blew it up?"

"Too late, Alessandro. We fired at them then, but they took the truck back up there where you see it."

Alessandro glanced over the top of the barricade out across the dry valley.

"Carlos? Where are the binoculars?"

"In the back. I'll get them."

Sánchez stood up uncertainly and walked slowly to the sedan. He leaned into the rear, fumbling on the floor. The driver's seat was torn, and the blood had begun to thicken on the dusty floor carpeting. He carried the field glasses to the barricade and squatted next to the militia leader.

"Why is it that you shoot at us and not at the mine guards, idiot? What if you had killed one of us, eh?"

The man wet his lips and shook his head, muttering. Sánchez touched the pistol slung on his hip. The leader of the militia drew back, baring his teeth. He spread his hands, palms up, and shrugged. Sánchez drew his pistol free and cocked the hammer.

"I think you need a lesson, *hombre*. You don't know what to shoot at. Maybe you'll wait until we turn our backs and then start shooting again, eh? Maybe you are not with the Movement at all! Let's see."

Alessandro reached out his left hand, almost absently, and pushed the pistol muzzle down toward the ground.

"Leave him alone, Carlos. He made a mistake."

"A mistake? He made two mistakes. Three mistakes! There was no one back on the road to warn the barricade. If we had been soldiers or the Guards, these men would have been wiped out. Can a man who doesn't know the difference between a telephone and a detonator be allowed to—"

"I said let him alone. That's enough, Carlos. There are miners over there. When did they arrive? Before the others blew up the bridge?"

"No, Alessandro, later."

"Was there shooting?"

"No. The miners have no guns."

"Is Ramos with them?"

"No."

"And no fighting. That's curious. The guards didn't try to drive them away, and the miners didn't try to get the guns from the guards."

The leader shrugged again, watching Sánchez. He cleared his throat.

"Well, maybe they don't have orders, either. What are simple men to do without orders?"

"Shoot the wrong people, that's what they do."

"Carlos. Listen, man, even the simplest of men doesn't need to be ordered to fight for his freedom. Does a bird have to be ordered to escape from his cage?"

"Well . . ."

"The bird doesn't take anything, *amigo*. He restores what is his by right of birth. He struggles to be free and then he is free. No one has to *tell* him. What have telephones to do with freedom, eh? But the bridge, that's another story. You were sent up here to guard the bridge. But you didn't. The bridge is gone and now freedom will be more difficult to restore to the miners, to you and to me, to us all, the whole country. Do you understand what you have done?"

"Yes . . . Alessandro. Forgive me."

"I forgive *you*. But I do not forgive the mistake."

The man sighed. Sánchez put his pistol away, reluctantly, and squatted, sucking on his cigarette. Alessandro watched through the binoculars, then grunted.

"What is it?"

"He's over there. The one-armed one. With four or five of his men. Between the bridge and the guards. There seem to be plenty of miners. But they're scattered. In case of shooting. *Muy bien.* Now listen. I'm going to talk with the one-armed one. Have your men cover me. If the guards shoot at me, shoot back. If they shoot at the one-armed one or any of the miners, shoot back. I know they're out of range now. But they'll have to come forward. They can't see the one-armed one from where they are. Don't shoot at the truck. We want the truck if we can get it. How many guards are there? I count eight, plus the driver of the truck."

"There is one more. Ten in all."

"Can your men shoot?"

The militia leader jerked his head at the body lying face down in the sand beside the road.

"*Jovencito . . .*"

"Shoot well!"

Alessandro rose and swung easily over the barricade. He ran down the road and out onto the broken span of the bridge, his hands stretched high in the air. The militia leader whistled, and his men ran to the line of broken boxes, oil drums and wire. He gave an order, and rifle bolts clicked. The men knelt or sat, aiming across the valley. Sánchez drew his revolver and pointed it at the militia leader.

"If one bullet touches him, you're dead, patriot. *Comprendes?*"

The man shrugged and nodded.

"*Claro . . .*"

Sánchez looked over the wire. Alessandro stood out on the broken prong of the bridge, very close to the edge. When he moved his feet, bits of dirt and wood broke away and spilled into the air and were carried off by the cool wind. The breeze died down. Sánchez picked up the binoculars. The Indians had seen him and were coming down, sliding and scrambling from one clump of stunted pines to the next, heading for their side of the broken bridge. The men in khaki uniforms standing near the truck had not noticed. Now one of them turned and pointed. The men climbed quickly into the truck. Sánchez threw the safety catch off his pistol.

"Here they come."

"I see them."

"Look well. They may be the last thing you'll see."

Alessandro seemed to lean against the cool, driving air that poured down the valley. He spread his arms, his fingers. His loose shirt fluttered. He arched his back, watching the men moving down the far slope of the valley. The truck started up and moved down the road. The wind sucked at his words. He arched and flung each syllable across the broken span, leaning forward, his arms wide for balance, the dirt flaking off beneath his feet and streaming down the wind. He clenched his right fist and slashed his arm down through the air.

"*Xal-tal-pa!*"

The name rang off the dry rocks, echoed and faded. The leader of the militia grunted and smiled thinly. Sánchez nudged him with the pistol.

490

"You remember, eh?"

"The name? The machete that took off heads in the old days? I remember. I fought up here back then, too. I remember Manón Xaltalpa with his knife. He looked like a tree that has been burned. Thin and that black. I remember Alessandro's father Felipe, and Felipe's woman."

He patted the pistol with one dirty finger and glared at Sánchez.

"And I remember your father, too. *El Feo*. The three men and one woman. We didn't see much of you kids, though."

His lips parted in a thin smile, and he touched the pistol again. Sánchez jerked back, his finger on the trigger. The militia leader spat against the oil drum.

"But I know you, Sánchez. It doesn't make any difference to me if you've got a pistol or not. It was your father who needed a pistol, no? Just once. Just for a minute. A few seconds, even, eh?"

He laughed and pushed his rifle up on top of the oil drum, crouched and sighted down the barrel. Alessandro called again. He clenched his fist, raised it high and swept it through the cool wind that tore at him. The broken prong of the bridge sagged and swayed.

"Xal-tal-pa! Xal-tal-pa!"

His cry echoed, and then the shouts came from across the valley, faint at first and jumbled, then slowing, growing stronger, swelling into a guttural chant.

"Martín! Martín! Martín! Martín!"

Alessandro turned and waved at the men at the barricade. His teeth flashed in a smile, and the wind whipped his lank hair across his brow. The bridge cracked and groaned. The Indians swarmed down the far rocky slope, plunging recklessly toward the bridge. Alessandro flung his arms wide.

"Hear me, brothers! Rise and come to us! We are dying in the city in the fight to win freedom! Come to us! Fight with us, shoulder to shoulder! Leave the mines! Break out and climb on the iron cars! To Casanueva! To Casanueva! I will send our fighters to be with you there! Take the trenches, seize the rifles and grenades. Come with the iron cars as close to the city as you can! Then join us! We fight with guns, with bombs, with knives and with our teeth and bare hands! Before it is too late! Rise once again! For the name of Xaltalpa!"

The truck stopped a hundred yards from the bridge. Sánchez watched through the glasses. He could see the faces clearly, light-skinned, some with blue eyes, some with brown. The American and German guards, employed to protect the mines and to ride with the shipments of silver into the city. They scattered across the road and began shooting. The first bullets bit into the dirt near Alessandro's feet. He did not move. The men behind the barricade muttered and shifted. The leader lifted his head and glanced down the ragged line.

"Shut up! Shut your mouths and wait until I say begin shooting."

The miners milled uncertainly, scattering in small groups and dashing away from the broken bridge. Alessandro's voice sang off the stones as he arched and flung his torso forward, driving his words through the wind at them.

"Don't run and leave us, brothers! We have come to help set you free. Together we will fight to make all of Costa Plata free! They shoot at me, the foreigners! See!"

The bullets kicked dust around him. One spout snapped up between his heels, spraying his crotch with dirt. A fragment of the wooden guard rail buzzed off, falling down into the dry valley below. Sánchez watched the truck grind slowly down the hill. The guards crouched and ran beside it. He nudged the leader.

"Here they come. Now, man, start shooting!"

The militia leader shrugged contemptuously. Sánchez saw a heavily built Indian burst from a clump of weeds and cactus. He climbed on a boulder and raised his right fist. His left sleeve was empty, cut off below the elbow.

"There he is!"

"Martín! Martín! Martín! We hear you!"

"Where is Ramos, man?"

"In the mines."

"Will you rise? For the love of God and Costa Plata! For the memory of Manón Xaltalpa, rise and strike with us now! The time is short!"

Sánchez watched two of the guards kneel and work their rifle bolts. They were turned toward a small cluster of miners scrambling for the shelter of a dry creek bed. Their chests jerked back when their rifles kicked. They loaded and aimed at Alessandro.

"Ramos refuses! He hears voices that say to him to lead the people north, away from the fighting!"

Bullets spanged off the boulder, and the one-armed man slipped down off it, into the shelter of the lumpy mass.

"Brothers, do you not hear my voice? And the voice of my dead father? And the cry of victory from the throat of Manón Xaltalpa? Do you hear the voices of all your fathers who fought for freedom once before?"

The scattered miners slowed and hesitated. Their one-armed leader shook his fist.

"We hear and listen, Alessandro!"

"Then, rise! Rise and join us. Pay no attention to Ramos. He hears voices because he is mad! Those who listen to him are mad! Listen to the voices of the dead calling for you to be men!"

The miners began to cheer, a thin, wind-shredded sound. The guards bunched together and rushed for the boulder, shooting from the hip, without aiming. One of the miners spun around and fell in the road. The militia leader pounded on the oil drum.

"Now, *chicos,* give it to them!"

The volley cracked, the bolts snicked, throwing the spent brass cases, and snicked, driving fresh cartridges into the chambers. Three of the guards were down. The second volley was ragged, like someone breaking sticks for a fire. The one-armed miner whirled and bellowed, a machete shining in his fist. The miners seized up stones and pieces of wood, snatched knives out from under their shirts and hefted short, sharp picks. They swarmed up the face of the rocky cliff. Five of the guards lay in the road, two more dragged toward the rutted ditch; the others fired blindly and ran for the truck. The militia leader touched Sánchez.

"Put that thing away. Look and tell us how it goes. Hey, Paco, don't shoot!"

Sánchez pressed the binoculars against his face. The plastic cylinders ringed his eyes and made them water. He blinked.

"They're finishing them off. Got the guns now. One of them in the ditch is still fighting, swinging his rifle. Uh. Three on top of him. They're climbing over the truck. One-arm is there. The door of the cab is open. They've got him out."

Sánchez lowered the glasses. His face was pale. The image of the flashing machete glittered behind his watering eyes. He coughed and stood up.

"It's over."

The militiamen jumped up and fired off another ragged volley and cheered. The miners across the valley swung their new weapons and shouted back. The militia leader took the pistol from Sánchez's hand and thrust it into the holster.

"A thing like that's no good at that range, *hombre*. Better take the hammer off cock, eh?"

Sánchez nodded, looking at Alessandro. He stood, leaning against the cool river of air that rushed down the valley. The wind frilled and tugged the sleeves of his shirt. His left shoulder was stained. He raised his right arm in salute.

"*Bravo, hermanos, bravo!* Now you have your new Xaltalpa! Now rise and strike with us! *Por la patria y la libertad! Viva Xaltalpa! Abajo Vizarra! Arriba Costa Plata!*"

"We are coming, Alessandro! We rise at last to fight! *Libertad o muerte! Arriba el Movimiento Liberal! Arriba Costa Plata!*"

Alessandro waved farewell. The miners swarmed into the truck, fired their new rifles in the air and cheered again. Alessandro walked up the rubble-strewn road to the barricade. His face was pale and set; his mouth curled down at the left corner. He waited until the militiamen cleared a path through the wire. Sánchez saw that his eyes were glassy with pain. He shouldered through the militiamen. Alessandro glanced at him and shook his head warningly.

"*Nada,* Carlitos, it's nothing. . . . Now, *chicos,* you did well! The Movement is proud of you. I am proud of you. Your brothers across the valley owe their lives to your good shooting. But there is not much left here to shoot at, eh?"

He pointed across the valley. A low cloud of dust drifted on the wind, concealing, then exposing, the bodies sprawled in the road. Sánchez stared at the stain seeping through the left sleeve of Alessandro's shirt and the tunic he had tugged on to hide it. The leader of the militia grinned and helped Alessandro thrust his right arm into the other sleeve and draw the tunic on over his shoulders. The sweat stood out on Alessandro's face. The militiamen laughed and slapped each other on the back. Alessandro looked at them.

"Since there is nothing left here, comrades, you had better go hunting. Strike right across the mountains for Casanueva. General Gómez has some of his soldiers in the trenches there. You will meet more comrades. Tell them what you saw and did today. Tell them to leave the mountains and move on Casanueva. When the trains from the mines reach there, attack! Attack! Never mind about prisoners. We can't feed them and can't spare the men to guard them. Just collect weapons. Now hear me. You must understand. Collect the rifles, pistols, whatever they've got. If you run into machine guns, attack by the flank. Don't throw grenades. We want those guns, understand? By the flank, then, crawling on your stomachs. And don't be pigs. Give the guns to the miners. Distribute them at the station and get on the trains. Go on the trains as far as you can, and when you get off, start shooting. I would lead you, but . . . I must return to the city . . . and—Carlos—"

Sánchez thrust out his hand and seized Alessandro's cold fingers, then gripped his good shoulder, bracing him.

"Hell, that's clear enough for these boys, Alessandro! They know what to do. Fight, that's what! And they'll do it! Over the mountains to Casanueva, fight and win, join with the miners and drive right on for the city. I will be in full command of the western sectors of the city. You men know me. Carlos Sánchez. Our leader will command the central assault on the palace. When the sun goes down, the real fighters of Costa Plata will show Vizarra and his pimps who's got balls, eh, *chicos?* So don't waste time. March to Casanueva. Another force will advance from the sanatorium. With the miners to help you, you'll squash the soldiers of Gómez like so many balls of dung. *Viva Alessandro! Arriba Costa Plata!"*

The men pressed and jostled, shouting and singing. Alessandro stiffened and forced a smile, his teeth grinding. Sánchez put him in the front seat and laid the binoculars in his lap, then ordered two riflemen into the rear seat, ignoring the bellowed protests of the leader. The men heaved the sedan away from the barricade. Sánchez crossed himself furtively and stamped on the starter. The engine whirred and caught, belching exhaust fumes. Alessandro raised himself and saluted. Sánchez saluted and let in the clutch. The command car rumbled up the hill, back toward the city. Sánchez slammed the window sealing off the driver from the rear seat, then turned to Alessandro.

"In the shoulder, *jovencito?"*

"Yes. Right in the meat. Right through, but maybe the shoulder bones are broken."

"You need a doctor, right away."

"Drive fast, Carlos. There's a member of the Movement at a *finca* not too far away. Maybe ten kilometers, southeast. A cattle boss. He went to medical school at the university before they threw him out.

495

Maybe we can find him. This tunic is so tight . . . it helps to stop the bleeding."

Sánchez lifted his rump, wrenched and squirmed, fighting to hold the heavy sedan on the road with one hand, while he pulled his belt free. He braked to a stop and opened the window.

"Keep your eyes open, back there. I think I saw something. I've got to check the radio here."

The two militiamen nodded and thrust their rifles out the rear windows. Sánchez punched holes in his belt with the tip of a pocket knife and bent over Alessandro.

"I'm going to put this around your arm. It may not do too much good, but we've got to do something. Tight, like this. Hurts, eh?"

"Some, Carlos, not bad."

"So. Every five minutes or less, loosen it. Can you do it with one hand? Like that. Good. Now, slide your hand into the tunic, between the buttons. That's it . . . *mierda,* he's out . . ."

Sánchez slipped Alessandro's belt off and fastened it around the wounded man's neck, a crude sling. His own belt he cinched tight and held the loose end in his hand. It was clumsy, but he could steer and free and tighten the tourniquet at the same time. He tapped on the window, grinned and let in the clutch.

Sánchez drove slowly, but the sedan jolted and bounced. Alessandro's lids fluttered with pain. Sánchez dragged on the loose belt end, counted to three hundred, and released it. Alessandro muttered and struggled, trying to throw off the belt sling. Sánchez took the first cattle path that seemed to him to run approximately southeast. The two militiamen drank a *bota* of brandy and then fell asleep, wrapped in each other's arms. The sedan rushed down a rutted track out onto the floor of a valley. The grass had been burned black and the scorched pasture was dotted with the bloated bodies of cattle. In the distance Sánchez saw a low building, the *finca,* or at least a farmhouse of some sort. The valley was smooth and the air smelled of ashes. He drove swiftly, straight for the building. When the sedan was still two kilometers from the *finca,* the motor sputtered, roared fitfully, stuttered and stopped. Sánchez threw out the clutch, and the command car coasted smoothly on, slower and slower, then stopped, steaming, near a fire-bitten clump of olive trees. Alessandro sat up, winced and looked at Sánchez.

"What's the matter? Why are we stopping?"

Sánchez shrugged and smiled bitterly.

"We're . . . we're out of gasoline, Alessandro."

"Ah, madre mía . . ."

"And this place has been hit, too. Probably by our people, but still. Maybe they're around. The two in back can help me look. We'll get some horses, maybe. Can you ride, do you think?"

"I can ride. To get back to the city by five o'clock, I'll ride a pig, a goat, a barn rat, anything . . ."

"Bien. I'll leave one of these heroes with you and take the other. Eh, tsst! You!"

"Diga?"

"We're going for a walk. Come on."

Alessandro watched the two men leave, Sánchez in front, holding his pistol. The wound in his shoulder had stiffened to a steady pang that dizzied him. Even the effort to turn on the radio was too much. The militiaman in the rear seat was nervous, convinced they had been betrayed, abandoned. The pain stunned Alessandro into a kind of stupor. He shook his head when the man babbled, but the effort blurred his vision and made his head ring. The militiaman shouted, and Alessandro opened his eyes. Sánchez was riding toward the sedan, leading a lean, saddle-galled mare with one cropped ear. Sánchez was mounted on a fat, dappled burro.

17

"ANITA?"

There was no answer. It was very quiet in the dressing room. The entire building was quiet. Footsteps sounded in the corridor, then stopped.

"Anita, is that you?"

The footsteps went away. Lucía muttered and reached for a package of cigarettes. There were no matches in the top drawer of the table, and her lighter sparked but would not catch. She dropped the lighter in the drawer and flung the cigarette on the floor. She walked to the sofa and sat down, got up and walked back to the dresser. She found the bottle of pills and shook two into her hand, hesitated and put one back in the bottle. The glass on the sink was empty. She turned on the cold water. The faucet gasped out a thin trickle of rusty mud. The hot water didn't work either. She put the pill on her tongue and tried to swallow. It felt as big as a peach stone. She gagged softly and spat the pill into the wastebasket, crossed the room and sat down on the sofa. She stood up and walked to the door, unlocked it and opened it a few centimeters.

"Anita?"

Her voice echoed down the long corridor. She stood for a moment, one hand holding the top of her dressing gown closed at her throat. At the end of the long corridor were three studios. Usually they were busy, the doors shut and guarded, the red bulbs burning. Now the three doors stood open. The corridor was usually filled with pages, worried-looking writers making final changes in some script before the program went on, studio musicians lounging and smoking between shows. Now no one moved. The cold air felt damp, dead. She slammed the door and listened to the echo batter away and fade to silence.

Her purse was on one arm of the sofa. She opened it and took out the two envelopes. One contained a neat stack of reales, Anita's salary for two months, the other a letter of recommendation stating that for five years, seven months and three weeks Anita Bosoño had been an exemplary personal maid, honest, sober, reliable and skilled at hairdressing and minor clothing repairs and alterations. She stared at the envelopes and replaced them in her purse.

The hanger swung back and forth on the hook high on the door. Lucía looked at her wristwatch. Anita had taken the blue silk dress away more than three-quarters of an hour ago, to sponge and press the rear panels and to mend the hem in one place. Nearly four o'clock. Perhaps she was chatting with one of the old women in the wardrobe section.

Lucía looked at the folding table. The remains of her lunch lay scattered on the plates, a half-eaten cutlet, some salad, flabby now, floating in a puddle of oil, a few crusts of bread and an empty cup of coffee. She opened her purse again and looked for matches, but found only a lipstick, a comb, a handkerchief, a small vial of perfume and the small brown manila packet containing her passport, a letter of credit drawn on a Swiss bank and two safe-deposit-box keys. Malata had handed the packet to her as he helped her into the sedan. Anita had been with her then. Where was she now?

Four o'clock. The Gabriela show, a program of fashions, society notes, soft piano background music and a guest. The woman was popular, although she had no talent whatever, except for talking. The young shopgirls had taken to imitating Gabriela's breathless little laugh. Even Anita did it, and it was annoying.

She turned on the radio. The rehearsal wasn't until five o'clock anyway. Something to kill the time.

She sat on the edge of the sofa, swinging one leg, her fingers twisted together in her lap. She separated her hands, looked at her nails, grimaced and found an emery board on the dresser. She tapped the radio with her hand. The set was old and took a few minutes to warm up. Absurd that she should have to put up with such a thing in her own private dressing room on the third floor of the Radio Costa Plata building itself. She would mention it to the general manager as soon as Anita came back. She would dress and go directly to his office. Perhaps he might offer her a drink in the executive's lounge. If not, she would demand to be taken there.

The radio set sputted twice.

"Alessandro! Alessandro! Christ, have pity on us, man! Make them stop! I don't want to die . . . I don't want to die!"

The volley smashed once, then again, the machine guns firing at once, the racket pouring out of the radio speaker in a sustained roar. She dropped the emery board and listened. The radio set crackled. A man's voice came on, bored and husky.

"Four hundred. Four hundred. Are you listening, Alessandro? Are you listening, Carlos Sánchez? Can you hear them scream? You can stop this now, at any moment. Pick up the nearest telephone. The central lines are being kept open to Security Police headquarters. Are you listening to them, Alessandro? Carlos Sánchez, your father still lives. How much longer will he live? Only you can save him. Only you can stop this. In one hour another hundred people will be dead. One hundred men and women and children, traitors to their country, their faith, their fellow citizens. Only you can stop it. Only you . . ."

She snapped off the radio and held her hands to her face. She felt nothing, not horror, not loathing. At first she had not believed it. The broadcasts were some sort of cruel joke, a political trick to fool the revolutionaries. But since the three o'clock broadcast, when the rebels shells fell on the quais and blew up an oil storage tank, and the announcer had snatched the microphone from old Sánchez and had screamed for someone to shoot back—it was no joke. It was happening. Where were they broadcasting from now, the *plaza de toros*, where Anita said the chauffeur had told her the hostages were being kept? It was terrible, terrible. Unbelievable. And the radio. You couldn't leave it alone. At the end of the three o'clock broadcast she had promised herself not to listen any more. But at four? The rehearsal for her own program wouldn't begin exactly at five. No. A few minutes after. Her accompanist, the director and the engineers would all be listening to the radio. And she would listen, too. That was what was terrible. You could listen to it, you *had* to listen to it, but you felt nothing. Not sorry, not even glad it was somebody else dragged shrieking out to stand in front of the guns instead of you. It was easier to imagine yourself crouching down, feet braced against the tripod legs, staring through the sights at the faces, deaf to their cries, waiting for the command and then slowly, deliberately, pressing the hard steel tongue of the trigger.

She stood up and shivered. What things to think! Was it because everything was over? Because tonight, after the broadcast, the car was to return, to take her to the airport where the plane waited to fly her to Mexico City? Never to come back. Never. Never to be alive. The others stood wailing before the machine-gun snouts. She would sing before a microphone.

She rushed to the door and tore it open. She leaned out into the hall, her hair swinging over her face, the cords in her neck standing out as she screamed.

"Anita! Anita!"

⸸

Fingel's head ached as though his derby had shrunk and clamped his skull in a circle of steel. He leaned against the stained and sticky bar, his legs shaking. The owner of the *taberna* shrugged.

"I tell you no one is here. Look, look around. I am of the Movement. Why should I lie? I believe you, man. But no one is here. Not Ramos. Not Alessandro."

"But I have a message to deliver."

The owner raised a dirty, wine-tinged hand. His hand trembled.

"No messages. No one wants to hear them. No one wants to hear."

"But do you know where they are?"

"No."

"Was Ramos here?"

"No."

"Was anybody here?"

"Yes. The one with one arm."

"One arm."

"*Sí, sí.* Like this. See? Only one arm. The one that goes from the hospital to the mines. Three times he has passed and stopped here. Today. Perhaps two hours before the radio—"

"Two hours ago?"

"Nearly three now. Before him the others, foreigners in uniforms."

"Guards from the mines?"

"*Extranjeros.* In uniforms. Then he with one arm."

"But where did they go?"

"Comrade, who knows? They come, they go. I am a patriot. But this is a tavern, not an information office."

Fingel groaned. His eyes felt filled with sand, his tongue thick and sour. He shrugged.

"I will wait for them. Or until we have news. Someone will come, eh?"

"*Quién sabe?* Who knows?"

"What time is it?"

The owner sloshed a glass in a pail of gray water. He shook his head.

"But what is the hour?"

"Nearly two o'clock, may God rip off their balls . . . ."

Fingel placed his briefcase on the bar and leaned on it. He tried to smile.

"I came in a car from the city."

"The ones in uniforms came in a truck."

"Ah? Well, we got lost in the hills."

The owner looked at Fingel and shook his head.

"Comrade, we are all lost now. In the hills, in the city, everywhere. *Siempre perdidos, siempre jodidos.*"

Fingel clucked his tongue, caught himself and frowned, worried and puzzled. The owner rubbed the glass on his apron and gnawed a toothpick. Fingel's stomach gurgled.

"Can . . . can one eat here?"

"People eat here. Drink wine here. Beer."

"Mineral water?"

"No mineral water."

"*Gaseosa?*"

"*Sí.*"

502

The owner chewed his toothpick and set the glass behind the bar on a low splintered shelf near the radio. He hesitated, then moved the glass to the other end of the shelf, passing before Fingel without looking at him. Fingel was afraid the man would leave him alone. He snatched his briefcase off the bar and trotted after the owner.

"*Por favor, una gaseosa.*"

"*Muy bien . . .*"

Fingel smiled faintly and leaned against the bar. The owner opened a bottle, brought the glass and poured the drink into it. Fingel looked at the glass and coughed once. The drink was tepid, the taste of lemon metallic. He swallowed most of it and smacked his lips. Two men, their sheepskin coats slung around their shoulders, watched him. They drank red wine in small wooden cups. Fingel glanced at them quickly and turned back to the bar. He sipped the *gaseosa,* making it last. He leaned forward and jerked his head at the two men.

"Are they patriots, those two?"

"They look at sheep all day long. Who knows what they are?"

"I . . . I'm hungry. Have you soup?"

"Bean soup."

"Meat?"

"Lamb chops."

"Is it clean? Good meat?"

"You are not in the city now, comrade. It's meat, that's all."

"Oh, good. I mean, that's fine. Some meat, then."

"Fried potatoes. A small lettuce. Goat cheese. Apricots."

"Potatoes and apricots."

"No cheese?"

"*No, gracias.*"

"*Tinto* or *blanco?*"

"No wine. No wine."

The owner shrugged and walked out through the door that led to the kitchen. He shouted at someone. Fingel carried his glass and the briefcase to the table nearest the bar, dusted the stool with his handkerchief and sat down. His stomach roiled. He gazed enviously at the little dish of olives on the table before the two men. They ate olives, grinding the pits and sucking noisily, then spat the stones on the floor. Fingel cautiously opened his briefcase and looked inside. He still couldn't believe it. He drew out the copies and stared at

General Vola's scrawled name. His own handwriting straggled below the line. He shook his head. His fingers touched the greasy bills Vola had given him. He stroked them gently, watching the two men out of the corner of his eye. They might be bandits. In the mountains, you never knew. What a commission! What would they say, though? A salesman as beneficiary? Had it happened before? No doubt there were many such happy meetings between clients and salesmen, between clients who appreciated the prompt service, the waived medical examination. And they were comrades, brothers and friends, as the general had said. Fingel closed the briefcase and drew the straps firm, fussing with the buckles. He sipped his drink. His stomach gurgled.

The owner brought the soup in a wooden bowl and set down a tin spoon.

"No wine?"

"No, *gracias.*"

The two men muttered to themselves. The owner turned to leave. Fingel wondered what time it was. He suddenly felt lonely, abandoned in a dirty tavern with bandits and lukewarm soup and a tin spoon.

"*Patrón,* turn on the radio. I would like to hear some music. Some nice dance music."

The owner turned slowly, his mouth open. His face flushed slowly.

"You make a joke? A city joke?"

"A joke? No. Some dance music."

"Dance music? You want to hear how they dance in the city?"

The owner seemed to be talking over Fingel's shoulder to the two shepherds. One of the men stood and slouched out through the open door of the *taberna.* Fingel clutched the spoon and drew his briefcase closer. The owner shook his fist.

"No, señor! The radio doesn't march. It is broken."

Fingel tried to smile. The man was angry because he had refused to buy wine. Why not? A small glass, even two glasses, perhaps. It might settle his stomach. A little wine was said to be good for you. Fingel shrugged.

"But the radio was marching when I came in here . . ."

The owner spat on the floor. The shepherd came back into the tavern and walked quickly up to the bar. He spoke a few words in the mountain dialect. The two men stared at each other. The owner lurched in the direction of the doorway, then caught himself. Fingel cleared his throat.

"I would like some wine. *Tinto* . . . with the meat."

The owner set his fists on his hips and gnawed his lip. He nodded once, as though making up his mind. The shepherd backed away from the bar.

"First he wants to hear dance music from the city, this one. Now he wants red wine with his meat."

Fingel sensed that he was being accused. The low, rank-smelling room was thick with his guilt. The second shepherd stood up, turning over his wine cup with one clumsy hand. He propped himself on the table, both clenched fists with knuckles down on the scarred boards. He breathed slowly, loudly, his eyes fixed on Fingel. The owner walked stiffly the length of the bar, raised the flap and reached out to a row of bottles. He snatched one up by the neck. Fingel gagged.

"And now he wants to drink *tinto,* this one!"

The owner walked over to the radio set, still holding the bottle by the neck. Fingel glanced quickly at the open door. He could make it outside before the shepherd would be able to reach him. The owner lifted the bottle and smashed it down four times, pausing between each shattering blow. Fingel blinked at the ruined set, a jumble of broken tubes, twisted wire and bits of wood. Wine streamed onto the floor. The owner turned and leaned across the bar. He held the jagged neck of the bottle out toward Fingel. His eyes glittered. He nodded, once.

"The radio is broken, señor, you see? It doesn't march."

The shepherd did not move. Fingel hugged his briefcase and ran for the door. The shepherd closed his eyes as Fingel burst past him.

The air was clear and cool. Fingel ran heavily, blindly, down the path toward the car where the driver waited for him. He stumbled on rock and roots. Pain stitched in his side. He looked back at the tavern and fell. He lay in the path, winded and stunned. His briefcase had burst, and the mountain wind scattered his papers. He groaned and fingered his shoulder, then his head. He had lost his derby. He crawled from side to side, shivering and glancing over his shoulder. The tavern was silent. The wind rattled his papers. He found his derby and carefully prodded the dent out of the crown. He set it on his head and gingerly wiped his face and eyes.

They were standing twenty paces away. He counted them. Twelve men. And the first shepherd. All but the shepherd held rifles. They were dark, windburned men with tough, dirty beards and earth-colored clothes. They did not move, did not seem to breathe. Ground mist swirled around their boots and leggings, hiding them, until the figures loomed legless, floating in the cold clouds. The mountain wind sucked the papers from Fingel's numb fingers, scattering the evidence introduced in his behalf. He dropped his head at the instant the shepherd extended his arm, pointing. Fingel waited. It was no good. They had come to judge him and now to take it away from him, his life.

The volley crashed and echoed off the wind-worn rocks. The militiamen carefully gathered up the papers and the briefcase and took them along as they crossed the shrouded scarps, marching to Casanueva.

☨

The mine shaft ran nearly level from the elevators to the end of the worked-out vein of ore and there rose, supported by timber balks, to form a large hall a half mile beneath the surface of the earth. The floor was a nubbled plane of broken stone, trenched where the ties for the pushcart railway had rotted out. The hall was dark and warm. Before the pick-cut face of the abandoned vein a boulder bulked, too massive to be broken and carted to the surface. A large iron box rested on a jut of the boulder, shoulder high. The hall damped the sound of low voices; the soft crush of sandals shifted on the floor. Five hundred men, small and brown, the drillers, shovelers, gang foremen, ore breakers, sluicemen and mule drivers, squatted staring at the huge stone. The lamps fixed to their helmets played over the face of the vein and the boulder and on the face of Ramos.

He raised his arms and hooked his fingers, as though gathering the small, shifting beams, as though the hundreds of lights soaked through the flesh of his palms and seeped into his chest. The dark chips of his eyes glittered. His voice grated like dry rocks rubbed together.

"Little brothers, hear me. Hear *me*. Now you know what passes in the city. One hundred die every hour. And one hundred will die every hour until Alessandro gives himself to Vizarra. Only then will the killing stop."

A thick, blurred sound rose and sank away, blotted up by the darkness. Ramos touched his chest with the fingers of his right hand, tapping his heart.

"Alessandro is my servant. I am his master, and he labors with

506

death in the city out of love for me. But his servants have no love for him. They are men of the *campo,* children and city blacks. The worst of men. Men of no tribe, no blood. All they hear and understand is the tongue that speaks of silver. Their ears curl only to the ring of coins. Alessandro speaks to them, since it is my wish, of freedom. And they do not hear him. They hear only the chink of coins, for their hearts are purses and hold silver, not blood. This is bad, little brothers. Bad. But we must endure it. We can endure it, as we have lived through all manner of things together. I have told Alessandro to speak of freedom, but there is talk only of the silver to pay his greedy servants in their turn. It is bad, brothers, but it is so."

The miners began a low, sullen crooning. They swayed, squatting on their haunches, one man nudging the man beside him into motion. The beams of their helmet lamps slid from side to side, back and forth, the shafts of light crossing, touching and amplifying in an instant of focus, then breaking past, running across the face of the vein, hesitating and sliding back. Ramos, dazzled and half blinded, blinked and raised his palm for silence.

"Would you go to the city to die? No. Would you send your brothers to the city to die? No. Would you send your fathers and your sons? No. Would you follow any man there? No. But we must do something. Little brothers, what is to be done?"

Ramos dropped his hand and waited. His hand, hooked like a tool, swung limp against his thigh. The miners muttered together. No man rose from his squatting posture to speak. Their high-cheekboned faces turned again toward Ramos. Their dark eyes, a thousand dark eyes, stared at him.

The hall was hushed. The beams of light played on the boulder and the iron box. Ramos dropped his hand on the box, a single thud like the beat of a heart.

"Come then! Yesterday was the day of the papers and the giving of money to you. And for four days now you have not worked, but held together talking like monkeys. Still, I spoke with them and made them give you money for no work that you might live. You have your money. Your women have money. The men of all your crews and their wives have money. Now you are to bring the money and put it in this box. Everyone must bring all his coins and all his paper money. All of it. You see, my brothers? I put my money into the holy box of freedom."

Ramos extended his hand and dropped coins into the iron chest.

"There. I who was poor am now without all money. My hands are empty, and my pockets, too, but my heart is filled with gladness, for I know that I have done as a man must who wishes to be free. Come, now, little brothers, show me your faith."

The miners did not move. They sat still, packed shoulder to shoulder, hip to hip, the beams from the lamps fixed on their helmets playing on the boulder and the iron box. They began to croon again, but in a plaintive minor key, a little melodic lament that quivered and rose above them and faded, only to begin again. Ramos looked out at the crouched bodies facing him. Someone in the back, on the left side, was leading the singing, the old dirge for the dying, the wordless chant to charm evil spirits away. Ramos flexed his fingers. His voice darkened with menace. His eyes glittered as he searched the faces. But the lights beat against his eyes. He could not see.

"Have not my plans worked before? Who spoke with the whites and got more money for you? Who caused the new houses and the clinic to be built? Who aided the strong and caused the cowardly and the weak and the false among you to vanish? I, Ramos! I have served you, lived among you, spoken for you. Now I . . . Alessandro needs money. So come forward now, one by one, and put your coins in the holy box of freedom."

He tried to see into their faces. He stepped forward, and the front row shrank back, their helmets tipped low over their faces. The dirge rose and swelled, echoing in a guttural murmur. The miners pressed together, their hands clasping their upper arms in the posture of mourning and of war council. Sweat stung in Ramos's eyes. He turned and snatched the iron coffer from the stone lip and set his palm against the great boulder. His lips slid back, uncovering his teeth.

"Little brothers, I have spoken. But, my brothers, you have not listened. When that happens, I grow angry, because I feel the Dark One whisper in my head. You know what he says, my brothers. Yes, you know. The Dark One grows angry, and I feel his rage. Who among you does not remember the little brothers who have been called beneath the rock by the Dark One? Who has ever seen those brothers again? It was by the power given to me by the Dark One that the rock was moved, that the brothers went beneath the rock. They will not come back. They go to the Dark One. And now I feel that the

Dark One is angry. He . . . yes, he is calling to me, telling me to move away the rock!"

The miners shrank together. Some began to whistle in terror. Ramos whirled and rushed away from the boulder. His long hair snapped in wet strands across his face. His lips fixed in a strained grin. His voice grew choked, and his body thrashed, his arms flailing wildly. The lament sprang up again, louder, stronger, swelling to defiance.

"I feel his anger. The Dark One . . . that hangs in the pit . . . moves his wings! He wishes . . . to wheel . . . with slow flight . . . on wet wings over all your houses!"

Ramos stumbled slowly backward toward the boulder. Sweat streamed down his contorted face. His arms flailed and suddenly stiffened. The miners whistled and crooned. Their helmets clicked together and the lights swung and jerked. Ramos gripped his right wrist with his left hand and wrestled with himself. Slowly, one by one, his fingers slipped from his twisting wrist. His right hand was sucked against the stone, palm flat, his arm shivering. The miners shrieked once and fell silent. Ramos looked at them.

"The Dark One has moved my hand. And I have touched the stone. He has given to me the power to move the rock, the only power he himself does not have. Now the Dark One asks for the gift of blood. Of blood. Oh, what little brother has not loved me? Who among us has not feared the Dark One? He swells with rage and I can hear . . . just now . . . just hear his wet wings sliding, unfolding. And the rock begins to tremble!"

The great boulder shifted slightly, grinding and rocking. Ramos turned his face up to the ceiling and with his free hand tore at his face, raking his cheeks until the blood flowed. The miners lifted the dirge, howling now like animals. Ramos shrieked above them.

"I cannot hold the rock! I cannot keep the Dark One down! For the sake of your wives and children, let the little brother who loves me not, who fears not the Dark One, be put forward from among you! Now, before the Dark One slips out to fly, to fly, to fly over all your houses!"

In the back, on the left side, a man slowly rose. Ramos heard the soft crush of gravel beneath the miner's sandals. He strained to see. The helmet lights dazzled him. He ground his knuckles against his

509

smarting eyes. He saw the man, taller, broader in the chest and shoulders, the pale shirt and canvas trousers. The empty sleeve.

"So. So you have come back. Then come here to me."

The one brown arm, thick and sinewed, reached slowly up and the strong fingers picked daintily at the switch on his helmet light. The light went out. Ramos stood, his palm still against the boulder. His head snapped from side to side and his long hair lashed. A cry tore from his throat. Another arm lifted. A light went out. Then another. And another. A thin, transparent stream of saliva ran from the corner of Ramos's mouth. Small fingers twitched, and two, seven, a dozen, thirty helmet lights flicked out. The beams playing on the boulder vanished; the dazzle faded from Ramos's eyes and the humid darkness rushed in. The dirge for the dying swelled up again, stronger and stronger.

"The Dark One calls for blood! Give him to me! Give him to me!"

In the dank, vaulted chamber, the switches clicked and chitted and the long, bright streams of light vanished. The darkness flowed toward Ramos. He lunged forward, and before his face a section of men, legs bent, faces stiff, one arm raised, vanished, and there was only breathing blackness. He ran to the left, his hooked hands outstretched, roaring, and the lights rushed away from him, tittering. He spun and blackness blotted before his face. Beneath their feet as they rose, a slow, gathering, forceful shift, the crushed stones softly muttered. The crooning dirge for the dying washed against him, rising in the blackness, pressing for the boulder. Ramos screamed as the first small, hard hands touched him, plucking at his flesh.

The dirge sank and died away. The blackness breathed and waited. No foot stirred the crushed stone floor. The lid of the iron box clopped shut. A flint knife clinked and shattered against the boulder.

A helmet light snapped on. His one good arm was pasted with blood and dust to the elbow. He walked slowly away from the great stone, his face dazed, his dark eyes dull. The others shrank back, both palms raised, turned out to save him from evil spirits. He walked through the hall beneath the surface of the earth, and the stones grated beneath his steps and slow drops fell from his fingers. The lamps were snapped on, one by one. When he reached the elevators, he walked in a bobbing wash of yellow light and his shadow ran on long before him. He stepped into the cage and turned to face them. He balled his slippery fingers, raised his arm and drew in the dank, dark air of the cavern. His arm fell, striking the blow. It was the ancient, unforgotten sign. The cry barked from their throats.

"*Xal-tal-pa!*"

☩

The door opened smoothly, silently. Vizarra did not turn around. He sat in a straight wooden chair, one foot on the floor, the other propped on the piano stool. He wiggled his toes and winced.

"Yes? Is that you, Doctor?"

"I am sorry, Your Excellency. The doctor, for some reason, went to the palace. He has been sent on out here."

Vizarra grunted. He had been holding his boot on his lap. He knocked it to the floor. Malata bent and picked it up, his fingers brushing the supple leather.

"He is a fool, that Swiss."

"Excellency, I don't—"

"I say he is a fool. Send him to me at once. As soon as he arrives."

"Yes, Excellency."

Malata did not move away. Vizarra waited for a few seconds, then sighed.

"Well, what is it?"

"It can wait, Excellency. Perhaps it would be better. You should take something to eat."

"Eat? You idiot! Here I can't walk with the gout, and you tell me to eat! What is it? Out with it!"

"There are several messages, Excellency."

"So? Save the worst for the last. Begin."

"Zamal has established radio contact with staff headquarters. He has reached the mines and has taken over there."

"Good. Took him too long to get there. But the workers have left."

Malata blinked and set the boot down beside the piano stool. Vizarra scowled and pulled out his watch.

"How did you know, Excellency? Someone at Staff telephoned?"

"No one telephoned. I just know they left. On the trains that were captured, right?"

"Correct, Excellency. The troops at Casanueva have been notified and they will—"

"Be overrun. The miners outnumber them at least ten to one. Tell

511

Zamal to remain in command at the mines, put two trucks on the tracks, two gun crews in each truck. Send them down the tracks to Casanueva. That's the fastest way to get there. The trucks are to be driven between seventy and eighty kilometers per hour, or as fast as they will go. It will minimize the jarring from the railroad ties. The machine gunners will hit the miners from behind . . . with luck. Go on."

"The officials at the mines are deeply disturbed."

"Tell them to go to hell. Or back to America."

"There was a fight between some guards and a rebel band. Up in the mountains. Sometime this afternoon. Ten employees of the mining concession were killed."

"Not Costa Platans?"

"No, Excellency, most unfortunately not. Six Americans, two Germans and two Canadians . . . um, Danforth and Miller."

"Why do you mention their names?"

"The officials have sent telegrams, Excellency. To Washington, Berlin and Ottawa. And Switzerland."

"To Geneva?"

"To the League of Nations, Excellency."

Vizarra closed his eyes. The pain seemed to spread from his foot up his leg, into his belly and chest, finally to his brain. Each pang stitched across his skull, on the inside, whipping and weaving a cap beneath the bone. He rocked slowly, groaning. Malata stood watching him. The spasm passed. Vizarra opened his eyes.

"God damn them! God damn them!"

Malata nodded slowly and cleared his throat. Vizarra unclenched his fists and waved for Malata to continue.

"There was another foreigner involved in the incident somehow."

"Yes? Who, the King of England? President of United States Steel? Chairman of a Swiss chocolate company?"

"A Frenchman, it seems."

"*Madre mía,* now the French are in on it!"

"Three Costa Platans were also killed in this incident. The owner of the tavern and two shepherds. All members of the insurgent movement. They were executed as traitors."

"Good. Go on."

"That clinic . . . you remember, Excellency?"

"Of course I remember! What about it?"

512

"It was surrounded. Some street fighting. The place was taken."

"Have the patients removed to Our Lady of the Sorrows. Arrest the doctors and interns. Let the nurses go and all children under the age of twelve."

"This has been done, sir. But the head of the hospital was Manfred Herzler, the chief of engineers from the mines."

"What in the name of God was he doing there?"

"He insists that he operated the clinic at the specific request of His Grace."

"The archbishop? Huh! Well, was Herzler killed?"

"Slightly wounded. Resisting arrest. He has been hospitalized. O'Conner is checking his story."

Vizarra snorted and cracked his knuckles.

"O'Conner is checking with the archbishop? I'd like to see and hear that."

Malata said nothing. Vizarra stared at his foot for a moment, then lifted his gaze and looked at the piano.

"O'Conner is no longer useful to us."

"No, Excellency?"

"No. He is stupid. Also he is an American. When this business is over, get rid of him."

"You mean pay him off, Excellency."

"Yes. Get him out of the country. There is no reason to do anything else. Someone will take care of that for us."

"I understand."

"I'm sure you do. Well, now is the time for the worst news. What is it?"

"We have received a cable from Livermore and one from Dunkel and one from our people in Nicaragua."

"So? Go on."

"Three gunboats are sailing from Nicaragua. They carry a contingent of United States Marines. A cutter and a frigate have been ordered out of Jamaica by the Royal Navy. They will be here soon, Excellency."

"I know how far it is to Nicaragua. And to Jamaica."

"Our cipher man informs us that both America and Great Britain plan to lodge protests with the League of Nations."

"Let them. The reason is that we have failed to protect foreign nationals, eh?"

"That is correct."

"Correct? Of course it's correct! And it's true. What do they expect me to do, eh? Well, what of Livermore and Dunkel?"

"They offer aid, Excellency."

Vizarra raised his head and grinned. Malata smiled and nodded.

"Aid? Oh, no, Julio. Come, you're joking!"

"Not at all, sir. They offer aid."

"They know, of course, that we are aware of what they offered Alessandro? Of course they do. They must. The *Guardacostas* have been following that freighter they sent. Does Dunkel mention the Monroe Doctrine?"

"He does, Excellency."

Vizarra tipped back his head and began to laugh. His chest shook and tears spilled from his eyes. He clutched himself and looked with streaming eyes at Malata and began to laugh again. He sat up, wincing and snorting, thumping his chest and wiping his damp cheeks.

"Christ, they forget nothing, these foreigners! Herzler is binding wounds for the archbishop, Livermore is showing the—what is it?— the Union Jack, and the *Yanqui* is saving us from whom . . . the Swiss Navy? They offer us *aid*. God, what a joke! What a joke. We are a very backward people, Julio, very backward. We have so much to learn. We remain preoccupied with honor. We must learn diplomacy! Yes, that's it. Diplomacy. The proper mixture of honor, threats and lying. The British are the greatest liars in the world. With them it's an art. Well, since they don't seem to use it for love, one must expect to discover it in their foreign policy, eh?"

"I beg your pardon, Excellency, but this is of the utmost seriousness!"

"Seriousness? Why, of course it is. That's what I'm saying. How neatly they have done it! I am laughing at them, Julio, because it is a little too early and a little too sad to laugh at myself. Ah, but you don't see it."

"Excellency, they mean to invade us!"

"Of course they do."

"And we will fight them?"

"You'd never fit in the British Foreign Office, Julio. You should see your face. You are white, absolutely white. Of course we shall not fight! Why fight? For what? What is there to fight about? They are sending troops and some ships, that's all."

"The sovereignty of Costa Plata . . ."

Vizarra sat up and glared at Malata, then bent, grunting, and picked up his boot. He waved it at Malata.

"Don't be stupid. Or if you must be stupid, be silent. Don't you think they want us to shoot? Just a few rounds from the guns down at the harbor. They want a better excuse than our failure to protect British and American citizens. It is all very neat, Julio. Decisions like this are made by gentlemen like Dunkel and Livermore and the other gentlemen of Amalgamated Fruit. They will offer this government aid and then send troops, or they will send troops and then declare that aid has been sent. After all, that freighter is still offshore. If Alessandro can reach it, our American and English friends will merely collect what they feel is theirs from a new government, that's all. You and I—why, Julio, we have nothing to do with it, really. It is Alessandro's problem. No, really. If he should win, why, they will arrest him and deport him, of course. And I will be restored. And one other minor change will be made."

Malata licked his lips and thrust his hands into his pockets.

"You mean me, Excellency?"

"Yes, Julio. You. O'Conner will take your place. The American, O'Conner."

Malata blinked once, his face twitching as though he had been struck.

"Then it will be necessary to—"

"Yes. Right away."

"Excellency, you really mean this? You plan to do nothing? The trade agreement! The future of the nation depends on it!"

"It did. For a few days it did. But that is over now. My golden dream. All my dreams are over. The night is ended. We are going to wake up soon. To an American alarm clock. And the new trade agreement is not worth the paper it's printed on. Section Eleven, as I remember. This government guarantees the safety of all foreign nationals and their dependents. Section Twelve states very simply that during the ninety-nine-year period this government will not nationalize, seize or appropriate the property of concessionaires. Now that is clear enough, no? But there are ten dead from the mines. And who is at the mines but Zamal? And what about the railroads? Our troops hold the station here and the marshaling yards. But Alessandro still has the locomotives and rolling stock. And what has happened to the office building of Livermore Lines Limited? A German religious fanatic has been using it as a clinic. And the Livermore docks and pier facilities? This afternoon they were shelled by the insurgents, one oil storage tank ignited and still burning. And you want us to fight them? No, Julio, no. The fighting is over and done with. Now we must consider the best terms of surrender."

"Surrender?"

"Absolutely. Write a telegram to Livermore and one to Dunkel. Say that we accept their aid, support or whatever. We would appreciate, moreover, a show of military strength, ideally several warships and a battalion or so of soldiers . . . to be used as auxiliary forces in conjunction with our own police, of course. Be vague. Don't let them know that we know, eh? But beg with them to do what they've already started to do. We will welcome them with open arms. And open legs, like a whore. Costa Plata the whore. She is on the ground. Climb on her and have your way . . ."

Vizarra stood up and rammed his foot into his boot, bent and tugged it, limped to the piano and smashed his fist down on the keys. The sound echoed off the walls. Vizarra turned, his face stiff with fury. The words, in a breathy, choked whisper, squeezed from between his lips.

". . . and when you have the little death in her, may she spit full in your mouth, gringo!"

He jammed his fist down again, pounding a jangled racket from the piano. His jowls shivered.

"And in yours, too, *Inglés!*"

"Excellency . . ."

Vizarra stared before him blindly, swaying on his bad foot, one corner of his mouth lifting with pain. He limped back to the chair and knocked it over with a swipe of his hand. Malata stared at the dull eyes in the red-rimmed sockets that turned toward him. Vizarra's voice was husky.

"All of it . . . all my life . . . now this . . . thrown to them . . . to the sharks by that kid. That little glob of turd! That . . . that *Alessandro!* From the moment that they shot Colleo there was no turning back! What is there in him that wants this? Eh? Tell me! Tell me! Now look at us! Like a whore in the dirt to be climbed on by every foreigner! And it's his fault! If he'd done nothing, waited . . . yes, waited just a little while, a few months, maybe a year or two. No more than that! After all . . . I'm old, I know it. I admit it. Yes,

516

I'm the Old Mule. I would have retired. And let them shoot me then, if they must have it so! But I would have ordered a general election. . . . Why couldn't he have seen that, the fool? The young, stupid, dangerous fool! He—yes, I swear it!—he could have been freely elected President! I . . . I would have seen to it! I would have prepared the ballots in his favor. I would even have said nothing against him! But now . . . look at what he has done and what he has made me do and what we have made of her together. The father and the son, the mother we have made a whore."

Vizarra sat down on the piano stool, his fists limp in his lap. Tears fell and sprinkled his knuckles. Malata watched, waited for several minutes and then coughed gently. Vizarra sat on the stool, unmoving, weeping silently on his hands. Malata slipped closer.

"Excellency?"

"In the telegram, Julio, express our sincerest regrets. About their people. Say that the mines will be turned back to them when the situation has stabilized. Also the railroads. Say, also, that we are fully prepared to negotiate reparations for all property damage under the terms of a new trade agreement. We deeply regret our failure to comply and abide by the terms of the document so recently signed. Be very formal and very humble. When you have it prepared, bring it to me. I may think of other things to say. I will hold her head in my arms while Alessandro holds her feet."

"Anything else, Excellency?"

"Yes. Order the shooting to stop at once. Release the hostages. Direct order to the Red Beret to surrender their arms."

"But, Excellency, Alessandro is still—"

"Let him fight. What can he win? The right to hold her feet, nothing more."

Vizarra's voice was flat, toneless. He sat staring at his wet hands and then began to chafe his fingers, as though chilled. Malata leaned over him, smiling slightly, his dark eyes shining with contempt. This old man, this grayhead with the bulging belly and the gout, the restless nights daubing his damp, pouchy eyes—this old man was done for, finally.

"You order a cease-fire, Excellency?"

"No. Just what I told you."

"Anything else?"

"Yes. Arrange an interview with His Grace. And I want a priest. Right away."

"Of course, Excellency. One thing."

Vizarra did not raise his head. He locked his hands together. Malata smirked with contempt.

"I will take care of O'Conner. Not for myself, you understand, but for Costa Plata. For the people."

"Good. The sooner the better."

"That leaves the position of director of the Security Police unoccupied, Excellency."

"It does. I know it."

Malata waited. Vizarra said nothing, did not move, sat staring at his damp knuckles.

"The position cannot remain unoccupied, Excellency. The foreigners will demand that the strictest security measures be taken, that the police cooperate in full with the detachment of troops."

"I know that, too."

"Someone must be appointed."

"Yes."

"Excellency, I—"

"You what, Malata?"

Vizarra lifted his head. His fingers curled into fists. Malata stepped back, his face expressionless.

"Excellency, I would like to volunteer to occupy that position. Without increase in pay."

"You?"

"As a temporary thing, if you wish—"

"A temporary thing?"

"I mean, why wait, Excellency? We should get rid of the man at once. Quietly. Discreetly. I can do it. I'll do it for you . . . for the people. It will be an act of patriotism, in fact, no?"

"Yes. Very patriotic."

"Then you agree? I am appointed to the position of director of Security Police. Thank you, Excellency. Thank you."

Vizarra stood up and set his fists on his hips. His red-rimmed eyes glittered and his jaw jutted. He raised his right hand and tapped Malata slowly on the chest with his stubby forefinger.

"Get rid of that *Yanqui* gangster. That's all. Nothing else, understand? There are no appointments being made here today. You have your work. Go and do it. I will take care of the Security Police. I will take care of Zamal and Lucca. I will take care of Sánchez and Ales-

518

sandro. I will take care of Livermore and Dunkel and their ships and their soldiers! And if you do not leave me and send a priest to me as I command, and fulfill all other orders and commands, I will take care of you with these two hands! Now get out, you . . . you . . . never mind what you are. I will see no one and speak with no one except staff headquarters and General Lucca."

"Yes . . . Excellency. Yes. I understand."

"Where is she now?"

"Who, Excellency?"

"That girl. That girl from the pueblo. The blind girl. Bring her here."

"Now?"

"Yes, now. At once! Find her. Call the Mother Superior. Have her come here with the priest. I want to see her."

Malata nodded his sleek head and backed away. Vizarra shrugged and snapped one finger on a piano key.

"Order dinner for two. To be served in the room off here."

"Yes, Excellency."

"With champagne. Two bottles. And when she arrives and when the priest leaves, I am not to be disturbed. Under any circumstances. Understand?"

"Perfectly, Excellency."

Vizarra touched the piano keyboard again and bent to listen to the sound. He looked at Malata and straightened.

"Tonight I will listen to the radio. I never listen to the radio alone. Never."

"Yes, Excellency."

"Julio?"

"Yes, Excellency?"

"I will consider your offer. Temporarily, however, the directorship of the Security Police will remain vacant. I will issue all orders to the police myself. But I will consider your offer."

"Yes, Excellency. Thank you."

Malata bowed and backed from the room. Vizarra touched the keyboard and smiled.

"Oh, yes, Julio, I will consider your offer, your very, very kind and patriotic offer . . ."

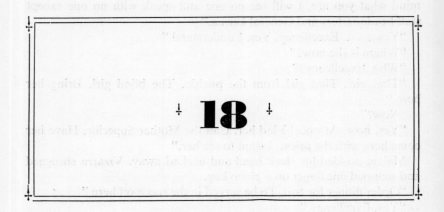

‡ 18 ‡

THE sun sank and burned dully through the rain clouds; the western wind drove across the *campo*. Dust whirled down the Avenida Vizarra, and the palm fronds slatted in the cool gusts. The streetlights went on in the eastern sector of the city from the Glorieta Colón to the palace hill. The smoke from the burning oil tank tilted and sank, spreading over the harbor, torn by the cold, thrusting wind. Five cafés were open by direct order of General Lucca, and the waiters hurried between the crowded tables carrying glasses of vermouth and beer. The men and women watched the sky and listened and waited. The cafés were quiet. The waiters moved very quickly between the tables and then stood together at the bar. The radio station had not broadcast in more than two hours. The rain came, falling hard, spattering on the torn, fluttering canopies, streaming down through the rents. The streetlights flickered and went off. The cafés emptied quickly. The waiters swept the tips into their pockets and dragged down the corrugated iron shutters. Three trucks filled with Lucca's Guards, the tires hissing, rolled past the wire stretched across the Glorieta Colón. Thunder rumbled up in the mountains, and the *serenos* ducked from doorway to doorway, locking up early. The bells boomed from the Cathedral of Santa Rosa. The rain lashed down from the dark, starless sky.

Voget's Red Brigade struck across the city toward the railroad yards, running through the rain, bent over at the waist, their rifles clutched against their chests, following the assault teams, four men each, two with grenades, the other pair staggering beneath the rain-soaked mattresses to fling over the barbed wire. The Guards began firing into the darkness, and a gasoline bomb splushed against a gondola car. Flames runneled over the ties, and the reek of creosote tainted the cold driving wind.

The gutted buildings of the university, gap-eyed jagged walls and rubble heaps, barricades of splintered desks pasted with soaked earth sprang up, touched by the long, yellow shaft of the searchlight beam from the roof of the administration building. Out of the trenches scraped across the athletic fields, scrambling and slipping, two waves, the survivors of the student cadres, surged through the clouds of drenching rain. Before they had advanced fifty meters, they slowed, dreamwalking in the gluey mud, the two lines wavering and bending. They began to sing the university hymn. The searchlight swept down the front line, and a machine gun stuttered. The students flopped in the mud and fired back. The second line, sliding and singing in hoarse, exhausted voices, moved through them. The first line loaded and rose, squinting against the rain. Olmega shouted, and the signal rocket slithered up into the dark, wind-whipped night and popped, a feeble sound, and the flare fizzed and died. Olmega tried to climb over the crumbling lip of the trench, but a professor of philosophy sitting on a crate of hand grenades reached out and held him fast. Olmega struggled, straining to see through the dark night and the rain. His teeth rattled together, and he slumped back into the trench. Bullets buzzed and whicked into the earth.

Alessandro saw the rocket and stood up slowly, drawing an automatic pistol from beneath his soaked tunic. He winced. His wound had stiffened. He stared down the long, empty boulevard. Across the street Sánchez crouched in another doorway. Twenty meters back, the two Belgians, Coco and Henri, headed a lumpy line of workers and soldiers that trailed to the end of the block and into an alley. The men, hunched and miserable, pressed against the dark housefronts and shuttered shops. Alessandro whistled and ran forward. He heard Sánchez shouting in a dull, weary voice. The men stood and ran forward toward the wire barricades strung across the Glorieta Colón.

The sewer cover lifted, stood on edge and wobbled like a huge coin down the slope, struck against an ammunition box and bongled, shivering down flat on the pavement. Two of the Guards stationed at the wire whirled and squeezed off shots into the darkness. A grenade rattled on the street and exploded. Along the barricade, the Guards turned and began firing blindly. Alessandro's men ran for the wire. The Guards swung back and forth, cursing and shooting. A dynamite charge whumped, and the front of a building buckled out, showering bricks and glass, sagged and smashed down on the barricade. A small head, neatly capped, bobbed in the dark pool of the open sewer hole. Captain Chinchón sprang up out of the hole and stood in the drenching rain, carefully adjusting his cape and stamping silt from his polished boots. His men swarmed up the ladder, their feet ringing on the iron rungs, squirmed out on the rubble-strewn pavement and spread across the street, firing at the broken barricade. Chinchón looked at his watch and put a silver whistle to his lips. At the signal, his men rose and trotted, humpbacked, to the barricade. A few shots crackled and a man's voice, close to Chinchón, groaned. An answering whistle floated over the heaped stones and tangled wire. Chinchón stood at attention as Alessandro, trailed by Sánchez and a dozen men, scrambled down the slope and trotted up to him. Chinchón saluted, clicked on his electric torch and pointed the beam at the open sewer hole.

"This way to the Palace Hotel."

Alessandro's teeth flashed. Chinchón gazed at the sling supporting Alessandro's left arm.

"Need help getting down?"

"No. You have the charges planted?"

"Just as you ordered. The others have already entered the building."

"She's up there?"

"Yes. And the program is scheduled to go on in a few minutes. We've got plenty of time. You have men enough to hold this position?"

"If you can send some of your own up to the next section of wire.

About twenty. Their password tonight is *Red Beret*. With luck they can walk right into the position. Then grenades."

Chinchón nodded and handed Sánchez the electric torch. Sánchez glared at him.

"Where's the truck? The getaway truck?"

"Waiting. My men will lead you to it."

"It had better be there, Chinchonito."

"Carlos! Come on, man!"

Chinchón frowned. He had been insulted, his loyalty and his skill challenged. He stalked away without saluting and ordered two of his men to bring back the sewer cover.

⸸

The studio was small. The engineer in his booth behind the pane of glass was no more than five paces from the end of the grand piano. He grinned at her and kissed his fingertips, the usual ritual, once every week, just before they went on the air. But tonight his face was gray with fatigue, and his lips twitched. During the rehearsal he had talked uncontrollably, repeating himself over and over. Since early afternoon he had been listening to the executions. Lucía stared at him. His mouth twisted, and he kept adjusting his earphones. The red bulb went on. She sat stiffly on the piano stool, listening, straining to catch the distant, bumping detonations in the dark streets outside the building. She tugged nervously at the sleeve of her white satin blouse. Anita had never returned. She had found her dress, dropped on the floor outside the wardrobe room. The announcer was talking, a new one tonight. Already she had forgotten his name. He was not quite sober and smiled too much. He had the second microphone near the door leading to the corridor.

" . . . to many, many kind requests, the popular romantic favorite, 'The Night of the Dove.' Señorita?"

Her fingers were stiff, clumsy. She glanced at them, repelled. She had bitten her nails. She did not know the introduction well enough and missed the top note of the chord, her little finger skidding off the black key, a half-tone flat. The announcer smiled at her. She swallowed, her throat ached suddenly, and began to sing:

> I stand alone and tremble in the night
> And long to know your heart, your strength, your soul.

> Tonight I'll dream my dreams till dawn,
> In all this darkness seek to find my goal.

She was singing badly, croaking like a raven. God, when would this program be over? When would she be able to get away from here, to the airplane waiting to take her away? Why did they write in, asking her to sing this stupid song? She hated it. Her fingers fumbled with the keys. She felt on the edge of tears. She made the G-minor seventh run and opened her mouth. The scream stuck in her dry throat. A man in a soiled army uniform was standing in the control room, holding a rifle in his hands. Her fingers staggered into a jangling discord. The engineer looked up. The man in the uniform jabbed the muzzle of his rifle into the engineer's back. The engineer sprang up, but the cord attached to his earphones shivered taut and he fell down over the control table. The man with the rifle slapped a card against the glass pane: CONTINUE SINGING.

She could not make her hands move. She bent forward toward her microphone and tried to sing, her voice breaking off into shrill, breathy whispers:

> This night I'll rush behind the clouds,
> Fly past the stars on wings of love.
> My lips will whisper what my heart has vowed,
> On this dark night, the night of the dove.

The corridor door opened. A pale young man with one arm in a sling walked in, followed by three other men in uniform. One of them, a dead cigar in his teeth, pointed a pistol at her. She sat frozen with terror. She saw the blur of motion as the engineer lunged up and threw the switch. The red bulb winked out. The man in the booth with him raised his rifle, hesitated, looking for a good spot, then drove the butt down on the back of his neck. The new announcer, his face white, began dragging the second microphone toward the open door, screaming into it.

"Help! Help, Security Police! They're here in the radio station! We are attacked! Help!"

The one with the sling moved, chopping down with his good hand, as the one with the pistol turned and fired. The slam of the shot blotted her short scream. The announcer staggered back, struck against the door and flopped in the corner, one leg kicking. The red light burned again. The air stank. The one with the sling looked at the second microphone. The cord was broken. He walked toward the piano, swept her sheet music off the extra chair and sat down beside her. She sat still, rigid, her arms crossed across her breasts. She moaned and lost control. The pistol barrel was only a foot from her head. She closed her eyes, sickened and ashamed.

Alessandro glanced at her, reached across her, wincing, and turned the microphone to his face. He hesitated for an instant, drew a deep breath, his eyes staring, dismayed, at Sánchez, and began to speak.

"People of Costa Plata. This is Alessandro Martín, speaking from Studio Four at Radio Costa Plata. Tonight is not a night for sentimental tunes, but a night to shout with the voices of men. I hereby proclaim the establishment of the People's Republic of Costa Plata. Men and women of the nation, we are free! Men of good faith from all foreign countries on our borders and overseas! From this moment understand that the People's Republic is the *de facto* government of the sovereign territories of Costa Plata, including all national waters to the three-mile limit. Violation of Costa Platan territorial rights will be regarded as an act of hostility against this government. The dictatorship of Rafael Vizarra no longer exists. People of Costa Plata, do not obey any decree issued by the toppled dictator, his murderers or the fascists of the Red Beret. Stand with us in this first hour of freedom. Help us to destroy the last vestiges of terrorism and tyranny. Volunteers, come to the central barracks, to the command posts at Jardín de Flores and barrio San Antonio. Fraternity, Federation and Freedom! Long live the officially proclaimed People's Republic of Costa Plata!"

Alessandro nodded, and the man in the booth threw the switch, then raised his rifle and pounded the butt down on the control panels. Alessandro stood up and snatched the pistol from Sánchez's hand.

"Why did you do that? Why, Carlos? You saw the light go off!"

"What does it matter? And don't yell at me like that!"

"Come on, let's get out of here. The streets outside are filled with O'Conner's men. Around the car, waiting for her. We'll just make it out through the steam tunnels before Chinchón's men set off the dynamite."

"You men! Out into the corridor! You . . . you spoke well, *jovencito*."

"I'll talk again, over the field transmitter . . . maybe. If this works, we'll have a few hours. If not . . . please get up now, señorita."

"Little one, she can't go in that dress."

Alessandro looked at the girl. She stared back at him, her mouth open.

"Where are your other clothes? Quickly, now!"

She shook her head. He was pale and needed a shave. His tunic was filthy, stiff with blood. He looked like an animal. He clamped his hand on her arm and dragged her away from the piano. Sánchez pounced on the pistol that clattered on the floor. He twisted up a knot of her hair.

"Get up, you little whore, or I'll blow your brains out!"

"Stop it, Carlos! Get away from her. Señorita, get up. Please."

"Please? Christ, kick her in the—"

"I can't."

"Why not?"

"I've . . . wet myself."

"You what? Oh. Well, huh. Well. Carlos, get the pants off that one over there. All right. Get up, now. We're not going to hurt you. You're going to come with us, that's all. Just for a little while. Then we'll let you go."

"Don't hit me!"

"Take off that dress. Right now."

She stared at him, terrified. It was true, what he had told her! They were going to rape her and then kill her when they were done.

Alessandro seized her shoulders and turned her around. He broke open the fastenings down the back of her long skirt, like a man in a hurry opening a poorly wrapped package. She gasped and clutched the ripped, soaked material around her thighs. A pair of tuxedo trousers flopped on the floor in front of her. Alessandro spoke. He was standing right behind her.

"Come, Carlos, don't be like that. *La pobrecita.* Poor kid, come on. He's turned around. No one's looking."

She stepped out of the ruined skirt and crouched, shivering and fumbling with the trousers. Suddenly she began to laugh.

"God, I'm soaked to the knees . . ."

She stood up, swaying, and felt his hand stuffing her blouse into the back of the pants.

"There. Turn up the cuffs. You see? They fit very nicely. What luck, eh? He was your size. Come along, please."

His slender fingers clamped around her wrist. He dragged her from the studio. The corridor was filled with armed men, some in a variety of uniforms, others in dirty street clothes. She ran beside him, running away from them, matching his strides. His face was set in a tight, pale grimace. The sling slapped against his belly. Sánchez pounded heavily behind, bellowing orders in his dead-sounding voice.

"Five minutes! Five minutes! Get out or up on the roof! The whole street out front is going up!"

Alessandro swerved and ran into the freight elevator. She jostled against him and a thin, squeaking cry burst from his clamped lips. He gripped her, and she found herself bracing, supporting him against the wall of the car, his narrow dark head resting against her shoulder. Sánchez crashed the grill shut and rammed over the lever. The elevator sank slowly.

"This is crazy, crazy!"

"Uhm?"

"He . . . he's all right, I think."

"I'm all right, yes. No, it will give us time. Until dawn. Until they come down from the mines."

He released her wrist and straightened. She stood between them, and the two men spoke around her. She breathed heavily and rubbed her wrist.

"Time? It's run out."

"No. The people will rise. Once more. One last time. A few hours only. Then the miners will reach Voget."

"It's too late . . ."

"No! Don't say that! You are the chief of state now, *hombre!* I've just made you the President."

"No . . . you didn't. You said nothing like that."

"I meant to. Maybe . . . it was . . ."

"What?"

"Because you shot him. I couldn't think clearly."

"I can. I say . . ."

"What, Carlitos? Tell me. Speak the truth. Say it."

"I say that the . . . I say that the people will rise with us again. One more time."

"With us . . . once more, if God wills it so."

"And someone shoots the Old Mule before dawn. We're down. Let's go."

They were in the basement of the building, running again down a gritty corridor, past the huge shapes of a steam condenser and generators. They slid across greasy steel plates, and Alessandro pounded his boot heel on a round metal cover. The hatch opened, and light shot up.

" 'Stá bien?"

"Sí!"

"Go ahead. The girl first."

She stared down the shaft. A vertical ladder ran down into some kind of tunnel floored with pipes and cables. A dirty face stared back up at her. She swallowed, hitched up the pants and swung her foot down to the first rung. Alessandro steadied her. His lips lifted in a shy smile.

"Be careful, señorita, don't fall. We can't get you another pair of pants, you know."

She jerked away from him, scowling, scrambled down the ladder and crouched in the tunnel. Voices echoed and wowed somewhere down the tunnel, and guns and equipment clanged on the pipes. The air was musty and damp. Alessandro slid down the ladder and reached his arm out for her. She ducked away.

"This is no game of tag, señorita. Get going."

He pushed her head into the tunnel. She began crawling, holding her breath. They were going to shut the tunnel at each end and bury her alive. Voices shouted incoherently. She saw a disc of light ahead and crawled toward it. Behind her he came dragging himself, his good hand slapping hard on the pipes. Twice his hard fingers brushed her ankles. Hands grabbed her at last and dragged her out into another room and dropped her on the dirty floor. It was very hot. She lay there gasping. She stared at the tunnel opening. Alessandro appeared, his dark hair plastered over his brow. The men in the room whooshed in relief and gently, tenderly drew him free and set him on his feet. They stood around him, grinning and proud. Alessandro smiled at them.

"Sánchez is stuck. His ass is too big."

The men laughed. Lucía snuffled her nose on the smeared cuff of her satin blouse and giggled. Alessandro saw her sitting on the floor. He flushed.

"Sorry, señorita . . ."

That seemed very funny, and she laughed out loud. The men stopped at once and stared at her. She looked from face to face, watching them, waiting, tensed, for the first one to move toward her. But there was nothing but curiosity in their faces. It took them a few seconds to remember that she was with them, then they turned back to their leader. Sánchez, red-faced and gasping, wriggled out of the tunnel. No one moved to help him. He stood up, very close to Alessandro.

"All right. Take her to the truck. You know where after that. But the regular driver goes there. With two guards. You make the telephone call to O'Conner. Get in the car, just as we said, and meet O'Conner at the Glorieta Colón. Have O'Conner understand clearly that he must bring your father first, then arrange for His Grace or—what's his name?—Monseñor Blanco to pass through our lines . . . no matter where our lines are. If the Glorieta position is lost again, Vizarra's troops must pull back. I want the Glorieta Colón clear, open from street to street. Make the exchange out in the open where our people can see. No one is to shoot O'Conner. And talk with him, *hombre,* like you never talked before. Make all kinds of demands, guarantees, pledges of safe conduct. Oh, I know, I know, O'Conner is O'Conner. But he must believe that we're going to . . . you know. You must buy us time, Carlos. Two or three hours. Then we'll delay getting her back to the lines. A two- or three-hour truce, a cease-fire. Our men will understand. And the people, Carlos?"

Sánchez wet his lips and pulled a cigar from the pocket of his tunic. He mumbled, then sensed the others staring at him, stood erect and looked around the sweltering room at them.

"The people will rise with us, one last time, for freedom. By that time the miners will be down here! We will have won!"

The men tried to cheer, a low rumbling, and slapped each other on the back. Lucía listened and watched, confused. Sánchez and Alessandro shook hands. Alessandro nodded.

"Let's blow the street. José, is the detonator rigged?"

"All wired."

The men rushed around. A cloud of sticky dust filled the room. They dove, one by one, into a narrow slot. She could hear them running. She sat still, choking in the dust, hardly able to see. Alessandro was gone. She touched her wrist where he had held her. Sánchez prodded her in the rear with his boot.

"Get up, *putita*."

One man walked in front, Sánchez behind her. They climbed two flights of metal stairs. A door opened, and rain splashed against her face. She felt the snout of the pistol against her back. The cold rain drenched her. They walked slowly across the alley. She hunched down. The rain poured into the dark slot of the alley. The truck was parked in the open doorway of a garage. Sánchez prodded her up into the cab and climbed in beside her. She sat shoulder to shoulder with Sánchez and the driver, the gearshift lever between her knees. That was why they made her put on pants. Well, she was wet from head to foot now, so what did it matter? She laughed softly. Sánchez lit his cigar and tossed away the match.

"No smoking, comrade. Orders of Capitán Chinchón."

"He eats what I leave in the tall grass, *amigo*. I give the orders here. Two minutes."

She was quite calm now. She sat holding her wrist. It would turn black-and-blue. She bruised easily. Sánchez blew out smoke. The driver muttered and fell silent. Then the rain-sluiced darkness jolted and shivered. An afterfall of broken stones, metal and glass. The rain spattered in the alley. The driver started the motor.

"That was it! Ten sticks right under the front entrance! The bastards never really even felt it, you know? Well, where to, General? They didn't tell me that."

Sánchez leaned forward, slamming her back against the seat, pinning her there. His cigar smoldered and she coughed weakly, suddenly frightened again.

"Not a general, *hijo. Jefe de Estado*. Chief of State of the People's Republic! Don Carlos Sánchez, hear me?"

"Of course, of course. I didn't mean . . ."

Sánchez leaned back and puffed his cigar.

"Take us to the central barracks, patriot. We're going to swap this little whore for my old man. *Nada por nada*. A bargain: nothing for nothing. And a safe-conduct for the archbishop, too. He wants to wash his burned hands in the font of the cathedral, see? *Nada por nada por nada*."

⊥

The heavy ammunition belt slithered through the loader's hands down into the metal box. The gunner grunted approval and settled himself, squirming on the broken stones of the floor. He stared into the flashlight beam. The captain bent toward him.

"All right?"

"*Sí, Capitán.*"

The captain walked away to the great boulder where Zamal stood. Two other men there knelt beside a portable searchlight. The captain butted one of the men in the back with his knee.

"The batteries? You've tested them?"

"*Sí, Capitán.*"

"The machine gun is ready, General."

Zamal nodded, gazing steadily down the tunnel toward the elevators. The captain turned the beam on the gunners. They flinched and shielded their eyes. They all felt the same. It was a queer place, this mine, this great chamber with the boulder. The darkness all around them had a smell, the damp soft odor of mold. The captain turned off his electric torch. He could feel it, as though the flesh from shoulder to shoulder had turned sensitive, almost seeing, like a damp sheet of film, the body sprawled at the base of the boulder. It seemed to leak through the darkness. They all felt it, the gun crew, the men with the light, himself. It lay there now in the absolute darkness and silence of the mine, the dead eyes glaring. The captain sensed that Zamal had drawn closer to him. The general seemed calm enough. But he must feel it, too. It was impossible not to. The face, the dead face, wore such an expression of surprise, of utter astonishment.

"Now all we do is wait for him, *Capitán.*"

The voice, so close to him, so soft and confiding, startled the captain. He nodded in the darkness and wiped his palms on his tunic. A small noise made him jump. Zamal coughed.

"A rat, my boy, that's all."

"Oh. A rat, sir?"

"That's all. The shafts are filled with them."

"Oh. You've been here before, sir?"

It made the captain's flesh crawl. For an instant he was positive that Zamal was not there, that the body beside the great stone had drifted through the darkness and hung over him. Before he could catch himself, he shrank away. Zamal's voice was calm, unnerving.

"Not for years. You don't have to whisper. We'll be able to hear the elevator. Yes. My father was a foreman here. Years ago, of course. This was the main shaft then. I used to bring him food and clean clothes. It got very hot, you see, all the men working here together. He used to sweat right through his clothes. If he didn't get dry clothes, he'd catch cold."

The captain grinned. It seemed absurd beyond measure that anyone at any time could have worried about catching cold in this place. Rats, though—that was different. How long before they'd be after the body lying huddled in the darkness?

"He was told, *Capitán?* You are certain of this?"

"Positive, sir. As soon as he got out of the car we could see that he was drunk. He asked at the smelter for Ramos. The men there had no orders, so they sent him to the house, you know. That was nearly a half hour ago."

"He was alone, though. Quite alone."

"Yes, alone. I could hear him yell about money."

"Capitán?"

"Sir?"

"I wouldn't stand there. You've shifted over. You're right in front of the light. Move."

"Sorry."

The captain shifted back toward the huge stone, forcing himself closer to Zamal. One of the men at the machine gun sneezed. The captain put his flashlight in the pocket of his tunic and buttoned the pocket. He could not stand holding the thing, not in this blackness. He held onto it, his thumb rubbing the switch through the fabric of his tunic. It made him feel better just to touch it, to know that he could have light with a single thrust of his thumb.

He swallowed. He remembered that he had forgotten to count the steps from the elevator shaft to the chamber. What if his torch had burned out, if the batteries had gone dead? In this air you could never tell. The thing might not work. After . . . after it was done, he would walk back to the elevators. But he might walk too far and fall into the shaft. The searchlight. Of course! They had the searchlight.

"You are certain you checked the batteries?"

"Eh? Oh, *sí, Capitán, sí.*"

He tried to stroll back to the boulder. Instead, he groped and shuffled, angry and afraid. His foot might touch the torn thing that lay at the base of the great rock. Zamal's purring voice, meditative and rebuking, licked at him.

532

"I am glad I decided to come down here. To see this done properly. These are . . . special conditions."

"Sir!"

One of the men at the searchlight, right underneath the captain, hissed the word. The captain stumbled back, grabbing for his flashlight. Zamal answered.

"I hear it, soldier. We all hear it."

The whine of the elevator shaft. The long, greasy cables like serpents looping down, the heavy weights rising as the cage dropped. The captain unbuttoned his tunic and struggled to control his voice. He muttered between his teeth. His hands were shaking uncontrollably. He was afraid that he would drop the light and then step on it.

"Ready, lights. Ready, gunners."

The elevator whined, a thin, distant sound. The door clattered as a boot struck it. The door clashed open. The captain held his breath. The others were doing the same. Faint footsteps crushed through the blackness, coming closer, stopping, coming on again. The captain strained to see until his face began to ache. When he saw the point of yellow light glimmer, he nearly cried aloud for joy. The gunner moved his hand. The captain heard a snick of oiled steel.

"Ramos!"

The sound boomed up through the blackness to the timbered ceiling and muffled back. The light came forward, slowly, flickering, wavering from one side of the shaft to the other.

"Ramos! *Ramos!* Vola has come for his money!"

The echoes gobbled in the dark, senseless sounds. The captain felt the urge to sneeze. He pressed the knuckle of his index finger against his nose and pushed up. The light came closer in a fluttering, crunching rush, then stopped. The captain, his breath caught, gripping his flashlight, stared at a jowly, unshaven face floating in the darkness like a mummer's mask. Zamal was breathing slowly, easily. The captain hated him. The blood thudded in his ears.

"*Ladrón!* Where are you, thief? Think you can cheat me?"

The light plunged down, fluttered, blued and nearly went out. The captain shoved at his nose, silently begging Zamal to give the order. He couldn't give the command himself. He would just sneeze.

Vola was on his knees, grunting and snuffling, scratching at the stones. He picked something up and brought it near the candle flame. The light gleamed on a silver disc, a coin.

"There! *Chiquita mía* . . . little honey one, five centavos. For me. Eh, Ramos, you swindler, you! I don't want these little ones! Where are my thousands? I know you're down here. They told me."

Vola crawled to the left, peering down and scrabbling at the rocks. He turned back, closer to the machine gun. He grinned and pushed the coin into his pocket, then stood up, swaying and blinking.

Now was the instant. The captain tore his hand from his face and drew a breath. The command stuck in his throat. Vola stumbled toward him. Less than fifty meters away.

The captain was bent over. He sneezed. The captain saw the fat, tear-blurred figure lurch erect.

"Who's there? Ramos? Ramos?"

Zamal spoke softly.

"Light."

The searchlight rammed its white bolt of brightness on Vola. He goggled, stupefied and squinting. The candle dropped from his hand. Zamal spoke again.

"Fire."

The machine gun exploded, hammering a numbing din, lashing smoke and bullets, flame dancing at the muzzle. Vola's body lifted, floating, his boots kicking the stones. The slugs tore at him, flinging him, turning him. He fell on his face. The machine gun spewed again. The body jittered and shifted. Bits of stone spanged off down the long tube of light. The captain watched them, amazed. Dust feathered around the body.

"Cease fire!"

The machine gun stopped at once. The captain's ears buzzed, and he swayed on his feet, still staring down the searchlight beam. He brought out his electric torch and pressed the switch on and off, on and off.

"*Capitán* . . ."

He nodded and unbuckled his holster. The pistol felt very heavy. He walked forward, flicking his flashlight on and off. He drew back the hammer. He did not look down when he squatted. He felt the muzzle bump and prod across the right shoulder, up the fat, yielding neck, then knock on the skull. He pressed the trigger. The pistol jogged in his hand. He straightened up and turned into the searchlight. The disc of light burned like a star. He closed his eyes and swayed in a red haze. Zamal spoke.

"All right. Throw him in the ore cart in the tunnel. The other one, too. Take the light up. Dismantle the gun and get it up. I'll be at the ingot vault. Report to me there, *Capitán*."

"But . . . but, sir, I am not regularly in command of this group. I—"

"Just clean this mess up, *hombre*. You can do that, can't you?"

"Yes, of course, sir."

The captain stepped out of the light. His foot dropped on something that rolled. He bent and picked up the candle Vola had carried. A thread of blue smoke rose into the air. The captain wet his fingers and snuffed the wick. He placed the candle in his pocket. Zamal walked up to him.

"Habit, my boy. Life is a habit. Living is a habit. The soldier does not have habits like that. He has the habit of dying. Understand?"

"Yes, sir."

"You have never seen a man killed before?"

"No, sir. Except for a training accident once."

"Only once? There should be more accidents on maneuvers. Accidents should be caused. In order to break the habit of living. Well, you saw him. He died well, did he not?"

"Yes, he died well."

"Throw the other one away somewhere. But bring Vola's body out to his sedan. We will take him to the military cemetery. We will bury him properly."

"Bury him?"

"Of course, *Capitán*. He was once my superior. And he died well."

"My God . . ."

"*Capitán?*"

"What, General?"

"How did you ever make captain? How?"

"I know about . . . radios, sir."

"You know about radios. Well, when you are done with this, send a message to staff headquarters. Say simply that Vola is dead. And the other one, too. Ramos."

The captain saluted. Zamal returned the salute and crunched away, striding down the shaft of light toward the elevator. The captain walked shakily back to the waiting soldiers. They grinned at him, despising him.

"Carry them out to the ore cart."

"Sí, Capitán . . ."

The captain took the candle from his pocket and flung it into the darkness. It struck and tumbled somewhere. He took out his flashlight again and turned the switch on and off, on and off. He had grown a new habit.

19

ALESSANDRO sat on the cot, staring at the bright blossom of flame within the glass lamp chimney. The top of the chimney was already sooted. He blinked slowly, aware only that time was passing, as silently and steadily as the burning flame. When all the oil was used, the wick would smolder and the light would go out. The cave would soon be completely dark.

The telephone stood on the low table, the line running off into the darkness beyond the circle of light. He gnawed his cheek, sucking in his lips. His left arm was crooked stiffly in the belt sling, his stained tunic draped over his shoulders. He scrubbed his dirty, unshaven face with his good hand and breathed slowly, drawing the dank, cold air into his chest. He glanced down at his left wrist. His watch was still strapped there, the crystal face shattered, the hands motionless. He fumbled with the strap, grainy with the dried salt of perspiration, freed the wristwatch and flung it on the table near the telephone. He looked at the three objects, pushed the broken watch over the table edge and heard it drop to the floor, turned the wick down and touched the telephone with his fingertips.

The sight of the telephone, so tempting, annoyed him. He stared at it deliberately for several moments, his fingertips just brushing the base. He moved his hand away and smiled. It was good to know that he would wait, that his body would not yet disobey his mind. A little surge of pride filled him and he damped it, forcing himself to bend awkwardly down to pick up the useless watch. His left shoulder panged. He sat up hastily, annoyed with himself for making so much of trifles. The important thing, the only important thing, was for the telephone to ring, for Carlos to call him, to say that they had purchased time, that the exchange would be made and *El Feo* set free. The old man knew the temptation of the telephone.

But Carlos had sent the girl out to the cave. To create still more delay? Not very likely. Carlos would be thinking of the Indians coming down from the mine. Whenever he was not thinking of himself. Perhaps it had not been wise to expose Carlos to such temptation. But who else could have been assigned to contact O'Conner for an exchange? The others were fighting. Only Carlos could be spared. Besides, it was his own father.

He turned slightly to look at her. She sat on another cot, smoking. Her presence annoyed him. He wanted *El Feo*. Or, for a discussion of final tactics, Voget. He noticed that she was wearing a heavy woolen sweater.

"Are you cold?"

"Yes."

"This isn't the Ritz in Paris."

He turned his back to her and listened. He could hear water dripping somewhere, like the distant sound of footsteps in the dark. The lamplight shone steadily. He spoke without looking at her.

"He should have taken you someplace else. Why bring you here?"

"I don't know. I don't care. How do you expect me to know what you don't know yourself? He put me in the truck, got into the car with O'Conner and drove off. To the Glorieta Colón, I suppose."

"Those were his orders, yes. Nothing was said about bringing you out here."

"Do you think I *want* to be here?"

"That's not the point. The point is whether or not I want you to *be* here."

"Then let me go."

"With pleasure. But at my convenience."

"I want to get away. From all of you. What have I ever done?"

"Who cares? It's what you will do that is important. Nothing else."

"I'll never come back to this country."

"I do not think you will be greatly missed."

"What time is it?"

He glanced automatically at his wrist and frowned.

"I said, what time is—"

"Please be quiet."

His shoulder ached steadily, a dull, stiff pang at the bones, deep in the flesh. Another scar to carry around. He pulled at his collar and ran the tips of his fingers over the slick welt beneath the curve of his jaw. That, that was luck. Five of us outside that village. Caught like rabbits by the Whites. Just luck that the rope was frozen. Dangling like a damned rabbit with a frozen rope sawing at my chin. The others already dead, frozen solid. Through the pines they came riding, a patrol of Budyenny's Red cavalry.

He shivered and stood up. He looked at her, puzzled. She shrank away from him, her hands to her face.

"There's a sheepskin in the box over there."

"I'm all right. I can wait as long as you can."

"Why don't they telephone? Why doesn't somebody call me to tell me something? How can I give orders? We should have brought the radio out here, set up an antenna outside the entrance. It is not merely inconvenient to forget the obvious; it is wrong, dangerously wrong. This business is too close, much too close. I did not allow us enough time."

He paced slowly back and forth, fingering the scar on his neck. He looked at the lantern and the telephone. The flare of the match she struck to light a cigarette made him start. He controlled the gesture, moved out his hand and caught up the lantern.

"Have you been here before?"

"No."

"These caves are famous, you know. The mosaics are unique. Here, see? The light's not very strong, but still . . . there. See?"

"I see."

"Centuries ago the Indians made these. Nobody knows where or how they developed the art. Imagine, mosaics here in Costa Plata. At the time of the late Roman Empire."

"They look like children made them."

"Exactly. This is Axoloqui. The colors are beautiful, no?"

"It's . . . indecent."

"Oh? I was just showing you. I meant nothing. Sorry to have wasted our time."

"Why bother to entertain a hostage?"

He set the lantern down on the table. His hand trembled. He pressed his fingers down on the rough surface of the table.

"Don't say that word."

"Aren't you going to shoot me?"

"You flatter yourself."

"Hostage. Those people on the docks. In the distillery. You have killed hundreds of them. Maybe thousands by this time."

He nodded, no longer really listening to her. Her voice bounded off the cave walls, shrill echoes, senseless with sudden fear.

"Why didn't you surrender?"

"Because Vizarra would shoot me."

"You deserve it."

"No doubt, but for different reasons."

"Murderer."

"I have been called more interesting names."

"Like what?"

"I call myself a revolutionary. It is what I call *myself* that matters."

"A revolutionary. Is a revolution like making love? Once you start, you can't stop?"

He grunted, slightly amused. A woman's view of politics is taken from a horizontal position.

"A revolution is an historical process. Certain forces—"

He broke off and shrugged his good shoulder. The telephone. Ring, damn you, ring. She said something in a sharp, angry voice. He sighed. Ring, ring and get her out of here.

"That just means that it's not your fault. And the people? Do they die for some historical process?"

"They just die."

She would not be silent. He tried not to hear her, but could not concentrate, could not shut her out.

". . . and that's just too bad, too bad for them, eh?"

"You wouldn't understand."

"Oh, yes. I understand. It's either Vizarra or you. That's what he told me. He understands you. Why didn't you just try to kill *him?* Leave the people alone."

"I am a revolutionary, not a terrorist. Now, for the love of God, shut your mouth, will you?"

He walked away from her to the edge of the circle of light, then back to the table and sat down. Her voice nipped at him.

"Why did all the others have to get killed? Why did they all have to die like animals?"

His fist slammed down on the table, and the angry words burst from him.

"Ask Vizarra!"

"You wanted . . . you *wanted* them killed."

He stared at his fist and carefully spread his fingers, then touched the tips to the rough tabletop, counting; first the little finger, then the fourth, the middle, then the index finger tapped down and the thumb beat. He moved his fingers slowly, counting, then faster and faster, until his hand made the light, quick imitation of a galloping horse, a runaway.

"That's absurd."

"It's true."

Before, that other time. There weren't enough to pay the debt. There are not enough yet. But soon there will be enough. And then . . . .

His fingers stilled. He sat on the cot, his head tipped back, staring. He stared, puzzled. Something was there. Out in the darkness. A pile, a heap, a mound of indistinct forms against the far wall of the cave. He blinked rapidly several times, and the dim image skidded from his brain. He wiped cold perspiration from his dirt-stiff brow. The sweat smeared the dirt to streaks. He stared again, but saw nothing. It was gone. No, there had been nothing there. It was fatigue, nothing more.

He stared briefly at the telephone.

"Will you hear it?"

"Eh? What?"

"I don't think so. Alessandro the Great is deaf."

"I am neither deaf nor . . . blind. I am *bored!* Why doesn't he call?"

"I know why. Because——"

"He owes me this. He must telephone! Soon. Now!"

"About what?"

"About . . . a trade agreement. Carlitos is arranging a trade agreement. Not like Vizarra's swindle, either. Thirteen years of organized theft and now he says, 'Here's a few reales for you people. Go have a drink and don't bother me.' "

"At least he did that for the people. What have you done? You still expect them to fight for you. Freedom or death and all that foolishness. There's been enough killing! I . . . I don't want to die!"

"Freedom must be purchased with death. There's never enough freedom—"

"And so there's never enough death. Not for you!"

Each death a coin to buy freedom. It takes a treasure to purchase a miracle. I have squandered a treasure to make a proper payment. But the unpaid balance was heavy. Such a father . . . *Mi padre vale mucho.* That poem. One rainy night in Belgrade I wrote it, so many years ago. And only now I know its meaning.

"What did you say?"

"Nothing."

"You were mumbling."

There. Against the wall, out in the darkness. Solid shapes, heavy things piled carelessly. Like sacks. Or like . . .

"What are you looking at?"

"Nothing."

"Nothing, eh? *Nada.* He always said that you were at least half anarchist. The Spanish dream, he called it. Every man alone, everyone out just for himself and everything in a mess. And keep the cafés open. The world can go to hell as long as there is enough coffee on the table. So you can look around and say that's the way God wants it."

Every man alone. Yet all heaped so?

He bent and drew a street map of the city out from beneath the cot, swept the dust off it with his palm and spread it beneath the warm light of the lamp. The familiar streets soothed him. He ran his fingers along the boulevards, circled the glorietas, his thumb skating on the nail. Here, from the north. The miners, a thrust so, no more than ten blocks, behind . . . yes, *behind* the university. Seal it off. Olmega would only have to hold the trenches. One column across into San Jerónimo and the two forces would join. The men would be together. He and Voget could then move—

She broke into a fit of hard, dry coughing. He glared at her, annoyed.

"How can I think with you—"

He watched her, astonished, as she flung something at him, then rose and ran across the floor, her loose men's pants flapping. Her cigarette—she had thrown that at him—patted near his foot in a weak spurt of orange bits. He did not sense what she meant to do until her head butted against his shoulder, jarring him back, washed with pain, the wincing breath drawing into his chest the scents of nicotine and perfume. Her hands, the nails beautifully trimmed with dirt beneath them, snatched at the map and pulled away a large piece. She half sat, half fell down on him. He rammed her off onto the dirt floor with his good hand and sagged against the table, dizzy with pain from the shock of her body. He glared dully, watching her hit hard, then scramble to her hands and knees. She struck out at him. He moved his good arm and amazingly plucked the piece of map from her fist. He stood up carefully. The pain probed down into his back muscles and smoldered in his left arm to the elbow.

"Get up."

"Go ahead! Take it and be damned! Read your map and what do you see? Nothing! There's nothing! Because you've failed! Like your father before you! No better than him! Worse!"

"Shut up, you little whore. Don't mention him."

He stepped toward her. She rose to a crouch and scragged the hair away from her face. Her pale lips puckered. He watched her spit at him and miss.

"And who was he, anyway, God?"

"Go sit down. You have a bad temper. How did Vizarra ever stand you?"

She looked at him uncertainly, her eyes bright with anger, nearly weeping. She turned and walked, holding up her man's pants, back to the cot and sat down heavily, hunched and shivering. He dropped the torn piece of map to the table. The air was filled with earthy-smelling dust that she had stirred. She blew her nose and laughed softly.

"Funny. We got on very well together."

"Two of a kind."

"Go read your stupid map."

Mi padre vale mucho. Was he God? No, but part of God. He was free and fought to make others free. And that is right, for God needs free men. Without free men, God is a cripple. He needs free men to work out His destiny. He gives the treasure and collects it again. Freedom is His miracle. My father knew that. But no miracle is free. I have paid, though. Nearly the full price. And I want the old man, *El Feo,* as the receipt. He will understand.

She said something.

"What?"

"I said, how's your arm?"

"All right."

"I didn't mean to hurt your arm."

"It's nothing."

"Well. I didn't mean to hurt it."

"No."

"So we just sit here and wait for the telephone to ring?"

"That's right."

"Maybe it will be God. Long-distance."

He felt himself grin. Carlitos or the old man. How long since they had talked? How long had it been? A few days, only. It was not possible.

She had lighted another cigarette and sat smoking nervously when he looked at her. Some of her defiance had come back.

"You don't believe me. That it's over. Finished."

"You are not General Lucca. Not Zamal. Not Gómez. Not Vizarra."

"You don't have a chance."

"When the miners strike into the city, we will have won. I was just working out the final commands. The city will fall. Finally."

"The people will not fight for you."

"They will fight for themselves. We are buying time for them to get ready."

"You believe in miracles."

"Not to believe in miracles argues a lack of imagination."

"Why doesn't the damned telephone ring, then? That would be a miracle."

"No, señorita. That would be a relief. Believe me."

"Does your arm hurt? Are you in pain?"

Pain. *El dolor. Mi padre vale mucho. La sangre me da dolor.* If it weren't for pain, what would Spaniards talk about? With the French it's love, with the English the weather.

"I must know what's going on out there! This is not tolerable! What has Carlitos done?"

She chuckled and tapped her cigarette.

"He's betrayed you."

"Perhaps. That would depend."

"You mean you *expected* him to?"

"I can tell what he thinks, most of the time. It matters little. If he has betrayed me and we win—"

"And if you lose?"

"We will not. But . . . just say, say that we do. What will it matter then to me what becomes of Carlos Sánchez? What will he have gained?"

"The same thing his father gained. His life."

He looked down at the telephone and touched it again.

If only I could talk with him. I could tell him that I know. That I've known for years. That I knew the instant I found them, dead together, up there in the mountains. That he had betrayed them. That he betrayed my father and my mother in order to protect, to save, not himself alone but *us*. Carlitos and me. I must tell him now that I have forgiven him. That I forgave him long ago. Forgave *him* . . . but not the betrayal. The sinner, not the sin. I could pick it up and call. But the line will be tapped. More likely cut. I should have gone myself. How stupid! Better to risk being shot by O'Conner's police in the Glorieta Colón than have dangled life in front of Carlito's nose. I trusted him once too often. Or have I? I am condemning him unheard . . . because this damned thing will not ring. I need the old man. Once more, I need him. To explain how I feel. That I know that instead of the quick, clean kill I deceived myself into believing we could effect, we have but bungled the butchery. Instead of the ritual sacrifice, I have merely maimed the animal, and now must watch helplessly while it stumbles in the sand, blowing blood from its nostrils, weak-knuckled and dull-eyed, but not hurt enough to die. Just hurt enough to suffer.

"Hey."

"Shut up, will you?"

"Is there something to drink in this hole? I'm freezing."

He hesitated, thinking. Yes. They had brought a box in from the truck when they left off the girl. There was a bottle or two, some clothing, a few bits of food and somebody's briefcase.

He walked into the darkness, groping beyond the bright pool of light, blindly. His boot struck a wooden crate, and he nearly fell. He squatted clumsily and fumbled in the box. His hand touched the cool cylinder of the bottle, a shaggy, damp sheepskin, the scraped leather of the briefcase. He gathered the objects slowly, awkwardly, hunching the briefcase up under his armpit, cradling the bottle in the crook of his wounded arm. When he picked up the briefcase, two glasses clinked. He forced them into his pockets, straightened and walked back to the girl.

"Here. Put this on."

"*Gracias.*"

The bottle was open. He set the glasses on the table.

"*Carlos Primero.* Typical. Carlos the First. Nothing but the best."

He filled the glasses and handed her one.

"*Salud.*"

"You're old-fashioned. We say 'Cheers' now. Like the English. Very chic."

"Oh."

"What's that, your newest book?"

"No."

"I've read your books, you know. Yes, all of them. And your poems, too."

Mi padre vale mucho . . .

"He had them in the library at the villa. He used to admire them, read them aloud."

"Am I supposed to be flattered?"

"I suppose not. Give me another drink. I want to feel numb. That's good stuff. Your friend Carlitos has good taste."

"Has he? He's an alcoholic, among other things."

"Then we'd get along. Old Sánchez was too serious for me."

Too serious. And he had the stuff of greatness. *Hombre,* but you've got to save it. You used it all up, and then what was left? Nothing. Nothing but the fear of death.

"Rafael used to torment him. He'd sit there and read one of your books aloud, see? Or I'd play the piano. One of the songs the people made from your poems. They were all forbidden, of course. And the tears would come to his eyes, old *El Feo.* He'd push his lips together.

He looked like an old horse. Until he went white around the mouth. Rafael would not let him even mention your name."

"That is why those like Vizarra must be destroyed. He practices cruelty with deliberation. And on a man noble enough to ruin himself and go on living in self-inflicted humiliation—"

"You're not listening. That's not polite. Give me another."

He drained his glass. The stuff rushed down into his chest like liquid gold. The tears sprang to his eyes. He groped for her glass.

"Huh! That stuff is strong."

"You don't like it?"

"Not much. When I'm with Carlos, I drink. Because he likes it. It makes him feel better if I drink, too. I don't have the head for it. Makes me dizzy. I don't like that. I don't like losing control. That happened to me once. A long time ago."

"I know. But did you lose control up there in the mountains? Or was that the way you really are?"

"What? Listen, why don't you just shut up and get drunk?"

"Yes, that's the way you are. If you had a knife now, you'd cut my throat. No knife. Going to beat me to death with that stupid briefcase, instead?"

"Shut up, you bitch!"

He flung the briefcase on the cot, drank his glass empty and sat down. He could feel the brandy in his blood. He scrubbed his watering eyes. He stared at her, wondering if she was trying to get him drunk.

"Vizarra knew it, too. He must have. That's why he ordered the hostages taken and shot. He was doing it for *you!* He called you his son."

"No!"

"Yes. He did it because he knew that you wanted them dead."

"That's not true!"

He sat for a moment, his mind racing, a jumble of thoughts, piling together in a confused heap, vague and blurred. He spoke and seemed to be listening to himself speak, but from a slight distance. He felt odd, ill.

"His . . . son. That's a . . . a filthy idea. My father was Felipe Martín. A *man,* not a mule. And she was a woman. And they came and tore her to pieces. And they came and hanged my father from a tree by one leg! They came and killed them like dogs. And like other dogs, the people up there did nothing. *Nothing!* They just watched. Before God and the Virgin I have forgiven them all . . . the soldiers. The betrayer. But not the others. No. What they did *not* do gives me the right. Yes, I have the right to take my vengeance. And I take it! And it is *sweet* . . . very sweet. Flesh for my flesh and blood for blood. The last one will be Vizarra. Him. And then . . . I stop."

"You . . . butcher."

"Yes. You are right. A butcher. And I have never confessed since that day in the mountains. I have never had on my tongue the wafer and the wine. They would have turned to dust and vinegar."

"And you expect some priest to . . ."

"Absolve me? Yes. Because I am repentant. But I cannot apologize. My revenge is honorable. Honorable. I will not apologize. Neither to man nor—"

The telephone tittered.

He started. The girl gasped. He snatched up the receiver.

"Carlos! Tell me that he's free. Put him on. I must tell him—What? . . . Oh . . . it's you . . ."

The voice was faint, the line crackled with static. But the voice spoke French with a Belgian accent.

"When are we getting out of here?"

He shook his head at her. She stood and walked to him, grabbed at the receiver. He swatted at her, but missed. He sat listening to the harsh, distant voice totaling the account.

"Ramos is dead. The student cadres were cut to pieces at the university. *Allô, allô?* I must retreat. In ten minutes we blow up the barracks here. The miners and the militia didn't make it. We have lost, Alessandro. *C'est fini . . .*"

"What's happened?"

He looked into her face and nodded slowly.

"You were right, señorita. Your Vizarra has won after all."

She looked down at him, saying nothing. She raised her glass. Her teeth clicked on the rim, and the brandy spilled down the front of the sheepskin jacket. She turned away and walked to the cot. He drew a deep breath.

"All right. Voget? Send a car to Boca Perro. To a man named Juanito. He's the leader of the fishing boat captains and smugglers there. Get as many of your people as you can out of the city at once. And I don't mean just Party members. Get Olmega's students on the boats. The freighter with the arms shipment should be at the rendezvous point. Too late there, too. Their next port of call is Buenos Aires. Listen. Your money is in the safe in the paymaster's office of the fishing cooperative in Boca Perro. The combination is six right, twice left to three, right again to seven. *Six, trois, sept. C'est ça.* In a big brown envelope. The rest has been banked for you in Antwerp, as we arranged. Coco's share can be given to his widow."

"*Ça va?* You're all right? How's the arm?"

"I'm all right, *hombre.* Right now I am organizing the rearguard action to cover your retreat. Carlos will be back *pronto.* We'll hold Boca Perro as long as we can. Just get them out of the country."

"*D'accord. Viva la revolución!*"

"What? Ah, yes. *Viva la revolución. Adiós,* Voget. You fought well and with honor. Costa Plata will remember you. I will submit a full report to your superiors in Moscow. Take care of Olmega. *Adiós . . . à bientôt.*"

He set the receiver down gently and drew a long breath, then struck the map of the city so that it sailed like a gaudy bat off into the darkness. Sour juices gushed into his mouth and clogged his throat. He spat on the floor.

"*El final* . . . thirteen years for nothing. He beat me. The Old Mule. They were brave. They fought with honor. And now . . . we have lost. *Lost.*"

He could not believe it. Like a bullet, the impact traumatized the flesh. His brain could know, but not yet feel. The agony would come not at once but soon, inevitable as fate.

"What . . . what will you do?"

"Do? What I said. Wait for Sánchez. Maybe we can get out on one of the boats. Carlitos, the old man and me. If not, we'll fight at Boca Perro."

He watched her. Her hands were shaking. She rose and walked to the table and refilled her glass, then his.

"Here. Drink this."

"I don't want it. Leave it there. For Carlitos, when he comes."

"He's never coming. It will be the others. O'Conner's police."

He shook his head.

"Even if he has betrayed me, he will come back. *Because* he has

549

betrayed me. You'll be all right. *El Feo,* too. They'll have no more use for him."

She bent close to him, staring, her dark eyes bewildered. He leaned away from her.

"Alessandro? You . . . you didn't think that you could get that old man free by bargaining with Rafael Vizarra for *me?"*

"Eh? Of course. Of course! The exchange should have taken place hours ago. Now it really doesn't matter . . ."

"Doesn't matter!"

She began to laugh, tight, brittle laughter like strips of metal gnashing together. He winced away from the sound. She stumbled back to the cot and fell on it, racked with hysteria, thrashing in a fit from side to side, screaming. He waited, stunned and helpless, then dragged himself erect and walked to her. He bent over her and shook her, gently at first, then hard, slamming her against the hard mattress. Tears ran out of her squeezed eyes. She caught a breath, laughed again, short, wrenching gasps, then stopped, exhausted. She lay on her back, staring up at him with tear-blinded eyes.

"Are you all right, señorita?"

She rolled her head weakly on the rough blankets and wiped her face on the clumsy sleeve of the sheepskin jacket. Her voice was weak, phlegmy.

"Oh, Alessandro, don't call me that. I'm only Vizarra's whore."

"I didn't mean to call you that."

"He . . . threw me out. You see? You tried to bargain with a worthless piece of goods. Vizarra was going to send me away to Mexico City tonight, by the last mail flight. He doesn't want me any more. So . . . see? It's *el final. El final* for both of us."

She sat up suddenly and fumbled out a cigarette. His legs felt suddenly weak. He sat down on the cot near her. He began to feel it, the first pangs of the wound, the rip of defeat.

"So Carlitos escaped me. All those years I drove him like a burro, ordering, insisting that he be a better man than he was. I made him live up to me. The bastard. I gave him pain. And got it back. The same coin. *Cara y cruz—"*

They both heard it at the same instant, the faint drone of engines.

"Is that—"

"No . . ."

He hesitated. Tell her. *Tell her, man.*

"That is the last mail flight to Mexico City."

She covered her face with her hands. Outside the cave, up in the night sky, the trimotor circled once over the smoldering, silent city, the wing lights winking, red and green, heading north for Mexico, the slow throb of engines fading, fading . . .

He sat beside her, his limbs slack. Feeble pains twitched in his shoulder and down his arm. He felt a great lassitude, a leaden slackness, pressing down on him.

It's too bad. This business has wrung me dry. They say a murderer feels this way. I never felt it before. Not like this. Raskolnikov went back and flung himself down on his sofa after putting the ax to the old pawnbroker. Now, now that it's finished and I know that it's finished, all I can think is . . . *too bad*. What if we'd won, and I saw Vizarra stretched dead now at my feet? What would I say then? *That's nice*. Something like that. How often we triumph—or fail— with nothing but banalities on our lips. I should be able to leave them something, some last few words, a phrase to covet like a relic. But . . . I have no words. None. Future historians will find me a dull type. I should grab up the lamp and soot the walls with some memorable utterance, or scratch on the stone of the altar until the blood runs there again. Instead, I say . . . *too bad*. Only *El Feo* would appreciate the irony of the poet struck dumb, the novelist unable to complete his autobiography. History can only condemn the artist weary beyond words.

"The truck is still outside, isn't it?"

"Yes. I ordered them to stay."

"But it doesn't matter now."

"But there's no point in your staying here."

"Is there any point in leaving? For either of us?"

"Eh . . . not for me. I'm sitting here trying to think of something noble. All my brain tells me is that my arm hurts. Not my heart, just my arm."

"I'm not going. I'm here. There's drink and *tabaco rubio*. In fact, I'll stay even if you leave."

"Señorita, women often mistake laziness for chivalry."

"When will they . . . come for us?"

He stood up and wandered across to the table.

"Want some more of this stuff?"

"Yes, please."

"Not too much. You'll get drunk."

"So what? I've been drunk plenty of times."

"Ah? How sophisticated."

She began to weep again, silently, so that for the time it took to raise the bottle and tilt it, he did not notice. She huddled on the cot, her hands in her lap, weeping silently, the clear drops rolling swiftly down her cheeks, falling on her knuckles. He stared at her, then picked the briefcase up off his cot, tucked it under his arm and carried the bottle over to her. He sat down beside her and sighed.

What a finish. *Jesucristo!* In a hole like an animal. One useless paw. A weeping woman. Waiting for the pack to dig me out. And then . . . the teeth.

"Señorita . . ."

"I'm sorry."

"I was not sympathetic. I spoke stupidly. I know something of your life. Enough to guess that how you lived before you went with Vizarra was enough to make you want to get drunk."

"Ya-ya . . . this is stupid. I never cried much before. Oh, it was better with him. He was . . . kind. Do you believe that?"

"Yes. Come, now, have a drink. First, dry your eyes. Here, take this."

She felt him push something into her hands She looked at it. A faded, worn piece of silk, stained and coated with grit. He took it back and shook it. It was a woman's scarf.

"Here. Keep it. I don't need it now."

She turned to him, stretched out her hands, and touched his drained and weary face. Her arms felt heavy and weak inside the bulky sheepskin. The shadows on his face masked his eyes. She pushed her trembling fingers into his stiff hair and drew his head toward her until his bitter mouth touched hers. She kept her eyes open and saw his lids flutter and, for an instant, close. He allowed himself to be kissed. Then he flung his good arm around her and hugged her with all his strength, holding her awkwardly, hard, his arm like a cable. The effort dragged his jaw open as he tried to drive what was left of his own strength into her. She felt his breath beat in her tangled hair.

"Are you so frightened, Lucía, that you won't even try to run? Come, be strong! Get out of here now. While you can!"

She pushed her face against his. His cheek was stubbled, gritty and cold. She muttered into the collar of his tunic.

"Where?"

He released her and pulled away, kicking idly at the briefcase. She watched him, trying to think of something to say, some way to thank him. She picked up the bottle and drank from it.

"That was . . . good of you. Maybe now my hands will stop shaking."

"I'm not very romantic."

She shrugged and smiled.

"Well, I could sing for you. Too bad there's no piano here. He wanted me to sing one of your songs for him on the radio tonight. But I was . . . interrupted. Eh, *hombre,* what will the people think, eh? *La Paloma de Costa Plata* giving a solo performance in a cave? *Escándalo público!"*

"No, not a scandal. Just . . . nothing. An absurdity."

"You never thought you'd lose, did you?"

"No. Never. I must be getting senile. I think I really believed that it was possible to live a life without anticlimax. And now . . . this. My mind is numb."

"Eh, my face is. I'm drunk . . . no, half drunk. I feel better."

"Look. Get out of here."

"No."

"I don't *want* you here!"

"Too bad. *Qué lástima!* Make me go, then."

"Look, if you think you're going to create some big scene, I can assure you that you'll be disappointed. This is Costa Plata, not Mayerling."

"Where's that? Out in the *campo,* isn't it?"

He made a snorting sound in his nose, picked up the briefcase and undid the straps. She tipped up the bottle and swallowed. The brandy flowed like hot honey into her. She felt gay, like singing, except that her teeth chattered.

"Huh . . . look at this stuff. A Hebrew prayer book, some money . . ."

"Good. I'll take that."

"What's this? A contract for . . . shoes and woolen goods. And a bunch of insurance policies. Insurance policies! There . . . you see? You see? He was right, that fat Englishman. Life *does* imitate art! This is perfect, *perfect.* Just what we need, no?"

"What fat Englishman? Livermore is very thin. They have no blood, the English. *Ni sangre ni leche."*

"Wilde. Oscar Wilde. A writer."

"A friend of yours?"

"Hardly. We've both been in jail, but the offenses were somewhat different. Here, sign right here."

She looked from the stiff sheets of paper he handed her to his grinning face.

"What are these things?"

"Can't you read? Don't you think it's funny?"

"No."

"Women have no sense of humor. They never laugh at the grotesque; they wash its face. Huh, I have no pen. I couldn't sign if I wanted to. Look here!"

"What?"

"This thing is signed by General Vola! That fat, drunken swine was buying insurance. Buying magic, like Chinchón told me. What's this other name? Fingel. Don't know him. Must be a friend of Vola's. Fingel, Fingel . . . I should know him."

"Here."

She lit a cigarette with shaking fingers and placed it between his pale lips. She tried to touch his face, but he jerked away. He blew smoke out his nose and grinned again at the pieces of paper. One corner was stained. He brought it close to his face. His hands jerked, and the contract fell to the floor of the cave.

"What's the matter?"

"Blood on it . . . dried blood."

"Listen, maybe we can make it still! Let's get out of here. We can get away. Together. You don't have to keep me or anything. I know I mean nothing to you. But I've got a lot of money. I mean I will have. In Switzerland. He put money there for me. In banks. I could help you. God, man, don't just sit there! Plenty of money. You could try again. Keep the Movement alive. And we'd be alive, too. Don't you want that? Alessandro, look at me. Please . . . help me!"

"There is only one sure way of keeping the Movement alive."

"But I don't want to die!"

"Then, go."

"Come with me, Alessandro. I beg you!"

"I must stay. I owe it to them, don't you see? But if you leave, you'll have a chance. I have a duty to stay. I want to stay because it is now the correct thing for me to do. And think how happy the historians will be. I must keep the Movement alive!"

"You won't leave."

"No, this is the proper place. In the famous *cuevas* of Costa Plata. Here . . . with my bottle of brandy, and I seldom drank. Cigarettes, and I seldom smoked. And my Hebrew book of prayers, and I cannot read them. And my insurance policies, and I cannot sign them."

"Oh, shut up, then."

"And with Lucía Bosola, Vizarra's mistress. Huh! I never did *that* very often, either. Ya-ya, but what they will make of me, eh?"

"Give me the bottle. I'm going to get drunk."

"Here."

"No . . . never mind."

"Go ahead. If that's what you want."

"That's all that's left. I think you're crazy."

"No. I am waking up. I can feel it!"

He stood up from the cot so suddenly that she nearly fell sideways. He stood straight and smiling, staring out into the darkness as though he saw something heaped against the wall. His eyes gleamed with a certain joy.

"Yes. Awake now, after *el sueño de la razón* . . . the sleep of reason that produces monsters."

"Where are you going? Don't leave me!"

"Just over here. To the telephone."

"You're not going to call? Don't surrender, don't!"

"Surrender? No. I am going to call old Sánchez. *El Feo.* I want my philosopher now. An old man, yes, but my Horatio all the same. I know that he held me in his heart. And now I want him to tell my story. For I, too, will leave a wounded name."

"How's your arm?"

"As good as it will ever be. Hello? *Oiga, oiga . . .*"

She sat on the cot, cuddling the bottle on her lap. She raised it and sipped slowly, steadily. He stood erect beside the table, calling fiercely, again and again. His voice echoed off the walls, the syllables tumbling together in a meaningless jumble of sound that went on and on, lapping and overlapping, beating back off the dark walls and off rumbling and dying, the chant springing up again and pounding on. She grew slowly rigid with fear. She saw his face, calm, intent, gilded by the lamplight. She saw his lips move, but she could not tell if he confessed or cursed. The sounds gobbled and boomed off the stone chamber, an unknown language, heavy with old menace and future threat, black syllables that stuttered in her ears, the quarreling voices of men and gods.

He set down the receiver and stood waiting until the echo tocked back like the sound of a blade dropped on an altar. He mused, motionless, waiting and listening.

She heard it. Men moving, a slow, stealthy shuffling, just within the entrance. Alessandro lifted the lamp.

"It's him. He's come back!"

Alessandro shook his head. He raised the lamp high. The flame played and sparkled on the thousands of bits of bright glass and polished stone. The frozen forms swung dazzling through the golden light, glittered chilly viridian, bold cobalt and hectic crimson, wheeling, gyring, blotted by vast, swooping shadows. The voice slammed off the stiff shield of Vigo.

"Alessandro!"

He beckoned to her. She rose, stupefied with fear and brandy, and wandered to his side. The golden light misted before her; the flame trembled and the figure of Axoloqui moved, his silver robe rippling as his fist groped for the woman of vapor, Onati.

He took the bottle from her and bashed it on the table, spraying brandy and glass. With the jagged neck in one hand, he bent forward carefully, lowered the lamp and huffed out the light. The careening figures vanished. There was just the dark.

She whimpered and fumbled closer until she stood behind him, sheltered, and there clung to him, her face against his shoulders. She bent with him when he crouched in the total darkness, alert and dangerous. She heard the clumsy footsteps scuff and clank across the cold stone floor. The cry died in her throat. She heard him whisper very softly.

"Here . . . here I am, *amigo*. Right here. But you'll have to come and get me. I will never give up now. And I will never apologize. *Never . . .*"

556

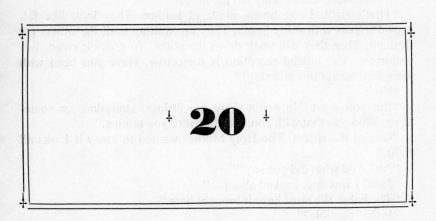

20

SHE sat on a low chair, her face toward the shattered window. He stood behind her, looking over her dark head, his hands resting on the back of the chair.

"Tell me, please, what they are doing."

"Oh, there are a great many men. Right in front, at the iron fence, about, oh, twenty Guards are rolling up the barbed wire and loading it into three trucks."

"Why do they call out? They're calling numbers."

"Yes. Those aren't the Guards. Regular soldiers. Two ordnance companies. They have set up long tables. Four—no, five—men are sitting there. When the member of the Red Beret steps up, he calls out his card number and one of the soldiers checks that with a party official. Then he lays down his rifle or pistol, whatever he has, and one of the soldiers calls out the serial numbers. That's entered on a separate list. Another group is stacking and checking the recaptured weapons."

"Oh."

"There is a water truck from the sanitation department. Right in the middle of the plaza."

"Yes. I heard them taking out the hoses."

"That's right. Long hoses, made of leather. They look like fat, brown snakes with shiny heads. They are waiting until the others get through. Then they will wash down the plaza. To make it clean. For tomorrow. The official reception is tomorrow. Have you been with your dressmaker this morning?"

"No."

"But you must. No doubt there are fittings, alterations or something. Who was that with you, then? I heard you talking."

"One of the sisters. The Holy Mother wanted to know if I was all right."

"Ah? And what did you say?"

"I said I was fine. I asked about—"

"The baby. We must have it brought here."

"Is that possible?"

"What? Of course. Everything is possible. Everything you want. Within reason, of course. To talk about going back to the sisters is not reasonable. To bring the child here to you is very reasonable. You will see the dressmaker."

"Must I?"

"Of course. The new dress will make you happy, no?"

"They are all alike to me, dresses."

"But not to me. Besides, don't you want to see . . . to meet the American and the English gentleman?"

"No, not really. Please, don't make me. His Grace will—"

"His Grace is still in the hospital. I am seeing him this afternoon, after the Cabinet meeting. I understand he is improving. Only Monseñor Blanco, his secretary, will be at the reception. And he is very quiet, Monseñor Blanco . . . for a priest. You have no reason to fear him."

"Oh, I'm not afraid. But they can see me. I would feel ashamed."

He moved his hands down to her shoulders and pressed with his fingers.

"From now on, you are not to be ashamed. What have you done to be ashamed, anyway?"

"It's a sin."

He bent down, the back of the chair striking his chest, until his lips nearly touched her ear.

"And the child? What was that? I have made arrangements for the child to be baptized, no? That ignorant priest in the pueblo—"

"No, he was a good man. Very good. It was the people there. They told him if he baptized the child, they would take it from me and kill it."

"So. Aren't you happier here than back in such a place?"

"I was very happy with the sisters."

"You will be happier here."

"As you say."

"Very well, do not attend the reception. Perhaps you are right. They will remember, the foreigners. It has been only such a short time. And it is best to proceed slowly. This is all new to you. I don't want to force you."

"Thank you."

"But there must be no more talk of the sisters. The baby will be brought here. One of the sisters may visit you one day each week. On Sunday. Every Sunday we will go to Mass together. Then you may receive one of the sisters. I suppose you have a favorite?"

"Yes."

"Do not receive her too often. No more than once each month."

"But—"

"There are certain things that you cannot do too often. The people will know. The orphanage is important to me. Certain people, if they know you receive one of the sisters too often, will stop their donations."

"But why?"

"Why? Because, that's why. You are not back in the pueblo now. Everything is different here. Much better for you. You do agree?"

"Yes."

He released her and straightened.

"Now, there was something else. What was it?"

"A loom."

"A loom? What for?"

"Could I have one? Oh, please . . ."

"What ever for?"

"That was how I earned my living. By weaving. I made the finest cloth. Of wool."

"All right. Just as long as you don't want the sheep, too."

"No. That would be very difficult. How would I feed them here?"

"That was a joke. I was joking."

"I'm sorry. I am stupid."

"No."

"Tell me what else is out there."

"Nothing else."

"But the ships in the harbor. Are they pretty?"

He gazed out across the city. The British frigate turned at anchor, a thread of smoke rising from the single tall funnel. The turrets were turned so that the guns pointed at the city. The naval ensign floated and rolled on the stern flagstaff. Lighters circled the vessel like water bugs, bringing the detachment of Royal Marines into the shattered docks. The American gunboats, two of them, low and squat, were moored near the jetty.

"Pretty. I think . . . yes, they are pretty. From here they look like children's toys. Very . . . harmless. I understand the English brought a band, too. You will hear some nice music tomorrow."

"One of them is very big. I heard the whistle. It sounded big and sad."

"That's the *Silver Princess,* a big liner. She's tied up to the company pier. She calls here every eighteen days for freight, mail and passengers. Today, well, is unusual. You see, they turned back at Panama."

"And they . . . where are they now?"

"Who?"

"My maid told me . . . from the light pole. They were there at dawn. I heard the soldiers and the police and the others shouting. They said terrible things. Are they there?"

He looked at the iron streetlamp. The two ropes dangled, swaying in the light, moist breeze. The ends had frayed. Sand had been thrown on the pavement.

"No . . . they are not there. I had them sent away."

"To the cemetery?"

"What for? No, not to the cemetery. Do you expect them to lie in state in the cathedral? I just had them sent away, that's all."

"And the miners?"

"Yes, they're out there."

"I could hear them, too. They were singing, but I couldn't make out the words."

"You hear very well. You hear . . . too much, perhaps."

"And must I be deaf, too?"

"No, I only meant . . ."

He felt himself flush and bit his lip. When the rap sounded on the door, he left her without speaking. He opened the door and stepped into the salon. Malata bowed slightly and walked over to the table. The map had been removed. At the far end of the room, plasterers and carpenters were repairing the pocked walls and ceiling. A new carpet lay rolled in the center of the room. Malata gestured at the workmen.

"I have spoken to the foreman, Excellency. Everything will be ready. They will work all through the night. But nothing can be done about the shell hole. The mason must cut new stones. I have suggested that one of the tapestries be taken from the dining hall and hung up to conceal it. The new chandelier will be installed this afternoon."

"Very good. Now, send someone to find out about looms. The kind women use to weave with in the pueblos."

"Yes, Excellency, one loom. The old-fashioned kind, I suppose."

"I suppose so. I am not in the textile business."

"Of course not, Excellency."

"Have it taken to the villa. Put it in the music room. See to it that the piano is removed."

"Remove the piano, Excellency? But for dancing parties, the orchestras will need—"

"There will be no dancing parties. There is no need for dancing parties and orchestras. Not any longer. Get a loom."

"Yes, Excellency."

"What have you there?"

"Documents to be approved before being released to the newspapers, Excellency."

"Write a decree lifting the censorship ban."

"I have taken the liberty . . . right here on top."

"Good."

Malata opened the folder and placed the typed sheets on the table. The Caudillo read them through and signed the first two, then sat back and stared at the plasterers up on the scaffolding.

"Where is he?"

"Still at security police headquarters."

"Notify him that he is the new Minister of Public Education. He is to be released and to come here before the Cabinet meeting. He will not, however, attend the Cabinet meeting. He will meet our foreign . . . guests."

"Very good."

"Give him, you know, my deepest sympathies and all the rest of it."

"Very good."

"How did the old man do it?"

"With his belt, Excellency. He stood on a chair and tied the end to the light fixture. The fixture pulled off the wall, but even so. He was very ugly, indeed, if I may say so. The body has been removed to the chapel."

"The chapel? But he can't be there. Take him to one of the places in the city."

"But, Excellency, look at the next sheet. You see? The doctor has made out the death certificate as heart failure."

"Just like him, the quack. Pay him off and get him on the ship. I want new doctors. Eye specialists. Find out about it."

"And *El Feo?*"

"He died of a heart attack. Have arrangements made for a funeral. A quiet funeral, but attended by all officials. I will make the young one's appointment after the service, dress him in the official sash and so on. A continuation, a sign of stability. The funeral will be held in three days. Two days. Now, this is O'Conner, eh?"

"Yes. He will be arrested tonight."

"Umm . . . *for evident collusion with the forces of rebellion and anarchy.* General Lucca will take care of this."

"He has been informed. O'Conner will be on the next freighter bound for Brazil. Four men will go with him. He will not arrive in Brazil."

"Pay him off handsomely, Julio. A hundred thousand, at the least. Record the serial numbers of the bills. The four agents will be responsible for seeing it deposited in the national treasury. Make that very clear."

Malata bowed and waited. The Caudillo bent over the documents. He read slowly, his lips moving. Malata saw the blood flush his forehead. Vizarra looked up, his face congested with rage. He stabbed the sheet of paper with one thick finger.

"What . . . what is this? What is the meaning of this piece of filth!"

"I'm afraid I don't understand, Excellency."

"This . . . *medical report!*"

"Well, already the people believe that she and Alessandro were . . . well, you understand, a rumor only, but I thought—"

"You? You think? You thought what?"

"The story has already started, Excellency. That they were lovers. That, in fact, they were there, in the cave, for a rendezvous. For . . . sentimental purposes. Now, of course, this reflects on . . . on yourself, Excellency, and so I thought that—"

"On me? It reflects on *me?*"

"I instructed the doctor to perform a post-mortem examination. The report speaks for itself. There is no evidence that the . . . that anything happened. That they had been making love."

Vizarra curled his fingers into fists and slowly stood up. Malata backed up two paces and wet his lips.

"You mean to tell me that you turned her body over to that doctor? To be mauled? To be poked? To be—"

"It was all completely scientific, Excellency . . ."

Vizarra picked up the sheet of paper and tore it into pieces, wadded the fragments and flung them into the wastebasket. He leaned across the table, his voice clotted, his lips set like a knife slash.

"You little swine! You filthy-minded ghoul! Get out of here! Get out! Leave Costa Plata and never come back. Never! Within forty-eight hours!"

Malata inclined his sleek head and drew a piece of paper from his jacket.

"You will regret this, you know."

"I should have done it years ago! What's that?"

"Why, my pay voucher. You'll sign it, of course."

"No!"

"Forty-eight hours is a long time. A lot can happen in two days. To Mr. Dunkel the American, for instance. Or Livermore. If word reached O'Conner in time . . . it would be very regrettable. Clear proof that you are incapable of governing Costa Plata. Of protecting the lives of foreign nationals. A lot can happen in forty-eight hours. Often, people change their minds. Yes, change their minds in forty-eight hours."

"Get out of here. You . . . *animal!*"

Malata bowed and glided across the floor. Vizarra slumped down in his chair and twisted his fingers together. He stared at the pay voucher. He fumbled out a cigar and lit it with shaking hands. He felt the plasterers up on the scaffold staring at him. He raised his head and growled at them.

"Get on with your work up there!"

He rose and limped slowly across the room. He stared out into the Plaza Mayor. The Indians still stood there, a little herd of them, bunched together at the far end of the plaza, staring fixedly at the two frayed ropes that dangled from the iron branch of the streetlamp. Vizarra smoked and stared out through the new, putty-smeared window. They were so passive, so patient, the miners. He picked out their leader, a powerful young man with one arm. How long would they stay out there, standing so silently, their eyes staring at the ropes, their faces blank, expressionless, rapt like worshipers at a shrine? The Caudillo shook his head.

"He's gone. He's gone. You came too late . . . or too early."

⸸

The motor thudded and the single screw threshed slowly, grinding the slick swells. The trawler rolled heavily. Already the seabirds, the solemn gulls and black-capped terns, had wheeled back, shrieking, for the low shore. Four more trawlers pushed across the green satin water, spinning out white wakes like lace. The *Guardacostas'* patrol boat fired again, a puff of smoke from the one-pounder on the bow. The plume of spray shot up, two hundred meters behind the last trawler. Olmega listened for the pop of the shot. He pushed his arm free from the blanket and set his thumbnail between his teeth and snapped it at the patrol boat.

"Cabronazos! Hijos de la puta grande!"

Voget grinned and took off his cap. He sat on a coil of greasy rope, part of the trawl rig.

"We made it, *copain*. There's the freighter, see?"

"Yes, *we* made it. With two hundred back on the beaches."

Voget shrugged.

"You always leave some on the beaches, kid. That's the way it is. But they'll be waiting for us when we come back."

"When we come back. Yes. But when? When will that be?"

"Well, we've got to see the comrades in Antwerp. Then Paris. Go to Stockholm. Then Moscow. I have to report. And you'll come along. It's winter in Moscow. Or will be when we get there. You'll get over the fever, kid. It's cold in Moscow."

"Will I? Will I get over it? I don't think so . . ."

Olmega sat in the tangled net, wrapped in his blanket, his revolver still strapped on his hip. He looked back at the shore, a low green smudge. Farther north, smoke like threads spun up into the sky and diffused. Beneath the sun lay the broken city and beyond that the misted jags of the sierra. He pointed them out to Voget.

"Next time there will be no beach and people left there. When we come back, we'll begin the fight up there, high in the mountains."

"We'll see, comrade."

"Yes, comrade, we'll see . . . I'll see, anyway. From the mountains to the sea."

✝

Down the long stone tunnels the dark water poured unceasingly, a black roaring flood. She knelt in the gloom, kneading and pounding, soaking and bleaching, rinsing the stains away. She spread the sopped garments out very carefully: an army tunic, a pair of tuxedo pants and a white satin blouse. *Tía Ajo* picked up her long stick with the iron claw fixed on the end and pushed the dim, heavy lump of the sheepskin jacket out into the stream. The water sucked it through the rusty grate. She bent and picked up a belt and two boots and threw them, one after the other, into the cold, dark flood.

✛ THE STATUE ✛

THE east side of the Plaza de la Revolución is formed by the old Gálvez brandy distillery, now the *Museo de la Hecatombe.* The glass cases containing a woman's torn dress, eighteen pairs of children's shoes, a rusty black shawl, broken eyeglasses and a white cane line three walls. The fourth, pitted shoulder high with bullet holes, is blank. In the center of the room stand a Browning .30-caliber machine gun and a portable army radio transmitter. On the floor, from the muzzle of the machine gun to the blank wall, four hundred and twelve rosaries are laid out in the form of a cross.

Outside, in the center of the plaza, stands the statue, raised on a concrete pedestal six and one-half meters high. The figure is cast in five thousand, six hundred and eighty-two kilograms of bronze and stands eleven meters above the pedestal. The face is almost without features, a hint of eyes, a fold of metal for the nose, no ears and a hole for the mouth. The right arm is extended, pointing. At the left leg, in a squatting position, is the figure of a young woman. That face, entirely without features, is turned upward as though dumbly pleading. The city taxi drivers tell the same joke to every tourist. They slow the cab at the monument, point out the figures, wait a few seconds and then explain that Alessandro is saying, *"Down the hall, señorita. The first door on your left. You can't miss it."*

The anniversary of Alessandro's death is a national holiday in Costa Plata. The President of the Republic, accompanied by the Ambassador of the United States, the British Consul, the cardinal with his withered, crippled hands and the Minister of State Security, lays a wreath at the foot of the monument and then delivers a very long speech. The American Ambassador comments every year that his nation contributed the concrete that forms the pedestal of the monument. The British Consul reads a statement in Spanish concerning the balance of trade. The cardinal gives the benediction, and the band, at a signal from General Lucca, plays the national anthem, followed by the revolutionary hymn. Not many in the crowd know the words to the hymn. The conclusion of the annual ceremonies is always unsatisfactory, despite belligerent editorials in the city's newspapers. The crowd begins to flow away down the Avenida Carlos Sánchez toward the cafés long before the muted singing comes to an end.

"Dios, qué calor! Sangría, before I die of the heat! I thought he'd never shut up. Worse than his father."

"Worse than anyone's father."

"He's new, the *Yanqui.* What's it say? Hendricks. Funny name. Did you see his shirt? Little buttons on the collars. Like this. Little buttons. Why is that?"

"Chico, to hold up his shirt. Let's have a beer."

"Of course, Papa remembers. No, it's just the way they made it. It just looks like a bridge. No, Papa didn't blow up any bridges. It just looks like they're on a broken bridge. It was in a cave."

"Every time I look at it, I cry. It's so sad. A real romance. And I pray. For him, you know. Not for her."

"I don't know why I go. It's an offense, really. The whole thing stinks to the heavens. What a farce! There they are, up in the mountains this very minute. Only last week they cut the road north of Casanueva and held it for two days."

"What's two days? A few discontented shepherds, that's all."

567

"That's all it will take, *amigo,* believe me. I've been in for three years now. What can they do? We're a democracy, right? You heard him, didn't you? They haven't made an arrest in six months."

"Six months from now, we'll hang him by *his* heels. Right from Alessandro's hand, the bastard."

"Naturally, for you and me. And all the members of our class. We understand. Certain things must be said. I don't think it's at all cynical. One must consider the low level of literacy. People believe what they are told. So, someone must tell them. Who better than the *Presidente* himself?"

"*Coño!* Remember the day they got him? Coming out of the race-track. *Brrrrt!* One dead mule. And three days later, we have this one. He who can't walk through the doors of the national palace."

"He can. Yes, he can. *Coño!* I saw him. True, he has to turn sideways so his horns don't bump, but what the hell?"

"It is only fitting that once a year we commemorate his life and his death. Our noblest tradition. I mean, every other country has some-one. It's a sign of political maturity."

"I don't see why they close the cinemas. It's so hot. And there's a good film at the Olympic."

"It's disgusting. They ought to pull it down. No wonder they left off the faces. If it had been realistically done, it would have been pornographic. I would forbid the children to walk by it."

"They were afraid. That's why there's no faces. If they looked like you or like me, why, we'd think . . . you know what we'd think. That we were like he was. That we were bigger and better. That we didn't have to beg from Washington or London or anywhere."

"The arm points to the mountains. And when they come down, you know what they're going to do? Put a bend in the arm. So it beckons. Now it just points."

"Psst. Shut up, will you! Ai-yah, look at the lollos on that one! And me weaned at the age of two."

"For two years they have been reclaiming the land in the sierra with irrigation projects. What has happened? Thievery, arson and anarchy. All his ideas. The irrigation program is not only a scientific failure, it's simply a method of watering the Communists."

"Did you see? No banners, no demonstrations this year. Malata's really cracking down. Seventeen arrested last night out at the univer-sity."

"It makes me weep. Well, so I'm old and sentimental. But they were good people, both of them. I know it. I wish he'd include them in his benediction."

"I could hardly hear him. How thin and white he is."

"My dear, he's ancient. And he came back from Rome with jaundice. His hands. He can't move any of his fingers. Still. Think how many doctors have seen him. Slick and shiny. Just like gloves. Let's have a sherbet."

"No. Your father doesn't know anything about it. Of course I was alive then. It was all other people. I never took any interest in politics. My father wasn't even a member of the party."

"My brother's wife's sister's husband works at the library. Well, they got him. You know what for? The suppressed letters. No, the final edition. From him to Sánchez. There were seven copies in the cage in the basement. They checked. There were only four. So they arrested him. For losing three volumes of Alessandro's letters."

"It is all a lot of sentimentality. Like last year. Some idiot jumps off the top of the stadium, wrapped in the flag, shouting his poetry. And why? Because we lost a football game to Peru. *Camarero! Una cerveza.*"

"My boy, there was no one like him. This is truth, so listen. He was like a shooting star in the night sky. *Zzzzosh!* Ah! Like that. For a little while . . . how short a time, too . . . everything was bright, burning and clear. He lit the skies for us, from the mountains to the sea. And brighter, always brighter, every minute, until you couldn't bear to look. Then gone, snuffed out in the darkness. But with shooting stars . . . you've seen them, sure you have . . . why, they burn on in the brain after they've gone out. A little spot of red."

"Say what you will, he brought us progress. He threw us forward. So, we landed on our faces. So what? We got up again, didn't we? New buildings, new schools, new cars."

"Old problems, old ideas, old wounds like running sores. Nothing has changed. He might just as well have been stillborn. Show me a peasant with three hectares of land and I'll show you a peasant picked out by Sánchez, living in a house paid for by Lucca, told what to say by Malata, shaking hands with the American Ambassador for a photographer. The latifundia are still as they were. The rich still own the *campo*. So now we drill oil offshore with towers. Does E-S-S-O spell *República de Costa Plata?* Not in my newspaper, *hombre.*"

"We live in a dream. An air-conditioned dream. The truth was as he saw it. Alone, free and poor. Better to be poor, to live in rags, he said, than to sit in silk at a tyrant's feet, jingling your stick, your fool's bells."

"A complete fool. His father a syphilitic, his mother a woman of the streets. His relationship with those Belgians is too obvious to deserve comment. Thank God Sánchez is a decent, reasonable fellow. No *caballero,* I grant you, but no hairy anarchist, either."

"It's the face. If only that great thing had a *face.* Then I could understand. Allendyce back in London has Nelson to look at. Hendricks has Lincoln. My Jaime was at Georgetown, you know. International scholarship. We saw Washington. I spent nearly two hours in the Lincoln Memorial. Dolores went back to the hotel with the children. Even Jaime was bored. He goes to an American school on a scholarship, and he can't stay with his father for a few minutes to look at Lincoln's statue. My father taught philosophy at the old university and died there. My older brother was wounded in the streets and bled to death. Look at me. You think I look pretty? With this face? I got my face fighting with Alessandro. *With* him, *hombre,* not *for* him. Well, I got my face. So I stood looking up at Lincoln. And I asked Jaime. Yes, I named him for the kid who shot Colleo. Dolores hates the name. I said, why don't we have a face for Alessandro? He was just a young man. *El Jovencito.* Didn't he have a face? Why didn't they ask me? I could have drawn them a picture. Yes, that would have looked like him, too. The face of a man. You know what Jaime said? Oh, the sculptor was Japanese. They understand the ideal better than we do. It's more aesthetic, is that the word? More aesthetic. You know what I did? I gave him one. Right in the face. Right there in the Lincoln Memorial. Paff! And you know what he did? He joined the Communists. Hah! I think he's got guts, that kid. Even with his face covered up with a beard."

"Dignity. That's what we lack. National dignity. We're like children. Politics for us is a license to steal, nothing more. The foreigners who come here. What do they see? The kids pissing in the streets outside the new Hilton. We're a century behind."

"He was right. The future is ours. It belongs to us. No more dictation from the North. Take their money and the hell with them."

"Nothing comes to the people. Sánchez has millions in Switzerland."

"Throw the gringos out, I say. I nearly puke every year. Not from the sun, either. From the speeches they make."

"I was there that night in the sanatorium. I'll never forget it, never. For a few minutes he made us all feel capable of everything. Everything. *Chico,* for five minutes I was a god! I could fly, I tell you! I have never been so good, so strong, before or since. That's why we died for him. Like rats. We knew we were done for. That last night. How it rained! We went for the barricade at Colón. *Wooom!* Up went the dynamite. I ran for the wire, right behind him. Man, we were floating. We were ten meters tall and our feet never touched the ground. I got one in the leg and another in the belly, and I swear to Santa Rosa, I never felt a thing. Those bullets, they were like drops of honey."

"At least he went in a good way, that one. They say they had to pull them apart. They wouldn't stop doing it. He begged for them to let him finish. That's the way to go, eh?"

"He was a saint. All he cared for was the people. But they failed him. At the very end, when only another few hours was needed, just to hold on until the miners arrived. He begged them. He gave them their freedom. And they were afraid."

"There is nothing more dangerous than a bourgeois fanatic. They who have had that background never understand the real proletariat. They are the dilettantes of disaster and pull everything down on their heads. He was as middle-class as Napoleon or Hitler."

"A Trotskyite deviationist. The Party has condemned his name to silence. Olmega issued a manifesto three days ago. You haven't read it? Then you may still be subjected to ideological contamination, comrade."

"If we must be governed, and I grant that we must, let us have no Vizarras, no Alessandros. Let us be governed by those neither below nor above us. Right on our level. Let us be governed by Sánchez, now and forever. We are not capable of more, nor do we deserve less. Let us embrace our fate. And have another vermouth. With lots of ice."

"Vizarra made the trains run on time and he was a good Catholic. Alessandro was an atheist and blew up everything."

"It's all the fault of the Americans, anyway."

"He, alone of all men, did us honor. He believed in us. He taught us to dream. The right dreams, the wrong dreams, that's not so important as the fact of dreaming. He said, 'Stand up and be men. Know that you have honor. Your rights are God's wishes. Your freedoms are not mortal. Together we will rebuild, because we are, you and I, more than ordinary men. The worst they can do is kill us.

And for what? For being men.' And what did he do? Like Prometheus, he watched us burn our fingers. We thought that the smell of burning flesh was a holy sacrifice. That we would all wear the red hats of cardinals. And we fell with him and made ruins. But we learned. We didn't have to drag ourselves on our bellies. And we weren't able to stand erect. He taught us to crawl, perhaps, but to believe that we might one day stand. He didn't sacrifice us. Neither did Vizarra. We sacrificed ourselves. We burned our fingers with Alessandro's match. He knew he was going to fail because he knew we would fail him, all of us, in one way or the other, that he himself would fail to live up to his own visions because he could not. To know that and to act in spite of it—that's what he taught us. And what some—a few of us, no more—have learned."

"He's down there, preaching land reform. So many liters of brimstone apiece. The wealthy must not be tormented more frequently than the poor. Liberalize the inferno or else!"

"In Heaven they have windmills, *amigo*. Nowhere else."

"But he died in the cave, man. Where the pictures are on the walls."

"And you know what he's saying to her? No? *Down the hall, señorita. The first door on your left. You can't miss it.*"

In the center of the plaza stands the statue raised on a concrete pedestal six and one-half meters high. The figure is cast in five thousand, six hundred and eighty-two kilograms of bronze and stands eleven meters above the pedestal. The face is almost without features. The right arm is extended, pointing.